THE PARASOL PROTECTORATE VOLUME TWO

ALSO BY GAIL CARRIGER

THE PARASOL PROTECTORATE (SFBC Omnibus Edition)

Soulless; Changeless; Blameless

THE PARASOL PROTECTORATE VOLUME TWO

HEARTLESS; TIMELESS

GAIL CARRIGER

This is a work of fiction. All of the characters, organizations and events portrayed in this novel are either products of the author's imagination or are used fictitiously and are not to be construed as real. Any resemblance to actual events, locales, organizations, or persons, living or dead, is entirely coincidental.

Publication History: Orbit mass market, July 2011

Publication History: Orbit mass market, March 2012

First SFBC Printing: March 2012

Selected by Rome Quezada, Senior Editor

Published by arrangement with
Orbit
Hachette Book Group
237 Park Avenue
New York, NY 10017

Visit The SFBC online at http://www.sfbc.com

ISBN 978-1-61793-780-4

Printed in the United States of America.

Contents

HEARTLESS

The Parasol Protectorate: Book the Fourth

Acknowledgments

Sometimes the necessaries are not something that can be researched. With grateful thanks to those who, wittingly or unwittingly, found themselves tutoring my madness: Mom for the holly; Willow for the dates; Rachel my mistress of the emotional red herring; Erin coma goddess; the Iz of continuity; and Phrannish the best wing-chick evah!

PROLOGUE

P Is for Preternatural

Notation to the Records, Subject P-464-AT, Alexia Tarabotti

Archivist: Mr. Phinkerlington, junior clerk, aethographic transmission specialist, second class

Subject P-464-AT is with child, sire unknown. Subject removed from London. Subject detached from Shadow Council. Position of muhjah vacant.

Notation to the Notation to the Records, Subject P-464-AT, Alexia Tarabotti

Archivist: Mr. Haverbink, field agent, recognizance and munitions expert, first class

Subject P-464-AT's pregnancy confirmed as direct result of union with Subject W-57790-CM, werewolf. Impregnation duly verified by scientists in good standing and by Italian Templars (preternatural breeding program discontinued circa 1805). (Please note: Templars classified as Threat to the Commonwealth of the Highest Order, yet their research in this is rated Unimpeachable.) Subject P-464-AT reinstated as muhjah.

Addendum to the Notation to the Notation to the Records, Subject P-464-AT, Alexia Tarabotti

Archivist: Professor Lyall, field agent, secretary prime (aka Subject W-56889-RL)

Werewolf howlers consulted on progeny. Child most likely a soul-stealer (aka *skin-stalker* or *flayer*).

Templar records reported to indicate this implies ability to be both mortal and immortal. Potentate, Lord Akeldama (aka Subject V-322-XA), concurs. Subject P-464-AT says she believes "the horrible man said something along the lines of . . . a creature that can both walk and crawl and that rides the soul as a knight will ride his steed." (Please note: suspect "horrible man" is reference to Florentine preceptor of the Knights Templar.)

Only previous recorded example of a soul-stealer was Al-Zabba (aka Zenobia, Queen of the Palmyrene, no subject number). Understood to be related to Subject V-322-XA, Akeldama. (He won't reveal the details—you know vampires.) Zenobia most likely result of union between Vampire Queen and Male Preternatural (subjects unknown). It is thus impossible to say if her abilities will be comparable to those of the forthcoming Subject P-464-AT progeny, as this child is the result of Female Preternatural and Alpha Werewolf union. In either case, type of manifestation unknown.

Suggest new classification for progeny: M for metanatural.

Additional Addendum for Consideration: Vampires clearly desire progeny eliminated, at expense of Subject P-464-AT. It is this archivist's belief that it is in the best interest of the Commonwealth to see this child born, for scientific purposes if nothing else. Have consulted with Subject V-322-XA, Akeldama, and believe we have a solution to vampire negativity.

CHAPTER ONE

In Which Lady Alexia Maccon Waddles

Five months! Five months you—dare I say it—*gentlemen* have been sitting on this little scheme of yours and only now you decide to inform me of it!" Lady Alexia Maccon did not enjoy being surprised by declarations of intent. She glared at the men before her. Fully grown, and a goodly number of centuries older than she, yet they still managed to look like shamefaced little boys.

The three gentlemen, despite identical expressions of sheepishness, were as dissimilar as men of fashion and social standing could possibly be. The first was large and slightly unkempt. His perfectly tailored evening jacket draped about massive shoulders with a degree of reluctance, as if it were well aware that it was worn under sufferance. The other two existed in far more congenial partnerships with their apparel, although, with the first, dress was a matter of subtlety and, with the second, a form of artistic, nigh declamatory, expression.

Lady Maccon was not looking fearsome enough to inspire feelings of embarrassment in any gentleman, fashionable or no. Perilously close to her confinement at almost eight months, she had the distinct appearance of a stuffed goose with bunions.

"We didna want to worry you overly," ventured her husband. His voice was gruff in an attempt at calm solicitude. The Earl of Woolsey's tawny eyes were lowered, and his hair might actually have been dampened.

"Oh, and the constant vampire death threats are so very restful for a woman in my condition?" Alexia was having none of it. Her voice was shrill enough to disturb Lord Akeldama's cat, normally a most unflappable creature. The chubby calico opened one yellow eye and yawned.

"But isn't it the most *perfect* solution, my little lilac bush?" exalted Lord Akeldama, petting the cat back into purring, boneless relaxation. The vampire's discomfiture was the most manufactured of the three. There was a twinkle in his beautiful eyes, however downcast. It was the twinkle of a man about to get his own way.

"What, to lose possession of my own child? For goodness' sake, I may be soulless and I am, admittedly, not precisely maternal, but I am by no means heartless. Really, Conall, how could you agree to this? Without consulting me!"

"Wife, did you miss the fact that the entire pack has been on constant bodyguard duty for the past five months? It's exhausting, my dear."

Lady Maccon adored her husband. She was particularly fond of the way he strode about shirtless in a fit of pique, but she was finding she didn't actually like him at the moment—the fathead. She was also suddenly hungry, a terrible bother, as it distracted her from her irritation.

"Oh, indeed, and how do you think I feel being on the receiving end of such constant supervision? But, Conall, *adoption*!" Alexia stood and began to pace about. Or, to be more precise, waddle fiercely. For once, she was blind to the gilded beauty of Lord Akeldama's drawing room. *I should have known better than to agree to a meeting here,* she thought. *Something untoward always occurs in Lord Akeldama's drawing room.*

"The queen thinks it's a good plan." That was Professor Lyall joining the fray. His was probably the most genuine regret, as he disliked confrontation. He was also the one truly responsible for this plot, unless Alexia was very wrong in her estimation of his character.

"Bully for the ruddy queen. Absolutely not—I refuse."

"Now, Alexia, my dearest, be reasonable." Her husband was trying to wheedle. He wasn't very good at it—wheedling looked odd on a man of his proportions and monthly inclinations.

"Reasonable? Go boil your head in reasonable!"

Lord Akeldama tried a new tactic. "I have already converted the room next to mine into a positively charming nursery, my little *pomegranate* seed."

Lady Maccon was really quite shocked to hear that. She paused in her wrath and her waddling to blink at the vampire in surprise. "Not your second closet? Never that."

"Indeed. You see how *seriously* I am taking this, my dearest petal? I have relocated *clothing* for you."

"For my child, you mean." But Alexia was impressed despite herself.

She looked to Lyall for assistance and tried desperately to calm herself and behave as practically as possible. "And this will stop the attacks?"

Professor Lyall nodded, pushing his spectacles up with one finger. They were an affectation—he had no need of them—but they gave him something to hide behind. And something to fiddle with. "I believe so. I have not, of course, been able to consult with any queens outright. The hives refuse to admit to an extermination mandate, and BUR has not yet determined how to prove definitively the vampires are"—he coughed gently—"trying to kill your child. And by default, you."

Alexia knew that the Bureau of Unnatural Registry was handicapped by a combination of paperwork and proper appearances. That is to say, because it was the enforcing body for England's supernatural and preternatural subjects, it had to seem at all times to be obeying its own laws, including those that guaranteed the packs and the hives some level of autonomy and self-governance.

"Monsieur Trouvé's homicidal mechanical ladybugs?"

"Never did trace the vampires' agent in Europe."

"The exploding gravy boat?"

"No appreciable evidence left behind."

"The flaming Mongolian poodle?"

"No connection to any known dealer."

"The poisoned dirigible meal that Mr. Tunstell consumed in my stead?"

"Well, given the general foulness of food while floating, that could simply have been a coincidence." Professor Lyall removed his spectacles and began to clean the clear lenses with a spotless white handkerchief.

"Oh, Professor Lyall, are you making a funny? It doesn't suit you."

The sandy-haired Beta gave Lady Maccon a dour look. "I am exploring new personality avenues."

"Well, stop it."

"Yes, my lady."

Alexia straightened her spine as much as her protruding belly would allow and looked down her nose at Professor Lyall where he sat, legs crossed elegantly. "Explain to me how you have arrived at this solution. Also, given that you have not proposed this scheme to the hives, how do you know with such confidence that it will stop this annoying little tick they seem to have developed wherein they continually try to murder me?"

Professor Lyall looked helplessly at his coconspirators. Lord Maccon, with a wide grin, slouched back into the golden velvet settee, making it creak in protest. Neither Lord Akeldama nor any of his drones were built to Lord Maccon's scale. The couch was overwhelmed by the experience. It had this in common with a good deal of furniture.

Lord Akeldama merely continued to twinkle unhelpfully.

Clearly surmising that he had been left out to dry, Professor Lyall took a long breath. "How did you know it was my idea?"

Alexia crossed her arms over her very ample chest. "My dear sir, give me *some* credit."

Professor Lyall put his glasses back on. "Well, we know that the vampires are afraid of what your child could be, but I think they are wise enough to know that if raised with the proper precautions, even the most natural-born predator will behave in an entirely civilized fashion. You, for example."

Alexia raised an eyebrow.

Her husband snorted derisively.

Professor Lyall refused to be intimidated. "You may be a tad outrageous, Lady Maccon, but you *are* always civilized."

"Hear, hear," added Lord Akeldama, raising a long-stemmed glass and then taking a sip of the pink fizzy drink within.

Lady Maccon inclined her head. "I shall take that as a compliment."

Professor Lyall soldiered bravely on. "It is vampire nature to believe that any vampire, even—you'll pardon the insult, my lord—Lord Akeldama, will instill the correct ethical code in a child. A vampire father would ensure the baby is kept away from the corruption of Americans, Templars, and other like-minded antisupernatural elements. And, of course, you, Lord and Lady Maccon. Simply put, the hives will feel like they are in control, and all death threats should stop as a result."

Alexia looked at Lord Akeldama. "Do you agree with that prediction?"

Lord Akeldama nodded. "Yes, my *dearest* marigold."

The earl was beginning to look less annoyed and more thoughtful.

Professor Lyall continued. "Lord Akeldama seemed the best solution."

Lord Maccon wrinkled his nose at that and huffed derisively.

Professor Lyall, Lord Akeldama, and Alexia all pretended not to hear.

"He is more powerful than any other rove in the area. He has a goodly number of drones. He is centrally located, and as potentate, he carries the authority of Queen Victoria. Few would dare interfere with his household."

Lord Akeldama tapped Lyall playfully with the back of one hand. "Dolly, you flatterer, you."

Professor Lyall ignored this. "He is also your friend."

Lord Akeldama looked up to his ceiling, as though contemplating possible new canoodling for the painted cherubs depicted there. "I have also implied that because of a certain unmentionable incident this winter, the hives owe me a debt of honor. My potentate predecessor may have taken matters into his own lily-white hands, but *the fact remains* that the hives should have exerted some control over his activities on their behalf. His kidnapping of *my droney poo* was *utterly* inexcusable, and they are very well aware of that *little* fact. I hold a blood debt and intend to bite them back with this arrangement."

Alexia looked at her friend. His posture and demeanor were as relaxed and frivolous as ever, but there was a hardness about his mouth that suggested he actually meant what he was saying. "That is a rather serious statement coming from you, my lord."

The vampire smiled, showing fang. "Better revel in the experience, my little *cream puff.* It will probably never occur again."

Lady Maccon nibbled at her lower lip and went to sit in one of Lord Akeldama's more upright chairs. She found it tricky these days to extract herself from couches and love seats and preferred simply not to get involved with plushy furniture.

"Oh, I can't think." She rubbed at her belly, annoyed at the fuzziness in her own brain, the persistent product of lack of sleep, physical discomfort, and hunger. She seemed to spend all her time either eating or dozing—sometimes dozing while eating and, once or twice, eating while dozing. Pregnancy had given her a new window into the human capacity for consumption.

"Oh, blast it, I'm positively starving."

Instantly, all three men proffered up comestibles extracted from inner waistcoat pockets. Professor Lyall's offering was a ham sandwich wrapped in brown paper, Lord Maccon's a weather-beaten apple, and Lord Akeldama's a small box of Turkish delight. Months of training had seen the entire werewolf household running attendance on an increasingly grumpy Alexia and learning, to a man, that if food was not provided promptly, fur might fly, or worse, Lady Maccon would start to weep. As a result, several of the pack now crinkled as they moved, having desperately stashed snacks all about their personage.

Alexia opted for all three offerings and began to eat, starting with the Turkish delight. "So you are genuinely disposed toward adopting my child?" she asked Lord Akeldama between bites, and then looked at her husband. "And *you* are willing to allow it?"

The earl lost his amused attitude and knelt before his wife, looking up at her. He put his hands on her knees. Even through all her layers of skirts, Alexia could feel the wide roughness of his palms. "I'm taxing BUR and the pack to keep you safe, wife. I've even contemplated calling in the Coldsteam Guards." Curse him for looking so handsome when he came over all bashful and sincere. It quite undid her resolve. "Not that I would do it any differently. I protect my own. But Queen Victoria would be livid if I pulled military strings in a personal matter. Well, more livid than she already is over my killing the potentate. We must be clever. They're older and craftier and they'll keep trying. We canna continue on like this for the rest of our child's life."

Perhaps he has learned something about pragmatism being married to me, Alexia thought. *Oh, but why'd he have to turn all sensible now?* She tried desperately not to fly into a tizzy over his unilateral handling of the situation. She knew that it cost Conall a terrible price to admit to any kind of inability. He liked to think he was all-powerful.

She cupped his cheek with her gloved hand. "But this is *our* baby."

"Do you have a better solution?" It was an honest question. He was genuinely hoping she could think up an alternative.

Alexia shook her head, trying not to come over mawkish. Then she firmed up her mouth. "Very well." She turned to Lord Akeldama. "If you intend to take possession of my child, then I'm moving in, too."

Lord Akeldama didn't miss a beat. He opened his arms wide as though to embrace her. "Darlingest of Alexias, *welcome* to the family."

"You do realize I may have to take up residence in your other closet?"

"Sacrifices, sacrifices."

"What? Absolutely not." Lord Maccon stood and glared down at his wife.

Lady Maccon got *that* look on her face. "I'm already in London two nights a week for the Shadow Council. I'll come in on Wednesday and stay through to Monday, spend the rest of the week at Woolsey."

The earl could do math. "Two nights? You'll give me two nights?! Unacceptable."

Alexia wouldn't budge. "You're in town on BUR business most evenings yourself. You can see me then."

"Alexia," said Lord Maccon on a definite growl, "I refuse to petition for visiting rights with my own wife!"

"Tough cheese. I am also this child's mother. You are forcing me to choose."

"Perhaps, if I may?" Professor Lyall interjected.

Lord and Lady Maccon glowered at him. They enjoyed arguing

with each other almost as much as they enjoyed any other intimate activity.

Professor Lyall called upon the sublime confidence of the truly urbane. "The house adjacent is to let. If Woolsey were to take it on as a town residence, my lord . . . ? You and Lady Maccon could maintain a room here at Lord Akeldama's but pretend to live next door. This would keep up the appearance of separation for when the child arrives. You, Lord Maccon, could spend meals and so forth with members of the pack while they are in town. Of course, parts of the month everyone would have to return to Woolsey for security purposes, and there's hunting and runs to consider. But it might work, as a temporary compromise. For a decade or two."

"Will the vampires object?" Alexia rather liked the idea. Woolsey Castle was a little too far outside of London for her taste, and those buttresses—positively excessive.

"I don't believe so. Not if it is made absolutely clear that Lord Akeldama has complete parental control, proper documentation and all. And we manage to keep up pretenses."

Lord Akeldama was amused. "Dolly, *darling*, so deliciously unprecedented—a wolf pack living directly next to a vampire such as *moi*."

The earl frowned. "My marriage was also unprecedented."

"True, true." Lord Akeldama was on a roll. He swept to his feet, dumping the cat unceremoniously off his lap, and began sashaying about the room. This evening he wore highly polished oxblood boots and white velvet jodhpurs with a red riding jacket. It was all purely decorative. Vampires rarely rode—most horses would have none of it—and Lord Akeldama disdained the sport as disastrous to one's hair. "Dolly, I *adore* this plan! Alexia, *sugar drop*, you must make over your town house to complement mine. Robin's-egg blue with silver detailing, don't you think? We could plant lilac bushes. I do so *love* lilac bushes."

Professor Lyall was not to be sidetracked. "Do you believe it will work?"

"Robin's-egg blue and silver? Of course. It will look *divine*."

Alexia hid a smile.

"No." Professor Lyall possessed infinite patience, whether dealing with Lord Maccon's temper, Lord Akeldama's purposeful obtuseness, or Lady Maccon's antics. *Being a Beta,* Alexia figured, *must be rather like being the world's most tolerant butler.* "Will having your vampire residence adjacent to a werewolf pack work?"

Lord Akeldama raised his monocle. Like Lyall's spectacles, it was entirely artificial. But he did love the accessory so. He had several, set with different gemstones and in different metals to match any outfit.

The vampire regarded the two werewolves in his drawing room through the small circle of glass. "You are rather more civilized under my dear Alexia's tutelage. I suppose it could be tolerated, so long as I do not have to dine with you. And, Lord Maccon, might we have words on the proper tying of a cravat? For my sanity's sake?"

Lord Maccon was nonplussed.

Professor Lyall, on the other hand, was pained. "I do what I can."

Lord Akeldama looked at him, pity in his eyes. "You are a brave man."

Lady Maccon interjected at this juncture. "And you wouldn't mind Conall and myself occasionally in residence?"

"If you see to the cravat situation, I suppose I could surrender yet another closet to the cause."

Alexia swallowed down a broad grin and tried to be as serious as humanly possible. "You are a noble man."

Lord Akeldama tilted his head in gracious acceptance of the accolade. "Whoever thought I would have a werewolf living in my closet?"

"Hobgoblins under the bed?" suggested Lady Maccon, allowing her grin to emerge.

"La, *butterball*, I should *be* so lucky." A gleam entered the vampire's eyes, and he brushed his blond hair flirtatiously off his neck. "I suppose your pack must spend a good deal of time underdressed?"

The earl rolled his eyes, but Professor Lyall was not above a little bribery. "Or not dressed at all."

Lord Akeldama nodded in pleasure. "Oh, my darling boys are going to *love* this new arrangement. They often take a keen interest in remarking upon the activities of our neighbors."

"Oh, dear," muttered Lord Maccon under his breath.

Biffy remained unmentioned, although everyone was thinking about him. Alexia, being Alexia, decided she would bring the taboo subject out into the open. "Biffy is going to be pleased."

Silence met that statement.

Lord Akeldama assumed a forced lightness of tone. "How *is* the newest member of the Woolsey Pack?"

In truth, Biffy was not adjusting as well as anyone would like. He still fought the change each month and refused to try shifting of his own volition. He obeyed Lord Maccon implicitly, but there was no joy in it. The result was that he was having trouble learning any modicum of control and had to be locked away more nights than not because of this weakness.

However, not being inclined to confide in a vampire, Lord Maccon only said gruffly, "The pup is well enough."

Lady Maccon frowned. Had she and Lord Akeldama been alone, she might have said something to him of Biffy's tribulations, but as it was, she let her husband handle it. If they, indeed, moved in to Lord Akeldama's neighborhood and home, he would find out the truth of the matter soon enough.

She made a dictatorial gesture at Conall.

Rather like a trained dog—although no one would dare suggest the comparison to any werewolf—Lord Maccon stood, offering both his hands. He hoisted his wife to her feet. During the last few months, Alexia had taken to using him thus on multiple occasions.

Professor Lyall stood as well.

"So it's decided?" Alexia looked at the three supernatural gentlemen.

They all nodded at her.

"Excellent. I shall have Floote make the arrangements. Professor, can you leak our relocation to the papers so that the vampires find out? Lord Akeldama, if you would use your very own special distribution methods as well?"

"Of course, my little *dewdrop.*"

"At once, my lady."

"You and I"—Lady Maccon grinned up at her husband, immersing herself, albeit briefly, in his tawny eyes—"have packing to do."

He sighed, no doubt contemplating the pack's reaction to the fact that their Alpha was about to reside, at least part of the time, in town. The Woolsey Pack was not exactly renowned for its interest in high society. No pack was. "How do you manage to drag me into such situations, wife?"

"Oh"—Alexia stood on tiptoe and leaned in to kiss the tip of his nose, balancing her belly against his strong frame—"you love it. Just think how terribly dull your life was before I came into it."

The earl gave her a dour look but ceded the point.

Alexia nestled against him, enjoying the tingles his massive body still engendered in her own.

Lord Akeldama sighed. "You lovebirds, how will I endure such flirtations constantly in my company? How déclassé, Lord Maccon, to love your *own* wife." He led the way out of his drawing room and into the long arched front hallway.

Inside the carriage, Lord Maccon scooped his wife against him and planted a buzzing kiss on the side of her neck.

Lady Maccon had initially thought Conall's amorous attentions would diminish as her pregnancy progressed, but she was happily mistaken. He was intrigued by the alterations of her body—a spirit of scientific inquiry that took the form of her being unclothed as often as he could arrange it. It was a good thing this was the season for such activities; London was experiencing quite the nicest summer in an age.

Alexia settled against her husband and, grabbing his face in both hands, directed his kissing toward her mouth for a long moment. He gave a little growl that was almost a purr and hauled her closer. Her stomach got in the way, but the earl didn't seem bothered.

They spent a half hour or so thus pleasantly occupied until Alexia said, "You really don't mind?"

"Mind?"

"Living in Lord Akeldama's closet?"

"I've done more foolish things for love in the past," he answered, rather unguardedly, before nibbling on her ear.

Alexia shifted against him. "You have? What?"

"Well, there was this—"

The carriage bucked and the window above the door shattered.

The earl immediately shielded his wife from the flying glass with his own body. Even fully mortal, his reactions were fast and military sharp.

"Oh, doesn't that just take the sticky pudding?" said Alexia. "Why is it *always* when I'm in a carriage?"

The horses screamed and the coach lurched, coming to a rattling halt. Something had definitely spooked the beasts into rearing against their traces.

In classic werewolf fashion, Lord Maccon didn't wait to see what it was but burst out the door, changing form at the same time to land in the road a raging wolf.

He's brash, thought his wife, *but terribly handsome about it.*

They were outside of London proper, following one of the many country lanes toward Barking that would eventually branch off to Woolsey Castle. Whatever had startled the horses seemed to be giving Lord Maccon a bit of stick. Alexia poked her head out to see.

Hedgehogs. Hundreds of them.

Lady Maccon frowned and then looked closer. The moon was only half full, and though it was a clear summer night, it was challenging to make out the particulars. She reassessed her first impression of the roly-poly attackers. These were far bigger than hedgehogs, with long gray spines. They reminded her of a series of etchings she'd once seen in a book on Darkest Africa. *What had that creature been named? Something to do with pig products? Ah, yes, a porcupine.* These looked like porcupines. To her utter amazement, they also seemed to be able to eject their spines at her husband, embedding them into his fur-covered flesh.

As each wickedly barbed spine hit, Conall howled in distress and bent to yank the projectile out with his teeth.

Then he seemed to partly lose control of his back legs.

Numbing agent? wondered Alexia. *Are they mechanical?* She grabbed her parasol and stuck the tip of it out the broken window. Firming her grip with one hand, she activated the magnetic disruption emitter with the other by pulling down on the appropriate lotus leaf in the handle.

The animals continued to attack Conall with no slowing or reaction to the invisible blast. Either the parasol was broken, which Alexia doubted, or the creatures had no magnetic parts. Perhaps they were as biological as they initially appeared.

Well, if they are biological . . . Lady Maccon took out her gun.

The earl had objected to his wife carrying firearms, until the vampires orchestrated the gravy-boat attack. After that, he took Alexia out behind Woolsey Castle, ordered two members of his pack to run about holding trenchers over their heads, and showed her how to shoot. Then he'd gifted her with a small but elegant gun, American made and delectably deadly. It was a .28 caliber Colt Paterson revolver, customized with a shorter barrel and a pearl handle—the former for ease of concealment and the latter to match Lady Maccon's hair accessories.

Alexia named the gun Ethel.

She could hit the Woolsey pot shed at six paces if she concentrated, but anything smaller or farther away was rather beyond her skill level. This didn't stop her from carrying Ethel, usually inside a reticule made to match her gown. However, it did stop her from pointing Ethel at any of the creatures near her husband. She could just as easily damage him as them.

Conall had managed to pull out most of the spines embedded in his body, but new and freshly equipped porcupines only fired at him again. Alexia tried to stop herself from panicking, as those projectiles might, just possibly, be silver tipped. However, while he seemed a tad overwhelmed and groggy, none had managed to hit him in any vital organs. Not yet. He was snapping and snarling, trying to get his deadly jaws about the creatures, but they seemed to move remarkably quickly for such pudgy animals.

In the interest of scientific experimentation, Alexia fired Ethel out the carriage window at a porcupine nearer to the edge of the undulating herd. Proximity and density combined to result in her actually hitting one. Not the one she'd aimed at, but . . . The animal in question fell heavily to one side and began to slowly bleed, thick black blood, the kind of blood emitted by vampires. Alexia wrinkled her nose in disgust. Once in her past, a certain wax-faced automaton had also oozed such blood.

Another shot rang out. The coachman, a newer claviger, was also firing on their attackers.

Lady Maccon frowned. Were these porcupines already dead? *Zombie porcupines?* She snorted at her own flight of fancy. *Surely not.* Necromancy had long since been disproved as mere superstitious folderol. She squinted. They did seem to have oddly shiny quills. *Wax perhaps? Or glass?*

Alexia's gun was outfitted with sundowner bullets, although no one had authorized her to carry them. Conall had positively insisted, and Alexia was not one to stand against him on matters of munitions. Undead or not, the porcupine she had shot stayed down. That was something to note. Although, truth be told, sundowner bullets would work just as well on any normal porcupine. Still, there were positively masses, and Conall had fallen once more to his side, writhing and howling under the swarm of quills.

Alexia put away Ethel and armed herself with her parasol once more. She poked it fully out the carriage window, opened it up, and then in one practiced movement flipped it about so that she held the tip, her fingers poised on the deadly dial there. Her husband would take some time to recover from the resulting injuries, and she loathed causing him pain, but sometimes circumstances warranted extreme measures. Making very certain she was dialing to the second and not the first or third position, she sprayed out a mixture of lapis solaris diluted in sulfuric acid. The liquid, designed to combat vampires, was still strong enough to burn any living creature—causing severe pain at the very least.

The mist floated out, coating the porcupines. The unmistakable smell of burning fur permeated the air. Her husband, now almost entirely covered in the creatures, avoided most of the spray as the porcupines took the brunt of the falling acid.

Eerily, they made no noise. The acid burned through the fur covering their faces but had little effect on the quills that continued to jab into Lord Maccon. The parasol sputtered and the spray turned to a dribble. Alexia shook it, flipped it up, and caught it in reverse before closing it.

With a roar so loud it was guaranteed to shake the porcupines in their boots, had they been wearing any, her husband shook off the creatures and reared back, as though luring them to follow him. Perhaps he was not so disabled as he pretended. Perhaps he was trying to draw them away from Alexia.

Struck with a sudden inspiration, Lady Maccon yelled to her lupine spouse, "My love, lead them off. Go for the lime pit." She remembered Conall complaining to her about running into the pit by accident only a few nights previous, singeing all the hair off of his forefeet.

Lord Maccon barked his agreement, understanding her completely—as Alpha, he was one of the few who held on to his wits when he lost his skin. He began backing off the road and down the gully toward the nearby pit. If the creatures had any wax components at all, the lime should at least seize them into immobility.

The porcupines followed.

Alexia had only a moment of reprieve to appreciate the macabre sight of a wolf luring away a flock of porcupines like some Aesop's version of the Pied Piper. A thud resounded on the driver's box on the outside of the carriage. Something far larger than a porcupine had hit the claviger coachman and knocked him out. Seconds later, for speed was always their strong point, the parasol was bashed out of Alexia's grasp and the carriage door yanked open.

"Good evening, Lady Maccon." The vampire tipped his top hat with one hand, holding the door with the other. He occupied the entrance in an ominous, looming manner.

"Ah, how do you do, Lord Ambrose?"

"Tolerably well, tolerably well. It is a lovely night, don't you find? And how is your"—he glanced at her engorged belly—"health?"

"Exceedingly abundant," Alexia replied with a self-effacing shrug, "although, I suspect, unlikely to remain so."

"Have you been eating figs?"

Alexia was startled by this odd question. "Figs?"

"Terribly beneficial in preventing biliousness in newborns, I understand."

Alexia had been in receipt of a good deal of unwanted pregnancy advice over the last several months, so she ignored this and got on to the business at hand.

"If you don't feel that it is forward of me to ask, are you here to kill me, Lord Ambrose?" She inched away from the carriage door, reaching for Ethel. The gun lay behind her on the coach seat. She had not had time to put it back into its reticule with the pineapple cut siding. The reticule was a perfect match to her gray plaid carriage dress with green lace trim. Lady Alexia Maccon was a woman who liked to see a thing done properly or not at all.

The vampire tilted his head to one side in acknowledgment. "Sadly, yes. I do apologize for the inconvenience."

"Oh, really, must you? I'd much rather you didn't."

"That's what they all say."

* * *

The ghost drifted. Floating between this world and death. It felt like being trapped in a coop, a cage for chickens, and she a poor fat hen kept to lay and lay and lay. What could she provide but the eggs of her mind? Nothing left. No more eggs.

"Bawk, bawk!" she clucked.

No one answered her.

It was better—this was better, she had to believe—than nothingness. Even the madness was better.

But sometimes she was aware of it, the reality of her coop, and the substantial world around it. There was something very wrong with that world. There were parts of it missing. There were people acting indifferent or incorrect. There were new feelings intruding that had no right to intrude. No right at all.

The ghost was certain, absolutely certain, that something must be done to stop it. But she was nothing more than a specter, and a mad one at that, drifting between undead and dead. What could she do? Who could she tell?

CHAPTER TWO

Wherein Alexia Will Not Be Flung

Lord Ambrose was an exceptionally well-formed gentleman. His perpetual expression was one of pensive hauteur exacerbated by aquiline features and brooding dark eyes. Alexia felt that he had much in common with a mahogany wardrobe that belonged to Mrs. Loontwill's great-grandfather and now resided in embarrassed austerity among the frippery of her mother's boudoir. That is to say, Lord Ambrose was immovable, impossible to live with, and mostly filled with frivolities incompatible with outward appearance.

Lady Maccon moved toward her gun, finding the spacious carriage difficult to navigate with her attention focused on the vampire in the doorway and her mobility hampered by the infant in her belly. "Terribly forward of the countess to send you, Lord Ambrose, to do the deed."

Lord Ambrose made his way inside. "Ah, well, our more subtle attempts seem to be wasted on you, Lady Maccon."

"Subtlety usually is."

Lord Ambrose ignored her and continued with his explanation. "I am her *praetoriani.* When you want something done properly, sometimes you must send the best." He lunged toward her, supernaturally fast. In his hands he held a garrote. Alexia would never have thought the most dignified of the Westminster Hive capable of wielding such a primitive assassin's weapon.

Lady Maccon might be prone to waddling of late, but there was nothing wrong with the mobility of her upper extremities. She ducked to avoid the deadly wire, grabbed for Ethel, swung about, pulling the hammer back in the same movement, and fired.

At such close range, even she could hit a vampire full force in the shoulder, surprising him considerably.

He paused in his attack. "Well, my word! You can't threaten me, you're pregnant!"

Alexia pulled the hammer back again. "Take a seat, won't you, Lord Ambrose? I believe I have something to discuss with you that might change your current approach. And I shall aim for a less-resilient part of your anatomy next."

The vampire was looking down at his shoulder, which wasn't healing as it ought. The bullet hadn't passed through but had gone into the bone and lodged there.

"Sundowner bullets," explained Lady Maccon. "You're in no mortal danger from a mere shoulder injury, my lord, but I shouldn't leave the bullet in there if I were you."

Gingerly, the vampire settled back against the plush velvet seat. Alexia had always thought Lord Ambrose the pinnacle of what a vampire ought to look like. He had a full head of glossy dark hair, a cleft chin, and, currently, a certain air of childish petulance.

Lady Maccon, never one for shilly-shallying even when her life wasn't in danger, got straight to the point. "You can stop with all your uncouth attempts at execution. I have decided to give this child up for adoption."

"Oh? And why should that make any difference to us, Lady Maccon?"

"The lucky father is to be Lord Akeldama."

The vampire lost his sulky expression for one of genuine shock. He most certainly hadn't expected such a bizarre revelation. The surprise sat upon his face as precariously as a mouse on a bowl of boiled pudding.

"Lord Akeldama?"

Lady Maccon nodded, sharply, once.

The vampire raised one hand and fluttered it slightly from side to side in a highly illustrative gesture. "Lord Akeldama?"

Lady Maccon nodded again.

He seemed to recollect some of his much-vaunted vampire gravitas. "You would allow your progeny to be raised by a vampire?"

Alexia's hand, still clutching her gun, didn't waver one iota. Vampires were tricky, changeable creatures. No sense in relaxing her guard, for all Lord Ambrose seemed to have relaxed his. He still held the garrote in his other hand.

"The potentate, no less." Alexia reminded him of Lord Akeldama's relatively recent change in political status.

She watched his face closely. She was giving him an out and knew that he must *want* an out. Countess Nadasdy, Queen of the Westminster

Hive, would want one. All the vampires had to be uncomfortable with this situation. It was probably why they kept bungling the assassination attempts; their little hearts simply weren't in it. Oh, not the killing—with vampires, that was but one step up from ordering a new pair of shoes. No, they would want to get out of having to kill an Alpha werewolf's mate. Lady Maccon's death at vampire hands, whether provable or not, would bring a whole mess of trouble down upon the hives. Trouble of the large, hairy, and angry variety. It was not that the bloodsuckers thought they would lose a war with werewolves; it was simply that they knew it would be bloody. Vampires hated to lose blood—it was troublesome to replace and always left a stain.

Lady Maccon pressed the point, figuring that Lord Ambrose had had enough time to cogitate her revelation. "Surely you can do nothing but approve so tidy a solution to our current predicament?"

The vampire pursed his full lips over his fangs. It was the very elegance of Alexia's proposal that had him seriously considering it. They both knew that. "You would not contemplate allowing Countess Nadasdy to be the infant's godmother, would you?"

Alexia placed a hand on her belly, taken aback. "Well," she hedged, trying for the most courteous response, "you know I should be delighted, but my husband, you must understand. He is already a little flustered by Lord Akeldama's parental undertaking. To add your hive into the mix might be more than he could stomach."

"Ah, yes, the sensitivities of werewolves must be taken into account. I always forget that. I can hardly countenance his approval of the scheme in the first place. He is amenable to this arrangement?"

"Unreservedly."

Lord Ambrose gave her a look of disbelief.

"Ah, well," Lady Maccon made light of the situation. "My dearest spouse has some reservations as to Lord Akeldama's ideas on schooling and, uh, proper dress, but he has approved the adoption."

"Remarkable powers of persuasion you possess, Lady Maccon."

Alexia was rather flattered he should think it all her idea, so she did not bother to correct him on the matter.

"You will make it fully legal, put the adoption in writing, file it with the Bureau?"

"Indeed. I understand Queen Victoria is agreeable. Woolsey is intending to lease the house adjacent to Lord Akeldama's to keep an eye on the child. You must allow me some level of motherly concern."

"Oh, yes, yes, entirely understandable. In writing, you said, Lady Maccon?"

"In writing, Lord Ambrose."

The vampire put his garrote away in a waistcoat pocket. "Given such a proposed arrangement, Lady Maccon, you will excuse me for the time being? I should return to Westminster at once. It is taxing to be so far away as it is, and my queen will want this new information as quickly as supernaturally possible."

"Ah, yes. I thought the hive's range extended only to parts of London proper."

"*Praetoriani* has some advantages."

With a gleam of pure mischief in her brown eyes, Lady Maccon remembered her manners. "You are certain you won't stay? Take a drop of port? My husband keeps a small stash in the carriage amenities compartment for emergencies."

"No, thank you kindly. Perhaps at some future date?"

"Not the whole killing thing, I hope? I should like to put that well behind us."

Lord Ambrose actually smiled. "No, Lady Maccon, the port. After all, you are taking a house in town. You will be in our territory now, won't you?"

Alexia blanched. Westminster Hive did hold sway over the most fashionable parts of London. "Why, yes, I suppose I will."

Lord Ambrose's smile became less friendly. "I will bid you good evening, then, Lady Maccon."

With that, he let himself out of the carriage, tossed her parasol in, and vanished into the night. Mere moments later, Lord Maccon, looking none the worse for his porcupine-herding activities, let himself back inside and unceremoniously swept Alexia into his arms. He was naked, of course, and Alexia had no time to reprimand him for not changing out of his clothing before he shifted form. Yet another jacket ruined.

"Where were we?" he rumbled into her ear before nibbling on it. He slid his arms about her, as far as they would reach, which admittedly wasn't far these days, and rubbed up and down her back.

Lady Maccon's increasing girth had rendered most bed sport impossible, but this did not stop them from what Conall affectionately referred to as *playing.* Despite Alexia's protestations that she was in perfect health, modern medical science banned connubial relations during the final months, and the earl refused to risk his wife's well-being. He had, Alexia discovered much to her distress, unanticipated powers of resistance.

She slid her gun out from between them and pushed it away along the bench. Time enough to tell her husband about Lord Ambrose later. If she told him now, he'd get all flustered and distracted. At the moment, *she* preferred to be the cause of both his flustering and his distraction.

"No lasting harm, my love?" She slid her hands along his sides, enjoying the silkiness of his skin just there and the way he writhed under her touch.

"Never." He kissed her mouth in a heated embrace.

Alexia wondered that even after so many months of marriage she still could get utterly lost in kissing her husband. It never became unexciting. It was like a rich milky tea—comforting, revitalizing, and delicious. Though she wasn't certain how he would take such an analogy, Alexia Maccon was *very* fond of tea.

She touched his chin with both hands, encouraging him to kiss deeper.

Moving house, thought Lady Maccon, *must be the world's most incommodious undertaking.*

She, of course, was not being allowed to physically help, although she did toddle about pointing at objects and indicating where they should go. She was enjoying herself immensely. Her husband and coconspirators having sallied off about their own business several days ago, she felt much like a chubby general in sole possession of a field of glittery battle, directing a mass invasion of foreign soil. Although, after having to mediate a head-to-head between Boots and Biffy over the efficaciousness of velvet decorative pillows, she suspected generals had it easier. Conall and Professor Lyall had arranged for her dominion over the relocation operation in order to distract her, but as she was well aware of the manipulation and, as they were well aware that she was well aware, she might as well have fun.

What made it particularly pleasant was that it had to be covert. They didn't want it known that Lord and Lady Maccon were actually taking up residence *inside* Lord Akeldama's house. The vampires had only reluctantly agreed to the Maccons moving in *next door,* frightened that a werewolf and a preternatural might unduly influence the rearing of a child, even one under Lord Akeldama's care. Further intimacy was strongly discouraged. Thus, they had made it look as though Lady Maccon were seeking refuge from the chaos by taking tea at Lord Akeldama's, while her belongings were moved into the rented accommodations adjacent. Alexia's personal effects were taken up one flight of stairs, down a hall, and out onto a balcony. They were then tossed over to Lord Akeldama's balcony—the balconies being a short distance apart and conveniently hidden by a large holly tree. Her private possessions were then carried down another hall, up another flight of stairs, and eventually into her new residential closet. This involved a good deal of ruckus, especially when it was furniture being tossed. *Thank goodness,* reflected Alexia, watching Biffy catch her favorite armoire with ease, *for supernatural strength.*

Lady Maccon's minions in this elaborate charade were three younger members of Woolsey's pack: Biffy, Rafe, and Phelan (Biffy as catcher and the other two as porter and chucker, respectively); the ever-efficient Floote; and a positive bevy of Lord Akeldama's drones scuttling about arranging everything *just so.*

After overseeing the tossing, Alexia repaired to monitor the arrangement of her new sleeping chamber. Lord Akeldama's third closet was quite spacious, almost the size of her bedchamber back at Woolsey. Admittedly, there were no windows, and there were gratuitous hooks, shelves, and rails covering the walls. But there was also enough room for a large bed (specially commissioned by Lord Akeldama to accommodate Lord Maccon's frame), a dressing table, and several other bits and bobs. Conall would have to make do without his dressing chamber, but since he was prone to wandering around underdressed, anyway, Alexia suspected this would not affect his habits detrimentally. The lack of a proper valet concerned her for about five seconds before she realized no drone of Lord Akeldama's would allow her husband passage through their hallways in anything less than tip-top, wrinkle-free condition.

Biffy was in his element, free to wander once more the luxurious, colorful, and somewhat effervescent corridors of his former master. Of all Alexia's acquaintances, Biffy was the most thrilled by the new cohabitation scheme. He was far more comfortable bustling about hanging Alexia's hats on hooks than he had been for the last five months at Woolsey Castle. One might even have described him as gay, no longer weighed down by the sport destiny had made of his afterlife.

The drones couldn't have been more excited if Queen Victoria were gracing them with her presence. A female in their midst, a baby in their future, and a room to decorate in the interim—pure heaven. After a brief scuffle over repapering the walls, it was decided, wholly without Alexia's say-so, that a new carpet and some additional lighting were sufficient to brighten up the closet.

Once Covert Operation Fling Furniture was concluded, the two other werewolves jumped easily from one balcony to the other and came to see if there was anything further their Alpha female wished of them. There was a good deal more, as she readily informed them. She desired the bed be moved slightly to the right and her armoire moved to the other side of the room, and then back again. Also the drones wished to inquire as to the werewolves' opinion on the matter of stacking Lady Maccon's hatboxes, and the correct order in which to hang Lord Maccon's cloaks.

By the end, Rafe wore the long-suffering look of an eagle being ordered about by a flock of excited pigeons.

Floote heralded completion by coming in with the last of Lady Maccon's most prized possessions: her parasol, dispatch case, and jewelry box.

"What do you think, Floote?"

"It's rather glossy, madam."

"No, not that. What do you think about the whole arrangement?"

They had been organizing and packing for several days, and Floote had taken charge of leasing the house adjacent to Lord Akeldama's (although not, much to the vampire's disappointment, repainting it), but Alexia had not found the time to consult with him on his opinion of the scheme itself.

Floote looked grave and very much the butler. He was ostensibly Lady Maccon's personal secretary and librarian now but had never been one to let go of good training. "It is a unique solution, madam."

"And?"

"You have always done things differently, madam."

"Will it work?"

"Anything is possible, madam," was Floote's noncommittal answer. Very diplomatic was Floote.

It was well into the night and no longer quite the time for social calls, even among the supernatural set, when Lord Akeldama's doorbell sounded, interrupting Alexia's conversation and the drone's bustling.

Emmet Wilberforce Bootbottle-Fipps—whom everyone, including Lady Maccon when she forgot herself, called Boots—trotted off in a flutter of green velvet frock coat to see who would call at such an hour. Lord Akeldama didn't always keep a butler; he said his drones needed the practice. Whatever that meant.

Alexia thought of something she had better see dealt with before it slipped her mind and became inconvenient. "Floote, would you please see about some very discreet carpenters to build a bridge between the balconies?"

"Madam?"

"I realize that they are hardly more than a yard apart, but my stability is not what it once was. It seems likely we must persist in this charade of actually living in the one abode while sneaking into the other. I refuse to be hurled willy-nilly between houses, no matter how strong my husband or how diverting he would find the attempt. Clothing isn't always enough of a barrier to preternatural contact, and I should hate to be the victim of unreliable catching, if you take my meaning."

"Perfectly, madam. I shall see to the builders directly." Floote kept a remarkably straight face for a man having heard such a preposterous statement come out of the mouth of an overly pregnant aristocrat.

Boots reappeared wearing a look of mild shock under his sculpted topiary of muttonchops. "The caller is for you, Lady Maccon."

"Yes?" Alexia held out her hand for a card.

There was none forthcoming, only Boots's shocked statement. "It is a *lady,* what!"

"They do happen, Boots, much as you would prefer to deny it."

"Oh, no, sorry 'bout that. I mean to say, how'd she know you were here?"

"Well, if you told me which lady, I might be able to elucidate."

"It's a Miss Loontwill, Lady Maccon."

"Oh, fiddlesticks. Which one?"

Miss Felicity Loontwill sat in Lord Akeldama's drawing room in a dress of sensible heathered tweed with only one layer of trim and six buttons, a hat with minimal feathers, and a gray knit shawl with a ruffled collar.

"Oh, my heavens," exclaimed Lady Maccon upon seeing her sister in such a state. "Felicity, are you quite all right?"

Miss Loontwill looked up. "Why, yes, of course, sister. Why shouldn't I be?"

"Is there something amiss with the family?"

"You mean, aside from Mama's predilection for pink?"

Alexia, blinking in flabbergasted shock, lowered herself carefully onto a chair. "But, Felicity, you are wearing last season's dress!" She lowered her voice, in genuine fear that her sister might be deranged. "And *knitwear.*"

"Oh." Felicity wrapped the ghastly shawl tighter about her neck. "It was necessary."

Lady Maccon was only further shocked by such an unexpected statement. "Necessary? Necessary!"

"Well, yes, Alexia, do pay attention. Have you always been this frazzled, or is it your unfortunate condition?" Felicity lowered her voice conspiratorially. "Necessary because I have been *fraternizing.*"

"You have? With whom?" Alexia became suspicious. It was very late at night for an unmarried young lady of quality to be cavorting about unchaperoned, especially one who kept daylight hours and whose parents shunned association with the supernatural set.

"I am wearing *tweed.* With whom else? Some poor unfortunates of the middle class."

Lady Maccon would have none of it. "Oh, really, Felicity, you can hardly expect me to believe that you have had anything whatsoever to do with the lower orders."

"You may choose to believe it or not, sister."

Alexia wished for a return of her ability to stride about and loom threateningly. Sadly, striding was several months behind her, and should she attempt to loom, she would undoubtedly overbalance and pitch forward in graceless splendor. She settled for glaring daggers at her sibling. "Very well, then, what are you doing here? And how did you know to find me at Lord Akeldama's residence?"

"Mrs. Tunstell told me where to find you." Felicity looked with a critical eye at the golden magnificence surrounding her.

"Ivy? How did Ivy know?"

"Madame Lefoux told her."

"Oh, she did, did she? And how—"

"Apparently someone named Professor Lyall told Madame Lefoux your relocation was taking place this evening and that you would hole up at Lord Akeldama's, in case there were any orders pending delivery. Have you commissioned a new hat, sister? From that crass foreign female? Are you certain you should be patronizing her establishment after what happened in Scotland? And who is this Professor Lyall person? You haven't taken up with *academics,* have you? That cannot possibly be healthy. Education is terribly bad for the nerves, especially for a woman in your state."

Lady Maccon grappled for some appropriate response.

Felicity added, in a blatant attempt at distraction, "Speaking of which, you *have* gotten tremendously portly, haven't you? Is increasing supposed to cause you to swell quite so much as all that?"

Lady Maccon frowned. "I believe I have increased, as it were, to the maximum. You know me—I always insist on seeing a thing done as thoroughly as possible."

"Well, Mama says to make certain you don't get angry with anyone. The child will end up looking like him."

"Oh, really?"

"Yes, emotional mimicking they call it, and—"

"Well, that's no trouble. It will simply end up looking like my husband."

"But what if it is a female? Wouldn't that be horrible? She'd be all fuzzy and—"

Felicity would have continued but Lady Maccon lost her patience, a thing she was all too prone to misplacing. "Felicity, why are you visiting me?"

Miss Loontwill hedged. "This is quite the remarkable abode. I never did think I should ever see inside of a vampire hive. And so charming and gleaming and full of exquisite collections. Almost up to my standards."

"This is not a hive—there is no queen. Not in the technical definition of the word. I will not be so easily detoured, Felicity. Why have you shown up at such a time of night? And why would you undertake such pains to discover my whereabouts?"

Her sister shifted on the brocade settee, her blond head tilted to one side and a small frown creased her perfect forehead. She had not, Alexia noticed, modified her elaborately styled ringlets to match her lowbrow outfit. A row of perfect flat curls were gummed to her forehead in the very latest style.

"You have not paid the family much mind since your return to London."

Lady Maccon considered this accusation. "You must admit, I was made to feel rather unwelcome prior to my departure." *And that is putting it mildly.* Her family had always been a mite petty for her taste, even before they unilaterally decided to expel her from their midst at the most inconvenient time. Since her ill-fated trip to Scotland and subsequent dash across half the known world, she had simply elected to avoid the Loontwills as much as possible. As Lady Maccon, denizen of the night, who fraternized with werewolves; inventors; and, horror of horrors, actors, this was a relatively easy undertaking.

"Yes, but it's been positively months, sister! I did not think you the type to hold a grudge. Did you know Evylin has renewed her engagement to Captain Featherstone-haugh?"

Lady Maccon only stared at her sister, tapping one slipper lightly on the carpeted floor.

Miss Loontwill blushed, looking toward her and then away again. "I have become"—she paused as though searching for the correct way of phrasing it—"involved."

Alexia felt a tremor of real fear flutter through her breast. *Or is that indigestion?* "Oh, no, Felicity. Not with someone unsuitable? Not with someone middle class. Mama would never forgive you!"

Felicity stood and began to wander about the gilded room showing considerable agitation. "No, no, you misconstrue my meaning. I have become involved with my local chapter of the"—she lowered her voice dramatically—"National Society for Women's Suffrage."

If Lady Maccon hadn't already been sitting down, she would have had to sit at such a statement. "You want to vote? You? But you can't even decide which gloves to wear of a morning."

"I believe in the cause."

"Poppycock. You've never believed in anything in your whole life, except possibly the reliability of the French to predict next season's color palette."

"Well. Still."

"But, Felicity, really this is so very common. Couldn't you start up a ladies aid society or an embroidery social? *You?* Politically minded? I cannot deem such a thing feasible. It has only been five months since I met with you last, not five years, and even then you could not change your character so drastically. A feathered bonnet does not molt so easily as that."

At which juncture, and without any warning whatsoever, Lord Akeldama wafted into the room smelling of lemon and peppermint candy and sporting a playbill of some risqué comedy from the West End.

"Alexia, pudding, how *are* you faring this fine evening? Is moving house tragically unsettling? A relocation can be such a *trial* on one's finer feelings, I always find." He paused artfully on the threshold to put down his opera glasses, gloves, and top hat on a convenient sideboard. Then he raised his silver and sapphire monocle to one eye and regarded Felicity through it.

"Oh, dear me, pardon the intrusion." His keen eyes took in the dated dress and the effusive curls of Alexia's visitor. "Alexia, my dove, you have some sort of *company*?"

"Lord Akeldama. You remember my sister?"

The quizzing glass did not lower. "I do?"

"I believe you may have met one another at my wedding festivities?" Alexia was in no doubt that her esteemed host knew *exactly* who Felicity was from the very moment he entered the room—possibly before—but he did dearly love a performance, even if he had to put one on himself.

"I did?" The vampire was dressed to the height of fashion for an evening out. He wore a midnight-blue tailcoat and matched trousers, quite subdued for Lord Akeldama, or so it would seem at first glance. The careful observer soon noted that his satin waistcoat was silver, blue, and purple paisley in an excessively bold print, and he wore gloves and spats of the same material. Alexia had no idea how he thought to carry off such an outrageous ensemble. Whoever heard of patterned gloves, let alone spats? Then again, no ensemble had ever yet gotten the better of Lord Akeldama, nor was one likely to.

He certainly had the right to look askance at Felicity. "I did! Miss Loontwill? But you are so very much altered from when we last met. How has such a transformation been effected?"

Even Felicity had not the gumption to stand up to Lord Akeldama armed with a monocle. She crumbled in the face of the majestic authority of his perfectly tied and still fluffy—despite an evening's activities—cravat with its ostentatiously large sapphire pin. "Oh, well, you see, my lord, I've had a, ur, meeting and simply didn't have the time to change. I thought to catch my sister before she retired, on a matter of some delicacy."

Lord Akeldama did not take the hint. "Oh, yes?"

"Felicity has joined the National Society for Women's Suffrage," Alexia said placidly.

The vampire proved instantly helpful. "Oh, yes? I understand Lord Ambrose is a frequent contributor."

Alexia nodded her understanding at last. "Lord Ambrose, is it? Oh, Felicity, you do realize he is a vampire?"

Miss Loontwill tossed her curls. "Well, yes, but an *eligible* vampire." She glanced at Lord Akeldama from under her lashes. "And I am getting ever so old!"

He was instantly sympathetic. "Of course you are. You are already what? All of eighteen?"

Miss Loontwill sallied on. "But then I was quite taken with the rhetoric."

Alexia supposed a young lady so swayed by the Parisian fashion papers might be persuaded by a decent oratory display.

Felicity continued. "Why shouldn't we women vote? After all, it's not as though the gentlemen have done so wondrous a job of things with their stewardship. I do not intend to offend, my lord."

"No offense taken, my little *buttercup.*"

Uh-oh, thought Alexia, *Felicity has been given an epithet. Lord Akeldama likes her.*

The vampire continued. "I find such struggles adorably commendable."

Felicity began pacing about in a manner Alexia had to admit not unlike her own good self when seized with a particularly inspired argument. "My point precisely. Don't you want the vote, Alexia? You cannot be content to allow that buffoonish husband of yours to speak for you in matters political. Not after the way he has behaved in the past."

Alexia declined to mention at this juncture that she already had the vote, and it was one of only three on Queen Victoria's Shadow Council. Such a vote as this counted a good deal more than any popular ballot might. Instead, she spoke a different truth. "I have never given the matter much thought. But this still does not explain how you have ended up on Lord Akeldama's doorstep."

"Yes, little snowdrop." Lord Akeldama took up a perch on the arm of the settee, watching Felicity as a parrot might watch a drab little sparrow that had strayed into his domain.

Miss Loontwill took a deep breath. "It is really not my fault. Mama did not endorse my endeavors with regards to Lord Ambrose. So I have been liberating myself from the house after bedtime by means of the servant's entrance. You used to have some success with this approach, Alexia. Don't think I didn't know. I believed I could accomplish such a thing undetected."

Alexia was beginning to understand. "But you miscalculated. I had help. Floote's help. I cannot imagine Swilkins being sympathetic to the Ambrose cause."

Felicity grimaced in agreement. "No, you are perfectly correct. I did not realize how vital the approbation of one's butler is in allowing for nocturnal autonomy."

"So let us get to the crux of the matter. Has Mama tossed you out?"

Felicity got that look on her face that said whoever was at fault in this scenario it was probably Felicity. "Not exactly."

"Oh, Felicity, you didn't. You walked out?"

"I thought, since you were taking a house in town, perhaps I might come to stay with you for a little while. I understand the company will not be nearly so refined or elegant as that to which I am accustomed, but . . ."

Lord Akeldama's forehead creased ever so slightly at *that* statement.

Lady Maccon cogitated. She would like to encourage this new spirit of social-mindedness. If Felicity needed anything in her life, it was a cause. Then she might stop nitpicking everyone else. But if she stayed with them, she would have to be taken into their confidence regarding the living arrangements. And there was another thing to consider. Should Felicity be exposed to a werewolf pack in all its ever-changing and overexposed glory while still unmarried? *This is the last thing I need right now. I can't even see my own feet anymore. How can I see that my sister is properly chaperoned?* Alexia had found pregnancy relatively manageable, up to a point. That point having been some three weeks ago, at which juncture her natural reserves of control gave way to sentimentality. Only yesterday she had ended breakfast sobbing over the fried eggs because they *looked at her funny.* The pack had spent a good half hour trying to find a way to pacify her. Her husband was so worried he looked to start crying himself.

Alexia copped out, embarrassed to have to do so in front of Lord Akeldama. "I shall have to consult my husband on the subject."

The vampire jumped in with alacrity. "You could stay here with me, little bluebell."

Felicity brightened. "Oh, why—"

Lady Maccon put her foot down. "Absolutely not." Of all the people Felicity should not be overexposed to, it was Lord Akeldama, on the basis of cattiness alone. If left together for too long, the two of them might actually take over the civilized world, through sheer application of snide remarks.

A tap sounded on the drawing room door.

"Now what?" wondered Alexia.

"Come in! We are unquestionably *at home,*" sung out Lord Akeldama.

The door opened and Boots and Biffy entered. Both were looking dapper and well put together as behooved a current and former drone of Lord Akeldama's, although Biffy had a certain aura that Boots lacked. Biffy was still the same pleasant-mannered fellow with a partiality for modish attire and the figure to show it off, but something had altered. There was a slight smudge on his cheekbone that no drone of Lord Akeldama's would ever show to his master. However, seeing the two stand together, Alexia didn't think it was entirely the smudge's fault. There was no vampire sophistication to Biffy anymore—no high-society shine, no sharpened edge. Instead he sported a slight air of embarrassment that Alexia suspected all werewolves felt deep down. It sprung from the certain knowledge that once a month he would get naked and turn into a slavering beast whether he liked it or not.

Lord Akeldama's inquisitive expression did not waver. "*Darlings!*" he said to the two of them, as though he had not seen them in years. "What exciting tidbits have you brought me?"

Miss Loontwill looked with interest at the two young men. "Oh," she said, "I remember you! You helped my sister plan her nuptials. You had that marvelous idea about a groom's cake. Stylish, two cakes. Especially for my sister's wedding—she is so very fond of food."

Biffy knew his duty and hurried forward to bow over Felicity's proffered hand. "Sandalio de Rabiffano, at your service, miss. How do you do?"

Alexia, who until that moment had never before heard Biffy's real name, gave Lord Akeldama a startled look. The vampire stood and wandered innocently over to her chair. "Spectacularly Spanish, wouldn't you say? Moorish blood some ways back."

She nodded sagely.

Biffy returned Felicity's hand. "I cannot take credit for the cake, miss. It's an odd little American custom."

Felicity flirted outrageously. "Oh, well, we won't tell anyone *that*, now, will we? Are you still in Lord Akeldama's employ?"

A brief flash of hurt passed over Biffy's pleasant face. "No, miss. I've been transferred to your sister's household."

Miss Loontwill clearly thought this a most beneficial arrangement. "Oh, have you, *indeed*?"

Alexia interrupted any continued flirtation. "Felicity, go next door and wait for me in the front parlor. Order tea if you must. When my husband returns, I'll discuss your request with him."

Felicity opened her mouth again.

"Now, Felicity." Lady Maccon was at her most dictatorial.

Much to everyone's surprise, including Felicity's, Felicity went.

Lord Akeldama tilted his head at Boots and gave a little nod after the retreating girl. With no verbal exchange required, Boots trotted obediently after Felicity. Biffy looked on wistfully. Alexia surmised that he was not yearning for Felicity's continued company but was regretting the fact that he could no longer obey Lord Akeldama's commands.

She brought him back around sharply. No sense in letting him dwell. "Biffy, did you have something to tell me or Lord Akeldama?"

"You, my lady. I am pleased to report that you have been successfully moved. The new house awaits your perusal and, hopefully, approval."

"Excellent! I should—Oh wait. Lord Akeldama, I keep meaning to ask. And while I'm in your company, if I may?"

"Yes, my little *syllabub*?"

"Do you recall, I was describing those porcupines to you? Or overgrown hedgehogs, or whatever their species inclination, from several nights ago? I was thinking, they were also ever so slightly vampiric in propensity. Their speed and their old dark blood and their susceptibility to the lapis solaris. Is that possible, do you think—vampire porcupines?"

Lord Akeldama's eyes lit with amusement. "Oh, my dearest girl, what *will* you think of next? Weregoats? Be on your guard, for at full moon they shall creep into your coat closet and eat up all your shoes!"

Biffy hid a smile.

Alexia was not in the mood to be mocked.

Lord Akeldama recovered his much-vaunted poise. "My darling *toffee button*, you can be quite the widgeon upon occasion. Animals do not have souls. How could they possibly? Next thing you know, I'll be petitioning Countess Nadasdy to bite old fatty there so I can have company into my dotage." He gestured to his cat. The chubby creature had delusions of being a vicious hunter but could never master anything more taxing than a pillow tassel. Or, on one recent and memorable occasion, one of Ivy's hats. Lady Maccon shuddered at the recollection. Why had she thought she could bring Ivy to tea with a vampire? Her dearest friend may have taken to the stage of late, but she was still not ready for intimate exposure to Lord Akeldama's brand of drama. Nor was Lord Akeldama entirely capable of withstanding intimate exposure to one of Ivy's hats. After that tea, Alexia had been forced to admit that Lord Akeldama and Ivy Tunstell were like plaid and brocade, utterly incompatible even in complementary colors.

At which juncture someone else came into Lord Akeldama's drawing room, only this time without announcement of any kind save a minor bellow.

"Good gracious me," said Lord Akeldama, sounding like some dowager countess of old Georgian inclination. "What has my house become? Charring Cross Station?"

Biffy looked to Lady Maccon, resplendent in her tent-like gown of eyelet lace and blue satin bows. "More akin to a dirigible landing green, I should think, my lord."

Alexia, who found her condition even more ridiculous than anyone else, was moved to smile at such a comparison. She had, of late, been feeling inflated.

Lord Akeldama chuckled softly. "Ah, Biffy, I have missed you, my dove."

The individual who had entered, unannounced and unbidden, observed this exchange with a frown.

Lord Akeldama turned upon him with mild censure in his sharp blue eyes. "Lord Maccon, if you are to stay here, and I believe *that* is settled for the moment, we really must train you in the fine art of knocking before entering a room."

The earl was gruff in his embarrassment. "Oh, yes. Upon occasion, I find it hard to remember details of etiquette." He swirled his cloak off. It landed on the back of a side chair before sliding off and falling to the floor.

Lord Akeldama shuddered.

"Lord Akeldama. Wife. Pup." Lord Maccon nodded. His tawny eyes concerned, he moved to bend over Alexia. "Everything still corked up?" he asked her in one ear.

"Yes, yes, don't fuss, Conall." Alexia would have none of it.

"Everything else squared away?"

"I was just about to perform the inspection. Hoist me up, would you, please?"

The earl grinned, braced himself, and offered her one massive hand. Alexia grasped it in both of hers and he levered. At her preternatural touch, he lost supernatural strength, but he was still powerful enough to handle Alexia—even in her inflated dirigible state.

"We will have to be *seen* going next door, I suppose. And we will have to determine a way to sneak back into this house later tonight."

"Such skulking and folderol, all for the sake of appearances," grumbled Lord Maccon.

Alexia bristled. She'd been through quite a hellish time when her husband had booted her from his bed and company. Society had ostracized her all because she *appeared* to have been indiscreet. "Appearances are everything!"

"Hear, *hear,*" agreed Lord Akeldama.

"Very well, wife. We must determine how to get you from our balcony to Lord Akeldama's."

He wore an expression Alexia suspected greatly. She glared at him. "You will find me a gangplank, thank you very much. I will not be flung, husband."

Lord Maccon looked a tad surprised at that. "Did I indicate I intended any such activity?"

"No, but I *know* how you get."

Conall was nonplussed by such an unwarranted accusation.

Alexia continued. "Oh, yes, and I should warn you. There's a surprise waiting for us in our new front parlor."

Lord Maccon grinned wolfishly. "Is it a nice surprise?"

"Only if you're in a very good mood," hedged his wife.

* * *

The ghost was in that space again, that insubstantial void. She thought she might float there forever if she could simply stay still. Still as death.

But reality intruded. Reality from her own mind, however little of it was left. "You have to tell someone. You have to tell them. This is wrong. You are mad and yet even you know this is wrong. Put a stop to it. You have to tell."

Oh, how inconvenient, when one's own brain starts issuing instructions.

"Who can I tell? Who can I tell? I am only a hen in a chicken coop."

"Tell someone who can do something. Tell the soulless girl."

"Her? But I don't even like her."

"That's no excuse. You don't like anyone."

The ghost hated it when she was sensible with herself.

CHAPTER THREE

Matters Ghostly

"Oh, really, must you?" was Lord Maccon's considered opinion, expressed to his wife upon seeing her sister in residence, as if Felicity were some sort of unfortunate digestive complaint Alexia had recently developed.

Lady Maccon ignored her sister, who sat waiting patiently in the parlor, and instead took in her new surroundings. The drones and the werewolves had done Woolsey Pack proud. Their new town house was quite filled to bursting with tasteful furniture, pleasingly arranged and minimally decorated. As the abode was intended to serve as a way station for those of the pack who had business in town, most personal items and vital survival necessities such as dungeons and clavigers were left back at Woolsey Castle. The result was that the new house had the look of a gentleman's club, rather than a private residence (but a nicely up-market gentleman's club). Lord Maccon muttered that it reminded him of one of the sitting rooms in the House of Lords. But he was muttering for the sake of it, and everyone knew it. Thick curtains kept harmful sunlight out, and thick, plush rugs kept heavy footfalls and claw scrapes to a minimum.

For the time being, Floote was to resume the post of butler to the secondary residence. He had not even batted an eye at this temporary demotion back to domestic staff. Alexia suspected that he had missed his former authority over the household and accompanying ability to monitor all business occurring within it. Personal secretary might be a higher position, but it did not carry with it quite the range of a butler's command over gossip.

The front parlor, where Felicity sat, was decked out in rich chocolate brown leather and cream twill, with only a small touch of brass here and there for accent—the filigree of a gas lamp, the fringe on a tablecloth, a large Oriental floor vase to hold Alexia's parasols, and a periscopic shoe-drying stand in front of the fireplace.

It was exactly the opposite of Lord Akeldama's brocade-and-gilt splendor.

Lady Maccon was impressed. "Floote, where did you find such lovely furnishings at such short notice?"

Floote looked at Alexia as though she had asked him the secrets of his daily ablutions.

"Now, now, wife. If Floote prefers to be thought a conjurer, who are we to inquire as to his sleight of hand? We must preserve a sense of wonder and faith, eh, Floote?" Lord Maccon slapped the dignified gentleman amiably on the back.

Floote sniffed. "If you say so, sir."

Lord Maccon turned to his wife's sister, sitting in demure silence and drab gray, both so utterly out of character as to garner even Lord Maccon's notice.

"Miss Felicity, has somebody died?"

Felicity stood and bobbed a curtsy at the earl. "Not that I am aware, my lord. Thank you for inquiring. How do you do?"

"There's something rather singular about your appearance this evening, isn't there? Have you done something different with your hair?"

"No, my lord. I'm simply a tad underdressed for visiting. Only, I had a favor to ask my sister and it couldn't possibly wait."

"Oh, did you?" The earl turned his tawny eyes on his wife.

Alexia tipped her chin up and to one side. "She wants to come stay with us."

"Oh, she does, does she?"

"Here."

"Here?" Conall took his wife's point exactly. They could hardly have Felicity stay in their new town house and not actually be living there themselves. What if that information got out? Felicity would be known to have resided with a pack of werewolves and no chaperone.

"Why not at Woolsey? Bit of country air? Looks like she could do with it." Lord Maccon grappled for a better solution.

"Felicity has involved herself in some"—Alexia paused—"questionable charitable work here in town. She seems to believe she may require our protection."

Lord Maccon looked confused. As well he might. "Protection . . . protection from whom?"

"My mother," replied his wife, with meaning.

Lord Maccon could understand *that* and was about to demand additional details when a ghost materialized up through the plush carpet next to him.

Under ordinary circumstances, ghosts were too polite to simply appear in the middle of a conversation. The better-behaved specters took pains to drift into front hallways at the very least, where a footman might notice and inquire as to their business. In a startling fashion, this one wafted into existence out of the center of the new rug, directly through the bouquet of flowers depicted there.

Lord Maccon exclaimed. Lady Maccon let out a little gasp and firmed her grip on her parasol. Floote raised one eyebrow. Felicity fainted.

Alexia and Conall looked at each other for a moment and then left Felicity slumped over in her chair by mutual and silent agreement. Alexia's parasol did have a small bottle of smelling salts among its many secret accoutrements, but this ghost required immediate attention with no time to revive troublesome sisters. The Maccons turned the full force of their collective attention onto the specter before them.

"Floote," asked Lady Maccon slowly, so as not to startle the creature, "did we know this house came with a ghost? Was that in the leasing documentation?"

"I don't believe so, madam. Let me ascertain the particulars." Floote glided off to find the deeds.

The ghost in question was rather fuzzy around the edges and not entirely cohesive in the middle either. She must be close to poltergeist state. When she began speaking, it became abundantly clear that this was indeed the case, for the ghost's mental faculties were degenerated and her voice was high and breathy, sounding as though it emanated from some distance away.

"Maccon? Or was it bacon? I used to like bacon. Very salty." The ghost paused and twirled about, trailing misty tendrils through the air. These eddied in Lady Maccon's direction, pulled by the preternatural's attraction for ambient aether. "Message. Missive. Mutton. Didn't like mutton—chewy. Wait! Urgent. Or was that pungent? Important. Impossible. Information."

Lady Maccon looked at her husband curiously. "One of BUR's?"

The Bureau of Unnatural Registry kept a number of mobile ghost agents—exhumed and preserved bodies with tethered specters that could be placed in select locales or near key public institutions for information-gathering purposes. They took pains to have a noncorporeal communication network in place, where each ghost's tether crossed over the limits of at least one other's. This stretched the length and breadth of London, although it was not able to cover the city in its entirety. Of course, it had to be updated as its members went insane, but such maintenance was practically second nature to BUR's spectral custodians.

The werewolf shook his shaggy head. "Not that I know of, my dear. I'd have to look at the registry to be certain. I've met most of our noncorporeal recruits at least once. Don't think this one is under contract at all, or someone would be taking far better care of the body." He braced himself in front of the ghost, arms stiff by his side. "Hallo? Listen up. Where are you tethered? This house? Where is your corpse? It needs looking to. You are drifting, young lady. Drifting."

The ghost looked at him in puzzled annoyance and floated up and down. "Not important. Not important at all. Message, that's what's important. What was it? Accents, accents, everywhere these days. London's full of foreigners. And curry. Who let in the curry?"

"That's the message?" Lady Maccon didn't like to be out of the loop, even if the loop was inside some nonsensical ghost's head.

The ghost whirled to face Alexia. "No, no, no. Now, no, what? Oh, yes. Are you Alexia Macaroon?"

Alexia didn't know how to respond to *that*, so she nodded.

Conall, useless beast, started laughing. "Macaroon? I love it!"

Both Alexia and the ghost ignored him. All of the ghost's wavering attention was now focused on Lady Maccon. "Tarabitty? Tarabotti. Daughter of? Dead. Soulless. Problem? Pudding!"

Alexia wondered whether all this verbal rigmarole was related to her father or to herself, but she supposed in either context it was accurate enough. "The same."

The ghost twirled about in midair, pleased with herself. "Message for you." She paused, worried and confused. "Custard. No. Conscription. No. Conspiracy. To kill, to kill . . ."

"Me?" Alexia hazarded a guess. She thought it might be a safe bet: someone was usually trying to kill her.

The ghost became agitated, straining at her invisible tether and vibrating slightly. "No, no, no. Not you. But someone. Something?" She brightened suddenly. "The queen. Kill the queen." The specter began to sing. "Kill the queen! Kill the queen! Kill the quee-een!"

Lord Maccon stopped smiling. "Ah, that's torn it."

"Good. Yes? That's all. Bye-bye, living people." The ghost then sank down through the floor of their new parlor and vanished, presumably back the way she had come.

Floote returned to the room at that juncture to find a silently shocked Lord and Lady Maccon staring at each other.

"No documented apparitions come tethered to this house, madam."

"Thank you, Floote. I suppose we should see to . . . ?" Alexia did not need to continue. The ever-resourceful Floote was already tending to Felicity with a scented handkerchief.

Lady Maccon turned to her husband. "And you should—"

He was already clapping his top hat to his head. "On my way, wife. She has to be within tether radius of this house. There should be a record of her somewhere in BUR's files. I'm taking Professor Lyall and Biffy with me."

Alexia nodded. "Don't be out too late. Someone needs to help get me back into Lord Akeldama's house before morning, and you know all I seem to do these days is sleep."

Her husband swept over in the manner of some Gothic hero, cloak flapping, and administered a loud kiss both to her and then, to her utter embarrassment, to her protruding stomach before dashing off. Luckily, Floote was still seeing to Felicity, so neither witnessed the excessive display of affection.

"I suppose that makes Felicity the least of our concerns."

The sun had just set, and the Maccons were awake, across the temporary gangplank from Lord Akeldama's house, and downstairs in their own dining room. The conversation had not changed from that of the night before; it had only paused for Conall to conduct some slapdash investigations and then catch half a day's sleep.

Lord Maccon glanced up from his repast. "We must take any threat against the queen seriously, my dear. Even if my efforts so far have proved unproductive, that does not mean we can treat the ravings of a ghost with flippancy."

"You believe I am not concerned? I've alerted the Shadow Council. We have a special meeting called for this very evening."

Lord Maccon looked disgruntled. "Now, Alexia, should you be involving yourself in this matter at such a late stage?"

"What? The rumor has only just been reported! I understand you and Lyall got lengths ahead yesterday after I went to bed, but I hardly think—"

"No, wife. I mean to say, you are not exactly up to your usual galavanting about London with parasol at the ready, now, are you?"

Alexia glanced down at her overstuffed belly and then got *that* look on her face. "I am entirely capable."

"Of what, waddling up to someone and ruthlessly bumping into them?"

Lady Maccon glared. "I assure you, *husband,* that while the rest of me may be moving more slowly than has previously been my custom, there is nothing whatsoever wrong with my mental capacities. I can manage!"

"Now, Alexia, *please* be reasonable."

Lady Maccon was willing to concede somewhat due to the nature of her state. "I promise that I will not take any unnecessary risks."

Her husband did not miss the fact that this statement would have to bow to his wife's definition of the term *necessary.* He was, therefore, not at all reassured. "At least take one of the pups with you on your investigations."

Lady Maccon narrowed her eyes.

The earl wheedled. "I should feel much better knowing someone had care of your physical safety. Even if the vampires are abstaining—and we've no guarantee yet that they are—you do tend to get yourself into certain predicaments. Now, it's not that I think you are incapable, my dear, simply that you are currently much less mobile."

Alexia did have to admit his reasoning. "Very well. But if I am to troll about with a companion, I want it to be Biffy."

The earl did not approve this selection at all. "Biffy! He's a new pup. He can't even control the change. What good could he possibly be?"

"It's Biffy or nobody." *Typical of my husband to see only Biffy's limitations as a werewolf and not his admirable abilities as a human.*

For the young dandy was, indeed, quite accomplished. Much to Lord Maccon's disgust, he had taken over many of the duties of lady's maid to his new mistress. Alexia had never bothered to hire a replacement for Angelique. Biffy's taste was impeccable, and he had a real eye for which hairstyles and fabrics would suit her best—better than Angelique, who had been good but rather more daringly French than Lady Maccon liked. Biffy, for all his audacious inclinations when it came to his own apparel, knew how to be sensible when it came to a lady who scurried around whacking at automatons and climbing into ornithopters.

"It isn't a wise choice." Lord Maccon's jaw was set.

No one else had yet joined them at the dining table. It was a rare thing in a pack to enjoy any privacy outside the bedroom. Alexia took advantage of their seclusion. She scooted toward her husband and rested her hand atop his on the fine lace tablecloth.

"Biffy has had Lord Akeldama's training. That is a skill set that branches away from being merely a dab hand with the curling tongs."

The earl snorted.

"I am not only thinking of my own comfort in this matter. He needs some kind of distraction, Conall. Haven't you noticed? Five months and he's still not settled."

The earl twisted his lips slightly to one side. He had noticed. Of course he had. He noticed everything about his wolves. It was part of his most essential being, to hold the pack together as a single cohesive entity. Alexia had read the papers; scientists called it the soul's intrinsic cross-linking of the essential humors, the enmatterment of aether. But she could also guess the truth of it: that just as vampires and ghosts became tethered to a place, so werewolves became tethered to a pack. Biffy's all too frequent melancholy must hurt Conall terribly.

"How will allowing him to accompany you help?"

"Am I not also part of this pack?"

"Ah." The earl turned his hand over to grip his wife's in a compliant caress.

"If you ask me, it is not so much Biffy who cannot find his place as Woolsey not giving him the right place to find. You are all thinking of him as you would any new werewolf. He's not, you understand? He's different."

Conall, remarkably, did not jump immediately to the defensive. "Yes, I'm aware. Randolph and I were recently discussing this very thing. But it cannot simply be a matter of Biffy's preferences. We werewolves are as experimental in our tastes as the vampires, if a little more reserved about the expression of them. And there's always Adelphus. He's willing."

Alexia made a disgusted noise. "Adelphus is always willing. Biffy does not need a lover, husband—he needs a purpose. This is a matter of culture. Biffy has come to you out of vampire culture. *Lord Akeldama's* vampire culture."

"So what do you recommend?"

"Woolsey has managed to accept me into its midst and I am by no means standard werewolf fare." Alexia played with her husband's fingers, threading and unthreading them with her own.

"But you are female."

"Exactly!"

"You are suggesting we treat Biffy as if he were a woman?"

"I am suggesting that you think about him as if he had married in from the outside."

Lord Maccon gave this due consideration and then nodded slowly.

Lady Maccon realized he must be very troubled by Biffy's unhappiness to listen to her suggestions with so few protestations.

Alexia squeezed his hand once more and then let go, returning to her meal of apple fritter and boiled arrowroot pudding with melted butter and currant jelly. Of late, her taste in comestibles had leaned ever more in the saccharine direction. Now she ate almost exclusively of the pudding course at any meal. "You think there's a chance you might lose him, don't you?"

Her husband did not answer her, which was an admission in and of itself. Instead he busily began tackling a veritable heap of fried veal cutlets.

Lady Maccon chose her next words with care. "How quickly can loner status be established?" She did not want to be perceived as doubting her husband's Alpha abilities. Men, even immortal ones, had fragile egos on certain subjects. Such egos could be as delicate and as messy as puff pastry. Though rather less palatable with tea. *Ooh, tea.*

"Wolves can go solitary at any time, but it is usually for a specific reason and occurs within the first few years of metamorphosis. Howlers say it has something to do with early bonding to the Alpha. Often it means the unbonded is too much Alpha himself. I don't believe Biffy falls into this category, but that is the only thing currently in our favor."

Alexia thought she spotted the real source of her husband's concern. "If Biffy becomes a loner, you don't believe he would survive. Do you?"

"Loners are unstable. They brawl constantly. Our new pup is not a fighter, not like that." Her husband's lovely eyes were pained and guilty. This mess with Biffy was his fault. Unintentionally his fault, but Lord Conall Maccon was not the kind of gentleman who shifted blame merely because they were all victims of circumstance.

Alexia took a breath and then dove for the kill. "Then you really should give him to me for a while. I'll see what I can do. Remember, I can tame him if I have to, if he loses control and goes to wolf." She wiggled ungloved fingers at her husband.

"Very well, wife. But you are to check in with either me or Randolph as to his progress."

As the earl said this, Professor Lyall wandered into the dining room. The Beta was his usual unassuming self—his sandy hair neatly combed; his angular features arranged into a nonthreatening expression; his demeanor quiet, self-effacing, and utterly forgettable. It was an aura that Alexia was beginning to suspect Professor Lyall had cultivated for decades.

"Good evening, my lady, my lord." The Beta assumed his seat.

A maid appeared at his elbow with fresh tea and the evening's paper. Professor Lyall was the type of man to have *that* kind of relationship with the domestic staff. Even newly hired and after only a day's residence, they were already providing exactly what he required without need for any time-wasting orders. Between him, Floote, and Biffy, there would never be a single upset in the running of the Maccon household. It was a good thing, too, for the indomitable Lady Maccon had other things to occupy her time and attention. The running of her household was best left to the gentlemen. Although, she did indicate to the maid that she, too, required tea.

"Professor Lyall, how are you this evening?" Alexia saw no reason why familiarity with an individual ought to breed familiarity of manner, except with her husband, of course. Even though she had been living, off and on, among the Woolsey Pack for almost a year, she never relaxed on courtesy.

"Tolerably well, my lady, tolerably well." Nor, indeed, did Professor Lyall, who was remarkably civilized for a werewolf and seemed particularly respectful of all codes of politeness and gracefulness of manner.

Now that she had both of them at her table, Lady Maccon directed the two werewolves back onto the weighty matter of the queen's life. "So, gentlemen, anything come out of BUR on the threat?"

"Not an aetheric sausage," complained the earl.

Professor Lyall shook his head.

"Must be the vampires," said Lord Maccon.

"Now, husband, why would you say that?"

"Isn't it always the vampires?"

"No, sometimes it's the scientists." Lady Maccon was referring obliquely to the disbanded Hypocras Club. "And sometimes it's the church." Now she was thinking of the Templars. "And sometimes it's the werewolves."

"Well, I say!" Lord Maccon stuffed another cutlet into his mouth. "I can't imagine you actually defending the vampires. They've been trying to kill you for months."

"Oh, Conall, do swallow first. Then speak. What kind of example is that for our child?"

The earl looked around as though trying to see if the little being had somehow been born without his notice and was now staring at him with an eye toward modeling its behavior upon his.

Lady Maccon continued. "Simply because the vampires are perennially trying to murder me doesn't mean they are trying to murder the queen as well, now, does it? One would think their resources would be somewhat taxed, if nothing else. Besides, what could possibly be their motive? The queen is a progressive." She was moved to defend her stance further. "I thought your lot was supposed to have long memories. Correct me if I'm wrong, Professor Lyall, but didn't the last major threat to Queen Victoria's life emanate from the Kingair Pack?"

"Really, Lady Maccon, couldn't it wait until I've at least finished my first cup of tea?" The Beta looked put upon.

Alexia said nothing.

Professor Lyall put down his tea pointedly. "There was that over-eager Pate fellow with the walking stick some twenty years ago or so. Completely mutilated Her Majesty's favorite bonnet. Shocking behavior. And there was that disgruntled Irishman with the unloaded pistol before that." He helped himself to a small serving of smoked kipper but paused before digging in. "And the reputed incident a few years back with John Brown." The Beta considered his kipper as though it held all the answers. "Come to think on it, they've all been remarkably ineffective."

Her husband snorted. "Notoriety mongers, the lot of them."

Alexia puffed out her cheeks. "You know what I mean. Those were all isolated incidents. I mean planned cohesive plots backed by serious intent."

The maid reappeared with more tea and an extra cup for Lord Maccon. Who sneered at it.

Professor Lyall's face sobered. "Then, no, Kingair was the last."

A delicate subject, indeed, as Kingair was Lord Maccon's former pack, and they had betrayed him in order to attempt the ghastly deed. He had killed his Beta and moved to London to challenge for Woolsey as a result. Like politics, or personal dressing habits, this was not proper meal-time conversation.

Professor Lyall, a man of much delicacy, seemed to find the subject particularly uncomfortable. After all, Woolsey had ultimately benefited from the assassination attempt. Their previous Alpha was reputed to be a man of petty disposition and profound temper, and Lord Maccon was considered one of the better werewolf leaders. The best, if Alexia had anything to say on the subject. Which she did. Often.

The bell sounded in the front entranceway, and Professor Lyall glanced up gratefully. There came a rumble of voices as Floote answered the door. Alexia couldn't make out who it was, but her husband and his Beta had werewolf hearing and their reactions—a slight smile from Lyall and a disgusted frown from Conall—gave her a pretty decent idea.

"Peaches!" Lord Akeldama wafted in on a wave of Bond Street's best pomade and a lemon-scented eau de toilette. Alexia's pregnancy had had a strange effect on her sense of smell, rendering it far more acute. She imagined she was getting some limited idea of how werewolves felt with their supernatural abilities in that arena.

The vampire, resplendent in a silver tailcoat and bright yellow waistcoat only one or two shades darker than his hair, paused in the doorway. "Isn't this delightfully *cozy*? How perfectly *splendid* that I can simply pop next door and visit you all à la table!"

"And how nice that you are not a hive queen to be so entirely confined to your own home," replied Alexia. She gestured for the vampire to draw up a chair. He did so with a flourish, shaking out his napkin and placing it in his lap, although he would, everyone knew, take no food.

Professor Lyall tilted his head at the teapot. When Lord Akeldama nodded, the Beta poured him out a cup. "Milk?"

"Lemon, if you would be so kind."

Lyall raised his eyebrows in shock but signaled one of the maids to run and see to this odd request. "I thought most vampires didn't tolerate citrus."

"Dolly, my pet, I am most assuredly not *most vampires.*"

Professor Lyall did not pursue this, as he had a more pressing question in mind. "It has occurred to me to worry about this scheme of ours. I understand it is a delicate subject, but this last winter you did swarm, did you not? Because of that spot of bother with Biffy being stuck under the Thames."

"Yes, poppet, what of it?"

"That swarming isn't going to hinder the effectiveness of your residency now, is it? You understand I ask only with a mind toward the safety of the child and because I've no records pertaining to the consequences of a rove swarming. No insult is intended."

Lord Akeldama grinned. "Dolly, such a *careful* little creature, aren't you? But fret not—my house isn't technically a hive. I'm not bound by the same kinds of instincts. I can return to my previous residence without psychological upset. Besides, that was half a year ago. I'm well recovered from the experience by now."

Lyall did not look entirely convinced.

Lord Akeldama changed the subject. "So what say you, all my *lupine darlings*, to this new threat?"

Lord Maccon looked with shock at his Beta. "Randolph, you didn't!"

Professor Lyall did not flinch. "Of course not."

"Wife?"

Alexia swallowed her bit of pudding. "He knows because, well, this *is* Lord Akeldama. You are going to have to get accustomed to it, my dear."

"Thank you, darling *plum nubbin*, for your faith in my meager resources."

"Of course, my lord. So?"

"Ah, *dandelion fluff,* I regret that I have not yet formed a ready opinion as to the nature and origin of these latest twitterings."

A footman appeared with the lemon, and Lyall poured the vampire a cup of tea. Lord Akeldama sipped it delicately.

Lord Maccon snorted. "You haven't lacked for a ready opinion in the whole of your very long life."

The vampire tittered at that. "True, but those expressed traditionally concern matters of dress, not politics."

Floote came in with Alexia's dispatch case. "You're due at the palace shortly, madam."

"Oh, my, yes, look at the time. Thank you, Floote. My parasol?"

"Here, madam."

"And perhaps a bite to take along?"

Floote handed her a sausage roll wrapped in checked cloth, having anticipated just such a request.

"Oh, thank you, Floote."

The earl looked up hopefully. Wordlessly Floote handed him another sausage roll. The earl downed it in two satisfied bites, even though he had just finished a rather large meal. Floote and Lyall exchanged knowing looks. It had become quite the task to keep both Lord and Lady Maccon fed these days.

Lady Maccon leaned forward onto the table, bracing against it with both hands, pleased to live in a household that did not favor the spindly furniture so in vogue with ladies of quality. By dint of some sizable effort, she managed to almost hoist herself to her feet before losing her balance and lurching back down.

"Oh, for goodness' sake," she cried out in abject frustration. The gentlemen all leaped to her assistance. Lord Maccon made it to her first. Which was probably a good thing. With her preternatural touch, none of the others present would have been of any use. They were all too slight in their mortal forms to handle her clumsiness.

Having gained her feet and some measure of her dignity, Alexia said, "I really must say, I am finding my own proportions quite vulgar."

Lord Maccon hid his smile. "Not all that much longer, my dear."

Alexia hated it when he called her his dear. "Really, it can't occur soon enough." She waved off Floote's offer of a cloak and accepted a light shawl instead. It was plenty warm enough even without the wrap, but formalities must be observed. Then she gathered up her case and parasol.

Biffy appeared at her elbow, bloodred tailcoat in place, pure white cravat emphasizing his pleasant features, and matched red top hat on his head. He may have had to sacrifice a good many things to take up his new role as a werewolf, but he had refused to sacrifice his tailor.

"I am to act as escort this evening, my lady?"

"Oh, yes, Biffy dear. How did you know?"

Biffy gave her a look remarkably similar to the one always worn by Lord Akeldama when he was asked such a question.

Alexia nodded her understanding and then looked to the vampire. "Share a carriage, my lord potentate?"

"Why not?" Lord Akeldama sucked down the last of his tea, stood, performed an exaggerated bow to the two werewolves still at the dining table, and offered his arm to Alexia. She took it and they swept from the room, Biffy trailing faithfully after.

As they left, Lady Maccon heard her husband say to Lyall, "How long do you imagine we are going to have to keep up this place of residence?"

"Until the child is grown, I suppose," responded the Beta.

"God's teeth, it's going to be a long sixteen years."

"I imagine you'll survive it relatively unscathed, my lord."

"Randolph, you and I both know there are things far worse than death."

Alexia and Lord Akeldama exchanged smiles.

* * *

"Did you tell her?" asked the first ghost, stretched as far as she could, shimmering in and out of existence with the strain of her extended tether.

"I told her." The second ghost bobbed up and down in the air above the street. She was a little more substantial, a little closer to home. "I told her what I could remember. I told her to put a stop to it. Are we done now?"

They were both lucid, strangely lucid, for two so near the end of enmatterment. It was as though the afterlife were giving them this one chance to fix things.

"We're done," said the first ghost. Both of them knew she wasn't referring to their plan or to their relationship but to their inevitable demise. "Now only I must wait."

CHAPTER FOUR

Where Tethered Specters Meet

Lady Maccon, muhjah, and Lord Akeldama, potentate, were allowed through the entrance to Buckingham Palace with very little ceremony. It was not one of their scheduled visits, but Lord Akeldama and Lady Maccon were regulars and, as such, required only minimal perusal. They were also favorites, or Lady Maccon was. Lord Akeldama was generally regarded by members of both the military and the constabulary with whom he had congress as *challenging in large doses.* However, the castle guards were diligent, hardworking lads with a care to their royal duties. Lady Maccon's neck was checked for bite marks and her dispatch case for illegal steam devices. She yielded up her parasol without question. Alexia would rather have them confiscate it than have to explain how it worked. Lord Akeldama's clothing was far too tight for any hidden weaponry, but the guards did check his top hat before allowing him to proceed.

Biffy was not permitted entrance, despite the extraordinarily royal color of his jacket. He was pronounced, with much forcefulness, as being *not on the register.* However, Biffy was of such a pleasant disposition that he was content to remain behind at the entrance for the duration of the council. Alexia distinctly heard him say, in lilting tones, "Such a big hat you have, Lieutenant Funtington!" to one of the stoic-faced palace guards.

"Incorrigible child," she said to Lord Akeldama with a smile of affection.

"I would say I taught him everything he knows, but Biffy's a natural." Lord Akeldama nodded his approval.

They made their way into the meeting chamber to find the dewan already pacing about in a tizzy. Queen Victoria was not there. The queen did not attend most Shadow Councils. She expected to be informed of anything significant but otherwise was uninterested in the minutiae.

"Threat to the queen, I hear." The dewan was a large gruff individual who reminded Alexia of her husband, in character if not in appearance or manner. Not that she would ever tell this to either of them. He held state as the Earl of Upper Slaughter but no longer boasted the country seat to accompany the title. Similarly, he had the demeanor of a leader without a pack. This freedom from responsibility both as lord and Alpha made the dewan the most powerful autonomous werewolf in all England. And, even though he was not quite as big as Conall Maccon, it was generally acknowledged by all—including said Conall Maccon—that Lord Slaughter could give even that most feared of Alphas a fight for his fur. Thus, the dewan and Lord Maccon tended to circle each other, both in and out of polite company, rather like two tugboats drawing freight—widely and with much tooting.

"Indeed." Alexia's practical side was pleased at the two Alphas' respective similarities, because constant exposure to her husband had given her the necessary skills for handling the dewan.

She and Lord Akeldama wafted—or, in Alexia's case, toddled—in and took seats at the long mahogany table, leaving the dewan to continue his pacing unmolested.

Lady Maccon snapped open the lid of her dispatch case and extracted her harmonic auditory resonance disruptor. The spiky little apparatus looked like two tuning forks sticking out of a bit of crystal. While Alexia rummaged about for further necessities, Lord Akeldama tapped one fork with his finger, waited a moment, and then tapped the other. This resulted in a discordant, low-pitched humming, amplified by the crystal. It would prevent their conversation from being overheard.

"Serious, do you think? This threat? One to be taken seriously?"

The dewan ought to have been handsome with his dark hair and deep-set eyes, but his mouth was a little too full, the cleft in his chin a little too pronounced, and his mustache and muttonchops excessively aggressive. This facial hair had initially given Alexia much distress. Why? was the question. Most gentlemen went clean-shaven into immortality's long night. Poor Biffy had had to wait in scruffy purgatory until Alexia returned home from her European tour and turned him mortal long enough to shave. Professor Lyall had reportedly been kind and sympathetic during that most trying of times.

Lady Maccon took out her notes on the ghostly event and closed her dispatch case. She had attempted to remember and transcribe everything the specter said to her. "The threat came to me via a ghost messenger. I think we must treat it with slightly greater significance than we would some blundering daylight opportunist with a taste to become the next darling of the anarchist press."

Lord Akeldama added, "And, my *sweetlings*, if a supernatural told of the threat to a preternatural, it is likely that something or someone equally unnatural is involved."

The dewan sucked at his teeth. "Very serious."

Lord Akeldama sat back and rested the tips of his long white fingers on the table before him. It was a gesture oddly reminiscent of his predecessor.

Alexia continued. "Greatly mysterious as well. My husband says that BUR records show nothing on this ghost. We've been unable to locate either her or her corpse since she delivered the message." Alexia had no compunction about involving the two disparate arms of Her Majesty's supernatural supervisory operations, nor tapping into the advantages afforded by her position as wife to BUR's chief officer. So far as she was concerned, bureaucratic restrictions were all very well in their place, but they couldn't be allowed to limit efficiency. So while BUR was supposed to handle enforcement and the Shadow Council deal with legislative issues, Alexia was actively causing the two to become ever more entangled.

This was largely held to be one of the reasons Queen Victoria had appointed her muhjah in the first place.

The dewan was suspicious. "Why was the message delivered to *you*? And why use a ghost? Most are instinctively afraid of you because of what you are and what you can do."

Lady Maccon nodded. Even when she was properly introduced to ghosts, they treated her with decided wariness. "Valid points. I don't know. If anyone, it should have been brought to the attention of my husband. He's the official channel."

"The fact that you are the muhjah is not well known around town except by the hives. A standard ghost would not have had access to information divulging your state and position and would not have known that you have the queen's ear. So, there is even less reason to tell you under such circumstances."

Alexia looked over her notes. "Perhaps it has something to do with my father."

The dewan paused in his pacing. "God's teeth, why should it?"

"The ghost muttered something about 'daughter of Tarabotti.' As though she were specifically driven to find me because of my name."

"Perhaps the ghost knew Alessandro Tarabotti in life, my little *dipped biscuit.*"

Alexia nodded. "Perhaps. Regardless, if the threat is coming from the supernatural element, who do we like as suspects?"

Lord Akeldama immediately said, "I know one or two darling little lone werewolves who've been getting restless." He tilted his head and snapped his teeth together a couple times.

The dewan countered with, "There are some rove vampires with sharp fangs."

Lady Maccon was having none of this kind of scapegoat prejudice. "I think we ought to take everything into consideration and assume that it could also be a hive or a pack that is involved."

Lord Akeldama looked cagey and the dewan uncomfortable.

The dewan said, "Oh, very well, but what kind of lead do we have?"

"Only the ghost. I have to find her, and soon, for she was getting rather unsubstantial."

"Why you?" demanded the dewan.

"Clearly it has to be me. I was the one she was looking for, so I am the one she will converse with. Either one of you might do more harm than good. I'm already concerned that my husband is blundering about without my supervision."

Lord Akeldama laughed. "Thank heavens he never hears you talk like that, *petunia.*"

"What makes you think he doesn't?" Alexia continued her line of reasoning. "A ghost left untended, no preservation enacted, in the dead of summer. How long would the specter remain sane under such conditions?"

The dewan answered, "Only a few days."

"And if she were given regular formaldehyde treatments?"

"Several weeks."

Alexia pursed her lips. "That is a rather broad window."

Lord Akeldama smoothed his fingertips over the tabletop. "Did she have any kind of accent, my petal?"

"You mean was she foreign?"

"No, snowdrop. I mean, could you make out her *place* in society?"

Lady Maccon considered this. "Good but not particularly well educated. I should say perhaps upstairs staff? Which could explain why she did not get proper preservation, burial . . . or registry with BUR." Alexia was smart enough to carry the line of reasoning full unto its undignified potential. "So I am looking for a shopgirl or perhaps a housekeeper or cook. One who has died within the past two weeks. Few or no family members. And within a tethering radius of the potentate's town house."

Lord Akeldama shook his head in distress. "You have my deepest sympathies."

Alexia knew this for the sham that it was. Lord Akeldama liked to pretend he attended only the best parties and fraternized with only the right kind of people. His drones were certainly drawn from the highest society had to offer. But Biffy, in his day, had unexpectedly turned up in more unsavory locales than a housekeeper would ever frequent, and Lord Akeldama would never make his drones go anywhere in London he had not vetted first himself.

The dewan kept the conversation on course. "But, Muhjah, that's hundreds of houses, not to mention shops, private clubs, and other places of interest."

Lady Maccon considered Madame Lefoux's underground contrivance chamber, just outside the radius of inquiry. "In addition, it does not take into account cellars or attics built with subterfuge in mind. And it assumes strangers will tell me if someone within their household has recently died. Nevertheless, can you think of a better approach?"

Neither Lord Akeldama nor the dewan could.

The infant-inconvenience kicked out in apparent punctuation to this statement. Lady Maccon made an *oof* noise, glared down at her stomach, then cleared her throat when the others looked at her inquiringly.

"Do we inform the queen in the meantime?" Now that they had some kind of plan, the dewan seemed to feel that pacing about was no longer necessary. He came to sit at the table.

Lord Akeldama took a stand at that. He always took a stand over control of information. "Not just yet, I think, fluffy. Not until we have more concrete evidence. All we have now are the mutterings of a mad ghost."

Lady Maccon, a mite suspicious of his motives, nevertheless had to agree with his point. "Very well, I'll investigate those residences that look to be nighttime inclined, as soon as we have finished here. I'll sleep tomorrow morning and continue in the afternoon with the daylight households."

Lord Akeldama winced and then took a deep breath. "This may be distressing to hear, my flower, but I'm afraid it simply *must* be said. I am loathe to advocate such an *onerous* thing, but as you are searching for someone beneath you, you might want to dress down accordingly."

Lady Maccon winced, thinking of Felicity and her knitwear. "Are you suggesting that I pretend to be a *servant*?"

"I am so very sorry, *dumpling*, but you might have greater success with subterfuge." The vampire's eyes welled with tears at the necessity of having to recommend such a horror.

Alexia took a deep breath to firm her resolve. "Oh, the actions I must undertake for my country."

So it was that Lady Maccon, dressed in some menial rags of ill design and shapeless cut, accompanied by Biffy in the guise of husband, became far more familiar with her new neighborhood than she had previously imagined possible. Biffy looked more uncomfortable in his baggy, lower-class Sunday best than Alexia had ever seen him in evening garb, no matter how tight the breeches or how high the collar. Nevertheless, he threw himself wholeheartedly into the role of out-of-work butler with pregnant housekeeper wife. At each new door, they asked politely after places recently vacated. At each they were treated with a modicum of compassion by the respective butlers—partly due to Alexia's condition but mostly due to the excellent references they were able to provide from one Lady Maccon of Woolsey Castle.

Still, after the eleventh cup of tea, they turned reluctantly back toward Lord Akeldama's street, none the wiser as to any recent deaths that might have gone to ghost. Although, they had received, much to Alexia's surprise, the offer of positions in the respectable town house of a minor baronet.

The infant-inconvenience, normally a fan of tea in any form, objected to such a quantity as was consumed upon visiting a succession of possible employers who treated prospective staff in accordance with all standards of common decency. Alexia positively sloshed as she walked. She gripped Biffy's arm, partly from necessity and partly from the need to keep him human should the rising sun beat their return home. She was moved to ask him something that had been somewhat troubling her of late. "Lord Akeldama takes his tea with lemon?"

Biffy nodded, looking down at her, curious as to where she was going with the conversation.

"It never occurred to me until Professor Lyall brought it up, but this is rather peculiar a preference in a vampire. I was under the impression there were problems with fangs and citrus."

Biffy smiled but said nothing.

Lady Maccon persisted. "Need I remind you where your loyalties now lie, young Biffy?"

"As if I could forget?" Biffy checked the lay of his collar in a nervous gesture. "Ah, well, it's no particular secret of the commonwealth. He spent several decades, as I understand it, building up a tolerance."

"Good gracious me, why?"

"Simply something to do, I suppose."

"That sounds more like the Lord Akeldama of the fashion rags than the Lord Akeldama you and I know."

"Of course, my lady. Truth?"

Alexia nodded.

"He likes to use lemon on his hair—says it adds brightness and shine. He's terribly vain." Biffy's smile was tinged with longing.

"Oh, I know." Alexia looked once more to her companion and then, with Lord Akeldama's colorful town house in sight, pretended exhaustion and slowed their walk even further.

"Biffy, my dear, I am worried about you."

"My lady?"

"I had a recent delivery of new fashion plates from Paris, and you hardly glanced at the hairstyles. My husband tells me you are still having difficulty controlling the change. And your cravat has been tied very simply of late, even for evening events."

"I miss him, my lady."

"Well, he is now living adjacent. You can hardly miss him all that much."

"True. But we are no longer compatible—I am a werewolf; he is a vampire."

"So?"

"So we cannot dance the same dance we used to." Biffy was so sweet when he tried to be circumspect.

Alexia shook her head at him. "Biffy, and I mean this in the kindest way possible: then you should *change the music.*"

"Very good, my lady."

Lady Maccon got very little sleep that day, partly due to the physical repercussions of too much tea and partly due to an unexpected visit from Ivy Tunstell early in the afternoon. Floote woke her with a gentle touch, a sincere apology, and the deeply troubling information that Miss Loontwill had taken it upon herself to entertain Mrs. Tunstell in the front parlor. They were awaiting Lady Maccon's pleasure. Alexia half fell, half rolled out of bed, leaving her poor husband, equally disturbed by her now-chronic restlessness, to sleep.

It being daylight, Biffy was still abed, so she had to ask Floote to assist in buttoning her dress. The butler paled in horror at the very idea and went to corral one of Lord Akeldama's drones in his stead. Boots proved willing to undertake the distasteful task. Although, it seemed to leave him unexpectedly breathless. Lady Maccon was beginning to learn that Boots was ever willing to undertake anything she asked of him.

Floote then managed to balance her, by sheer strength of will, across the short gangplank between balconies.

Downstairs, Felicity was looking more herself, having sent for her things that morning on the assumption that no objections could be found to her assuming permanent residence in her sister's house. She wore a dress of modern cut with a shirtwaist-style top in turquoise satin trimmed in lace and complemented by matching turquoise rosettes on a white muslin skirt. A demure black bow was tied about her neck à la cravat, and black trim peeked forth between the flounces of the sleeves and at the center of the rosettes. The dress was new, expensive, and very stylish.

Mrs. Ivy Tunstell, by contrast, wore a visiting gown from two summers prior, its bustle a little too large and its design a little too bold. Unfortunate Ivy, having married a common theatrical, had to make over her existing gowns rather than order new ones.

For once, however, she did not seem to mind but was weathering Felicity's conversation, which could be nothing but barb-tipped under the circumstances of an over-bustled dress, with complacent demeanor and atypical presence of mind. Either Ivy did not realize she was being insulted, or she had some more interesting matters occupying her thoughts.

Lady Maccon took a deep breath and entered the parlor.

"Oh, sister, you do keep such peculiar hours in this household of yours," commented Felicity, noticing her first.

Ivy hopped to her feet and tripped over to blow kisses at Alexia's face. It was a repulsively Continental habit that she had adopted since her marriage. Lady Maccon blamed overexposure to the stage, or possibly her sometime employment in Madame Lefoux's hat shop where the French propensity for familiar mannerisms, particularly between ladies, was encouraged beyond the pale.

"My dearest Ivy, how do you do? What an unexpected visit."

"Oh, Alexia, how perfectly splendid of you to be in residence. I was so afraid"—Ivy lowered her voice dramatically—"that you might be in your confinement. Your silhouette is alarmingly advanced. I am not intruding, am I? No, you would be abed. Even you would not receive callers at such a time. Have you been drinking enough tea? Very good for ladies in your condition, is tea."

Lady Maccon took a moment to allow the wash of Ivy's chatter to cascade over her much in the manner that dandelion seeds fly on the winds of inconsequentiality. "Pray, do not trouble yourself on my behalf, Ivy. As you see, I am still ambulatory. Although, I will admit that it is a little problematic getting *into* motion these days. I do apologize for keeping you waiting."

"Oh, pray, do not concern yourself. Felicity was quite proficient a substitute."

Lady Maccon raised her eyebrows.

Ivy nodded in a conspiratorial way to indicate she was being entirely sincere. Her copious dark ringlets bobbed about. Her marriage had had little effect on her girlish preferences in hairstyles. It was probably just as well she had made a less-than-favorable match, for the wives of actors were rather expected to be eccentric in the matter of appearance.

At this juncture Felicity rose. "If you will excuse me, ladies, I have a meeting to attend."

Lady Maccon looked after her sister in shock as she left with neither a remark as to Alexia's corpulence nor to Ivy's substandard attire. "I wonder if she will change her dress again."

Ivy swished back over to the settee and collapsed onto it dramatically. "Change? Why should she? That was a perfectly splendid day gown."

"Ivy, did you not notice something peculiar about Felicity's demeanor?"

"Should I have?"

"She was awfully nice, wasn't she?"

"Yes."

"To you."

"Yes."

"And to me."

"Yes, why"—a pause—"come to think on it, that *is* peculiar."

"Isn't it just?"

"Is she in poor health?"

"My dear sister has *joined a society.*" Lady Maccon pursed her lips and pretended coyness.

This was lost on Mrs. Tunstell, who said only, "Well, there you have it. Constructive occupation and attention to good works can have just such a beneficial effect on peevish young ladies. Either that or she has fallen in love."

Alexia could hardly find the words to explain in a manner that Ivy would comprehend. "It is a feminine-advocacy association."

Ivy gasped and clutched at her bosom. "Oh, Alexia, what a thing to say out loud!"

Lady Maccon realized that Ivy might be right—they were heading into highly indecorous, not to say dangerous, territory. "Well, of course"—Alexia cleared her throat ostentatiously—"do tell me, what business is it that has brought you to call this afternoon, my dear Ivy?"

"Oh, Alexia, I do have quite the surfeit of delightful news to relate. I hardly know where to start."

"The beginning, I find, is usually the best place."

"Oh, but, Alexia, that's the most overwhelming part. It is all happening at once."

Lady Maccon took a firm stance at this juncture—she rang for Floote. "Tea is obviously necessary."

"Oh, my, yes," agreed Ivy fervently.

Floote, having anticipated just such a request, came in with tea, treacle tart, and a bunch of grapes imported at prodigious expense from Portugal.

Lady Maccon poured the tea while Ivy waited, fairly vibrating with her news but unwilling to begin recitation until her friend had finished handling the hot liquid.

Alexia placed the teapot carefully back on the tray and handed Ivy her cup. "Well?"

"Have you noticed anything singular about my appearance?" Ivy immediately put the cup down without taking a sip.

Lady Maccon regarded her friend. If a brown dress could be called glaring, Ivy's could be so described. It boasted an overdress and bustle of chocolate satin with a pure white skirt striped, like a circus tent, in the same shade. The accompanying hat was, of course, ridiculous: almost conical in shape but covered with what looked to be the feathers of at least three pheasants mixed in with a good deal of blue and yellow silk flowers. However, none of these extremes of dress were unusual for Mrs. Tunstell. "Not as such."

Ivy blushed beet red, apparently mortified by what she must now relate given Alexia's failed powers of observation. She lowered her voice. "I am very eager for the tea." This garnered no response from the confused Alexia, as Ivy wasn't drinking it. So Ivy soldiered bravely on. "I am—oh, dear, how to put this delicately?—anticipating a familial increase."

"Why, Ivy, I didn't know you expected any kind of inheritance."

"Oh, no." Ivy's blush deepened. "Not that kind of increase." She nodded significantly toward Alexia's portly form.

"Ivy! You are pregnant!"

"Oh, Alexia, really, must you say it so loudly?"

"Felicitations, indeed. How delightful."

Ivy moved the conversation hurriedly onward. "And Tunny and I have decided to form our own dramatic association."

Lady Maccon paused to reinterpret this confession. "Ivy, are you saying you intend to establish an acting troupe?"

Mrs. Tunstell nodded, her curls bouncing. "Tunny thinks it a good plan to start a new family of players as well as a new family, as he is keen on saying."

A family, indeed, Alexia thought. Having left the werewolf pack, Tunstell must be trying, in his own way, to build a new pack for himself. "Well," she said, "I do wish you all the best luck in the world. However, Ivy—and I do not mean to be crude—how have you managed to gather the means to fund such an undertaking?"

Ivy blushed and lowered her eyes. "I was dispatched to consult you on just such a subject. I understand Woolsey is quite enthusiastic in its patronage of artistic endeavors. Tunny implied you even had some capital invested in a circus!"

"Indeed, but, Ivy, for obvious reasons, those are in the interest of furthering the pack. Claviger recruitment and so forth. Tunstell has voluntarily severed any such connection."

Ivy nodded glumly. "I thought you would say as much."

"Now, wait just a moment. I'm not so feeble a friend as to abandon anyone, especially you, my dear, when in need." Lady Maccon frowned in thought. "Perhaps I could dip into my own coffers. You may not be aware, but my father left me rather well set up, and Conall is quite generous with a weekly allowance. We have never discussed my personal income, but he seems disinterested in my financial affairs. I am convinced he shouldn't object if I were to become a patron of the arts. Why should Woolsey have all the fun?"

"Oh, Alexia, really? I couldn't ask such a thing of you!" protested Ivy in a tone that suggested this had been her objective in calling all along.

"No, no." Alexia was becoming rather entranced with the proposal. "I think it a capital idea. I wonder if I might ask a rather odd favor in return?"

Ivy looked amenable to anything that might further her husband's goal. "Oh, please do."

Alexia grappled with how exactly to phrase this next question without exposing too much of her nature to her dear friend. She had never told Ivy of her preternatural state, nor of her post as muhjah and the general investigative endeavors that resulted.

"I find myself curious as to the activities of the lower orders. No insult intended, my dear Ivy, but even as the mistress of your own troupe, and clientele notwithstanding, you will have a certain amount of contact with less savory elements of London society. I would appreciate . . . information . . . with regards to these elements on occasion."

Mrs. Tunstell was overcome with such joy upon hearing this that she was moved to dab at one eye with an embroidered handkerchief. "Why, Alexia, my dear, have you undertaken an interest in *scandal mongering* at last? Oh, it is too much. Too wonderful."

Even prior to her marriage, Miss Ivy Hisselpenny's social position had prevented her from attending events of high standing, while Miss Alexia Tarabotti had suffered under the yoke of just such events. As far as Ivy was concerned, this yielded up a poor quality and quantity of gossip. The Alexia of her girlhood had not been curious about the interpersonal relationships of others, let alone their dress and manners.

The handkerchief lowered and Ivy's face became suffused with a naive cunning. "Is there anything in particular you wish me to look out for?"

"Why, Ivy!"

Mrs. Tunstell sipped her tea coquettishly.

Lady Maccon took the plunge. "As a matter of fact, there have been rumors of late with regards to a threat upon a certain peer of the realm. I cannot say more, but if you wouldn't mind?"

"Well, I did hear Lord Blingchester's carriage was to be decommissioned."

"No, Ivy, not that kind of threat."

"And the Duchess of Snodgrove's chambermaid was so incensed recently that she indicated she might actually not affix her hat properly for the midsummer ball."

"No, not quite that either. But this is all intriguing information. I should appreciate your continued conversation and company even after your evolved circumstances."

Ivy closed her eyes and took a small breath. "Oh, Alexia, how kind of you. I did fear . . ." She flipped open a fan and fluttered it in an excess of sentimental feeling. "I did fear that once Tunny and I launched this endeavor, you would be unwilling to continue the association. After all, I intend to perhaps take on some small roles myself. Tunny thinks I may have dramatic talent. Being seen to take tea with the wife of an actor is one thing, but taking tea with the actress herself is quite another."

Lady Maccon shifted forward as much as possible and stretched out a hand to rest softly atop Mrs. Tunstell's. "Ivy, I would never even consider it. Let us say no more on the subject."

Ivy seemed to feel the time had come to move on to yet another pertinent bit of news. "I did have one other thing to relate to you, my dear Alexia. As you may have surmised, I have had to give over my position as assistant to Madame Lefoux. Of course, I shall miss the society of all those lovely hats, but I was there just the other evening when a very peculiar event occurred. Given your husband's state, I immediately thought of you."

"How very perspicacious." Much to her own amazement, Lady Maccon had found that Mrs. Tunstell, a lady of little society and less apparent sense, often had the most surprising things to relate. Knowing well that the best encouragement was to say nothing, Alexia drank her tea and gave Ivy a dark-eyed look of interest.

"Well, you should never believe it, but I ran into a scepter in the street."

"A scepter . . . what, like the queen's?"

"Oh, no, you know what I mean. A ghost. Me, can you imagine? Right through it I went, all la-di-da. I could hardly countenance it. I was completely unnerved. After I had recovered my capacities, I realized the poor thing was a tad absent of good sense. Subsequent to much inane burbling, she did manage to articulate some information. She seemed peculiarly attracted to my parasol, which I was carrying at night only because my business with Madame Lefoux had taken longer than expected. Otherwise, you understand, I have always found your habit of toting daytime accessories at all hours *highly* esoteric. Never mind that. This ghost seemed peculiarly interested in my parasol. Kept asking about it. Wanted to know if it *did* anything, apart from shield me from the sun, of course. I informed her flat out that the only person I knew who boasted a parasol that extruded things was my dear friend Lady Maccon. You remember I saw yours emit when we were traveling in the north? Well, I told this to the ghost in no unceremonious terms, at which point she got most stimulated and asked as to your current whereabouts. Well, since she was a ghost and, as such, tethered within a shortened area of the location, I saw no reason not to relay your new address to her. It was all very odd. And she kept repeating the most peculiar turn of phrase, regarding a cephalopod."

"Oh, indeed? What exactly did she say, Ivy?"

" 'The octopus is inequitable,' or some such drivel." Ivy looked as though she might continue her discussion, except at that moment she caught sight of Felicity through the open parlor door.

"Alexia, your sister appears to be most unbalanced. I am quite convinced I just observed her wearing a lemon-yellow knit shawl. With a fringe. Going out into public. I cannot countenance it."

Lady Maccon closed her eyes and shook her head. "Never mind that now, Ivy."

"Convinced, I tell you. How remarkable."

"Anything more about the ghost, Ivy?"

"I think it might have had something to do with the OBO."

This comment brought Alexia up short. "*What did you just say?*"

"The Order of the Brass Octopus—you must have heard of it."

Lady Maccon blinked in shock and put her hand to her stomach where the infant-inconvenience kicked out in surprise as well. "Of course I have heard of it, Ivy. The question is, how have *you*?"

"Oh, Alexia, I have been working for Madame Lefoux for positively ages. She has been traveling overmuch of late, and her appearance can be very distracting, but I am not so unobservant as *all that.* I am well aware that when she is in town, she undertakes fewer hat-orientated activities than hat-focused ones. She runs an underground contrivance chamber as I understand it."

"She told you?"

"Not exactly. If Madame Lefoux prefers to keep things a secret, who am I to gainsay her? But I did look inside some of those hatboxes of hers, and they do not always contain hats. I did inquire as to the specifics, and Madame Lefoux assured me it was better if I not become involved. However, Alexia, I wouldn't want you to think me ignorant. Tunny and I do talk about such things, and I have eyes enough in my head to observe, even if I do not always understand."

"I apologize for doubting you, Ivy."

Ivy looked wistful. "Perhaps one day you, too, will take me into your confidence."

"Oh, Ivy, I—"

Ivy held up a hand. "When you are quite ready, of course."

Alexia sighed. "Speaking of which, you must excuse me. This news about the ghost, it is of no little importance. I must consult my husband's Beta immediately."

Ivy looked about. "But it is daylight."

"Sometimes even werewolves are awake during the day. When the situation demands it. Conall is asleep, so Professor Lyall is probably awake and at his duties."

"Is a cephalopod so dire as all that?"

"I am afraid it might be. If you would excuse me, Ivy?"

"Of course."

"I shall inform Floote about the little matter of my patronage. He will set you up right and proper with the necessary pecuniary advance."

Ivy grabbed at Lady Maccon's hand as she passed. "Oh, thank you, Alexia."

Alexia was as good as her word, going immediately to Floote and issuing him with instructions. Then, in the interest of economy and perhaps saving herself a trip to BUR, she casually asked, "Is there a local OBO chapter in this area? I understand it is quite the secret society but thought perhaps you might know."

Floote gave her a meditative look. "Yes, madam, a block over. I noticed the marking just after you began visiting with Lord Akeldama."

"Marking, Floote?"

"Yes, madam. There is a brass octopus on the door handle. Number eighty-eight."

CHAPTER FIVE

The Lair of the Octopus

Number 88 was not a very impressive domicile. In fact, it was one of the least elegant in the neighborhood. While its immediate neighbors were nothing when compared to Lord Akeldama's abode, they still put their very best brick forward. They acknowledged, in an entirely unspoken way, that they were denizens of the most fashionable residential area in London and that architecture and grounds should earn this accolade. Number eighty-eight was altogether shabby by comparison. Its paint was not exactly peeling, but it was faded, and its garden was overgrown with herbs gone to seed and lettuces that had bolted.

Scientists, thought Alexia as she made her way up the front steps and pulled the bell rope. She wore her worst dress, altered to compensate for her stomach and made of a worsted fabric somewhere between dishwater brown and green. She couldn't remember why she'd originally purchased the poor sad thing—probably to upset her mother. She had even borrowed one of Felicity's ugly shawls, despite the fact that the day was too warm for such a conceit. With the addition of a full white mob cap and a very humble expression, she looked every inch the housekeeper she wished to portray.

The butler who answered her knock seemed to feel the same, for he did not even question her status. His demeanor was one of pedantic pleasantness, exacerbated by a round jolliness customarily encountered among bakers or butchers not butlers. He sported a stout neck and a head of wildly bushy white hair that called to mind nothing so much as a cauliflower.

"Good afternoon," said Alexia, bobbing a curtsy. "I heard your establishment was in need of new staff, and I have come to inquire about the position."

The butler looked her up and down, pursing his lips. "We did lose our cook several weeks ago. We have been doing fine with a temporary, and we certainly don't wish to take on someone in your condition. You can understand that." It was said kindly, but most firmly, and meant to discourage.

Alexia stiffened her spine. "Oh, yes, sir. My lying-in shouldn't be a day over a fortnight, and I do make the best calf's-feet jelly you will ever taste." Alexia took a gamble with that. The butler looked like the kind of man who liked jelly, his shape being of the jelly inclination already.

She was right. His squinty eyes lit with pleasure. "Oh, well, if that is the case. Have you references?"

"The very best, from Lady Maccon herself, sir."

"Indeed? How comprehensive is your knowledge of herbs and spices? Our gentlemen residents, you understand, are mostly bachelors. Their table requirements are simple, but their extracurricular requests can be a tad esoteric."

Alexia pretended shock.

The butler made haste to correct any miscommunication. "Oh, no, no, nothing like that. They simply may ask for quantities of dried herbs for their experiments. They are all men of intellect."

"Ah. As to that, my knowledge is unequaled by any I have ever met before or since." Alexia was rather enjoying bragging about things about which she knew absolutely nothing.

"I should find that very hard to believe. Our previous cook was a renowned expert in the medicinal arts. However, do come in, Mrs. . . . ?"

Alexia scrabbled for a name, then came up with the best she could at short notice. "Floote. Mrs. Floote."

This butler didn't seem to know *her* butler, for his expression did not alter at the improbability of such a pairing as Floote and Alexia. He merely ushered her inside and led her down and into the kitchen.

It was like no kitchen Alexia had ever seen. Not that she had spent much time in kitchens, but she felt she was at least familiar with the general expectations of such a utilitarian room. This one was pristinely clean and boasted not only the requisite number of pots and pans, but also steam devices, one or two massive measuring buckets, and what looked like glass jars filled with specimen samples lining the counters. It resembled the combination of a bottling factory, a brewery, and Madame Lefoux's contrivance chamber.

Alexia made no attempt to disguise her astonishment—any normal housekeeper would be as surprised as she upon seeing such a strange cooking arena. "My goodness, what a peculiar arrangement of furnishings and utensils."

They were alone in the kitchen, and it was just that time of the afternoon when most household staff had a brief moment to satisfy their own concerns before the tea was called for.

"Ah, yes, our previous cook had some interest in other endeavors apart from meal preparation. She was a kind of intellectual herself, if you would allow such a thing in a female. My employers sometimes encourage aberrant behavior."

Alexia, having spent a goodly number of years immersed in books and having attended many Royal Society presentations, not to mention her intimacy with Madame Lefoux, could indeed allow such things in females, but in her current guise forbore to say so. Instead, she looked around in silence. Only to notice a prevalence of octopuses. They were positively everywhere, stamped onto jar lids and labels, etched into the handles of iron skillets, engraved onto the sides of copper pots, and even pressed into the top of a vat of soap set out to harden on a sideboard.

"My, someone certainly has an affection for cephalopods." Alexia waddled over, all casualness, to examine a row of very small bottles of dark brown glass and mysterious content. They were corked up, each cork boasting a small glass octopus pressed into it in a range of colors. Otherwise, there was no mention made of the content.

She reached to pick one up only to find that the butler, in the silent manner customary to the breed, had sidled up next to her. "I should not, Mrs. Floote, if I were you. Our previous cook had an interest in rather more hazardous forms of distillery and preservation as well."

"What happened to the good lady, sir?" Alexia asked with a forced lightness in tone.

"She stopped. If I were you, I should take particular care with that yellow octopus there."

Alexia moved hurriedly away from the whole row of little bottles, suddenly feeling that they were precariously placed on their shelf.

The butler looked her up and down. "There are many stairs in this house, you understand, Mrs. Floote? You will not be able to remain in only the kitchen. How am I to be convinced you are capable of your duties?"

Alexia seized upon this as a perfect opportunity to further her investigations. "Well, I am interested in seeing the accommodations, should you choose to engage my services. If you would be so kind as to show me to the staff quarters, I can demonstrate my mobility."

The butler nodded and gestured her toward a back staircase that wound up through the house to the attic apartments. The room he eventually shepherded her into was a tiny, cramped cell that still contained some remnants of its previous occupant, just as Alexia had hoped.

More small brown bottles and a few curious-looking vials lay about. A handkerchief was spread across the windowsill, upon which bunches of herbs lay drying.

"Of course, we will clear out these quarters prior to new occupation." The butler curled his lip as he looked around.

Small cloth-bound notebooks were scattered here and there; several were quite dusty with neglect. There were also bits of scrap paper and even what looked to be some kind of ledger.

"Your previous cook was literate, sir?"

"I warned you she was peculiar."

Alexia took another look around and then, thinking rapidly, maneuvered toward the small bed. "Oh, dear, perhaps those stairs were a tad much given my present condition. I seem to be feeling rather overstimulated." She collapsed onto the bed, leaning back dramatically and almost overbalancing. It was a paltry performance.

Nevertheless, the butler seemed convinced. "Oh, I say, Mrs. Floote. This simply isn't on. Really, we can't consider anyone who—"

Alexia cut him off by groaning and clutching at her stomach significantly.

The man blanched.

"Perhaps if I could have a little moment to recover, sir?"

The butler looked like he would prefer to be anywhere else but there. "I shall fetch you a glass of water, shall I? Perhaps some, er, jelly?"

"Oh, yes, capital idea. Do take your time."

At which he hurried out.

Immediately, Alexia lurched upright, an exercise that made up in efficiency what it lacked in dignity, and began searching the room. She found very little memorabilia with regards to the occupant's personality, but there were even more notebooks and mysterious bottles tucked away in the bedside drawer and the wardrobe. She tucked anything that looked to be secret or significant into the stealth pockets of her parasol. Then, knowing she must limit herself, she took what seemed to be the most recent notebook and one that looked to be the oldest and most dusty, along with a neatly printed ledger and bundled them up in Felicity's shawl. The parasol was clanking slightly and drooping from its excess load, and she thought the knitwear bundle must look very suspicious, but when the butler returned, he was so overjoyed to find her recovered he didn't notice either.

Alexia decided to make good her escape. Saying she felt weak and had best hurry home before nightfall, she moved toward the door. The butler led her downstairs, declining to offer her the position, despite her calf's-foot jelly, but suggesting she call round in several months when she had recovered from her inconvenience, jelly apparently being quite the alluring prospect.

He was just letting her out when a voice stopped them both in their tracks. "Well, gracious me. Miss Tarabotti?"

Alexia clutched her loot closer to her breast, closed her eyes, and took a deep breath. Then she looked upward.

The gentleman walking slowly down the staircase toward her was an iconic example of the scientific species. His gray muttonchops were untended, his eyes bespectacled, and his attire too far into tweed for midsummer and midtown. Unfortunately, Alexia was all too familiar with that face.

"Why, Dr. Neebs! I thought you were dead."

"Ah, not quite. Although Lord Maccon did do his level best." The man continued down the steps, moving with a pronounced limp probably sustained during that last battle in the Hypocras Club's exsanguination chamber. As he closed in upon her, Alexia noted his eyes were very hard behind those spectacles.

"In which case, shouldn't you be serving a sentence for intellectual misconduct?"

"I assure you, it has been served. Now, I think perhaps you should come with me, Miss Tarabotti."

"Oh, but I was just leaving."

"Yes, I am certain you were."

The butler, at a bit of a loss, was looking back and forth between them.

Alexia backed toward the open door, lifting up her parasol in a defensive position and pressing her thumb against the appropriate lotus petal in the handle, arming the tip with one of the numbing darts. She wished she had not left Ethel behind; guns, by and large, were far more threatening than parasols.

Nevertheless, Dr. Neebs looked at it with wary respect. "Madame Lefoux's work, isn't that?"

"You know Madame Lefoux?"

Dr. Neebs looked at her as though she were an idiot. *Of course,* thought Alexia, *this is a chapter of the Order of the Brass Octopus. Madame Lefoux is also a member. I did not realize the Order was reabsorbing the Hypocras Club. I must tell Conall.*

The scientist tilted his head to one side. "What are you about, Miss Tarabotti?"

Alexia faltered. Dr. Neebs was not to be trusted, of that she was certain. Apparently, he felt much the same about her, for he issued a sharp instruction to the butler.

"Grab her!"

Luckily, the butler was confused by the proceedings and did not understand how his role had suddenly become one of ruffian. He was also holding a glass of water in one hand and a jar of calf's-foot jelly in the other.

"What? Sir?"

At which juncture Alexia shot the scientist with a numbing dart. Madame Lefoux had armed the darts with a high-quality, fast-acting poison that had some affiliation with laudanum. Dr. Neebs pitched forward with an expression of shock on his face and collapsed at the base of the staircase.

The butler recovered from his inertia and lunged at Alexia. Lady Maccon, clumsy at the best of times, lurched to the side, waving her parasol wildly in a wide arc and managing to strike the butler a glancing blow to the side of the head.

It was not a very accurate hit but it was violent, and the man, clearly unused to anything of the kind, reeled away looking at her with an expression of such disgruntlement that Alexia was moved to grin.

"Why, Mrs. Floote, such indecorous behavior!"

Alexia armed her parasol and shot him with a second numbing dart. His knees gave out and he crumpled to the floor of the foyer. "Yes, I know. I do apologize. It is a personal failing of mine."

With that, she let herself out into the street and lumbered off, clutching her plunder and feeling very furtive and rather proud of her afternoon's achievement.

Unfortunately for Lady Maccon, there was absolutely no one to appreciate her endeavors when she returned home. Any werewolves in town were abed, Felicity was still out (not that Alexia could confide in *her*), and Floote was off tending to some domestic duty or another. Disgruntled, Alexia set herself up in the back parlor to examine her misappropriated loot.

The back parlor was already her favorite room. It had been made over with quiet card parties in mind: cream and pale gold walls, ornate dark cherry furniture, and royal blue curtains and coverings. The several small tables were marble topped, and the large chandelier boasted the very latest in gas lighting. It was just that kind of soulful elegance that soulless Alexia could never hope to achieve on her own.

She set the bottles aside to give to BUR for analysis and picked up the ledger and journals with interest. Two hours later, stomach growling and tea cold and forgotten at her elbow, she put them back down again. They had been as absorbing as only the highly private musings of a complete stranger can be. They were illuminating as well, in their way, although not with regards to the current threat to the queen's life. Of that there was no mention at all, nor was there any concrete evidence to implicate the OBO.

The ledger proved to be a record of transactions, mainly sales the cook had made to various individuals, everything encoded with symbols, initials, abbreviations, and numbers. After reading the journals as well, Alexia surmised that the cook must have been an honorary OBO member. Her interests were focused on those concoctions that one could not purchase easily from apothecary or pharmacist. Such liquids, for example, as Madame Lefoux incorporated into Alexia's parasol and perhaps other potions even more deadly.

The most recent journal, unfinished and unhelpful, articulated only the increasingly disorientated views of an aging woman who seemed to be succumbing to a brew of her own fabrication, either involuntarily or out of a derangement of the spirit. There was no way to determine whether she was, indeed, the ghost who had come to warn Lady Maccon, but it was as good a lead as any.

However, it was the older journal that drew her attention. One particular entry was dated some twenty years ago. It mused with interest over a new order—for ingredients to be sent by post in separate allotments, for sake of security, to a werewolf pack in Scotland. The connection between time and location caused Alexia to ruminate over her husband's anguished retelling of a certain betrayal. The same betrayal that would cause him to abandon the Kingair Pack and then take over Woolsey. He had been so very cut up about it. "I caught them mixing the poison," he had said. "Poison, mind you! Poison has no place on pack grounds or in pack business. It isna an honest way to kill anyone, let alone a monarch." She realized there was no way to prove a connection, but coincidence in date was good enough for her. This *must* be an accounting of the order for the poison that long ago was meant to kill Queen Victoria.

"Astonishing," she said into the empty room, rereading the incriminating passage. Absentmindedly, she picked up her teacup and sipped. The liquid being cold, she placed it back down with a grimace. She quickly ascertained that the remainder under the cozy was equally tepid and pulled the bell rope.

Floote materialized. "Madam?"

"Fresh tea, please, Floote. There's a dear."

"Certainly, madam."

He vanished, reappearing in a miraculously short time with a freshly brewed pot and, much to Lady Maccon's delight, a small wedge of tempting-looking cake.

"Oh, thank you, Floote. Is that lemon sponge? Marvelous. Tell me, are any of the men awake yet?"

"I believe Mr. Rabiffano and the professor are just rising."

"Mr. Rabiffano, who is . . . ? Oh, Biffy! Not my husband, then?"

"Difficult to tell, madam, him being in the other house."

"Ah, yes, of course, how silly of me." Lady Maccon went back to her perusal of the little journal.

"Will there be anything else, madam?"

"The question is, Floote, why order the toxins from London? Why not patronize the baser elements who supply such pernicious needs closer to home?"

"Madam?"

"I mean, Floote, hypothetically, why special-order poison from one destination only to eventually transport it back to do the dastardly deed? Although, I suppose the queen might have been visiting Scotland at the time. But still, why all the way from town?"

"Everyone orders from London, madam," replied Floote most decidedly, even though he had no idea as to the specifics of her question. "It is the fashion."

"Yes, but if one were afraid of being caught?"

Floote seemed to feel he might participate in the discussion even without full possession of the necessary facts. "Perhaps one wanted to be caught, madam."

Lady Maccon frowned. "Oh, no, I hardly think—" She was cut off by the arrival of Professor Lyall, who looked his normal unremarkably dapper self, despite having just arisen.

He stuck his head around the corner of the door in some surprise, evidently unsure of what to make of his mistress's encampment.

"Lady Maccon, good evening. How are you?"

"Professor Lyall. Oh, Floote, do carry on."

Floote wafted away, giving Lyall a very significant look, as though to say, *She is in one of her moods—tread with caution.*

Heeding the unspoken advice, the werewolf let himself in hesitantly. "You are in the back parlor, Lady Maccon?"

"Just as you see."

"Not the front?"

"I like the wallpaper. I have had a most illuminating day, Professor Lyall."

"Oh, dear. Have you, indeed?" The gentleman settled down into a chair near his Alpha female. At a nod from Lady Maccon, he helped himself to tea. Floote, being Floote, had thought to provide more than one cup. "I have not yet read the evening papers. Is that going to signify, my lady?"

Lady Maccon frowned. "I doubt it. I don't think the constabulary were alerted to my activities."

Professor Lyall forbore to mention that this indicated there might have been a need for such action. "Well?"

In as flattering a manner as possible, Lady Maccon detailed her afternoon's shenanigans. As she did so, Professor Lyall's face creased with worry.

"On your own? In your state?"

"I'm perfectly capable."

"Yes, indeed. You even managed to use your condition to your advantage. But I thought you were meant to take Biffy with you on these jaunts. Himself ordered it."

"Well, yes, but this couldn't wait for evening. And such interesting evidence I have uncovered. Now where did I put my pen?" She began patting about her lap—what there was left of it—in annoyance.

Professor Lyall produced a stylographic pen from his waistcoat and passed it to her. Alexia nodded her thanks.

"You really believe that this new threat has some connection to the old Kingair attempt?" he asked while she made a note in the margin of one of the journals.

"It seems likely."

"Your evidence appears to be circumstantial at best."

"Never discount serendipity. Would you be so kind as to have some of these potions analyzed? Also, I should like to see BUR's report regarding the Kingair failed assassination and my husband's subsequent challenge for Woolsey Alpha, plus any corresponding postings in the popular press."

Professor Lyall looked rather pained. "If you insist, my lady."

"I do."

"Give me a few hours to organize everything? The laboratory will take some time with those samples—several days, at least—but I shall bring the other items you requested back with me."

"Oh, no need. I shall jaunt to BUR after I call on Madame Lefoux and file the appropriate requisition forms myself."

"Ah, had you intended—?"

"Not until I traced this OBO connection. Of course, Genevieve would have had nothing to do with OBO operations twenty years ago, being only a small child, but still it is worth making inquiries. She knows *things*. Not to mention the fact that Ivy ran into a ghost in that area the other night. Can't possibly be the same ghost—no tether stretches so far—but there must be a connection to our mysterious messenger."

"If you must, my lady. But this time do please take Biffy with you."

"Of course. I shall be glad of the company. Shall we go in to supper?"

Professor Lyall nodded gratefully and they arose to make their way to the dining room.

"What ho, wife?"

Conall Maccon thumped down the stairs looking far more pulled together than Alexia had ever seen him in all their acquaintance. His cravat, a becoming ethereal azure that perfectly complemented his tawny eyes, was tied Nabog style over unusually high collar points. His shirt was tucked to perfection, his waistcoat seamless, and the sleeves of his jacket just so. As a direct result, he was also looking rather uncomfortable.

"My goodness, husband. How handsome you are this evening! Did the drones get hold of you?"

The earl give his wife a very telling stare before sweeping down upon her and planting a kiss on her lips right in front of the embarrassed gazes of Lyall, Floote, and a small number of household staff.

Alexia's limited mobility prevented her from any evasive maneuvers. Like some wanton hussy, she could do nothing but endure his amorous attentions with blushes and sputterings of delighted horror.

He pulled back finally. "Excellent, best way to start one's evening. Wouldn't you agree, gentlemen?"

Professor Lyall rolled his eyes at his Alpha's antics, and Floote bustled quickly off about his business.

They entered the dining room. During the course of Alexia's conversation with Professor Lyall, most of the rest of the current town residents—two werewolves and a few assorted clavigers—had arisen and assembled around the table. They all stood politely as Lady Maccon seated herself before returning to prior conversation or consumption, depending upon personality. Biffy, seated slightly apart from the others, was pretending deep absorption in the latest issue of *Le Beaux Assemblée,* otherwise known as *Beau's Court and Fashionable Magazine Addressed Particularly to the Gentleman of Leisure.* Lord Maccon frowned at him, but the dandy didn't seem to notice.

Alexia helped herself to a bowl of stewed fruit, plum pudding, and custard. After some conversation with her husband on domestic matters, she turned his attention to her own recent investigations.

"You didn't!"

"I most assuredly did. And now I have need of the carriage. I should like to visit Madame Lefoux before calling at BUR for the documentation Professor Lyall promised me."

Lord Maccon gave his Beta a repressive look.

Professor Lyall shrugged, as though to say, *You married her.*

"Alexia," Lord Maccon said in a drawn-out growl, "you know I am not comfortable with that particular incident resurfacing. I shouldn't like you to be stirring up trouble over an event well and truly settled."

Lady Maccon, perfectly understanding that the nature of his growl was not one of anger but of distress, put down her fork and placed her hand over his. "But you must acknowledge that if there is a connection, we should pursue all avenues of investigation. I promise to keep my attention focused on the relevant details and not be distracted by personal curiosity."

Lord Maccon sighed.

Lady Maccon lowered her voice, although she was perfectly well aware that she was surrounded by beings with supernatural hearing who could discern every word she said. "I know this is a subject that pains you, my love, but if we are to get to the root of this matter, you must see that there may indeed be a correlation."

He nodded. "But have a care, please, my heart? I fear you are messing with matters best left undisturbed."

A stillness in the crinkling of Professor Lyall's evening paper seemed to indicate the Beta was entirely in agreement with his Alpha on this point.

Alexia nodded and let go of her husband. She glanced up and across the table. "Biffy, would you be amenable to accompanying me this evening as I make my rounds? I should appreciate the companionship of one more mobile than myself."

"Of course, my lady, delighted. What hat should I wear?"

"Oh, your town topper should suit us well enough. We shan't be going into society."

His face fell slightly at that. "Very good, my lady. Should I retrieve it now?"

"Oh, no, please finish your meal. No sense in wasting food in the pursuit of information. The one is far more vital than the other, despite what Lord Akeldama may think."

Biffy smiled slightly and continued on with the consumption of his raw steak and fried egg.

Madame Genevieve Lefoux was a woman of style and understanding. If that style leaned toward gentlemen's dress and mannerisms and if that understanding leaned toward scientific theory and practice, Lady

Maccon was certainly not the kind of person so in want of sensibility that she would critique a friend for such eccentricities. Some considerable intimacy had left Alexia with the distinct feeling that Madame Lefoux liked her and that she liked Madame Lefoux, but not a great deal more. Trust, for example, seemed still in question. Between them existed a friendship quite different from the one she shared with Ivy Tunstell. There was no discussion of the latest fashions or societal events. If asked, Alexia might say that she could not recall precisely what it was she and the French inventor did discuss, but whatever it was, it always left Alexia feeling intellectually stretched and vaguely exhausted—rather like visiting a museum.

Madame Lefoux had a new, pretty, young shopgirl behind the counter when they arrived at Chapeau de Poupe. Madame Lefoux's shopgirls were always young and pretty. This one seemed overset by the unexpected arrival of the grand Lady Maccon and was mightily relieved when her mistress, elegant and refined in gray tails and top hat, appeared to take over the management of such an august personage.

"My dear Lady Maccon!"

"Madame Lefoux, how do you do?"

The Frenchwoman grasped both of Alexia's hands and kissed first one and then the other of Alexia's cheeks. No air was left between lips and flesh, as was the custom among women of fashion, nor was this an extravagant gesture for fashion's sake. No, for Madame Lefoux, such a greeting was as natural as a handshake among American businessmen. Her actions were tender and her smile dimpled with genuine affection.

"What an unexpected pleasure! But are you certain you should be in public in your condition?"

"My dear Genevieve, you have been so long away I began to suspect you might never return to us. Then what should London do when in need of a new hat?"

Madame Lefoux acknowledged both the compliment and rebuke of Alexia's statement with a tilt of her dark head.

Lady Maccon noted, with some concern, that her friend was looking practically gaunt. Mostly composed of sharp angles, Madame Lefoux could never be described as full figured, but during her most recent travels, she had lost flesh she could not afford to lose. The inventor always had been more concerned with the pursuits of the mind than the body, but never before had her lovely green eyes sported such dark circles.

"Are you well?" asked Alexia. "Is it Quesnel? He is supposed to be home for the month, is he not? Is he being perfectly beastly?"

Madame Lefoux's son was a cheerful towheaded creature with an unfortunate nose for mischief. There was no malice to his actions, but his mere presence resulted in a kind of microcosmic chaos that kept his mother on edge whenever he was in residence.

Madame Lefoux flinched slightly and shook her head. "He did not make it home this time."

"Oh, dear! But then if not Quesnel, what could possibly be the matter? Truly, you do not look at all well."

"Oh, pray, do not concern yourself, Alexia. Some trouble sleeping, nothing more. How are you? I understand you have taken a residence in town. You certainly look amplified. Have you been maintaining a tranquil environment? I read recently that it is terribly important for the baby to be surrounded by peace. Knowing your disposition, this has me worried."

Alexia blinked at her.

Perceiving that her solicitude was unwelcome, the Frenchwoman moved hastily on. "Did you come to pick up Woolsey's new glassical order, or is this merely a social call?"

Lady Maccon accepted the conversational redirection. She respected her friend's need for privacy and her expertly cultivated aura of mystery. She also did not want to appear nosy. "Oh, is there an order? I suppose I could collect it. But, in actuality, there is a matter I should very much like to discuss with you." Alexia noticed the curiosity in the eyes of the new shopgirl. "In seclusion, perhaps?" And then, as she was not certain as to the extent of the shopgirl's knowledge, she confined her voice to a whisper. "Below?"

Madame Lefoux lowered her eyelashes and nodded gravely. "Of course, of course."

Alexia looked to her escort. "Biffy, will you find yourself entertainment enough here for a quarter of an hour, or should you prefer to run along to the Lottapiggle Tea Shop on Cavendish Square?"

"Oh, I can abide a while among such loveliness as this." The young werewolf waved a graceful gloved hand at the forest of dangling hats displayed all about him. He brushed his fingers along an exaggerated ostrich feather, much as a young girl would trail her fingertips through a fountain. "Beautiful brim rolling."

"I shan't be very long," replied his mistress before following her friend toward the back of the shop, where a door in the wall led to an ascension room that took them down to a passageway, underneath Regent Street, and into the inventor's much-vaunted contrivance chamber.

Madame Lefoux's laboratory might have been a great wonder of the world, if only because it was a wonder the Frenchwoman could ever find anything inside it. The massive, cavelike laboratory was not only messy, but it was also noisy. Alexia often thought that the only reason it could not be heard in the street above was that Regent was one of the busiest thoroughfares in London. Then she wondered if that was why Madame Lefoux had chosen this particular spot.

As ever, Lady Maccon took in her surroundings with a kind of reverence that was part appreciation, part horror. There were engines and mysterious constructs galore, some of them running, many of them disassembled into component parts. There were diagrams and sketches of larger projects strewn about, mostly aeronautical devices such as ornithopters, as aetheric travel was one of Madame Lefoux's specialties. It smelled of oil.

"Oh, my, is that a new commission?" Alexia picked her way slowly through the clutter, holding her skirts well out of the way of any possible grease stains.

Dominating the chamber was a partly assembled transport contraption. Or Alexia assumed it was a transport—as yet, it had no apparent wheels, rails, or legs. It was shaped like a massive bowler hat without a brim, so she supposed it might be an underwater conveyance. Inside were levers and pull cords, an operator's seat, and two small slits at the front for visibility. It was almost buglike and well outside of the Frenchwoman's ordinary principles of subtlety. Alexia's parasol with all its secret pockets and component parts was far more to Genevieve's taste. Traditionally, she did not go in for big and flashy.

"Something I've been working on of late."

"Is it armored?" Lady Maccon had an embarrassingly unladylike interest in modern technology.

"In part." Something in Madame Lefoux's tone warned Alexia off.

"Oh, dear, is it under contract from the War Office? I'm probably not supposed to know. I do apologize for asking. We shall say no more about it."

"Thank you." Madame Lefoux smiled in tired gratitude. Her dimples barely showed.

Government defense commissions were lucrative but not something one could speak of openly, even to the queen's muhjah. The inventor moved to take Alexia's hand, her own work-hardened by decades of tool use. Alexia could feel the roughness even through her gloves, along with a companion thrill she had grown to accept was part of the price of intimacy with this woman. Genevieve was so very *intriguing.*

"Was there something specific you wanted, my dear Alexia?"

Alexia hesitated and then, without subtlety, jumped right to the point. "Genevieve, do you know anything about the Kingair assassination attempt on Queen Victoria of twenty years ago? I mean, anything from the Order of the Brass Octopus?"

Madame Lefoux started in genuine surprise. "My goodness, what has brought you back around to that?"

"Let us say I made a contact recently who has led me into explorations of the past."

Madame Lefoux crossed her arms and leaned back against a coiled roll of brass plating. "Hmm. I personally know nothing. I would have been no more than thirteen at the time, but we could ask my aunt. I'm not certain how useful she might be but the attempt can't hurt."

"Your aunt? Oh you mean . . . ?"

Madame Lefoux nodded, her face sad. "She's finally undergoing diminished spectral cohesion. Even with all my preservation techniques and chemical expertise, it was inevitable. However, she does have her lucid moments."

Alexia realized this must be the true source of Genevieve's distress. She was losing a treasured family member. The woman who had raised her. Genevieve may have a well-developed mystique, but she was not emotionally reserved and she loved deeply. Alexia moved to her friend and stroked her upper arm where the muscles tensed. "Oh, Genevieve, I am so very sorry."

The inventor's face crumpled slightly at the sympathy. "I cannot help but think that this is to be my fate, too. First Angelique and now Beatrice."

"Oh, surely not! You cannot be so confident you have excess soul." Alexia would have offered to ensure exorcism, but Genevieve had been so angry when she performed the service for Angelique.

"No, you are correct. I have been traveling, researching, studying, trying to find a way to extend my aunt's afterlife. But there is *nothing.*" Her tone was anguished, that of a scientist who sees a problem but no solution.

"Oh, but you have done your level best! You have given her *years,* far longer than any ghost has a right to expect."

"Years for what? Humiliation and madness?" Genevieve took a breath, then placed her hand over Alexia's where it stroked her arm, stilling the movement. "I do apologize, my lovely Alexia. This is not your burden. You still wish to speak to her?"

"Would she talk to me, do you think?"

"We can but try."

Lady Maccon nodded and attempted to shrug herself out of her normally regal posture, trying to be less overbearing and physically threatening. She didn't want to scare the ghost. Not that a woman in her corpulent condition boasted so fearsome a visage.

Madame Lefoux yelled, her normally melodious voice sharp, "Aunt, where are you? Aunt!"

Several moments later, a ghostly form shimmered into existence out of the side of a conveyer belt spool, looking grumpy.

"Yes, Niece, you summoned me?" Formerly Beatrice Lefoux had been in life an angular spinster of severe attitude and limited affection. She might once have been pretty but obviously never allowed herself, nor others, to enjoy that fact. There was much of her in Madame Lefoux, tempered by a level of good humor and mischief that the aunt had never bothered to cultivate. The specter was beginning to go fuzzy, not so badly as Alexia's ghostly messenger but enough for it to be clear she wasn't long for this world.

As soon as she spotted Lady Maccon, the ghost drew herself inward, appearing to wrap the drifting threads of her noncorporeal self closer, as a werewolf wraps his cloak around after shifting.

"Why, you have the soulless visiting you, Niece. Honestly, I don't know why you persist in such an association." The ghost's voice was bitter, but more out of habit than any real offense. Then she seemed to lose track of what she was saying. "Where? What? Where am I? Genevieve, why, you are so old. Where is my little girl?" She swirled in a circle. "You have built an octomaton? I said never again. What could possibly be so dire?" As she spoke, the ghost shifted between French and heavily accented English. Luckily, Alexia was tolerably competent in both.

Madame Lefoux, her expression stiff in an attempt to hide distress, snapped her fingers in front of her deceased aunt's face. "Now, Aunt, please pay attention. Lady Maccon here has something very serious to ask of you. Go on, Alexia."

"Formerly Lefoux, are you familiar with the attempt on Queen Victoria's life that took place in the winter of 1853? A Scottish werewolf pack was implicated. It was a matter of poison."

The ghost bobbled up and down in surprise, losing some small measure of control over bits of herself. An eyebrow detached from her forehead. "Oh, why, yes. Although not intimately, of course. Not from the actual assassination perspective but more from the sidelines. I lost one of my students because of it."

"Oh?"

"Why, yes. Lost her to the mist of the moor. Lost her to duty. So promising, so strong, so . . . wait. What were you asking? What are we discussing? Why must I forget things all the time?"

"The Kingair assassination attempt," Alexia prompted.

"Silly dogfight. Poor girl. Imagine having to take on that kind of responsibility. At sixteen! And over werewolves. Werewolves who planned a poisoning. So many things wrong with the very idea. So many things out of character. Out of the supernatural order. Was it ever put right, I wonder?"

Alexia pulled a measure of this rambling together. "Sidheag Maccon was your student?"

The ghost's head tilted. "Sidheag. That name is familiar. Oh, why, yes. So hard to finish in one way, so easy to finish in another. A strong girl, good at finishing. But then again, strength in girls is not so much valued as it ought to be."

Lady Maccon, as interested as she was in anything to do with her husband's great-great-great-granddaughter, now one of the only female werewolves in England and Alpha of the Kingair Pack, felt she must still steer the ghost back onto more relevant matters. "Did you happen to hear, at the time, whether there was a connection between the assassination attempt and the Order of the Brass Octopus?"

"Connection? Connection? Of course not."

Alexia was taken aback by the firm confidence in the ghost's voice. "How can you be so certain?"

"How can I not? Imagine such a thing. No, no, not against the queen. Never against Queen Victoria. We would have known. I would have known. Someone would have told me." Formerly Beatrice Lefoux swirled about in her distress, once more catching sight of Madame Lefoux's latest project. She paused as though hypnotized by the imposing thing. "Oh, Genevieve, I can't believe you would. I can't. Not for anything. Why, child, why? I must tell. I must convince . . ." She ended up facing Alexia once more and, as though seeing her for the first time, said, "You! Soulless. You will stop everything in the end, won't you? Even me."

Madame Lefoux pressed her lips together, closed her eyes, and gave a sad sigh. "There she goes. We won't get any more sense out of her this evening. I'm sorry, Alexia."

"Oh, no, that's quite all right. It wasn't precisely what I was hoping for, but it has convinced me that I must contact Lady Kingair as soon as possible. I must convince my husband's old pack to reveal the details of the original plot. Only they can fully unravel this mystery. I can't believe that the OBO was not involved, but if your aunt says so with such conviction, only the source of the threat itself can reveal the truth of the matter."

"And, of course, my aunt was never a member of the Order."

"She wasn't?" Alexia was genuinely surprised.

"Absolutely not. Women weren't allowed to join back in her day. It's difficult enough now." The French inventor, one of the smartest people Alexia had ever met, reached behind her neck to finger the octopus tattoo that lay hidden there, just under the curls of her scandalously short hair. Alexia tried to imagine Genevieve without her secret underground world. Impossible.

Alexia said, "I shall have to send someone to Scotland. I don't suppose . . . ?"

Madame Lefoux looked even more unhappy. "Oh, no. I am sorry, my dearest Alexia, but I cannot afford the time. Not right now. I have this"—she waved a hand at the monstrous thing she was building—"to finish. And my aunt to think of. I should be with her, now that the end is near."

Lady Maccon turned to the inventor and, because she seemed to need it more than anything else, embraced her gently. It was awkward given Alexia's belly but worth it for the slight lessening Alexia could feel in Genevieve's stiffened shoulders. "Would you like me to send her on?" she asked in a hushed voice.

"No, thank you. I am not yet ready to let her go. You understand?"

Alexia sighed and released her friend. "Well, worry not on this particular matter. I will get to the bottom of it. Even if I have to send Ivy Tunstell to Scotland for me!"

Fated words that, as is often the case with frivolous speech, Alexia was going to come to regret.

CHAPTER SIX

In Which Mrs. Tunstell Proves Useful

Were they not recently moved into new accommodations, Lady Maccon might have made a different choice—one of Woolsey's older clavigers, perhaps. But the pack was in chaos over the relocation. They were nowhere near as tethered to a place as vampires, but werewolves were, in simple terms, tethered to each other and were creatures of profound habit. Such arbitrary reorganization ruffled the fur. Solidarity and proximity became ever more necessary for the pack's continued cohesion. Were BUR not occupied with its own investigation as to the current threat against Queen Victoria, Alexia might have tapped Haverbink or another experienced investigator. And, finally, were the Shadow Council supplied with its own agents, the muhjah would have had manpower to call upon. However, with none of these options readily available, Lady Maccon cast about herself and found that she had only one possible choice—as unlikely and as addlepated as that choice might be.

Mrs. Tunstell ran a tight household, despite overseeing her rented accommodations with a floppy hand and absentminded disposition. Her abode was clean and neat, and callers could be assured of a decent cup of tea or candy dish of raw meat, depending upon taste and inclination. Despite an interior resplendent in every shade of pastel, Ivy's home was a popular watering hole. As a result, the Tunstells had developed a name for themselves among the more esoteric members of the West End as agreeable hosts interested in a wide range of topics and ever willing to open their door to the friendly visitor. This meant that, at any given time, one was practically guaranteed to find some breed of indifferent poet or insipid sculptor in residence.

So it was that when Lady Maccon called around teatime that summer afternoon, a delighted Mrs. Tunstell welcomed her inside with assurances that while they had indeed adopted a stray poet, that versifier was quite firmly asleep and had been for the better part of three days.

Ivy's good-humored little face fell. "He drinks, poor man, to forget the pain of the embittered universe that subsumes his soul. Or do I mean sublimes his soul? Any-hoo, we've had to remove the tea quite forcibly from his grasp on more than one occasion. Barley water, says Tunny, is the only thing one should take when suffering such ailments of the emotional humors."

"Oh, dear," commiserated Alexia. "I suppose one might recover one's spirits out of desperation if all one had to drink was barley water."

"Exactly so!" Ivy nodded over her husband's evident sagacity on the application of revolting beverages to despondent poets. She motioned her friend into her front parlor, a diminutive room that boasted all the elegance of iced Nesselrode pudding.

Lady Maccon deposited her parasol into the small umbrella stand and made her way gingerly toward a wingback chair, careful not to upset any of the decorative objects strewn about. Her visiting dress was of flowing blue paisley with a stiffened quilted skirt. Designed to accommodate her increasing girth, it was much wider—and thus more dangerous to Ivy's receiving room—than the current trends dictated.

She sat heavily in the chair, sighing at the relief of getting the weight off her poor feet, which seemed to have swollen to near twice their original proportions. "Ivy, my dear, I was wondering if I might prevail upon you for a very great favor."

"Oh, Alexia, of course. You have only to ask and I shall do whatever."

Lady Maccon hesitated, wondering exactly how much to reveal. Ivy was a dear little soul, but was she reliable? She decided to buck up and take the plunge. "Ivy, have you ever wondered if there might, just possibly, be something slightly unusual about me?"

"Well, Alexia my dear, I never liked to say, but I have always wondered about your hat preferences. They have struck me as mighty plain."

Lady Maccon shook her head. The long blue ostrich feather of her not-at-all-plain hat wafted back and forth behind her. "No, not that, I mean . . . Well, dash it, Ivy, there's nothing for it."

Mrs. Tunstell gasped in enchanted shock at Lady Maccon's lowbrow language. "Alexia, you have been fraternizing with werewolves overmuch! Military men can be terribly bad for one's verbal concatenation."

Alexia took a deep breath and then blurted out, "I'm preternatural."

Ivy's dark eyes widened. "*Oh, no*! Is it catching?"

Alexia blinked at her.

Ivy donned a sympathetic expression. "Is it a terribly painful condition?"

Lady Maccon continued to blink.

Ivy put a hand to her throat. "Is it the baby? Will you both be well? Should I send for barley water?"

Alexia finally found her voice. "No, *preternatural.* You might know the term, as in *soulless*? Or curse-breaker. I have no soul. None at all. As a matter of fact, I can cancel it out in supernatural creatures given half a chance."

Ivy relaxed. "Oh, *that.* Yes, I knew. I shouldn't let it concern you, my dear. I doubt anybody minds."

"Yes, but . . . Wait, you knew?"

Ivy tut-tutted and shook dark ringlets at her friend in mock amusement. "Of course I knew—have done for simply ages."

"But you never mentioned a thing to me on the subject." Alexia was not often flummoxed. She found it an usual sensation and wondered if this was what Ivy felt like most of the time. Her friend's revelation did, however, give her some degree of confidence in her next move. Despite all her frivolities, Ivy could clearly keep a secret and, it turned out, was more observant than Alexia had previously given her credit for.

"Now, Alexia, I thought you were embarrassed about it. I didn't want to bring up an uncomfortable personal disability. I have more sensitivity and care for the feelings of others than that!"

"Ah, oh, well. Of course you do. Regardless, as a preternatural, I am currently engaged in some investigations. I was hoping to enlist your aid. It has to do with my husband's work." Alexia didn't want to tell Ivy absolutely everything, but she didn't want to fib outright either.

"For BUR? Espionage! Oh, really? How terribly glamorous." Ivy clasped yellow-gloved hands together in delight.

"To which end I was hoping to, well, induct you into a kind of secret society."

Ivy looked as though she had not heard anything so thrilling in all her life. "Me?" she squeaked. "Really? How *marvelous.* What's it called, this secret society?"

Alexia hesitated and then, recalling a phrase her husband had once offered up in the heat of annoyance, suggested tentatively, "The Parasol Protectorate?"

"Oooh, what a perfectly splendid name. So full of ornamentation!" Ivy practically bounced up and down on the lavender settee in her excitement. "Must I make a pledge, or memorize a sacred code of conduct, or engage in some pagan ritual or other?" Ivy had an expectant look on her face that suggested she would be very disappointed if this were not the case.

"Well, yes, of course." Lady Maccon floundered, trying to come up with something appropriate to the occasion. She couldn't make Ivy kneel, not in that dress—a periwinkle muslin day gown with an extremely long, tight bodice of the style favored by actresses.

After a moment's thought, Alexia stood laboriously and waddled over to the umbrella stand to retrieve her parasol. This she opened and placed point downward in the center of the room. Since the room was so very small, this did manage to take up most of the free space. Motioning Ivy to stand, Alexia handed her the handle and said, "Spin the parasol three times and repeat after me: I shield in the name of fashion. I accessorize for one and all. Pursuit of truth is my passion. This I vow by the great parasol."

Ivy did as she was told, face serious and concentrated. "I shield in the name of fashion. I accessorize for one and all. Pursuit of truth is my passion. This I vow by the great parasol."

"Now pick the parasol up and raise it, open, to the ceiling. Yes, just like that."

"Is that all? Shouldn't the vow be sealed in blood or something like?"

"Oh, do you think?"

Ivy nodded enthusiastically.

Alexia shrugged. "If you insist." She took back her parasol, snapped it closed, and twisted the handle. Two wickedly sharp spikes projected out of the tip, one of silver, the other of wood.

Ivy inhaled in appreciation.

Lady Maccon flipped the parasol about. Then she took off one of her gloves. After a moment's hesitation, Ivy did the same. Alexia nicked the pad of her thumb with the silver spike and then did the same for Ivy, who gave a little squeak of alarm. Then Alexia pressed their two thumbs together.

"May the blood of the soulless keep your own soul safe," intoned Alexia, feeling appallingly melodramatic but knowing Ivy would love this better than anything.

Ivy did. "Oh, Alexia, this is so very stirring! It should be part of a play."

"I shall have a special parasol made up for you, similar to mine."

"Oh, no, but thank you for the thought, Alexia. I couldn't possibly carry an accessory that emitted things all willy-nilly like that. Really, I'm much obliged, but I simply couldn't bear it. You, of course, manage to carry it off with aplomb, but it would be too vulgar on someone like me."

Lady Maccon frowned, but knowing her friend's true weakness, she made another suggestion. "A special hat, perhaps?"

Ivy hesitated.

"Madame Lefoux designed my parasol."

"Well, perhaps a small hat. One that isn't too oozy?"

Alexia smiled. "I am convinced that could be arranged."

Ivy bit her lip on a smile. "Oh, Alexia, a secret society. How marvelous of you. Who else is a member? Do we have regular meetings? Is there a covert signal so we should know one another at social gatherings?"

"Um, well, as to that, so far you are my first inductee, so to speak. I anticipate future members, though."

Ivy looked quite crestfallen.

Lady Maccon continued on hastily. "But you will have to operate and report in under a cipher, of course—for aetherograms and other secret messages."

Ivy brightened at that. "Oh, of course. What shall my cipher be? Something romantic yet subtle, I hope?"

Lady Maccon contemplated her friend while a series of rather silly names suggested themselves. Finally, she settled on one she knew Ivy would like, because it represented a style of headdress to which she was rather devoted but that Alexia might remember because it struck her as particularly Ivyish. "How about Puff Bonnet?"

Ivy's pretty face glowed with pleasure. "Oh, fabulous. Perfectly modish. And what's yours?"

Again, Alexia was ill prepared for the question. She cast about helplessly. "Uh. Oh, let me think." She grappled, running through her mind several of Lord Akeldama's epithets and some of her husband's more affectionate endearments. Nothing quite suited a secret society, at least not that she could admit openly to Ivy. Finally, she settled on the simplest she could think of. "You may refer to me as the Ruffled Parasol. That should do well enough."

Ivy clapped her hands. "Oh, excellent. Alexia, this is superb fun."

Lady Maccon sat back down. "Do you think we might have tea now?" she asked plaintively.

Ivy immediately rang the bell rope, and in short order a nervous young maid brought in a laden tea tray.

"Marvelous," said Lady Maccon in evident relief.

Ivy poured. "And now that I have been properly inducted into the Protectorate, what is my first assignment?"

"Ah, yes, the reason I came to visit in the first place. You see, there is a matter of national delicacy concerning an assassination attempt on

Queen Victoria. Some twenty years ago, members of the Kingair Pack tried to eliminate Her Majesty."

"Oh, no, really? Not those nice Scotsmen? They couldn't possibly do anything so treasonous. Well, except trot around displaying their knees for all to see, but nothing so calamitous as attempted regicide."

"I assure you, Ivy, this is the honest truth, universally acknowledged by those in a position to know such details." Lady Maccon sipped her tea and then nodded wisely. "Fact—my husband's previous pack tried to kill Queen Victoria by means of a poison. I need *you* to float back to Castle Kingair and ascertain the particulars."

Ivy grinned. She had developed, since her first trip with Alexia to Scotland, a most unladylike fondness for dirigible travel. Her current position in life did not allow her to indulge, but now . . .

Lady Maccon grinned back. "All I know is that the previous Beta spearheaded the plot and was killed. My husband left the pack as a result. Any further information could be invaluable to my current investigation. Do you think you are up to this task, even in your present condition?"

Ivy blushed at the very mention. "I am barely along, and you *certainly* cannot go."

Alexia patted her belly. "My difficulty exactly."

"Can I take Tunny with me?"

"I should hope you would. And you may tell him of your mission, although not your new position."

Ivy nodded. More pleased, Alexia suspected, by the need to keep one secret from her husband than by permission to reveal another.

"Now, Ivy, please pay particular attention to any information on the poison that was going to be used. I believe that may be key. I shall give you a crystalline valve frequensor for aetheric transmission to my personal transponder at Woolsey. At sunset you are to report in, even if you have uncovered nothing of interest. I should like to know you are safe."

"Oh, but, Alexia, you know how clumsy I am with gadgetry."

"You will do fine, Ivy. How soon can you leave? Naturally your expenses will be covered."

Ivy blushed at the mention of such unseemly matters as fiscal settlements.

Alexia brushed her friend's embarrassment aside. "I know one doesn't ordinarily talk of such matters, but you are operating under the umbrella of the Parasol Protectorate now, and you must be free to act in accordance with the needs of the organization, regardless of expense. Is that clear, Ivy?"

Mrs. Tunstell nodded, cheeks still hot. "Yes, of course, Alexia, but—"

"It is a good thing I am to be patroness of your acting troupe, as it is the perfect way to hide pecuniary advancements."

"Oh, yes, indeed, Alexia. But I wish you didn't insist on mentioning such things while we are eating—"

"We shall say nothing more on the subject. Can you leave directly?"

"Tunny has no performances on at the moment."

"Then I shall send Floote tomorrow with the necessary papers." Lady Maccon finished the last of her tea and stood. She was suddenly tired. It was as though she had been out and about most of the night, sorting out the problems of the entire empire. Which, in her way, she had.

Mrs. Tunstell stood as well. "To Scotland I go, investigating assignation attempts of the past!"

"Assassination," corrected Lady Maccon.

"Yes, that. I must find my extra special hairmuffs for dirigible travel. I had them made to match my own curls. They are rather stunning, if I do say so myself."

"Of that, I have no doubt."

Lady Maccon returned to her new house and then made her way across to Lord Akeldama's. Floote's builders produced exemplary work. They had constructed a small secret drawbridge between the two balconies that operated by way of a hydraulic lever. It flipped downward. At the same time an elaborate spring mechanism caused the railing on each balcony to fold away. This allowed Alexia to easily traverse from one building to the next despite encumbrances.

She retired to her closet with alacrity. She had been keeping remarkably odd hours recently, what with having to consult daylight folk yet living with the supernatural set. It was of little consequence, as the infant-inconvenience was making it increasingly arduous to sleep for any length of time without some part of her body going numb or some unmentionable function driving her out of bed. Really, pregnancy was the most undignified thing she had ever had to endure in all her life, and for several years Alexia Tarabotti had been a confirmed spinster living with the Loontwills—a most undignified state—so that was saying something.

She slept restlessly, shifting aside when her husband joined her only to be awakened fully just after sunset by someone banging on the closet door.

"Conall, there is someone at the door to our *bedroom*!" She shook her massive husband where he lay in a boneless pile next to her.

He snuffled softly and rolled over, trying to gather her in closer. He had to settle for patting her belly absently and burrowing into her neck.

Alexia arched against him as much as she was able, enjoying the affection and the movement of his lips against her skin. For such a scruffy man, he had very soft lips.

"Darling, light of my life, lord of my heart, there is someone at the door to our closet, seeking entrance. And I don't believe Lord Akeldama and his boys are awake yet."

The earl merely burrowed in against her with greater interest, apparently finding the flavor of her neck most intriguing.

The door shook and rattled as whoever it was seemed to be trying to physically force it open. But for all Lord Akeldama's frolicsome decorative choices, his town house was built with the supernatural in mind, the protection of his clothing being paramount. The door barely budged. Someone on the other side yelled, but a door so massive that it could withstand shoe thieves could also muffle even the loudest commentary on the subject.

Lady Maccon was becoming concerned. "Conall, get up and answer the door, do! Really, it sounds most pressing."

"I, too, have matters that are pressing and must needs be taken into hand."

Alexia giggled at the terribleness of both pun and innuendo. She was pleased her husband still thought her attractive, despite her beached-whale state, but was finding it increasingly awkward to accommodate him. The spirit was willing but the flesh was swollen. Still, she enjoyed the compliment and understood that there was no real demand behind the caresses. The earl knew her well enough to realize she valued his desire almost as much as his love. After a lifetime of feeling ugly and unworthy, Alexia was now tolerably assured that Conall genuinely did want her, even if they could do nothing about it at present. She also understood that he was expressing his conjugal interest partly out of knowledge of her own need for such assurances. A werewolf and a buffoon, her husband, but wonderfully caring once he'd blundered into the way of it.

And yet, someone was still torturing their poor door. Conall blinked awake, his tawny eyes wide and direct. He kissed the tip of his wife's long nose and, with a massive sigh, rolled out of bed and lumbered over to the door.

Alexia, sleepy lidded, admired his backside, then shrieked, "Conall, robe! For goodness' sake."

Her husband ignored her, throwing open the door and crossing his arms over a wide, hairy chest. He was wearing not one stitch of clothing. Alexia sank down under the covers in mortification.

She need not have worried; it was only Professor Lyall.

"Randolph," grumbled her husband, "what's all the ruckus about?"

"It's Biffy, my lord. Best come quickly. You're needed."

"Already?" Lord Maccon swore a blue streak, his blistering language the result of military service combined with a creative imagination. After a glance about the room, he seemed to decide that changing his form would be faster than getting dressed. He began to shift, the musculature underneath his skin rearranging, the hair on his head migrating downward and turning into fur. Quick enough, he dropped to all fours. Then he dashed out and down the hall, presumably to leap the gap between houses and see to whatever had gone wrong. Alexia caught sight of the brindled tip of his fluffy tail as he skidded out of sight without even a nod in her direction.

"What is it, Professor?" she demanded imperiously before her husband's Beta could follow in his Alpha's wake. It was rather unlike Professor Lyall to disturb them with such forcefulness. It was equally rare for there to be any issue so in need of the earl's attention that his second could not delay the matter or handle the preliminaries himself.

Professor Lyall turned back to the dim interior with a reluctant droop to his posture. "It's Biffy, my lady. He really is not handling the curse well this month. He fights it too much, and the more he fights it, the more painful it is."

"But it's over a week until full moon! How long will he suffer such bouts of early physiological disjunction?" *Poor Biffy. It is so embarrassing—premature transfluctuation.*

"Difficult to say. Could be years, could be decades of losing nights around full moon until he has better control. All new pups are like this, although they are not often taken so suddenly or so badly as Biffy. Usually it is only a few days before the moon. Biffy's cycle is off."

Alexia winced. "And you could not . . . ?"

Backlit by the expensively bright gas lighting of Lord Akeldama's hallway, it was impossible to make out the werewolf's expression. Even if she could, knowing Professor Lyall, his face would not reveal much.

"In the end, I am only a Beta, Lady Maccon. When a werewolf is in wolf form, moonstruck and rampaging, there is nothing that can calm or control him except an Alpha. You must have realized by now that there is much more to Alpha than being simply big and strong. There is power of restraint and wolf-form intelligence as well."

"But, Professor Lyall, you are very restrained all the time."

"Thank you, Lady Maccon. There can be no higher compliment to a werewolf, but mine is a matter of self-control only. That does others little good."

"Except that you lead by example."

"Except that. And now I should leave you to get dressed. I believe we may expect your results from BUR shortly."

"My results?"

"Those little OBO bottles of mysterious liquid."

"Ah, yes, fantastic! Will you please arrange for Floote and I to have the carriage after supper? I must visit Woolsey's library as soon as possible."

The Beta nodded. "I have a feeling it will already be commissioned. We'll have to take Biffy to the countryside for his confinement. His most recent inabilities have resulted in some rather disastrous redecoration of your back parlor."

"Oh, no, really? And after the drones did such a lovely job with it."

"We had to lock him somewhere, and that room has no windows."

"I understand. But claw marks are murder on wallpaper."

"Too true, Lady Maccon."

Professor Lyall drifted away and, because he was Professor Lyall, managed to corral one of Lord Akeldama's drones, just awakened, to help Lady Maccon dress.

Boots stuck his head in before catching sight of Lady Maccon still abed. The head instantly retreated and a back was presented in the doorway.

"Oh, dear me, most sorry, Lady M. Can't be me. Couldn't handle it a second time. Not that noble. I'll go rustle up someone a little more suitable to assist you. Shall I? Be back in a jiff."

Mystified, Alexia began the laborious process of squirming herself around and lurching by stages out of bed. She was just standing when Lord Akeldama came traipsing merrily into the room. "Top of the evening to you, my *blooming* marigold! My lovelorn little Boots said you could use a bit of twisting up, and I thought since I was awake I might avail myself of your *delicious* company and provide much-needed assistance simultaneously."

Lord Akeldama himself was not yet properly dressed for the evening. His affected monocle was absent, as were the obligatory spots of rouge on his alabaster cheeks and the ridiculous spats about his ankles. Nevertheless, even in his least formal attire, Lord Akeldama excelled.

"But, my dear friend, your knees!"

He was wearing royal blue breeches of watered silk, a damask waistcoat of white and gold, and a quilted velvet smoking jacket ornamented with brandenbourgs. His trousers were of such very fine quality, Alexia was quite aghast that the vampire should even consider playing at lady's maid, for he might have to kneel—on the floor!

"Oh, phooey, you know me, darling—always open to an adventure *à la toilette.*"

Lord Akeldama was a man who Lady Maccon very much doubted had had much to do with dressing—or undressing—ladies on a regular basis, yet he seemed more than equal to the task. In the early days of her pregnancy, Alexia might have managed it herself, rejecting her corset and selecting a carriage dress or some other gown that fastened up the front. However, at this point, she couldn't even see her own feet, let alone touch them. So she acquiesced to this very strange new form of servant.

"I suppose it was courteous of Professor Lyall to think to send someone in. But really, if a gentleman who is not my husband is to see me bare, why not him?"

Lord Akeldama sashayed over to her, scooping up her underthings along the way. He tittered at the very idea. "Oh, my darling *pea blossom,* your professor might enjoy it a little too much. Like my poor Boots. And they are both gentlemen of principle." His hands began nimbly dealing with ties and buttons.

"What could you possibly be implying, my lord?" Lady Maccon asked this from within a chemise partly stuck over her head.

The vampire pulled the fine muslin down and smoothed it out over her belly with a little pat. His other hand was on her naked arm, and the contact turned him human in that moment. His fine, sharp fangs vanished, his pale white skin flushed slightly peach, and his lustrous blond hair lost a mote of its brilliance. He grinned at her, his face more effeminate than ethereal. "La, *honeysuckle,* you are well aware that we *here* are all, in our own special way, *deviants* in our penchants."

Lady Maccon thought about Lord Akeldama's drawing room with all its gilt and tassels. Even knowing this was not the vampire's point of reference, she nodded. "Oh, yes, I noticed."

Lord Akeldama rarely shrugged, for this upset the fall of his jacket, but he looked as though he would have at this juncture. Instead, he flounced over to the side of the room where Alexia's clothing hung on a long rack and began perusing various gowns, eyeing each with a discerning eye.

"Not that one," said Alexia when he paused overlong, considering a green and gold stripe.

"No?"

"The décolletage is too low."

"My dearest girl, this is a good design point, not a bad one. You should accentuate your best *features.*"

"No, honestly, my lord, these days I—how to put this?—overflow. It's terribly incommodious." Alexia made a kind of flip-forward gesture with both hands at her bosom area. Always substantial, that particular region had expanded to near scenic proportions over the last few months. Lord Maccon was delighted. Lady Maccon found it ridiculous. *As if I weren't well enough endowed to start with!*

"Ah, yes. I do see your point, *periwinkle.*" He moved on.

"You were saying, about Professor Lyall?"

"What I mean to articulate, *honey bee*, is that there are *levels* of deviation. Some of us are, shall we say, more *experimental* than others in our tastes. In some, I believe it is a matter of boredom, in others it is nature, and for still others it is indifference." The vampire's tone of voice was filled with the usual airy flippancy, but Alexia had a feeling this was something he had studied much over the centuries. Also, Lord Akeldama never doled out information without good reason.

The vampire continued to prattle on as he sorted through her wardrobe without looking up at her, as though he were having a conversation with the dresses. "So few are lucky enough to love where they will. Or unlucky, I suppose." Finally, he selected a walking outfit comprised of a ruffled purple skirt, cream blouse, and square cropped Spanish jacket in mauve. Despite the fact that there was very little trim, something about it clearly appealed to him. Alexia was delighted with this choice, as the outfit coordinated with one of her favorite hats, a little mauve bowler with a purple ostrich feather.

He brought it over to her and held it up, nodding. "Excellent palette for your coloring, my *little Italian pastry.* Did our Biffy help you order this?" Without waiting for confirmation, he continued his previous discussion with studied casualness. "Your Professor Lyall is one of those."

"One of the indifferent ones?"

"Ah, no, petal, one of those who has no particular preferences."

"And Boots?" Alexia held very still as the vampire moved around behind her, very much like a real maid, and began lacing up the back of the skirt.

"Boots is another one."

Lady Maccon thought she understood what he was trying to say but was determined to ensure things were as clear as possible. Lord Akeldama may enjoy prevarications and euphemisms, but no one had ever accused Alexia of being coy. "Are you telling me, my lord, that Boots enjoys the *company* of both men and women?"

The vampire came back around to the front and cocked his head to one side, as though more interested in the fit of the jacket than their conversation. "I know, peculiar of him, isn't it, my little *pigeon*? But I and mine, possibly more than anyone else in London, do not presume to judge the predilections of others." He bent forward to tidy the fall of the bow at Alexia's neck. Then he had her sit while he fussed with stockings.

"Well, I should never venture to question your assessment of Boots's taste, but really, you must be mistaken in Professor Lyall's nature. He's in the military, for goodness' sake!"

"I take it you have heard very little on the subject of Her Majesty's Royal Navy?" The vampire moved on to her shoes. Her feet were so swollen she no longer fit into any of her boots, much to his disgust. "Imagine wearing a walking dress with dancing slippers!"

"Well, it's not as though I *walk* all that much anymore. But, my dear lord, I can't believe it. Not Professor Lyall. You must misconstrue."

Lord Akeldama became motionless, his head bent over one of her kid slippers. "Oh, little lilac bush, I *know* I do not."

Lady Maccon stilled herself, frowning down at the blond head bent so diligently at her feet. "I have never seen him favor anyone of either sex. I had thought it was a part of being Beta, to love the pack at the expense of every other romance. Not that I have met many Betas. It is not a personality trait, then? Has he not always been so reticent?"

Lord Akeldama stood and came back behind her, beginning to toy with her hair.

"You arrange a lady's ensemble rather well, for an aristocrat. Don't you, my lord?"

"We all came from somewhere originally, *buttercup*, even us vampires. Of course, your Professor Lyall and I have never run in the same circles, and until you came into our lives, I must admit I never paid him much mind." The vampire frowned and a look of genuine disfavor crossed his beautiful face. "This may yet prove to be a rather catastrophic oversight. As bad as that brief period wherein I became enamored of a lime-green overcoat." He shuddered at the unpleasantness of the memory.

"Surely it cannot be so awful as all that. It is *only* Professor Lyall of whom we speak."

"*Exactly*, my plum puff. So few of us can be so easily dismissed as an *only*. I've done some inquiring. They say he never quite recovered from a broken heart."

Alexia frowned. "Oh, do *they*?"

"An embarrassing affliction in an immortal, broken-heartedness, wouldn't you say? Least of all in a man of sense and dignity."

Lady Maccon gave her friend a sharp look through the looking glass as he pinned one of her curls into place. "No, I should say instead *poor Professor Lyall.*"

Lord Akeldama finished with her hair. "There!" he pronounced with a flourish. He held up a hand mirror for her to look at the back. "I haven't our lovely Biffy's skill with the curling tongs, so a simple updo will have to suffice. I apologize for such ineptitude. I should add one or two rosettes or a fresh flower, just here."

"Oh, simple is absolutely splendid, and anything is better than what I could do for myself. I shall take your advice about the flower, of course."

The vampire nodded, took the mirror back, and placed it on the armoire. "And . . . how is Biffy?" The very flatness in the vampire's words alerted Alexia to the importance of this oh-so-casual question.

"He is still upset at having to give up snuff." Lord Akeldama smiled only slightly at her attempted lightheartedness, so Alexia adopted his serious tone. "Not as well as he could be. My husband thinks, and I am inclined to agree with him, there is something holding him back. Pitiable, for Biffy did not ask for the lupine afterlife, but he must learn to accept it."

Lord Akeldama's perfect mouth twisted slightly.

"I am given to understand there is a matter of control. He must learn to master the shift rather than allow it to master him. Until he does, there are all sorts of restrictions. He cannot go out during the day or he may be permanently damaged, he must be kept near silver for simply ages around the moon, and no sweet basil within smelling distance. It's all quite tragic."

Lord Akeldama stepped back and then spoke as though she had never answered his question. "Ah, well, I must bid you adieu, *my dearest girl.* I have my own toilette to see to. There is a most licentious music hall show opening this *very* evening, and I have a mind to attend in full regalia." He made his way toward the door in the sweeping manner much favored by an operatic villain when exiting stage left.

Lady Maccon was not fooled.

"My lord." Alexia's voice was soft and gentle, or as soft and as gentle as she could make it, being not a woman generally in command of such feminine wiles. "On our subject of brokenheartedness, should I now be saying *poor Lord Akeldama?*"

The vampire left without dignifying that with a reply.

Lady Maccon lowered the balcony drawbridge and made her way into Woolsey's town home and down the stairs. Walking a gangplank when one cannot see one's feet was a tad nerve-racking, but Alexia Maccon was a woman of forthright character and firm principle, not to be defeated by a mere fat belly. She encountered Felicity, obviously recently returned from one of her unmentionable jaunts, for she was once more attired in knitwear. They had no chance for idle conversation, thank goodness, for the house was in a veritable uproar.

Still, Felicity would not allow Alexia to pass without some commentary. "Sister! What is that tremendous ruckus in the back parlor?"

"Felicity, you did know, when you prevailed upon my hospitality, that this was the den of werewolves, did you not?"

"Yes, but to behave like animals? Surely that's not polite."

Lady Maccon narrowed her eyes, tilted her head, and gave her sister a look and the time to contemplate what she had just said.

Felicity sputtered. "You mean to say? Changed! Here! In town? How unspeakably shameful!" She turned to walk with her sister back down the stairs. "May I see?"

Lady Maccon wondered if she did not prefer the cuttingly nasty Felicity of previous incarnations.

"No, you most certainly may not! Really, what has gotten into you of late? You are not at all yourself."

"Is it so unlikely that I should wish to improve myself?"

Alexia fingered the dull gray shawl draped over her sister's faded dress. "Yes. Yes, it is."

Felicity huffed in annoyance. "I must go change for supper."

Lady Maccon looked her up and down, emitting a lip curl that was, quite frankly, remarkably Felicity-like. Sometimes, although not too often, there came an indication that they were, indeed, related. "Yes, I do believe you must."

Felicity wiggled her shoulders and emitted the "Oh, la," of an insult being shaken off, and proceeded back up to the best bedroom, which she had, naturally, commandeered as her own.

Lady Maccon waddled on down, one careful stair at a time. The urgency of the noises below made her increasingly annoyed by her own inability to move with any kind of alacrity. *Really this is simply too ridiculous! I'm trapped by my own body.* She attained the main hall only to find that the door to the back parlor was locked and shaking. Professor Lyall and two clavigers were milling about unhappily, crowding the passageway with masculine concern.

"Why aren't you at supper?" demanded Lady Maccon imperiously. "I am certain Floote and the staff have gone to substantial lengths to provide."

Everyone stilled and looked at her.

"Go on, go eat," she said to them, as though they were small children or pet dogs.

Professor Lyall raised a quizzical brow at her.

Lady Maccon lowered her voice. "Biffy wouldn't want anyone to see."

"Ah." Then the Beta, obedient to his mistress's will, followed his fellows into the dining room, shutting the door behind him.

Lady Maccon let herself into the back parlor. Which was an absolute mess. Lord Maccon, now a massive brindled wolf—quite handsome, Alexia always thought, even in lupine form—was squared off against a younger, lankier animal. Biffy's fur was a deep chocolate color, much the same as his hair, except for his stomach and up to the ruff, which was oxblood. His eyes were yellow and crazed.

Lord Maccon barked at his wife authoritatively. Lord Maccon was always barking at his wife, the form of his body mattering not one jot.

Alexia dismissed the commanding tone. "Yes, yes, but you must admit I can be quite useful under such circumstances as these, even in my less-than-nimble state."

Lord Maccon growled in evident annoyance.

Biffy caught Lady Maccon's scent and turned instinctively to hurl himself at her, a new threat. The earl twisted to place his own body in the way. The slighter wolf charged full tilt into his Alpha. Biffy reeled, shaking his head and whining. Lord Maccon feinted toward him, teeth nipping, backing him flush against the now mostly destroyed chaise.

"Oh, Conall, look at this room!" Lady Maccon was displeased. The place was in chaos—furniture overturned, drapes shredded, and one of the cook's precious journals had been bitten into and slobbered all over.

"Oh, doesn't that just take the biscuit! That's evidence, that is." Alexia's hand was to her breast in distress. "Oh, dear, I suppose I ought to have kept it with me." She couldn't really blame Biffy, of course, but it was vexing. She toddled her way toward him, stripping off her gloves.

Biffy continued to snap and slather in her direction, growling in uncontrollable rage, the cursed monster of folklore made flesh and fur before her.

Alexia tsked at him. "Really, Biffy, must you?" Then she used her best Lady Maccon voice. "Behave! What kind of conduct is this for a gentleman!"

Alexia was Alpha, too, and the commanding tone sunk in. Biffy mellowed his snapping frenzy. Some measure of sense entered his yellow eyes. Lord Maccon seized the opportunity and charged, clamping down hard on the other wolf's neck, bearing him down to the floor by sheer superiority of mass.

Lady Maccon approached and looked down at the tableau. "It's no good, Conall. I can't bend down to touch him without falling over."

Her husband let out a snort of amusement. Then, with a casual flick of his head, he hurled the young wolf upward. A surprised Biffy landed on his back on the chaise lounge, scrambling to right himself and attack once more.

Lady Maccon grabbed his tail. He jerked in surprise, enough to overbalance her so that she fell with an *oof* onto the chaise next to him. In that same instant, the power of her preternatural touch forced him back into human form. Even as Biffy's tail retreated, Alexia reached for a paw with her other hand.

In very short order, a naked Biffy lay sprawled in a most undignified way upon the chaise lounge with his foot firmly grasped by his mistress. Since contact with Alexia made him mortal, with all the physical responses such a state entailed, it was not unsurprising to find him blushing crimson in humiliation.

Alexia, while sympathetic to his plight, maintained her grasp and noted, with scientific detachment, that his blush went *all the way* down. *Remarkable.*

Her husband's growl drew her attention back to him. He, too, was back in his human form and naked.

"What?"

"Stop looking at him. He's bare."

"So are you, husband."

"Yes, well, you can look at me all you like."

"Yes, well. Oh." Lady Maccon clutched suddenly at her stomach with her free hand.

Conall's mild jealousy translated instantly to overbearing solicitude. "Alexia! Are you ailing? Oh, you shouldna hae come in here! It's too dangerous. You fell."

Biffy sat up, also concerned. He tried to extract his ankle, but Lady Maccon refused to let go. "My lady, what is wrong?"

"Oh, stop it! Both of you. The infant is simply kicking up a fuss over such sudden activity. No, Biffy dear, we must stay in contact, however indecorous you find it." Biffy offered her his hand instead of his foot. Alexia accepted the exchange of prisoners.

"Shall I ring for Floote?" suggested Biffy, blushing slightly less now that he had something to be worried about that wasn't his own shame.

Alexia hid a smile. "You should find that rather difficult, as you seem to have chewed up the bell rope."

Biffy looked around, blushing again. He covered his face with one hand, peeking through open fingers as though he couldn't stand to look, yet was unable to drag his eyes away. "Oh my ruffled bacon! What have I done? Your poor parlor. My lord, my lady, *please* forgive me. I was not myself. I was in thrall to the curse."

Lord Maccon was having none of it. "That's the problem, pup. You were yourself. You continue to refuse to accept that."

Lady Maccon understood her husband's meaning and tried to phrase it in a more sympathetic manner. "You must begin to accustom yourself to being a werewolf, Biffy dear. Even attempt to enjoy it. This continued resistance is unhealthy." She looked around. "Mainly to my furniture."

Biffy looked down and nodded. "Yes, I know. But, my lady, it's so undignified. I mean to say, one must strip before shifting. And then after . . ." He looked down at himself, attempting to cross his legs. Lord Maccon took sympathy on him and tossed him a velvet throw pillow. Biffy placed it into his lap gratefully. Alexia noted her husband took no such pains himself.

Biffy's blue eyes were wide. "Thank you, my lady, for bringing me back. It hurts, but it is worth anything to be human again."

"Yes, but the question is, how are we to get you dressed while I maintain contact?" Alexia wanted to know, ever practical.

Lord Maccon grinned. "Something can be arranged. I shall call Floote in, shall I? He will know how to manage." In the absence of the bellpull, Conall strode out into the hall, yelling for the butler.

Mere moments later, Floote appeared. He took in the wretched condition of the room, furniture everywhere, and the entirely unfurnished condition of two of its occupants without even the flicker of an eyelid.

"Sirs. Madam."

"Floote, my man," said the earl jovially. "We will need someone to see to this room. It's a wee bit messy. A re-covering of the chaise, I think; repairs to the wallpaper and curtains; and a new bell rope. Oh, and Biffy here needs to be dressed without letting go of my wife's paw."

"Yes, sir." Floote turned to see to the matter.

Lady Maccon cleared her throat and looked meaningfully at her husband, up and down and then up again.

"What? Oh, yes, and send one of the clavigers next door for some kit for me as well. Deuced inconvenient, but I suppose I may need garments at some point tonight."

Floote vanished and then reappeared in due time carrying a stack of clothing for Biffy. The young werewolf looked as though he would like to object to the butler's selection but didn't want to cause any more of a fuss. It did seem that Floote had chosen the most somber attire possible out of all of the dandy's peacocklike closet. Biffy's bottom half was seen to rather simply. After which Floote suggested the young man kneel at the edge of the chaise lounge and Lady Maccon touch the back of his head while shirt, waistcoat, jacket, and cravat were summarily dealt with. Floote handled everything with consummate skill, an ability Alexia attributed to his many years as valet to her father. Alessandro Tarabotti, by all accounts, had been a bit of a dandy himself.

While Floote, Alexia, and Biffy performed their complicated game of knotted parts on the chaise, a claviger arrived with apparel for Lord Maccon. The earl threw it on in an arbitrary way, showing all the attention to detail a ferret might employ if called upon to decorate a hat. Lord Maccon believed that if his trousers were on his legs, and something else was on his torso, he was dressed. The less done after that, the better. His wife had been startled to find that in the summertime, he actually went around their room barefoot! Once—and only once, mind you—he even attempted to join her for tea in such a state. *Impossible man.* Alexia put a stop to *that* posthaste.

Professor Lyall stuck his head in to see if everything was sorted.

"Ah, good. You've managed matters."

"Doesn't she always?" grumbled her husband.

"Yes, Professor Lyall?" asked Alexia.

"I thought you should know, my lady, those results you wanted came in from our laboratory at BUR."

"Yes?"

"On those little vials you, uh, found?"

"Yes?"

"Poison. All of them. Different kinds, different effectiveness levels. Some detectable, some not as such. Mostly for mortals but one or two that might put even a supernatural under the weather for some time. Nasty stuff."

CHAPTER SEVEN

The Werewolves of Woolsey Castle

Having to keep Biffy mortal made for a pretty incommodious several hours. Ordinarily, Lady Maccon, even pregnant, could manage a meal and a carriage ride with aplomb, but when one must stay attached in some manner to a dandy, even the most mundane tasks become an exercise in complexity.

"It's a good thing I enjoy your company, Biffy. I can't imagine having to handle daily tasks with someone less agreeable affixed. Like my husband, for example." Alexia shuddered at the very idea. She enjoyed having Conall affixed to her, but only for a limited amount of time.

The husband in question looked up at his lady with a grumbled, "Oh, thank you verra much, wife."

They were sitting in the carriage together. Woolsey Castle loomed on the horizon—a sizable blob in the moonlight. Lady Maccon, being a woman of little artistic preference, regarded her domain with an eye toward its practicality as an abode for werewolves rather than an architectural endeavor. Which was good, as it was rather more of an architectural tragedy. Those unfortunate enough to happen upon it during daylight could tender only one compliment—that it was pleasingly situated. And it was, atop rising ground in extensive, if slightly unkempt, grounds with a cobbled courtyard and decent stables.

"Oh, you know perfectly well what I mean, husband. We've had to stay attached before, but customarily only when violence was imminent."

"And sometimes for other reasons." He gave her his version of a seductive look.

She smiled. "Yes, dear, exactly."

Biffy said, being on his best behavior, "Thank you for the compliment, my lady, and I do apologize for the inconvenience."

"So long as there are no more zombie porcupines, we should do very well."

"Shouldn't be," said her husband. "Seems the hives have officially declared a cease-fire. Hard to tell truth with vampires but they appear to be pleased with the idea of Lord Akeldama adopting our child."

"Well, at least someone is."

Woolsey Castle was no castle at all but a large Georgian manor house augmented by mismatched Gothic-style flying buttresses. On her most recent trip to Italy, Lady Maccon had encountered a bug—a creature larger than her thumb that flew upright, like an angel, with a nose like an elephant, horns like a bull, and multiple wings. It stayed aloft in an erratic up-and-down manner as though it were remembering, occasionally, that a bug of its size and shape ought not to be able to fly. Woolsey Castle was built, in principle, upon much the same lines as that bug: improbably constructed, exceedingly ugly, and impossible to determine how it continued to stay upright or, indeed, why it bothered to do so.

Since Lord and Lady Maccon had set forth to their country seat with no warning, their unanticipated arrival at Woolsey threw the residents into a tizzy. Lord Maccon swept into the bevy of sprightly young men who'd congregated in the courtyard, taller than most by a head, and carved a path before him, scythelike.

Major Channing, Woolsey's Gamma, strode down from his sanctum and out the front door to greet them, still knotting his cravat and looking as though he had only just arisen, despite the lateness of the hour. "My lord, you were not expected until full moon."

"Emergency trip. Have to stick certain persons down the dungeon sooner than anticipated." There were rumors as to the original owner's use of Woolsey's dungeon, but regardless of initial intent it had proved ideal for a werewolf pack. In fact, the whole house was well suited. In addition to a well-fortified holding area and brick walls, there were no less than fourteen bedrooms, a goodly number of receiving parlors, and several precarious-looking but fully functional towers, one of which Lord and Lady Maccon utilized as their boudoir.

Channing waved a hand at a gaggle of clavigers, directing them to help with luggage and assist in extracting Lady Maccon from the carriage. The earl was already cocking an ear to a murmured report from one of his pack. He left his wife to see to Biffy, secure in the knowledge that if nothing else, Alexia was good at setting a gentleman in his proper place, even if that place be a dungeon.

Lady Maccon, happy to lean upon Biffy, for exhaustion was beginning to take its toll once more, made her way down into the dungeon and saw the young dandy safely into one of the smaller cells. Two clavigers accompanied them, carrying the requisite amount of silver-tipped and silver-edged weaponry, just in case Lady Maccon lost her grip.

Alexia did not want to let go, for Biffy's face was pale with the imminent terror of transformation. It was an agonizing process for all werewolves to endure, but the new ones had it the worst, for they were not yet accustomed to the sensation, and they were forced into it more frequently by their own lack of control.

Biffy clearly did not care to leave contact with the safe haven of her preternatural skin, but he was too much the gentleman to say. He would be more mortified to impose upon her for the duration of an entire night than to transform into a rampaging monster.

Alexia averted her eyes and kept her hand to the back of his head, her fingers buried in his thick chocolate brown hair, while the clavigers stripped him and clapped silver manacles about his elegant wrists. Conscious of his fading dignity, she kept a stream of irreverent chatter mostly concerning matters fashionable and decorative.

"We are ready, my lady," said one of the clavigers, arms full of clothing, as he exited the prison cell. The other stood outside the silver-plated bars, ready to slam the door as soon as Lady Maccon came through.

"I am sorry," was all Alexia could think to say to the young man.

Biffy shook his head. "Oh, no, my lady, you have given me unexpected peace."

They stretched apart, fingertips just touching.

"Now," said Lady Maccon, and she broke contact, moving as fast as she could in her condition through the door and into the viewing hall.

Biffy, mindful of any damage he might do before she could touch him again, threw himself away in that same instant, using all his regained supernatural strength and speed, before the change descended upon him.

Alexia found the werewolf transformation an intellectually fascinating occurrence and enjoyed watching it, as one might enjoy dissecting a frog, but not in the younger werewolves. Her husband, Professor Lyall, and even Major Channing could manage shifting form with very little indication as to the pain accompanying the experience. Biffy could not. The moment they broke contact, he began to scream. Lady Maccon had learned over the past several months that there is no worse noise in the universe than a proud, kind young man suffering. His scream evolved into a howl as bones and organs broke and re-formed.

Swallowing down bile and wishing she had wax to stopper her ears, Alexia firmly took the arm of one of the clavigers and ushered him toward the stairs and up into the comforting hullabaloo of the pack, leaving the other to stand solitary vigil over a broken man.

"You really want that?" she asked her escort.

The claviger did not try to hedge. Everyone knew Lady Maccon to be direct in her conversation and intolerant of shilly-shallying. "Immortality, my lady, is nothing to treat lightly, no matter the package or the price."

"But at such a cost as that?"

"I would be choosing it, my lady. He did not."

"And you wouldn't prefer trying for vampire instead?"

"To suck blood for survival and never see the sun again? No, thank you, my lady. I'll take my chances with the pain and the curse, should I be so lucky as to have the choice."

"Brave lad." She patted his arm as they attained the top of the stair.

The hubbub resulting from the sudden arrival of Alphas in their midst had settled down into the pleasant boisterous hum of pack in full play. There was some discussion of going hunting, others thought a game of dice was in order, and a few were advocating a light wrestling match. "Outside," grumbled Lady Maccon mildly upon hearing *that*.

At first, Alexia had thought she would never acclimatize to living with over a dozen grown men—she, who had been reared with only sisters. But she rather enjoyed it. At least with men, one always knew where they were located, great yelling, galumphing creatures that they were.

She flagged down Rumpet, the pack butler. "Tea in the library when you have a moment, please, Rumpet? I have some research to undertake. And, would you be so kind as to ask my husband to attend me when he has the time? No hurry."

"Right away, my lady."

The library was Alexia's favorite room and personal sanctuary. However, this evening she intended to use it for its actual purpose—research. She headed toward the far corner, where behind a massive armchair she had carved out some space on the shelves for her father's collection. He had favored tiny leather-covered journals of the type used by schoolboys to keep accounts—navy blue with plain covers dated in the upper left corner.

From what his daughter had gleaned, Alessandro Tarabotti had not been a very nice person. Practical, as all preternaturals are, but without the ethical grounding Alexia had managed to cultivate. Perhaps this was because he was male, or perhaps it was the result of a childhood spent in the wilds of Italy far from the progressive posturing of England. His journals began the autumn of his sixteenth year, during his first term at Oxford, and ended shortly after his marriage to Alexia's mother. They were sporadic at best, constant for weeks and then absent of a single word for months or years. They were mainly concerned with sexual exploits, violent encounters, and long descriptions of new jackets and top hats. Nevertheless, Alexia turned toward them hopefully, hunting out any possible mention of an assassination attempt. Sadly, the journals stopped some ten years before the Kingair plot. She allowed herself only a brief time to get lost in her father's tidy handwriting—amazed, as always, to note how similar that writing was to her own—before pulling herself back and turning her attention to other books. She whiled away the rest of the night thus occupied. Her reverie was disturbed only by Rumpet bringing in an endless supply of fresh tea and, at one point, by Channing, of all people.

"Why, Lady Maccon," he said, unconvincingly. "I was simply looking for—"

"A book?"

Major Channing Channing of the Chesterfield Channings and Lady Alexia Maccon had gotten off on the wrong foot and never managed to stabilize their relationship—despite the fact that he had, on more than one occasion, saved her life. As far as Alexia was concerned, Major Channing was uncomfortably good-looking—a strapping blond with icy-blue eyes, marked cheekbones, and imperiously arched brows. He was a true soldier to the bone, which might not have been so bad a thing had not his nobility of profession been augmented by an arrogance of manner and toothiness of accent so extreme only the bluest of the blue-blooded individuals ought to foist such upon others. As to Channing's opinion of his mistress, the less said on the subject the better, and even *he* was wise enough to understand *that.*

"What are you researching, my lady?"

Alexia saw no reason to hide. "The old Kingair assassination attempt on Queen Victoria. Do you remember any of it?" Her tone was sharp.

The Gamma could not quite disguise the look of concern that suffused his face. Or was that guilt? "No. Why?"

"I think it might be relevant to our current situation."

"I hardly think *that* likely."

"Are you certain you remember nothing?"

Channing evaded the question. "Any success?"

"None. Dash it."

"Well"—Channing shrugged and made his way nonchalantly back

out of the library, without a book—"I think you're on the wrong track. No good can come of meddling in the past, my lady." Only Channing could put on such an air of dismissive disgust.

"Meddling! I like that."

"Yes, you do," said the Gamma, closing the door behind him.

After that, no one else intruded upon Alexia's investigations until some few hours before dawn, when her husband came thumping in.

She looked up to see Conall watching her fondly, propping up a bookshelf with one massive shoulder.

"Ah, finally remembered me, have you?" She smiled, her eyes soft and dark.

He strode over and kissed her gently. "Never forgot. Simply misplaced while handling matters of pack and protocol." He tugged playfully at a dark curl that had escaped to lie against her neck in a loose whorl.

"Anything of import?"

"Nothing that should concern you." He had learned enough to add, "Although I'm happy to relay the inconsequential details, should you wish to hear them."

"Oh, no thank you. Do restrain yourself. How is Biffy?"

"Not so good. Not so good."

"I'm afraid your brand of roughness is not working as it ought to pull him into the pack."

"You may be right. I am troubled, my love. I have never faced the problem of a reluctant werewolf before. Of course, in the Dark Ages they had to deal with this kind of thing all the time. Lord knows how they managed it. But our Biffy is such a unique case in this modern time of enlightenment that even I canna fix . . ." He paused, struggling for the right words, almost stuttering. "I canna fix his unhappiness."

He cleared himself some space among the piles of books and manuscripts around his wife and settled next to her, flush against her side.

Alexia took his big hand in both of hers, stroking the palm with her thumbs. Her husband was a gorgeous lout of a man, and she could not but admit she adored both his size and his temperament, but it was his caring motherhenishness she loved best of all. "I hold them both in the highest of esteem, but Biffy has become overly Byronic. He really must endeavor to fall out of love with Lord Akeldama."

"Oh? And how does one fall out of love?"

"Unfortunately, I have absolutely no idea."

The earl was learning to have a good deal of faith in his capable wife. "You will think of something. And how is my delicious wife? No ill effects from your tumble earlier this evening?"

"What? Oh, onto the chaise? No, none at all. But, husband, I am having very little success on the matter of this threat to the queen."

"Perhaps the ghost was mistaken or misheard. We have not considered that. She was close to poltergeist phase."

"That's possible. And it might be possible that there is no connection to the Kingair attempt."

Lord Maccon growled in irritation.

"Yes, I am well aware that you hate to be reminded."

"Every man hates remembering failure. But we werewolves are the worst of the lot on the subject. I cannot believe there is a connection."

"It is my only avenue of inquiry."

"Perhaps you can leave it for the moment. I require your presence."

Alexia bristled at the commanding tone. "Oh, yes?"

"In bed."

"Oh. Yes." Alexia relaxed and smiled, allowing her husband to help her to her feet.

Alexia slept on the far side of the bed from Conall. This was not because he was a restless sleeper. In fact, he was as still as any supernatural creature, though not quite so dead-looking as a vampire, and he snored softly. And, though Lady Maccon would never admit it to anyone, not even to Ivy, she was a bit of a cuddler. She simply didn't want him vulnerable while he slept. Also, given his irreverence for physical appearance, she was in constant fear that should she touch him all night long, he would grow a beard and then neglect to shave.

On this particular day's rest, the infant-inconvenience allowed Lady Maccon to doze only fitfully on her side, facing the tower window. Which was why she was partly awake when the burglar entered.

There were many things wrong with a thief breaking into Woolsey Castle in the middle of the day. First, what thief in his right mind travels all the way to Barking to perform a break-in? Prospects were much better in London. Second, why bother with Woolsey Castle, a den of werewolves? Just down the road was a small but wealthy ducal estate. And third, why aim for one of the challenging tower windows and not a downstairs parlor?

Nevertheless, the masked form clambered over the sill with graceful economy of movement and stood, light and balanced on his feet, silhouetted against the thick curtains that could not entirely block out the full afternoon sun. He inhaled sharply upon seeing Lady Maccon up on one elbow staring at him. Clearly, he expected to find the room abandoned.

Lady Maccon was far less reticent. She let out a scream that might have raised the dead, and in this case did.

Her husband was no pup who, required by recent metamorphosis and weak control, must sleep solid the entire day through. Oh, no, he *could* be awakened. It was simply that when he was very tired, it took a mighty loud noise. Not much of a screamer as a general rule, Alexia's lung capacity was nevertheless sufficient to the task and produced a trumpeting kind of yell. Once emitted, however, it did not, as one might expect, bring domestic staff and clavigers running. It had taken only one or two highly embarrassing incidents for the denizens of Woolsey Castle to ignore any and all strange noises produced by Lord and Lady Maccon during their slumbering hours.

Still, one angry husband was sufficient to meet Lady Maccon's needs.

The burglar darted to one side of the room, running for Alexia's armoire. There he opened several drawers, finally extracting a sheaf of papers. These he stuffed into a sack. Alexia rolled from the bed, cursing her own lack of mobility, and charged toward him at the same time as her husband. Conall, made clumsy by the full sun, deep sleep, and the unexpectedness of the event, got his feet caught in the bedclothes and pinwheeled widely in a circle like some large and eccentric ballet dancer, before righting himself and lurching at the intruder. *That'll teach him to steal the coverlet,* thought his wife in satisfaction.

Choosing wisely, the burglar went for Alexia, the weaker link, pushing her aside. She kicked out. Her foot met flesh, but not hard enough. All that resulted was Alexia losing her balance and tumbling backward onto the floor, twisting her ankle in the process.

The intruder dove for the open window. Literally dove right through, for he managed to unfold some kind of metal reinforced cape that became a parachute. This carried him gently down the five stories to the ground. Without registering his wife's predicament, floundering about on the floor, Lord Maccon leaped after.

"Oh, no, Conall, don't you dare—" But Alexia's admonishment met only empty air, for he had already jumped out of the window. A werewolf could take such a fall and survive, of course, but not without substantial damage, especially during daylight.

Greatly concerned, Alexia crawled and squirmed her way across the floor, then used a stool and the windowsill to haul herself upright, balancing precariously on her good foot. Her husband had angled his leap to land on the rooftop of the castle keep; he then lowered himself some three stories to the ground and dashed after the culprit. Naked.

The wrongdoer, however, was equipped to escape at speed. He had a mono-wheel cycle, rigged up with a small steam propeller, that carried him away across the landscape at a remarkably rapid pace.

The sun was full in the sky, so Lord Maccon was unable to change into his wolf form, and even as fast as a werewolf could be after sunset, it was probably not sufficient to catch up to that wheel. Alexia watched Conall run a goodly distance before coming to this realization and stopping. Sometimes his hunter instinct took a while to defuse.

She tsked in annoyance and turned to glare at her armoire, a mile away and impossible to get at without crawling, trying to determine what exactly had been stolen. What on earth had she stashed in that drawer? She certainly hadn't looked at whatever it was since she unpacked after her wedding. So far as she could remember, it had been full of old letters, personal correspondences, party invitations, and visiting cards. Why on earth would anyone want to steal *that*?

"Really, husband," she said from her post by the window when he got around to climbing back up the many flights of stairs to their sleeping chamber, "how you manage to jump about like some deranged jackrabbit without any permanent damage is a mystery to me."

Lord Maccon snorted at her and went to sniff suspiciously at her armoire. "So, what was in that drawer?"

"I can't readily recall. Some society missives from before we were married, I believe. Can't imagine what anyone would want with those." She frowned, trying to dig her way through the mire of pregnancy-addled wits.

"You'd think they'd be after your dispatch case if it was classified paperwork they wanted."

"Exactly so. What did you smell?"

"A bit of grease, probably from that parachute contraption. Nothing else significant. And you, of course—the whole armoire smells of you."

"Mmm, and how do I smell?"

"Vanilla and cinnamon baked puff pastry," he answered promptly. "Always. Delicious."

Alexia grinned.

"But not of child. I've never been able to smell the bairn. Neither has Randolph. Odd that."

Alexia's grin faded.

Her husband returned to his examination of the drawer. "I suppose the constabulary will have to be called."

"I don't see why. It was only the odd bit of paperwork."

"But you kept them." The earl was confused.

"Yes, but that doesn't mean they were important."

"Ah." He nodded his understanding. "Like all your many pairs of shoes."

Alexia chose to ignore this. "It must be someone I know who stole it. Or arranged for the theft."

"Hmm?" Lord Maccon slumped thoughtfully onto the bed.

"I saw him enter. He was after that drawer in particular. I don't think he was expecting us to be here—he seemed more than usually startled to see me. He must be intimate with our family, or acquainted with some member of Woolsey staff, to know where our room is located and that we were not supposed to be in residence."

"Or it is meant to throw us off the scent. Perhaps he stole something else or did something that has nothing to do with those papers."

Alexia pondered, still standing on one foot, like an egret, propped back against the windowsill. "Or he is after some important item to use for blackmail. Or something to give to the popular press. There has been remarkably little scandal since you and I reconciled. I wouldn't put that kind of thing past old Twittergaddle and the *Chirrup*."

"Well, idle speculation is getting us nowhere. Perhaps he got the wrong room or the wrong drawer. Now, why are we not both back in bed?"

"Ah, yes, there is some difficultly there. My ankle, you see, no longer appears to be functioning as designed." Alexia gave Conall a weak smile, and he noticed, for the first time, her awkward stance.

"God's teeth, why?" The earl strode over to his wife and offered his own substantial form instead of the windowsill. Alexia transferred her weight gratefully.

"Well, I did take a little bit of a tumble just now. Seems I have twisted my ankle."

"You never . . . ? Wife!" He half carried her to the bed before bending over to examine her foot and lower leg carefully. His hands were impossibly gentle, but still Alexia winced. The joint was already starting to swell. "I shall call for a surgeon immediately! And the constabulary."

"Oh, now, Conall, I scarcely think that necessary. The surgeon, I mean. You may, of course, summon the police if you think it best, but I hardly require the services of a physician for a twisted ankle."

Lord Maccon entirely ignored this and marched from the room, already yelling at the top of his considerable lungs for Rumpet and any claviger who might be awake.

Lady Maccon, ankle throbbing dreadfully, tried to go back to sleep, knowing that in very short order her room would be swarming with surgeons and policemen and that her dozing time would be drastically curtailed.

As predicted, Alexia got very little respite that day, which barely made much difference, as she was forced to rest that night after the surgeon pronounced her unfit to walk. She was confined to her bed with a splint and barley water and told that on no account was she to move for an entire week. Worse, she was also told that she was to lay off tea for the next twenty-four hours, as imbibing any hot liquid was bound to increase the swelling. Alexia called the doctor a quack and threw her bed cap at him. He retreated, but she knew perfectly well that Conall and the rest of Woolsey would see that his instructions were obeyed to the letter.

Lady Maccon was not the kind of woman who could be easily confined to bed for seven hours, let alone seven days. Those who knew her well were already dreading her confinement, and this, so close to that fated time, was seen as a preliminary test as to both her behavior and everyone else's ability to cope with it. It was pronounced, by Rumpet and Floote much later in some private butler musings, to be an abject failure on all counts. No one survived it intact, least of all Alexia.

By the second day, she was chafing, to put it politely. "Queen Victoria could be in imminent danger and here I lie, confined to my bed by that fool of a physician because of an *ankle.* It is not to be borne!"

"Certainly not with any grace," muttered her husband.

Lady Maccon ignored this and continued with her ranting. "And Felicity—who is keeping an eye on Felicity?"

"Professor Lyall has her well in hand, I assure you."

"Oh, well, if it's Professor Lyall. He can handle you—I have every confidence in his ability to restrain my sister." Her tone was petulant, for which she wasn't entirely to be blamed, being grimy, sore, and stationary. Nor was her lying-in translating to actual rest. She was too far along for the infant-inconvenience to permit anything more than a few fitful minutes of shut-eye at a time.

"Who says he can handle me?" The earl looked most offended by this blight on his independence.

His lady wife arched an eyebrow at him as if to say, *Oh, now, Conall, really.* She continued on to a new worry, without further disparagement of such frivolous masculine dignity. "Have you had the lads check the aethographic transmitter every evening at sunset? You remember, I'm expecting some very important information."

"Yes, dear."

Alexia twisted her lips together in contemplation, trying to come up with something else to gripe about. "Oh, I do hate being cooped up." She picked at the blanket draped over her belly.

"Now you know how Biffy feels."

Lady Maccon's temper softened at the mention of the dandy. "How is he?"

"Well. I have taken your suggestion under advisement, my dear, and I am trying a gentler approach—less firmness of manner."

"Now *that* I should like to see."

"I have been sitting and talking him through the change at sunset. Rumpet suggested some light music might help as well. So I have Burbleson—you remember Catogan Burbleson, that new musically minded claviger we recruited last month?—playing violin all the while. A nice soothing piece of European fluff. Hard to tell if any of this is helping, but my efforts don't seem to be making the poor boy feel any worse."

Alexia was suspicious. "Is young Catogan any good on the violin?"

"Rather."

"Well, perhaps he could come play a bit for me, then? I must say, Conall, it is exceedingly dull being bedridden."

Her husband grunted at that—his version of a sympathetic murmur.

Eventually, the earl resorted to pulling Floote back from London in order to cater to Alexia's whims. No one could manage Lady Maccon quite so well as Floote. As a result, most of Woolsey's library and a goodly number of newspapers and Royal Society pamphlets took up residence about Alexia's bed, and her imperious bell ringing and strident demands ebbed slightly. She began receiving hourly reassurances that Queen Victoria was under guard. Her Majesty's Growlers, special werewolf bodyguards, were on high alert, and in deference to the muhjah's conviction that werewolves might be a risk factor, there was also a rove vampire and four Swiss guards in attendance at all times.

Lord Akeldama sent Boots around with not only inquiries as to Lady Maccon's health, but also a small spate of useful information. The ghosts around London seemed to be in turmoil, for they were appearing and disappearing and wafting here and there, whispering dire threats concerning imminent danger. If queried directly, none of them seemed to know exactly what was going on, but the ghostly community was certainly all aflutter about something.

Alexia went nearly spare at this information combined with the fact that she was unable to rush off to London at *that very moment* in order to continue inquiries. She turned from demanding to positively imperious and made life rather unbearable for those unfortunate enough to be at Woolsey. As full moon was just around the corner, older members of the pack were out running, hunting, or working in the moonlight hours and the youngsters were now locked in with Biffy. This meant only the household staff really had to suffer the yoke of Lady Maccon's impatience, and Floote, ever saintly, undertook the bulk of her amusement.

No one was particularly surprised when on the evening of the fifth day, even Floote's powers failed and Lady Maccon threw off her covers, put weight upon her ankle, which seemed perfectly functional, if a tad achy, and pronounced herself fit enough for a carriage ride into London. No, what surprised everyone was that she had lasted that long.

She had just persuaded a blushing claviger to help her dress when Floote appeared in the doorway clutching several pieces of paper and looking thoughtful. So thoughtful that he did not, initially, attempt to prevent her from her planned departure.

"Madam, the most interesting series of aetherograms have just come in through the transmitter. I believe they are intended for you."

Alexia looked up with interest. "You believe?"

"They are directed to the Ruffled Parasol. I doubt someone would actually attempt to communicate with an accessory."

"Indeed."

"From someone calling himself Puff Bonnet."

"Herself. Yes, go on."

"From Scotland."

"Yes, yes, Floote, what does she *say*?"

Floote cleared his throat and began to read. " 'To Ruffled Parasol. Vital information regarding super-secret subject of confabulation.' " He moved on to the next bit of paper. " 'Past persons of Scottishness in contact with mastermind of supernatural persuasion in London, aka Agent Doom.' " Floote moved on to the third bit of paper. " 'Lady K says Agent Doom assisted depraved Plan of Action. May have all been his idea.' " Moving on to the last one, he read out, " 'Summer permits Scots to expose more knee than lady of refinement should have to withstand. Hairmuffs much admired. Yours etc., Puff Bonnet.' "

Lady Maccon put out her hand for Ivy's correspondence. "Fascinating. Floote, send a message back thanking her and telling her she can return to London. Would you, please? And call up the carriage. My husband is at BUR tonight? I must consult with him immediately on the subject."

"But, madam!"

"It's no good, Floote. The fate of the nation may be at stake."

Floote, who knew well when he had no chance of winning an argument, turned to do as ordered.

CHAPTER EIGHT

Death by Teapot

"Why, Lady Maccon, I understood you to be confined to the countryside for two more days at the very least." Professor Lyall was the first to notice Alexia as she let herself into BUR's head office. The building was situated just off of Fleet Street and was a mite grimy and bureaucratic for Alexia's taste. Lyall and her husband shared a large front office, crammed with two desks, a changing closet, a settee, four chairs, multiple hat stands, and a wardrobe full of clothing for visiting werewolves. Since the Bureau was always untangling some significant supernatural crisis or another and didn't seem to employ a decent cleaning staff, it was also crammed with paperwork, metal aethographic slates, dirty teacups, and, for some strange reason, a large number of stuffed ducks.

Lord Maccon looked up from a pile of antiquated parchment rolls. His tawny eyes were narrowed. "She bloody well was. What are you doing here, wife?"

"I'm perfectly fine," protested Alexia, trying not to look as though she were leaning on her parasol for assistance in walking. Although, truth be told, she was grateful for its support, as her waddle had evolved into a lurching hobble.

Her husband, with a long-suffering sigh, came out from behind his desk and loomed over her. Alexia expected recriminations, but instead the big man administered an enthusiastic embrace by which masterful tactic he managed to maneuver her backward and down onto a chair in one corner of the room.

Bemused, Lady Maccon found herself firmly off her feet. "Well," she sputtered, "I say."

The earl took that as an excuse to give her a blistering kiss. Presumably to stop her from saying anything further.

Professor Lyall chuckled at their antics and then returned to quietly going about official business, papers rustling softly as he calculated and correlated some complex mathematical matter of state.

"I have just come by the most interesting bit of information," was Lady Maccon's opening gambit.

This statement effectively distracted her husband from any further admonishments. "Well?"

"I sent Ivy to Scotland to find out from Lady Kingair what *really* happened with that previous assassination attempt."

"Ivy? As in Mrs. Tunstell? What a very peculiar choice."

"I shouldn't underestimate Ivy if I were you, husband. She has discovered something."

Conall ruminated a brief moment on this absurd statement and then said, "Yes?"

"It wasn't simply that the poison was to come from London; there was a London agent involved, a *mastermind* if you would believe it. Ivy seems to think that this man orchestrated the whole attempt."

Lord Maccon stilled. "What?"

"Here you thought you had put the matter to rest." Alexia was feeling justifiably smug.

The earl's face became still—the quiet before the storm. "Did she provide any details concerning the identity of this agent?"

"Only that he was supernatural."

Behind them, Professor Lyall's paper rustling stopped. He looked over at them, his vulpine face sharpened further by inquisitiveness. Randolph Lyall's position at BUR was not held because he was Beta to Lord Maccon, but because of his innate investigative abilities. He had an astute mind and a nose for trouble—literally, being a werewolf.

Lord Maccon's temper frothed over. "I knew the vampires had to be involved somehow! The vampires are always involved."

Alexia stilled. "How do you know it was vampires? It could have been a ghost, or even a werewolf."

Professor Lyall came over to participate in the conversation. "This is grave news."

The earl continued to expound. "Well, if a ghost, she would have long since disanimated, so we're well out of luck there. And if a werewolf, he must have been a loner of some kind. Most of those were killed off by the Hypocras Club last year. Damned scientists. So I suggest we start with the vampires."

"I had already reached a similar conclusion myself, husband."

"I'll go to the hives," suggested Professor Lyall, already heading for a hat rack.

Lord Maccon looked as though he would like to protest.

His wife put a hand to his arm. "No, that's a good idea. He is far more politic than you. Even if he isn't strictly gentry."

Professor Lyall hid a smile, clapped his top hat to his head, and walked briskly out into the night without another word, merely touching the brim in Lady Maccon's direction before departing.

"Very well," grumbled the earl. "I'll go after the local roves. There's always a chance it could be one of them. And you—you stay right here and keep off that foot."

"*That* is about as likely as a vampire going sunbathing. I am going to call upon Lord Akeldama. As potentate, he must be consulted on this matter. The dewan as well, I suppose. Could you send a man to inquire if Lord Slaughter could attend me this evening?"

Figuring that Lord Akeldama would at least ensure that his wife remain seated for some length of time in pursuit of gossip if for no other reason, the earl made no further protest. He cursed without much rancor and acquiesced to her request, sending Special Agent Haverbink off to alert the dewan. Lord Maccon did, however, insist upon seeing her to Lord Akeldama's abode himself before pursuing his own investigations.

"Alexia, my *poppadom*, what are you doing in London this fine evening? Aren't you supposed to be abed reveling in the romanticism of a weakened condition?"

Lady Maccon was, for once, not in the humor to entertain Lord Akeldama's flowery ways. "Yes, but something highly untoward has occurred."

"My dear, how *perfectly splendid*! Do sit and tell old Uncle Akeldama all about it! Tea?"

"Of course. Oh, and I should warn you, I have invited the dewan over. This is a matter for the Commonwealth."

"Well, if you insist. But, my *dearest flower,* how ghastly to consider that such a mustache must shadow the clean-shaven grandeur of my domicile." Lord Akeldama was rumored to insist that all his drones go without the dreaded lip skirt. The vampire had once had the vapors upon encountering an unexpected mustache around a corner of his hallway. Muttonchops were permitted in moderation, and only because they were currently all the rage among the most fashionable of London's gentlemen-about-town. Even so, they must be as well tended as the topiary of Hampton Court.

With a sigh, Alexia settled herself into one of Lord Akeldama's magnificent wingback chairs. The ever-considerate Boots rushed over with a pouf on which to rest her throbbing ankle.

Lord Akeldama noticed him and thus the fact that they were not alone. "Ah, Boots, my *lovely* boy, clear the room, would you, please? Oh, and bring me my harmonic auditory resonance disruptor. It's on my dressing table next to the French verbena hand cream. There's a dear."

Boots, resplendent in his favorite forest-green velvet frock coat, nodded and vanished from the room. He reappeared shortly thereafter pushing in a laden tea trolley upon which lay the expected assortment of delicacies and a small spiky device.

"Will there be anything else, my lord?"

"No, thank you, Boots."

Boots turned his attention eagerly onto Lady Maccon. "My lady?"

"No, thank you, Mr. Bootbottle-Fipps."

Remarkably, her use of his proper name seemed to cause the young dandy some embarrassment, for he blushed and backed hurriedly out of the room, leaving them alone save for a plethora of gold-tasseled throw pillows and the fat calico cat purring placidly in a corner.

Lord Akeldama flicked the forks of the auditory disruptor, and the low-pitched humming sound commenced, the sound of two different kinds of bees arguing. He situated the device carefully in the center of the trolley. The cat, who had been lying on her back in a highly undignified sprawl, rolled over, stretched languidly, and ambled toward the drawing room door, disgruntled by the noise. When her lashing tail and obviously presented backside were ignored, she yowled imperiously.

Lord Akeldama rose. "Your servant, Madam Pudgemuffin," he said, letting her out of the room.

Lady Maccon calculated that she and her host were on familiar enough terms for her to pour her own tea. She did so while he dealt with the demanding feline.

The vampire resumed his seat, crossing one silken leg over the other and rocking the crossed foot back and forth slightly. This was a gesture of impatience when exhibited by any ordinary human, but with Lord Akeldama it seemed to express suppressed energy rather than any particular emotional state. "I used to love pets, my dove, did you know? When I was mortal."

"Did you?" Alexia encouraged cautiously. Lord Akeldama rarely spoke of his life *before.* She was afraid of saying more and thus forestalling further confidences.

"Yes. It is greatly troubling that I am now left with only a cat for company."

Alexia refrained from mentioning the plethora of fashionable gentlemen who seemed to be ever in, out, and about Lord Akeldama's domicile. "I suppose you might consider keeping more than one cat."

"Oh, dear me, *no.* Then I should be known as *that vampire with all the cats.*"

"I hardly think that ever likely to become your defining characteristic, my lord." Alexia took in her host's evening garb—black tails and silver trousers, coupled with a corseted black and silver paisley waistcoat and silver cravat. The neckwear was pinned with a massive silver filigree pin, and the monocle dangling idly from one gloved hand was silver and diamond to match. Lord Akeldama's golden hair was brushed to shiny butter yellow glory, fastened back in such a way that one long lock was allowed to artfully escape.

"Oh, *clementine,* what a splendid thing to say!"

Lady Maccon took a sip of tea and firmed up her resolve. "My lord, I do hate to ask this of you especially, but will you be completely serious with me for a moment?"

Lord Akeldama's foot stopped rocking and his pleasant expression tightened. "My darling girl, we have known each other many years now, but such a request breaches even the bonds of *our* friendship."

"I meant no offense, I assure you. But you remember this matter I have been investigating? How the current threat on the queen's life has led me to dredge up a certain uncomfortable assassination attempt of the past?"

"Of course. As a matter of interest, I have some rather *noteworthy* information to relay to you on the subject. But, please, ladies first."

Alexia was intrigued but spoke on as etiquette demanded. "I have heard from Scotland. It seems that there was an agent here in London who apparently concocted the whole dismal plot. A supernatural agent. You wouldn't know anything of this, would you by any chance?"

"My dearest girl, you cannot possibly think that I—"

"No, actually, I don't. You enjoy gathering information, Lord Akeldama, but very rarely seem to put it to any active use, aside from furthering your own curiosity. I fail to see how a botched assassination attempt could have anything to do with your unremitting inquisitiveness."

"Quite logical of you, *buttercup.*" Lord Akeldama smiled, showing his fangs. They glistened silver in the bright gas lighting, matching his cravat.

"And, of course, you would never have botched it."

The vampire laughed—a sharp sparkling sound of unexpected delight. "So kind, my little crumpet, *so kind.*"

"So, what do you make of it?"

"That twenty years ago, some supernatural or other, in London, was trying to kill the queen?"

"My husband thinks it must be a vampire. I'm inclined to suspect a ghost, which would leave the trail cold, of course."

Lord Akeldama tapped one fang with the edge of his monocle. "I dare say your last option is best."

"Werewolves?" Alexia looked into her teacup.

"*A werewolf,* yes, my gherkin."

Alexia put down her cup and then flicked the two sounding rods on the harmonic device to encourage greater auditory disruption. "A loner I suppose, which leaves me in the same situation as a ghost. Most of the local loners were eliminated by the Hypocras Club's illegal experiments last year." She poured herself a second cup of tea, added a small dollop of milk, and lifted it to her lips.

Lord Akeldama shook his head, looking unusually pensive. The monocle stopped tapping. "You are missing a piece in this game, I think, *butterball.* My instincts are inclined to say pack, not loner. You don't know what the local pack was like at that time. But I remember. Oh, yes. There were rumors all over town. Nothing proven, of course. The last Alpha wasn't right in the head. A fact kept well away from public and press, and from daylight musings for that matter, but a *fact*, nonetheless. What he was doing to earn that reputation, well . . ."

"But even twenty years ago, the local pack was . . ." Alexia sat back, sentence unfinished, hand instinctively and protectively pressed upon her belly.

"Woolsey."

Alexia mentally catalogued the Woolsey Pack members. Aside from her husband and Biffy, *all of them* were holdovers from the previous Alpha. "Channing," she said finally. "I'll wager it was Channing. He certainly didn't like the idea of my investigating the past. Interrupted me in the library just the other day. I'll need to check the military records, of course, find out who was in England at the time and who was billeted overseas."

"Good girl," approved the vampire. "Nice and thorough, but I have something more for you. That cook who worked for the OBO who you were investigating? The little poisoner?"

"Oh, yes. How did you know about her?"

"*Please,* darling." He gestured with the monocle toward himself, as if pointing a finger.

"Oh, of course. I apologize. Do go on."

"She preferred a tannin-activated dosing mechanism. Very hard to detect, you understand. Her preferred brand of poison at the time was stimulated by the application of hot water and a chemical component most commonly found in tea."

Alexia put down her teacup with a clatter.

Lord Akeldama continued, eyes twinkling. "It requires a specialized automechanical nickel-lined teapot. The teapot was to arrive as a gift for Queen Victoria, and the first time she drank from it—death." The vampire made a gesture with two slim, perfectly manicured fingers curving down toward his own neck, like fangs. "Your little ghost may have supplied the poison, but teapots of that type were made by only one specialty manufacturer."

Lady Maccon narrowed her eyes. Coincidence was a fateful thing. "Let me guess, Beatrice Lefoux?"

"Indeed."

Alexia stood, slowly and cautiously by degrees but with evident firmness of intent, leaning upon her parasol. "Well, this has been most edifying, Lord Akeldama. Most edifying. Thank you. I must be on my way."

Right at that moment, there was a scuffle in the hallway and the door to the drawing room burst open to reveal the dewan.

"What is the meaning of such a summons as I just received?" He barreled into the room all loud bluster, bringing along an odor of London night air and raw meat.

Lady Maccon waddled past him as though the summons had nothing whatsoever to do with her. "Oh, hello, Dewan. The potentate will be happy to explain everything. Please excuse me, my lords. Important business." She paused, searching for an excuse. "Shopping. I'm certain you understand. Hats. Very critical hats."

"What?" said the werewolf. "But you directed me to attend you! Here, Lady Maccon! At the house of a *vampire*!"

Lord Akeldama stood up from his consciously relaxed posture as though he might try to waylay Lady Maccon.

Alexia waved at them both cheerily from the doorway before hobbling out and into her waiting carriage. "Regent Street, please, posthaste. Chapeau de Poupe."

Lady Maccon barely glanced at the hats. She headed straight through the shop past the sputtering attendant in a, it must be said, very grand *Lady* Maccon–like manner. "I shall make my own way," she said to the fretful girl, and then, "*She* is expecting me." Which was, of course, an outfight fib but served to mollify the chit. Luckily, for all concerned, the shopgirl had the presence of mind to flip the CLOSED sign and shut the door before anyone could observe Lady Maccon's disappearance into the wall.

Madame Lefoux was in her contrivance chamber, looking, if possible, even more gaunt and unwell than when Alexia had seen her last.

"My dear, Genevieve! I thought I was the one meant to be laid up. You look as though you could use a week's rest. Surely this new project cannot be so vital you must damage your health over its completion."

The inventor smiled wanly but barely glanced up from her work, concentrating on some engine schematic rolled out on a metal crate before her. The massive bowler-hat contraption she was still building loomed behind her, looking more of-a-piece. It was at least three times Lord Maccon's height, with its podlike driving chamber now seated atop multiple tentacle-like supports.

Alexia thought perhaps her friend's intense focus on work was a necessary distraction from her aunt's terminal condition. "Goodness me, quite a fearsome thing, is it not? How do you intend to get it out of the chamber, Genevieve? It will never fit through that passageway of yours."

"Oh, it's only loosely assembled. I shall take it out in pieces. I have an arrangement with the Pantechnicon to utilize a warehouse for the final stage of construction." The Frenchwoman stood, stretched, and turned to face Lady Maccon full-on for the first time. She scrubbed her grease-covered hands with a rag and then came over to greet her guest properly. A soft kiss was pressed lovingly against Alexia's cheek, and Alexia was reminded of her friend's consistently solicitous care in the past.

"Are you certain there is nothing you wish to talk about? I assure you I am the soul of discretion; it should go no further. Is there nothing I can do to help?"

"Oh, my dearest lady, I wish there were." Madame Lefoux moved away, elegant shoulders hunched.

Alexia wondered if there might not be some other component to her friend's unhappiness. "Has Quesnel been asking about his real mother again?"

Genevieve and she had discussed such matters in the past. Angelique's violent death was deemed too much for an impressionable young boy. As was the former maid's identity as his biological mother.

Madame Lefoux's soft chin firmed. "*I* am his real mother."

Lady Maccon understood such defensiveness. "It must be hard, though, not telling him about Angelique."

Genevieve dimpled wanly. "Oh, Quesnel knows."

"Oh, oh, dear. How did he . . . ?"

"I should prefer not to talk about it just now." The inventor's face, always tricky to read, shut down completely, her dimples vanishing as surely as poodles after a water rat.

Alexia, saddened by such icy reticence, nevertheless respected her friend's wishes. "I actually have a matter of business to consult you on. I recently learned something of your aunt's past activities. She undertook the manufacture of special automated teapots, I understand, very special ones. Nickel plated?"

"Oh, yes? When was this?"

"Twenty years ago."

"Well, I should hardly remember that myself, I'm afraid. You may be correct, of course. We can attempt to converse with my aunt on the subject or look through her records. I warn you, she is difficult." She switched to her perfect musical French. "Aunt Beatrice?"

A ghostly body shimmered out of a wall nearby. The specter was looking worse than last time, her form barely recognizable as human, misty with lack of cohesion. "Do I hear my name? Do I hear bells? Silver bells!"

"She has gone to poltergeist?" Alexia's voice was soft in sympathy.

"Unfortunately, almost entirely. She has some lucid moments. So not yet completely lost to me. Go ahead, try." Genevieve's voice was drawn with unhappiness.

"Pardon me, Formerly Lefoux, but do you recall a special order for a teapot, twenty years ago. Nickel plated?" Alexia relayed some of the other details.

The ghost ignored her, drifting up toward the high ceiling, floating about the head of her niece's massive project, extending herself so that she became a crude kind of tiara.

Genevieve's face fell. "Let me go check her old records. I think I may have kept them when we moved."

While Madame Lefoux fussed about a far corner of her massive laboratory, Formerly Lefoux drifted back down to Alexia, as if drawn against her will. She was definitely beginning to lose control over noncorporeal cohesion, the end stages before involuntary disanimus. As her mental faculties failed, she was forgetting she was human, forgetting what her own body once looked like. Or that was what the scientists hypothesized. Mental control over the physical was a popular theory.

The ambient aether feathered hazy tendrils off the ghostly form, carrying them toward Lady Maccon. Alexia's preternatural state fractured some of the remaining tether of the ghost's body, pulling it apart. It was an eerie thing to watch, likes soap suds in water curling down a sink.

The ghost seemed to be observing the phenomenon of her own destruction with interest. Until she remembered her selfhood and tugged back, gathering herself inward. "Preternatural!" she hissed. "Preternatural female! What are you—Oh, oh, yes. You are the one who will stop it. Stop it all. You are."

Then she became distracted by something unseen. She swirled about, drifting away from Alexia, still muttering to herself. Behind her murmuring voice, Alexia could make out the high keening wail that all her vocalizations would eventually dissolve into—the death shriek of a dying soul.

Alexia shook her head. "Poor thing. What a way to end. So embarrassing."

"Wrong track. Wrong track!" Formerly Lefoux garbled.

Madame Lefoux returned, walking right through her aunt she was so lost in thought. "Oh, oops, sorry, Aunt. I do apologize, Alexia. I can't seem to locate the crate where I stashed those records. Allow me some time and I'll see what I can find later tonight. Would that do?"

"Of course, thank you for the attempt."

"And now, if you will excuse me? I really must return to work."

"Oh, certainly."

"And you must return to your husband. He's looking for you."

"Oh? He is? How did you know?"

"Please, Alexia, you are wandering around out of bed, with a limp, grossly pregnant. Knowing you, I'm quite certain you are not meant to be. Ergo, he must be looking for you."

"How well you know us both, Genevieve."

Lord Maccon was indeed looking for his errant wife. The moment her carriage drew up before their new town residence, he was out the front door, down the steps, and scooping her up into his arms.

Alexia withstood his solicitous attentions with much forbearance. "Must you make a scene here in the public street?" was all she said after he had kissed her ardently.

"I was worried. You were gone much longer than I expected."

"You thought to catch me at Lord Akeldama's?"

"Well, yes, and instead I caught the dewan, for my pains." This was growled out in a very wolfish manner for a man whose husbandly duties rendered him not a werewolf at that precise moment.

The earl carried his wife into their back parlor, which five days' absence had seen adequately refurbished, if not quite up to Biffy's exacting standards. Alexia was convinced that once recovered from this month's bone-bender, the dandy would see to it the room was brought back up to snuff.

Lord Maccon deposited his wife into a chair and then knelt next to her, clutching one of her hands. "Tell me truthfully—how are you feeling?"

Alexia took a breath. "Truthfully? I sometimes wonder if I, like Madame Lefoux, should affect masculine dress."

"Gracious me, why?"

"You mean aside from the issue of greater mobility?"

"My love, I don't think that's currently the result of your clothing."

"Indeed, well, I mean *after* the baby."

"I still don't see why you should want to."

"Oh, no? I dare you to spend a week in a corset, long skirts, and a bustle."

"How do you know I haven't?"

"Oh, ho!"

"Now stop playing games, woman. How are you really feeling?"

Alexia sighed. "A little tired, a lot frustrated, but well in body if not spirit. My ankle is paining me only a little, and the infant-inconvenience has been remarkably patient with all my carriage rides and poodling about." She contemplated how to raise the subject of Lord Akeldama's thoughts on the matter of the queen. Finally, knowing she had little inherent delicacy of speech and that her husband had none at all, she decided he would probably appreciate directness.

"Lord Akeldama thinks the London mastermind of your Kingair plot was a Woolsey Pack member."

"Does he, by George?"

"Now, stay calm, my dear. Think logically. I know that is difficult for you. But wouldn't someone like Channing take—"

Lord Maccon shook his head. "No, not Channing. He would never—"

"But Lord Akeldama said that the previous Alpha was not right in the head. Couldn't that have had something to do with it? If he ordered Channing to—"

Lord Maccon's voice was sharp. "No. But Lord Woolsey himself? That *is* an idea. Much as I hate to admit it. The man was mad, my dear. Utterly mad. It can happen that way, especially to Alphas when we get too old. There's a reason, you know, that we werewolves fight amongst ourselves. I mean aside from the etiquette of the duel. Especially Alphas.

We shouldn't be allowed to live forever—we go all funny in the brain. Or that's what the howlers sing of. Vampires do, too, if you ask me. I mean, you only have to look at Lord Akeldama to realize he's . . . but I digress."

His wife reminded him of where they were in the conversation. "Lord Woolsey, you were saying?"

Lord Maccon looked down at their joined hands. "It can take on many forms, the madness—sometimes quite harmless little esoteric inclinations and sometimes not. Lord Woolsey, as I understand it, became deviant. Even brutal in his"—he paused, looking for the right word that might not shock even his indomitable wife—"tastes."

Alexia contemplated this. Conall was an aggressive lover, demanding, although he could be quite gentle. Of course, with her, he had no real teeth to do damage beyond a nibble or two. But there had been one or two times, early on in their courtship, when she had wondered if he might not actually think of her as food. She had also read overmuch of her father's journals.

"You mean, conjugally violent?"

"Not precisely, but from what I have been told, he was inclined to derive pleasure from sadistic activities." Lord Maccon actually blushed. He could do that while touching her. Alexia found it little-boy endearing. With the fingers of her free hand, she stroked through his thick dark hair.

"Gracious. And how did the pack manage to keep such a thing secret?"

"Oh, you'd be surprised. Such proclivities are not confined to werewolves alone. There are even brothels that—"

Alexia held up a hand. "No, thank you, my dear. I should prefer not to know any additional details."

"Of course, my love, of course."

"I am glad you killed him."

Lord Maccon nodded, letting go of his wife's hand, then standing and turning away, lost to his memories. He fiddled with a little cluster of daguerreotypes arranged on the mantelpiece. That quick, feral quality was back to his movements, a supernatural facet of his werewolf self. "As am I, wife, as am I. I have killed many people in my day, for queen and country, for pack and challenge; rarely do I get to say I am proud of that part of my afterlife. He was a brute, and I was fortunate indeed that I was just strong enough to see him eliminated, and he was just mad enough to make bad choices during the passion of battle. He allowed himself to enjoy it too much."

Lord Maccon's head suddenly cocked—supernatural hearing making out some new sound that Alexia could not discern.

"There is someone at the door." He put down the image he had been toying with and turned to face the entrance, crossing his arms.

His wife picked up her parasol.

* * *

The ghost was confused. She spent a good deal of her time confused these nights. She was also alone. Everyone had gone, to the very last, so that she floated in her madness, losing her afterlife into silence and aether. Threads of her true self were drifting away. And there was no friendly face to sit with her while she died a second time.

She remembered that there was something unfinished. Was it her life?

She remembered there was something she still needed to do. Was it die?

She remembered that there was something wrong. She had tried to fix it, hadn't she? What should she care for the living?

Wrong, it was all wrong. She was wrong. And soon she wouldn't be. That was wrong, too.

CHAPTER NINE

In Which the Past Complicates the Present

A knock came at the back parlor door, and Floote stuck his debonair head around the side. "Madame Lefoux to see you, madam."

Lady Maccon placed her parasol carefully to one side, pretending her husband had not just given her due warning. "Ah, yes, show her into the front parlor, would you, please, Floote? I'll be in shortly. We simply can't have company in this room yet—it's not decent."

"Very good, madam."

Alexia turned back to her husband, beckoning with one hand to get him to come help her stand. He did, bracing himself.

"Oomph," she said, attaining her feet. "Very well, I shall add Lord Woolsey to our ever-growing list of suspects who are now dead and thus useless. Death can be jolly well inconvenient, if you ask me. We can't possibly prove his involvement."

"Or what bearing it might have on this new threat to the queen." The earl placed a casual arm about his wife, assistance couched in a more Alexia-acceptable act of affection. Nearly a year of marriage and he was finally learning.

"True, true." His wife leaned against him.

Another knock sounded at the back parlor door.

"What now!" growled Lord Maccon.

Professor Lyall's sandy head popped in this time. "You're wanted, my lord, on a matter of pack business."

"Oh, very well." The earl helped his wife waddle down the hallway. He abandoned her at the door to the front parlor and then followed his Beta out into the night.

"Hat, my lord," came Professor Lyall's mild rebuke, a disembodied voice from the darkness.

Conall came back inside, scooped a convenient top hat off of the hall stand, and disappeared outside again.

Alexia paused at the door to the front parlor. Floote had left it slightly ajar, and she overheard conversation drifting from within, Madame Lefoux's mellow voice and that of another, clear and erudite, confident with age and authority.

"Mr. Tarabotti had significant romantic success. I often wondered if the soulless weren't dangerously attractive to those with too much soul. You, for example, probably have excess. You like her, don't you?"

"Oh, really, Mr. Floote, why this sudden interest in my romantic inclinations?"

Lady Maccon started at that. She might have recognized Floote's voice, of course, except that she had never heard him string so many words together at once. It must be admitted, she had privately doubted his ability to formulate a complete sentence. Or at least his willingness to do so.

"Be careful, madam." The butler's voice was stiff with rebuke.

Alexia flushed slightly at the very idea of her staff taking such a tone with a *guest*!

"Is it my care you are concerned with or Alexia's?" Madame Lefoux seemed well able to withstand such a grave breach in domestic protocol.

"Both."

"Very well. Now, would you be so kind as to check up on Her Highness? I am in a bit of a rush and the evening isn't getting any longer."

At this juncture, Lady Maccon made a great blundering noise and entered the room.

Floote, unflappable, backed away from his intimate proximity to the French inventor as though it were the most natural thing in the world.

"Madame Lefoux, to what do I owe the pleasure of your company? I seem to have just left you." Alexia made her way laboriously across the room.

"I have that information you were looking for. About the teapots." The inventor handed over a sheaf of old parchment paper, yellowed about the edges, thick and ridged, marked by hand and the assistance of a straight edge into some sort of ledger. "It's in my aunt's code, which I am certain you could decipher if you wished. But essentially it indicates that she had only one order for the teapot invention that year, but it was a big one. It didn't come through any suspicious channels. That's the intriguing part. It was a government order, out of London, with funds originating in the Bureau of Unnatural Registry."

Lady Maccon's mouth opened slightly, then snapped shut. "Ivy's

Agent Doom was at BUR?" She sighed. "Well, I suppose that puts Lord Woolsey to the top of my suspect list. He would have held my husband's position at the time."

Floote, in the act of shutting the door behind himself, paused on the threshold. "Lord Woolsey, madam?"

Alexia looked at him, all big-eyed and innocuous. "Yes. I'm beginning to think he must have had a hand in the Kingair assassination attempt."

Madame Lefoux looked entirely uninterested at this. Her present concerns must be outweighing any curiosity over the past. "I do hope the information will be of some use, Alexia. When you're finished, could I please have those records back? I like to keep these things in proper order. You understand, don't you?"

"Of course."

"And now, I hate to be so abrupt, but I must get back to it."

"Of course, of course. Do try to get some rest, please, Genevieve?"

"I'll rest when the souls do," quipped the inventor with a shrug. Then she left the room, only to return a moment later. "Have you seen my top hat?"

"The gray one out in the hall?" Lady Maccon's stomach fell in a way that had nothing whatsoever to do with the child.

"Yes."

"I believe my husband may have accidentally absconded with it. Was it *special*?"

"Only in that it was my favorite hat. I can't imagine it fit him. Must be several sizes too small."

Lady Maccon closed her eyes at the very idea. "Oh, he must look quite a picture. I do apologize, Genevieve. He is so very bad about these things. I'll have it sent over as soon as he returns."

"Oh, no trouble. I do, after all, own a hat shop." The inventor flashed a dimpled smile, and Alexia felt a strange bump of pleasure at the sight. It had been so long since Genevieve had smiled fully.

Floote saw the Frenchwoman to the door, but before he could even attempt to resume his regular duties, Lady Maccon called him back into her presence.

"Floote, a moment of your time."

Floote came to stand before her, wary. His face, as always, was impassive, but Alexia had learned over the years to watch the set of his shoulders for clues as to his real feelings.

"Floote, I wouldn't wish to be an eavesdropper, not on my friends or my staff—that is, by rights, your provenance. However, I couldn't help but overhear some bit of your conversation with Madame Lefoux before I entered this room. Really, I didn't know you had it in you. Several sentences in a row. And some of them quite sharp."

"Madam?" The shoulders twitched.

Floote really didn't have much of a sense of humor, poor man. Lady Maccon stopped teasing him and moved on to the meat of the matter. "You were discussing my father, weren't you?"

"In a manner, madam."

"And?"

"Madame Lefoux pays you a good deal of conspicuous attention."

"Yes. I always figured it was her *way.* If you take my meaning."

"I do, madam."

"But you think it is something more?"

His shoulders tensed and Floote looked, if such a thing were to be conceived, uncomfortable. "I have made observations over the years."

"Yes?" Having a conversation with Floote was about as easy as explaining the formulation of the counterbalance theorem to a bowl of macaroni pudding.

"On the nature of preternatural interactions, if you would, madam."

"Yes, I would. Go on."

Floote spoke slowly, choosing his words with care. "I have arrived at certain conclusions."

"Concerning what, exactly?" *Coaxing, coaxing,* thought Alexia. Never her strong point in a conversation, letting others take their time getting to a point. Still, the company of Lord Akeldama had taught her much in the way of it.

"There may be attraction between those who have excess soul and those who have none at all, madam."

"You mean preternatural and supernatural?"

"Or preternatural and natural folk with supernatural potential."

"What kind of attraction?" asked Lady Maccon rather injudiciously.

Floote raised an eloquent eyebrow.

"Did my father—" Alexia stopped, trying to come up with the correct phrasing. This was a strange sensation for her, thinking before she spoke. Her husband was much the same way or they might never have tolerated each other. Floote was notoriously reluctant to talk about his former employer, citing classified protection of international relations and the safety of the empire. Lady Maccon tried again. "Did my father exercise this appeal on purpose?"

"Not to my knowledge." Suddenly Floote switched topics, volunteering information in a most unexpected and un-Floote-like manner.

"Do you know why the Templars gave up their preternatural breeding program, madam?"

Alexia's brain tried to change gears, a steam engine caught on the wrong track. "Uh, no."

"They never could entirely control preternaturals. It's your pragmatism. Your kind cannot be persuaded by faith; pure logic must be applied."

Alexia's very pragmatic nature was confused as to why normally taciturn Floote was telling her this, and right now. "Is that what happened to my father? Did he lose faith?"

"Not exactly faith, madam."

"What do you mean, precisely, Floote? Enough shilly-shallying."

"He engaged in an exchange of loyalties."

Alexia frowned. She was beginning to suspect there were far fewer coincidences in life than she had previously believed. "Let me guess. This occurred about twenty years ago?"

"Nearer to thirty, but if you are asking if the three events are linked, the answer is yes."

"My father rejecting the Templars, his death, and the Kingair assassination attempt? But when the Kingair Pack tried to kill the queen, he was already dead."

"My point exactly, madam."

A loud crashing and banging came at the front door. Lady Maccon would have liked to query Floote further, but pressing noises seemed to be calling on his butler attentions.

Floote glided out, all calmness and dignity, to see what the fuss was about. Whoever it was, however, pushed past him and came rushing into the front parlor, crying, "Lady Maccon! Lady Maccon, you are needed most urgently!"

The intrusion resolved itself into the form of two of Lord Akeldama's boys, Boots and a young viscount by the name of Trizdale. They were overwrought and disheveled—conditions highly out of character for any of Lord Akeldama's drones. One sleeve of Boots's favorite green jacket was torn, and Tizzy's boots actually looked to be scuffed in places. *Scuffed, indeed!*

"My goodness me, gentlemen, has there been an *incident?*"

"Oh, my lady, I can hardly bear to say it. But we are being assaulted!"

"Oh, my." Lady Maccon signaled them to come closer. "Don't stand there gawping—help me to rise. What can I do?"

"Well, my lady, we are under attack from a werewolf!"

Alexia paled considerably. "In a vampire's abode? Deary me! What is this world coming to?"

Boots said, "That's just the thing, my lady. We thought it best to fetch you. The creature is on a bender."

Lady Maccon grabbed up her parasol and her reticule. "Of course, of course. I'll come directly. Lend me your arm, please, Mr. Bootbottle-Fipps."

As quickly as possible, the two young dandies helped Alexia to waddle out the front door and along the path past the lilac bushes into Lord Akeldama's house.

The arched and frescoed hallway was packed with concerned-looking young men, several of them worse off than Boots and Tizzy. Two were even missing their cravats. A truly startling thing to see. They were milling about and talking in obvious trepidation, at a loss but eager to do something.

"Gentlemen!" Lady Maccon's shrill feminine voice cut through the masculine hubbub. She raised her parasol on high as though about to conduct a concert. "Where is the beast?"

"Please, mum, it's our master."

Alexia paused in perplexity and lowered her parasol slightly. Lord Akeldama was a vampire, but no one would ever refer to him as a *beast*.

The dandies continued in a chorus of explanations and objections.

"He's gone and locked himself in the drawing room."

"With *that* monster."

"I should never wish to question our lord's choices, but *really!*"

"So ill-kempt. I'm convinced its fur had split ends."

"Said he could handle it."

"For our own good, he said. Not to let anyone in."

"I'm not *anyone.*" Lady Maccon pushed her way through the throng of perfectly tailored jackets and high white collars, as one of those particularly chubby terriers might clear a path through a pack of poodles.

The young men gave way until she was faced with the gilt door, painted with white and lavender swirls, that led into Lord Akeldama's infamous drawing room. She took a deep breath and knocked loudly with the handle of her parasol.

"Lord Akeldama? It's Lady Maccon. May I enter?"

From behind the door came the sound of scuffling and possibly Lord Akeldama's voice. But no one actually bid her entrance.

She knocked again. Even under the most dire of circumstances, one didn't simply go bursting into a man's private drawing room without sufficient provocation.

A particularly loud crash was all the response she got.

Alexia decided that *this* could be considered sufficient provocation and slowly turned the knob. Parasol at the ready, she waddled in as quick as she could, closing the door firmly behind her. Just because she was disobeying Lord Akeldama's orders didn't mean the drones could as well.

Her fascinated gaze fell upon quite the tableau.

Lady Maccon had witnessed an altercation between a vampire and a werewolf once before, but it had been inside a moving carriage and had rather rapidly relocated from carriage to road. Also, back then, the two opponents had genuinely been trying to kill each other. This was different.

Lord Akeldama was locked in single combat with a werewolf. The wolf was definitely trying to kill him, jaws snapping and all his supernatural strength bent on the vampire's destruction. But Lord Akeldama, while fighting the wolf off, did not seem to be enthusiastic about killing him. For one thing, his favored weapon, a silver-edged glaive that masqueraded as a piece of gold plumbing, was still in its customary place above the mantelpiece. No, Lord Akeldama seemed to be employing mostly evasive strategies, which only served to frustrate and anger the wolf.

The beast lunged for the vampire's elegant white neck, and Lord Akeldama dodged to the side, flicking out one arm in a blasé manner, as if flapping a large handkerchief at a departing steamer. It was a gesture that, for all its casualness, still lifted the werewolf up and entirely over the vampire's blond head to land on his back near the fireplace.

Alexia had never had the chance to observe Lord Akeldama fight before. Of course, one knew Lord Akeldama must be *able* to fight. He was rumored to be quite old, and as such must be at least capable of combat. But this was akin to knowing, academically, that his chubby calico house cat was capable of hunting rats—the actual execution of the task always seemed highly improbable and possibly embarrassing for all concerned. Thus, she now found herself quite intrigued by the display before her. And soon discovered that she was wrong in her initial assumption.

Far from any discomfit or awkwardness, Lord Akeldama fought with a nonchalant lazy efficiency, as though he had all the time in the world on his side. Which Alexia supposed he did. His advantage was in speed, eyesight, and dexterity. The wolf had strength, smell, and sound to rely on, but he was inexperienced. The werewolf hadn't an Alpha's skill, either, which Lord Maccon had once described to his wife as fighting with soul. No, this wolf was moon mad. His jaws snapped and his claws speared surfaces without regard to logic or expense. The vampire's perfectly elegant drawing room was faring no better than Alexia's back parlor. He was also getting saliva all over the pretty throw cushions.

It would have been an entirely uneven match except that Lord Akeldama really was trying not to hurt Biffy.

Because that was who it was: Biffy, chocolate brown fur with an oxblood stomach.

"How on earth did you get out of the Woolsey dungeon?"

No one answered her, of course.

Biffy charged Lord Akeldama. The vampire seemed to flash spontaneously from one side of the room to the other, leaving the werewolf to complete his leap with no quarry at the end of it. Biffy landed on a gold brocade chair, overturning it so that its legs stuck up, shockingly bare, into the air.

The werewolf noticed Lady Maccon's presence first. His nostrils flared. His hairy head swiveled around to cast a yellow-eyed glare in her direction. There was none of Biffy's soft blue gentleness in those eyes, only the need to maim, feast, and kill.

Lord Akeldama was only seconds behind noticing that they had company. "Why, Alexia, my *little cowslip*, how kind of you to call. Especially in your present condition."

Alexia played along. "Well, I had nothing better to do of an evening, and I did hear you needed help in entertaining an unexpected guest."

The vampire gave a little chuckle. "La so, my custard. As you see. Our company is a *tad* overwrought. Methinks he could use some good cheer."

"I do see. Is there any way in which I may provide assistance?"

While this conversation took place, Biffy charged at Alexia. She barely had time to arm her dart emitter before Lord Akeldama interposed, protecting her gallantly.

He took on the brunt of the attack. Biffy's claws scraped down the vampire's legs, tearing silk trousers to ribbons and gouging deep into the muscle. Old black blood seeped out. At the same time, the werewolf's jaws locked about Lord Akeldama's upper arm, biting clean through the meatiest part. The pain must have been phenomenal, but the vampire merely shook the wolf off, as a dog will shake off water. Even as Alexia watched, Lord Akeldama's wounds began to heal.

Biffy launched himself at the vampire once more, and together they grappled, Lord Akeldama always just that split second faster and a whole lot craftier so that even with all the predatory advantages afforded by the werewolf state, Biffy could not break the vampire's hold nor his will when both were set so firmly against him.

Alexia said, "I've been meaning to have this little chat with you, my lord. Some of your young gentlemen friends do seem to get overly clingy, don't you find?"

The vampire puffed out a breath of amusement. His hair was coming loose from its ribbon, and he appeared to have lost his cravat pin.

"My *darling pumpkin blossom,* it is not my intent to engender such gripping affection, I assure you. It is purely by accident."

"You are too charismatic for your own good."

"*You* said it, my dabble-duck, not I." Once more the vampire managed to use grip and speed to lever the wolf off of him and hurl the creature across the room, away from Alexia. Biffy landed full against the wall and slid down, taking several watercolors with him. He crashed to the floor, the paintings now lying amidst shards of glass and gilt frames. He shook himself and stumbled dizzily to his feet.

Alexia fired the parasol. Her dart struck home and the werewolf collapsed back. He seemed to wobble, losing control of bits of himself, but then, quicker than any vampire Alexia had ever shot, fought against the effects of the drug and regained his feet. She wondered if Madame Lefoux's last batch of numbing agent was up to snuff or if it was simply less effective on werewolves.

Lord Akeldama flitted to one side, catching the wolf's attention and directing his next charge away from Lady Maccon.

Alexia said, deciding on a new tactic, "If you think you could hold him steady, my lord, I might be able to manage a calming touch. You know, some lads these days simply require a female to administer discipline."

"Of course, my plum, of course."

Biffy hit Lord Akeldama broadside, and in the same movement, the vampire turned all affectionate, instead of tossing him away. Wrapping both his arms and legs about the wolf, Lord Akeldama used the beast's own momentum to tumble them both to the lush carpet. In an amazing feat of wrestling, the vampire got one elbow about Biffy's muzzle, his hand closing firmly over the nose. With his other arm, he locked down the forelegs. With his legs, Lord Akeldama secured Biffy's hindquarters. It was a remarkable exhibition of agility and flexibility. Alexia was duly impressed, having wrestled a bit with her husband. Lord Akeldama was clearly very experienced in the matter of intimate tussling.

Alexia knew the vampire would not be able to pin the werewolf thus for very long. In the end, Biffy was stronger and would break free, but Lord Akeldama did have the beast momentarily confused.

She waddled up and, casting her own safety to the winds, leaned forward, not unexpectedly losing her balance. She landed fully atop both supernatural creatures, ensuring her bare hands were in contact with Biffy but turning both men mortal in her enthusiasm.

It was a very odd sensation, for in such a position, Alexia was uncomfortably aware of Biffy's body changing from wolf to human. She could feel the slide of muscle and bone beneath her protruding belly as he shifted. It was eerily like the feel of her child kicking underneath her own skin.

Biffy howled with the pain of it, directly into Alexia's ear. A howl that turned to a scream of agony, then a whimper of remembered suffering, and finally little snuffles of acute embarrassment. Then, as he came to the horrific realization of what he had almost done, he turned to his former master.

"Oh, dear, oh, dear. Oh dear." It was a litany of distress. "My lord, are you well? Did I cause any permanent injury? Oh look at your trousers! Oh, mercy. I am so sorry."

Lord Akeldama's healing was paused midway so that the claw marks were still visible under the tattered ribbons of his silken britches.

" 'Tis but a scratch, my pet. Do not trouble yourself so." He looked down at himself. "Well, several scratches, to be precise."

At this juncture, Alexia was forced into a realization that rather shook the foundations of her universe: there are some circumstances that even the very best manners could not possibly rectify. This was one such situation. For there she lay, pregnant and out of balance, atop a pile consisting of one overdressed vampire and one underdressed werewolf.

"Biffy," she said finally, "to what do we owe the pleasure of your visit? I was under the impression you were otherwise contained this evening." It was a valiant attempt, but even such talk as this could not mask the awkwardness.

Lord Akeldama attempted to unwind himself from Biffy and extract himself from Alexia without the aid of supernatural strength. When this was finally accomplished, he stood, dashed to the door to reassure his drones of his undamaged state, and sent one of them to fetch clothing.

Biffy and Alexia helped each other to rise.

"Are you unharmed, my lady?"

Alexia did a quick internal check. "It would appear so. Remarkably resilient, this baby of mine. I could use a bit of a sit-down, though."

Biffy helped her to an ottoman—one of the few pieces of furniture in the room not overturned—her hand firmly clasped in his. They sat and stared off into space, grappling with how best to handle their predicament. Lord Maccon might be a blustering instrument of rudeness, but he did have his uses in dispersing awkward silences. Alexia handed Biffy a shawl, only slightly saliva-ridden. He set it gratefully in his lap.

She tried not to look, of course she did, but Biffy did have a rather nice physique. Not nearly so splendid as her husband's, but not everyone could be built like a steam engine, and the young dandy had kept himself well in hand before metamorphosis, for all his frivolous pursuits.

"Biffy, were you secretly a Corinthian?" Alexia wondered out loud before she could stop herself.

Biffy blushed. "No, my lady, although I did enjoy fencing rather more than some of my compatriots might consider healthy."

Lady Maccon nodded sagely.

Lord Akeldama returned, looking not a whit put out. His brief sojourn among his drones had resulted in hair and neck cloth back to crisp and pristine order and a new pair of satin trousers. *How do they do it?* wondered Alexia.

"Biffy, *duckling*, what a surprise your visiting little old *me* at this time of moon." He handed his former drone a pair of sapphire-colored britches.

Biffy blushed, pulling them on with one hand. Alexia took polite interest in the opposite side of the room. "Yes, well, I wasn't entirely in my right faculties, my lord, when I made the decision to, uh, call. I think I simply, well, instinctively"—he glanced at Lady Maccon from under his lashes—"headed home."

Lord Akeldama nodded. "Yes, my *dove*, but you have missed the mark. Your home is next door. I know it's easy to be confused."

"Too easy. Especially in my altered state."

They were speaking about Biffy's werewolfness as one would an evening's inebriation. Alexia looked back and forth between the two of them. Lord Akeldama had taken a seat opposite his former drone, his eyes heavy-lidded, his posture informal, revealing nothing.

Biffy, too, was beginning to assume his old dapperness, as though this were actually a social call. As though he were not half naked in a vampire's drawing room. As though he had not just tried to kill them both.

Lady Maccon had always admired Lord Akeldama's ability to remain patently unruffled by the world about him. It was as commendable as his never-ending efforts to ensure that his own small corner of London was filled with nothing but beauty and pleasant conversation. But sometimes, and she should never say such a thing openly, it smacked of cowardice. She wondered if the immortal's avoidance of life's ugliness was a matter of survival or bigotry. Lord Akeldama did so love to know all the gossip about the mundane world, but it was in the manner of a cat amusing himself among the butterflies without a need to interfere should their wings get torn off. They were only butterflies, after all.

Lady Maccon felt it behooved her, just this once, to point out the wounded wingless insect before him. Soullessness may confer practicality, but it did not always confer caution. "Gentlemen, you may place my abruptness at the door of my current condition, but I am not in the mood to tolerate idiosyncrasies. Circumstances have placed us all in an untenable position. No, Biffy, I do not mean your unclothed state—I mean your werewolf one."

Both Lord Akeldama and Biffy looked at her, mouths slightly agape.

"The time has come to move onward. Both of you. Biffy, your choices were taken from you, and that is regrettable, but you are still an immortal—and not dead—which is more than most can say." She turned her baleful look upon the vampire. "And you, my lord, must let go. This is not some contest you have lost. This is life, or afterlife, I suppose. For goodness' sake, stop wallowing, both of you."

Biffy looked duly chastised.

Lord Akeldama sputtered.

Lady Maccon tilted her head in such a way as to dare him to deny the truth in her words. He was certainly old enough to know himself; whether he cared to admit such a fault out loud remained to be seen.

The two men looked at each other, their faces tight.

It was Biffy who closed his eyes a long moment and then nodded briefly.

Lord Akeldama lifted one white hand and trailed two fingers down the side of his former drone's face. "Ah, my boy. If it must be so."

Lady Maccon could be merciful, so she moved the conversation on. "Biffy, how did you get out of Woolsey's dungeon?"

Biffy shrugged. "I don't know. I can't remember much when I'm a wolf. Someone must have unbolted the cell door."

"Yes, but why? And who?" Alexia looked suspiciously at Lord Akeldama. Was he meddling?

The vampire shook his head. "Not me or mine, I *assure* you, blossom."

A loud knock sounded at the door to the drawing room, all the warning they got before it burst open and two men came stomping in.

"Well," said Alexia, "at least he knocked first. Perhaps he's learning."

The earl strode across the room and bent to kiss his wife's cheek. "Wife, thought I would find you here. And young Biffy, too—how are you, pup?"

Lady Maccon looked to her husband's Beta, gesturing at Biffy with her free hand. "The pack business that took you away?"

Professor Lyall nodded. "He led us a merry chase before we traced him here." He tapped his nose, indicating the method of tracking.

"How'd he get out?"

Professor Lyall tilted his head, which was as good as he would get to admitting that he had no idea.

Alexia nudged her husband in Biffy's direction. He shot her a brief glance out of resigned tawny eyes and then crouched down in front of the half-naked dandy. It was a very servile position for an Alpha. He lowered his voice to a soft growl, of the kind meant to be comforting. It's terribly difficult for a werewolf to be comforting—especially an Alpha dealing with a reluctant pack member. The instinct is to subdue and discipline.

Alexia nodded at him encouragingly.

"My boy, why did you run here?"

Biffy looked up at the ceiling and then back down again. He swallowed, nervous. "I don't know, my lord, some instinct. I'm sorry, but this is still home to me."

Lord Maccon looked at Lord Akeldama, predator to predator. Then he turned back to his pack member.

"It has been six months, many moons, and still you are not settling. I know this was not the end you wanted, but it is the end you have been given. Somehow we must make this work."

No one missed the *we.*

Alexia was extremely proud of her husband at that moment. *He can be taught!*

He took a deep breath. "How can we make this easier for you? How can I?"

Biffy looked utterly startled to be asked such a question by such a man. "Perhaps," he ventured, "perhaps I could be allowed to take up permanent residence here, in town?"

Lord Maccon frowned, glancing at Lord Akeldama. "Is that wise?"

Lord Akeldama stood as though totally disinterested in the entire conversation. He walked to the other side of the room and stared down at his torn watercolor paintings.

Professor Lyall stepped in to fill the breach. "Young Biffy might benefit from a distraction. Some form of employment, perhaps?"

Biffy started. He was a gentleman, born and bred; honest work was a little beyond his frame of reference. "I suppose I could try it. I've never had proper employment before." He spoke as though it were some kind of exotic cuisine he had not yet sampled.

Lord Maccon nodded. "At BUR? After all, you have contacts within society that might prove useful. I am in a position to see you well settled with the government."

Biffy looked somewhat intrigued.

Professor Lyall came around to stand before Alexia, next to her crouching husband. His normally passive face showed genuine concern for the new pack member, and it was clear that he had put thought into how Biffy might be better integrated.

"We could come up with a suitable range of duties. Regular occupation might help you acclimatize to your new position."

Lady Maccon looked, really looked, at her husband's second for the first time in their acquaintance. At the way he stood, shoulders not too straight, gaze not too direct. At the way he dressed, almost to the height of style but with a studied carelessness, the simple knot to his cravat, the reserved cut to his waistcoat. There was just enough not perfect about his appearance as to make him forgettable. Professor Lyall was the type of man who could stand in the center of a group and no one would remember he was there, except that the group would stay together because of him.

And then, right there, holding on to the hand of a half-naked dandy, Alexia discovered the piece of the puzzle she had been missing.

CHAPTER TEN

Ivy's Agent Doom

"It was you!"

It had taken well over two hours to configure the wine cellar of the new house to hold Biffy for the remainder of the evening without damage to either the wine, the cellar, or, most importantly, Biffy. They would have to devise a better long-term solution if he was to take up permanent residence in town. They left Lord Maccon coaching him through the change, arms wrapped about him, gruff voice keeping him calm.

Alexia had pigeon-holed Lyall and practically dragged him into the back parlor, giving Floote very strict instructions that under no circumstances were they to be disturbed by anyone. Now she was busy waving her parasol wildly in his direction.

"You're Agent Doom! How ninnyhammered of me not to have seen it sooner! You rigged the whole thing back then. The whole Kingair attempt. And that was the point, of course, that it should be only an *attempt.* It was never meant to succeed. The queen was never meant to die. The point was to convince the Kingair Pack to turn against their Alpha, to give him a reason to leave. You needed Conall to come to London so he could challenge Lord Woolsey. The Alpha who had gone mad." The parasol inscribed ever increasing wiggles in the air in her enthusiasm.

Professor Lyall turned away, walking to the other side of the room, his soft brown boots making no noise on the carpet. His sandy head was bent only slightly. He spoke to the wall. "You have no idea what a blessing it is, to have a capable Alpha."

"And you are Beta. You would do whatever it took to keep your pack together. Even arrange to steal another pack's leader. Does my husband know what you did?"

Lyall stiffened.

Alexia answered her own question. "No, of course he doesn't know. He needs to trust you. He needs you to be his reliable second just as much as you need him as leader. Telling him would defeat the very action you took; it would disturb the cohesion of your pack."

Professor Lyall turned to face her. His hazel eyes were tired, for all they were set in that eternally young face. There was no pleading in them. "Are *you* going to tell him?"

"That you were a double agent? That you destroyed his relationship with his old pack, with his best friend, with his homeland, to steal him for Woolsey? I don't know." Alexia put a hand to her stomach, suddenly exhausted by the events of the past week. "It would destroy him, I think. Treachery from his Beta, his lynchpin. A second time."

She paused, looking him full in the face. "But to keep this information from Conall, to share in your deception? You must know that this puts me in an untenable position as his wife."

Professor Lyall avoided her direct gaze, wincing slightly. "I had no choice. You must see that? Lord Maccon was the only werewolf in Britain capable of taking on Lord Woolsey and winning. When Alphas go bad, my lady, it is sickening. All that concentrated attention to pack cohesion and all that protective energy turns rotten—no one is safe. As Beta, I could shield the others but only for so long. Eventually, I knew his psychosis would leak out, encompassing them as well. Such a thing can drive an entire pack to madness. We don't talk of it. The howlers don't sing of it. But it occurs. I am not trying to excuse myself, you understand, simply explain."

Alexia was still stuck on the horror of having such knowledge when her husband did not. "Who else knows? Who else knew?"

A knock sounded and then immediately the door crashed open.

"Oh, for goodness' sake, doesn't anyone wait to be bidden entrance anymore?" cried Alexia in vexation, whirling to face the intruder, parasol quite definitely at the ready. "I said *no one* was to disturb us!"

It was Major Channing Channing of the Chesterfield Channings.

"And what are you doing here?" Lady Maccon's tone was far from welcoming, but her parasol relaxed into a safer position.

"Biffy is missing!"

"Yes, yes, you're late. He turned up next door, got into a tussle with Lord Akeldama, and now Conall has him down in the wine cellar."

The Gamma paused. "You have a crazed werewolf in your wine cellar?"

"You can think of a better place to stash him?"

"What about the wine?"

Lady Maccon abruptly lost interest in dealing with her husband's Gamma. She turned back to Professor Lyall, who was looking cowed. "Does *he* know?"

"Me? Know what?" Channing's beautiful ice-blue eyes were the picture of innocence. But his eyelids flickered as he took in Alexia's militant attitude and Professor Lyall's intimidated demeanor, the latter as out of character as the former was standard. Everyone was accustomed to Professor Lyall skulking about in the background, but he did that with an air of quiet confidence, not shame.

The major looked back and forth between the two, but instead of leaving them to their private discourse, he turned, slammed the door, and wedged a seat under the handle.

"Lyall, your disruptor, if you would?"

Professor Lyall reached into his waistcoat and pulled out a harmonic auditory resonance disruptor. He tossed the small crystal device to Channing, who set it atop the chair in front of the door and then quickly flicked the two tuning forks, activating the discordant humming.

Only then did he approach Lady Maccon. "*What do Iknow?*" He asked it as though he could predict her answer.

Alexia looked at Lyall.

Channing cocked his head. "Is this about the past? I told you no good could come of your meddling."

Lyall raised his head, smelling the air. Then he turned to look at Channing.

For the first time, Alexia realized the two men were probably old friends. Sometime enemies, of course, but only in the manner of those who have been too long in each other's company, possibly centuries. These two had known each other far longer than either had known Lord Maccon.

"You know?" Lyall said to the Gamma.

Channing nodded, all patrician beauty and aristocratic superiority as compared to Professor Lyall's studied middleclass inoffensiveness.

The Beta looked at his hands. "Did you know all along?"

Channing sighed, his fine face becoming suffused with a brief paroxysm of agony. So brief Alexia thought she had imagined it. "What kind of Gamma do you take me for?"

Lyall laughed, a huff of pain. "A mostly absentee one." There was no bitterness to the statement, simply fact. Channing was often away fighting Queen Victoria's little wars. "I didn't think you realized."

"Realized what, exactly? That it was occurring? Or that you were taking the brunt of it so he'd stay off the rest of us? Who do you think kept the others from finding out what was really going on? I didn't approve of you and Sandy—you know I didn't—but that doesn't mean I approved of what the Alpha was doing either."

Alexia's previous self-righteousness disintegrated under the implication of Channing's comments. There was more to Lyall's manipulations than she had realized. "Sandy? Who is Sandy?"

Professor Lyall twisted his lips into a little smile. Then he reached into his waistcoat—he always seemed to have everything he needed in that waistcoat of his—and pulled out a tiny leather-covered journal, navy blue with a very plain cover dated 1848 to 1850 in the upper left corner. It looked achingly familiar.

He walked softly across the room and handed it to Alexia. "I have the rest as well, from 1845 on. He left them to me on purpose. I wasn't keeping them intentionally away from you."

Alexia could think of nothing whatsoever to say. The silence stretched until finally she asked, "The ones from after he abandoned my mother?"

"And from when you were born." The Beta's face was a study in impassivity. "But this one was his last. I like to keep it with me. A reminder." A whisper of a smile crossed that deadpan face, the kind of smile one sees at funerals. "He didn't have an opportunity to finish it."

Alexia flipped the journal open, glancing over the scribbled text within. The little book was barely half full. Lines jumped out at her, details of a love affair that had altered everyone involved. Only as she read did the full scope of the ramifications come into focus. It was rather like being broadsided by a Christmas ham.

Winter 1848—for a while he walked with a limp but would not tell me why,

said one entry. Another, from the following spring, read:

There is talk of a theater trip on the morrow. He will not be permitted to attend, of that I am convinced. Yet we both pretended he would accompany me and that we should laugh together at the follies of society.

For all the tight control of the penmanship, Alexia could read the tension and the fear behind her father's words. As the entries progressed, some of his sentences turned her stomach with their brutal honesty.

The bruises are on his face now and so deep sometimes I wonder if they will ever heal, even with all his supernatural abilities.

She looked up at Lyall, attempting to appreciate all the implications. Trying to see bruises almost twenty-five years gone. From the stillness in his face, she supposed they might be there—well hidden, but there.

"Read the last entry," he suggested gently. "Go on."

June 23, 1850

It is full moon tonight. He is not going to come. Tonight all his wounds will be self-inflicted. Time was once, he would spend such nights with me. Now there is no surety left for any of them except in his presence. He is holding his whole world together by merely enduring. He has asked me to wait. Yet I do not have the patience of an immortal, and I will do anything to stop his suffering. Anything. In the end it comes to one thing. I hunt. It is what I am best at. I am better at hunting than I am at loving.

Alexia closed the book. Her face was wet. "You're the one he's writing about. The one who was maltreated."

Professor Lyall said nothing. He didn't need to respond. Alexia was not asking a question.

She looked away from him, finding the brocade of a nearby curtain quite fascinating. "The previous Alpha really was insane."

Channing strode over to Professor Lyall and placed a hand on his arm. No more sympathy than that. It seemed sufficient. "Randolph didn't even tell Sandy the worst of it."

Professor Lyall said softly, "He was so old. Things go fuzzy with Alphas when they get old."

"Yes, but he—"

Lyall looked up. "Unnecessary, Channing. Lady Maccon is still a lady. Remember your manners."

Alexia turned the small slim volume over in her hand—the end of her father's life. "What really happened to him, at the last?"

"He went after our Alpha." Professor Lyall removed his spectacles as though to clean them, but then seemed to forget he had done so. The glasses dangled from his fingers, glinting in the gas lamplight.

Channing seemed to feel further explanation was necessary. "He was good, your father, very good. He'd been trained by the Templars for one purpose and one purpose only—to hunt down and kill supernatural creatures. But even he couldn't take on an Alpha. Even an insane, sadistic bastard like Lord Woolsey was still an Alpha with a pack at his back."

Professor Lyall put his spectacles down on a side table and rubbed a hand across his forehead. "I told him not to, of course. Such a waste. But he was always one to pick and choose listening to me. Sandy was too much an Alpha himself."

Alexia thought for the first time that Professor Lyall and Lord Akeldama shared some mannerisms. They were both good at hiding their emotions. To a certain extent, this was to be expected in vampires, but in werewolves . . . Lyall's reserve was practically flawless. Then she wondered if his very quiet stillness were not like that of a child climbing into hot water, afraid that every little movement would only make things hotter and more painful.

Professor Lyall said, "Your father's death taught me one thing. That something needed to be done about our Alpha. That if I had to bring down another pack to do it, so be it. At the time, there were only two wolves in England capable of killing Lord Woolsey. The dewan and—"

Alexia filled in the rest of his sentence. "Conall Maccon, Lord Kingair. So it wasn't simply a change of leadership you were after; it was self-preservation."

One corner of Lyall's mouth quirked upward. "It was revenge. Never forget, my lady, I'm still a werewolf. It took me nearly four years to plan. I'll admit that's a vampire's style. But it worked."

"You loved my father, didn't you, Professor?"

"He was not a very good man."

A pause. Alexia thumbed through the little journal. It was worn about the edges from countless readings and rereadings.

Professor Lyall let out a little sigh. "Do you know how old I am, my lady?"

Alexia shook her head.

"Old enough to know better. Things are never good when immortals fall in love. Mortals end up dead, one way or another, and we are left alone again. Why do you think the pack is so important? Or the hive, for that matter. It is not simply a vehicle for safety; it is a vehicle for sanity, to stave off the loneliness. Our mistrust of loners and roves is not only custom, it is based on this fact."

Alexia's brain buzzed with all these new revelations, but finally the whirling settled on one thing. "Oh, lordy, Floote. Floote knew."

"Some, yes. He *was* Sandy's valet at the time."

"Is it you who are keeping him quiet?"

Professor Lyall shook his head. "Your butler has never taken his orders from me."

Alexia looked at the little journal again, stroking the cover, and then offered it back to Lyall. "Perhaps you will let me read it in its entirety sometime?"

The Beta's eyes crinkled up, wincing as though he might cry. Then he swallowed, nodded, and placed the book inside his waistcoat pocket.

Alexia took a deep breath. "So, back to the crisis at hand. I suppose neither of you is currently planning to kill Queen Victoria, even in jest?"

Two almost simultaneous head shakes met that question.

"Are you telling me I've been on the wrong track all this time?"

The werewolves looked at each other, neither of them willing to risk her wrath.

Alexia sighed and extracted the sheaf of paper Madame Lefoux had given her from her reticule. "So this is entirely useless? No connection between the last attempt and this one. Pure coincidence that the poisoner you were going to use, Professor, happened to die in service to the OBO. And that she possibly then became a ghost who delivered a warning to me."

"Looks like it must be, my lady."

"I don't like coincidences."

"Now that, my lady, I can't help you with."

Alexia sighed and stood, using her parasol as a crutch. "Back to the beginning, I suppose. Nothing for it. I shall have to return these papers to Madame Lefoux." The child inside her kicked mightily at the very idea. "Perhaps tomorrow night. Bed first."

"A very sensible idea, my lady."

"None of that from you, Professor, thank you very much. I'm still miffed. I understand why you did it, but I *am* miffed." Alexia began making her way painstakingly to the door, prepared to climb upstairs and across the balcony bridge into her closet boudoir.

Neither werewolf tried to help her. She was clearly not in the mood to be coddled. Lyall did touch her arm as she passed. The action turned him mortal for a moment. Alexia had never had an opportunity to see him mortal before. He looked much the same as he did when immortal—perhaps there were more lines about his mouth and at the corners of his eyes—but he was still a pale vulpine man with sandy hair—utterly unremarkable.

"*Are* you going to tell Conall?"

Alexia turned around slowly and leveled a decided glare in his direction. It told him, in no uncertain terms, exactly how she felt about this state of affairs. "No, no, I'm not. Damn you."

And then, with as much dignity as was possible given her condition, she waddled from the room, like some unbalanced galleon under full sail.

Only to run into Felicity in the hallway. It was like trundling full tilt into a pillar of molasses, the conversation likely to be sticky and the individual attractive only to creepy-crawlies. Alexia was never prepared to run into her sister, but on such a night as this when the chit should be fast asleep, it really was *beyond.*

Felicity, for her part, was bleary-eyed and wearing nothing but a highly ornamented nightgown, the excess material of which she clutched, with artful trembling hands, to her breast. Her hair was a tousle of golden curls that cascaded over one shoulder, a ridiculous pink bed cap perched precariously atop her head. The nightgown, too, was pink, a foulard with printed magenta flowers, replete with ruching, frillings, a quantity of lace trim, and a particularly large ruff about the neck. Alexia thought Felicity looked like a big pink Christmas tree.

"Sister," said the tree, "there is a most impressive rumpus emanating from the wine cellar."

"Oh, go back to bed, Felicity. It's only a werewolf. Really. You'd think people never had monsters in their cellars."

Felicity blinked.

Channing came up behind Alexia. "Lady Maccon, might I have a private word, before you seek your rest?"

Felicity's eyes widened and her breath caught.

Alexia turned around. "Yes, well, if you insist, Major Channing."

A sharp elbow met her protruding belly. "Introduce us," hissed Felicity. Her sister was looking at the Gamma with much the same expression as that which entered Ivy Tunstell's eyes when faced with a particularly hideous hat, which is to say, covetous and lacking in all elements of good judgment.

Alexia was taken well aback. "But you are in your night attire!" Felicity only gave her a big-eyed head shake. "Oh, very well, Felicity. This is Major Channing Channing of the Chesterfield Channings. He is a werewolf and my husband's Gamma. Major Channing, do please meet my sister, Felicity Loontwill. She is human, if you can believe such a thing after ten minutes' conversation."

Felicity tittered in a manner she probably thought was musical. "Oh, Alexia, you so like to have your little jokes." She offered her hand to the handsome man before her. "I do apologize for my informal state, Major."

Major Channing clasped it elegantly in both of his, bowing with evident interest, even daring to brush his lips across her wrist. "You are a picture, Miss Loontwill. A picture."

Felicity blushed and took back her hand more slowly than was proper. "I should never have thought *you* a werewolf, Major."

"Ah, Miss Loontwill, it was eternal life as a gallant soldier that called to me."

Felicity's eyelids fluttered. "Oh, a soldiering man through and through, are you, sir? How romantic."

"To the bone, Miss Loontwill."

Alexia felt she was about to be sick, and it had nothing to do with her pregnancy. "Really, Felicity, it is the middle of the night. Don't you have one of your meetings tomorrow?"

"Oh, yes, Alexia, but I should never wish to be rude in fine company."

Major Channing practically clicked his heels. "Miss Loontwill, I cannot deny you your beauty rest, however unnecessary I might feel it. Such loveliness as yours is already so near to perfection it can require no further assistance in that regard."

Alexia tilted her head, trying to determine if there was an insult buried in all that flowery talk.

Felicity tittered again. "Oh, really, Major Channing, we hardly know one another."

"Your meeting, Felicity. Rest." Alexia tapped her parasol pointedly.

"Oh, la, yes, I suppose I should."

Lady Maccon was tired and out of temper. She decided she had a right, under such circumstances, to be difficult. "My sister is an active member of the National Society for Women's Suffrage," she explained sweetly to Major Channing.

The Gamma was taken aback by this information. No doubt in all his long years he had never encountered a woman of Felicity's ilk—and her ilk was in very little doubt after even a few seconds of acquaintance—who would be involved in such a thing as politics.

"Really, Miss Loontwill? You must tell me more about this little club of yours. I can hardly believe a woman of your elegance need dabble in such trifles. Find yourself a nice gentleman to marry and he can do such fiddling things as voting for you."

Rather suddenly, Alexia felt like she might want to join the movement herself. Imagine such a man as Major Channing thinking he had any inkling of what a woman might want. *So condescending.*

Felicity's eyelashes fluttered as though doing battle with a very fierce wind. "No one has asked me yet."

Lady Maccon marshaled her displeasure. "Felicity, bed, now. I don't care one jot for your finer feelings, but I need my rest. Channing, help me up the stairs and we shall have our little confidence."

Felicity reluctantly undertook to do her sister's bidding.

Major Channing, even more reluctantly, took Alexia's arm. "So, my lady, I wanted to—"

"No, Major, wait until she is well away," cautioned Lady Maccon.

They waited, making their way slowly up to the next floor.

Alexia finally deemed it safe, but still she spoke in a very low voice. "Yes?"

"I wanted to say, about that business with our Beta. Randolph is different from the rest of us wolves, you do realize? Your father was the love of his life, and we immortals don't say such a thing lightly. Oh, there were others before Sandy—mostly women, I'll have you know." Channing seemed to be one of the few immortals Alexia had met who was concerned with such things. "But Sandy was the last. I worry. It was a quarter of a century ago."

Lady Maccon frowned. "I have other pressing concerns at the moment, Major, but I will give the matter my due attention as soon as possible."

Channing panicked. "Oh, now, I'm not asking you to matchmake, my lady. I'm simply pleading for leniency. I could not confide such fears to Lord Maccon, and you are also our Alpha."

Alexia pinched at the bridge of her nose. "Could we talk about this tomorrow evening, perhaps? I really am quite done in."

"No, my lady. Have you forgotten? Tomorrow is full moon."

"Oh, blast it, it is. What a mess. Later, then. I promise not to take any rash action with regards to the good professor without due consideration as to the consequences."

Channing clearly knew when to retreat from a battle. "Thank you very much, my lady. As to your sister, she is quite a peach, is she not? You have been hiding her from me."

Lady Maccon would not be goaded. "Really, Channing, she is practically"—she paused to do some calculations—"one-twentieth your age. Or worse. Don't you want some maturity in your life?"

"Good God, no!"

"Well, how about some human decency?"

"Now you're just being insulting."

Alexia huffed in amusement.

Channing raised blond eyebrows at her, handsome devil that he was. "Ah, but this is what I enjoy so much about immortality. The decades may pass for me, but the ladies, well, they will keep coming along all young and beautiful, now, won't they?"

"Channing, someone should lock you away."

"Now, Lady Maccon, that transpires tomorrow night, remember?"

Alexia did not bother to warn him off her sister. Such a man as Channing would only see that as a challenge. Best to pretend not to care. Felicity was on her own with this one. Lady Maccon was exhausted.

So exhausted, in fact, that she didn't awaken when her husband later crawled in next to her in their bed. Her big, strong husband who had spent the night holding on to a boy afraid of change. Who had coached that boy through a pain Conall could no longer remember. Who had forced Biffy to realize he must give up his love or he would lose all of his remaining choices. Her big, strong husband who curled up close against her back and cried, not because of what Biffy suffered but because he, Conall Maccon, had caused that suffering.

Alexia awoke early the next evening to an unfamiliar sense of peace. She was not, by and large, a restful person. This did not trouble her overmuch. But it did mean that peace was, ironically, a slightly uncomfortable sensation. It drove her fully awake, sharp and sudden, once she had recognized and identified it. Her husband had slept pressed against her the whole day through, and she had been so very tired even the inconvenience of pregnancy had awakened her only a few times. She luxuriated in the pleasure of Conall's broad, comforting presence. His scent was of open fields, even here in town. She reflected whimsically that he was the incarnation of a grassy hill. His face was rough with a full day's growth. It was a good thing they were now encamped in Lord Akeldama's house. If any household were to employ the services of an excellent barber, it was this one.

Alexia pushed aside the bedding, the better to examine her personal territory with greater thoroughness. She smoothed her hands along her husband's massive shoulders and chest, resting fingertips at the notch in the base of his throat. She petted him as though he were in wolf form. She rarely got to indulge in such a luxury; usually her preternatural touch turned him back to human before she even got in one good scratch. Sometimes, though, and no one had ever been able to tell her why, she could put on her gloves and pet his thick brindled coat, even tug on his velvety ears with no shifting. *Yet another mystery of my state,* she thought. It had happened once in Scotland, and then a few other times during the winter months. These days, however, her preternatural abilities seemed to be amplified. He went human simply by being close to her. *I wonder if it has something to do with the pregnancy. I should do some experiments and see if I can isolate the conditions.* Before her marriage, she'd never spent much time in the company of supernaturals, apart from Lord Akeldama, and she had never had the opportunity to really study her own abilities.

But in the interim, she would continue petting whatever form he presented her with. She trailed her hands back over his chest, threading fingers through the hair there, tugging slightly, and then down along his sides.

A rumbling snuffle of amusement met this action.

"That tickles." But Conall did not make any move to prevent her continued explorations. Instead, he picked up his own hand and began smoothing it over her protruding belly.

The infant-inconvenience kicked in response, and Conall twitched at the sensation.

"Active little pup, isn't he?"

"She," corrected his wife. "As if any child of mine would dare be a boy."

It was a long-standing argument.

"Boy," replied Conall. "Any child as difficult as this one has been from the start must, perforce, be male."

Alexia snorted. "As if *my* daughter would be calm and biddable."

Conall grinned, catching one of her hands and bringing it in for a kiss, all prickly whiskers and soft lips. "Very good point, wife. Very good point."

Alexia snuggled against him. "Did you manage to settle Biffy?"

Conall shrugged, an up and down of muscle under her ear. "I spent the remainder of last night with him. I think that helped mitigate the trauma. It is hard to tell. Regardless, by this point, I should be able to sense him."

"Sense, what do you mean, sense?"

"Difficult to articulate. Do you know that sensation you get when there is someone else in the room, even if you cannot see them? For us Alphas, pack members are a little like that. Whether we are in the same room or not, we simply know the pack is there. Biffy, he isn't a part of that yet. So he isn't part of my pack."

Alexia was struck with a moment of inspiration. "You should encourage him and Lyall to spend more time together."

"Now, Alexia, are you trying to matchmake?"

"Maybe."

"I thought you said Biffy did not need to be in love, he needed to find his place."

"Perhaps, in this matter, Biffy is not the half of the equation who needs to be in love."

"Ah. How did you know Randolph might favor . . . ? Never mind, I don't want to know. It would never work. Not those two."

Alexia took mild offense. Biffy and Lyall were both such good men, so personable and kindly. "Oh, I don't know about that. They seem eminently suited."

Lord Maccon looked up at the ceiling. Clearly he was trying to come up with a delicate way to phrase this. "They are both, uh, too much the Beta, if you take my meaning."

Alexia didn't. "I don't see how that can be an objection."

Lord Maccon obviously felt he could not go into the matter any further without spoiling what little was left of his wife's feminine delicacy, so he grappled for a means of changing the subject. Only to recall exactly what night this was.

"Oh, bugger it. It's full moon, isna it?"

"Indeed it is. Good thing we're all cozied up together, isn't it, my dear?"

Lord Maccon pursed his lips, trying to decide what to do. He had not intended to sleep the whole day through but had wanted to be on his way back to the dungeons before moonrise. "I left orders for Lyall and Channing to transport Biffy back to Woolsey before sunset, but I really should get there myself."

"Too late now—the moon is up."

He grunted, annoyed with himself. "Would you mind terribly taking the journey with me? The wine cellar here might hold a new pup, but it won't hold me. And I should be with him, tonight of all nights. Even moonstruck myself, my presence will soothe him. Besides, I can't imagine you want to stay attached to me all night."

Alexia blinked at him flirtatiously. "You know, under more slender circumstances, I wouldn't mind spending an evening thus occupied, but I really must be getting on with this investigation. I need to return some paperwork to Madame Lefoux, and I'm back to square one questioning the ghosts. I do wish this pregnancy didn't make me so abstracted. I keep missing things, and I shouldn't have allowed myself to be so easily sidetracked by history."

Lord Maccon didn't bother trying to argue. Given her ankle and her pregnancy, his wife was in no condition to do any such thing as continue an active inquiry. It was full moon. What could he do to see her safe except have her tailed? Which, naturally, he'd been doing for the past five weeks. For one moment, he did consider coming up with some kind of excuse to keep her at Woolsey even while he, himself, was incapacitated.

Instead, he growled out, "Very well. But, please, take some precautionary measures?"

Lady Maccon grinned. "Oh, my love, but that is so very boring."

Lord Maccon growled again.

Alexia kissed the tip of his nose. "I'll be good, I promise."

"Why is it that I am always at my most terrified when you say that?"

* * *

Above the ghost, under a full moon, the living celebrated being alive.

Mortals trotted about in shoes and corsets made to limit movement, fashion for prey. They drank (becoming pickled as any gherkin) and puffed at cigars (becoming smoked as any kipper), behaving like the food they were. Silly, thought the ghost, that they couldn't see such simple comparisons.

Immortals saluted the full moon with blood, some in crystal glasses, others by tearing into meat and howling. Aside from the ancient Greeks and their long-ago offerings, there was no blood for ghosts. Not anymore.

The ghost could hear herself crying. Not the herself that still remembered what being herself meant. Some other part of her, the part that was fading into aether.

She wished she had studied more on the nature of the supernatural and less on the nature of the technological world. She wished her passions had taken her into a learning that would allow her to tolerate the sensation of disanimus with dignity. But there was no dignity in death.

And she was alone. Perhaps that was not so bad, under such ignominious circumstances?

Still, where were the scientific pamphlets that taught a woman how to listen to herself die?

CHAPTER ELEVEN

Wherein Hairmuffs Become All the Rage

Lady Maccon accompanied her husband home to Woolsey Castle and saw him safely locked away in its well-fortified dungeons. He shared a cell with Biffy, both of them tearing into the walls of their impenetrable prison—and into each other. They would do no permanent damage, but still Alexia could not watch. As with most things in life, Lady Maccon preferred the civilized exterior to the dark underbelly (with the exception of pork products, of course).

"This is an odd world I have become part of, Rumpet." The Woolsey butler was helping her back to the carriage to return to town. Woolsey's formal coach was fitted out with full-moon regalia: ribbons tied to the top rails, crest newly polished, a matched set of parade bays hitched to the front. Lady Maccon gave the nose of one a pat. She liked the bays; they were steady, sensible horses with high prances and the general temperaments of gormless newts. "And I used to think werewolves were such simple, basic creatures."

"In some ways, madam, but they are also immortal. Dealing with eternity requires a certain complexity of spirit." The butler handed her up into the carriage.

"Why, Rumpet, have you been hiding the soul of a philosopher under that efficacious exterior?"

"What butler isn't, madam?"

"Good point." Lady Maccon signaled the coachman to drive on.

London at full moon was a different city entirely from any other time of the month. For this one night, out of default or desire, the vampires ruled. Hives throughout England hosted parties, but the biggest occurred in London proper. Roves were at liberty to roam undisciplined and unmonitored. It wasn't that the werewolves necessarily kept vampire largess in check, just that with guaranteed werewolf absence, the vampires had the autonomy to be that little bit more toothsome than normal.

It was also an excuse for the daylight folk to dance the night away. Or, in the case of the conservatives who wanted nothing to do with immortals and their ilk, to dirigible the night away. Most of the Giffard fleet was afloat at full moon, running short-haul tourist jaunts above the city. Some were rented out for private parties; others simply took advantage of the moonlight and the festivities to run special offers at high expense for the fashionable to display their latest floating attire. A few airships were outfitted with firework display apparatuses, shooting off colorful explosions of red and yellow sparkles, like hundreds of shooting stars, into the sky.

It was always a challenging night for BUR. Several core staff were werewolves—three from Woolsey, two from HM Growlers, and one new loner. A number of clavigers also held commissions. All were conspicuous by their absence. Top that off with the vampire agents away enjoying the revels, and full moon left the Bureau understaffed and unhappy about it. There were a few contract ghosts paying very close attention to what went on during the extravagances, but they couldn't exactly provide physical enforcement if such became necessary. That left the mortal agents at the fore during moon time, spearheaded by the likes of Haverbink—capable, tough, working-class men with a taste for danger and an ear for trouble. Of course, the potentate's drones were also out and about, but they couldn't be trusted to report their findings to BUR, even if the rumors were true and Lord Maccon was sleeping in Lord Akeldama's closet.

Lady Maccon liked full moon. There was something irrepressibly celebratory about it. London came alive with excitement and dark ancient mysteries. Admittedly, there were fangs and blood and equally acrimonious things, but full moon also brought with it blood-sausage pies, candy sugar wolves, and other tasty treats. Lady Maccon was easily ruled by her stomach into approval of any event. It was the poor quality of the comestibles, not the company, that caused her to continually refuse invitation to most public assembly rooms. The rest of the ton thought this snobbish and approved. They did not realize it was solely based on the shabbiness of the provisions.

Apart from the food and the pleasant aspect of dirigibles silhouetted against the moon, Alexia also enjoyed the fact that a night ruled by vampires meant everyone was in their best looks and tip-top manners. While her own taste was, frankly, pedestrian, Lady Maccon did enjoy seeing what all the peacocks had arranged to drape themselves with. In the better parts of London, one could run into almost anything: the latest evening gowns from Paris, floating dresses to the extremes of practicality from the Americas, and the fullest, most complex cravat ties imaginable. One could witness a veritable cornucopia of visual delights merely by driving through the crowded streets.

If Alexia had not been so enthralled, with her face pressed firmly to the carriage window, she would have missed the porcupine. But she was and so she didn't.

She banged on the roof of the carriage with her parasol, sharp and loud. "Halt!"

The coachman pulled the bays up, right there in the middle of the busy thoroughfare—aristocracy had its privileges and Woolsey's carriage was crested.

Lady Maccon lifted up the speaking tube she'd recently had installed and belled through to the box.

The coachman picked up his receiver. "Yes, madam?"

"Follow that porcupine!"

"Certainly, madam." In his years of service to Lord Maccon, the poor man had received far more ludicrous requests.

The carriage lurched to the side, causing Alexia to drop her end of the tube, which swung from its heavy metal cord and whacked her in the arm. There was no highspeed chase—for which Alexia was grateful, as she'd had quite enough of those to last a lifetime, thank you very much!—because the porcupine, which happened to be on a lead like a little dog, was moving at a sedate pace often interrupted by curious bystanders. The creature was obviously out for a stroll for that purpose, to attract interest and attention on a night practically designed for such displays of eccentricity and ostentation.

Eventually, traffic allowed the carriage to pull a little ahead of the porcupine and stop. The coachman came around and let Lady Maccon down in time for her to accost the owner.

"Ah, pardon me, madam," said Lady Maccon to the young lady in charge of the porcupine before realizing that they were already acquainted. "Why, Miss Dair!"

"Goodness me, Lady Maccon? Should you be in public in your condition? You are looking most encumbered." The vampire drone seemed genuinely surprised to see her.

"But it is a lovely evening to be out, as you obviously realize, Miss Dair."

"Indeed, the moon has got his cravat on."

"If you don't mind my asking, what on earth are you doing strolling the streets of London with a zombie porcupine?"

"Why shouldn't I be enjoying the company of my new pet?" Miss Mabel Dair, renowned actress, was exactly the type of original female to elect to keep a pet porcupine, but Lady Maccon would have none of it.

"New pet, indeed! A whole herd of those nasty creatures attacked me and my husband only recently."

The actress paused, a look of defensiveness suffusing her pretty face. "Perhaps the inside of your carriage, Lady Maccon, might be a better place for this conversation?"

Mabel Dair boasted a stylish figure, if a little round, with an arrangement of curves that cemented her appeal firmly among a specific class of fashionable gentlemen. And, if the rumors were to be believed, one very fashionable woman, Countess Nadasdy. Miss Dair had risen to prominence and become the reigning darling of the West End via the Westminster Hive's unflagging support. She'd engaged in no less than three continental tours and garnered a considerable amount of popularity in the colonies as well. She had copious blond curls done up in high piled coques of the very latest style, and her face was pleasingly sweet. She gave off an entirely unwarranted air of innocence, for Miss Dair was a woman of strong character—an excellent rider, a dab hand at cards, and a personal friend to the countess as well as being her drone. She also had very good taste in evening dresses. A woman not to be taken lightly, porcupine or no.

She and her pet climbed inside the Woolsey carriage, leaving her escort to shadow them on the street. Lady Maccon turned her attention from the actress to the porcupine. It looked very like those that had attacked her husband, which is to say, not exactly alive.

"An undead porcupine," insisted Lady Maccon with conviction.

"Ah, yes, I see how you might make that kind of assessment, but no. That is not possible, as it was never alive." The actress settled herself in the facing seat next to Alexia, smoothing out the silk skirts of her green gown as she did so.

"It can't be mechanical. I tried a magnetic disruption emission on them and nothing resulted."

"Oh, did you? Well, it's worth knowing Albert here has been field tested against one of the best. I should like to see the emitter you used."

"Yes, I wager you would." Alexia made no move to show her anything whatsoever about her parasol or its armament. She gestured at the porcupine, which had settled into a kind of crouch at the actress's feet. "May I?"

Mabel Dair considered the request. "If you must." Then she bent and lifted the little creature up to the bench between them so that Lady Maccon could examine it at her leisure.

At such close range, it became clear rather quickly that there was no way it had been, or ever would be, alive. It was a construct of some kind, its inner workings covered over in skin, fur, and spines that made it *look* like a porcupine.

"I thought mechanimals were outlawed."

"This is not a mechanimal."

"It has been made without any ferric parts? Inspired, indeed." Lady Maccon was duly impressed. She was no Madame Lefoux, to be able to understand the construct's makeup fully in the space of only a few minutes' examination, but she was well enough versed in scientific literature to know she held some very advanced technology in her grasp.

"But why use such skill merely to create a pet?"

Mabel Dair shrugged, an elegant little movement, refined so as not to disturb the fall of her gown. "The extermination mandate has been retracted. Your relocation and adoption agreement was quite a masterly maneuver in the great game. My mistress was impressed. Not that I am admitting to anything, of course, but those first porcupines were highly experimental. They were not as effective as we had hoped, so she has let me make a pet of one of the few we have left."

"Ingenious technology." Lady Maccon continued her examination of the little creature. There were small clips behind each of its ears that, when pressed, popped open to reveal some of the inner workings in the brain area.

"I supposed it would have been far more dangerous had it been a real African zombie." She tapped at one of the faux bones. "Remarkable. I take it the hive has filed all the appropriate licensing with the patent office? Must be one of the countess's pet scientists, since I haven't read anything from the Royal Society on the subject. Is it designed specifically to withstand a magnetic disruption?" Then she noticed that the porcupine had ceramic and wooden moving parts held together with string and sinew, greased with some kind of dark waxy liquid. Alexia had misinterpreted this as blood, but closer inspection revealed it to be of exactly the same type as that found in the Hypocras Club's automaton. "Oh, dear. Did you get hold of some of the Hypocras Club's reports? I thought BUR put a lockdown on those."

"Only you, Lady Maccon, would draw such a connection." Miss Dair was beginning to look a little nervous.

At that juncture, it occurred to Lady Maccon to ask, "Why are you in my carriage, Miss Dair?"

The actress recovered her poise. "Ah, yes, well, Lady Maccon, there has been a breach in social etiquette, and it was only when you accosted me in the street that I realized it. I know the countess would want me to rectify the situation. You must believe, we understood that on full-moon nights you were otherwise occupied or we should never have neglected you."

"What *are* you on about?"

"This." Miss Dair handed Alexia an embossed invitation to a full-moon party taking place later that night.

The Maccons and the Nadasdys always invited each other to their respective festivities. The Westminster vampires, out of tether and hive bounds, had never been able to visit Woolsey Castle, and the countess herself, of course, could not leave her house. But Lord and Lady Maccon had visited her on several occasions, always staying exactly as long as was polite and no longer. Vampire hives were not comfortable places for werewolves to be, particularly Alpha werewolves, but the social niceties must be observed.

Alexia took the invitation reluctantly. "Well, thank you, but I have a busy schedule, and at such late notice, please understand I will try to put in an appearance but—"

Miss Dair continued making the excuses for her. "In your current condition, that would be difficult. I understand perfectly and the countess will as well. But I didn't want you to think we were slighting you in any way. Case in point, I have been instructed by my mistress to inform you, should we encounter each other, that we are officially delighted with your new living arrangements and wish it to be known outright that there are no hard feelings. Or"—she paused delicately, her actress training becoming apparent—"consequences."

As if they were not the ones who had been actively trying to kill me! Lady Maccon, in a huff, said pointedly, "Likewise. Perhaps next time if your lot told me why they were trying to exterminate me from the start, much unnecessary chaos could be avoided. Not to mention loss of porcupine life."

"Yes, indeed. What did happen to them?"

"Lime pit."

"Oh. Oh! Very good, Lady Maccon. I should never have thought of that."

"Is this little creature still armed with the projectile spines? Some kind of numbing agent, I assume."

"Yes, but not to worry—he's quite tame. And it is for my protection and not any ulterior motive."

"I am very glad to hear it. Well, Miss Dair, can I take you to your destination, or would you prefer to walk? I can see you might wish to display your pet to advantage. Your mistress is looking to profit by the new technology, isn't she?"

"You know vampires."

Normally polite company wouldn't mention pecuniary matters, but Miss Dair was only an actress, so Alexia said, "You'd think owning half the known world would be enough for them."

Mabel Dair smiled. "Control, Muhjah, comes in many different forms."

"Indeed it does, indeed it does. Well . . . ," Lady Maccon picked up the speaking tube and addressed her coachman. "Pull up here, please. My companion wishes to alight."

"Very good, my lady," came the tinny reply.

The carriage pulled to the side, allowing Miss Dair and her porcupine to disgorge themselves and continue their promenade.

"Perhaps we will enjoy the pleasure of your company later tonight, Lady Maccon."

"Perhaps. Thank you for your scintillating conversation, Miss Dair. Good night."

"Good night."

They parted, many a reveler now curious as to the relationship between a werewolf's wife and a vampire drone. The rumors were out concerning Biffy. Was Lady Maccon trying to poach yet another key player from the vampire's camp? New gossip was set in motion. And that, too, Alexia realized, might have been all part of Miss Dair's scheme in visiting with her.

She spoke once more into the tube. "Chapeau de Poupe, if you please."

It was early still, so far as the night's festivities were concerned. No establishment of worth in all of London would dare be closed on such an evening. Thus Lady Maccon was unsurprised to find Madame Lefoux's hat shop not only open but also occupied by multiple ladies of worth and their respective escorts. The hats, suspended on their long cords from the ceiling, swayed to and fro, but without imparting their usual aura of undersea calm. There was too much clatter and bustle (in both senses of the word) for that. Alexia was surprised to find that Madame Lefoux herself was not in residence. For all her more atypical pursuits, the inventor normally made a point of putting in an appearance in her shop on busy nights. Half the reason the ladies chose to frequent Chapeau de Poupe was on the off chance they might encounter the scandalous proprietress in all her top-hatted glory.

In her absence, Lady Maccon trundled in and stood, confused. How was she to make her way to the contrivance chamber without someone seeing her? She respected Madame Lefoux's wish to keep the chamber, its activities, and its entrance a secret from the general public. But with what seemed to be at least half said general public milling about in the shop, how was Alexia to return the papers and consult the inventor on the nature of the porcupines without being observed? Alexia Maccon was many things, but stealthy was not one of them.

She made her way to the counter—an attractive high table painted white to add to the modern atmosphere that was a hallmark of Madame Lefoux's refined taste.

"Pardon me?" Lady Maccon used her best, most imperious tone.

"I'll be right with you, madam," chirruped the girl who stood there. She was all bright chatter and false friendliness, but her back remained quite firmly presented. She was busy rustling through stacks of hatboxes.

"I don't mean to interrupt your work, young lady, but this is an urgent matter."

"Yes, madam, I am certain it is. I do apologize for the delay, but as you can see, we are a little understaffed this evening. If you wouldn't mind waiting just one more moment."

"I must see Madame Lefoux."

"Yes, yes, madam, I know. *Everyone* wishes the personal attention of the madame, but she is unavailable this particular evening. Perhaps one of the other ladies might be of assistance?"

"No, really, it must be Madame Lefoux. I have some important paperwork to return to her."

"Return? Oh, did the hat not suit madam's needs? I *am* sorry."

"Not a hat. Nothing to do with hats." Lady Maccon was getting impatient.

"Yes, certainly, if madam would simply wait. I shall be at your service momentarily."

Alexia sighed. This was getting her nowhere. She moved away from the counter and took a slow turn about the room, utilizing her parasol as a kind of cane and exaggerating her limp so that sympathy drove those ladies out of her way who did not already know her face and rank. This maneuver garnered her more attention, rather than less, and she was left with a distinct feeling of inertia.

Madame Lefoux's hats were of the latest style, a number of them too daring for any save Ivy and her ilk. Cabinets displayed other accessories as well—mob caps, sleeping caps, hair pins, and bands all decorated beautifully. There were reticules of varying shapes and sizes; gloves; and dirigible accessories such as velvet ear protectors, skirt ties, weighted hem inserts, and the finest in color-tinted glass goggles. There was even a line of masquerade goggles trimmed with feathers and flowers.

And, last but not least, a rack displaying Ivy Tunstell's hairmuffs, designed for the fashionable young lady who wished to keep her hair untangled and her ears warm while still sporting the latest ringlets. They had gone somewhat out of favor recently, having enjoyed a brief spate of popularity during the winter months, but were still on display in deference to Mrs. Tunstell's finer feelings.

Alexia completed her circuit of the shop and came to a decision. Given that any kind of stealth was out of the question, she must opt for her only alternative—making a fuss.

"Pardon me, miss."

The same shopgirl was still rummaging behind the counter. Really, how long did it take to find a hatbox?

"*Yes,* madam, I will be right with you."

Lady Maccon reached down inside herself for her most regal, difficult, aristocratic nature. "I will *not be ignored,* young lady!"

That got the girl's attention. She actually turned around to see who this interfering female was.

"Do you know who I am?"

The young woman gave her the full once-over. "Lady Maccon?" she hazarded a guess.

"Indeed."

"I had been warned to keep an eye out for you."

"Warned? Warned! Were you, indeed? Well, now I am here and . . . and . . ." She floundered. It was terribly hard to be angry when one wasn't. "I have a very grave matter to discuss with your patroness."

"I told you, madam, and I do apologize, but she is not available this evening, even for you."

"Unacceptable!" Alexia was rather pleased with both the word choice and her execution. Very commanding, indeed! *That's what living with werewolves will do for a girl. Now where to go from here?* "I'll have you know I have been swindled! Absolutely swindled. I will have none of it. I shall call on the constabulary. You see if I don't."

By this time, Lady Maccon and the now-trembling shopgirl had attracted the attention of the entire establishment, both patrons and hire.

"I came here looking for hairmuffs. I hear they are *the thing* for dirigible travel, and I desire a set that matches my hair, and what do I find? Not a single pair of the appropriate shade. Where are they all?"

"Well, you see, madam, we are currently out of the darker colors. If madam would like to put in an order—"

"No, madam would *not* like! Madam would like a set of the hairmuffs right this very moment!" At this juncture, Alexia contemplated stamping her foot, but that was probably excessively dramatic, even for this audience.

Instead, she waddled over to the muff display stand near the shop window. She grabbed a cluster of her own curls, artfully arranged over the shoulder of her blue and green plaid visiting dress, and waved them at the stand. Then she backed off as though physically repulsed by the mismatch.

"You see?" She stood away and pointed with the tip of her parasol at the offending hairmuffs.

The shopgirl did see. So, in fact, did all the other ladies present. What they saw was that Lady Maccon, only a few days from her confinement, had still extricated herself from bed and the bosom of her husband's affection in order to come to this very shop to buy hairmuffs. They must, perforce, be *back en mode.* Lady Maccon, wife to the Earl of Woolsey, was known to fraternize with the trendsetters and fashion leaders of the ton. She herself might prefer more practical garb, especially in her present state, but if she was buying hairmuffs, then Lord Akeldama approved the accessory. If Lord Akeldama approved, then the vampires approved, and if the vampires approved, well, that was simply it: hairmuffs must be *the living end.*

Suddenly, every lady in that shop had to have a set of Mrs. Tunstells' *Hairmuffs for the Elevated Lady Traveler.* They all stopped admiring whatever hat they were fawning over and swarmed the little stand. Even those who had absolutely no intention of ever setting foot on board a dirigible suddenly were in a mad passion to own hairmuffs. For what became fashionable for floating descended to the ground—witness the craze for decorative goggles.

Lady Maccon was swarmed by a gaggle of bustled and trussed ladies, all grabbing for the muffs, squealing at each other while they tried desperately to snatch the colors that matched their own coiffures. There was even a little pushing and some shortness of breath. It was practically a rout.

The shopgirls obligingly descended into the milieu as well, notepads out, trying to convince the ladies not to purchase right away but to place an order for the appropriate color and perhaps multiple styles and different-size ringlets as well.

In the resulting chaos, Lady Maccon extracted herself and lurched, as stealthily as was within her limited capacity, to the very back of the shop. Here, in a shadowed corner under an attractive display of gloves, was the handle to the entrance to the ascension chamber. She activated it, the hidden door swinging quietly open. Alexia noted with relief that the chamber was already at the upper level waiting for her. She clambered inside, drawing the door to the shop closed behind her.

After many months of friendship, not to mention parasol maintenance and aethographor repairs, Alexia was more than familiar with the operation of Madame Lefoux's ascension chamber. What once had upset her stomach and frightened her was now standard procedure on her visiting rounds. She flipped the lever that operated the windlass machine and did not even stumble when the contraption landed with a jarring thud.

Lady Maccon waddled down the passageway and thumped loudly at the contrivance chamber door.

Silence.

Figuring that Madame Lefoux probably could not hear her knock, for inside the chamber was always a cacophony of mechanical noises, she let herself in.

It took her a long moment of scanning over all the piles of machinery, but she eventually became convinced that Madame Lefoux really was not in residence. Nor was her new contraption. The shopgirl had not lied in the interest of social niceties. Madame Lefoux was definitely unavailable. Alexia pursed her lips. Genevieve had said something about relocating in order to put the finishing touches to the latest invention. Alexia debated trying to remember where and following her there or simply leaving the papers behind. *They'll probably be safe enough.* She placed them on a nearby metal tabletop and was about to depart when she heard something.

Alexia had no werewolf's hearing to be able to note some strange noise among the rattling, humming, hissing clatter. Even without the Frenchwoman in residence, some machines never ceased their activity. But she definitely heard another sound, an underlying keen to the rattles that might, or might not, be human in origin.

It might also be a very excited mouse.

Lady Maccon contemplated not getting involved. She also contemplated not using her parasol—after all, some of the machines in that chamber might be engaged in some delicate feat of manufacturing that could not afford to be paused midclatter. In Alexia's case, contemplation was never signified by more than a pause before performing the action she would have taken, contemplation or no.

She took her parasol firmly in hand, raised it high above her head, and activated the magnetic disruption emitter by pulling down on the appropriate lotus leaf in the handle with her thumb.

Silence descended—the unnatural silence of work stilled midmotion. If Alexia had been a fanciful girl, she would have said it was like time freezing, but she wasn't, so she didn't. She merely listened for the one sound that didn't stop.

It came, a low keening wail, and Alexia realized that she was familiar with just such a noise. Not a sound made by the living, but still a sound *made* rather than a sound *manufactured.* It was the intermittent sharp cry of second-death, and Alexia had a pretty good guess as to who was suffering it.

CHAPTER TWELVE

Formerly Beatrice Lefoux

"Formerly Lefoux. Formerly Lefoux, is that you?" Alexia tried to make her voice gentle.

The silence stretched and then the faraway screaming came again.

There was something inexorably sad about the sound, as though it were that much worse to die a second time. It moved even Lady Maccon's practical heart. "Formerly Lefoux, please, I will not harm you. I promise, I can bring you peace, if you would like, or simply be here with you. I promise, no soulless touch unless you request it. Don't be afraid. There's nothing I could do. I don't even know where your body is kept."

The magnetic disruption wore off at that juncture, and the contrivance chamber sprang back into humming, clanking motion. Right next to Alexia's head, a contraption that looked like a tuba, a sleigh, and a mustache trimmer cobbled together let out the most amazing sound of reverberating flatulence. Lady Maccon started in disgust and moved hurriedly away.

"Please, Formerly Lefoux, I should very much like to ask you something. I need your help."

The ghost materialized into existence out of a massive glass valve to Alexia's left. Or, more properly, she materialized as much as she was able into existence, which wasn't all that much anymore. Bits of her were now drifting off in spiraling fuzzy tendrils. Her shape was no longer human, but more cloudlike, as little wisps of her noncorporeal form fought against the aether currents. Many of those currents were now centered in on Lady Maccon, so the ghostly parts were carried toward Alexia. The vampires called preternaturals *soul-suckers*, but science was coming around to thinking of them more as aether absorbers.

This particular phenomenon of her physiology was only really visible when she shared the room with a dying ghost.

"Soulless!" screamed Formerly Lefoux once she had found her voice, or possibly, found her voice box. She spoke in French. "Why are you here? Where is my niece? What has she done? What have you done? Where is the octomaton? What. What? Who is that screaming? Is that me? How can that be me *and* this be me, talking to you? You. Soulless? What are you doing here? Where is my niece?"

It was like some broken symphony destined to repeat the same few lines of music over and over again. The ghost was caught up in a loop of reasoning. Periodically, Formerly Lefoux interrupted herself to cry out, a long low moan of agony to accompany the wail of second-death. Whether it was pain of the spirit or pain in truth was difficult to tell, but it sounded to Alexia not unlike poor Biffy being forced into werewolf shift.

Alexia straightened her spine. Before her lay her preternatural duty, staring her in the face. That didn't occur very often. Under ordinary circumstances, she would have asked Genevieve for permission, but the inventor was gone. She had abandoned her poor aunt in this state. The ghost was suffering.

"Formerly Lefoux," she said politely, "I am in the unique position to offer you . . . that is, I could . . . Oh, dash it, would you like an exorcism?"

"Death? Death! Are you asking me if I want death, soulless? To not exist at all." The ghost twirled like a child's toy, spiraling all the way up to the beams of the contrivance chamber ceiling. The tendrils of her fleshless body swirled around like the feathers of one of Ivy's more excitable hats. Floating far above, the ghost became contemplative. "I have served my time. I have taught. Not many get to say that. I have touched lives. I have finished them all. And I have done it after I died as well." She paused and drifted back down. "Not that I like children all that much. What can a ghost do? When my niece, my lovely intelligent girl, became enamored of that awful woman. All I taught her was gone. Then the boy. Just like his mother. Devious. Who thought I should end up teaching a boy child? And now. Look what it has all come to. Death. My death, and a soulless offering me succor. Unnatural. All of it. Preternatural girl, what good are you to me?"

"I can give you serenity." Lady Maccon's eyebrow was quirked. Really, ghosts in near poltergeist phase did ramble most awfully.

"I don't want peace. I want hope. Can you give me that?"

Sympathy, so far as Alexia was concerned, only went so far. "Very well, then, this is getting disturbingly philosophical. Formerly Lefoux, if you'd rather not have my aid in the matter of your existence, or lack thereof, I should probably be on my way. Do try not to wail so loudly. They will hear you in the street above, and then BUR will be called. Frankly, the Bureau really doesn't need this kind of additional work on full moon."

The ghost floated back down. For a moment, she recollected herself, switching from French to heavily accented English. "No, wait. I will . . . What will I? Oh, yez, I will show you. Follow me."

She began bobbing slowly across the room. She had no concern for obstacles or pathways through the devices, instruments, and tools of Madame Lefoux's collection, merely floating in a straight line. Alexia, who was more substantial in every understanding of the word, made her cumbersome way after. She lost sight of the ghost on more than one occasion, but eventually they ended up in a corner of the massive room, next to a large barrel that rested on its side and was marked with the logo of a well-respected pickled onion manufacturer.

As Formerly Lefoux neared the barrel, she became more and more substantial, until she was almost her old self—the ghost Alexia had first met nearly half a year ago. A tall, gaunt, severe-looking older woman, in clothing years out of date and small spectacles, who bore a marked resemblance to Madame Lefoux. There might even once have been dimples.

The keening wail was much louder here, although it still seemed to be coming from some distance away, with an echo as though emanating from the bottom of a mine.

"I do apologize. I can't stop that," said the ghost at Alexia's wince.

"No, you wouldn't be able to. Your time has come."

The ghost nodded, an action that was visible now that she had managed to gather herself into better order. "Genevieve gave me a long afterlife. Few ghosts are so fortunate. They usually have only months. I had years."

"Years?"

"Years."

"She is a truly brilliant woman." Alexia was properly impressed.

"Yet she loves too frequently and too easily. I couldn't teach her that lesson. So much like her father. She loves you, I think, a little. More, if you had given her the opportunity."

The discussion had gotten away from Alexia again. This was often the case with ghosts—no more control over conversation than of their own forms. "But I'm married!"

"All the best ones are. And that son of hers."

Lady Maccon looked down at her own belly. "Everyone should love their child."

"Even if he is a wild creature born to another woman?"

"Especially then."

The ghost let out a dry laugh. "I can see why you two are friends."

It was in thinking about Genevieve's love life (a thing, Alexia must admit, she tried desperately not to do, as it was so preposterously captivating) that Alexia put everything together. Not fast enough, of course, because the wails were getting louder, and nearer. Even a ghost such as Formerly Lefoux, with such strength of character and mental fitness, could not resist her own demise when it was fated.

Alexia asked, "Is there something wrong with Genevieve?"

"Yes." It was said on a hiss. The ghost was shaking, shivering in the air before her, as though riding atop an ill-balanced steam engine.

"That machine, the one she was building, it wasn't a government commission, was it?"

"No." The ghost began spinning as she vibrated. The tendrils were back, drifting away, floating into the air—puffs of selfhood carried away. Her feet were almost entirely disintegrated. While Alexia watched, one of Formerly Lefoux's hands detached and began drifting toward her.

Lady Maccon tried to dodge the hand, but it followed her. "It's the kind of contraption that could break into a house, isn't it? Or a palace?"

"Yes. So unlike her, to build something brutish. But sometimes we women get desperate." The screaming was getting louder. "Right question, soulless. *You aren't asking me the right question.* And we are almost out of time." Her other hand detached and wafted toward Alexia. "Soulless? What are you? Why are you here? Where is my niece?"

"It was *you* who activated the ghost communication network, wasn't it? Did *you* send me the message, Formerly Lefoux? The one about killing the queen?"

"Yessss," hissed the ghost.

"But why would Genevieve want to kill the—"

Alexia was cut off midquestion as Formerly Lefoux burst apart, like a rotten tomato thrown against a tree. The ghost exploded noiselessly. Parts of her drifted off in all directions at once, a spread of white mist wafting all around and through the machinery of the contrivance chamber. Then, showily, all those bits began drifting in Alexia's direction—eyes, eyebrows, hair, a limb or two.

Alexia couldn't help herself; she let out a scream of shock. There was no going back now. Formerly Beatrice Lefoux had gone to full poltergeist. It was time for Lady Maccon to fulfill her duty to queen and country and perform the required exorcism.

She approached the barrel of pickled onions. It lay on its side, and it was a very big barrel. She checked around the back where multiple coils and tubes were coming out, hooked into some interesting-looking lidded metal buckets. Either Madame Lefoux was particularly interested in the quality of her pickled onions or . . .

Alexia knew well her friend's style and design aesthetic, so she looked for any small protrusion or unusual sculptural addition to the barrel, something that might be pressed or pulled. On the end of the barrel facing the wall, she found a small brass octopus. She pushed against it. With a faint clunking noise, the wood of the pickle barrel slid away, like that of a rolltop desk, revealing that there were, unsurprisingly, no onions inside. Instead it housed a coffin-sized fish tank filled with a bubbling yellow liquid and the preserved body of Beatrice Lefoux.

The formaldehyde, for that is what the liquid must be, had done its job. There was also clearly some way in which the bubbling injections of gas were allowing the ghost to still form a noncorporeal self while not losing too much flesh to decomposition. Alexia was caught by the genius of the invention. It was one of the great trials of ghostly employment, that specters would stay sane only so long as their bodies could be preserved, but that they could not form a tether and apparition if that body was immersed fully in a preservation liquid. Madame Lefoux had invented a way around this conundrum by having air bubbling through the formaldehyde in enough quantity to permit a tether, while allowing the flesh to stay submerged and preserved. No wonder Formerly Lefoux had enjoyed such a long afterlife.

But even such ingeniousness as this, the height of scientific breakthrough, could not save a ghost in the end. Eventually the body would decay enough so that it could no longer hold the tether; the ghost would lose cohesion and succumb to second-death.

Alexia thought she might mention this tank to BUR. They would probably want to order a few for their more valuable spectral agents. She wondered if the gas injections had something to do with the explosive nature of Formerly Lefoux's poltergeist state. In any event, the tank's work was completed. Alexia had to devise a way inside.

The screams were now deafening. Formerly Lefoux's misty body parts were centering on Alexia, attaching themselves to the exposed skin of her arms, face, and neck, like body part burrs. It was repulsive. Alexia tried to brush them off, but they merely transferred to her wrist.

There seemed no way into the tank. Madame Lefoux had never intended to open it once it was built.

Lady Maccon was getting frantic to stop the screaming. She was also becoming increasingly aware of time wasted. She must get out of the contrivance chamber and stop Madame Lefoux's mad scheme to build a monster to kill the queen. Why would Genevieve, of all people, want to do such a thing?

Desperate, she flipped her parasol, hefted it as far behind her back as her condition would allow, and swung it around with all her might. She hit the side of the glass tank with the hard pineapple-looking handle. The tank cracked and then broke, spilling the yellow fluid and with it a strong, suffocating scent. Lady Maccon backed away hurriedly, lifting her ruffled skirts out of the toxic liquid. Her eyes began burning and watering. She coughed as the sensation moved to her throat, and she tried to breathe in shallow gasps. Luckily, most of the liquid was absorbed quickly by the hard, compact dirt of the contrivance chamber floor.

The body inside flopped over and against the cracked side of the tank, one hand dangling out through the broken glass. Quickly, Alexia tugged off her glove and stepped up to it. She touched the cold dead hand once, flesh to flesh, and just like that, it was over.

The wailing stopped. The body part wisps vanished—mist gone to aether. All that remained was the clanking sound of Madame Lefoux's machines in motion and the empty air.

"May you find your stillness, Formerly Lefoux," said Alexia.

She looked ruefully at the mess before her: broken glass, fractured tank, dead body. She abhorred such untidiness, but she had no time to see to the cleanup. Best to contact Floote on the matter as soon as she found some time.

With that, she turned away and waddled back out of the chamber and into the passageway. She hoped the clientele above her was still arguing over hairmuffs, for she had no time to scheme her way around exposing Madame Lefoux's secret entrance this time. She must stop her friend from imprudent action. And, more importantly, she desperately needed to find out why. Why Madame Lefoux, such an intelligent woman, would try to do something so dull-witted as mount a frontal attack on Buckingham Palace in order to kill the Queen of England.

Fortunately, the hairmuff obsession was still in full sway. Almost no one noticed Lady Maccon scuttle, like some kind of gimpy goose, out of the door in the wall. She then made her way through the myriad of dangling hats and out of the shop. A few remarked upon the smell of formaldehyde, and one or two noted her ladyship's undignified ascension into the depths of her fancy carriage, but few thought to connect the two. However, the head shopgirl did, and made a note to tell the mistress everything, before returning to the sudden increase in hairmuff orders.

Lady Maccon remembered what Madame Lefoux had said about relocation. She'd arranged to utilize space in the Pantechnicon. Alexia was unaware of the location of the warehouse consortium. Being a matter of *trade,* it was not something Lady Maccon *ought* to know. Sometimes Madame Lefoux's engineering interests led her into the most peculiar parts of London. Alexia had, of course, heard of the Pantechnicon but had never had occasion to visit such a thing as the facility in which Giffard's Incorporated housed and maintained its dirigible fleet. The Pantechnicon stored and distributed a good deal of furniture as well. The very idea of a lady of good breeding visiting such a place. There would be tables lying about, on their sides, naked! Not to mention *flaccid* dirigibles! Alexia shuddered at the very idea. However, sometimes the muhjah had to go where Lady Maccon would not, and so she gave the order and trusted her driver to know the location, which turned out to be Belgravia, a deeply suspect part of London.

After clattering for some time down one cobbled street after another, having passed through the worst and most raucous crowds of the West End and moving toward Chelsea, the carriage drew to a stop. Lady Maccon's speaking tube rang imperiously.

She picked up the listening trumpet. "Yes?"

"Motcomb Street, madam."

"Thank you." *Never heard of it.* She looked suspiciously out the carriage window. What Lady Maccon had never quite fathomed was how extraordinarily large the Pantechnicon had to be in order to accommodate both flaccid dirigibles and naked tables. She was in front of a massive caterpillar of warehouses. Each one resembled a barn, only bigger, being several stories high with arched metal roofs. Alexia assumed these must somehow open or come off in order to accommodate the dirigibles. The street was dimly lit by the flickering yellow glow of torchlight rather than by the steady white of gas, and the area was bereft of humanity. This was a part of the city that catered to day dealers, workers of transport and industry who loaded and unloaded their contraptions and carriers under the light of the sun. It was not a place for the likes of Lady Maccon to be traipsing about on full moon.

But Alexia was not going to let a little thing like the dark emptiness of an alleyway prevent her from proceeding with her intent to assist a friend in dire need of sensible council. So she alighted from the carriage, Ethel in one hand and her parasol in the other. She waddled slowly along the row of gigantic structures, listening at the door of each, standing on tiptoe to peer in at small dingy windows—the only means of viewing the interior. She rubbed the grimy coating on leaded glass with her soiled glove. The Pantechnicon appeared to be as abandoned as the street. There was no sign of Madame Lefoux or her contraption.

Then, finally, inside the last building in the row, Alexia caught sight of a spark of light. Inside, Madame Lefoux, or the person she assumed must be Madame Lefoux, wore a glass and metal bucket over her head, like the offspring of a medieval knight's helmet and a fishbowl. She was also wearing the most hideous pair of coveralls and was busy with a flaming torch, welding great slabs of metal together. Her giant mechanical construct had taken its final form, and Alexia could not help but emit a little gasp of amazement at the sight of the monstrous thing.

It was colossal, at least two stories high. The brimless bowler-hat portion now rested atop eight articulated metal tentacles that hung down like pillars, but if Lady Maccon knew Madame Lefoux, each would be able to move independently of the others. A remarkable creature, indeed. It looked like nothing so much as a massive upright octopus on tiptoe. Alexia wondered what it said about her current state that this comparison made her hungry. *Ah, pregnancy.*

She banged on the window to attract Madame Lefoux's attention, but the French woman clearly could not hear, for she did not pause in her activities.

Lady Maccon circumnavigated the building, looking for an entrance. It had massive loading doors street-side, but these were bolted firmly shut. There must be a smaller, more convenient, one-person door somewhere about the place.

Finally, she found it. It, too, was locked. She whacked at it with her parasol in frustration, but brute force was also ineffectual. Not for the first time, Alexia wished she knew how to pick a lock. Conall had frowned most severely upon that particular request and on her proposed venture into Newgate Prison in order to hire the necessary criminally minded individual as instructor.

She went back round to the front and considered breaking one of the lower windows; while it was too small to climb through, even if she were not eight months pregnant, she could at least yell. A massive noise interrupted her right before she was about to swing the parasol.

The building began shaking slightly, the metal roof creaking most terribly, and the two great loading bay doors clattered against their hinges. Gouts of steam billowed from beneath the doors and around the edges. Metal screeched and the trundling thrumming sound of a steam engine in full operation emanated from within. Alexia backed away from the door. The sounds began to get louder and louder and the doors shook with more vigor. More steam puffed forth.

It was getting closer.

Lady Maccon waddled as fast as she could away from the doors, and just in the nick of time, too, for they burst open, crashing against the sides of the building in a great splintering of wood, left to hang askew on their hinges.

A gigantic tiptoeing octopus came through, looking almost as though it floated atop the cloud of steam that gushed forth from under its mantle to swirl about its tentacles. The doors were not quite tall enough to permit an easy exit, but this didn't seem to trouble the creature. It simply took a chunk of the roof off with its head. Tiles fell and splintered, dust wafted up, and steam wafted down as the world's biggest automated cephalopod tentacled its way into the London street.

"The octomaton, I presume. I see Genevieve didn't quite get the size measurements right," said Alexia to no one in particular.

The octomaton didn't notice Lady Maccon, a rotund little being far below in the shadows, but it spotted her carriage. It raised up one tentacle and took careful aim. A burst of fire came pouring out the tip. The beautifully matched horses (chosen for appearance and docility around werewolves rather than for bravery) panicked, as did the stunned coachman (chosen for precisely the same reasons). All three took off at high speed. The carriage careened wildly around a street corner, ribbons trailing merrily behind it, and disappeared into the night.

"Wait!" cried Lady Maccon. "Come back!" But the conveyance was long gone. "Oh, bother. Now what?"

The octomaton, untroubled by Alexia's cry or predicament, began to make its way up the street away from her, following the carriage. Lady Maccon raised her parasol and pulled at the special lotus leaf in the handle, activating the magnetic disruption emitter. Even aimed directly at the massive creature, it had absolutely no effect. Either Madame Lefoux also had access to the vampire's porcupine technology, or she had installed some kind of defensive shield to protect her creation from Alexia's armament. Alexia was not surprised; after all, the Frenchwoman was not so thickheaded as to build one weapon that could so easily be defeated by another of her own design. Especially if she knew Alexia was on the case and might very well find her out.

Alexia switched to Ethel, raising and firing the gun. The bullet bounced harmlessly off the octomaton's metal exterior. It left behind a dent, but once again, the massive creature did not register her tiny efforts against it.

It proceeded down the street in a not-very-dignified manner. Madame Lefoux had not gotten the en pointe tentacle balance quite right. Windows rattled as it passed, and periodically it staggered slightly to one side, crashing into and partly destroying the sides of buildings. At last, rounding the corner away from the Pantechnicon, it lurched into one of the streetlamps, an old-fashioned brassier-style torch, tipping it onto the thatched roof of a storage shed. Almost immediately the shed caught fire, and the flames began to spread. Metal roof notwithstanding, it presently became apparent that even the Pantechnicon could not resist the blaze.

Alexia was at a loss. None of her parasol's special abilities were designed to deal with fire. In her current state, she reckoned her best option was to beat an undignified retreat to safety. After all, she was practical enough to know when there was little even she could do to rectify such a situation. She turned south, toward the river.

As she limped along, Alexia's mind whirled with confusion. Why would Madame Lefoux build such a creature? She was, by and large, a woman of subtlety in both life and art. Why was she heading north and not due east to Buckingham? Queen Victoria never left the safety of her palace on full moon—it was simply too wild a night for her staid sensibilities. If Madame Lefoux had designs on the queen, she was going in the wrong direction. Alexia frowned. *I am clearly missing something. Either something Genevieve said, or did not say, or something Formerly Lefoux said or did not say. Or . . .*

Lady Alexia Maccon stopped in her very solid tracks and hit her forehead with the butt of her hand. Fortunately, it was the hand that held Ethel, not the hand that held her parasol, or she might have done herself damage.

"Of course! How could I be so silly? I have *the wrong queen.*"

Then she started walking again, her mind now calculating in a steel-traplike fashion—that is, if the trap were of the spring-loaded, not-very-sensitive variety. Lady Maccon was not one to do too many things at once, especially not right now, but she was tolerably convinced she could handle bipedal motion and thought at the same time.

The original ghostly messenger had never specified Queen Victoria, and neither had Formerly Lefoux. Genevieve Lefoux and her octomaton weren't after the monarch of the empire; oh, no, they were after a hive queen. That made far more sense. Genevieve had never liked the vampires, not since they corrupted Angelique (although she was always content enough to take their money). Given their rocky history, again over that troublesome violet-eyed French maid, Alexia would wager good money Genevieve was after Countess Nadasdy. This made sense given the northward direction of her tentacleing, toward Mayfair. Somehow, Madame Lefoux had deduced the whereabouts of the Westminster Hive.

Another mystery. The location of a hive was a guarded secret. Lady Maccon herself knew of it, of course, but that was only because . . .

"Oh, Alexia, you idiot!" *The burglary at Woolsey!* Madame Lefoux must have been the thief, stealing those old missives because among them was Alexia's original invitation from Countess Nadasdy to visit the hive. It had been delivered to her by Mabel Dair in Hyde Park the afternoon after Alexia killed her first vampire. It contained the address of the hive house, and Alexia had foolishly never thought to destroy it. *When did I tell Genevieve that story?*

Lady Maccon cast desperately about the empty street. She had to reach the Westminster Hive, and fast. Never before had she resented the infant-inconvenience more than at this moment, not to mention her dependence on horse-drawn transport. She even had an invitation that would get her in the door, but no way to get there in time to warn them of imminent tentacled doom. She was stranded in the wilds of Belgravia!

She waddled faster.

The fire was spreading and whooshing behind her. The once-dim alley was alight with a flickering orange and yellow glow. The din of collapsing buildings and roaring flames was added to by the loud clanging bell of an approaching fire engine. One of the dirigibles must have spotted the blaze and drop-messaged the appropriate authorities. If anything, this made Alexia move faster. The last thing she needed was to be detained trying to explain her presence at the Pantechnicon. It also reminded her to look up to see if she could spot a dirigible.

Sure enough, there were several headed sedately in her direction, having caught sight of the fire and redirected their lazy circling toward an intriguing new attraction. They were safely above the conflagration, not yet in the aether but high enough to avoid any risk associated with even the most massive of ground fires.

Lady Maccon waved her parasol commandingly and yelled, but she was a mere speck far below, unless someone had a pair of Shersky and Droop's latest long-distance binoculars. Since her marriage, Alexia had adopted a more respectable and somber color palette than that of the pastel-inclined unattached young lady. This made her even less visible in the flickering shadows of Motcomb Street.

It was then that Alexia noticed that the Giffard symbol (a shaping of the name that turned the *G* into a massive red and black balloon) on a nearby warehouse was modified with a kind of starburst pattern at its end and a phrase underneath that read PYROTECHNIC DIVISION LTD. She stopped, turned on her heel, and headed for a nearby lamppost. With barely a pause for consideration, she hauled off, took careful aim, and threw her parasol hard at the torch section. The parasol, spearlike, crashed into the lamp and brought both it and the hot coals inside down to the ground with a clang.

Lady Maccon huffed her way over to the coals, retrieved her now-slightly-scorched and sooty accessory by its tip, and, holding it like a mallet, used the chubby handle to hit one particularly nice-looking coal along the street toward the Giffard pyrotechnic warehouse. It was a excellent thing, reflected Alexia at that juncture, that she was good at croquet. At a nice distance, she took careful aim and, with a kind of scooping action, struck the wedge of coal hard. It arced splendidly upward, crashing through the window of the warehouse in a most satisfactory manner.

Then she waited, long, slow counts, hoping the coal had managed to hit upon something reliably explosive.

It had. A popping, cracking noise came first, then some whizzing and whirling sounds, and finally a series of loud gunshots. The doors and windows of the warehouse exploded outward, pushing Alexia backward. Instinctively, she popped open her parasol to shield herself as the world around her turned into a smoking cornucopia of brightly flashing lights and loud noises. The entire stockpile of what she imagined must be a very expensive collection of gunpowder display sparkles and sky-lighters exploded, shimmering and flashing in an ever-increasing series of flares.

Lady Maccon cowered in the road—there was really no other way of putting it—behind her open parasol, trusting in the durability of Madame Lefoux's design to protect her from the worst of it.

Eventually, the popping detonations slowed, and she began to register the heat of the real fire as it crept down Motcomb Street toward her. She coughed and waved her parasol. The moonlight made the residual smoke silvery white, as if a thousand ghosts were collected around her.

Alexia, eyes watering, blinked and tried to take shallow, steady breaths. Then, through the dispersing smoke, a massive upside-down shepherdess-style bonnet appeared, hovering some two stories above the ground and heading toward her. As the smoke vanished, the cumbersome form of a small private dirigible bobbed into view above the bonnet, proving that it was, in fact, not a hat at all but the gondola portion of the air conveyance. The pilot, some miracle worker of the first order, navigated the small craft down toward Lady Maccon, lowering it carefully between the rows of buildings while battling to keep it away from the flames of the burning Pantechnicon.

CHAPTER THIRTEEN

The Octopus Stalks at Moonlight

It was Giffard's smallest craft, short-range and generally hired only for classified recognizance or personal pleasure jaunting. The gondola portion, even more strongly resembling a shepherdess's hat upon close inspection, was big enough for only five people. The model was based off of Blanchard's original balloon. It had four dragonfly-like wing rudders, sprouting below the passenger section. There was a small steam engine and propeller at the back, but the captain had to steer by means of multiple levers and tillers, making him perform a frantic dance. In usefulness, it resembled those small Thames crossing barges so favored by the criminally minded. Giffard had come out with a whole fleet recently, at luxury prices, so the affluent could invest in private air transport. Alexia found them undignified, not the least because there was no door. One had to actually clamber over the edge of the gondola to get inside. Imagine that, fully grown adults clambering! But when one was stranded in an alley with a burning Pantechnicon and a rampaging octomaton, one really couldn't afford to be picky.

Two of the figures inside the hat leaned over the edge, pointing at her.

"Yoo-hoo!" yodeled one of them jovially.

"Over here! Quickly, gentlemen, please, this way!" replied Alexia at full volume, waving her parasol madly.

One of the gentlemen touched the brim of his top hat at her (no tipping was possible with a hat tied down for air travel). "Lady Maccon."

"By George, Boots! How the deuce can you possibly tell that there is Lady Maccon?" queried the other top-hated gentleman.

"Who else would be standing in the middle of a street on full-moon night with a raging ruddy fire behind her, waving a parasol about?"

"Good point, good point."

"Lady Maccon," came the yell. "Would you like a lift?"

"Mr. Bootbottle-Fipps," said Alexia in exasperation, "ask a silly question . . ."

The dirigible gondola bumped softly down, and she toddled over to it.

Boots and the second young dandy, who proved to be Viscount Trizdale, hopped nimbly out and came to assist her. Tizzy was a slight, effete young blond with an aristocratic nose and a partiality for the color yellow. Boots had a bit more substance in physicality and taste, but not much.

Lady Maccon looked from one to the other of the two gentlemen and then at the side of the gondola that she must now scale. With great reluctance and knowing she had no other choice, she put herself into their well-manicured hands.

No one, later that evening, nor ever again so long as any of them lived, mentioned what had to be done in order to get a very pregnant Lady Maccon into that passenger basket. There was some heaving, and a good deal of squeaking (both from Alexia and Tizzy), and hands might have had to be placed upon portions of the anatomy pleasing to neither Alexia nor her rescuers. Suffice it to say that Lady Maccon had cause to be grateful Lord Akeldama insisted that his drones undertake some sporting activity, for all their fashionable proclivities.

Alexia landed upon her bustle, legs slightly in the air. Gravity being even more forthright than Lady Maccon, she flailed about before managing to roll to one side and climb laboriously to her feet. She had a rather severe stitch in her side, a few bruises on her nether regions, and she was flushed with heat and exertion, but everything else, including the child, seemed to be in working order. The two young men jumped back inside after her.

"What are you doing here?" Lady Maccon demanded, still in shock that her plan to signal for help had actually worked. "Did my husband put a tail on me? What is it with werewolves and tails?"

Tizzy and Boots looked at each other.

Finally Boots said, "It wasn't entirely the earl, Lady Maccon. Our lord asked us to keep an eye on you this evening as well. He indicated things might come to pass on full moon that required additional recognizance in this part of London, if you take my meaning."

"How on earth would he know to do a thing like that? Oh, forget I asked. How does Lord Akeldama know anything?" Logic returned along with dignity, and Alexia took stock of her change in circumstances.

Boots shrugged. "Things *always* come to pass on full moon."

Without having to be directed, the pilot was already taking the small craft back up, away from fire and smoke. He was a diminutive man, clean-shaven, with a snubbed nose and a mercurial expression. His cravat was very well tied and it coordinated perfectly with his waistcoat.

"Don't tell me." Alexia looked him up and down. "This dirigible happens to be owned by Lord Akeldama?"

"If that's what you desire, my lady, we won't tell you." Boots looked guilty, as though he were somehow failing her in this request.

Lady Maccon twisted her lips together in thought. The infant-inconvenience kicked at her mightily, and she clutched reflexively at her stomach. "I hate to do this to you, gentlemen, but I find myself in desperate need to call upon Westminster Hive, as quickly as possible. How fast does this contraption go?"

The pilot gave her a cheeky grin. "Oh, you'd be surprised, my lady. Very surprised. Lord Akeldama had this little beauty retrofitted by Madame Lefoux. That he did."

"I didn't know they had professional dealings with each other." Lady Maccon arched an eyebrow.

"I understand this was a first commission. The very first. Lord Akeldama was delighted with her work. Quite delighted. As, indeed, am I. Can't try floating himself, poor man." The pilot looked as though he really felt genuinely sorry for the vampire's inability. "But he's had this beauty put through her paces around the green, and I assure you, that Frenchwoman is a miracle worker. A miracle worker, I say. The things she can do with aeronautics."

"She did comment once that it was her specialty at university. And, of course, there's always Monsieur Trouvé and the ornithopter."

The pilot looked up from his activities with a gleam of interest. "Ornithopter you say? I'd heard the French were branching out. My goodness, what a sight that must be."

"Yes." Lady Maccon's voice was low. "Better to see in action than to use oneself, if you ask me." She raised her voice. "About this dirigible going faster? It's very important that I put in an appearance within the next few minutes. Why don't you show me the full extent of this lovely craft's paces?"

Another grin met that request. "Just point me in the appropriate direction, my lady!"

Alexia did so, gesturing north. They were already above the rooftops, the fire well behind them. She toddled to the edge and looked down: Hyde Park was to their left and a little ahead, while Green Park and the

Palace Garden lay spread behind them and to the right. Even so high, she could hear the howling of Queen Victoria's personal werewolf guard, the Growlers, locked away in one special wing of Buckingham below.

She indicated a point ahead and slightly to the right, between the two parks—the center of Mayfair. The pilot pulled down hard on a doorknob-ended lever, and the craft lurched in that direction, faster than Alexia had thought dirigibles could go. Madame Lefoux's touch, indeed.

"Does she have a name, Captain?" she yelled into the rushing air.

Both the interest and the title earned Lady Maccon a great deal of loyalty from the young pilot. "'Course she does, my lady. Himself calls her *Buffety,* for the rocking motion, I suspect. She's on the registry as *Dandelion Fluff Upon a Spoon.* Don't know as I can rightly explain that one."

Tizzy tittered knowingly. Lady Maccon and the pilot looked at him, but the young lordling seemed disinclined to elaborate.

Lady Maccon shrugged. "I suppose Lord Akeldama names in mysterious ways."

Boots, his eyes on Alexia's other hand, which was still wrapped protectively about her swollen belly, inquired solicitously, "Is it the child, Lady Maccon?"

"The reason for our urgency? Oh, no. I have an invitation to attend Countess Nadasdy's full-moon party, and I am late."

Boots and Tizzy nodded their full understanding of this grave social necessity. All speed was indeed called for.

"We shall make haste, then, my lady. We wouldn't want you to arrive beyond the fashionable hour."

"Thank you for your understanding, Mr. Bootbottle-Fipps."

"And the fire, my lady?" Boots's muttonchops fluffed up in the breeze.

Alexia batted her eyelashes. "Fire? What fire?"

"Ah, is that how it is?"

Lady Maccon turned to look once more out of the gondola. She could make out the massive form of the octomaton, careening through the corner of Hyde Park behind Apsley House directly below them. But with another pull on that lever, *Dandelion Fluff Upon a Spoon* surged ahead and on into Mayfair, leaving the rampaging octopus far behind. The drones, having noticed the great crashing beast, made little warbling noises of distress before insisting Alexia tell them *all about it.*

The Westminster Hive house was one of many similar fashionable residences. It stood at the end of the block and a little apart from the row, but nothing else distinguished it as special or supernaturally inclined. Perhaps the grounds were a little too well tended and the exterior a little too clean and freshly painted, but no more or less than that customarily afforded by the very wealthy. It was a good-enough address, but not too good, and it was large enough to accommodate the countess, the primary members of her hive, and their drones, but not too large.

On this particular full moon, it was busier than usual, with a number of carriages pulling in at the front and disgorging some of the ton's very highest and most progressive politicians, aristocrats, and artists. Alexia, as muhjah, knew (although others might not) that the assembled were all in the vampire's enclave, or employ, or service, or all three. They were attired in their very best, collars starched high, dresses cut low, britches tight, and bustles shapely. It was a parade of consequence—Countess Nadasdy would allow nothing less.

High floating was assuredly a fashionable way to arrive at a party, the latest and greatest, some might say. But it was not at all convenient for a street already clogged with private carriages and hired hansoms. As the dirigible neared, a few of the horses spooked, rearing and neighing. Ground conveyances crashed into one another in their efforts to clear space, which resulted in a good deal of yelling.

"Who do they think they are, arriving like that?" wondered one elderly gentleman.

Vampires enjoyed investing in the latest inventions, and they did have trade concerns, most notably with the East India Company, but they were traditionalists at heart. So, too, were their guests. For no matter how modish the private pleasure dirigible might be in principle, no one approved of it disturbing their own dignified arrival with its puffed-up sense of novelty. Dignity aside, the dirigible was going to land whether they liked it or not, and consequently, space was eventually made. The gondola bumped down in front of the hive house's wrought-iron fence.

Lady Maccon was left in a quandary. She now had to get out over the side of the passenger basket. She could conceive of no possible way her exit would be any less humiliating than her entry. She did not want to go through such a process again, let alone in front of such august bodies as those now glaring at her. But she could swear she heard the crashing sound of the octomaton, and she really had no time to spare for anyone's decorum, even her own.

"Mr. Bootbottle-Fipps, Viscount, if you would be so kind?" She puffed out her cheeks and prepared herself for mortification.

"Of course, my lady." The ever-eager Boots stepped over to assist her. Tizzy, it must be admitted, moved with less alacrity. As they prepared to boost her (there really was no other way of putting it) over the edge of the gondola (at which juncture she foresaw landing on her much-abused bustle yet again), a savior appeared.

No doubt alerted by the disapproving cries and exacerbation of activity in the street, Miss Mabel Dair emerged from the hive house, dramatically silhouetted against the crowded, well-lit interior. She paused, center stage, on the front stoop. She wore an evening gown the color of old gold with a low square neckline, trimmed with loops of black lace and pink silk roses. There were fresh roses in her hair and her bustle was full—the more risqué trends out of Paris with the smaller bustle and form-fitting bodice were not for her. No, here, under her mistress's guarded eye, even an actress like Miss Dair dressed demurely.

Lady Alexia Maccon, at the side of a dirigible passenger basket, looked as though she was in imminent danger of not playing by the rules.

Miss Dair yelled from the step, using her stage voice to cut through the noise of the crowded street. "Why, Lady Maccon, how delightful. We did not expect you. Especially not in so elaborate a transport."

"Good evening, Miss Dair. It is rather smart, isn't it? Unfortunately, I seem to be having difficulty getting out."

Miss Dair bit her lower lip, hiding a smile. "Let me fetch some help."

"Ah, yes, thank you, Miss Dair, but I *am* in a wee bit of a hurry."

"Of course you are, Lady Maccon." The actress turned back into the house, signaling with a sharp gesticulation of a satin-gloved hand. Mere moments later, she turned and traipsed down the steps followed by a veritable herd of dignified-looking footmen, all of whom took to the lifting and depositing of Lady Maccon as they would any household task, with gravely serious faces and not one flicker of amusement.

Once Alexia had attained her freedom, Boots touched his hat brim with one gray-gloved hand. "A very good evening to you, Lady Maccon."

"You won't be joining me?"

Boots exchanged a telling look with Mabel Dair. "Not at this particular party, my lady. We would make things"—he paused delicately—"prickly."

Lady Maccon nodded her understanding and gave the matter no further thought. There are some places where, despite their universal skills at being ubiquitous, even Lord Akeldama's drones could not go.

Mabel Dair offered Lady Maccon her arm. Alexia took it gratefully, although she firmed her grip on her parasol with her free hand. She was, after all, entering a hive house, and despite the strictures of polite society, vampires had never looked upon her, and her soullessness, with any degree of acceptance. On every prior occasion but one,

Lady Maccon had visited this hive with her husband. Tonight she was going in alone. Miss Mabel Dair may have her arm, but Alexia knew very well that the actress did *not* have her back.

Together the two women entered the party.

The house itself had not changed from when Alexia visited it that first time. Inside, it was far more luxurious than its exterior suggested, although all displays of prosperity were tasteful, without a hint of vulgarity. Persian carpets still lay thick and soft, in coordinating shades of deep red, their patterns subtle, but they were difficult to see as so many top boots and evening slippers trod over them. Striking paintings still hung on the walls, masterworks ranging from contemporary abstract pieces to one relaxed, porcelain-skinned lady that could only be by Titian. But Alexia only knew they were there because she had seen them before; this time as she wended her way through the throng, coiffured comb-outs and flowered headdresses obscured her view. The lavish mahogany furniture was actually being sat upon, and the many stone statues of Roman senators and Egyptian gods had become nothing more than stony members of the milling throng.

"My goodness me," yelled Alexia at her escort over the loud chatter. "This is quite the crush."

The actress nodded enthusiastically. "The countess is supposed to make a very important announcement this evening. Everyone, and I do mean *everyone,* accepted her invitation."

"Announcement, what kind of . . . ?"

But Miss Dair's attention was back to pushing their way through the throng.

One or two people recognized Alexia—heads tilted in her direction, faces perplexed. "Lady Maccon?" came the confused acknowledgment of her presence, accompanied by small nods. She could hear the gossipmongers whirling away like so many steam engines gearing up to explode. *What was the wife of an Alpha werewolf doing there? And so far along in her pregnancy. And alone! On full moon!*

As they pressed on, Alexia became aware of a presence shadowing them through the crowd. Just as a tall, thin man accosted Miss Dair from the front, a person behind them cleared his throat.

Lady Maccon turned to find herself face-to-face with a nondescript gentleman, so nondescript in countenance as to be challenging to describe. His hair was just this side of brown, and his eyes just that side of blue, combined with an arrangement of other features neither striking nor interesting. He wore unremarkable but stylish clothing, all of which suggested a level of premeditated obscurity that reminded her irresistibly of Professor Lyall.

"Your Grace," she said warily in greeting.

The Duke of Hematol did not smile, but that might have been because he did not wish to show her his fangs just yet. "Lady Maccon, what an unexpected pleasure."

Alexia glanced at Miss Dair, who was engaging in a hushed and rather forceful conversation with Dr. Caedes, another member of Countess Nadasdy's inner circle. He was a tall, thin vampire who Alexia always thought looked like a parasol without its fabric cover, all points and sharp angles. He *unfolded* rather than walked. He did not look pleased.

The duke was more subtle and better able to hide his feelings over Lady Maccon's unanticipated presence. Alexia wondered where Lord Ambrose, the last member of this little band, was stashed. Probably near the countess, as he acted as her *praetoriani.* At a party as crowded as this, the queen would want her pet bodyguard as close as possible.

"We did not expect you on this particular night, Lady Maccon. We had assumed you would be assisting your husband with his"—a calculated pause—"disability."

Alexia narrowed her eyes and fished about in her reticule, coming up with the required card. "I have *an invitation.*"

"Of course you do."

"It is most urgent I speak with your mistress immediately. I have some vital information to impart."

"Tell it to me."

Alexia put on her most superior Lady Macconish expression and looked him up and down. "I think *not.*"

The vampire stood his ground.

He was not a very large man. Alexia figured if push came to shove, she could probably take him on even in her current state. Being soulless had its uses. She removed her gloves.

He watched this movement with concerned interest.

"No need for that, Lady Maccon." If he was as much like Professor Lyall as Alexia believed, physical conflict would not be his preferred solution to any given confrontation. He looked up toward the storklike doctor and gestured sharply with his chin. The other vampire reacted with supernatural swiftness, grabbing Miss Dair's arm and melting away into the crowd, leaving Lady Maccon with a new, far less attractive, escort.

"It really is most vital that I see her as soon as possible. She may be in grave danger." Alexia left her gloves off and tried to impress upon the vampire her urgency without being too threatening.

The duke smiled. His fangs were small and sharp, barely present, as subtle as the rest of his projected image. "You mortals are always in a hurry."

Lady Maccon gritted her teeth. "This time it is in *your* best interest—really, it is."

The duke looked at her closely. "Very well, come with me."

He led her through the crowd, which thinned as they left the main hallway that serviced the drawing room, parlors, dining hall, and receiving area. They rounded a corner into a part of the house Alexia loved, the museum of machinery, where the history of human innovation was displayed with as much care as the marble statuary and oil paintings of the public areas. The duke moved at a sedate pace, too sedate for Alexia, who, even pregnant and knowing she was going beyond the bounds of proper etiquette, pushed past him. She scuttled by the very first steam engine ever built and then past the model of the Babbage Engine with barely a glance to spare for either feat of human ingenuity.

The vampire hurried to catch up, pushing past her in turn when they reached the stairs, leading the way up rather than, as had occurred on previous occasions, into the back parlor that was the countess's preferred sanctuary. This was a special evening, indeed. Lady Maccon was being let into the high sanctum of the hive. She had never before been allowed *upstairs.*

There were drones strategically placed on the staircase, all attractive and perfectly dressed, looking like they might be guests at the party, but Alexia knew from the way they watched her that they were as much fixtures in the house as its Persian rugs. Only more deadly than the rugs, one supposed. They did nothing, however, as Lady Maccon was in the company of the duke. But they did watch her carefully.

They arrived at a closed door. The Duke of Hematol knocked, a pattern of taps. It opened to reveal Lord Ambrose, as tall, as dark, and as handsome as any milk-water miss might wish her own personal vampire to be.

"Lady Maccon! How unexpected."

"So everyone keeps pointing out." Alexia tried to barge past him.

"You can't come in here."

"Oh, for goodness' sake, I mean her no harm. Truth be told, quite the opposite."

An exchange of glances occurred between Lord Ambrose and the duke.

"She is part of this new order. I think we must believe her."

"You used to think Walsingham was right!" Lord Ambrose accused his compatriot.

"I still do. But in character, she is no more her father's daughter than Lord Maccon is Lord Woolsey's successor or Lord Akeldama is Walsingham's."

Lady Maccon glared. "If you mean that I think for myself and make my own choices, then you are spot-on. Now, I must see the countess immediately. I have—"

Lord Ambrose didn't budge. "I must take possession of your parasol."

"Absolutely not. We may need it shortly, especially if you don't let me in. I tell you I have—"

"I must insist."

"Let her in, Ambrose dear." Countess Nadasdy had a voice as warm as butter and just as greasy. She could fry people with that voice, if she wanted to.

Immediately, Lord Ambrose moved out of Alexia's direct line of sight, revealing the interior of the chamber. It was a very-well-appointed boudoir, complete with not only a massive canopied bed, but also a full sitting area and other highly desirable accoutrements. There was the latest and most sophisticated in exsanguination warmers, an overlarge teapot for storing blood with multiple spouts and tubing attached. Both the pot and the tubes wore knitted tea cozies, and there was a warming brazier underneath to keep the vital liquid moving through the tubes.

The countess was indeed *at tea.* Her version being a lavish affair, complete with lace-covered tea trolley set out with teacups and matched teapot of fine china painted with little pink roses and edged in silver. There were pink and white petits fours that no one was eating and cups of tea that no one was drinking. A three-tiered serving dish of silver held a tempting display of finger sandwiches and sugared rose petals, and there was even a small platter of . . . could it be? *Treacle tart!*

Lady Maccon was excessively fond of treacle tart.

The assembled drones and guests were all dressed in shades of white, pale green, and pink to accessorize the decor. Elegant Greek urns held massive arrangements of flowers—pale cream roses with pink edges and long leaf ferns. It was all very well coordinated, perhaps too well, as a scientific etching of an animal compares to the real thing.

A second tea trolley was also prominently displayed, similarly draped in a fine lace cloth. It was one of the lower styles meant for front parlors and afternoon visiting hours. Upon it lay the supine form of a young lady, dressed to match the china in a white damask evening gown with pink flowers. Her throat was bare and exposed, and her fine blond hair was piled high and off of her neck.

The countess, it would appear, had a very particular definition of high tea.

"Oh, dear. I do hate to interrupt you at mealtime," said Lady Maccon, not at all apologetically. "But I have the most important information to impart."

She waddled forward, only to have her way blocked yet again by Lord Ambrose. "My Queen, I must protest, a soulless in your inner sanctum. While you are at table!"

Countess Nadasdy looked up from the young girl's fine white neck. "Ambrose. We have been over this before." Alexia had never thought the Westminster queen entirely suited the role of vampire. Not that Lady Maccon's opinion mattered much. If the rumors were to be believed, Countess Nadasdy had been suiting the role for over a thousand years. Possibly two. But, unlike Lord Ambrose, she simply didn't look the part. She was a cozy little woman—short and on the plump side. Her cheeks were round and rosy, and her big eyes sparked. True, the blush was mercuric and the eyes sparkled with belladonna and calculation, not humor, but it was hard to feel threatened by a woman who looked like the living incarnation of one of Lord Akeldama's shepherdess seduction paintings.

"She is a hunter," protested Lord Ambrose.

"She is a *lady.* Aren't you, Lady Maccon?"

Alexia looked down at her protruding belly. "So the evidence would seem to suggest." The baby inside of her moved around as though to punctuate the statement. *Yes,* said Alexia to it internally, *I don't like Lord Ambrose either. But now is not the time for histrionics.*

"Ah, yes, felicitations on the imminent event."

"Let us hope not all *that* imminent. Incidentally, my apologies, venerable ones. Until recently, you seem to have found the advent of my progeny discombobulating."

"Exactly, My Queen, we cannot have that—"

Lady Maccon interrupted Lord Ambrose by the simple expedient of prodding his ribs with her parasol. She aimed exactly for that point in the rib cage that the ticklish find most discomposing. Not that vampires got ticklish, so far as Alexia was aware, but it was the principle of the thing. "Yes, yes, I know you still would prefer it if I were dead, Lord Ambrose, but never mind that now. Countess, listen to me. You have to get away."

Lord Ambrose moved and Lady Maccon proceeded toward the hive queen.

The countess dabbed at a bit of blood on the side of her mouth with a white linen handkerchief. Alexia barely caught a hint of fang before they were tucked away behind perfect cupid's bow–shaped lips. The countess never showed fang unless she meant it. "My dear Lady Maccon, what *are* you wearing? Is that a *visiting* gown?"

"What? Oh, yes, sorry. I hadn't intended to come to your lovely gathering, or I would be more appropriately dressed. But, please listen, you must leave now!"

"Leave this room? Whatever for? It is one of my particular favorites."

"No, no, leave the house."

"Abandon my hive? Never! Don't be foolish, child."

"But, Countess, there is an octomaton heading in this direction. It wants to kill you and it knows the location."

"Preposterous. There hasn't been an octomaton in a dog's age. And how would it know where to find me?"

"Ah, yes, well, as to that. There was this break-in, you see—"

Lord Ambrose bristled. "Soul-sucker! What have you done?"

"How was I to remember one little invitation from way back?"

The countess went momentarily still, like a wasp atop a slice of melon. "Lady Maccon, who is it that wants to kill me?"

"Oh, too many to choose from? I am similarly blessed."

"Lady Maccon!"

Alexia had hoped not to reveal the identity of the culprit. It was one thing to warn the hive of imminent attack; it was quite another to expose Madame Lefoux without first understanding her motives. *Well, perhaps if my* friend *had let me in on her reasoning, I might not now be forced into this situation. But in the end, I am muhjah, and I must remember that my duty is to maintain the solidarity of the peace between humans and supernatural folk. No matter Madame Lefoux's grounds, we cannot have a hive arbitrarily attacked by an inventor. It is not only impolitic, it is impolite.*

So, Lady Maccon took a deep breath and told the truth. "Madame Lefoux has built the octomaton. She intends to kill you with it."

The countess's big cornflower-blue eyes narrowed.

"What!" That was Lord Ambrose.

The Duke of Hematol made his way over toward his queen. "I told you no good would come of taking in that French maid."

The countess held up a hand. "She's after the boy."

"Of course she is after the boy!" The duke's voice was harsh with annoyance. "Dabble in the affairs of mortal women and this is what transpires. Octomaton at your doorstep. I warned you."

"Your complaint was recorded by the edict keeper at the time."

Lady Maccon blinked. "Quesnel? What has he to do with any of this? Wait." She tilted her head and gave the countess a look. "Did you kidnap Madame Lefoux's son?"

Alexia often felt it wasn't possible for a vampire to look guilty. But the countess was giving the expression a fair facsimile.

"Why? I mean, for goodness' sake." Lady Maccon shook her finger at the hive queen as though the ancient vampire were a very naughty schoolgirl caught with her hand in the jam jar. "Shame on you! Bad vampire."

The countess tsked dismissively. "Oh, really. There's no cause for condescension, soul-sucker. The boy was promised to us. In her will, Angelique named the hive guardian to her child. We didn't even know he existed until that moment. Madame Lefoux wouldn't hear of it, of course. But he *is ours.* And we never let go of what is rightfully ours. We didn't kidnap him. We *retrieved* him."

Lady Maccon thought of her own child, now promised away to Lord Akeldama in order to keep them both safe from fang interference and assassination attempts. "Oh, really, Countess. *I mean to say!* What is it with you vampires? Don't you ever relax your machinations? No wonder Genevieve wants to kill you. Kidnapping. That's very low. Very low, indeed. What could you possibly want with the boy anyway? He's a terrible scamp."

The countess's round, pleasant face went very hard. "We want him because he is *ours*! What more reason do we need? The law is on our side in this. We have copies of the will."

Lady Maccon demanded details. "Does it name the hive, or you specifically, Countess?"

"Me alone, I believe."

Lady Maccon cast her hands heavenward, although there was no one up there for her to appeal to. It was an accepted fact that preternaturals had no spiritual recourse, only pragmatism. Alexia didn't mind; the latter had often gotten her out of sticky situations, whereas the former seemed highly unreliable when one was in a bind. "Well, there you have it. With no legal recourse, Genevieve only has to see you dead in order to get her child back. Plus, she has the added pleasure of killing the woman who corrupted her lover."

The countess looked as though she had not thought of matters in such a way.

"You cannot be serious."

Alexia shrugged. "Consider her perspective."

The countess stood. "Good point. And she is French. They get terribly emotional, don't they? Ambrose, arm the defenses. Hematol, send out runners. If it really is an octomaton, we are going to need additional military support. Get me my personal physician. Oh, and bring out the aethertronic Gatling gun."

Lady Maccon could not help but admire the countess's command of the situation. Alexia herself was sometimes known, among members of the pack, as *the general.* Of course, the gentlemen in question believed their mistress unaware of this moniker. Alexia preferred it that way and would periodically go into fits of autocratic demands simply to ascertain if she could get them to grumble about it when they thought she couldn't hear. Werewolves tended to believe all mortals slightly deaf.

As the countess set about putting her people in order, her meal, left to lie on the tea table in soporific languor, stirred. The young blonde raised herself slowly up onto her elbows and looked about foggily.

"Felicity!"

"Oh, dear, Alexia? What on earth are *you* doing here?"

"Me! Me?" Lady Maccon was reduced to sputtering. "What about you? I'll have you know, sister mine, that I came here because I had an invitation to the party!"

Felicity wiped delicately at the side of her neck with a tea cloth. "I didn't know you ran in the countess's circles."

"You mean, supernatural circles? My husband is a werewolf, for goodness' sake! Must you keep forgetting that tiny little detail?"

"Yes, but on full-moon night, shouldn't you be with him? And aren't you terribly far along to be out in public?"

Lady Maccon practically growled. "Felicity. My presence here is not of concern. But yours most certainly is! What on earth are you doing allowing a vampire—and not just any vampire, mind you, but the ruddy Westminster queen herself—to feed on you? You're . . . you're . . . not even chaperoned!" she sputtered.

Felicity's expression became hard and calculating. Alexia had seen that look before but had never given it much credence beyond smallness of mind. However, this time she had the upsetting realization that she might have underestimated her sister. "Felicity, *what have you done?*"

Felicity gave a humorless little smile.

"How long has this relationship been going on?" Alexia tried to think back. When had her sister first started wearing high-necked dresses and lace collars?

"Oh, Alexia, you can be so dim-witted. Since I met Lord Ambrose at your wedding, of course. He very kindly said that I looked like just the type of creative and ambitious young lady who would have excess soul. He asked if I would like to live forever. I thought to myself, well, *of course* I have excess soul. Mama is always saying what a good artist I would be, should I ever try, and what a good musician I would be, should I ever learn to play. And, most assuredly, I should like to live forever! Not to mention be courted by Lord Ambrose! Then what should the other ladies have to say?"

Lady Maccon ground her teeth together. "Felicity! What have you done? Oh, gracious me, it was you who stole my journal on the dirigible to Scotland, wasn't it?"

Felicity looked archly up at the ceiling.

"You leaked my pregnancy to the press intentionally, didn't you?"

Felicity gave a delicate little shrug.

Alexia was quite disgusted with her sister. To be stupid was one thing; to be stupid and evil yielded up untidy consequences. "Why, you conniving bit of baggage! How could you? To your own flesh and blood!" She was also scandalized. "Do pull your dress up. What a neckline!" Alexia was so out of temper, in fact, she nearly forgot that they were all in danger from a rampaging two-story octopus. "And?"

Felicity pursed her lips and looked at the ceiling.

"Go on!"

"Oh, really, sister, there is no need to take that tone of voice with me. All Lord Ambrose wanted was a few reports on your activities and health now and again. Well, and the journal. Until this recent change of address—then we thought if I were to take up residence with you, well, you know . . . And I've been visiting with the countess only now and again, let her have a little nibble, relay some information. No harm done. She's perfectly lovely, isn't she? Quite the motherly sort."

"Aside from the neck biting?" Sarcasm was, of course, the lowest form of discourse, but sometimes Alexia couldn't resist such temptation as her sister offered. That was probably how Countess Nadasdy felt. *Which explains those ugly shawls Felicity's been wearing. She's been hiding her neck.*

They both turned to watch the countess as she conferred with two of her drones. She was moving lightning fast from one task to the next, preparing to defend her territory with both might and cunning and, if Alexia's eyes were to be believed, a tin of what looked to be pickled herring. The vampire queen had the demeanor and appearance of some sort of small, quick hedge bird—a tit, perhaps. If a tit could kill you with a mere nod of its little feathered head.

"Felicity. What did you tell her about me?"

"Well, anything I could think of, of course. But really, Alexia, your activities are very dull. I fail to see why anyone should be interested in you or that child of yours."

"You would."

With her hive busy mustering up troops, the countess flitted back over, sat down, and looked as though she intended to return to tea.

Lady Maccon narrowed her eyes, marched the last few feet to the beautiful cream brocade settee, and placed a very firm and very bare hand on the vampire queen's forearm. Alexia was a good deal stronger than a proper English lady ought to be, and the countess was suddenly ill equipped to shake off such a grip.

"No more tea." Alexia was quite decided on this point.

The countess looked from her to her sister. "Remarkable, isn't it? Sisterhood, I mean. One would never guess it to look at you."

Alexia rolled her eyes, let go of the countess's arm, and gave her a look of mild reproach. "My sister cannot possibly have been an effective spy."

The vampire queen shrugged and reached for her tea—the ordinary kind. She sipped at the bone china cup delicately, taking no pleasure or sustenance from the beverage.

Waste of perfectly good tea, thought Alexia. She looked at Felicity. But, then, the countess probably thought Felicity was a waste of perfectly good blood.

Her sister assumed a dramatically relaxed pose atop the tea trolley, her face petulant.

Alexia reached for a treacle tartlet and popped it into her own mouth.

"You have been conducting some interesting investigations recently, Lady Maccon," said the vampire queen slyly. "Something to do with your father's past, if what your sister has relayed is true. And a ghost. I know you are adverse to my advice, but trust me, Lady Maccon, it would be best not to delve too deeply into Alessandro Tarabotti's records."

Alexia thought about Floote, who always seemed to know more about her father than he was willing to tell her. Or was allowed to tell her.

"Did you vampires somehow have my father classified? Do you have my butler under a gag order? And now you are corrupting my sister. Really, Countess Nadasdy, why go to such lengths?" Lady Maccon put her hand back onto the vampire queen's arm, turning her mortal once more.

The countess flinched but did not pull away. "Really, Lady Maccon, must you? It's a most unsettling sensation."

At which juncture Lord Ambrose turned and saw what was occurring on the couch.

"Let go of her, you soul-sucking bitch!" He charged across the room.

Alexia let go and raised her parasol.

"Now, Ambrose, no harm done." The countess sounded placid but her fangs were showing slightly.

Felicity was looking back and forth between the players around her with increasing befuddlement on her pretty face. Since Felicity often wore such a look whenever attempting to understand any conversation not directly concerning herself, Alexia saw no reason to explain. The last thing Felicity needed to know was that her older sister was anything more than a bother. *That is, assuming Felicity still doesn't know I'm preternatural. Right now it's difficult to put anything past her.*

Lord Ambrose looked as though he would very much like to strike Lady Maccon.

Still holding the parasol at the defensive, Alexia reached inside her reticule and withdrew Ethel. She then lowered the parasol to reveal the gun now pointed at the vampire.

"Back away a little, if you would, Lord Ambrose. You are making me feel most unwelcome."

Lord Ambrose did as he was told with a snorted, "You *are* unwelcome."

"Do I have to keep reminding everyone? I had an invitation!"

"Alexia, you have a gun!" exclaimed Felicity, horrified.

"Yes." Lady Maccon relaxed back into the settee and allowed the gun to waver slightly over toward the countess. "I should warn you, Lord Ambrose, my aim is not very accurate."

"And is that gun loaded with . . . ?" He did not finish the sentence. He did not need to.

"I should never, of course, admit to the fact that Ethel here is equipped with sundowner bullets. But a few may have *accidentally* made it from my husband's stock into my own. Can't imagine how."

Lord Ambrose backed farther away.

Alexia looked with annoyance at her sister. "Get off the tea trolley, Felicity, do. What a place for a young lady to be sitting. Do you have any idea what kind of trouble you are in?"

Felicity sniffed. "You sound just like Mama."

"Yes, well, *you* are beginning to *act* like Mama!"

Felicity gasped.

Lord Ambrose made a move forward, thinking Lady Maccon's attention distracted.

Ethel swung once more toward the countess. Alexia's hand was remarkably steady. "Ah, ah, ah."

The vampire backed away again.

"Now," said Alexia, "I do so hate to do this to you all. But really, our safest bet would be to get out of here. And quickly."

The countess shook her head. "You may leave, of course, Lady Maccon, but—"

"No, no, both of us, I insist."

"Foolish child," said the Duke of Hematol, coming back into the room. "How can anyone know so little of vampire edict and sit the Shadow Council? Our queen cannot leave this house. It is not a matter of choice—it is a matter of physiology."

"She could swarm." Lady Maccon swung her gun once more toward the vampire queen.

Lord Ambrose hissed.

Lady Maccon said, "Go on, Countess, swarm. There's a good vampire."

The duke let out an annoyed sigh. "Save us all from the practicality of soul-suckers. She can't swarm on command, woman. Queens don't just up and swarm when told they have to. Swarming is a biological imperative. You might as well tell someone to spontaneously combust."

Alexia looked at Lord Ambrose. "Really? Would that work on him?"

At which juncture the most tremendous crash reverberated through the house, and guests at the party below started screaming.

The octomaton had arrived.

Lady Maccon gestured with her gun in an arbitrary manner. "*Now* will you swarm?"

CHAPTER FOURTEEN

In Which Lady Maccon Mislays Her Parasol

The countess jumped to her feet. So, too, did Felicity. Lord Ambrose decided Lady Maccon was no longer the greatest threat in his world and turned toward the racket.

"Now would be an excellent time," prodded Alexia.

The countess shook her head in exasperation. "Swarming is not something one chooses. I know this is difficult for you to understand, soul-sucker, but not everything is the result of conscious thought. Swarming is instinct. I have to know, deep down in my soul on a supernatural level, that my hive is no longer safe. Then I would have to source a new hive, never to return to this one. Now is not that time."

The house fairly rattled on its foundations as another mighty crash rent the air.

"Are you convinced of that?" wondered Alexia.

Something was literally tearing its way through the building, as a child will rip paper twists to get at the sugar candy inside. *Tasty vampire candy. Mmm.*

Felicity started to scream.

"Where did you stash Quesnel, Countess Nadasdy?" Lady Maccon raised her voice to carry over the din.

The countess was distracted by the commotion. "What?"

"I was simply suggesting you might want to retrieve him. Have him with you, and soon."

"Oh, yes, excellent plan. Hematol, would you fetch the boy?"

"Yes, my queen." The duke, having only just appeared, looked reluctant to obey; no vampire wishes to leave the side of his queen when she is in danger. But a direct order was a direct order, so he bowed perfunctorily and scurried off.

Yet another crash sounded. The door burst open. Dr. Caedes, a number of the footman-drones, and several other hive vampires ran into the room. Mabel Dair was the last inside, slamming the door behind her. The actress's beautiful gold gown was ripped, and her hair had fallen down about her face. She looked as though she were just about to perform Ophelia's death scene to a packed audience.

"My queen, you would not believe the monster down there! It is horrible! It ripped right through the wall, the one with the Titian. And it broke the bust of Demeter."

The countess was obligingly sympathetic to the trauma. "Come to me, my dear."

Mabel Dair ran to her mistress, knelt at her feet, and buried her face in the vampire's full skirts. Her hands were trembling where they gripped the fine taffeta material.

Alexia was tempted to clap. *Spectacular performance*!

The queen set one perfect white hand atop Miss Dair's cascading blond curls and looked to her hive. "Dr. Caedes, report! What is the octomaton's armament? Is it standard to the earlier model?"

"No, my queen, it seems to have been modified."

"Fire?"

"Yes, but only one tentacle. And the customary wooden blades. But a third seems to be able to shoot stakes. And the fourth has bullets."

"Go on. That's only four."

"It hasn't yet used any of the others yet."

"If this is Madame Lefoux we are dealing with, she'll have armed every single tentacle with something deadly. That's how she thinks."

Alexia couldn't help but agree. Genevieve was like that about her gadgets—the more uses the better.

The wall on the opposite side of the room shook. They heard a horrible, wrenching, tearing, crashing noise. It was the sound of metal and wood and brick colliding. The entire wall before them was ripped asunder. Once the dust settled, the domed head of the octomaton became visible, balanced atop its many tentacles. The creature scrabbled for purchase within the rubble of what had once been one of London's most stylish residences. The silver light of the moon and the bright gas of the streetlamps lit up the gleaming metal hide of the mechanical creature. Alexia could just see the fleeing forms of the countess's party guests in the street below.

Alexia raised her parasol and stood. She pointed the frilly accessory at the octomaton accusingly. "Genevieve, I do hope you didn't kill anyone."

But if Madame Lefoux was in there, guiding the creature, she did not acknowledge Lady Maccon. She had one intended target and one target only—Countess Nadasdy.

A gigantic tentacle wormed its way up into the room and hit out at the vampire queen, trying to crush her. Alexia preferred to lead with an airborne offensive, but Madame Lefoux was opting for hand-to-hand—or was that hand-to-tentacle?—combat. Possibly to protect as many innocents as she could.

The queen, supernatural in speed and cunning, simply dodged out of the way of the massive metal thing. But she was well and truly trapped, for there were no other doors out of that room, and half of her house was now destroyed.

Felicity let out another scream and then did the most sensible thing she could do under the circumstances—she fainted. At which point, everyone else did an equally sensible thing and ignored her.

Lord Ambrose charged. Alexia had no idea what he intended to do or how he intended to do it, but he seemed bent on something. He leaped, impossibly fast and high, landing atop the head of the creature, where he began trying to scrabble for a way inside. *Ah, going for the brains of the operation.*

Lady Maccon figured that was a pretty intelligent plan, but the vampire was thwarted in his attempts to pull off the hatch of the dome. He tried to punch through the helmet-like mantle, but Madame Lefoux was a master worker in such matters. The head was practically seamless, with no possible way of getting in from the outside, not even for a vampire. She had given herself slits to see out of, but those slits were just big enough to peer through; they were not sufficiently large for a vampire to get his fingers inside and pry open the casing.

A tentacle whipped around and with a casual gesture brushed Lord Ambrose off as if he were a crumb. The vampire fell past the edge of the floor where the wall once had stood, grabbing wildly and missing, and disappeared out of sight. Only to reappear moments later, simply leaping up from one story to the next until he was back inside.

This time Lord Ambrose dove for the root of one of the tentacles, trying to tear it off the body. Relying on all his strength, he attempted to forcibly rip away the ball bearings and pulleys that directed the thing's movements. Nothing. Madame Lefoux always thought in terms of supernatural strength and designed her devices accordingly.

While Lord Ambrose was thus occupied with a direct attack, several of the more courageous drones also charged the octomaton. These were swept aside with little more than the perfunctory wave of a free tentacle. Others made their way to their queen, standing in a protective huddle between her and the mechanical beast. One of the vampires was loading the pickled herring, which seemed to actually be some kind of ammunition, into an aethertronic Gatling gun. He cranked the belt through, and the machine spat the shiny fish at the octomaton in a *rat-tat-tat* of automated fire. The fish sizzled and stuck where they hit, eating angry holes into the octomaton's protective plating.

Another tentacle crept into the room, which now seemed to be filled with writhing metal octopus arms. This one raised up slowly, like a snake. Its tip opened with a snap, and it shot a blast of fire at the group surrounding Countess Nadasdy.

Drones screamed, and the countess, fleet and fast, leaped to the side, carrying two of them with her. She would try to rescue any she could from the flames, much as Conall would do with his clavigers under similar circumstances.

Knowing it was probably futile, Alexia put her gun back in her reticule and activated the magnetic disruption emitter in her parasol, aiming it at the octopus. As before, there was no reaction to the invisible blast, although the Gatling gun seized up. The tentacle swung around, spraying fire over the boudoir. The canopy over the handsome four-poster bed caught and flamed up to the ceiling. Alexia popped open her parasol and raised it before her like a shield, protecting herself from the blast.

Upon lowering it, she found that all was chaos and dust, with the smell of burning and the sound of screaming around her. Yet another tentacle slithered into the room. She had a sinking feeling that this one might actually be a real threat. Madame Lefoux was done playing. Alexia knew what her parasol was capable of where vampires were concerned, and this particular tentacle dripped an ominous liquid out of its tip—a liquid that sizzled when it hit the carpet and burned a hole where it landed.

Lapis solaris, unless Alexia missed her guess. It was one of the most deadly weapons in her parasol, and a favorite among those who opposed vampires. The danger was that it had to be diluted in sulfuric acid, and that could kill most anyone else as well as damage a vampire.

"Genevieve, don't! You could injure innocents!" Alexia was scared, not just for the hive but also for the drones and her sister, who all seemed to be in the line of squirt.

"Countess, please, you must draw her away. People will die." Lady Maccon turned her plea on the endangered vampire queen.

But Countess Nadasdy was beyond reason. All her efforts were now focused on protecting herself and her people from annihilation.

The Duke of Hematol reappeared, carrying an undersized grubby boy child in his supernaturally strong arms. If possible, the duke moved even faster than the queen had, coming to a stop before her and thrusting Quesnel's kicking form into her grasp. Everything stilled.

Quesnel was hollering and thrashing, but upon seeing the octomaton, he seemed more afraid of it than the vampires. He squealed and clutched reflexively at Countess Nadasdy's neck with one skinny, smudged arm.

The octomaton could not fire without risk of injury to the boy. No modern science had yet devised a weapon, apart from sunlight, that could harm a vampire without also harming a human. One of the tentacles, already falling with deadly force toward the vampire queen, veered away at the last minute, landing with a crash on the laden tea trolley, which had managed to survive the chaos until that moment. It crumpled in half under the blow, spinning fine china, treacle tart, and finger sandwiches in all directions.

So far as Alexia was concerned, that was *the last straw.* The infant-inconvenience inside her beat a tattoo of encouragement as she strode forward and whacked at the metal tentacle with her parasol and all her might. "Genevieve! Not the treacle tartlets!"

Whack, whack, whack. Twang!

It was, of course, a futile effort. But it made Alexia feel better.

The tentacle's tip flipped open, and a tube popped forward and out, becoming a bullhorn like those favored by circus ringmasters. The octomaton raised this to one of the slits in its eye. Madame Lefoux spoke into it.

Or at least it sounded like Madame Lefoux. It was odd to hear her cultured, slightly accented, mellow feminine voice coming out of such a big, bulbous creature. "Give me my son and I will leave you in peace, Countess."

"Maman!" yelled Quesnel to the octomaton. Realizing it was his mother and not some nightmarish monster, he began struggling in the vampire queen's arms. To absolutely no avail; she was much, much stronger than he would ever be. The countess merely clutched the boy tighter.

Quesnel began yelling in French. "Stop, Maman. They haven't hurt me. I'm fine. They've been very kind. They feed me sweets!" His pointy chin was set and his voice imperious.

Madame Lefoux said nothing more. It was clear they were at an impasse. The countess was not going to let go of the boy, and Madame Lefoux was not going to let them go anywhere.

Alexia edged toward her sister, sensing that very soon the queen would have no recourse but flight. Leaving Felicity behind in this building was, unfortunately, not really feasible, appealing as the idea might be.

The house swayed on its foundation. Over half of it was now gone, with only the back section still intact, and there was very little holding that in place. The frame and supports were failing. Alexia had often thought London houses were built with far less structural integrity than even her cheapest bustle.

She waddled closer to the vampire queen, careful not to touch her. "Countess, I know you said practicality wouldn't come into it, but this would be an excellent time to swarm, if you could but try."

The countess turned eyes upon Alexia that were dilated black with fear. She drew her lips back in a shriek of wrath, exposing all four of her fangs: Feeders and Makers, the second set being ones that only a queen had. Very little of the sense was left in the woman's face. In this particular arena, clearly vampires could end up like werewolves, creatures of emotion, dependent only on the little that was left of their soul to save them.

Lady Maccon was not normally an indecisive individual, but in that second she wondered if she might have chosen the wrong side in this little battle. Even though Madame Lefoux was rampaging through London in a highly unlawful and destructive manner, the countess was behaving like nothing more than a child snatcher. Alexia knew she had the capacity to end this. She could reach out and touch the vampire, turn her human and utterly vulnerable and unable to hold on to the wiry and gyrating Quesnel.

She hesitated, for Alexia could not escape logic, even in crisis. The only diplomatic faux pas worse than a hive queen dying at the hand of a scientist would be if she did so at the hand of Lady Maccon, soulless, muhjah, and werewolf lover.

As if to settle the matter, a tentacle came crashing toward them. It knocked Alexia back. She tripped and stumbled on her weakened ankle and, for what felt like the millionth time that evening, fell back upon her bustle.

She landed next to Felicity and so wiggled over to her and slapped her about the face for a bit. Finally, her sister blinked blue eyes open.

"Alexia?"

The infant-inconvenience was rather sick of this kind of overactive, not to say violent, treatment on behalf of its mother. It thrashed in protest, and Alexia lay back suddenly with an "oof" of distress.

"Alexia!" Felicity may actually have been a little worried. She had never seen her older sister show any sign of weakness. Ever.

Alexia struggled to sit back up. "Felicity, we have got to get away from here."

Felicity helped Alexia to rise, just in time for them to see Lord

Ambrose and two other vampires leap at the octomaton in one tremendous coordinated charge. They draped and strapped down a sheet of fabric, what looked to be a very large tablecloth, over the monster's head. Smart maneuver, for it momentarily blinded Madame Lefoux on the inside. She could neither steer nor attack. The tentacles flailed futilely.

With the octomaton temporarily disabled, the countess sprang into action. So did her drones. They all ran to the open side of the building, the countess moving at speed and clutching Quesnel tight to her breast. Without hesitation, she leaped over the edge and down to the rubble. Quesnel let out a holler of fear at the plunge, quickly followed by what could only be a whoop of exhilaration.

Alexia and Felicity tottered to the edge after them and looked down. Three stories. There was no way *they* could jump and survive, and there was no other apparent way to get down.

However, they did have an excellent perspective on the carnage and could watch the countess and her vampires race between the tentacles of the octomaton and dash away into the moonlit city, swarming at last. The drones followed a little more judiciously, climbing down out of what was left of the house by degrees and then running after, unable to keep up with the supernatural speed of their mistress.

The octomaton screamed, or Madame Lefoux did, and set its flaming tentacle to burn away the tablecloth that obscured its vision. As soon as it was gone, it took the inventor only a moment to realize that her quarry had escaped. Only Alexia and her sister still stood in the swaying building—a structure that was clearly about to come tumbling down.

The monster turned to track the fleeing vampires. Then it crashed off through the streets, heedless of who or what it crushed. Madame Lefoux either hadn't seen Alexia's plight or didn't care to help her. Alexia hoped fervently it was the former, or her friend was indeed more heartless than she had ever thought possible.

"Bugger," said Lady Maccon succinctly.

Felicity gasped at her language, even under such trying circumstances.

Alexia looked at her sister and said, fully knowing that Felicity wouldn't understand what she was talking about, "I'm going to have to arrest her, in the end."

The hive house yielded to gravity, tilting forward in a slow, reluctant creak.

The two women slid toward the edge. Felicity shrieked, and Alexia, in classic fashion given the tenor of her evening, lost her balance and tumbled forward, also yielding to gravity. She went right over, scraping and scrabbling at the splintered floorboards.

She managed to just hang on. Her parasol fell, landing among wall fragments, bits of art, and torn carpet far below. Alexia dangled, desperately holding on to the side of a wooden beam that stuck slightly out above the abyss.

Felicity had hysterics.

Lady Maccon wondered how long her grip was going to hold, grateful she'd removed her gloves. She was rather strong, but it had been a very long week and she wasn't up to her prepregnancy standards. Plus she was carrying a sizable amount of extra weight.

Well, she thought philosophically, *this is a very romantic way to die. Madame Lefoux would certainly feel cut up about it. So that's something. Guilt can be very useful.*

And then, just when she thought all was lost, she felt a puff of air behind her neck and a tingling stirring of the aether.

"What ho!" said Boots. "Can I be of any assistance, Lady Maccon?"

The basket-shaped gondola of Lord Akeldama's private dirigible came down out of the sky like some kind of fat and benevolent savior.

Alexia looked over her shoulder at him from where she dangled. "Not especially. I thought I might simply hang about here for a while, see what transpired."

"Oh, don't fuss about her," yelled Felicity. "Help me! I'm far more important."

Boots ignored Miss Loontwill and directed the pilot to float in until the gondola section of the basket was just under Lady Maccon.

The building lurched at exactly that moment, and Alexia, with a cry, lost her purchase on the beam.

She landed with a thud inside the basket. Her feet failed her and she went backward, once more onto the bustle, which had very little resilience left after the evening's extensive abuse. After a moment's consideration, Alexia just flopped right there on her back. Enough was enough.

"Now me, now meee!" shrieked Felicity, and she seemed to have good cause, for the structure was indeed falling.

Boots looked the young woman up and down, no doubt taking in the bite marks on her white neck. The remains of the house might well be tumbling down that very moment, but he hesitated.

"Lady Maccon?" Boots was a very well-trained drone.

Alexia sucked at her teeth and looked up at her sister. "If we must."

The pilot gave the balloon some lift and it rose. Tizzy put out his arm politely, as though escorting Miss Loontwill in to dinner, and Felicity stepped off the ledge and into the dirigible with all the dignity of a terrified kitten.

The building crumbled behind her. The pilot pulled one of his propeller levers hard, and the airship let out a great puff of steam and surged forward, just in time to escape a large chunk of roof as the last of the hive house crumbled to the ground.

"Where to, Lady Maccon?"

Alexia looked up at Boots, who was crouched over her in evident concern. The child inside her was continuing to express its distress with the night's events. Lady Maccon could think of but one place to go, with her husband out of commission and the moon still high and bright above them. All of her normal hidey-holes were inaccessible: Madame Lefoux's contrivance chamber was out of the picture, and the Tunstells were still in Scotland.

BUR, she was confident, would already be investigating the scene of the destruction below or chasing the octomaton as it crashed through the city. BUR had an arsenal of weaponry at its disposal—their own aethertronic Gatling guns, mini-magnatronic cannons, not to mention Mandalson custard probes. Let *them* try to stop Madame Lefoux for a while. They probably wouldn't be any more successful than she, given the inventor's intellectual skills and mechanical abilities, but they might slow her down. Alexia, after all, had only a parasol. Then she swore, realizing that she didn't even have that anymore. It was lying below, probably buried under half a collapsed building. Ethel was secured in the reticule tied at her waist, but her precious parasol was gone.

"I'm certain you gentlemen would agree with me. It's at times like this that what a girl needs is some serious council on her attire."

Boots and Tizzy looked with deep concern at Alexia's sorry state of dress, her bustle flattened, her hem filthy, her lacy trim soot-covered and burned.

"Bond Street?" suggested Tizzy seriously.

Alexia arched a brow. "Oh, no, this is a profound clothing emergency. Please, take me to Lord Akeldama."

"At once, Lady Maccon, at once." Boots's face was suitably grave behind the muttonchops. The dirigible floated up a little higher and, with another violent puff of steam, set a brisk glide north toward Lord Akeldama's town house.

CHAPTER FIFTEEN

Where Dirigibles Fear to Tread

Lord Akeldama had arranged for a dirigible landing green to be built on the roof of his town house. It was shifted off to one side, allowing room for his aethographor's cuspidor-like receiver. Lady Maccon wondered that she had not noticed this before, but then she didn't spend much time investigating rooftops as part of her daily routine.

The dirigible touched down as light as a meringue. Given that bipedal motion hadn't been doing her many favors that evening, Alexia reluctantly clambered to her feet. Much to her delight, Lord Akeldama had made allowances for a dignified exit from the transport here at its home base. A drone bustled over with a specially designed peaked step ladder that flipped over the side of the gondola basket and then telescoped out to the required height on each side. This permitted one to climb up one side and down the other with great solemnity and aplomb.

"Why," wondered Alexia, "don't you float around already carrying that little ladder?"

"We thought nobody would be disembarking before we returned home."

Felicity climbed out after her sister and stood in haughty disapproval to one side. "What a way to travel! One can hardly countenance how acceptable floating has become. So unnaturally high up. And to land on a roof! Why, Alexia, I can see the tops of buildings. They are not landscaped properly!" All the while complaining, Felicity patted at her hair to ensure it hadn't been disturbed by air travel or her near-death experience.

"Oh, Felicity, do be quiet. I have had quite enough of your prattle for one evening."

Summoned by that secret instinct possessed only by the very best of servants, who always know when the mistress is in residence, Floote appeared at Alexia's elbow.

"Oh, Floote!"

"Madam."

"How did you know I would be here?"

Floote arched a brow as though to say, *Where else would you possibly end up on full-moon night but on Lord Akeldama's rooftop?*

"Yes, of course. Would you please take Felicity here back to our house and lock her in a room somewhere? The back parlor. Or possibly the newly configured wine cellar."

Felicity shrieked, "What?"

Floote looked at Felicity with an expression that was as close to a smile as Alexia had ever seen on his face—a tiny little crinkle at one corner of his mouth. "Consider it done, madam."

"Thank you, Floote."

The butler took a very firm grip on Felicity's arm and began leading her off.

"Oh, and, Floote, please send someone to check around the rubble of the Westminster Hive house right away, before the scavengers get there. I believe I accidentally dropped my parasol. And there might be some nice bits of art lying about."

Floote didn't even flinch at the knowledge that one of the most respected residences in London was now in ruins. "Of course, madam. I assume it is now permitted to give out the address?"

Lady Maccon gave it to him.

He moved smoothly off, dragging the protesting Felicity behind him.

"Sister, really, this is uncalled for. Is it the tooth marks? Is that what has you overset? There are only a few."

"Miss Felicity," Alexia heard Floote say, "do try to behave."

Boots, finished mooring down the dirigible, came up next to Alexia and offered her his arm. "Lady Maccon?"

She took it gratefully. The infant-inconvenience really was being quite troublesome at the moment. She felt as though she'd swallowed a fighting ferret.

"Perhaps you could take me to the, uh, closet, Mr. Bootbottle-Fipps? I feel I ought to lie down. Just for a moment, mind you. There is still a loose hive to deal with. I suppose I should try to determine where Countess Nadasdy has gone. And Madame Lefoux, of course. She should not be allowed to rampage."

"Certainly not, my lady," agreed Boots. Who clearly felt, as Alexia did, that rampaging under any circumstances was uncalled for.

They had barely made it off the roof and down the staircases toward Lord Akeldama's second best closet when a panting drone appeared before them. He was a tall and comely fellow with an affable face, a mop of curly hair, and a loose, floppy way of walking. He also had the most poorly tied cravat Alexia had ever seen within walking distance of Lord Akeldama. She looked with shock at Boots.

"New drone," Boots explained to Lady Maccon before turning amicably to face the young man.

"What ho, Boots!"

"Chip chip, Shabumpkin. Looking for me?"

"Rather!"

"Ah! Need a mo' to see her ladyship squared away properly."

"Oh, no, not just you, my dear chap. Looking for Lady Maccon as well. Care to follow?"

Alexia looked at the young man as though he had crawled from somewhere smelly. "Must I?"

" 'Fraid so, your ladyship. Himself has called an emergency meeting of the Shadow Council," explained the drone.

"But it's full moon—the dewan can't attend."

"Several of us pointed this out to him. Niggling detail, said he."

"Oh, dear. Not at Buckingham, I hope?" Alexia clutched at her stomach, appalled at the very idea of any further travel.

The dandy grinned. "In his drawing room, madam. Where else?"

"Oh, thank goodness. Have Floote follow me there, would you, please? Once he's finished with his current line of business."

" 'Course, Lady Maccon. My pleasure."

"Thank you, Mr., uh, Shabumpkin."

At which Boots straightened his spine, took a firmer grip on Alexia's arm, and guided her carefully down the next few sets of stairs and into Lord Akeldama's infamous drawing room. Once there, Shabumpkin nodded to them amiably and gangled off.

Lord Akeldama was waiting for her. Alexia was unsurprised to note that while she'd been dashing about London tracking an octomaton, the vampire had engaged in nothing more stressful than a change of clothing. He was wearing the most remarkable suit of tails and britches she had ever seen, candy-striped satin in cream and wine. This he had paired with a pink waistcoat of watered silk, pink hose, and pink top hat. His cravat, a waterfall of wine satin, was pinned with a gold and ruby pin, and matching rubies glittered about his fingers, monocle, and boutonniere.

"Can I get you anything, Lady Maccon?" offered Boots after seeing her safely ensconced in a chair, obviously concerned over her evident physical discomfort.

"Tea?" Alexia named the only thing she could think of that universally cured all ills.

"Of course." He vanished after a quick exchange of glances with his master.

However, when the tea was brought in some five minutes later, it was Floote who brought it, not Boots. The butler left quickly but Alexia was in no doubt he'd taken up residence very close to the outside of the door.

Lord Akeldama, in some distress, did not produce his harmonic auditory resonance disruptor, and Alexia did not remind him. She figured she might need Floote's advice on whatever occured next.

"So, my lord?" said she to the vampire, not at all up for dillydallying.

Lord Akeldama got straight to the point. Which was, in and of itself, a marker of his distress.

"My *precious* plum blossom, do you have *any* idea who is sitting in the back alleyway behind the kitchen *right this very moment?*"

Since Alexia was pretty darned convinced she would have spotted the octomaton from the roof, she took her second best guess.

"Countess Nadasdy?"

"Behind the kitchen! By my longest fang! I—" He interrupted himself. "Gracious me, *buttercup*, but how *did* you know?"

Even coping with the violent kicking and squirming in her tummy, Alexia couldn't help but smile. "Now you know how I always feel."

"She swarmed."

"Yes, *finally*. You wouldn't believe what it took to chivy her out of that place. You'd think she was a ghost, so tightly tethered as to never be separated from her fixing point."

Lord Akeldama sat down, took a deep breath, and composed himself. "*Darling* marigold, please don't tell me you're responsible for . . . you know." He fluttered one perfectly white hand in the air, like a dying handkerchief.

"Oh, no, silly. Not me. Madame Lefoux."

"Oh. Of course. Madame Lefoux." The vampire's expression was arrested, deadpan at this latest bit of information.

Lady Maccon swore she could see the cogs and wheels of his massive intellect whirring away behind that effete painted face.

"Because of the little French maid?" He finally hazarded a guess.

Lady Maccon was enjoying having the upper hand for once. She had never dared to hope that someday she would have more information in a crisis than Lord Akeldama.

"Ah, no—Quesnel."

"Her son?"

"Not exactly hers."

Lord Akeldama stood up from his casual lounging posture. "The little towheaded lad the countess has with her? The one who ripped my jacket?"

"That sounds like Quesnel."

"What's the hive queen doing with a French inventor's son?"

"Ah, apparently, Angelique left a will."

Lord Akeldama tapped one fang with the edge of his gold and ruby monocle, pulling all the threads together right before Alexia's eyes. "Angelique is the boy's real mother, and she left him to the tender care of the *hive*? Silly bint."

"And the countess stole him from Genevieve. So Genevieve built an octomaton and destroyed the hive house trying to get him back."

"Upon my word, that's escalating things rather much."

"I daresay it is."

Lord Akeldama stopped tapping and began swinging his monocle back and forth while he took up a slow pace about the room. His white brow creased in one perfect line between the eyebrows.

Lady Maccon rubbed her protesting belly with one hand and sipped tea with the other. For once, the magic liquid was unable to disseminate any beneficial effects. The child was not happy, and tea was not going to pacify the beast.

The monocle stilled.

Alexia straightened up in her chair expectantly.

"The question remains, what is to be done with an entire hive skulking in my back alley?"

"Have them in for tea?" suggested Lady Maccon.

"No, no, not possible, little cream puff. They can't come in here."

Vampires were peculiar about etiquette. "Buckingham Palace? That should be relatively secure."

"No, no. Political nightmare. Vampire queen in the palace? Trust me, *darling*, it is never a good idea to have too many queens in one place, let alone one palace."

"To be really safe and buy us some extra time, we really ought to get her out of London."

"She won't like that at all, but there is *sense* to the suggestion, bluebell."

"How long do we have? I mean to say, how long does a swarming usually last?"

Lord Akeldama frowned. Concerned over whether he should give her this information, she suspected, rather than over any possibility of his not having it. "A newly made queen has months to settle, but an old queen has only a few hours."

Lady Maccon shrugged. Only one solution readily presented itself. It was the safest place she knew of—defensible and secure.

"I will have to take her to Woolsey."

Lord Akeldama sat down. "If you say so, Lady Alpha."

There was something in his tone that gave Alexia pause. He sounded like that when he had recently purchased a particularly nice waistcoat. She couldn't understand why he should be so self-satisfied with this predicament. As her benighted husband would say, *vampires*!

Someone had to do something. They couldn't let the Westminster queen simply cool her heels in an alleyway behind Lord Akeldama's and Lord Maccon's respective houses. What a scandal if the papers ever found *that* out! Alexia very much hoped Felicity was locked away. "It will only be until we can determine what's to be done with her. And how to resolve this situation with Quesnel. Hopefully without destroying any other perfectly innocent buildings." Lady Maccon tilted back her head and yelled, "Floote!"

The rapidity of Floote's appearance suggested he had, indeed, been waiting just outside the door.

"Floote, how many carriages do we have in town?"

"Just the one, madam. Just arrived back in."

"Well, that'll have to do. Hitch up the goers and have it brought round to the back, please. I shall meet you there."

"A journey? But, madam, you are unwell."

"Can't be helped, Floote. I cannot justifiably send a hive of vampires into a den of werewolves alone and without diplomatic assistance. The clavigers would never allow it. No, someone has to go with them, and that someone has to be me. The staff at the castle won't listen to anyone else, not on full moon."

Floote vanished, and Lady Maccon stood and began to make her way with stilted awkwardness out of the drawing room and through Lord Akeldama's house. The vampire followed. About halfway, however, she held up a finger at her host.

The baby inside of her had shifted. It felt a little lighter somehow. Well, who was she to question such a helpful adjustment? She patted her belly approvingly. However, she also rocked from one foot to the other. The infant-inconvenience had come to rest on a certain portion of her anatomy.

"Uh, oh, dear. How embarrassing. I really must visit your . . . uh . . . that is . . . um."

If he could have blushed, Lord Akeldama would have. Instead, he took out a red lace fan from the inside pocket of his jacket and fanned himself vigorously with it while Alexia tottered off to see to the necessary business. She returned several long moments later, feeling better about all aspects of life.

Then she led the way onward through Lord Akeldama's house, behind the grand staircase and past the servants' stairs, through the kitchen, and out the back door. Lord Akeldama minced along solicitously after her.

Behind the house, past such shockingly vulgar objects as dustbins and a clothesline, the hive waited. Much to Lady Maccon's shock, there were gentlemen's undergarments on that clothesline! She closed her eyes and took a deep and fortifying breath. When she opened them again, she looked past the necessities into the delivery alley where a clot of vampires paced restlessly.

Countess Nadasdy was there with Dr. Caedes, Lord Ambrose, the Duke of Hematol, and two other vampires Alexia did not know by name. The hive queen was not in any condition to converse on any topic, mundane or otherwise. She was in obvious mental distress, her movements frenzied and her nerves overset. She paced to and fro, muttering and jerking at any noise. A startled vampire can leap to amazing heights and move at incredible speeds; this ability made the soft, round queen grasshopper-like. Sometimes she fought against one of her male counterparts as though trying to escape from the loose circle they formed around her. Occasionally, she would lash out at one of them, clawing at his face or biting hard into an exposed body part. The male vampire would only gentle her back into the center of the group, his wounds healed by the time she resumed her twitching.

Lady Maccon noted with relief that Quesnel had been transferred to Dr. Caedes's care. It was clearly not safe for a mortal to be near the queen. Alexia caught the young scamp's violet eye under his floppy thatch of yellow hair. He looked terrified. She gave him a wink and he brightened almost instantly. Theirs was not a long acquaintance, but she had once supported him in the matter of an exploding boiler, and he had trusted her implicitly ever since.

Alexia moved forward, only to pause, finding herself alone and Lord Akeldama left standing in a dramatic pose on the stoop behind her. Frankly, she had been surprised he even considered walking through the kitchen. He'd probably never even seen that part of his house before.

She turned back. "You aren't facilitating this conversation?" Never had she known Lord Akeldama to step aside when something significant was afoot.

The rove vampire chuckled. "My little *dumpling*, the countess would not tolerate my presence in her current condition. And I could hardly stand to endure such waistcoats as Dr. Caedes seems to favor these days. Not to mention the universal lack of headgear."

Alexia looked over the vampires with new eyes. It was true; the gentlemen seemed to have misplaced their top hats during the kerfuffle.

"No, no, my *cream puff*, this is *yours* to play now." He spared her a worried glance. She had not stopped clutching her protruding belly since she first reappeared in his drawing room. "If you are certain you can handle it with sufficient dexterity."

Lady Maccon took a fortifying breath, almost overbalancing. Responsibility was responsibility and no baby was going to prevent her from seeing everything right. Her world, currently, was in disarray. If Alexia Maccon was good at nothing else, she was good at putting things to rights and bringing order to the universe. Right now the Westminster Hive needed her managerial talents. She could hardly shirk her duty for so mere a trifle as pregnancy.

Without a backward glance at Lord Akeldama, she strode forward into the midst of the panicking hive. Or she would like to say she strode; it was more a gimpy kind of shuffle.

"Wait, Alexia! Where is your parasol?" Lord Akeldama sounded more concerned than she had ever heard him, devoid of both italics and pet names.

Lady Maccon gesticulated in an expressive way and yelled back to him, "Underneath what's left of the hive house, I suspect." Then she faced her muhjah duties full-on. "Right, you lot. I've had about enough of this waggish behavior."

Countess Nadasdy turned and hissed at her. Actually hissed.

"Oh, really." Lady Maccon was revolted. She looked at the Duke of Hematol. "Would you like me to sober her up?" She twiddled her naked fingers at him.

Lord Ambrose snarled and leaped, in one of those fantastic supernatural feats of athleticism, to place himself between Lady Maccon and his queen.

"Apparently not. Have you a better solution?"

The duke said, "We could not have her mortal and vulnerable, not in such an unprotected state."

Behind them, clattering through the alley behind the long row of town houses, the Woolsey carriage drew to a stop, the chestnut travelers hitched up rather than the parade bays. The countess leaped toward it as though it were some fearsome foe. Lord Ambrose held her back by snaking both arms around her from behind in an embarrassingly intimate gesture. It was only an old-fashioned gingerbread coach with a massive crest on its side and just that kind of superfluous decadence that would appeal to Lord Akeldama but that Lady Maccon had always felt was ever so slightly embarrassing for Woolsey. It was built to make an impression, not for speed or nimbleness. But Alexia hardly thought even such grandiose ugliness warranted a vampire attack.

"Well, then, as Lord Akeldama will not invite you in for tea and a sit-down, I was thinking I might suggest we retreat to Woolsey for the time being. Take refuge there."

All the assembled vampires, even the countess, who seemed to have only a limited ability to follow what was going on around her, paused to look at Lady Maccon as though she had just donned Grecian robes and begun hurling peeled grapes at them.

"Are you certain, Lady Maccon?" asked one of them, almost timidly for a vampire.

The doctor stepped forward, elongated and frail-looking, for all he held the struggling Quesnel as though the boy weighed no more than one of Madame Lefoux's automated feather dusters. "You are inviting us to stay, Lady Maccon? At Woolsey?"

Alexia did not see the source of their persistent confusion. "Well, yes. But I've only the one carriage, so you and the boy and the countess had best come with me. The others can run behind. Try to keep up."

Lord Ambrose looked at Dr. Caedes. "It is unprecedented."

Dr. Caedes looked at the Duke of Hematol. "There is no edict for this."

The duke looked at Lady Maccon, rolling his head from one side to the other. "The marriage was unprecedented, and so is the forthcoming child. She but maintains her brand of tradition." The duke moved toward his mistress. Cautiously, careful not to make any sudden movements.

"My Queen, we have an option." He spoke precisely, careful to enunciate each and every word.

Countess Nadasdy shook herself. "We have?" Her voice sounded hollow and very far away, as though emanating from the bottom of a mine. It reminded Alexia of something, but with the child inside her creating a fuss and the prospect of a long drive ahead, she couldn't remember what.

The countess looked to Lord Ambrose. "Who must we kill?"

"It is an offer freely given. An *invitation.*"

For a moment, Countess Nadasdy seemed to return to herself, focusing completely on the faces of her three most treasured hive members. Her supports. Her tentacles. "Well, let us take it, then. No time to spare." She looked around, cornflower-blue eyes suddenly sharp. "Is that *laundry*? Where *have* you brought me?"

With a nod to Lady Maccon, Lord Ambrose hustled his queen into the Woolsey carriage. Quicker than the mortal eye could follow, he ducked back out again, his movements made smoother without the need to monitor a hat. He leaped to the driver's box, unceremoniously dismissing the perfectly respectable coachman who sat there and taking up the reins himself. Lady Maccon arched a brow at him.

"Pardon me?"

"I once raced chariots," he explained with a grin that showed off his fangs to perfection.

"I do not think it is quite the same thing, Lord Ambrose," remonstrated Alexia.

Dr. Caedes and Quesnel climbed inside next. And then, reluctantly, Lady Maccon. She struggled a bit with the steps, and no vampire was willing to offer her any kind of assistance, no touching, not even for politeness' sake. Once inside, she was unsurprised to find that the vampires were seated together on one bench so that she must sit alone on the other.

Lord Ambrose whipped the horses up and they took off at a canter, far too fast for the crowded streets of London. The clattering on the cobbles was awfully loud, and the carriage seemed to gyrate around the turns far more than Alexia had noticed before. Her belly protested the swaying.

It ordinarily took just under two hours to reach Woolsey from central London, less time for a werewolf in full fur, of course. The Count of Trizdale once claimed to have run it in his highflyer coach in only an hour and a quarter. Lord Ambrose, it seemed, was intent on trying to break that record.

Within London, the streets were worn enough into ruts for relatively smooth travel, and even though he had been tethered to Mayfair for hundreds of years, Lord Ambrose knew the way. Plenty of time to study maps, Alexia supposed. They took the lesser used road toward West Ham. However, upon exiting the city, everything went awry.

Not that the evening's events prior to that moment had been all sugared violet petals. But still.

First, and worst, so far as Lady Maccon was concerned, they hit the dirt road of the countryside. It had never bothered her overmuch before, and the carriage was well sprung and padded inside. But the fast pace combined with more-than-was-normal jiggling did not amuse the infant-inconvenience. Fifteen minutes of that and Alexia felt a new bodily sensation commence—a dull ache in the small of her back. She wondered if she had damaged herself during one of the evening's many bustle-crushing dismounts.

Then they heard Lord Ambrose yell and smelled acrid smoke. Here, away from looming shadows of the city buildings and under the full moon's light, everything was much easier to see. Alexia watched through the window as one of their vampire escorts put on a burst of speed, drew alongside the carriage, and leaped. The coach lurched but did not slow, and there came the sound of the roof above them being beaten viciously.

"Are we on fire?" Lady Maccon shifted herself into a better position, drew down the window sash, and stuck her head out into the rushing air, trying to see behind them.

It might have been difficult for her to make out their enemy, had there been a man on horseback or another carriage behind them, but the thing skittering after them over the fields and between the hedgerows was doing so on eight massive tentacles. Well, seven massive tentacles—it had the eighth in front of it spurting fire at the carriage. It was also several stories high.

Alexia pulled her head back inside. "Dr. Caedes, I suggest you have your charge there show himself. It might prevent Genevieve from actually killing us."

The carriage lurched again and picked up speed. The vampire on the roof, having succeeded in beating out the flames, had jumped off. But they were moving nowhere near as fast as they had initially—the horses were tiring, if not becoming winded and destroyed by such cruel speed.

The octomaton was gaining on them, and Woolsey still a good distance away.

Dr. Caedes changed his grip on the boy and tried to force Quesnel to stick his head out of the carriage window. Quesnel was not at all inclined to do anything any of the vampires wanted. Alexia gave her friend's son an almost imperceptible nod, at which point he did as directed. He stuck not only his head but also one skinny arm outside, waving madly at the creature behind them.

The ache in Lady Maccon's back intensified and she felt her stomach lurch, wavelike. She'd never experienced such a sensation before. She let out a squeak of alarm and fell back against the padded wall of the coach. Then it was gone.

Alexia poked at her stomach with a finger. "Don't you dare. Now is most inopportune! Besides, arriving early to a party is disrespectful."

The octomaton fell back just far enough to allow the carriage to slow, but if Alexia knew Madame Lefoux, this was only giving the inventor time to come up with a new plan of attack. Genevieve must realize Alexia was also in the carriage and that they were headed to Woolsey. There was no other reason to be on that road at that time, for aside from everything else, no one traveled to Barking at night and no one *ever* traveled to Barking *at speed.*

"Oh, my goodness." Lady Maccon had the most uncomfortable feeling that she had lost some of her legendary control, over the physical, if not the mental. A wet sensation in her lower area indicated that her bustle, and quite possibly the rest of her dress, really was not going to survive this night. Then came that wavelike feeling again, starting at the top of her stomach and working its way down.

Dr. Caedes, who wasn't a real doctor, was nevertheless perceptive enough to see that the tenor of Lady Maccon's distress had changed.

"Lady Maccon, have you commenced? That would be most unfortunate timing."

Alexia frowned. "No, I absolutely forbid it. I will not—Oooh." She ended on a groan.

"I believe you have."

Quesnel perked up at this. "Bully! I've never seen a birth before." He turned big lavender eyes onto the now-sweating Lady Maccon.

"You're not going to tonight, either, young man," Alexia reprimanded between puffs of breath.

The countess, who was still twitchy as all get out and only partly paying attention to any conversation, looked with bright suspicious eyes at Alexia. "You can't. Not while I am here with you. What if *it* comes out and we have to touch it? Dr. Caedes, throw her out of the carriage at once."

Even with the strange wave sensation and a burgeoning pain, Alexia was quick enough to reach into her reticule and pull out Ethel before Dr. Caedes could stop her.

Not that he tried. Instead, he attempted to reason with the countess. "We can't, my queen. We need her to get us inside the house. She is our invitation."

Lady Maccon felt compelled to add, "And this is *my* carriage! If anyone is getting out, it's you!" She felt an additional downward pressure from the child inside her. "No, not *you*!" Then she looked wildly around. "This is not allowed," she said in a blanket kind of way, including both the imminent baby, the vampires, Quesnel, and the octomaton. She looked down at her belly. "I will not begin our relationship with disobedience. I get enough of *that* from your father."

The countess looked like she had eaten something foul, like a piece of fresh fruit. "I cannot be in proximity to an abomination! Do you know what might transpire?"

Now, this form of panic could be useful. "No, why don't you enlighten me?"

Too late. A crushing, grinding noise came from behind them. Alexia had no idea what the octomaton was up to, but when she stuck her head out of the window, she saw it was no longer following them. The carriage had turned off the main track, into the long weaving roadway that wended through Woolsey's grounds.

They were almost home.

Mere moments later, a tremendous crash came in front of them and the carriage slewed to one side and came to a rocking halt. Out of the window Alexia could see Woolsey just ahead atop its rise of ground, silvered under the moonlight, looking as though it had its own form of stone tentacles embodied in multiple flying buttresses.

It might as well have been a thousand leagues away, for the octomaton had felled a tree across the road before them. Lord Ambrose could not turn the carriage around, even if the high hedges permitted such a thing, for behind them the massive metal creature barred the way. The vampire escort, panting from their long run, instinctively formed a barrier before the coach, as though they could stop any attack by physically imposing themselves between the octomaton and their queen.

Alexia glanced around in desperation. She was among enemies, exhausted, and about to give birth. She was running out of options and would have to trust one of the vampires. Opening the carriage door, she yelled at the vanguard, "Your Grace, I have a proposition for you."

The Duke of Hematol turned to face her.

"We need some help, and we need a distraction if we are to make our destination."

"What do you suggest, Lady Maccon?"

"That we call out the hounds."

"And how do we do that? You definitely can't run to the castle from here, none of us can carry you to Woolsey, and no claviger will take the word of a vampire messenger."

"Listen to me. You tell them that Lady Maccon says it is *a matter of urgency.* The Alpha female requires her pack to attend her, regardless of their current state." *I will have to change the secret phrase now.*

"But—"

"It will work. You must trust me." She wasn't certain, of course. *A matter of urgency* was pack code for Lady Maccon acting as muhjah. She had rarely had to use the summons, and then only with a perfectly sane husband or Beta, never with only clavigers. Would the message even be understood?

The duke gave her one hard, long look. Then he whirled and ran, leaping the fallen tree with almost as much ease as a werewolf, heading directly for the castle, supernatural speed in full effect.

With one of their oldest and wisest gone and the great metal octopus looming above their unprotected queen, the vampires around Lady Maccon went ever so slightly insane themselves. Not as mad as the countess, but definitely wild. One of them charged the octomaton, only to be swept easily aside.

The metal creature raised up a tentacle to its eye slit, once more opening the tip and flipping out the bullhorn that allowed Madame Lefoux to speak.

"Give me Quesnel. You are out of options." There came a short pause. "I can hardly believe it of you, Alexia, helping vampires. They tried to kill you!"

Alexia stuck her head out of the door-side window of the carriage and yelled back, "So? Recently, you also tried to kill me. In my experience, murder could almost be an expression of affection." It took an enormous effort to yell, and she fell back into the carriage, moaning and clutching at her stomach. She hated to admit it, even to herself, but Alexia Maccon was afraid.

Then came the noise, an eerie blessing of a sound, one that Alexia had grown to love very much over the past year or so.

Wolves. Howling.

CHAPTER SIXTEEN

A Clot of Vampires

The Woolsey Pack was a large collective, a good dozen strong. And a dozen werewolves is like two dozen regular wolves in size alone. Normally, they were also one of the better-behaved packs. When other packs were feeling snide, they called Woolsey *tame.* But no werewolf behaves himself on full moon.

Lady Maccon knew very well that she was taking a grave risk. She also knew her smell would attract her husband. Even in the throes of full-moon's curse, he would run to her. He might try to kill her, but he would come. He was Woolsey's Alpha for a reason, with enough charisma to hold his pack and drag them with him, no matter how strong the need to break away and trail blood and raw meat across the countryside. They would all follow him, which meant he would bring them all to her.

So it proved to be.

They poured out the lower doors and windows of the castle, howling to the skies. They evolved into a kind of cohesive moving liquid, flowing down the hillside as one silvered blob, like mercury on a scientist's palm. The howling became deafening as they neared, and they were swifter than Alexia remembered, full of eternal rage at a world that forced such a cost of immortality upon them. Any human would flee, and Alexia could see that even the vampires were tempted to run away from the massive supernatural force charging toward them.

At the front ran the biggest of the lot, a brindled wolf with yellow eyes, intent on but one thing—a smell on the evening breeze. It was the scent of mate, and lover, and partner, and fear, and something new coming. Near to that, twining with it, was the scent of young boy, fresh meat to be consumed. Underneath was the smell of rotten flesh and old bloodlines—other predators invading his territory. Dominating it all was the odor of industry, a monstrous machine, another enemy.

Lady Maccon stepped out of the carriage and slammed the door behind her, placing herself before the boy and the queen, knowing that she would be the last possible defense, that if nothing else, she had her bare hands.

Her legs, however, refused to obey her. She found herself leaning against the door, wishing she had her parasol for leverage.

The pack was there. The blur of fur and teeth and tail turned into individual wolves. Lord Conall Maccon came to a sliding halt before his wife.

Alexia never quite knew how to handle her husband when he was in such a state. There was nothing of the man she loved in those yellow eyes, not during full moon. Her only hope was that he would perceive the octomaton as more of a threat than the vampires. That his driving instinct would be to defend territory first and eat later, thus ignoring her and Quesnel, who represented fresh meat.

Her hope proved to be the case, for Conall's yellow eyes flashed once, almost human, and he lolled his tongue out at her. Then the pack turned in a body and launched itself at the octomaton. One wolf per tentacle, the remaining four at the neck. Supernatural teeth were guided by instinct toward joints and arteries, even if those joints were made of ball bearings and pulleys and those arteries hydraulic steam-powered cables.

Alexia could only watch, admiring the grace in their amazingly high leaps. She held Ethel in one hand, but the gun dangled uselessly. She was nowhere near good enough to hit even something the size of the octomaton without also risking a wolf. The vampires made no move to help. This might have been because they were afraid a werewolf would take this ill and start attacking them, or it might be because they were vampires.

Lady Maccon could make out some of the pack by their markings. There was Channing, easiest to spot because of his pure white coat; and Lyall, smaller than the rest and more nimble, almost vampirelike in his speed and dexterity; and Biffy, darkest of all the pack with his ox-blood stomach fur, abandoned and utterly vicious in his movements. But Alexia's eye was ever drawn, again and again, to the brindled coat of the largest wolf as he leaped up and savaged some portion of the octomaton, landed, and then leaped again.

To have had any real effect, the wolves should have all concentrated on one tentacle together, or all gone for the neck, but they were moonstruck. Even under the best of circumstances, only a few werewolves fully retain their capacity for human intelligence while in wolf form. Full moon was not the best of circumstances.

The octomaton was built for many things but not, apparently, for a full-pack assault. True, it was well armored and mostly metal, but Madame Lefoux had not used any silver, so it was vulnerable, especially in such numbers. But the Frenchwoman was not remaining idle. Oh, no. Madame Lefoux had those vicious tentacles in play, spraying fire and shooting wooden stakes. Alexia knew it was only a matter of time before the inventor became desperate enough to once more bring out the tentacle that shot lapis solaris.

Then Lady Maccon caught sight of a white floating blob behind the top of the octomaton, sailing the aether breezes swiftly in her direction—a small private dirigible.

Another contraction hit her hard. Alexia doubled over and slid down the side of the carriage, slumping to the ground, leaving the door vulnerable to attack. It was the first time the wave sensation had actually hurt. Curling against the involuntary movements of her own body, she looked up and over to the east.

She couldn't help but cry out—not from the pain but from what she saw. There was a distinct pinking to the cold silvery blue of the night sky.

She had to get them all to the safety of the castle.

She looked to Lord Ambrose, now standing over her barring the door, defending his queen. "We must bring the creature down somehow, buy us enough time to get to Woolsey. *The sun is rising.*"

The vampire's eyes went black with fear. The sun would stop werewolves in their tracks, turning them back to human shape. It would slow some of the younger members, making them vulnerable, and it would do permanent damage to Biffy, who lacked the necessary control. But it would kill the vampires, every last one of them, even the queen.

Alexia thought of something. "Find me a litter, my lord."

"What, Lady Maccon?"

"Tear off the roof of the carriage or remove part of the driving box. With one vampire at either end, you could use it to carry me to Woolsey. No one would have to touch me, there would be no loss of strength. We could make a break for it."

"Strategic retreat. Excellent notion." He leaped atop the driver's box.

Lady Maccon heard a loud ripping noise.

Above, she saw a bright flash of orange light emanate from the side of the dirigible and a loud clang as a massive bullet hit and tore through the mantle of the octomaton. The creature lurched at the impact but did not fall.

Lord Akeldama had sent air support. Alexia had no idea what kind of weapon the drones had, possibly a tiny cannon, or an elephant gun, or an aethero-modified blunderbuss, but she didn't care. It fired again.

By the time the second projectile hit its mark, Lord Ambrose was back, as was the duke. They rested a wide board on the ground next to Alexia. She managed to slide and squirm her way onto it.

They lifted her up. The queen and Dr. Caedes, carrying Quesnel, leaped out of the top of the torn and burned carriage, jack-in-the-box-like, and took off toward Woolsey, jumping the felled tree. The countess looked particularly odd performing this maneuver with her flowered receiving gown and dumpy figure. Lady Maccon's vampire litter bearers followed. Alexia could do nothing more than grip the sides of the board, desperate not to tumble off. The leap over the fallen tree was pure torture, and she was convinced she would fall when they bumped down, but she managed to hold on.

The wolves were providing enough of a distraction so that Madame Lefoux in the octomaton did not at first see them break for the castle. By the time she did, sending flames blasting after them, they were well out of range.

There was no need to bang on Woolsey's main door; it was wide open, with many of the clavigers and household staff assembled on the front stoop, mouths agape. They had binoculars or glassicals pressed to their faces and were riveted by the battle below. At Lady Maccon's imperious wave, they made a corridor for the vampires to run through, right up to the entrance, at which point everyone stopped abruptly. They waited with a ritual solemnity uncalled for in such dire circumstances.

"What is it *now?*" Alexia was annoyed beyond all reason. She was carried right to the door, like a dressed pig on a dinner platter. *Any moment now,* she thought in a flight of fantasy, *Cook will appear with an apple to stuff into my mouth.*

Lord Ambrose rested the bottom of the board down and the duke tilted it up so that Lady Maccon had merely to slide gently to her feet, finding herself standing.

A quick gesture had her supported on both sides by two of Woolsey's largest clavigers. Thus she managed to hobble inside the entrance of her home.

Still the vampires waited on the front stoop, like some bizarre parody of orphaned puppies—soulful eyed, pathetically scruffy, deadly fanged, immortal orphaned puppies.

Lady Maccon turned ponderously. "Well?"

"Invite us in to stay, Alexia Maccon, Lady of Woolsey, mistress of this domicile." The countess's words were singsong and hymnlike. She clutched a wide-eyed, blubbering Quesnel tightly to her breast—no trace of the scamp left, just terrified boy.

"Oh, for goodness' sake, come in, come in." Alexia frowned, trying to think. They had a goodly number of rooms, but where would it be best to put a whole hive of vampires? She pursed her lips. "Best to get you lot down to the dungeon. It's the only place I can guarantee that there are absolutely no windows, and the sun *is* about to rise."

Rumpet came forward. "Lady Maccon, what have you done?"

The vampires traipsed solemnly into the house. Alexia pointed out the appropriate staircase and they filed wordlessly down.

"You have invited in a queen?" The butler, normally quite a florid man, was ashen.

"I have."

The Duke of Hematol gave her a tired smile as he passed, showing fang, acknowledging the butler's fear as his due. "We can never go back now, you realize, Lady Maccon? Once a queen swarms and relocates, it is forever."

Lady Maccon finally understood Lord Akeldama's smile and why he refused to invite the hive in for tea. Alexia had managed to get his greatest rival out of London, for good. Not only was he potentate, and in charge of his own ring of very specially trained young men, but also he would now be the sole leader of fashion left in central London.

And Lady Maccon was stuck with vampires in her basement. "Curses, I have been rather neatly played."

Another contraction hit her, and she had no more thought for her present domestic predicament. She suspected this was somewhat akin to the pain her husband felt upon changing shape.

Rumpet put out a hand to steady her. "My lady?"

"Rumpet, there is an octomaton on our doorstep."

"So I noticed, my lady. And half of BUR has just arrived as well."

Alexia looked. It was true. Several of BUR's human members, on the octomaton's trail out of London, had finally caught up. She thought she could see Haverbink's tall, strapping form. "Oh, God. The pack will turn on them, they're food." And even as she watched, one of the werewolves left off fighting Madame Lefoux's creature and charged one of the BUR agents. "We must protect them. Get the pack members back inside!"

"Indeed, madam."

"Call up the clavigers. Tell them to bring the necessary equipment and open the silver cabinet."

"Immediately, madam." The butler moved toward a nested triangular alcove formed by the staircase. Next to the large cowbell that he rang at mealtimes there dangled a silver chain. At the end of that chain was a silver key. Next to it was a special glass box containing a large horn. Rumpet broke the glass with one swift punch of his gloved hand. He placed the horn to his lips and blew.

Not the most dignified of sounds emanated forth, a kind of farting noise. But it rattled through the castle in a way that suggested the sound had been manufactured specifically to permeate rock. The clavigers instantly assembled around Rumpet in the hallway. Pack policy dictated that every pack member have at least two clavigers. Lord Maccon had six these days, and there were a few extras loitering about as well.

Rumpet used the key to open the silver cabinet, an old mahogany monstrosity that gave no clue as to its true contents. Inside, instead of the usual household valuables—candlesticks, baby spoons, and the like—was the claviger kit. Displayed in neat rows and on special hooks were silver manacles, enough pairs for every member of the pack; silver knives; a few precious bottles of lapis lunearis; and, most importantly, the fishing nets. These were spun of silver cord, weighted at the corners, and used to capture and weaken a wolf without damage. Dangling from little hooks in each door were fifty fine silver chains with fifty fine silver whistles.

The clavigers, grim-faced, armed themselves and took up the nets. Each put a whistle over his head. They were so high-pitched that no human ear could possibly make out the sound, but wolves and dogs were violently affected by the noise.

Alexia thought of something. "Try to bring in Biffy first. Remember he's still susceptible to pup-stage sun damage. Take care—he'll be the most vicious. Oh, my goodness, what will I say if he accidentally eats somebody?"

Six of the biggest and best clavigers ran to the stables, and Alexia heard the roaring sound of the steam-powered penny-farthing wagons starting. Two clavigers per wagon—one to steer and one to cast the net—they roared out and down the hillside, steam trailing in a white cloud behind them. The other clavigers ran after.

Lady Maccon witnessed very little of the battle after that. She leaned against Rumpet and tried to watch, but contractions kept distracting her, and the fighting below was nothing more to her unfocused mind than a puddinglike mass of clavigers, wolves, and steam from penny-farthings and an octomaton. Occasionally, a spurt of fire jetted into the air or a glittering waterfall of silver net was cast upward.

Eventually she gave up. "Rumpet, help me to the bottom of the stair."

The butler did so, and Alexia sank gratefully down onto the steps of the grand staircase. "Now, please go down and ensure that the vampires are locked in. The last thing we need is them on the loose."

"At once, my lady."

Rumpet disappeared and returned later, grim-faced.

"That bad?"

"They are complaining about the accommodations and demanding feather pillows, my lady."

"Of course they are." Alexia doubled over in pain as another contraction ripped through her. Dimly, she saw Lord Akeldama's dirigible float in to a graceful landing in the front courtyard of Woolsey. Boots and the airship company leaped agilely out of the basket and lashed the craft to a hitching post.

The first set of clavigers returned at that point, dragging a netted wolf with the aid of a penny-farthing wagon. It took four of them to get him up the steps and into the castle, even with the silver net burning him into submission. It wasn't Biffy, but it looked to be one of the other youngsters, Rafe.

Alexia's attention was refocused into moaning as her pains became, if possible, worse. She looked for Rumpet, but he was busy supervising the unloading, seeing to it that the young wolf was dragged down into the dungeon and locked away. Alexia spared a moment to hope that all the vampires had gone into one of the cells together, or things were about to get very complicated, indeed.

"Conall!" she yelled through the pain, even knowing he was in wolf form and that he would be the hardest to catch and the last to return home. "Where is he?" She was irrationally convinced that he should be with her right that very moment.

At which juncture, a wide, cool cloth was placed across her brow and a soft reliable voice said exactly the right thing. "Here, madam, drink this."

A cup was pressed against her lips and Alexia sipped. Strong, milky, and restorative, exactly how she liked it best. Tea.

She opened her eyes, previously screwed closed in anguish, to see the fine lined face of an elderly gentleman, nondescript and familiar. "Floote."

"Good evening, madam."

"Where did you come from?"

Floote gestured behind him where the dirigible was still visible through the open front door. Tizzy and Boots hovered in the doorway, looking at Alexia in horror and with an air that suggested they would rather be anywhere else but there.

"I caught a lift, madam."

"Eep!" squeaked Tizzy as he was pushed aside by another group of clavigers dragging another netted wolf home. *Hemming,* thought Alexia. *Had to be.* Only Hemming whined like that. They muscled their captive through the hallway and toward the dungeon stairs without need of an order from the panting and writhing Lady Maccon.

The previous group came back up, passing them on the stairs.

"Back out," ordered their Alpha female, "and concentrate on finding Biffy. The others can take the sun."

"I thought werewolves could withstand sunlight?" asked Boots.

Alexia moaned long and low before answering. "Yes. But not when still learning control."

"What'll happen to him if he doesn't make it in?"

Rumpet reappeared at that juncture. "Ah, Mr. Floote." He acknowledged his butler peer with a slight bow.

"Mr. Rumpet," replied Floote. And then, turning his attention back to Lady Maccon, "Now, madam, do concentrate and try to inhale deeply. Breathe through the pain."

Alexia glared at her butler. "Easy for you to say. Have you ever done this?"

"Certainly not, madam."

"Rumpet, did all the vampires get sorted?"

"Mostly, my lady."

"What do you mean, *mostly*?"

The conversation paused at that while everyone waited courteously for Lady Maccon to let out another part scream part howl of anger as the agony rippled through her body. They all pretended not to notice her thrashing. It was very polite of them.

"Well, a few of the vampires spread themselves about. So we'll have to put some of ours in with them."

"What's the world coming to? Vampires and werewolves sleeping together," quipped Alexia sarcastically.

One of the clavigers, a cheerful, freckled blighter who had performed Scottish ballads for the queen herself on more than one occasion, said, "It's quite sweet, really. They've snuggled up with each other."

"Snuggled? The wolf should be tearing the vampire apart."

"Not anymore, my lady. Look."

Alexia looked. The sun was up, its first rays cresting the horizon. It was going to be a bright, clear summer day. It was all too much, even for the most sensible preternatural. Lady Maccon panicked. "Biffy! Biffy's not yet inside! Quickly!" She gestured the clavigers. "Get me up. Get me out there. Get me to him! He could die!" Alexia was starting to cry, both from the pain and from the thought of poor young Biffy lying out there, burning alive.

"But, my lady, you're about to, well, uh, give birth!" objected Rumpet.

"Oh, that's not important. That can wait." Alexia turned. "Floote! Do something."

Floote nodded. He pointed to one of the clavigers. "You, do as she asks. Boots, you take the other side." He looked down at his mistress. Of course, Alessandro Tarabotti's daughter would be difficult. "Madam, whatever you do, don't push!"

"Bring blankets," yelled Lady Maccon at the remaining clavigers and Rumpet. "Rip those curtains down if you must. Most of the pack is out there naked! Oh, this is all so embarrassing."

Boots and the freckled claviger formed a kind of litter by linking their crossed arms and hoisted Lady Maccon up. She threw an arm around each, and the two young men part ran and part stumbled their way back out the door and down the seemingly endless hillside toward the carnage below.

The octomaton was down, the result of too many of its tentacles torn off during battle. As she neared, Alexia could see the now-naked bodies of the pack lying fallen—bloodied, bruised, and burned. Scattered among them were the severed tentacles of the octomaton plus some of its guts: bolts, pulleys, and engine parts. Here and there, a claviger or BUR member who hadn't moved fast enough was limping or clutching at a wounded limb, but thankfully none of them seemed seriously injured. The werewolves, on the other hand, lay floppy and nonsensical, like so much fried fish. Most of them looked like they were simply sound asleep, the standard reaction to full-moon bone-benders. But none were healing under the direct rays of the sun. Even immortality had its limits.

Clavigers were running around covering the ones they could with blankets and pulling others back toward the house.

"Where's Biffy?" Alexia couldn't see him anywhere.

Then she realized there was someone else she couldn't see, and her voice rose in terror to a near shriek. "Where's Conall? Oh no, oh no, oh no." Alexia's commanding tone turned into a chant of keening distress only offset by the need to scream as another contraction hit her. She loved Biffy dearly, but all her worry was now transferred to an even more important love—her husband. *Was he injured? Dead?*

The two young men carried her, tripping and faltering, in and around the wreckage until, near the great metal bowler hat that was the fallen head of the octomaton, an oasis of calm awaited them.

Professor Lyall, wearing an orange velvet curtain wrapped about him like a toga and still looking remarkably dignified, was marshaling the troops and issuing orders.

Upon seeing the amazing vision of his Alpha female, carried by two young men, in clear distress—both the lady and the young men—wending toward him, he said, "Lady Maccon?"

"Professor. Where is my husband? Where is Biffy?"

"Oh, of course, preternatural touch. Very good idea."

"Professor!"

"Lady Maccon, are you all right?" Professor Lyall moved closer, inspecting her closely. "Have you *started*?" He looked at Boots, who raised both eyebrows expressively.

"Where is Conall?" Alexia practically shrieked.

"He's fine, my lady. Perfectly fine. He took Biffy inside, out of the sun."

"Inside?"

"Inside the octomaton. With Madame Lefoux. Once she realized, she opened the hatch and let them in."

Lady Maccon swallowed down her fear, almost sick with relief. "Show me."

Professor Lyall led them to the octomaton's head, around one side, and then *rat-tat-tatted* on it diffidently. A door, previously invisible it was so seamlessly integrated into the octomaton's armor plating, popped open and Genevieve Lefoux looked out.

Lady Maccon wished fervently at that moment that she had her parasol with her. She would have greeted the Frenchwoman with one very hard whack to the head, friend or no, for getting them all into such a pickle. Justified or not, the inventor had caused everybody a good deal of unnecessary bother.

"Professor Lyall. Yes?"

"Lady Maccon, to see her husband." The Beta stepped aside to allow the Frenchwoman to catch sight of the sweating and clearly distressed Alexia and her improvised transport.

"Alexia? Are you unwell?"

Alexia was quite definitely *at her limit*. "No, no, I am *not*. I have been gallivanting all over London chasing you or being chased by you. I have watched the city burn and the hive house collapse and have fallen out of a dirigible—*twice*! I am in imminent danger of giving birth. And I have *lost my parasol*!" This last was said on a rather childish wail.

A different voice came from inside—deep, commanding, and tinged with a Scottish accent. "That my wife? Capital. She's just the thing to get the pup his legs back."

Genevieve's head disappeared with an "oof" as though she had been dragged forcibly backward, and Lord Maccon's head emerged instead.

The earl was looking perfectly fine, if a little sleepy. Werewolves usually slept the full day through after a full moon. It was testament to both Conall's and Lyall's strength that they were up and moving, although both were rather clumsy about it. Conall described being awake the night after as akin to playing tiddlywinks, drunk, with a penguin—confusing and slightly dreamlike. His hair was wild and unkempt, and his tawny eyes were soft and buttery, mellowed by battle and victory.

He caught sight of his wife. "Ah, my love, get inside, would you? No way to get Biffy back to safety without your touch. Good of you to come. Interesting choice of transport."

At which juncture, his wife threw back her head and screamed.

Lord Conall Maccon's expression changed instantly to one of absolute panic and total ferocity. He charged out of the octomaton and bounded to his mate. He tossed poor Boots out of his way with a mere flick of the wrist and took Lady Maccon into his own arms.

"What's wrong? Are you—You canna! Now isna a good time!"

"Oh, no?" panted his wife. "Well, tell that to the child. This is all *your* fault, you do realize?"

"My fault, how could it possibly . . . ?"

He trailed off as a different howl of agony came from inside the octomaton's head and Madame Lefoux looked back out. "Young Biffy could use your presence, my lord."

The earl growled in annoyance and made his way over to the door. He shoved Alexia inside first, following after.

It was very cramped quarters. Madame Lefoux had designed the guidance chamber for only two occupants, herself and Quesnel. Lord Maccon accounted for about that number on his own, plus the pregnant Alexia, and Biffy sprawled on the floor.

It took a moment for Lady Maccon's eyes to adjust to the inner gloom, but she saw soon enough that Biffy was burned badly down one leg. Much of the skin was gone—blistered and blackened most awfully.

"Should I touch him? He might never heal."

Lord Maccon slammed the door closed against the wicked sun. "Blast it, woman, what possessed you to come down here in such a state?"

"How is Quesnel?" demanded Madame Lefoux. "Is he unharmed?"

"He's safe." Alexia did not mention he was currently locked in a dungeon with a vampire queen.

"Alexia"—Madame Lefoux clasped her hands together and opened her green eyes wide and looked pleading—"you know it was my only choice? You know I had to get him back. He's all I have. She stole him from me."

"And you couldn't come to me for help? Really, Genevieve, what kind of feeble friend do you take me for?"

"She has the law on her side."

Alexia clutched at her stomach and moaned. She was being flooded by the most overwhelming sensation—the need to push downward. "So?"

"You are muhjah."

"I might have been able to come up with a solution."

"I hate her more than anything. First she steals Angelique, and now Quesnel! What right has she to—"

"And your solution is to build a ruddy great octopus? Really, Genevieve, don't you think you might have overreacted?"

"The OBO is on my side."

"Oh, are they really? Now that *is* interesting. That plus taking in former Hypocras members?" Alexia was momentarily distracted by the need to give birth. "Oh, yes, husband, I meant to tell you this. It seems the OBO is developing an antisupernatural agenda. You might want to look into—"She broke off to let out another scream. "My goodness, that *is* uncommonly painful."

Lord Maccon turned ferocious yellow eyes on the inventor. "Enough. She has other things to attend to."

Genevieve looked closely at Alexia. "True, that does seem to be the case. My lord, have you ever delivered a baby before?"

The earl paled as much as was possible, which was a good deal more than normal given he was holding on to his wife's hand. "I delivered a litter of kittens once."

The Frenchwoman nodded. "Not quite the same thing. What about Professor Lyall?"

Lord Maccon looked wild-eyed. "Mostly sheep, I think."

Alexia looked up between contractions. "Were you there when Quesnel was born?"

The Frenchwoman nodded. "Yes, but so was the midwife. I think I remember the principles, and, of course, I've read a good deal on the subject."

Alexia relaxed slightly. Books always made her feel better. Another wave washed through her and she cried out.

Lord Maccon looked sternly at Madame Lefoux. "Make it stop!"

Both women ignored him.

A polite tap came at the door. Madame Lefoux cracked it open.

Floote stood there, his back stiff, his expression one of studied indifference. "Clean cloth, bandages, hot water, and tea, madam." He passed the necessities in.

"Oh, thank you, Floote." The Frenchwoman took the items gratefully. After a moment's thought, she rested them on top of the comatose Biffy, since he was the only vacant surface. "Any words of advice?"

"Madam, sometimes even I am out of options."

"Very good, Floote. Keep the tea coming."

"Of course, madam."

Which was why, some six hours later, Alexia Maccon's daughter was born inside the head of an octomaton in the presence of her husband, a comatose werewolf dandy, and a French inventor.

CHAPTER SEVENTEEN

In Which We All Learn a Little Something About Prudence

Later on, Lady Maccon was to describe that particular day as the worst of her life. She had neither the soul nor the romanticism to consider childbirth magical or emotionally transporting. So far as she could gather, it mostly involved pain, indignity, and mess. There was nothing engaging or appealing about the process. And, as she told her husband firmly, she intended never to go through it again.

Madame Lefoux acted as midwife. In her scientific way, she was unexpectedly adept at the job. When the infant finally appeared, she held it up for Alexia to see, rather proudly as though she'd done all the hard work herself.

"Goodness," said an exhausted Lady Maccon, "are babies customarily that repulsive looking?"

Madame Lefoux pursed her lips and turned the infant about, as though she hadn't quite looked closely before. "I assure you, the appearance improves with time."

Alexia held out her arms—her dress was already ruined anyway—and received the pink wriggling thing into her embrace. She smiled up at her husband. "I told you it would be a girl."

"Why isna she crying?" complained Lord Maccon. "Shouldna she be crying? Aren't all bairns supposed to cry?"

"Perhaps she's mute," suggested Alexia. "Be a sensible thing with parents like us."

Lord Maccon looked properly horrified at the idea.

Alexia grinned even more broadly as she came to a wonderful realization. "Look! I'm not repelled by her. No feelings of revulsion at all. She must be human, not a preternatural. How marvelous!"

A tap came at the octomaton door.

"Yes?" Lord Maccon sung out. He'd decided to stop worrying about the child and was crouched down cooing over her and making silly faces.

Professor Lyall looked in. He'd apparently found the time to change out of the improvised toga and into perfectly respectable attire. He caught sight of his Alpha, who looked up and beamed proudly.

"Randolph, I have a daughter!"

"Felicitations, my lord, my lady."

Alexia nodded politely from her makeshift bed in the corner of the octomaton, only then noticing that she was resting against a pile of cords and springs, and there was some kind of valve digging into the small of her back. "Thank you, Professor. And it would appear that she is not a curse-breaker."

The Beta looked over at the child with a flash of academic interest but no real surprise. "She isn't? I thought preternaturals always breed true."

"Apparently not."

"Well, that is good news. However, and I do hate to interrupt the blessed event, but, my lord, we have several difficulties at the moment that could very much use your attention. Do you think we might repair to a more hospitable venue?"

Lord Maccon crouched over his wife and nuzzled her neck gently. "My dear?"

Alexia stroked his hair back from the temple with her free hand. "I'll give it a try. I would dearly love to be in my own bed."

Lady Maccon had to hold on to both her newborn child and Biffy as Lord Maccon carried her and Professor Lyall carried Biffy back up to the castle. At which juncture Conall declared that Woolsey *smelled rotten.*

Professor Lyall opened his mouth to explain but caught a sharp look from Alexia. So he refrained.

Predicting that his Alpha would find out soon enough on his own, the Beta carried Biffy down to a cell, tended to the pup's still-angry burns with a pat of butter, and chivied him in with the Duke of Hematol as the best of a bad lot of options.

Upstairs it was decided that Madame Lefoux should also be locked up.

"Put her into the one next to the countess and Quesnel," suggested Lady Maccon snidely to her confused husband. "Now, there will be an interesting conversation come nightfall."

"The countess? Countess who?"

Alexia contemplated letting Quesnel out—after all, the boy hadn't done anything wrong—but from previous experience, she saw no reason why having him underfoot might improve matters. Quesnel was an agent of chaos even at the best of times, and life was busy enough without his *help.* Plus, she suspected the best thing for him at the moment was some time with his maman.

"But I just delivered your child!" protested Madame Lefoux.

"And very grateful I am, too, Genevieve." Alexia was always one to give credit where it was due. "However, you rampaged through the streets of London in a massive octopus, and you are going to have to pay for your crimes."

"Preternaturals!" exclaimed the Frenchwoman, disgusted.

"At least this way you are near your boy. He was terribly upset by the attack," yelled Lady Maccon as her husband hauled the struggling inventor away.

Which was when Lord Maccon discovered the reason behind the funny smell. He had a hive of vampires living in his castle.

He came back upstairs fit to be pickled. "Wife!"

Lady Maccon had vanished.

"Floote!"

"She's gone upstairs, sir. To your chambers."

"Of course she has."

Lord Maccon stormed upstairs to find his wife abed, the babe asleep in the crook of one arm. The child had already proved herself perfectly capable of sleeping through both her mother's and her father's vocal exertions. *A very good survival trait,* thought Alexia, wincing as Conall clomped into the room.

"There are *vampires* in my dungeon!"

"Yes, well, where else was I supposed to stash them?"

"The countess swarmed?" The earl leaped to the only possible conclusion. "And you invited them in? *Here*?"

Alexia nodded.

"Great. Wonderful! Brilliant."

Lady Maccon sighed, a kind of sad, quiet noise that calmed Lord Maccon where her yelling would only have aggravated matters. "I can explain."

Conall came to kneel next to the bed, his anger dissipated by her uncharacteristic meekness. His wife must be very tired.

"Very well, explain."

Alexia relayed the events of the night, and by the time she reached the concluding pack-versus-octomaton battle, she was yawning hugely.

"What are we going to do now?" wondered her husband. Even saying it, Alexia could tell from his defeated expression that he was already facing up to the truth—for better or worse, Woolsey Castle now belonged to the Westminster Hive. Or rather, the Woolsey Hive.

Alexia saw him blink back tears and felt her heart clench. She hadn't meant to make such a grave error in judgment, but the deed was done. Her own eyes stung in sympathy.

He nodded. "I rather loved this old place, buttresses and all. But it hasna been my home all that long. I can break from it. The rest of the pack, they are going to be difficult. Ach, my poor pack. I've nae served them verra well these last few months."

"Oh, Conall, it's not your fault! Please don't worry. I'll think of something. I always do." Alexia wanted to find a solution right then and there just to wipe that horrible expression of disappointment off her husband's sweet face, but she could hardly keep her eyes open.

The earl bent and pressed a kiss to his wife's lips and then to his daughter's little forehead. Alexia suspected he was contemplating going back downstairs to check in with Lyall, as there was still a lot to be done that afternoon.

"Come to bed," said his wife.

"You two ladies do look verra peaceful. Perhaps just a little kip."

"Lyall has both Floote and Rumpet helping him. They could run the empire, those three, if they felt like it."

Lord Maccon chuckled and crawled in on Alexia's other side, settling his big body down into the feather mattress.

Alexia sighed contentedly and nestled against him, curled about the baby.

He snuffled once at the nape of her neck. "We need to find a name for the wee one."

"Mmm?" was his wife's only answer.

"I'm nae certain that's a verra good name."

"Mmm."

"Sorry to disturb you, my lord, but the vampires are asking for you." Professor Lyall's voice was quiet and apologetic.

Alexia Maccon came awake with a start to the feel of her husband shifting behind her. He was evidently trying to extract himself from the bed without disturbing her. Poor man, stealth of movement was not one of his stronger character traits. Not in human form at any rate.

"What time is it, Randolph?"

"Just after sunset, my lord. I thought it best to let you sleep the remainder of the day away."

"Oh, yes? And have you been awake the whole time?"

Silence met that.

"Ah. Right. You tell me the lay of the fur, Randolph, and then you go catch some rest."

Alexia heard a faint howling. The younger werewolves, still unable to control change so close to full moon, were back in their fur and imprisoned below for another night. Locked away with vampires.

"Who is seeing to them?" asked the earl as he, too, registered the sound.

"Channing, my lord."

"Oh, blast." All pretense at subtlety abandoned, Lord Maccon jumped out of bed.

This jiggled the baby. A thin, querulous wail started up from just under Alexia's chin. She started violently, for she had, until that moment, entirely forgotten about the child. Her child.

She opened her eyes and looked down. Half a day's intermittent rest had not improved the infant's appearance. She was red and wrinkly, and her face got all scrunched up when she cried.

Conall, obviously still under the impression that Alexia was asleep, hurried around the bed and scooped the tiny creature up. The whining turned to a little snuffling howl, and there in his arms instead of a child, lay a newborn wolf cub.

Lord Maccon nearly dropped his daughter. "God's teeth!"

Alexia sat up, not quite comprehending what she had just seen. "Conall, where's the baby?"

Her husband, mute in shock, proffered the cub at her.

"What have you done to her?"

"Me? Nothing. I simply picked her up. She was perfectly normal and then *poof*."

"Well, she's unquestionably cuter in that form." Alexia was prosaic.

"Here, you take her." Lord Maccon put the squalling furry cub back into his wife's arms.

At which juncture she promptly turned back into a baby. Alexia could feel the bone and flesh shifting under the swaddling clothes. It seemed to be relatively painless, for the infant's cries did not modulate to those of real distress.

"Oh, my." Alexia thought she sounded rather sedate, under the circumstances. "What *have* we gotten ourselves into?"

Professor Lyall's voice was awed. "Never thought I'd live to see a real skin-stalker born in my lifetime. Amazing."

"Is that what it means?" Alexia looked down at the child. "How extraordinary."

Professor Lyall smiled. "I guess it must. So, what's her name, my lady?"

Alexia frowned. "Oh, yes, *that.*"

Lord Maccon grinned, looking down at his wife. "With us for parents, we ought to call her Prudence."

Lady Maccon, however, did not seem to share the joke. "Actually, I rather like that. How about Prudence Alessandra, after my father? And then Maccon, because when Lord Akeldama adopts her, she's going to be an Akeldama."

Lord Maccon looked down at his daughter. "Poor little thing. That's a lot of names to live up to."

"My lord," interjected his Beta, "not that I don't see the importance of this particular matter, but can it wait? Biffy could use your proximity. And the vampires are kicking up quite the fuss. We've no justification for keeping them locked in the dungeon. What are we going to do about them?"

Lord Maccon sighed. "Sadly, it's not them we have to find what to do with—it's us. We can't stay living here, not with a hive in residence as well, and they can't leave. Not now. When you invited the countess in, Alexia, you gave them Woolsey Castle."

"Oh, no, surely not."

Professor Lyall sat down in a nearby chair. Alexia had never seen him look defeated before, but at that moment, Woolsey's Beta looked as close to crushed as any man she'd ever seen.

Lord Maccon looked grim. "Nothing else for it. We'll have to move the pack permanently into London. We will need to buy a second town house to accommodate us all and build dungeons."

Professor Lyall protested this decision. "Where will we run? How will we hunt? My lord, there is no such thing as an urban pack!"

"This is the age of industry, invention, and refined behavior. I suppose Woolsey really will have to learn to move with the times and become civilized." Lord Maccon was resolved.

Alexia looked at her child. "It would only be for sixteen years or so. Until Prudence is grown. Then we could look for a new territory. Sixteen years isn't all that long for a werewolf."

Professor Lyall did not look cheered by this shortening of his urban sentence. "The pack is not going to like this."

"I have made my decision," said his Alpha.

"The queen is not going to like this."

"We'll just have to persuade her it's in the best interest of the Crown."

"I think that's a very good idea," said Countess Nadasdy, entering the room at that moment, followed by Quesnel and Madame Lefoux.

Well, Alexia supposed, *it's her room now.*

"How did you three get out?" griped Professor Lyall.

The countess gave him a withering look. "Did you think I was queen of the vampires for nothing? We are the original inventors of the idea of a mistress of the domain. This is now my domain. No cell in all of Woolsey will hold me for long."

"Pish tosh. She can pick locks." Madame Lefoux crossed her arms and looked at the vampire queen witheringly.

"It was marvelous," added Quesnel, who seemed to be regarding Countess Nadasdy with real respect for the first time.

The countess ignored the Frenchwoman and her child and gave Alexia's baby a wary look. "Just keep that *thing* away from me."

Alexia rocked the newborn at her threateningly. "You mean this dangerous vampire-eating creature?"

The countess hissed and backed away, as though Alexia might throw baby Prudence at her.

Madame Lefoux wended her way to Lady Maccon's bedside to coo over the infant.

Countess Nadasdy said, "Woolsey is ours now, unfortunately. It is hardly to be countenanced. Me living near *Barking* in the *countryside.* Why, it is positively leagues away from everywhere."

Lord Maccon did not protest her claim. "We will need a few days to clear out. The youngsters of the pack can't be moved until the moon fades."

"Take all the time you need," said the vampire queen magnanimously. "But the soul-sucker and her abomination of a child must leave tonight." She twirled toward the door dramatically and then paused on the threshold. "And the boy is mine."

With that, she swept out, presumably to release the rest of her hive. "Oh," Alexia heard her say to no one in particular as she walked down the stairs, "simply *everything* will have to be redecorated! And those buttresses!"

Madame Lefoux stayed behind. She looked worn and tired from the events of the night before, not to mention her own trials. Quesnel was practically stuck to her side, his grubby little hand entwined with hers. Madame Lefoux had grease stains on her fingertips and a smudge on her chin.

"You can't let her take him away from me." The Frenchwoman appealed to the assembled dignitaries with anguished green eyes. "Please."

Now, Alexia's subconscious had apparently given this conundrum some thought while she dozed. For a solution instantly proposed itself. "Speaking as muhjah, there is nothing we can legally do to remove him from the hive. If Angelique's testament is as they say, and you never formally adopted Quesnel under British law, then her claim is valid and legally recognized in this country."

Madame Lefoux nodded morosely.

Alexia pursed her lips. "You know vampires and solicitors—practically indistinguishable. I'm sorry, Genevieve, but Quesnel belongs with Countess Nadasdy now."

Quesnel gave a little whimper at that statement. Madame Lefoux clutched him to her and looked wild-eyed at Lord Maccon. As though, somehow, he might save her.

Alexia continued. "Now, before you go off and build a gigantic squid, I should tell you that I also intend to give *you* to Countess Nadasdy, Genevieve."

"What!"

"It is the only viable solution." Alexia wished she had a judge's wig and a mallet, for she felt like she'd done rather well with this verdict. "Quesnel is what, ten? He comes into his majority at age sixteen. So, with Countess Nadasdy's approval—and I hardly think she'll object—you will serve as drone to the Westminster Hive for the next six years. Or, I should say, the *Woolsey Hive.* I can make a case with the queen and the countess not to press charges if such an indenture could be arranged instead. Given your distaste for the hive, this should be a rather fitting punishment. And you get to stay with Quesnel."

"Ah," said her husband proudly, "good plan. If we cannot bring Quesnel to Madame Lefoux, we bring Madame Lefoux to Quesnel."

"Thank you, my dear."

"This is a *terrible* idea!" wailed Madame Lefoux.

Alexia ignored this. "I suggest you take over Professor Lyall's sheep-breeding shed for your contrivance chamber. It is already rather well equipped and could easily be expanded."

"But—" protested Madame Lefoux.

"You can think of a better solution?"

"But I *hate* Countess Nadasdy."

"I suspect you have that in common with most of her drones and some of her vampires. I will have Floote draw up the necessary documentation and make the legal arrangements. Look on the bright side, Genevieve. At least you can temper the hive's influence over Quesnel. He will still have his maman to teach him how to make things explode and all the wisdom of the vampires at his fingertips."

Quesnel looked up at his mother, his big violet eyes pleading. "Please, Maman. I like to explode things!"

Madame Lefoux sighed. "I have gotten myself neatly enmeshed, haven't I?"

"Yes, you have."

"Do you think the countess will approve such a bargain?"

"Why shouldn't she? She gets patronage, patent, and control over your inventions for the next six years. Quesnel stays with you both. Plus, think of the havoc Quesnel could cause living in a hive house! Keep them all on their toes and out of London politics for a while."

Madame Lefoux brightened slightly at that suggestion.

Quesnel's face lit up. "No more boarding school?"

Professor Lyall frowned. "This shifts England's vampire power structures significantly."

Alexia grinned. "Lord Akeldama thought he'd have London under his purview. I am merely balancing the scales. Now my pack will be living in his territory full-time, and Countess Nadasdy has Madame Lefoux working for her."

Professor Lyall stood, still looking a little sad. "You are a very good muhjah, aren't you, Lady Maccon?"

"I like to be tidy about it. While we are on the subject, Madame Lefoux, when you have cleared out your contrivance chamber, I thought that might be a good space for us to build the pack a London dungeon."

Lord Maccon grinned. "It's big enough, and underground, and easy to secure. An excellent idea, my love."

Madame Lefoux looked resigned. "And the hat shop?" Even though the shop had been a front to cover over her more nefarious dealings, she'd always had an affection for the establishment.

Alexia cocked her head. "I thought Biffy might do. You remember, my dear, we discussed that he was in great need of useful employment, and such a venture might suit him better than a position at BUR."

This time it was Professor Lyall who smiled in approval. "Wonderful notion, Lady Maccon."

"My darling wife," said Lord Maccon, "you think of everything."

Alexia blushed at the compliment. "I try."

So it was that the werewolf pack formerly of Woolsey Castle became the first ever to claim an urban hunting ground. In the late summer of 1874, they officially changed their name to the London Pack and took up residence next door to the rove vampire and potentate, Lord Akeldama. Where they kept their full-moon dungeon no one knew, but it was noted with interest that the new pack seemed to have developed a keen interest in lady's headgear.

It was a landmark summer so far as the tattle-mongers were concerned. Even the most conservative of the daylight folk took interest in the doings of the supernatural set, for the werewolf relocation was but the half of it. The Westminster Hive, having swarmed for the only time in recorded history, relocated to the countryside and changed its name to Woolsey. No one dared comment on the unfashionable choice. It was immediately suggested the government build a train track between the hive's new location and London. Even though Countess Nadasdy herself could not live at the heart of style, at least style could visit the countess. Protective measures were put into place and the vampires seemed to feel that isolation balanced out a known location.

The scandal rags were delighted by the entire ruckus, including the carnage caused throughout the city on that full-moon night by what was reputed to be a massive mechanical octopus. The hive house destroyed! The Pantechnicon burned to the ground! Indeed, there was so much of interest to report that a few key elements escaped the press. The fact that Chapeau de Poupe changed proprietors went unremarked upon except by such true hat aficionados as Mrs. Ivy Tunstell. The fact that the Woolsey Hive gained a very prestigious and highly valuable new drone escaped all but the scientific community's notice.

"Very, very nicely played, *my little plum pudding*," was Lord Akeldama's comment to Lady Maccon a few evenings later. He was carrying a paper in one hand and his monocle in the other.

Alexia looked up from where she sat in her bed. "You didn't think I would let you get away with everything, did you?"

He was visiting her in his third best closet. Lady Maccon preferred to remain in bed for the time being. She was feeling a good deal recovered from her ordeal, but she felt she ought to lie low for a while. If people knew she was back in form, she might have to attend a meeting of the Shadow Council, and the queen was reputed to be *not amused* by all the kerfuffle. Also there was Felicity to consider.

"And where is *my* lovely Biffy?" wondered the vampire.

Alexia clucked at her baby and jiggled the girl up and down a bit. Prudence gurgled good-naturedly and then spit up. "Ah, he has taken charge of Madame Lefoux's hat shop. He always did have a remarkably good eye."

Lord Akeldama looked wistful. "Trade? Indeed?"

"Yes, it's proving to be a mellowing influence. And an excellent distraction." By the time Alexia had wiped the baby's chin with a handkerchief, the infant was fast asleep.

"Ah." The monocle twirled, wrapping itself around Lord Akeldama's finger until the chain was too short, at which point it began swinging in the opposite direction.

"You didn't actually want him to pine away and die, did you?"

"Well . . ."

"Oh, you are *impossible.* Come over here and hold your adopted daughter."

Lord Akeldama grinned and minced over to the side of the bed to scoop up the slumbering baby. So far Prudence was proving to be an unexpectedly docile child.

The vampire cooed over her in quite an excessive way, telling her how beautiful she was and what fun they were going to have shopping together, until he interrupted his own litany of italicized praise with an exclamation of discovery.

"Would you *look at that!*"

"What? What is it now?" Alexia leaned up in bed on one elbow.

Lord Akeldama tilted the child in her direction. Prudence Alessandra Maccon Akeldama had developed porcelain-white skin and a perfect set of tiny little fangs.

TIMELESS

The Parasol Protectorate: Book the Fifth

Acknowledgments

Phrannish read this last book during the middle of production. Rach read it a week after giving birth. Iz did her rounds ill, having just returned from Israel and in the process of buying a house. So for all my girls, with lives more grown-up than mine, this writer beast is eternally grateful that you put said lives on hold . . . one final time. My personal parasol protectorate, thank you. We must do it again sometime.

CHAPTER ONE

In Which There Is Almost a Bath and Definitely a Trip to the Theater

"I said no such thing," grumbled Lord Maccon, allowing himself, begrudgingly, to be trussed in a new evening jacket. He twisted his head around, annoyed by the height of the collar and the tightness of the cravat. Floote patiently waited for him to stop twitching before continuing with the jacket. Werewolf or not, Lord Maccon would look his best or Floote's given name wasn't Algernon—which it was.

"Yes, you did, my dear." Lady Alexia Maccon was one of the few people in London who dared contradict Lord Maccon. Being his wife, it might be said that she rather specialized in doing so. Alexia was already dressed, her statuesque form resplendent in a maroon silk and black lace evening gown with mandarin collar and Asian sleeves, newly arrived from Paris. "I remember it quite distinctly." She pretended distraction in transferring her necessaries into a black beaded reticule. "I said we should show our patronage and support on opening night, and you *grunted* at me."

"Well, there, that explains everything. That was a grunt of displeasure." Lord Maccon wrinkled his nose like a petulant child while Floote skirted about him, puffing away nonexistent crumbs with the latest in steam-controlled air-puffing dewrinklers.

"No, dear, no. It was definitely one of your affirmative grunts."

Conall Maccon paused at that and gave his wife a startled look. "God's teeth, woman, how could you possibly tell?"

"Three years of marriage, dear. Regardless, I've replied in the affirmative that we will be in attendance at the Adelphi at nine sharp in time to take our box. We are *both* expected. There is no way out of it."

Lord Maccon sighed, giving in. Which was a good thing, as his wife and Floote had managed to strap him into full evening dress and there was no way to escape that.

In a show of solidarity, he grabbed his wife, pulling her against him and snuffling her neck. Alexia suppressed a smile and, in deference to Floote's austere presence, pretended not to enjoy herself immensely.

"Lovely dress, my love, very flattering."

Alexia gave her husband a little ear nibble for this compliment. "Thank you, my heart. However, you ought to know that the most interesting thing about this dress is how remarkably easy it is to get into and out of."

Floote cleared his throat to remind them of his presence.

"Wife, I intend to test the veracity of that statement when we return from this outing of yours."

Alexia pulled away from Conall, patting at her hair self-consciously. "Thank you kindly, Floote. Very well done as always. I'm sorry to have drawn you away from your regular duties."

The elderly butler merely nodded, expressionless. "Of course, madam."

"Especially as there seem to be no drones about. Where are they all?"

The butler thought for a moment and then said, "I believe that it is bath night, madam."

Lady Maccon paled in horror. "Oh, goodness. We had best escape quickly, then, Conall, or I'll never be able to get away in time for—"

Clearly summoned by her fear of just such a delay, a knock sounded at Lord Akeldama's third closet door.

How Lord and Lady Maccon had come to be residing in Lord Akeldama's third closet in the first place was a matter of some debate among those privy to this information. A few speculated that there had been a negotiated exchange of spats and possibly promises of daily treacle tart. Nevertheless, the arrangement seemed to be working remarkably well for all parties, much to everyone's bemusement, and so long as the vampire hives did not find out, it was likely to remain so. Lord Akeldama now had a preternatural in his closet and a werewolf pack next door, but he and his drones had certainly weathered much worse in the way of neighbors, and he had certainly housed far more shocking things in his closet, if the rumors were to be believed.

For nigh on two years, Lord and Lady Maccon had maintained the appearance of actually living next door, Lord Akeldama maintained the appearance of still utilizing all his closets, and his drones maintained the appearance of not having full creative control over everyone's wardrobe. Most importantly, as it turned out, Alexia was still close enough to her child to come to everyone's rescue. Unforeseen as it may have been when they originally concocted the arrangement, it had become increasingly clear that the home of a metanatural required the presence of a preternatural or no one was safe—particularly on bath night.

Lady Maccon opened the closet door wide and took in the sorry sight of the gentleman before her. Lord Akeldama's drones were men of fashion and social standing. They set the mode for all of London with regards to collar points and spats. The handsome young man who stood before her represented the best London society had to offer—an exquisite plum tailcoat, a high-tied waterfall of white about his neck, his hair curled just so about the ears—except that he was dripping with soap suds, his neck cloth was coming untied, and one collar point drooped sadly.

"Oh, dear, what has she done now?"

"Far too much to explain, my lady. I think you had better come at once."

Alexia looked down at her beautiful new dress. "But I do so like this gown."

"Lord Akeldama accidentally touched her."

"Oh, good gracious!" Lady Maccon seized her parasol and her beaded reticule—now containing a fan; her opera glassicals; and Ethel, her .28-caliber Colt Paterson revolver—and charged down the stairs after the drone. The poor boy actually squelched in his beautifully shined shoes.

Her husband, with a grumbled, "Didn't we warn him against that?" came crashing unhelpfully after.

Downstairs, Lord Akeldama had converted a side parlor into a bathing chamber for his adopted daughter. It had become clear rather early on that bathing was going to be an event of epic proportions, requiring a room large enough to accommodate several of his best and most capable drones. Still, this being Lord Akeldama, even a room dedicated to the cleanliness of an infant was not allowed to be sacrificed upon the unadorned altar of practicality.

A thick Georgian rug lay on the floor covered with cavorting shepherdesses, the walls were painted in pale blue and white, and he'd had the ceiling frescoed with sea life in deference to the troublesome child's evident unwillingness to associate with such. The cheerful otters, fish, and cephalopods above were meant as encouragement, but it was clear his daughter saw them as nothing more than squishy threats.

In the exact center of the room stood a gold, claw-footed bathtub. It was far too large for a toddler, but Lord Akeldama never did anything by halves, especially if he might double it at three times the expense. There was also a fireplace, before which stood multiple gold racks supporting fluffy and highly absorbent drying cloths and one very small Chinese silk robe.

There were no less than eight drones in attendance, as well as Lord Akeldama, a footman, and the nursemaid. Nevertheless, nothing could take on Prudence Alessandra Maccon Akeldama when bathing was at stake.

The tub was overturned, saturating the beautiful rug with soapy water. Several of the drones were drenched. One was nursing a bruised knee and another a split lip. Lord Akeldama had tiny soapy handprints all over him. One of the drying racks had fallen on its side, singeing a cloth in the fire. The footman was standing with his mouth open, holding a bar of soap in one hand and a wedge of cheese in the other. The nanny had collapsed on a settee in tears.

In fact, the only person who seemed neither injured nor wet in any way was Prudence herself. The toddler was perched precariously on top of the mantelpiece over the fire, completely naked, with a very militant expression on her tiny face, yelling, "Noth, Dama. Noth wet. Noth, Dama!" She was lisping around her fangs.

Alexia stood in the doorway, transfixed.

Lord Akeldama straightened where he stood. "My *darlings*," he said, "tactic number eight, I think—circle and enclose. Now brace yourselves, my pets. I'm going in."

All the drones straightened and took up wide boxer's stances, forming a loose circle about the contested mantelpiece. All attention was focused on the toddler, who held the high ground, unflinching.

The ancient vampire launched himself at his adopted daughter. He could move fast, possibly faster than any other creature Alexia had ever observed, and she had been the unfortunate victim of more than one vampire attack. However, in this particular instance, Lord Akeldama moved no quicker than any ordinary mortal man. Which was, of course, the current difficulty—he *was* an ordinary mortal. His face was no longer deathless perfection but slightly effete and perhaps a little sulky. His movements were still graceful, but they were mortally graceful and, unfortunately, mortally slow.

Prudence leaped away in the manner of some kind of high-speed frog, her tiny, stubbly legs supernaturally strong but still toddler unstable. She crashed to the floor, screamed in very brief pain, and then zipped about looking for a break in the circle of drones closing in upon her.

"Noth, Dama. Noth wet," she cried, charging one of the drones, her tiny fangs bared. Unaware of her own supernatural strength, the baby managed to bash her way between the poor man's legs, making for the open doorway.

Except that the doorway was not, in fact, open. Therein stood the only creature who little Prudence had learned to fear and, of course, the one she loved best in all the world.

"Mama!" came her delighted cry, and then, "Dada!" as Conall's shaggy head loomed up from behind his wife.

Alexia held out her arms and Prudence barreled into them with all the supernatural speed that a toddler vampire could manage. Alexia let out a harrumph of impact and stumbled backward into Conall's broad, supportive embrace.

The moment the naked baby came into contact with Alexia's bare arms, Prudence became no more dangerous than any squirming child.

"Now, Prudence, what is this fuss?" remonstrated her mother.

"No, Dama. No wet!" explained the toddler very clearly, now that she did not have the fangs to speak around.

"It's bath night. You don't have a choice. Real ladies are clean ladies," explained her mother, rather sensibly, she thought.

Prudence was having none of it. "Nuh-uh."

Lord Akeldama came over. He was once more pale, his movements quick and sharp. "Apologies, my little dumpling. She got away from Boots there and hurled herself at me before I could dodge." He moved one fine white hand to stroke his adopted daughter's hair back from her face. It was safe to do so now that Alexia held her close.

Prudence narrowed her eyes suspiciously. "No wet, Dama," she insisted.

"Well, accidents will happen and we all know how she gets." Alexia gave her daughter a stern look. Prudence, undaunted, glared back. Lady Maccon shook her head in exasperation. "Conall and I are off to the theater. Do you think you can handle bath night without me? Or should we cancel?"

Lord Akeldama was aghast at the mere suggestion. "Oh, dear me no, *buttercup*, never that! *Not* go to the theater? Heaven forfend. No, we shall shift perfectly well here without you, now that we've weathered this one teeny-tiny upset, won't we, Prudence?"

"No," replied Prudence.

Lord Akeldama backed away from her. "I'll stay well out of range from here on, I assure you," continued the vampire. "One brush with mortality a night is more than enough for me. It's quite the *discombobulating* sensation, your daughter's touch. Not at all like your own."

Lord Maccon, who had been placed in a similar position on more than one occasion with regard to his daughter's odd abilities, was uncharacteristically sympathetic to the vampire. He replied with a fervent, "I'll say." He also took the opportunity of Prudence being in her mother's arms to ruffle his daughter's hair affectionately.

"Dada! No wet?"

"Perhaps we could move bath night to tomorrow," suggested Lord Maccon, succumbing to the plea in his daughter's eyes.

Lord Akeldama brightened.

"Absolutely not," replied Lady Maccon to both of them. "Backbone, gentlemen. We must stick to a routine. All the physicians say routine is vital to the well-being of the infant and her proper ethical indoctrination."

The two immortals exchanged the looks of men who knew when they were beaten.

In order to forestall any further shilly-shallying, Alexia carried her struggling daughter over to the tub, which had been righted and refilled with warm water. Under ordinary circumstances, she would have plopped the child in herself, but worried over the dress, she passed Prudence off to Boots and stepped well out of harm's way.

Under the watchful eye of her mother, the toddler acquiesced to full immersion, with only a nose wrinkle of disgust.

Alexia nodded. "Good girl. Now do behave for poor Dama. He puts up with an awful lot from you."

"Dama!" replied the child, pointing at Lord Akeldama.

"Yes, very good." Alexia turned back to her husband and the vampire in the doorway. "Do have a care, my lord."

Lord Akeldama nodded. "Indeed. I must say I had not *anticipated* such a challenge when Professor Lyall first suggested the adoption."

"Yes, it was foolish of all of us to think that Alexia here would produce a biddable child," agreed the sire of said child, implying that any flaw was Alexia's fault and that he would have produced nothing but the most mild-mannered and pliant of offspring.

"Or even one that a vampire could control."

"Or a vampire and a pack of werewolves, for that matter."

Alexia gave them both a *look*. "I hardly feel I can be entirely at fault. Are you claiming Sidheag is an aberration in the Maccon line?"

Lord Maccon tilted his head, thinking about his great-great-great-granddaughter, now Alpha werewolf of the Kingair Pack, a woman prone to wielding rifles and smoking small cigars. "Point taken."

Their conversation was interrupted by a tremendous splash as Prudence managed to pull, even without supernatural strength, one of the drones partly into the bath with her. Several of the others rushed to his aid, cooing in equal distress over his predicament and the state of his cuffs.

Prudence Alessandra Maccon Akeldama would have been difficult enough without her metanatural abilities. But having a precocious child who could take on immortality was overwhelming, even for two supernatural households. Prudence actually seemed to steal supernatural abilities, turning her victim mortal for the space of a night. If Alexia had not interfered, Lord Akeldama would have remained mortal, and Prudence a fanged toddler, until sunrise. Her mother, or presumably some other preternatural, was the only apparent antidote.

Lord Maccon had accustomed himself, with much grumbling, to touching his daughter only when she was already in contact with her mother or when it was daylight. He was a man who appreciated a good cuddle, so this was disappointing. But poor Lord Akeldama found the whole situation distasteful. He had officially adopted the chit, and as a result had taken on the lion's share of her care, but he was never actually able to show her physical affection. When she was a small child, he'd managed with leather gloves and thick swaddling blankets, but even then accidents occurred. Now that Prudence was more mobile, the risk was simply too great. Naked touch guaranteed activation of her powers, but sometimes she could steal through clothing, too. When Prudence got older and more reasonable, Alexia intended to subject her daughter to some controlled analytical tests, but right now everyone in the household was simply trying to survive. The toddler couldn't be less interested in the importance of scientific discoveries, for all her mother tried to explain them. It was, Alexia felt, a troubling character flaw.

With one last glare to ensure Prudence remained at least mostly submerged, Alexia made good her escape, dragging her husband behind her. Conall held his amusement in check until they were inside the carriage and on their way toward the West End. Then he let out the most tremendous guffaw.

Alexia couldn't help it—she also started to chuckle. "Poor Lord Akeldama."

Conall wiped his streaming eyes. "Oh, he loves it. Hasn't had this much excitement in a hundred years or more."

"Are you certain they will manage without me?"

"We will be back in only a few hours. How bad can it get?"

"Don't tempt fate, my love."

"Better worry about our own survival."

"Why, what could you possibly mean?" Alexia straightened and looked out the carriage window suspiciously. True, it had been several years since someone tried to kill her in a conveyance, but it had happened with startling regularity for a period of time, and she had never gotten over her suspicion of carriages as a result.

"No, no, my dear. I meant to imply the play to which I am being dragged."

"Oh, I like that. As if I could drag you anywhere. You're twice my size."

Conall gave her the look of a man who knows when to hold his tongue.

"Ivy has assured me that this is a brilliant rendition of a truly moving story and that the troupe is in top form after their continental tour. *The Death Rains of Swansea*, I believe it is called. It's one of Tunstell's own pieces, very artistic and performed in the new sentimental interpretive style."

"Wife, you are taking me unto certain doom." He put his hand to his head and fell back against the cushioned wall of the cab in a fair imitation of theatricality.

"Oh, hush your nonsense. It will be perfectly fine."

Her husband's expression hinted strongly at a preference for, perhaps, death or at least battle, rather than endure the next few hours.

The Maccons arrived, displaying the type of elegance expected from members of the ton. Lady Alexia Maccon was resplendent, some might even have said handsome, in her new French gown. Lord Maccon looked like an earl for once, his hair *almost* under control and his evening dress *almost* impeccable. It was generally thought that the move to London had resulted in quite an improvement in the appearance and manners of the former Woolsey Pack. Some blamed living so close to Lord Akeldama, others the taming effect of an urban environment, and several stalwart holdouts thought it might be Lady Maccon's fault. In truth, it was probably all three, but it was the iron fist of Lord Akeldama's drones that truly enacted the change—or should one say, iron curling tongs? One of Lord Maccon's pack merely had to enter their purview with hair askew and handfuls of clucking pinks descended upon him like so many mallard ducks upon a hapless piece of untidy bread.

Alexia led her husband firmly to their private box. The whites of his eyes were showing in fear.

The Death Rains of Swansea featured a lovelorn werewolf enamored of a vampire queen and a dastardly villain with evil intent trying to tear them apart. The stage vampires were depicted with particularly striking fake fangs and a messy sort of red paint smeared about their chins. The werewolves sported proper dress except for large shaggy ears tied about their heads with pink tulle bows—Ivy's influence, no doubt.

Ivy Tunstell, Alexia's dear friend, played the vampire queen. She did so with much sweeping about the stage and fainting, her own fangs larger than anyone else's, which made it so difficult for her to articulate that many of her speeches were reduced to mere spitting hisses. She wore a hat that was part bonnet, part crown, driving home the queen theme, in colors of yellow, red, and gold. Her husband, playing the enamored werewolf, pranced about in a comic interpretation of lupine leaps, barked a lot, and got into several splendid stage fights.

The oddest moment, Alexia felt, was a dreamlike sequence just prior to the break, wherein Tunstell wore bumblebee-striped drawers with attached vest and performed a small ballet before his vampire queen. The queen was dressed in a voluminous black chiffon gown with a high Shakespearian collar and an exterior corset of green with matching fan. Her hair was done up on either side of her head in round puffs, looking like bear ears, and her arms were bare. *Bare!*

Conall, at this juncture, began to shake uncontrollably.

"I believe this is meant to symbolize the absurdity of their improbable affection," explained Alexia to her husband in severe tones. "Deeply philosophical. The bee represents the circularity of life and the unending buzz of immortality. Ivy's dress, so like that of an opera girl, suggests at the frivolousness of dancing through existence without love."

Conall continued to vibrate silently, as though trembling in pain.

"I'm not certain about the fan or the ears." Alexia tapped her cheek thoughtfully with her own fan.

The curtain dropped on the first act with the bumblebeeclad hero left prostrate at the feet of his vampire love. The audience erupted into wild cheers. Lord Conall Maccon began to guffaw in loud rumbling tones that carried beautifully throughout the theater. Many people turned to look up at him in disapproval.

Well, thought his wife, *at least he managed to hold it in until the break*.

Eventually, her husband controlled his mirth. "Brilliant! I apologize, wife, for objecting to this jaunt. It is immeasurably entertaining."

"Well, do be certain to say nothing of the kind to poor Tunstell. You are meant to be profoundly moved, not amused."

A timid knock came at their box.

"Enter," yodeled his lordship, still chuckling.

The curtain was pushed aside, and in came one of the people Alexia would have said was least likely to visit the theater, Madame Genevieve Lefoux.

"Good evening, Lord Maccon, Alexia."

"Genevieve, how unexpected."

Madame Lefoux was dressed impeccably. Fraternization with the Woolsey Hive had neither a deleterious nor improving effect on her attire. If Countess Nadasdy had tried to get her newest drone to dress appropriately, she had failed. Madame Lefoux dressed to the height of style, for a man. Her taste was still subtle and elegant with no vampiric flamboyances in the manner of cravat ties or cuff links. True she sported cravat pins and pocket watches, but Alexia would lay good money that not a one solely functioned as a cravat pin or a pocket watch.

"Are you enjoying the show?" inquired the Frenchwoman.

"I am finding it diverting. Conall is not taking it seriously."

Lord Maccon puffed out his cheeks.

"And you?" Alexia directed the question back at her erstwhile friend. Since Genevieve's wildly spectacular charge through London and resulting transition to vampire drone, no small measure of awkwardness had existed between them. Two years on and still they had not regained the closeness they had both so enjoyed at the beginning of their association. Madame Lefoux had polluted it through the application of a rampaging octomaton, and Alexia had finished it off by sentencing Genevieve to a decade of indentured servitude.

"It is interesting," replied the Frenchwoman cautiously. "And how is little Prudence?"

"Difficult, as ever. And Quesnel?"

"The same."

The two women exchanged careful smiles. Lady Maccon, despite herself, liked Madame Lefoux. There was just something about her that appealed. And she did owe the Frenchwoman a debt, for it was the inventor who had acted the part of midwife to Prudence's grossly mistimed entrance into the world. Nevertheless, Alexia did not trust her. Madame Lefoux always promoted her own agenda first, even as a drone, with the Order of the Brass Octopus second. What little loyalty and affection for Alexia she still had must, perforce, be a low priority now.

Lady Maccon moved them on from the platitudes with a direct reminder. "And how is the countess?"

Madame Lefoux gave one of her little French shrugs. "She is herself, unchanging, as ever. It is on her behest that I am here. I have been directed to bring you a message."

"Oh, yes, how did you know where to find me?"

"The Tunstells have a new play, and you are their patroness. I admit I had not anticipated *your* presence, my lord."

Lord Maccon grinned wolfishly. "I was persuaded."

"The message?" Alexia put out her hand.

"Ah, no, we have all learned never to do *that* again. The message is a verbal one. Countess Nadasdy has received instructions and would like to see you, Lady Maccon."

"Instructions? Instructions from who?"

"I am not privy to that information," replied the inventor.

Alexia turned to her husband. "Who on earth would dare order around the Woolsey Hive queen?"

"Oh, no, Alexia, you misunderstand me. The instructions came *to* her, but they are *for* you."

"Me? Me! Why . . . ," Alexia sputtered in outrage.

"I'm afraid I know nothing more. Are you available to call upon her this evening, after the performance?"

Alexia, whose curiosity was quite piqued, nodded her acquiescence. "It is bath night, but Lord Akeldama and his boys must really learn to muddle through."

"Bath night?" The Frenchwoman was intrigued.

"Prudence is particularly difficult on bath nights."

"Ah, yes. Some of them don't want to get clean. Quesnel was like that. As you may have noticed, circumstances never did improve." Genevieve's son was known for being grubby.

"And how is he muddling along, living with vampires?"

"Thriving, the little monster."

"Much like Prudence, then."

"As you say." The Frenchwoman tilted her head. "And my hat shop?"

"Biffy has it marvelously well in hand. You should drop by and visit. He's there tonight. I'm certain he would love to see you."

"Perhaps I shall. It's not often I get into London these days." Madame Lefoux began edging toward the curtain, donning her gray top hat and making her good-byes.

She left Lord and Lady Maccon in puzzled silence, with a mystery that, it must be said, somewhat mitigated their enjoyment of the second act, as did the lack of any additional bumblebee courtship rituals.

CHAPTER TWO

Wherein Mrs. Colindrikal-Bumbcruncher Does Not Buy a Hat

Don't you believe this would suit the young miss better?" Biffy was a man of principle. He refused, on principle, to sell a huge tricolored pifferaro bonnet decorated with a cascade of clove pinks, black currants, and cut jet beads to Mrs. Colindrikal-Bumbcruncher for her daughter. Miss Colindrikal-Bumbcruncher was plain, dreadfully plain, and the bonnet was rather more of an insult than a decoration by contrast. The hat was the height of fashion, but Biffy was convinced a little gold straw bonnet was the superior choice. Biffy was *never wrong about hats*. The difficulty lay in convincing Mrs. Colindrikal-Bumbcruncher of this fact.

"You see, madam, the refined elegance complements the delicacy of Miss Colindrikal-Bumbcruncher's complexion."

Mrs. Colindrikal-Bumbcruncher did not see and would have none of it. "No, young man. The pifferaro, if you please."

"I'm afraid that is not possible, madam. That hat is promised elsewhere."

"Then why is it out on the floor?"

"A mistake, Mrs. Colindrikal-Bumbcruncher. My apologies."

"I see. Well, clearly we have made a *mistake* in patronizing your establishment! I shall take my custom *elsewhere*. Come, Arabella." With which the matron marched out, dragging her daughter in her wake. The young lady mouthed an apology behind her mother's back and gave the little gold straw bonnet a wistful look. *Poor creature*, thought Biffy, before returning both hats to their displays.

The silver bells attached to the front of the shop tinkled as a new customer entered. Some evenings those bells never seemed to stop. The store was increasingly popular, despite Biffy's occasional refusal to actually sell hats. He was getting a reputation for being an eccentric. Perhaps not quite so much as the previous owner, but there were ladies who would travel miles in order to have a handsome young werewolf refuse to sell them a hat.

He looked up to see Madame Lefoux. She carried in with her the slightly putrid scent of London and her own special blend of vanilla and machine oil. She was looking exceptionally well, Biffy thought. Life in the country clearly agreed with her. She was not, perhaps, so dandified in dress and manner as Biffy and his set, but she certainly knew how to make the most of somber blues and grays. He wondered, not for the first time, what she might look like in a proper gown. Biffy couldn't help it, he was excessively fond of female fashions and could not quite understand why a woman, with so many delicious options, might choose to dress and live as a man.

"Another satisfied customer, Mr. Biffy?"

"Mrs. Colindrikal-Bumbcruncher has the taste level of an ill-educated parboiled potato."

"Revolting female," agreed the Frenchwoman amiably, "and her gowns are always so well made. Makes her that much more vexing. Did you know her daughter is engaged to Captain Featherstonehaugh?"

Biffy raised one eyebrow. "And he's not the first, I hear."

"Why, Mr. Biffy, you talk such scandal."

"You wrong me, Madame Lefoux. I never gossip. I observe. And then relay my observations to practically everyone."

The inventor smiled, showing her dimples.

"How may I help you this evening?" Biffy put on his shopboy persona. "A new chapeau, or were you thinking about some other fripperies?"

"Oh, well, perhaps." Madame Lefoux's reply was vague as she looked about her old establishment.

Biffy tried to imagine it through her eyes. It was much the same. The hats still dangled from long chains so that patrons had to push their way through swaying tendrils, but the secret door was now even more well hidden behind a curtained-off back area, and he had expanded recently, opening up a men's hats and accessories section.

The Frenchwoman was drawn into examination of a lovely top hat in midnight blue velvet.

"That would suit your complexion very well," commented Biffy when she fingered the turn of the brim.

"I am sure you are right, but not tonight. I simply came to visit the old place. You have tended it well."

Biffy gave a little bow. "I am but a steward to your vision."

Madame Lefoux huffed in amusement. "Flatterer."

Biffy never knew where he stood with Madame Lefoux. She was so very much outside his experience: an inventor, a scientist, and middle class, with a marked preference for the company of young ladies and an eccentricity of dress that was too restrained to be unstudied. Biffy didn't like enigmas—they were out of fashion.

"I have recently come from seeing Lord and Lady Maccon at the theater."

Biffy was willing to play along. "Oh, indeed? I thought it was bath night."

"Apparently, Lord Akeldama was left to muddle through alone."

"Oh, dear."

"It occurred to me that we have switched places, you and I."

The French, thought Biffy, *could be very philosophical.* "Come again?"

"I have become a reluctant drone to vampires and you nest in the bosom of the Maccon home and hearth."

"Ah, were you once in that bosom? I had thought you never quite got all the way inside. Not for lack of trying, of course."

The Frenchwoman laughed. "Touché."

The front door tinkled again. *Busy night for new moon.* Biffy looked up, smile in place, knowing he made a fetching picture. He wore his very best brown suit. True, his cravat was tied more simply than he liked—his new claviger needed training—and his hair was slightly mussed. His hair was *always* slightly mussed these days despite liberal application of Bond Street's best pomade. One, apparently, had to bear up under such tribulations when one was a werewolf.

Felicity Loontwill entered the shop and wafted over to him in a flutter of raspberry taffeta and a great show of cordiality. She smelled of too much rose water and too little sleep. Her dress was very French, her hair was very German, and her shoes were quite definitely Italian. He could detect the odor of fish oil.

"Mr. Rabiffano, I was so hoping you would be here. And Madame Lefoux, how unexpectedly delightful!"

"Why, Miss Loontwill, back from your European tour already?" Biffy didn't like Lady Maccon's sister. She was the type of girl who would show her neck to a vampire one moment and her ankle to a chimney sweep the next.

"Yes. And what a bother it was. Two years abroad with absolutely nothing to show for it."

"No delusional Italian count or French marquis fell in love with you? Shocking." Madame Lefoux's green eyes twinkled.

The door jingled again and Mrs. Loontwill and Lady Evelyn Mongtwee entered the shop. Lady Evelyn headed immediately toward a spectacular hat of chartreuse and crimson, while Mrs. Loontwill followed her other daughter up to the counter.

"Oh, Mama, do you remember Mr. Rabiffano? He belongs to our dear Alexia's household."

Mrs. Loontwill looked at the dandy suspiciously. "Oh, does he, indeed? A pleasure to meet you, I'm sure. Come away, Felicity."

Mrs. Loontwill didn't even glance in Madame Lefoux's direction.

The three ladies then gave their undivided attention to the hats while Biffy tried to comprehend what they were about.

Madame Lefoux voiced his thoughts. "Do you think they are actually here to shop?"

"I believe Lady Maccon is not receiving them at present, so they may be after information." He looked suspiciously at the Frenchwoman. "Now that Felicity has returned, will she be rejoining the Woolsey Hive?"

Madame Lefoux shrugged. "I don't know, but I shouldn't think so. I can't imagine it holds much appeal, now that the hive is located outside London. You know these society chits—only interested in the glamorous side of immortality. She may find herself another hive. Or a husband, of course."

At which juncture Felicity returned to them, in clear defiance of her mother's wishes. "Mr. Rabiffano, how is my *dear* sister? I can hardly believe how long it has been since I saw her last."

"She is well," replied Biffy, utterly passive.

"And that child of hers? My darling little niece?"

Her face sharpened when she was being nosy, noted Biffy, rather like that of an inquisitive trout. "She, too, is well."

"And how is Lord Maccon? Still doting upon them both?"

"Still, as you say, doting."

"Why, Mr. Rabiffano, you have grown so dreary and terse since your accident."

With a twinkle to his eye, the dandy gestured at the little gold straw bonnet. "What do you think of this one, Miss Loontwill? It is very subtle and sophisticated."

Felicity backed away hurriedly. "Oh, no, mine is too bold a beauty for anything so insipid." She turned away. "Mama, Evy, have you seen anything to your taste?"

"Not tonight, my dear."

"No, sister, although that green and red toque makes quite the statement."

Felicity looked back at Madame Lefoux, on point. "How unfortunate that you are no longer in charge here, madame. I do believe that the quality may have fallen."

Madame Lefoux said nothing and Biffy took the hit without flinching.

"Do, please, give my sister and her husband my best regards. I do hope they remain blissfully enamored of one another, although it is terribly embarrassing." Felicity whirled to the French inventor. "And give the countess my compliments as well, of course."

With that, the rose-scented blonde led her mother and her sister out into the night with nary a backward glance.

Biffy and Madame Lefoux exchanged looks.

"What was *that* about?" wondered the inventor.

"A warning of some kind."

"Or an offer? I think I should return to Woolsey."

"You are turning into a very good drone, aren't you, Madame Lefoux?"

As she made her way out, the Frenchwoman gave him a look that suggested she preferred it if everyone thought that. Biffy hoarded away that bit of information. He had much to tell Lady Maccon when he saw her next.

Alexia and Conall arrived home from the theater prepared to go out immediately to call on the Woolsey Hive. One did not ignore an invitation from Countess Nadasdy, even if one was a peer of the realm. Alexia alighted from her gilded carriage in a flutter of taffeta and intrigue, marching into her town residence with strides of such vigor as to make the bustle of her dress sway alarmingly back and forth. Lord Maccon eyed this appreciatively. The tuck-in at his wife's waist was particularly appealing, emphasizing an area ideally suited to a man's hand, particularly if one had hands as large as his. Alexia turned in the doorway and gave him a look.

"Oh, do hurry." They were still making a show of living in their own house and so had to move swiftly up the stairs and across the secret gangplank into Lord Akeldama's residence in order to effect a change of attire.

Floote's dapper head emerged from the back parlor as they did so. "Madam?"

"Not stopping, Floote. We have been *summoned*."

"Queen Victoria?"

"No, worse—a queen."

"Will you go by rail or shall I have the groom switch to fresh horses?"

Alexia paused halfway up the grand staircase.

"Train, I think, please."

"At once, madam."

Prudence, much to everyone's delight, was down for her nap, nested with her head atop Lord Akeldama's cat and her feet tucked under the Viscount Trizdale's lemon-satin-covered leg. The viscount was looking strained, obviously under orders not to move for fear of waking the child. Prudence was wearing an excessively frilly dress of cream and lavender plaid. Lord Akeldama had changed into an outfit of royal purple and champagne to complement it and was sitting nearby, a fond eye to his drone and adopted daughter. He appeared to be reading a suspiciously embossed novel, but Alexia could not quite countenance such an activity in Lord Akeldama. To her certain knowledge, he never read anything, except perhaps the society gossip columns. She was unsurprised when, upon catching sight of them lurking in the hallway, the vampire put his book down with alacrity and sprang to meet them.

Together they looked at the lemony drone, calico feline, and plaid pile of infant.

"Isn't that just a *picture*?" Lord Akeldama was adrift on a sea of candy-colored domestic bliss.

"All is well?" Alexia spoke in hushed tones.

The vampire tucked a lock of silvery blond hair behind his ear in an oddly soft gesture. "*Excessively.* The puggle behaved herself after you departed, and as you can see, we had no further incidents of note."

"I do hope she grows out of this dislike for soap suds."

Lord Akeldama gave Lord Maccon a significant sort of once-over where he lurked behind his wife in the hallway. "My *darling* chamomile bud, we can but hope."

Lord Maccon took mild offense and sniffed at himself subtly.

"Conall and I have been summoned to visit Woolsey. You will manage without us for the remainder of the night?"

"I believe we may, *just possibly*, survive, my little periwinkle."

Lady Maccon smiled and was about to head upstairs to change her gown when someone pulled the bell rope. Being already in the hallway and hoping to keep Prudence from waking, Lord Maccon dashed to answer the door despite the fact that this was most unbecoming for a werewolf of his station, and it was someone else's house.

"Oh, really, Conall. Do try *not* to behave like a footman," remonstrated his wife.

Ignoring her, Lord Maccon opened the door with a flourish and a tiny bow—as behooved a footman.

Lady Maccon cast her hands up in exasperation.

Fortunately it was only Professor Lyall on the stoop. If any man was used to Lord Maccon's disregard for all laws of propriety and precedence, it was his Beta. "Oh, good, my lord. I was hoping to catch you here."

"Randolph."

"Dolly *darling*!" said Lord Akeldama.

Professor Lyall didn't even twitch an eyelid at the appalling moniker.

"You had a visitor, my lord," said the Beta to his Alpha, looking refined.

Alexia was confident enough in her assessment of Lyall's character to spot a certain tension. He displayed quick efficiency under most circumstances. Such forced calm as this indicated a need for caution.

Her husband knew this, too. Or perhaps he smelled something. He loosened his stance, prepared to fight. "BUR or pack business?"

"Pack."

"Oh, must I? Is it terribly important? We are required out of town."

Alexia interrupted. "I alone am required. You, as I understand it, my love, were simply coming along out of curiosity."

Conall frowned. His wife knew perfectly well that the real reason he wished to accompany her was for security. He hated sending her into a hive alone. Alexia waggled her reticule at him. As yet, there was no new parasol in her life, but she still carried Ethel, and the sundowner gun was good enough when pointed at a vampire queen.

"I'm afraid this is important," said a new voice from behind Professor Lyall, in the street.

Professor Lyall's lip curled slightly. "I thought I told you to wait."

"Dinna forget, I'm Alpha. You canna order me around like you do everyone else."

Alexia thought that a tad unfair. Professor Lyall was many things, but he was not at all tyrannical. That was more Conall's style. It might be better said that Professor Lyall *arranged* everyone and everything around him just so. Alexia didn't mind in the least; she was rather fond of a nice arrangement.

A woman moved out of the gloom of the front garden and into the light cast by the bright gas chandeliers of Lord Akeldama's hallway. Professor Lyall, polite man that he was, shifted to one side to allow their unexpected visitor to take center stage.

Sidheag Maccon, the Lady of Kingair, looked much the same as she had almost three years earlier, when Alexia had seen her last. Immortality had given her skin a certain pallor, but her face was still grim and lined about the eyes and mouth, and she still wore her graying hair back in one heavy plait, like a schoolgirl. She wore a threadbare velvet cloak that would do nothing to ward off the evening's chill. Alexia noted the woman's bare feet. Clearly, the cloak was not for cold but for modesty.

"Evening, Gramps," said Lady Kingair to Lord Maccon, and then, "Grams," to Alexia. Considering she looked older than both, it was an odd kind of greeting to anyone unfamiliar with the Maccon's familial relationships.

"Great-Great-Great-Granddaughter," responded Lord Maccon tersely. "To what do we owe this honor?"

"We have a problem."

"Oh, do *we*?"

"Yes. May I come in?"

Lord Maccon shifted, making an open-hand gesture back at Lord Akeldama, this being the vampire's house. Vampires were odd about inviting people in. Lord Akeldama had once muttered something about imbalance in the tether ratio after Lady Maccon entertained Mrs. Ivy Tunstell overly long in his drawing room. He seemed to have adjusted tolerably well to Prudence and her parents living under his roof, but after the Ivy tea incident, Alexia always made certain to entertain her guests next door, in her own parlor.

Lord Akeldama peeked over Lady Maccon's shoulder, standing on tiptoe. "I don't believe we have been introduced, young lady." His tone of voice said much on the subject of any woman darkening his doorstep with plaited hair, a Scottish accent, and an old velvet cloak.

Alexia pivoted slightly and, after a quick consideration, decided Lady Kingair was just lady enough to warrant the precedence, and said, "Lady Kingair, may I introduce our host, Lord Akeldama? Lord Akeldama, this is Sidheag Maccon, Alpha of the Kingair Pack."

Everyone waited a breath.

"I thought as much." Lord Akeldama gave a little bow. "Enchanted."

The female werewolf nodded.

The two immortals evaluated each other. Alexia wondered if either saw beyond the outrageousness of the other's appearance. Lord Akeldama's eyes gleamed and Lady Kingair sniffed at the air.

Finally Lord Akeldama said, "Perhaps you had best come in."

Alexia felt a surge of triumph at the achievement of such civilized discourse under such trying social circumstances. Introductions had been made!

However, her pleasure was interrupted by a high-treble query from behind them. "Dama?"

"Ah, I see *somebody* is awake. Good evening, my puggle darling."

Lord Akeldama turned away from his new acquaintance to look fondly down the corridor.

Prudence's little head poked out from the drawing room. Tizzy stood behind her, looking apologetic. "I *am* sorry, my lord. She heard your voices."

"Not to worry, my ducky *darling*. I know how she gets."

Prudence seemed to take that as an invitation and padded down the hallway on her little stubby legs. "Mama! Dada!"

Lady Kingair, momentarily forgotten, was intrigued. "This must be my new great-great-great-aunt?"

Alexia's forehead creased. "Is that correct? Shouldn't it be great-great-great-great-half sister?" She looked at her husband for support. "Immortality makes for some pretty peculiar genealogy, I must say." *No wonder the vampires refuse to metamorphose those with children. Very tidy of them.* Vampires preferred to have everything in the universe neat. In that, Alexia sympathized with their struggles.

Lord Maccon frowned. "No, I believe it must be something more along the lines of—"

He never finished his sentence. Prudence, seeing that there was a stranger among her favorite people, and assuming that all who came into her presence would instantly adore her, charged Lady Kingair.

"Oh, no, *wait*!" said Tizzy.

Too late, Alexia dove to pick up her daughter.

Prudence dodged through the legs of the adults and latched on to Lady Kingair's leg, which was quite naked under the velvet cloak. In the space of a heartbeat, the infant changed into a small wolf cub, muslin dress ripped to tatters in the process. The cub, far faster than a toddler, went barreling off down the street, tail waving madly.

"So that's what *flayer* means," said Sidheag, pursing her lips and arching her eyebrows. Her unnatural pallor was gone and the lines in her face were more pronounced—mortality had returned.

Without even a pause, Lord Maccon stripped smoothly out of his full evening dress in a manner that suggested he had been practicing of late. Alexia blushed.

"Well, welcome to London Town, indeed!" exclaimed Lord Akeldama, whipping out a large feather fan and fluttering it vigorously in front of his face.

"Oh, Conall, really, in full view!" was Alexia's response, but her husband was already changing midstride from human to wolf. It was done with a good deal of finesse. Even if it was done right there for all the world to see. Sometimes being married to a werewolf was almost too much for a lady of breeding. Alexia contemplated divesting Lord

Akeldama of his fan—her face was quite hot, and *he* no longer possessed the ability to blush. As if reading her mind, he angled about so that he could fan them both.

"That is a lovely fan," said Alexia under her breath.

"Isn't it marvelous? From a little shop I discovered off Bond Street. Shall I order one for you as well?"

"In teal?"

"Of course, my blushing pumpkin."

"I do apologize for my husband's behavior."

"Werewolves will happen, my pickled gherkin. One has to merely keep a stiff upper lip."

"My dear Lord A, you keep stiff whatever you wish—you always do."

"Doesn't it hurt her?" Lady Kingair asked rather wistfully as Alexia exited the vampire's house down the front stoop to stand next to her, watching as the massive wolf chased the tiny cub.

"Not that we can tell."

"And how long will this last?" Sidheag made a gesture up and down her own body, indicating her altered state.

"Until sunrise. Unless I intervene."

Sidheag held a naked arm out at Lady Maccon hopefully.

"Oh, no, not you. The preternatural touch has no effect on you anymore. You're mortal. No, I have to touch my daughter. Then immortality, sort of, well, reverberates back to you. Difficult to explain. I wish we understood more."

Professor Lyall stood off to one side, a tiny smile on his face, watching the chaos in the street.

Prudence tried to hide behind a pile of delivery crates stacked on one side of the road. Lord Maccon went after her, knocking the crates to the ground with a tremendous clatter. The wolf cub went for the steam-powered monowheel propped against the stone wall of the Colindrikal-Bumbcruncher's front yard. Mr. Colindrikal-Bumbcruncher was particularly fond of his monowheel. He had it specially commissioned from Germany at prodigious expense.

Prudence took refuge behind the spokes of the center area. Lord Maccon was having none of it. He wiggled one mighty paw through to get at her. The spokes bent slightly, Lord Maccon got stuck, and Prudence dodged out, pelting once more down the street. Her tail wagged even more enthusiastically at the delightful game.

Lord Maccon extracted himself from the monowheel, shaking loose and causing the beautiful contraption to crash over with an ominous crunch. Lady Maccon made a mental note to send a card of apology around to their neighbors as soon as possible. The unfortunate Colindrikal-Bumbcrunchers had suffered great travails over the past two years. The town house had been in Mr. Colindrikal-Bumbcruncher's family for generations. Its proximity to a rove vampire was well known and tolerated, if not exactly accepted. Just as all the best castles had poltergeists, so all the best neighborhoods had vampires. But the addition of werewolves to their quiet corner of London was *outside of enough*. Mrs. Colindrikal-Bumbcruncher had recently snubbed Lady Maccon in the park, and frankly, Alexia couldn't fault her for it.

She squinted at the Colindrikal-Bumbcruncher house, trying to see if an inquisitive face at a window might have observed Conall's transformation in Lord Akeldama's hallway. That would require an even more profound apology, and a gift. *Fruitcake, perhaps.* Then again, perhaps the sight of Lord Maccon's backside might warrant less of an apology, depending on Mrs. Colindrikal-Bumbcruncher's preferences. Lady Maccon was distracted from this line of thinking by Professor Lyall's shout of amazement.

"Great ghosts, would you look at that?"

Alexia could not recall Professor Lyall ever raising his voice. She whirled about and looked.

Prudence had reached a good distance away, near to the end of the street, where an orange-tinted lamp cast a weak glow on the corner. There she had turned abruptly back into a squalling, naked infant. It was very embarrassing for all concerned. Particularly, if her screams of outrage were to be believed, Prudence.

"Well, my goodness," said Alexia. "That's never happened before."

Professor Lyall became quite professorial. "Has she ever gotten that far away from one of her victims before?"

Lady Maccon was slightly offended. "Must we use that word? *Victim*?"

Professor Lyall gave her an expressive look.

She acquiesced. "Quite right, it *is* unfortunately apt. Not that I know of." She turned to look at Lord Akeldama. "My lord?"

"My darling *sweet pea*, had I known that if we simply let her run a little distance she would work herself out, I would have let her *gallivant* about at will."

Lord Maccon, still in wolf form, trotted over to pick up his human daughter. Possibly by the scruff of her neck.

"Oh, Conall, wait!" said Lady Maccon.

The moment he touched her, Prudence turned once more into a wolf cub, this time stealing her father's skin, and he was left to stand in the middle of the street, starkers. Prudence tore off back toward the house. Lord Maccon made to follow, this time in his lumbering mortal form.

Alexia, forgetting the delicacy of the Colindrikal-Bumbcrunchers' finer feelings, was seized with the spirit of scientific inquiry. "No, Conall, wait, stay there."

Lord Maccon might have disregarded his wife, particularly if he had any thought of his own shame or the dignity of the neighborhood, but he was not that kind of husband. He had learned all of Alexia's cadences and tones, and that one meant she was *on to something interesting*. Best to do as she asked. So he stood, watching with interest, as his little daughter dashed back the way they had come and then past the house in the opposite direction.

Just as before, at a distance from her victim, she turned back into a toddler. This time Lady Maccon went to retrieve her. *What must the surrounding households think of us? Screaming baby, wolf cub, werewolves.* Really, she would never put up with it herself were she not married into the madness. As she hoisted Prudence, she looked up to see Mr. and Mrs. Colindrikal-Bumbcruncher and their butler glaring daggers at her from their open front door.

Conall, with a little start, turned back into a wolf before heads turned in his direction and someone would be forced to faint. Knowing the Colindrikal-Bumbcrunchers, that someone would probably be the butler.

Sidheag Maccon began to laugh. Lord Akeldama hustled her swiftly inside, fanning himself with the feather fan.

Lord Maccon, once more a wolf, was in the door next. Alexia and her troublesome offspring followed, but not before she heard the Colindrikal-Bumbcrunchers' door close with a definite click of censure.

"Oh, dear," said Lady Maccon upon attaining the relative safety of Lord Akeldama's drawing room. "I do believe we have become *those* neighbors."

CHAPTER THREE

In Which Lord Maccon Wears a Pink Brocade Shawl

"I don't have much time," said Alexia, sitting down with Prudence cuddled in her lap. After her exhausting shape-changing laps up and down the street, the infant had done the most practical thing and fallen asleep, leaving her parents to handle the consequences.

"That was a remarkable display of whatnot," remarked Lady Kingair, settling herself gingerly into one of Lord Akeldama's highest and stiffest-looking wingback chairs. She drew her shabby velvet cloak closely about her and tossed her long plait behind her shoulder.

"And an interesting newfound aspect of your daughter's abilities." Professor Lyall looked as though he might like a notepad and a stylus of some kind to make a note for BUR's records.

"Or failing." Lady Maccon was not so certain she liked the idea of her invincible little daughter having this weakness. Given Alexia's own experience, it was more likely than not that someone, more probably several someones, would try to kill Prudence over the course of her lifetime. It was far less comfortable knowing that all they would have to do was determine the limits of her abilities.

"That's what it is, isn't it?" Alexia looked to Professor Lyall, the only one who might qualify as an expert so far as these things went. "It's a tether, much like a ghost's to her corpse."

"Or a queen's to her hive," added Lord Akeldama.

"Or a werewolf's to his pack," added Lord Maccon.

Lady Maccon pursed her lips and looked down at her daughter. The poor thing had inherited her mother's complexion and curly hair. Alexia hoped the nose would not follow. She brushed back some of that dark hair. "Why should she be any different, I suppose?"

Lord Maccon came over to his wife and placed his hand on the back of her neck, caressing the nape with his calloused fingers. "Even you have limits, my dear wife? Who would have thought?"

That wrested Alexia out of her maudlin humors. "Yes, thank you, darling. We must press on. Woolsey is calling. So, if Lady Kingair would like to inform us as to the nature of her visit?"

Lady Kingair, it seemed, was a tad reluctant to do so in Lord Akeldama's well-appointed drawing room surrounded by the expectant faces of not only her great-great-great-grandfather, but also his wife, his Beta, a very eccentric sort of vampire, that vampire's lemon-colored drone, a sleeping child, and a fat calico cat. It was more audience than any lady of quality should have to endure when paying a social call on family.

"Gramps, could we nae go somewhere more private?"

Lord Maccon rolled his eyes around, as if only now noticing the crowd. He was a werewolf, after all; he naturally acclimatized to the pack around him, even if that pack had gotten a little bizarrely dressed of late.

"Well, what I know, my wife and Randolph know. And, unfortunately, what Alexia knows, Lord Akeldama knows. However, if you insist, we could put out the drone." He paused while Tizzy tried to look as if butter wouldn't melt in his mouth, or on his trousers for that matter. "And the cat, I suppose."

Lady Kingair emitted an exhalation of exasperation. "Oh, verra well. To cut to the crux of it: Dubh has disappeared."

Lord Maccon narrowed his eyes. "That's not like a Beta."

Professor Lyall looked concerned by this news. "What happened?"

Alexia wondered if he and the Kingair Beta had ever met.

Sidheag Maccon was clearly searching for a way of putting it that would not make her seem in the wrong. "I sent him away to investigate some small matter of interest to the pack, and we havena heard back from him."

"Begin at the beginning," instructed Lord Maccon, looking resigned.

"I sent him to Egypt."

"Egypt!"

"To track down the source of the mummy."

Lady Maccon looked to her husband in exasperation. "Isn't that just like one of *your* progeny? Couldn't just let sleeping mummies lie, could she? Oh, no, had to go off, nosing about." She rounded on her several-times-removed stepdaughter. "Did it occur to you that I exhausted my parasol's supply of acid to destroy that blasted creature for a *very good reason*? The last thing we need is more of them entering the country!

Just look at the havoc the last one caused. There was mortality simply everywhere."

"Oh, really, no. I dinna want to collect another one. I wanted to find out the particulars of the condition. We need to know where it came from. If there are more, they need to be controlled."

"And you couldn't have simply suggested that to BUR instead of trying to manage the situation yourself?"

"BUR's jurisdiction is homeland only. This is a matter for the empire, and I had the feeling that *we* wolves needed tae see tae it. So I sent Dubh."

"And?" Lord Maccon's expression was dark.

"An' he was supposed tae report in two weeks ago. He never made the aethographic transmission. Then again last week. Still naught. Then, two days past, this came through. I dinna think it's from him. I think it's a warning."

She threw a piece of paper down on the tea table before them. It was plain parchment of the kind employed by transmission specialists the empire over for recording incoming aetherograms. Only, instead of the usual abrupt sentence, one single symbol was drawn upon it: a circle atop a cross, split in two.

Alexia had seen that symbol before, on the papyrus wrappings about a dangerous little mummy in Scotland and later hanging from a chain around the neck of a Templar. "Wonderful. The broken ankh."

Lord Maccon bent to examine the document more closely.

Prudence stirred, giggling in her sleep. Alexia tucked the blanket, one of Lord Akeldama's pink brocade shawls, more securely about her daughter.

Lord Maccon and Lady Kingair both looked at Alexia. Lord Maccon, it ought to be noted, was wearing another pink brocade shawl wrapped securely about his waist. It looked like a skirt from the East Indies. Alexia supposed her husband, being Scottish, was accustomed to wearing skirts. And he did have very nice knees. Scotsmen, she had occasion to observe, often did have nice knees. Perhaps that was why they insisted upon kilts.

"Oh, don't tell me I never told you about it?"

"You never told *me*, my little robin's egg." Lord Akeldama waved his closed feathered fan about in the air, inscribing the symbol he saw before him.

"Well, the ankh translates to 'eternal life' or so Champollion says. And there we see eternal life destroyed. What do you think it might mean? Preternaturals, of course. Me."

Lord Akeldama pursed his lips. "Perhaps. But sometimes the ancients inscribed a hieroglyphic broken to keep the symbol from leaking off the stone and into reality. When inscribed for that reason, the meaning of the hieroglyphic does not alter."

"But who would nae want immortality?" asked Sidheag Maccon. She had pestered her great-great-great-grandfather for years to be made into a werewolf.

"Not everyone wants to live forever," Alexia said. "Take Madame Lefoux, for example."

Lord Maccon brought them back around to the point. "So Dubh has gone missing, in Egypt? What do you want me to do about it? Isn't this a matter for the dewan?"

Lady Kingair cocked her head. "You are family. I thought you might make some inquiries without having tae involve official channels."

Lord Maccon exchanged looks with his wife. Alexia glanced significantly at Lord Akeldama's massive gilded cuckoo clock that dominated one corner of the room.

"We should be getting on," he said.

"I shall be fine without you, my love. I will take the train. Nothing unpleasant ever happens on the train," assured his wife.

Lord Maccon did not look reassured. Nevertheless, it was clear he was more concerned by troubles among werewolves than summons from vampires.

"Very well, my dear." He turned to Lady Kingair. "We had better adjourn to BUR headquarters. We will need the assets only the Bureau can provide."

Lady Kingair nodded.

"Randolph."

"I'm with you, my lord. But I prefer to travel a little more formally."

"Very well. We shall meet you there." At which Lord Maccon swooped down upon his wife, one hand firmly occupied in keeping the shawl secure about his midriff. "Please, be cautious, my love, train or no train."

Alexia leaned into his embrace. Uncaring for the watching eyes about them—everyone there was family, after all—she touched his chin with one hand and arched up into his kiss. Prudence, accustomed to such activity, did not move in her mother's lap. Conall disappeared out into the hallway to remove the pink brocade and change form.

Mere moments later, a shaggy wolf head peeked back into the room and barked insistently. With a start, Lady Kingair excused herself to follow him.

"My hallway," remarked Lord Akeldama, "has never before seen such *lively* action. And *that*, my sugarplums, is *saying* something!"

Lady Maccon left her daughter asleep in her adopted father's drawing room. She changed out of her evening gown and into a visiting dress of ecru over a bronze skirt with brown velvet detailing. It was perhaps too unadorned for a vampire queen, but it was eminently appropriate for public transport. She commandeered one of the drones to assist her with the buttons, seeing as Biffy—her *lady's valet*, as she liked to call him—was busy with his hats. She tucked Ethel into a brown velvet reticule, checking to ensure the gun was fully loaded with sundowner bullets. Alexia detested the very idea that she might have to actually *use* her gun. Like any well-bred woman, she vastly preferred merely to wave it about and make wild, menacing gestures. This was partly because her marksmanship was limited to sometimes hitting the side of the barn—if it was a very large barn and she was very close to it—and partly because guns seemed so decidedly *final*. Still, even if all she intended to do was threaten, she might as well be able to fulfill that threat adequately. Alexia abhorred hypocrisy, especially when munitions were involved.

She took a moment to lament her lack of parasol. Every time she left the house, she felt keenly the absence of her heretofore ubiquitous accessory. She had asked Conall for a replacement, and he had muttered mysterious husband-with-gifts-afoot mutters, but nothing had resulted. She might have to take matters into her own hands soon. But with Madame Lefoux indentured to the Woolsey Hive, Alexia was at a loss as to how to locate an inventor capable of producing work of such complexity and delicacy, not to mention fashion.

Floote materialized with two first-class tickets from London to Woolsey on the Tilbury Line's Barking Express.

"Lord Maccon will not be joining me, Floote. Are any of the men available to act as escort?"

Floote took a long moment to consider his mistress's options. Alexia knew she had tasked her butler with quite a conundrum. With drones, werewolves, and clavigers to choose from, distributed among two households and currently bumbling about most of London, there was quite the crowd for even a butler of Floote's cranial capacity to keep account of. All Alexia knew was that Biffy was working and that Boots was visiting relations in Steeple Bumpshod.

Floote took a small breath. "I'm afraid there is only Major Channing immediately available, madam."

Alexia winced. "Really? How unfortunate. Well, he will have to do. I can't very well travel by train alone, can I? Would you tell him I request his attendance as escort, please?"

This time it was Floote's turn to wince, which for him was a mere twitch of one eyelid. "Of course, madam."

He glided off, reappearing moments later with her wrap and Major Channing, the London Pack's toffee-nosed Gamma werewolf.

"Lady Maccon, you require my services?" Major Channing Channing of the Chesterfield Channings was a man who spoke the Queen's English with that unctuous precision instilled only by generations of the best schools, the best society, and an overabundance of teeth.

"Yes, Major, I must visit Woolsey."

Major Channing looked as though he would quite like to object to the very idea of accompanying his Alpha female into the countryside, but he knew perfectly well that Lady Maccon would ask for him only if she had no other alternatives. He also knew who was most likely to bear the brunt of Lord Maccon's wrath if she were allowed to travel alone. So he said the only thing he could say under such circumstances.

"I am, of course, at your disposal, my lady. Ready, willing, and able."

"Don't overdo it, Channing."

"Yes, my lady."

Lady Maccon eyed the Gamma's outfit with a critical eye. He was in his military garb, and Alexia wasn't entirely certain that was appropriate for calling on vampires. *But do we have time for him to change?* To give insult by being very late indeed or by bringing a soldier into the house of a vampire queen? Quite the conundrum.

"Floote, what time does our train depart?"

"In one half hour, madam, from Fenchurch Street Station."

"Ah, no time for you to change, then, Major. Very well, collect your greatcoat and let's be away."

They rode the train in an uncomfortable silence, Alexia pondering the night out the window and Major Channing pondering an exceedingly dull-looking financial paper. Major Channing, Alexia had discovered much to her shock, was interested in figures, and as such was bursar to the pack. It seemed odd for a man of breeding and snobbery to dally with *mathematics*, but immortality did strange things to people's hobbies.

Some three-quarters of an hour into their journey, they consumed some very nice tea and little crustless sandwiches provided by an obsequious train steward who seemed very well aware of the dignity of Major Channing and rather less of that of Lady Maccon. As she nibbled her cucumber and cress, Alexia wondered if this were not one of the reasons she disliked the major so very much. He was awfully good at being aristocratic. Alexia, on the other hand, was only good at being autocratic. Not quite the same thing.

Alexia became increasingly aware of a prickling sensation at the back of her neck, as though she were being scrutinized carefully. It was a most disagreeable sensation, like stepping one's bare foot into a vat of pudding.

Pretending travel fatigue, she arose to engage in a short constitutional.

There were few other occupants in first class, but Alexia was startled to find that behind them and across sat a man in a sort of floppy turban. That is to say, she was not startled that there was someone else in the carriage but that a man was in a *turban*—most irregular. Turbans were well out of fashion, even for women. He seemed unduly interested in his daily paper, suggesting he had, until very recently, been unduly interested in something else. Lady Maccon, never one to take anything as coincidence, suspected him of observing her, or Major Channing, or both.

She pretended a little stumble as the train rattled along and fell in against the turbaned gentleman, upsetting his tea onto his paper.

"Oh, dear me, I *do* apologize," she declaimed loudly.

The man shook his damp paper in disgust but said nothing.

"Please allow me to fetch you another cup? Steward!"

The man only shook his head and mumbled something low in a language Alexia did not recognize.

"Well, if you're quite sure you won't?"

The man shook his head again.

Alexia continued her walk to the end of the car, then turned about and returned to her seat.

"Major Channing, I do believe we have company," she stated upon reseating herself.

The werewolf looked up from his own paper and over. "The man in the turban?"

"You noticed?"

"Hasn't taken his eyes off you most of the ride. Bloody foreigners."

"You didn't think to tell me?"

"Thought it was your figure. Orientals never like to see a lady's assets."

"Oh, really, Major, must you be so crass? Such language." Alexia paused, considering. "What nationality would you say?"

The major, who was very well traveled, answered without needing to look up again. "Egyptian."

"Interesting."

"Is it?"

"Oh, Major, you do so love to annoy, don't you?"

"It is the stuff of living, my lady."

"Don't be pert."

"Me? I wouldn't dream of it."

No further incidents occurred, and when they alighted at their stop, the foreign gentleman did not follow them.

"Interesting," said Alexia again.

The Woolsey Station, a new stopover, was built at considerable expense by the newly relocated Woolsey Hive with an eye toward encouraging Londoners to engage in country jaunts. The greatest disappointment in Countess Nadasdy's very long life was this exile to the outer reaches of Barking. The Woolsey Hive queen had commissioned the station to be built and even allocated a portion of Woolsey's extensive grounds. From the station, visitors could catch a tiny private train, conducted by a complicated tram apparatus without an engineer. The location of the hive was no longer a not-very-well-kept secret. The vampires seemed to feel some sense of security in the country, but they were still vampires. There was no longer a road leading directly to Woolsey; there was only this special train, the operation of which was tightly controlled by drones at the castle terminus.

Lady Maccon approached the contraption warily. It looked like a chubby flat-bottomed rowboat on tracks, with a fabric-covered interior and two massive parasols for protection from the elements. Major Channing helped her to step inside and then followed, settling himself opposite. At which juncture they sat, staring at the scenery so as not to look at each other, waiting for something to happen.

"I suppose they must be alerted to the fact that we have arrived." Alexia looked about for some kind of signaling device. She noticed that off to one side of the bench sat a fat little gun. After subjecting it to close examination, she shot it up into the air.

It made a tremendous clap. Major Channing started violently, much to Alexia's satisfaction, and the gun emitted a ball of bright white fire that floated high up and then faded out.

Alexia looked at the weapon with approval. "Ingenious. Must be one of Madame Lefoux's. I didn't know she dabbled in ballistics."

Channing rolled his ice-blue eyes. "That woman is an inveterate dabbler."

They had no further time to consider the gun, for the rowboat jolted once, causing Alexia to fall back hard against one of the parasol supports. It was Major Channing's turn to look amused at her predicament.

They rolled forward, first at quite a sedate pace and then at increasing speed, the tracks running up the long, low hill to where Woolsey Castle crouched, a confused and confusing hodgepodge of architecture.

Countess Nadasdy had done what she could to improve the Maccons' former place of residence, but it did little good. The resulting building merely looked grumpy over the indignity of change. She'd had it painted, and planted, and primped, and festooned, and draped to within an inch of its very long life. But it was asking too much of the poor thing. The result was something akin to dressing a bulldog up like an opera dancer. Underneath the tulle, it was still a bowlegged bulldog.

Major Channing helped Alexia out of the tram, and they made their way up the wide steps to the front door. Alexia felt a little odd, pulling the bell rope at what once had been her home. She could only imagine what Major Channing felt, having lived there for goodness knew how many decades.

His face was stoic. Or she thought it was stoic; it was difficult to tell under all that handsome haughtiness.

"She certainly has made"—he paused—"adjustments."

Lady Maccon nodded. "The door is painted with silver swirls. Silver!"

Major Channing had no opportunity to answer, for said door was opened by a beautiful young maid with glossy ebony hair, decked out in a frilled black dress with crisp white shirt and black pin-tucked apron front. Perfect in every way, as was to be expected in the countess's household.

"Lady Maccon and Major Channing, to see Countess Nadasdy."

"Oh, yes, you are expected, my lady. I'll inform my mistress you are here. If you wouldn't mind waiting one moment in the hall?"

Lady Maccon and Major Channing did not mind, for they were busy absorbing the transformation the countess had enacted upon their former abode. The carpets were now all thick and plush and blood red in color. The walls had been repapered in pale cream and gold, with a collection of fine art rescued from the wreckage of the hive's previous abode on prominent display. These were luxurious changes that neither appealed to a werewolf's taste nor suited his lifestyle. One simply did not live with Titian paintings and Persian rugs when one grew claws on a regular basis.

Major Channing, who hadn't seen the place since the pack left it, arched one blond eyebrow. "Would hardly have thought it the same house."

Lady Maccon made no answer. A vampire was oiling his way down the staircase toward them.

"Dr. Caedes, how do you do?"

"Lady Maccon." Dr. Caedes was a thin, reedy man, with a hairline paused in the act of withdrawal and an interest in engineering, not medicinal matters, despite his title.

"You know Major Channing, of course?"

"We may have met." The doctor inclined his head. He did not smile nor show fang.

Ah, thought Alexia, *we are to be treated with respect. How droll.* "My husband would have attended your summons, but he was called away on urgent business."

"Oh?"

"A family matter."

"I do hope it is nothing serious?"

Alexia tilted her head, playing the game of reveal with aplomb. She had been some time now a member of the Shadow Council and was a quick study in the fine art of conversing upon matters of great importance yet saying nothing significant. "More bedraggled, I suspect. Shall we proceed?"

Dr. Caedes backed down, having to follow the niceties of conversation that he and his kind had insinuated into society. "Of course, my lady. If you'd care to follow me? The countess is awaiting you in the Blue Room."

The Blue Room, as it turned out, was the room formerly occupied by the Woolsey Pack's extensive library. Alexia tried to hide her distress at the destruction of her favorite retreat. The vampires had stripped it of its mahogany shelving and leather seats and had papered it in cream and sky-blue stripes. The furniture was all cream in color with a decidedly Oriental influence and, unless Alexia was very much mistaken, Thomas Chippendale originals.

Countess Nadasdy sat in an arranged manner, draped to one side over the corner of a window seat. She wore an extremely fashionable and extraordinarily elaborate moss-green receiving dress trimmed with pale blue, the skirt tied back so narrowly that Lady Maccon wondered at the queen's ability to walk about, and the sleeves were so tight Alexia very much doubted the vampire could lift her arms at all. Biffy had tried to foist such absurdities upon Alexia, but only once, at which juncture she insisted that mobility was not to be sacrificed for taste, especially not with a child like Prudence dashing about. Biffy hunted down daringly cut fluid styles influenced by the Far East for his mistress to wear instead and said no more about it.

The countess had the ample figure of a milkmaid who had partaken too freely of the creamy results of her labors, which did not suit the style of the dress at all. Alexia would never have said a word, but she shuddered to think of Lord Akeldama's opinion on such a figure in such attire. She planned, of course, to describe it in detail to her dear friend as soon as possible.

"Ah, Lady Maccon, do come in."

"Countess Nadasdy, how do you do? You are adjusting to rural life, I see."

"For a girl with as unsullied a nature as I, the countryside is unobjectionable."

Lady Maccon paused, verbally stymied by the countess using the words *unsullied* and *girl* to describe herself.

The vampire queen glanced away from Lady Maccon's ill-disguised discomposure. "Thank you, Dr. Caedes. You may leave us."

"But, My Queen!"

"This is a matter for Lady Maccon and I, alone."

Alexia said quickly, "Countess, may I present Major Channing?"

"You may. Major Channing and I are already acquainted. I'm sure he won't mind allowing us a few moments of privacy?"

Major Channing looked like he would mind, but realizing that Dr. Caedes was about to leave his queen with a preternatural decided it was all in good faith.

"I shall be just outside the door, my lady, should you need anything."

Alexia nodded. "Thank you, Channing. I'm convinced all will be well."

So Alexia found herself alone in a blue room with a vampire queen.

After Felicity and Madame Lefoux departed, the shop turned into a frenzy of fashionable ladies in pursuit of hats, but Biffy's staff of assorted shopgirls had it well under control. He did a quick lap to ensure no lady was purchasing anything that did not suit her coloring, complexion, demeanor, station, or creed. He then left his accessories to the tender mercies of Britain's shopping public and retired down to the contrivance chamber to catch up on necessary paperwork. He was engaged at first, it must be admitted, in beautifying said paperwork by trimming the corners and adding necessary swirls and flowers to the text.

It had all happened rather organically. Because he was there most nights, and the contrivance chamber was the new dungeon for Lord Maccon's wolves, Biffy had assumed responsibility for a good deal of pack organization. Professor Lyall didn't seem to mind. In fact, he rather approved, so far as Biffy could tell. He wondered if the professor, after decades of sole stewardship, was relieved to have someone else take on part of the burden.

Since Madame Lefoux had removed all her machines, instruments, and gadgets, the contrivance chamber was a good deal more cavernous. Biffy thought it could use some nice rose-patterned wallpaper and a brocade cushion or two. But, given that its new purpose was as a full-moon prison, there was no point in wasting wallpaper on werewolves.

The dandy circled the huge room slowly, imagining himself swanking about a massive ballroom in one of Paris's fancy hotels—except he was checking the security of the pulley system, not waltzing with worldly Parisian ladies in obscenely large headdresses. Everything seemed to be secure. Gustave Trouvé had done an excellent job. The massive cages, iron coated in a silver wash, were strong enough to hold even Lord Maccon, yet they rose to the ceiling via a cranking mechanism that even the weakest claviger could operate. Biffy looked up contemplatively at the bottoms of the cages and wondered if he might not turn them into some kind of chandelier. Or at least ornament them with some ribbons and a tassel or two.

He settled behind his small desk in one corner of the room. There was pack business to attend to: a puzzle over one of the new recruits and a petition from a loner for one of his clavigers to be put up for metamorphosis. Several hours later, he stood, stretched, and packed away his work. He considered the fact that all around town, plays were ending, clubs were filling with smoke and chatter, and the gentlemen follies were at large. Perhaps he might change and catch the last of the evening's entertainment before sunrise. He had been required, by dint of association, to give over some of his dandified ways after becoming a werewolf, but not all of them. He fingered delicately the unruly curls of his hair. Some young men about town had recently assumed a certain level of scruff and simulated messiness. Biffy liked to think it was his influence.

The pack town house was dark. Everyone was taking advantage of the lures that London had to offer with little risk of accidental change for the youngsters or chronic boredom for the elders. He was making his way upstairs when he caught a smell, an unusual one not ordinarily associated with his abode. Something spicy and exotic and—he paused, trying to think—*sandy.* He turned, tracking with small short sniffs, following the alien scent toward the back of the house and the servants' domain.

Biffy heard the murmur of voices, his fine wolf hearing alerting him even through the shut kitchen door. Men's voices, one of them deep and authoritative, the other higher and more lilting. The first sounded familiar, but it was difficult to tell who it was, as they both were speaking in a foreign tongue Biffy couldn't quite place.

The conversation ended and the outer door to the kitchen opened and shut, letting in the sound of the back alley and a brief whiff of rubbish. Lightning fast, Biffy nipped into the shadows under the staircase at the far side of the hall, watching for the other party of the conversation.

Floote emerged from the room. The butler did not notice Biffy, merely gliding about his duties.

Biffy stood a long time in the dark, thinking. Then he realized what language it had been. Interesting that Lady Maccon's pet butler spoke fluent Arabic.

"Well." Alexia stood before the queen of the Woolsey Hive and narrowed her eyes at the woman. "Here I am, Countess, at your disposal. How can I help?"

"Now, Lady Maccon, is that any way to address your betters?" Countess Nadasdy didn't move from her stiff pose.

Alexia privately suspected, due to the tightness of the dress, that she couldn't.

"You have taken me away from an evening with my family, Countess."

"Yes, on the subject of which, we understood Lord Akeldama would have primary care for the abomination and yet . . ." The vampire let her words trail off.

Alexia understood perfectly. "Yes, and he does. Prudence lives with him. And please refer to my daughter by her name."

"But you live next door and visit quite frequently, I understand."

"It is necessary."

"A mother's love or a child's affliction?" The countess widened her cornflower-blue eyes significantly.

"Someone has to cancel her out."

The countess grinned suddenly. "Difficult is she, the soul-stealer?"

"Only when she isn't herself."

"Fascinating way of putting it."

"You simply must learn to relax your standards, Countess, or Prudence could run ragged all over London, even getting so far as Barking." Alexia, nettled that she had been offered neither seat nor tea, allowed some of her annoyance to creep into her voice. "Is this the nature of your summons or did you have something particular you wished to discuss with me?"

The vampire queen reached out to a small side table. Alexia was certain she heard the dress creak. The queen gestured Alexia to come closer, using a small scroll of parchment she had resting there.

"Someone wishes to meet the abomination."

"What was that? I'm afraid I didn't quite catch it. Wishes to meet *who*, did you say?" Alexia looked pointedly out a nearby window.

Countess Nadasdy showed fang. "Matakara wishes to meet your child."

"Mata-who? Well, many people wish to meet *Prudence*. Why should this particular person signify to any—"

The countess interrupted her with a sharp gesture. "No. You misunderstand. Matakara, queen of the Alexandria Hive."

"Who?"

"Oh, how can you be intimate with so many immortals, yet be so ignorant of our world?" The countess's beautiful round face became pinched in annoyance. "Queen Matakara is the oldest living vampire, possibly the oldest living creature. Some claim over three thousand years. Of course, no one knows the actual number with any certainty."

Alexia tried to fathom such a vast age. "Oh."

"She has shown a particular interest in your progeny. Generally speaking, Queen Matakara hasn't shown an interest in anything *at all* for five hundred years. It is a great honor. When one is summoned to visit her, one does not delay."

"Let me get this perfectly clear. She requires *me* to travel, to *Egypt*, with *my* daughter, on *her* whim?" Lady Maccon was, perhaps, less impressed than she ought to be by the interest of such an august body.

"Yes, but she would prefer if the reason for your journey were not publicly known."

"She wants me to travel to Egypt with my daughter under subterfuge? You have heard of my daughter's antics, have you not?"

"Yes."

Alexia huffed out a breath in exasperation. "Not asking very much, is she?"

"Here." The countess passed her the missive.

The sum of the request, or more properly the order, written in a slightly stilted manner that suggested the writer's first language was not English, was indeed as had been discussed.

Alexia looked up from it, annoyed. "Why?"

"Because she desires it, of course." Clearly Queen Matakara had the same kind of superior social power over the countess as the Queen of England did the Duchess of Devonshire.

"No, I mean to ask, why should I inconvenience myself with a trip?"

"Ah, yes, preternaturals, so very practical. I understand Egypt is lovely this time of year, and I believe there is something more that you have overlooked."

Alexia read the letter again and then flipped it over. There was a postscript on the reverse side. "I believe your husband is missing a werewolf. And you are missing a father. I can help you with both."

Alexia folded the parchment carefully and tucked it into her reticule, next to Ethel. "I'll prepare to leave at once."

"My *dear* Lady Maccon, I surmised that might be the case." The countess looked sublimely pleased with herself.

Alexia sneered. Nothing was more annoying than a self-satisfied vampire, which, given that seemed to be their natural state, was saying something about vampires.

A great hullabaloo out in the corridor heralded some kind of emergency. There was a good deal of yelling and then a banging at the door to the Blue Room.

"I left orders not to be disturbed!" yelled the queen, moved to irritated vocalization, if not actually moved to, well, move.

Said orders, however, were clearly to be disregarded, for the door burst open and in stumbled Dr. Caedes, Major Channing, and Madame Lefoux. They were carrying between them an exquisite young woman with dark hair, whose eyes were closed and body ominously floppy. Her perfection was marred by a great gash at the back of her head that bled copiously.

"Oh, really! I just had this room made over," said Countess Nadasdy.

CHAPTER FOUR

Several Unexpected Occurrences and Tea

It's Asphodel, My Queen. Riding accident."

The vampire queen made a beckoning motion with two fingers. "Bring her to me."

The three carried the drone over to her mistress. The girl's breathing was shallow, and she did not move.

"Dead drones are so inconvenient. Not to mention the hassle in finding an adequately fit, able, and attractive replacement."

"I think you should try for the bite, My Queen."

Countess Nadasdy looked at her vampire companion skeptically. "You do, do you, Doctor? I suppose it has been a while since I took the gamble."

The door crashed open once more and Mabel Dair appeared in the aperture, resplendent in a bronze riding gown with red trim. The actress swept into the room. "How is she?"

Miss Dair sashayed across the thick carpet and cast herself forward to kneel on the floor next to Countess Nadasdy and the injured drone. "Oh, poor Asphodel!"

Alexia had to give the actress credit for a moving performance.

Madame Lefoux stepped forward and bent to press Miss Dair's shoulders soothingly. "Come away, *chérie*. There's nothing we can do for her now."

Mabel allowed herself to be gentled into a standing position and away from the hive queen. "Oh, you will try, please, won't you, mistress? Asphodel is such a sweet girl."

The queen wrinkled her nose and looked back down. "I suppose she is quite pretty. Very well, bring me my sippy goblet."

Dr. Caedes sprang into action. "At once, My Queen!" He vanished from the room.

While they waited for him to return, Alexia turned to the new arrivals. "Good evening, Madame Lefoux. Miss Dair."

"Lady Maccon, how do you do?" replied the actress. Hands were clasped to her trembling bosom, and the bulk of her attention was still centered on the dying girl.

Madame Lefoux merely tipped her head in Alexia's direction and gave her a small, tight smile. Then she returned her attention to the actress, placing a solicitous arm about the woman's waist.

Dr. Caedes returned, bearing a small silver goblet with some kind of lid attached to the top. It looked like those cup attachments designed for gentlemen with mustaches. He passed it to the queen, who took it in one hand.

"Prepare the girl."

Dr. Caedes grabbed the comatose woman by the shoulders and shifted her into his mistress's lap. His supernatural strength made the task an easy one, even had the girl not been relatively slight. He turned her head so that she rested with the side of her neck exposed.

The queen took a drink from the goblet, swished the contents around in her mouth, and paused, an intense look of contemplation on her face. Then Countess Nadasdy bared her teeth, both the longer regular fangs, the feeders, and the smaller fangs to either side, the makers. Alexia wasn't quite certain on the logistics of vampire metamorphosis. They were secretive about the details, and rarely were scientists, save their own, permitted to observe. But she knew the current theory held that feeders sucked the blood out while makers pumped blood in, so metamorphosis occurred by process of the queen literally giving her own blood over to the new vampire.

The countess opened her mouth wide. The makers were dripping perfect drops of dark blood, almost black. Alexia wondered if the contents of the sippy goblet acted as a catalyst.

Dr. Caedes bent and looked into his queen's mouth. "I believe we may proceed, My Queen."

Lady Maccon could only hope that the vampire metamorphosis process was less brutal than the werewolves. Her husband had practically eaten Lady Kingair whole in order to change her. It was most indelicate. The last thing Alexia wanted was to witness the vampire version of a three-course meal.

"Should we be watching this? Isn't unbirth a matter for family intimates only?" Alexia asked Major Channing on a hiss.

"I think we are remaining as witnesses apurpose, my lady. She wants to prove her strength." The major seemed not at all perturbed by the prospect.

"Does she? Why? Did I look as though I doubted it?"

"No. But our Alpha has managed two successful metamorphoses in the past three years. That has got to smart something awful for the vampires."

"You mean, I have stumbled into some kind of eternal tiddlywinks match? Who can make the most immortals? What are you people, schoolroom children?"

Major Channing tilted his hands, palms up, in supplication.

"Oh, for goodness' sake," said Alexia, and then hushed, for the countess was biting down at last.

It was a good deal more elegant than with the werewolves at first. Countess Nadasdy sank her feeder fangs deep into the flesh of the girl's neck and then kept going until she was far enough in for the maker fangs to sink in as well. She cradled both arms about the woman and leaned back so that she was held up to her mouth like a tea sandwich. The girl's slack white face tilted toward the small audience. Countess Nadasdy closed her eyes, assuming an expression of ecstatic bliss. She moved not one muscle, except that Alexia could see a strange up and down fluttering in her neck, like a cow regurgitating its cud, only faster, smaller, and in both directions.

Asphodel remained limp in her mistress's arms for a long while, until her whole body jerked—once. Alexia jumped in reaction, as did Major Channing. Madame Lefoux gave them both a quelling look.

Asphodel's eyes popped open, wide, startled, looking directly at the observers. Then she began to scream. It was a deep, drawn-out cry of agony. Her pupils dilated, darkening and changing color, extending outward until her entire eyeball was a solid deep red.

The girl's eyes began to bleed. Drops of blood leaked out, running down the sides of her face and dripping off her nose. Her screams became gargles as blood began to pour out of her mouth, muffling the cries.

Dr. Caedes said, "Enough, My Queen. It isn't taking. There will be no making this one over."

The hive queen only continued to suck, her expression beatific. Her arms were beginning to lose their hold, however, and she was sagging over the girl.

Dr. Caedes stepped forward and ripped Asphodel off of his queen's fangs. Under normal circumstances, Alexia suspected he would not have been able to do so. All vampires were strong, but queens were reputed to be the strongest of them all. However, the countess's beautiful eyes, when they finally opened, were sunken with exhaustion.

Dr. Caedes yanked the maid from the countess's grasp and threw her to the floor like a used dishrag. The girl convulsed one final time and stilled.

Alexia went to bend over her solicitously, careful not to touch her in case, somehow, this was all as it was meant to be, and preternatural contact might interfere with the process of metamorphosis. The girl, however, was motionless. Lady Maccon looked up from her crouch at Major Channing. The werewolf shook his blond head.

Dr. Caedes spoke into the shocked quiet of the Blue Room. "My Queen, it did not take. You need to feed and restore your strength. Please, put the makers away. I will call in the drones."

Countess Nadasdy turned an unfocused gaze onto her vampire companion. "Didn't it work? Another one gone. How unfortunate. I shall have to buy a new dress, then." She looked around, catching sight of the fallen girl and Lady Maccon bent over her. She laughed. "There's nothing you can do, soul-sucker."

Alexia stood, feeling queasy.

There was blood everywhere. Soaked into the countess's green gown, splattered across the cream and blue carpet, and pooling under the body of the unfortunate girl. It was really more than any lady should have to tolerate when making a social call.

Dr. Caedes gestured Mabel Dair forward. "See to your mistress, Miss Dair."

"Certainly, Doctor. At once." Mabel ran to the countess, her golden curls bouncing, and offered up her wrist.

Dr. Caedes followed, reaching around to support his queen's head. "Now remember, only feeders. You are weak, My Queen."

Countess Nadasdy drank for a long time from the actress's wrist, everyone watching in silence. Mabel Dair stood still and quiet in her beautiful bronze dress, but soon the rose bloom on her perfect round cheeks began to fade.

Dr. Caedes said gently, "Enough, My Queen."

Countess Nadasdy did not stop.

Madame Lefoux strode forward. Her movements were angular and sharp under the impeccable cut of her evening jacket. She grabbed Miss Dair's arm above the wrist and jerked it off the vampire queen's teeth, causing both women to gasp in surprise.

"He said enough."

The countess glared at the Frenchwoman. "Don't you dare dictate to me, *drone*."

"Haven't you had sufficient blood for one evening?" The inventor gestured with her hand at the body and the mess that resulted.

Countess Nadasdy licked her lips. "And yet, I am still hungry."

The Frenchwoman lurched away. Dr. Caedes stopped her by placing his hands on her shoulders. "You don't want the queen to take from Miss Dair anymore, do you, Madame Lefoux? Offering yourself in her place, are you? That's very generous. Especially considering how cautious you have been with your blood since you came to us."

Madame Lefoux pushed her hair back behind her ears, defiantly. She'd let it grow longer since becoming a drone, but it was still too short for a woman. She offered up her wrist without protest. The countess sank in her fangs. Madame Lefoux looked away.

"Perhaps the major and I should make our farewells," suggested Alexia, uncomfortable witnessing Genevieve's pretend disinterest. At which juncture they did, leaving Madame Lefoux dismissive, Mabel Dair drained, Dr. Cedes distracted, and the countess still at tea.

Fenchurch Street wasn't Alexia's favorite station. It was too close to the London Docks and, of course, the Tower of London. There was something about the Tower, with all its ghosts that would not be exorcized, that gave her the squirms. It was as if they were dinner guests who had overstayed their welcome.

Lady Maccon and Major Channing alighted. It was the quietest time of the night, so there were no porters to be found. Lady Maccon sat in the first-class waiting room alone, impatient, while Major Channing went to see about a hackney.

A man unlike any Alexia had ever encountered burst in through the door just after Channing vanished out of sight. Alexia knew there were such people about London, but not in her part of the city! His hair was long and shaggy. His face was sunburned like that of a sailor. His beard was ferocious and untended. However, Alexia did not fear him, for the man appeared to be in a state of extreme distress, and he knew her name.

"Lady Maccon! Lady Maccon."

He spoke with a Scottish accent. His voice was vaguely familiar, for all that it was faint and cracked. For the life of her, Alexia couldn't place that gaunt, cooked-lobster face, not under all that unkempt.

She looked down her nose at the man. "Do I *know* you, sir?"

"Yes, my lady. Dubh." He cracked a weak smile. "I'm a mite different from when you saw me last."

The werewolf could not be but understating the case. Dubh had not been a particularly handsome or agreeable man, but now he was positively unsightly. A Scotsman, to be sure, and Alexia acknowledged her preferences seemed to lean in that direction. In the past, the man had not behaved much to Alexia's taste, having engaged in a bout of fisticuffs with Conall that destroyed most of a dining room and an entire plate of meringues. "Why, Mr. Dubh, what has brought about such a need for the barber? Are you unwell? Have you been the victim of an anarchist outrage?"

Alexia made to move over to him, for he had propped himself against the jamb of the door and seemed likely to slide right down it and fold up upon the floor.

"No, my lady, I beg you. I could not stand your touch."

"But, my dear sir, let me summon help. You have been much missed. Your Alpha is here in London looking for you. I could send Major Channing to fetch—"

"No, please, my lady, only listen. I have waited to catch you alone. 'Tis a matter for you alone. Your household . . . your household is nae safe. It is nae contained."

"Do go on."

"Your da . . . what he did . . . in Egypt. You need tae stop it."

"What? What did he do?"

"The mummies, my lady, they—"

A gunshot fired clear and sharp in the silence of the station. Lady Maccon cried out as a bloom of red blood appeared on Dubh's chest. The Beta looked utterly surprised, raising both hands to cup over the wound.

He pitched forward, facedown, showing that he had been shot in the back.

Alexia clasped her hands together and willed herself to stay away, although all her instincts urged her to help the injured man. She yelled out at the very top of her lungs, "Major Channing, Major Channing, come quickly! Something *untoward* has occurred."

The Gamma came dashing in using speed only supernaturals could achieve. He immediately crouched over the fallen werewolf.

He sniffed. "Kingair Pack? The missing Beta? But what is he doing *here*? I thought he went missing in Egypt."

"It appears he recently returned. Look—beard, tan, loss of flesh. He's been mortal for some length of time. Only one thing does that to a werewolf."

"The God-Breaker Plague."

"Can you think of a better explanation? Except, of course, that he is back here, in the country. He should be a werewolf once more."

"Oh, he is, or I wouldn't be able to smell the pack in him," answered Major Channing with confidence. "He's not mortal, only very, very weak."

"Then he's not dead?"

"Not yet. We'd better get him home and the bullet out or he might well be. Take care, my lady. The assailant may still be out there. I should go first."

"But," said Alexia, "I have Ethel." She withdrew the small gun from her reticule and cocked it.

Major Channing rolled his eyes.

"Onward!" Alexia trotted out of the waiting room, eyes alert for movement in the shadows, gun at the ready.

Nothing happened.

They made it to the waiting hackney easily. Major Channing offered the driver triple the fare for double the speed. They would have made it back home in record time had there not been a fire in Cheapside that caused them to double back and go around.

Once home, a single yell from Lady Maccon brought all the werewolves and clavigers running. It was getting near to dawn, so the house was full, clavigers waking up and werewolves preparing for bed. The injured Kingair Beta caused quite a hubbub. He was taken carefully inside and into the back parlor, while runners were sent to BUR to fetch Lord Maccon and Lady Kingair.

Dubh was looking worse, his breath rasped. Alexia was genuinely concerned for his survival. She sat down on the couch opposite, feeling utterly ineffectual, as she could not even pat his hand or wipe his brow.

Floote appeared at her elbow. "Trouble, madam?"

"Oh, Floote, yes. Where have you been? Do you know anything that could help?"

"Help, madam?"

"He's been shot."

"We should try to get the bullet out, madam, in case it is silver."

"Oh, yes, of course, do you—"

"I'm afraid not, madam, but I will send for a surgeon directly."

"Progressive?"

"Naturally, madam."

"Very good. Please do."

Floote nodded to a young claviger who jumped eagerly forward, and the butler gave him the address of a physician.

"Perhaps, madam, a little air for the invalid?"

"Of course! Clear the room, please, gentlemen."

All the worried-looking clavigers and werewolves filed out. Floote walked quietly off and returned moments later with tea.

They sat in silence, watching as Dubh's breathing became fainter.

Their reverie was interrupted by a clatter at the door, indicating Lord Maccon had returned.

Alexia hurried to meet her husband.

"Alexia, are you unwell?"

"Of course not. Did the runner explain what has transpired?"

"Dubh appeared, found you at the train station, tried to tell you something, and was shot."

"Yes, that's about the whole of it."

"Dashed inconvenient."

Lady Kingair pushed up next to her great-great-great-grandfather. "How is he?"

"Not well, I'm afraid. We have done what we can, and a surgeon has been sent for. Follow me." Alexia led the way into the back parlor.

They entered to find Floote bent over the injured man. The butler's normally impassive face was creased with worry. He looked up as they burst in and shook his head.

"No!" cried Lady Kingair, her voice ringing in distress. She shoved the butler aside to bend over her Beta. "Oh, no, Dubh."

The werewolf was dead.

Lady Kingair began to weep. Full shaking sobs, the grief of an old friend and longtime companion.

Alexia turned away from such naked emotion to find her husband's face also suffused with sorrow. She forgot that Dubh had been a part of his pack as well. Not so close as a Beta back then, but still, werewolves lived a long time and pack members were always valued. There had been no love lost personality-wise, but a dead immortal was never to be taken lightly. It was a tragedy of lost information, like the burning of the Library of Alexandria.

Alexia went to Conall and held him close, wrapping her arms tightly about him, not caring that others could see. Taking charge of the situation—everyone needed a hobby and that was Alexia's—she guided her husband gently to a large armchair and saw him seated. She sent Floote for a dram of formaldehyde and directed a claviger to fetch Professor Lyall. Then she made her way out into the hall to confirm what the waiting werewolves had already guessed from Lady Kingair's cry—that they had lost one of their own.

CHAPTER FIVE

Under Cover of Thespians

Needless to say, there was a good deal for Lady Maccon to take care of before she could broach the matter of Queen Matakara with her husband. No one got much sleep that day, except perhaps Biffy. The newest of the London Pack seemed to have come home, raised his eyebrows at the unholy hubbub, and, very sensibly, gone to bed with the latest copy of *Le Beaux Assemblée*.

Lady Maccon spent the morning finding a black dress for herself, black waistcoats for the pack, and mourning bands for the staff. Dubh hadn't exactly been family, but he had died in her house, and she felt that proper respects ought to be paid. BUR was in an uproar and the clavigers were all aflutter with the drama, so she had to keep an eye to them as well.

When evening finally did arrive, Lady Kingair insisted on departing immediately with Dubh's body for Scotland. However, she stated that she would be returning after the burial in all due haste to sort the matter of his murder out to her satisfaction. Her tone cast aspersions over the English's ability to properly tend to such matters. The abruptness of her departure left Lord and Lady Maccon standing dumbly in the hallway, staring at one another, exhausted by lack of sleep. When the knock came at their front door, they were entirely unprepared to meet Lord Akeldama's painted face, nor a chipper Prudence sitting happily on Tizzy's hip just behind him.

"Dada! Mama!" greeted their daughter.

"Oh, darling, good evening!" said her mother, trying to look pleased. "Lord Akeldama, Viscount Trizdale, do come in."

"Oh, no, thank you kindly, *pudding cheeks*. We thought we'd go for a little stroll in the park. I can't believe we will benefit from this delightful weather much longer. The puggle and I were wondering if you darlings would care to accompany us?"

"Oh, how kind. I do apologize, my lord, but we've had rather a trying day."

"So my little droney poos informed me. It was all go here last night *and* all day today, I understand. Someone had a *serious* accident. Not to mention the fact that *you* paid a visit to Woolsey Hive, my *dear* Alexia. But, my fabulous darling, *all black*? Surely that couldn't possibly be necessary?"

Lady Maccon faced this onslaught with composed grace until the very end. "Oh, good gracious me, Woolsey! Conall, my dear, I entirely forgot! I must talk with you about that directly. Yes, as you say, Lord Akeldama, very busy. I'm sorry to be so abrupt but I really am quite exhausted. Perhaps tomorrow night?" Alexia wasn't about to give the vampire the satisfaction of any further information.

Lord Akeldama knew when he was being dismissed. The vampire tilted his head graciously, and he and Tizzy returned to the street where an enormous pram awaited Prudence's pleasure. Lord Akeldama had had the contraption made shortly after the adoption was made official. It was a Plimsaul Brothers Perambulator Special Class. It had penny-farthing-style wheels, in brass, and a leather carriage gilded in gold and trimmed with an excessive number of swirls. The handle could be adjusted for height, and from it dangled a porcelain plate with the name *Proud Mary* in flowery scroll. There was a crank for raising and lowering the affixed protective parasol—also good for inclement weather. The pram—rather optimistically, felt Alexia—converted to take more than one child at a time. Lord Akeldama had ordered it designed with removable interior lining, lace trim, and ribbons. He had then commissioned a full set made in every possible color so as to match any outfit he might wear. In the light of the gas streetlamp, Alexia could just make out that they were all in teal and silver this evening. Prudence was in a darling cream lace dress and Tizzy in a complementary shade of pale gold. The nursemaid trailed behind looking put-upon. Somehow the vampire had even gotten her to don a teal ribbon in solidarity.

They paraded off. No doubt the vampire was prepared, nay delighted, to stop and be admired by many a curious bystander. It was likely to be a very slow amble about the park. Lord Akeldama did so enjoy making a spectacle of himself. Luckily, signs were beginning to indicate that Prudence felt similarly on the subject. Two peas in a very sparkly pod.

Lady Maccon grabbed her husband by the arm, practically dragging him into their back parlor and closing the door firmly behind her.

"Oh, Conall, something else has happened, and in the horror of Dubh's unfortunate demise, I entirely forgot to tell you. I witnessed Countess Nadasdy try to metamorphose a new queen yesterday eve."

"You never!" Lord Maccon was shaken slightly out of his melancholy. He patted the seat next to him, and Alexia came willingly over to settle beside him.

"It was all a rather rushed affair. One of her drones had an accident. The countess failed the attempt, but it was fascinating, from a scientific standpoint. Did you know the feeder fangs go in first? Oh, and there was blood everywhere! But I get ahead of myself. That's not the important part. Now, where did I put my reticule? Oh, bother. I must have dropped it when I pulled out Ethel at the station." She tsked at herself. "Never mind, I think I can remember the sum of the note."

"Note? What are you on about, my dearest?" Lord Maccon was watching his wife in fascination. Alexia so rarely got flustered; it was charming. It made him want to grab and pull her close, stroke her into stopping all her verbal fluttering.

"Countess Nadasdy summoned me to visit Woolsey because Prudence and I have been summoned, commanded even, to visit the queen of the Alexandria Hive herself."

Lord Maccon stopped thinking about the fineness of his wife's figure. "Matakara? Indeed?" He looked impressed.

Alexia was surprised. Her husband was rarely impressed by anything to do with vampires. In fact, Lord Maccon was rarely impressed by anything period, except perhaps Lady Maccon on occasion.

"She commands us to attend her in Egypt as soon as possible. *In Egypt*, mind you."

Lord Maccon didn't flinch at the outrageousness of such a demand, only saying, "Well, I shall have to accompany you, if that is the case."

Alexia paused. She had her story all prepared. Her explanation as to why she should go. She was even formulating a plan to disguise her reason for traveling. Yet, here her husband went just knuckling under and wanting to go with her. "Wait, what? You aren't going to object?"

"Would it signify if I did?"

"Well, yes, but I would still go."

"My love, one does not deny Queen Matakara. Not even if one is Alpha of the London Pack."

Alexia was so surprised she handed her husband his own argument—the one she had been prepared to battle. "You don't want to stay and see to the murder investigation?"

"Of course I do. But I would never allow you to go to Egypt alone. It's a dangerous land and not simply because of the God-Breaker Plague.

Lyall, Channing, and Biffy are rather more capable than I like to admit. I'm certain they can handle everything here, including Lady Kingair and a dead werewolf investigation."

Alexia's jaw dropped. "Really, this is too easy. What—" She paused. "Oh, I see! You want to investigate what Dubh was up to in Egypt—what he found out there—don't you?"

Lord Maccon shrugged. "Don't *you*?"

"Do you think Lady Kingair was lying to us about why she sent him?"

"No, but I do think he must have uncovered something significant. And why you in particular? Why not his pack?"

"This all has to do with my father. Dubh started to say something to that effect right before he was shot, and Queen Matakara's note intimated she knew secrets about my father. He spent some time in Egypt, I understand from his journals. Unfortunately, he seems never to have written anything down during those times. Although, he met my mother when he was over there."

Lord Maccon blinked. "Mrs. Loontwill traveled to Egypt?"

"I know, astonishing to think on, isn't it?" Alexia grinned at her husband's obvious confusion.

"Very."

"So, I should plan the trip? The vampires can't possibly object to us taking full charge of Prudence for a month or two. After all, it is at *their* behest."

"Vampires object to everything. They will probably want to send a drone as monitor."

"Mmm. Also, it'll be slower with you along, my love. I was hoping to travel by Dirigible Postal Express, but with a werewolf we'll have to go by sea." She patted her husband's thigh to modulate any insult inherent in the words.

He covered her hand with his large one. "The Peninsular and Oriental Steam Navigation Company has a new high-speed ship direct to Alexandria out of Southampton that takes ten days. It also crosses various dirigible flight paths, so we can get regular mail drops. Lyall can keep me informed on the Dubh investigation while we journey there."

"How very well informed you are, husband, on travel to Egypt. One would almost think you anticipated the jaunt."

Lord Maccon avoided explaining by asking, "How do you propose to disguise the purpose of our journey?"

Alexia grinned. "Let me rest for a bit. I'll make a midnight call, determine if the other party is amenable, and let you know later."

"My dearest love, I hate it when you come over mysterious. It indicates that I will be made uncomfortable by the results."

"Pish-tosh, you love it. It keeps you on your very estimable toes."

"Come here, you impossible woman." Conall grabbed his wife and held her close, kissing her neck and then her lips.

Alexia perfectly understood the nature of the caress. "We should go to bed directly, my love, have a sleep."

"Sleep?"

Alexia was extremely susceptible to that particular tone in her husband's voice.

They made their way up the stairs in their own home and then out and across the little drawbridge into Lord Akeldama's town house, where they kept their secret bedchamber in his third best closet. Alexia did not summon Biffy, instead allowing Conall to fumble with her buttons and stays, far more patient with his fiddling than she ordinarily was. He managed her dress, corset, and underthings in record time, and she made short work of his clothing. Alexia had learned her way around a man's toilette after only a week or so of marriage. She had also learned to appreciate the warmth of Conall's bare flesh against her own. Terribly hedonistic of her, such unconditional surrender, and she should never admit such a thing to anyone. There was something about connubial relations that appealed, sticky as they might be. She found her husband's touch as necessary to her daily routine as tea. Possibly more difficult to give up.

Alexia let Conall swoop her up and deposit her onto the big feather mattress, following her down into the puffy warmth. Once there, however, she gently but firmly took the control from him. Most of the time, because her husband was a dear bossy brute in the best possible way, she let him take charge in the matter of bed sport. But sometimes he must be reminded that she, too, was an Alpha, and her forthright nature would not permit her to always follow his lead in any part of their life together. She knew, given Dubh's death, that Conall needed to be cared for, and she needed to look after him. The evening called for gentleness, long smooth caresses, and slow kisses, reminding them both that they were alive and that they were together. She wanted to make him believe through her touch that she wasn't going anywhere. Their customary rough, joyful, nibbling passion could wait until she had made her point as firmly as she could, in a language Conall understood perfectly.

Ivy Tunstell received Alexia Maccon in her sitting room. The advent of twins into Mrs. Tunstell's life had affected neither the decoration of her house, which was pastel and frilly, nor of herself, who was more so. How she and her husband afforded a nursemaid Alexia would never be so gauche as to ask. With such an addendum to their household staff, Ivy's domestic bliss and stage appearances were little affected by the unexpected double blessing. As a matter of fact, she looked, behaved, and spoke much as she had before she married.

Ivy's children, unlike Alexia's daughter, seemed unpardonably well behaved. On those few occasions when they had had occasion to meet, Lady Maccon had said the customary "goo," and the babies had cooed and batted their overly long eyelashes back until someone came and took them away, which was all that one could really ask of babies. Alexia found them charming and consequently was perversely glad they were abed when she arrived.

"My dearest Alexia, how do you do?" Mrs. Tunstell greeted her friend with genuine pleasure, hands outstretched to clasp both of Alexia's. She drew Lady Maccon in to blow air kisses at either cheek, an affectation Alexia found overly French but was learning to accept as a consequence of time spent in the company of thespians.

"Ivy, my dear, how do you do? And how are you enjoying this fine evening?"

"I am quite reveling in the commonplace refinement of family life."

"Oh, ah, yes, and how is Tunstell?"

"Perfectly darling as ever. You know, he married me when I was but a poor and pretty young thing. All that has changed since then, of course."

"And the twins?" Born some half a year after Prudence, they were named Percival and Primrose, but more commonly called Percy and Tidwinkle by their mother. Percy was, of course, understandable, but Alexia had yet to understand how Tidwinkle evolved from Primrose.

Ivy smiled her sweet mother's-little-angels smile—accompanying the expression with a sigh of devotion. "Oh, the *darlings*. I could just eat them up with a spoon. They are asleep, sweet, precious things. And your little Prudence, how is she?"

"A tremendous bother and holy terror, of course."

Mrs. Tunstell tittered at that. "Oh, Alexia, you are too wicked. Imagine talking about one's own child in such a manner!"

"My dearest Ivy, I speak only the barest of truths."

"Well, I suppose young Prudence *is* a bit of a mixed infant."

"Thank goodness I have help or I'd be practically run off of my feet, I tell you!"

"Yes," Ivy said suspiciously. "I'm sure Lord Akeldama is invaluable?"

"He is taking Prudence for a stroll in the park as we speak."

Ivy gestured Alexia to sit and sent the maid for tea.

Alexia did as she was bid.

Ivy settled herself happily opposite her friend, delighted as always that dear Lady Maccon still afforded her any time at all. There was such a large disparity in their consequence as a result of marriage, no matter how much Alexia tried to convince Ivy otherwise, that Ivy always felt she was being honored by the continued acquaintance. Even a position as intimate as fellow member of a secret society and spy was not enough to reconcile Mrs. Tunstell to the fact that Lady Maccon, wife of an earl, came to take tea with her . . . in Soho! In *rented* apartments!

Still, it did not stop Mrs. Tunstell from reprimanding said Lady Maccon gently on the subject of Lord Akeldama. The man was, after all, too outrageous for fatherhood. The vampire side of his character being, in Ivy's universe, far less a thing than his scandalous comportment and flamboyant dress. Even her fellow actors were not so bad. "Couldn't you have gotten yourself a nice nursemaid, Alexia dear? For stabilization of the vital emotional humors? I can recommend them highly."

"Oh, Lord Akeldama has one of those as well. His humors are quite stable, I assure you. It makes no flour for the biscuit in the end with my daughter. Prudence requires all hands to man the forward deck, if you take my meaning. Twice as difficult as her father, even on his best days."

Ivy shook her head. "Alexia, really, you do say the most shocking things imaginable."

Lady Maccon, knowing such pleasantries might continue in this vein for three-quarters of an hour or more, moved on to a topic more in alignment with her visit. "I managed to catch the opening of your new play the night before last."

"Did you, indeed? How kind. Very patronly of you. Did you enjoy it?" Ivy clasped her hands together and regarded her friend with wide, shining eyes.

The maid came in with the tea, giving Alexia a moment to properly phrase her reply. She waited while Ivy poured and then took a measured sip before replying. "As your patroness, I approve most heartily. You and Tunstell have done me proud. A unique story and a most original portrayal of love and tragedy. I can safely say, I am convinced London has never seen its like before. Nor will it again. I thought the bumblebee opera dancer sequence was . . . riveting."

"Oh, thank you! It warms the cudgels of my heart to hear you say such a thing." Ivy positively beamed, her copious dark ringlets quivering in delight.

"I was wondering how long you're scheduled to run this performance at this particular venue, and whether you had considered taking it on tour?"

Ivy sipped her tea and considered the question with all seriousness. "We have only a week in our contract. We had intended merely to test the waters with this new style, with an eye toward expanding to a larger venue if it went over well. Why? Have you something in mind?"

Lady Maccon put down her teacup. "Actually, I wondered if you might consider"—she paused for dramatic effect—"Egypt?"

Mrs. Tunstell gasped and put one small white hand to her throat. "Egypt?"

"I believe the Egyptian theatergoing public might find *The Death Rains of Swansea* truly moving. The subject matter is so very exotic, and I understand there is a lady of means in residence there who is particularly interested in performances of this kind. Had you thought to take the production outside of London?"

"Well, yes, Europe of course. But all the way to Egypt? Do they have tea there?" Ivy wasn't looking wholly opposed to the jaunt. Ever since her trip with Alexia to Scotland, Mrs. Tunstell had rather a taste for foreign travel. Alexia blamed the kilts.

She pressed her advantage. "I would, of course, fund the expedition and make the necessary arrangements."

"Oh, now, Alexia, please, you embarrass me." Ivy blushed but did not refuse the offer.

"As your patroness, I feel it my duty to spread the deeply moving message inherent in your play. The bumblebee dance alone was a masterpiece of modern storytelling. I do not think we should deny it to others merely because of distance and questionable beverage options."

Mrs. Tunstell nodded, her pert little face solemn at this profound statement.

"Besides"—Alexia lowered her voice significantly—"there is also a matter for the Parasol Protectorate to handle in Egypt."

"Oh!" Ivy was overcome with excitement.

"I may call upon you in your capacity as Agent Puff Bonnet."

"If that is the case, I shall speak to Tunny and we shall take measures and make preparations immediately! I shall need more hatboxes."

Alexia blanched slightly at this ready enthusiasm. The Tunstells' acting troupe numbered nearly a dozen, plus assorted sycophants. "Perhaps we could narrow the scope of your production down slightly? This is a delicate matter."

"Such a thing *might* be possible."

"Down to, perhaps, only you and Tunstell?"

"I don't know. There is the wardrobe to consider. Who will look after that? And one or two of the supporting roles are perfectly vital to the story. And what about the twins? I couldn't possibly leave my beloved poppets. We will need our nursemaid along, as I couldn't manage without her. Then there is . . ."

Mrs. Tunstell continued to prattle on and Alexia let her. After a good long negotiation, Ivy concluded she could narrow her entourage down to ten, Tunstell and the twins not included, and she would collect the names and paperwork and send them on to Floote as soon as possible.

It was decided that they could leave by the end of the next week, all details being finalized. Lady Maccon departed feeling that the hard part was over and that all she need do now was persuade her husband as to the sensibleness of hiding themselves in plain sight among a bunch of actors.

She sent a note round to Countess Nadasdy instructing her to tell Queen Matakara that if the Alexandria Hive were to express particular interest in seeing a performance of *The Death Rains of Swansea*, it might also get a visit from Lord and Lady Maccon and their unusual child. Queen Matakara was to demand the play be performed before her in person, in her own home, and to that end was asking the Tunstells' Acting Troupe a la Mode to travel to Egypt specially. Alexia and Conall would be invited along as patrons.

By the time Lady Maccon had completed this task, the pack was home and a general ruckus of large men had resulted. Conall stuck his head round the doorjamb to say there was nothing new concerning Dubh and did she know where Biffy had gotten to?

Alexia replied that, no, she didn't and would he please come in and let her explain her plan before he gallivanted off again. He did, and she did, and after a good deal of grumbling, he accepted the necessity of traveling under cover of thespians.

"And now," announced Alexia, "I am going to have a chat with Lord Akeldama. I want his perspective on this summons from Queen Matakara, and I should inform him of my imminent protracted absence from the Shadow Council. He will have to handle the dewan on his own."

"If you think it necessary."

"My dear, you really must come around to the fact that Lord Akeldama knows useful things. Things even you and BUR don't know. Plus, he is Prudence's legal guardian. If we wish to take her out of the country, even at a vampire's request, we must ask his permission. It is the way of things."

Lord Maccon gestured her on magnanimously, and Alexia took herself next door without further ado.

Upon waking that evening Biffy was understandably bothered to hear of Dubh's death. However, it was a middling bother. He had never met the man, and, if the rumors were to be believed, he hadn't missed out on much. Besides, it was difficult to mourn the loss of anyone who had spent a good deal of his life in Scotland. Biffy was tolerably more disturbed by the fact that he had developed a cowlick while asleep that would not lie flat no matter what he did.

Biffy wondered if this attitude might be considered crass. He wouldn't want to be thought crass. It was simply that he still felt disconnected from his werewolf brethren. They had little conversation that did not revolve around sports or ballistics. Major Channing had a well-tied cravat, but really, even Biffy could not forge a relationship based solely upon attractive neck gear.

Biffy skirted off early to see to the hat shop and returned for a midnight snack to find Lord and Lady Maccon out and those few others still in residence dressed in black waistcoats. With a sigh, he went to change, disliking Dubh more for the alteration in his wardrobe than the poor man probably deserved.

He was picking idly at a plate of kippers when Professor Lyall wandered in, spotted him, and said, "Oh, good, Biffy, just the man I was looking for."

Biffy was startled. Professor Lyall had always been scrupulously kind to him, but other than doling out responsibility for the contrivance chamber and associated paperwork, the Beta had had very little to do with Biffy. Taking care of Lord Maccon was a full-time job, a fact Biffy understood all too well. He was such a very large and fearsome man, and so very scruffy. Biffy was part afraid of the Alpha, part in awe, and part driven by a pressing need to get him to a tailor.

He swallowed his bit of kipper and rose slightly out of his seat in deference to rank. "Professor Lyall, how can I be of service?" Biffy was hoping someday to learn the secret of the Beta's tame coiffure. It showed such admirable restraint.

"We're hitting a spot of bother getting anything substantial in the way of onlookers from Fenchurch Street. I was wondering if perhaps you might have some contacts in that area, from your before days?"

"Lord Akeldama did have me visit a pub near there upon occasion. One of the barmaids might remember me."

"Bar*maids*? Very well, if you say so."

"Would you like me to inquire now?"

"Please, and if you wouldn't mind some company?"

Biffy looked the Beta over—quiet, unassuming, with excellent if understated taste in waistcoats and a generally put-upon expression. Not the type of company Biffy would have chosen in his past, but that was the past. "Certainly, Professor, delighted." Perhaps they might discuss the matter of controlling cowlicks.

"Now, Biffy, don't tell fibs. I know I'm not up to your standards."

If he still had the capacity, Biffy would have colored at that bold statement. "Oh, sir, I should never even hint that you were anything but ideally suited to—"

Professor Lyall cut him short. "I was only teasing. Shall we?"

Biffy finished his last mouthful of kipper, wondering if the Beta generally teased at table. Then he stood, grabbed his hat and cane, and followed the professor out into the night.

They walked in silence for a long moment. Finally Biffy said, "I was wondering, sir."

"Yes?" Professor Lyall had a very gentle voice.

"I was wondering if perhaps your appearance were not as calculated to be unobtrusive as that of Lord Akeldama's drones, only in a far more subtle way." Biffy saw white teeth flash in a quick smile.

"Well, it is a Beta's job to take to the background."

"Did Dubh do that?"

"Not as I understood it. But he was a far fly from a true Beta. Lord Maccon killed his Kingair Beta for treason before he left the pack. Dubh stepped in because there was no one better."

"What an awful mess that must have been."

Next to him, Professor Lyall's footsteps paused one infinitesimal minute. Without his supernatural hearing, Biffy never would have caught the hesitation. "For the Kingair Pack? Yes, I suppose it was. You know, at the time, I never even gave them a thought. The Woolsey Pack had its own problems."

Biffy had heard the rumors. He had also done his best to learn the history of his pack. "The Alpha prior to Lord Maccon had gone sour, I understand."

"That's a rather elegant way of putting it—as though he were curdled milk."

"You didn't like him, sir?"

"Oh, Biffy, don't you think you could call me Randolph by now?"

"Goodness, must I?"

"Everyone else in the pack does."

"Doesn't make it palatable. Can I rename you?"

"How very Lord Akeldama of you. Not Dolly, though, please."

"Randy?"

Sour silence greeted that.

"Lyall, then. Are you going to answer my question, sir, or avoid it?"

Lyall cast him a sharp look. "You're right. I didn't like him."

Biffy felt a small frisson of horror. "Do *all* Alphas go sour?"

"All of the old ones, I'm afraid. Fortunately, most of them die fighting off challengers. But the really strong ones, the ones who live past three or four hundred, they all go—as you say—sour."

"And how old is Lord Maccon?"

"Oh, don't you worry about him."

"But he'll get there?"

"I suspect he might be one of the ones who does."

"And you have a plan?"

Professor Lyall gave a small huff of amusement. "I believe *he* does. You believe ours is a far more ugly world than that of the vampires, don't you, young pup?"

Biffy said nothing at that.

"Perhaps they simply hide it better. Had you considered that?"

Biffy thought of his dear Lord Akeldama, all light heart, pale skin, and sweet fanged smiles. Again, he said nothing.

Professor Lyall sighed. "You're one of us now. You made it through the first few years. You're controlling the change. You're taking on pack responsibility."

"Barely. Have you seen the way my hair is behaving of late? Practically scruffy."

They hailed a hansom cab and slung themselves inside. "Fenchurch Street, please, my good man, the Trout and Pinion Pub."

The fly got them there in good time, and they alighted before a questionable-looking establishment. For this part of town, near the docks, being more of a mind to cater to the daylight folk, it was quiet late at night. Nevertheless, the pub looked unfortunately popular.

The locals quieted at the advent of strangers, especially one dressed as flawlessly as Biffy. A murmur of suspicious talk circulated as they made their way to the bar.

The barmaid remembered Biffy. Most women of her class did. Biffy was a good tipper and he never groped or expected anything. Plus he dressed so well he tended to make a favorable impression on females of the species.

"Well there's my fine young gentleman, and ain't it been an age since I clapped eyes on you last?"

"Nettie, my dove"—Biffy put on his most extravagant mannerisms—"how are you this *delightful* evening?"

"Couldn't be better, ducky. Couldn't be better. What can I get you boys?"

"Two whiskeys, please, my darling, and a little of your company if you have a mind."

"Make that three and I'll sit on your knee while we drink 'em."

"Done!" Biffy slapped down the requisite coin, plus a generous gratuity, and he and Lyall made their way over to a small side table near the fire.

Nettie hollered back for a replacement barmaid, then joined them, carrying the three whiskeys, sloshed into tumblers. She settled herself, as threatened, on Biffy's knee, sipping her drink and twinkling hopefully at both men. She was a buxom thing, perhaps more round than Lyall favored, if Biffy was any judge of the man's taste, but of very pleasant disposition and inclined to chatter once steered in the correct direction. Her hair was so blond and fine as to be almost white, as were her eyebrows, giving her an expression of uninterrupted wonder that some might have taken for stupidity. Biffy had yet to determine whether this was actually the case.

"So, how's the pub fared since I visited last, Nettie my dove?"

"Oh, well, let me just tell you, love. Old Mr. Yonlenker—you remember, the bootblack down the block?—tried to clean his own chimney just last week, got himself wedged right proper for two days. They had to use lard to get him out. And then . . ." Nettie chattered on about all the various regulars round the neighborhood for a good twenty minutes. Biffy let the wave of gossip wash over him. Professor Lyall paid dutiful attention and Biffy asked enough questions to keep her going.

Finally he prodded gently, "I hear there was a bit of a flutter at the station the other night."

Nettie fell obligingly into the trap. "Oh, wasn't there ever? Gunshots! Young Johnny Gawkins round Mincing Lane said he's sure he saw a man taking off by private dirigible! Round these parts, can you imagine? And then of course there was the fire, same night. Can't say as how the two are linked, but I ain't saying they're not, neither."

Biffy blinked, confounded for a moment. "Young Johnny say anything about the man's looks?"

"Gentlemanly, think he said. Though nothing up to your standards, of course, me young buck. You sure ain't half curious about it, aren't ya?"

"Oh, you know me, Nettie, terrible one for scandal-mongering. Tell me, has Angie Pennyworth had her baby yet?"

"Not as how! Twins I tell you! And her without two pennies to rub together, and no da never did come forward. Crying shame, that's what I say. Though of a certainty an' we're all thinking it's *you know who*." The barmaid gestured with her pale head at a skinny lad lurking in the far corner, nursing a pint.

"Not Alec Weebs? Never!" Biffy was appreciatively shocked.

"Oh, believe it." Nettie settled herself in for another round.

Biffy gestured at the replacement barmaid for more whiskey.

Professor Lyall nodded at Biffy imperceptibly in approval. A gentleman in a private dirigible wasn't much to go on since the recent upsurge in dirigible popularity, but it was better than nothing. And at least there were records of dirigible sales. That narrowed their suspect list.

CHAPTER SIX

In Which the Parasol Protectorate Acquires a New Member

Lord Akeldama was back from his walk, Prudence was down for her nap, and Tizzy and the nursemaid were relieved of their duties for the moment. The vampire was holding court in his drawing room with a small collection of drones arrayed around him, a bottle of champagne on the end table, and the fat calico cat on his lap. Truth be told, Lord Akeldama had transformed into rather a homebody since becoming a father, much to London's surprise. This was because home had become, under Prudence's influence, even more exciting than the social whirl of the ton. Besides, Lord Akeldama had nothing but time; he could afford a few decades to play at parenting. He had, after all, never indulged in such an experience before. When one was a vampire as long-lived as he, new experiences were hard-won, difficult to find, and treasured—like good-quality face powder.

"Alexia, my *dearest* custard cup, how *are* you? Was it a perfectly *horrid* night?"

"Pretty much horrid, yes. And how was your stroll in the park?"

"We were the statement of the hour!"

"Of course you were."

The drones amicably made room for Alexia to sit, standing prettily while she did so. They then returned to their own chattering, leaving their master and his visitor to carry on together. However, Alexia was very well aware that ears were perked. Lord Akeldama's drones were trained in such a way as to suit their own intrinsic natures, and in the end, one could never take the love of gossip out of a soul once embedded there. They were as much interested in Lord Akeldama's secrets as they were in everyone else's.

"Lord Akeldama, do you think we might have a little word, in confidence? I have had a rather interesting summons and I could use the benefit of your advice."

"Of course, my *dearest girl*! Clear the room, please, *my darlings.* You may take the champagne."

The drones rose and trooped obligingly out, closing the door behind them.

"Ah, the dears, they are probably all pressed in a huddle with their collective ear to the jamb."

"Prudence and I have been summoned to visit Queen Matakara, in Egypt. What do you make of *that*?"

Lord Akeldama was not as awed as Lady Maccon might have hoped. "Ah, my dearest *sugar drop*, I am only surprised it has taken her so long. You aren't *actually* considering going, are you?"

"Not to put too fine a point on it, but yes. I've always wanted to see Egypt. There is also a pack matter Conall wishes to investigate there. I have even devised a cover story."

"Oh, Alexia, my rose hip, I *really* wish you wouldn't. Not Egypt. It's not a nice place, so hot and smelly. Full of tourists in muted colors. The puggle might be endangered. And I, of course, could not accompany you."

"Endangered by bad smells and muted colors?"

"Not to mention local dress. Have you seen what they wear in that country? All loose and flowy, *abominable* concessions to comfort and practicality." Lord Akeldama's hand floated up and out in the air in a simulation of the flutter of robes worn by exotic tribesmen. He lowered his voice. "There are too many secrets and too few immortals to keep them."

Alexia pressed further. "And Queen Matakara, have you ever met her?"

"In a manner of speaking."

Lady Maccon looked at her friend sharply. "What manner?"

"A very long time ago, my dearest pudding drop, you might say she was *responsible for everything*."

Alexia gasped. "Oh my giddy aunt! She *made* you!"

"Well, darling, there is no need to put it so crassly as all that!"

So many questions cluttered Alexia's mind at this revelation that her head very nearly did take to spinning. "But how did you get *here*?"

"Oh, silly child. We can move long distances, for a short period of time, right after metamorphosis. How else do you think vampires managed to migrate all over the world?"

Alexia shrugged. "I suppose I thought you simply expanded outward in ever-increasing circles."

Lord Akeldama laughed. "There would have to be considerably more of us for that, my darling sugar lump."

Lady Maccon sighed, then asked the best question she could, given Lord Akeldama's evasiveness. "What *can* you tell me about Queen Matakara?"

The vampire raised his gem-studded monocle and looked at her through the clear glass. "Not quite the right question, sweetling."

"Oh, very well. What *will* you tell me about Queen Matakara? Given that I will be taking your adopted daughter into her hive whether you like it or not."

"Hard line, my little *marmalade pot*, but better. I will tell you that she is very old, and her concerns are not that of the shorter lived."

"No advice at all, not even for Prudence's sake?"

The vampire looked at her, a slight smile on his face. "You are not above playing all the cards you have been dealt, are you, my darling girl? Very well. You want my advice? Don't go. More than that? Be careful. What Queen Matakara *says* is never the whole truth, and what Queen Matakara *is* has been hidden by the sands of time. It is not that she no longer cares to win; it is that she does not play the game at all. For you and I, my dear, who live for such petty diversions, this is practically impossible to comprehend."

"Then why ask to see Prudence? Why involve herself?"

"There you have the *real* danger, my clementine, and the *real* question, and, of course, there is no way for us to understand the answer."

"Because she is outside of our understanding?"

"Precisely."

"Unusual woman."

"You haven't yet seen the way she dresses."

While Lyall tracked down dirigible possession records, and Lord Maccon dashed about looking for clues, Lady Maccon planned her trip. Or, to be precise, she told Floote what she wanted and he made the necessary arrangements and procurements. The Tunstells were accounted for, and much to Alexia's disgust, Countess Nadasdy insisted on sending one of her drones along as ambassador for the English hives.

"She only wants to keep an eye on *me*," she objected to Floote while they contemplated which traveling gowns were best suited to an Egyptian climate. "Do you know who she's sending? Of course you do."

Floote said nothing.

Lady Maccon cast her hands up into the air in exasperation and began pacing about the room, gesticulating wildly in accordance with her Italian heritage.

"Exactly! Madame Lefoux. That woman simply cannot be depended upon. I'm surprised the countess trusts her so far as she can throw her. Although, I suppose being a vampire, she could throw her quite far. Then again, perhaps she is sending her along because she doesn't trust her. I mean, who is Genevieve favoring these days? Me, the vampire, the OBO, or herself?"

"A woman of conflicted loyalties, madam."

"To say the least! She must live a very complicated life. I'm certain I could never be so duplicitous."

"No, madam, not in your nature. I shouldn't let it concern you."

"No?"

"You can be guaranteed of at least one thing, madam. This time she doesn't want you dead."

"Oh, yes? How can I know this?" Alexia huffed, and sat on her bed, her lace robe floating out around her in a waterfall of opulence. "You know, Floote, I really enjoyed her company. That's the difficulty."

"You still do, madam."

"Don't be familiar, Floote."

Floote ignored this, in the manner of long-time family retainers everywhere. "It will be good for you to have someone like her along, madam."

"Like what? What do you mean, Floote?"

"Sensible. Scientific."

Alexia paused. "Are you speaking as my butler or as my father's valet?"

"Both, madam."

Floote's face was, as always, practically impossible to read. But after days of packing and organizing, Lady Maccon was beginning to get the distinct impression that he did not approve of Egypt.

"You don't want me to go, do you, Floote?"

Floote paused, looking down at his hands, perfectly gloved in white cotton, as was appropriate to upstairs staff.

"I made Mr. Tarabotti two promises. The first was to keep you safe. Egypt is not safe."

"And the second?"

Floote shook his head ever so slightly. "I can't stop you, madam. But *he* wouldn't want you to go."

Alexia had read her father's journals. "I have done a great deal in my life he would not have approved of. My marriage, for one."

Floote went back to packing. "He would want you to live as you wished, but not in Egypt."

"I am sorry, Floote, but it's time. If you won't tell me the missing parts of my father's life, perhaps someone there will." Alexia had always thought Floote's loyalty was absolute. Floote had stayed with her pregnant mother when Alessandro abandoned them. He had changed her nappies when she was a babe. He had left the Loontwill household to attend Alexia after her marriage to a werewolf. Now, she thought for the first time, perhaps it was his loyalty to her dead father that was unshakable and she was merely a proxy player.

Later that night, when her husband came home, Alexia curled against him rather more fiercely than she ordinarily might. Conall knew his wife well enough to sense the confusion and offer physical comfort of the kind she had given him only a few evenings earlier. In his touch, Alexia found reassurance. She also realized that with both Conall and Ivy along, she was leaving her home interests unsupervised. Lyall owed his loyalty to Lord Maccon, and she considered him an unreliable source ever since she found out he was behind the Kingair assassination attempt. Lord Akeldama's motives were always his own. Who did that leave her?

Things remained excitedly on the go all that week. Biffy carved out what time he could for his precious hats but nevertheless found himself drawn into the excitement of Dubh's murder investigation and Egyptian travel. He simply couldn't abstain. He was overly intrigued by the affairs of others.

He did manage to return to his duties as lady's valet. He rather adored Lady Maccon, and had from the moment she first appeared in Lord Akeldama's life. She had such an endearingly practical way of looking at the world. He had once described her to a colleague as the type of female who was born a grande dame. Everyone and everything had a proper place or she would see they were put into one of her own devising. Although she did require his guidance in the manner of her toilette. So far as Biffy was concerned, that, too, was an admirable quality in a lady. He enjoyed being needed, and Lady Maccon would be lost without him.

Which was precisely what she said as he fussed about with her hair. "Oh, Biffy, how do you do it? So lovely, you know I should be utterly lost without you."

"Thank you very much, my lady." Biffy finished cleaning the curling tongs and placed them into a drawer, standing back to take a critical look at his masterwork.

"That will do, my lady. Now, what would you like to wear this evening?"

"Oh, something sensible I think, Biffy. I won't be doing anything more exciting than packing."

Biffy went to look at her row of dresses. "How are preparations coming along for the trip?" He selected a day gown of cream striped in red with a cuirasse bodice of black velvet and a matched black underskirt. He paired this with a forward-tilting wide-brimmed hat with masculine overtones counteracted by a great array of feathers. Alexia thought the hat a little much but bowed to Biffy's judgment and allowed herself to be trussed up.

"Admirably, I believe. All of us should be prepared to leave the day after tomorrow. I am rather looking forward to it."

"I do hope you enjoy yourself."

"Thank you, Biffy. There was one more thing. I was wondering if I might prevail upon you. That is . . ." Lady Maccon paused, as though embarrassed or unable to find the words.

Biffy immediately left off fastening all the copious small buttons at the back of her gown and circled around to stand next to her, meeting her eyes via the looking glass. "My lady, you know you have only to ask."

"Oh, yes, of course. But this is a matter of some delicacy. I want it to be your own choice. Not one driven by pack or status."

She turned so they could look at each other face-to-face and took one of his hands in hers. He felt the effect of her touch instantly, an awareness of mortality, a dimming of his supernatural senses. It was a little like dropping out of the aether into the lower atmosphere, a sinking sensation in the stomach. He had learned to ignore the feeling. What with dressing and arranging Lady Maccon's hair, he experienced it frequently.

"I have a little private consortium. I was wondering if, perhaps, you might be persuaded to join."

Biffy was fascinated. "What kind of consortium?"

"A sort of secret society. I will, of course, require a vow of silence."

"Naturally. What do you call yourselves?"

"The Parasol Protectorate."

Biffy smiled. "I am enthralled by the concept of a society named after an accessory. Do go on, my lady."

"I am afraid you would be only our third member. Currently, the society consists of myself and Ivy Tunstell."

"Mrs. Tunstell?"

"She was rather invaluable in a matter of some considerable delicacy just before Prudence was born."

"What is the purpose of this society?"

"I suppose the root of the Protectorate is to seek truth and protect the innocent. In as polite and well accessorized a way as possible, of course."

"That seems quite glamorous enough to me." Biffy was rather taken with the idea of being in a club with the estimable Lady Maccon. It sounded most diverting. "Do I make a pledge?"

"Oh, dear. I did invent one for Ivy, but it is a tad ridiculous."

"Splendid."

Lady Maccon giggled. "Very well. Fetch me one of those parasols, please. I'm afraid the original pledge required my special parasol, but one of those will do as a replacement."

"Your *special parasol*, my lady?"

"Oh, just you wait. I'll have something made for you. Perhaps a particular top hat?"

"Particular?"

"Lots of hidden gadgets, concealed compartments, covert weaponry, and the like."

"What a horrid thing to do to a perfectly nice top hat!"

"Cane, then?"

Biffy tilted his head in consideration. Then he remembered Lord Akeldama's gold pipe that was actually a glaive. "Perhaps a cane. Now, about that pledge?" He was not about to allow Lady Maccon to deny him ready amusement.

His mistress sighed. "If you insist, Biffy. Spin the parasol three times and repeat after me: I shield in the name of fashion. I accessorize for one and all. Pursuit of truth is my passion. This I vow by the great parasol."

Biffy couldn't help it; he started to laugh, but he did as he was bid.

"Do try to keep a straight face," said his mistress, although she said it around her own grin. "Now pick the parasol up and raise it open to the ceiling."

Biffy did as instructed.

"Ivy insisted we seal the vow in blood, but I hardly think that necessary, do you?"

Biffy raised his eyebrows. It was fun watching Lady Maccon squirm.

"Oh, I had no idea *you* would be so difficult. Very well." She retrieved a small knife from her armoire. It was not silver, so in order to make the cut, she had to hold on to Biffy's wrist with her bare hand, keeping him mortal.

"May the blood of the soulless keep your own soul safe," she intoned, cutting a tiny slice in the pad of her thumb and then in his and pressing the two together.

Biffy had a moment of panic. What might her preternatural blood do to his werewolf blood? But the second she let go, his cut healed instantly, leaving no remnant mark behind.

"Now, Mrs. Tunstell goes by the sobriquet Puff Bonnet."

Biffy let out an uncontrolled bark of laughter.

"Yes, yes. Well, I go by Ruffled Parasol. What would you like your moniker to be?"

"I suppose it ought to be another accessory of some kind?"

Lady Maccon nodded.

"How about Wingtip Spectator?"

"Perfect. I will inform Ivy of your indoctrination."

"And now, my lady, I assume there is a reason for your recruiting me at this particular time?"

Lady Maccon looked at him. "You see, Biffy? That's what I mean. You are an adorably smart thing, aren't you?"

Biffy raised an eyebrow.

"I require someone to monitor London while Ivy and I are abroad. Keep me informed as to the nature of the murder investigation. Keep an eye on Channing's behavior—and Lyall's for that matter. And the vampires, of course."

"Tall order, my lady. Professor Lyall?"

"Everyone has secrets Biffy, even Lyall."

"Especially Professor Lyall, my lady. I'd say he is keeping a goodly number of everyone else's secrets as well as his own."

"You see, what did I say? Perceptive. Now, there will be irregular dirigible mail during our steamer crossing. I'll provide you with a schedule of the ones you'll need to utilize, depending on where we are. After that, I intend to set up an aethographic connection to the public access transmitter in Alexandria. I have the valve frequensor codes here, and I will give them mine. Thereafter, you will have to send all messages in code. I'll send you the first one just after sunset the day after we arrive—London sunset. Please coordinate the timing and be ready to receive. Lord Akeldama trained you in the use of an aethographic transmitter?"

"Of course." Biffy had known the workings of every single transmitter since the technology first came to London those many years ago. "This is going to be delightful fun, isn't it, my lady?"

At that, Lady Maccon put an arm about his waist and leaned her head on his shoulder. "That's the spirit!"

"Oh, dear heavens, Ivy, must you bring so many hats?"

They had let the entire first-class coach for the short haul from

London to Southampton, where their steamer awaited the tides. Lady Maccon stood next to her husband on the platform waiting to board.

Mrs. Tunstell was wearing a traveling gown of pale pink and apple-green stripes, trimmed with multiple blue trailing ribbons. Her hat was a great tower of feather puffs, pink and green, through which peeked the heads of stuffed bluebirds and more ribbons. In addition to her hatboxes, of which she took the greatest care and supervision, Mrs. Tunstell was accompanied by her husband, her children, their nursemaid, the wardrobe mistress, the prop master, a set designer, and six supporting cast members. Being actors, the whole lot of them performed the simple act of loading and boarding a train with all the pomp and circumstance of a three-ring circus.

Everyone was a flutter of broad gestures, eye-searing attire, and loudly projected voices. Tunstell was his usual cheery redheaded self, the excitement of travel merely causing him to grin more broadly at the world. Alexia wouldn't exactly accuse Tunstell of being the kind of man who wrote sonnets, but his britches were overly tight and in a vocal plaid, his top hat was purple, and his traveling coat was scarlet. In fact, his entire outfit seemed an impressionistic take on riding out for the hunt. Biffy, who had come to the station to see them off, looked as though he might faint at the very sight of it and took his leave quite hurriedly.

Alexia carried Prudence in her naked arms, waiting until the sun was properly up, at which juncture she could hand the squirming toddler off to her husband without fear of any furry recriminations. It was a great embarrassment to be seen in public without her gloves, but she was taking absolutely no chances. They had a train to catch. Prudence simply couldn't be allowed to delay matters by turning wolf and running off.

There had been a very tearful good-bye before they left their house. Lady Maccon held Prudence close while Lord Akeldama peppered his puggle with kisses. Tizzy, Boots, and all the other drones made their farewells as well, doling out an excessive number of coos and coddles to Prudence, as well as small gifts for the journey. Lady Maccon was beginning to suspect her child of being rather spoiled. All this excitement caused Prudence to come over tetchy for the duration of the ride to Waterloo Station. Alexia had only just gotten her settled when they were summarily immersed in the chaos of the Tunstells' acting troupe.

Of course, Prudence was beaming in delight at all the drama and color. She was very much Lord Akeldama's daughter in this and clapped her chubby little hands when Mrs. Tunstell ordered the porter to fit all her hatboxes inside the train car at once and the poor man went tumbling backward, hats flying everywhere.

"Stay!" Mrs. Tunstell ordered her hats.

"Oh, really, Ivy. Let the porter handle things. The man knows what he is doing. Get your party settled." Alexia was as annoyed as her daughter was delighted.

"But, Alexia, my hats, they simply can't be left to just anyone. It's the collection of a lifetime."

Lady Maccon told a calculated fib in order to expedite matters. "Oh, but, Ivy, I do believe I see the nursemaid trying to attract your attention from within. Perhaps the twins—"

Mrs. Tunstell immediately forgot all about her precious hats and climbed hurriedly up into the train to see if her little angels were indeed suffering any possible distress.

Unlike Prudence, the Tunstell twins were apparently bored by the prospect of foreign travel. Perhaps their ennui was brought on by near constant exposure to the theatrical lifestyle. Primrose was quietly entranced by all the trim and sparkle about her, clearly her mother's daughter. Periodically tiny arms would wave out from her bassinet, reaching for a feather or a particularly gaudy bow. Percy, on the other hand, had spit up obligingly all over the lead villain's velvet cape and then gone to sleep.

"Alexia, Lord Maccon. Good morning." A warm, faintly accented voice came wafting from behind them.

Alexia turned. "*Madame Lefoux*, you made it in good time, I see."

"As if I would miss this for the world, *Lady Maccon*."

"As you can see, it is quite the kerfuffle," Alexia said. They watched as the last of Ivy's entourage made their way on board, leaving a mound of luggage behind on the platform.

"Conall, tip the porters well, would you, please?" Lady Maccon prodded her husband into coping with the mountain.

"Of course, my dear." Lord Maccon wandered over to see to the logistics.

Alexia shifted Prudence to her other hip. "Prudence, this is Madame Lefoux. I don't believe you have met since your arrival into this world. Madame Lefoux, may I introduce Prudence Alessandra Maccon Akeldama?"

"Dama?" queried Prudence at that.

"No, dear, Lefoux. Can you say Lefoux?"

"Foo!" pronounced Prudence with great acumen.

The Frenchwoman shook Prudence's pudgy little hand solemnly. "A pleasure to make your acquaintance, young miss."

"Foo Foo," replied Prudence with equal gravitas. Then, after giving the lady dressed as a gentleman a very assessing look, she added, "Btttpttbtpt."

The inventor brought along only a small portmanteau for the journey and a hatbox Alexia remembered as being a hatbox only on the surface. Underneath it was a cleverly devised toolkit.

"Expecting trouble, are you, Genevieve?" Alexia forgot to be formal, falling all too quickly into the familiarity bred by a previous journey made together across Europe—a time when she and the inventor had been friends rather than cautious acquaintances.

"Of course. Aren't you? No parasol, I see. Or not a *real* one."

Alexia narrowed her eyes. "No. Mine happened to get destroyed when a certain person brought a certain hive house down around everyone's ears."

"I *am* sorry about that. Things got a touch out of hand." Madame Lefoux dimpled hopefully.

Alexia was having none of it. "Sorry isn't good enough. I *lost* my *parasol.*" She practically hissed it. The absence still rankled.

"You might have said something. I could easily have made you a replacement. The countess has me very well set up."

Alexia arched her eyebrows.

"Ah. You don't trust me now that I belong to the Woolsey Hive. May I remind you that you put me there?"

Alexia sputtered.

"Dada," said Prudence, warning them both.

Lord Maccon had seen to the luggage. "Well, ladies, Madame Lefoux, shall we? The train is about to depart, and I believe everyone is aboard, save us." It took him a moment to sense the tension between his wife and her erstwhile friend.

"Now, now, what's all this about?"

"Foo!" pointed out Prudence.

"Yes, poppet, so I see."

"Your wife is still missing her parasol."

"Ah. My dear, I did order you a new one, but it is taking far longer than I expected. You know how scientists can be."

"Oh, thank you, Conall! I did think it might have slipped your mind."

"Never, my dear." He bent and kissed her on the temple. "Now, if that settles matters?"

The sun peeked up, outside the station but definitely rising. The train sounded its horn, loud and long, and the engine began to ramp up, belting bouts of smoke and steam out onto the platform like a sudden, smelly fog.

Lord Maccon grabbed Madame Lefoux's portmanteau and tossed it up into the coach to the waiting steward. His strength was taxed by the rising sun, but not so much as to make even a large piece of luggage much of a burden. He took Prudence from his wife. His daughter wrapped chubby arms about him in delight. Prudence was growing to love daylight, since she associated it with hugging her father. In addition, her aunt Biffy and her uncle Lyall were more likely to scoop her up and twirl her around when the sun was up.

"Dada," she said approvingly. Then she leaned forward toward his ear, as if to tell him a secret, and spouted a whole stream of incomprehensible babbling. Alexia figured this was Prudence's version of gossip. It was probably quite interesting and informative, had it actually been composed of words.

"Prudence, darling," said her mother as she climbed up into the train. "You must learn to use proper English. Otherwise, you can't possibly hope to be understood."

"No," said Prudence, most decidedly.

Madame Lefoux seemed to find this terribly amusing, for Alexia heard her chuckle behind her as she, too, climbed inside the coach.

The Tunstells' troupe had already struck up a rousing chorus of "Shine Your Buttons with Brasso," an extremely bawdy tune entirely ill-suited to the first-class compartment of the Morning Express to Southampton.

Lady Maccon looked at her husband as if he might be one to justify such behavior.

He shrugged. "Actors."

Prudence, lacking in all sense of dignity and decorum, squeaked in delight and clapped along with the song.

Madame Lefoux immersed herself in some papers from the Royal Society, humming along.

Tunstell demanded ale, despite it being early morning. One of the young ladies from the supporting cast began to dance a little jig in the aisle.

"What will the steward think of us?" said Alexia to no one in particular. "This is going to be a very long trip."

CHAPTER SEVEN

Biffy Encounters a Most Unsatisfactory Parasol

In the years that followed, when Lady Maccon had occasion to recall that nightmare morning, she would shudder at the horror of it all. She who has not traveled in the company of ten actors, three toddlers, a werewolf, and a French inventor cannot possibly sympathize with such torture. The chaos of the train station was a mere appetizer to the main course of utter insanity that was the Maccon party's attempt at boarding the steamer at Southampton. Miraculously, they managed to do so with few actual casualties. Ivy lost one of her hatboxes to the briny deep and had a fit of hysterics. The man playing the villain, a fellow named Tumtrinkle, barked his shin on the side of the entrance ramp, an occurrence that, for some strange reason, caused him to sing Wagnerian arias at the top of his lungs to withstand the pain for the next three-quarters of an hour. The wardrobe mistress was in a panic over the proper treatment of the costumes, and the set designer insisted on handling all of the backdrops personally, despite the fact that he had a dodgy back and a limp. One of the understudies was not pleased with the size and location of her room and began to cry, claiming that in her country, ghosts were tethered near water, so she could not possibly be in a room that overlooked the ocean . . . on a boat. Percy spit up on the captain's lapel. Primrose ripped a very long feather out of a lady passenger's hat. Prudence squirmed out of her father's grasp at one point, toddled over to the railing, and nearly fell over the edge.

Lady Maccon felt, if she were the type of woman to succumb to such things, a severe bout of nerves might have been called for. She could quite easily have taken to her apartments with a cool cloth to her head and the worries of the world far behind her.

Instead, she oversaw the loading of the mountain of luggage with an iron fist, distributed cleaning cloths to the captain and Percy, rescued and returned the feather to its rightful owner, sent a steward to Ivy's room with restorative tea, insisted Tunstell comfort the hysterical understudy, distracted the wardrobe mistress and set designer with questions, corralled her daughter with one arm and her frantic husband with the other, and all before the steamer tooted its departure horn and lurched ponderously out into a dark and choppy sea.

Finally, once everything was settled, Alexia turned to Conall, her eyes shining with curiosity. "Who did you order it from?"

Lord Maccon, exhausted, as only a man can be when put in sole charge of an infant, said, "To what could you possibly be referring, my dear?"

"The parasol, of course! Who did you order my new parasol from?"

"I took a good hard look at the available options, since Madame Lefoux was off the market, and thought we needed someone who at least knew something of your character and requirements. So, I approached Gustave Trouvé with the commission."

"My goodness, that's rather outside his preferred practice, is it not?"

"Most assuredly, but out of fond regard, he took the order anyway. He has, I am afraid to say, encountered some difficulty in execution. Hasn't Madame Lefoux's touch with accessories."

"I should think not, with a beard like that. Are you quite certain he is up to the task?"

"Too late now—the finished product was supposed to arrive just before we departed. I left instructions with Lyall to send the article on as soon as it appeared. It was meant to be a surprise."

"Knowing Monsieur Trouvé's taste, I'm certain it still will be. But thank you, my love, very thoughtful. I have felt quite bereft these past few years. Although, thank goodness, I have had very little need of it."

"Comparative peace has been nice." Conall moved Prudence, who had dozed off, to drape more artistically over one massive shoulder and shifted closer to his wife. They stood at the rear of the ship, watching the cliffs of England retreat into the mist.

"But?"

"But you have been getting restless, my harridan. Don't think I haven't noticed. You wanted to come to Egypt for a bit of excitement, if nothing else."

Alexia smiled and leaned her chin on his vacant shoulder. "You'd think Prudence would be excitement enough."

"Mmm."

"And don't place this all on me—you're harking after some adventure yourself, aren't you, husband? Or have you Egyptian interests?"

"Ah, Alexia, how do you know me so well?"

"Are you going to tell me?"

"Not yet."

"I loathe it when you do that."

"It's only fair. You practice the same policies, wife. Case in point: were you going to tell me about Biffy?"

"What about him?"

"You said something to him before we left. Didn't you?"

"Good gracious me, how could you possibly know that? Biffy has far too much circumspection to reveal anything to you."

"I know, my dear, because he changed. There was a lightness about him. He fit correctly into the pack, a role he has been reluctant to fill heretofore. What did you do?"

"I gave him a purpose and a family. I told you all along that was what he needed."

"But I tried that with the hat shop."

"I guess it had to be the right purpose."

"And you aren't going to tell me any more until I tell you about my reason for visiting Egypt."

"My love, now it is *you* who knows *me* too well."

Lord Maccon laughed, jiggling Prudence quite violently. Fortunately, much like her father, she was difficult to awaken.

It was a gray, wintry day, and there was little to see now that they had taken to the open ocean.

Alexia was beginning to feel the chill. "So long as we understand each other. And now let's get our daughter inside. It's a mite cold out here on deck, don't you think?"

"Indubitably."

Biffy felt the absence of his Alphas as a kind of odd ache. It was difficult to describe, but the world was rather like a tailored waistcoat without buttonholes—missing something important. It wasn't as though he could not function without buttonholes; it was simply that everything felt a little *unfastened* without them.

He returned from the station in good time only to find a stranger at the door to his hat shop. A well-rounded stranger with a narrow wooden box tucked under one arm, an indifferent mode of dress, and an abnormally proactive beard. From the quantity of dust about his person, Biffy surmised the man had been traveling. Without spats, he noticed in alarm. There was a certain cut to the stranger's greatcoat that suggested France, and from the weathered appearance of the garment, Biffy deduced he must have come by train directly from the Dover landing green, on the Channel Dirigible Express out of Calais.

"Good evening, sir," said Biffy. "May I help you at all?"

"Ah, good evening." The man had a jovial way of speaking and a French accent.

"Are you looking for Madame Lefoux, perhaps?"

"Cousin Genevieve, no. Why would you think . . . ? Ah, yes, this used to be her shop. No, I am in search of Lady Maccon. I have a delivery for her. This was the address given with the commission."

"Indeed? Is it something for the London Pack perchance?"

"No, no. For her specifically, at Lord Maccon's request."

Biffy unlocked the shop door. "In that case, you had best come in, Mr. . . . ?"

"Monsieur Trouvé, at your service." The Frenchman doffed his hat, his button eyes twinkling, apparently at the mere pleasure of being asked to introduce himself.

Biffy felt the bushiness of his beard became less offensive in a man who seemed so very good-natured.

"Pardon me for a moment. I must see to the lights." Biffy left the Frenchman at the entrance and flitted quickly about in his practiced nightly ritual of turning up the gas in all the lamps and straightening gloves and hair-muffs from the day's activities. His head girl was good, but when she closed the shop for supper, she never left things quite up to his exacting standards. He remembered talking with Lady Maccon about her journey through Europe after Lord Maccon's unfortunate distrust of her moral fiber. At the time, he had been locked in a massive egg beneath the Thames. Later, however, Lady Maccon had related her side of the story, and it had included this French clockmaker, one Monsieur Trouvé. He was also the man who had designed the cages in the contrivance chamber below.

He completed his circuit of the shop and returned to his visitor.

"You are said by experts to be the last word on the subject of clocks. And I have heard of your exploits as relates to a certain ornithopter, the *Muddy Duck*. It is a pleasure to make your acquaintance."

The Frenchman threw his head back and let loose an infectious peal of laughter. "Yes, of course. It has been so long since I saw either Lady Maccon or Cousin Genevieve that I thought I might make the trip to London myself with the goods. An excuse for socializing, yes?"

"I am afraid you've missed them both. They left only a few hours ago for Southampton."

"Oh, how unfortunate. Will they be back soon?"

"Regrettably, no. They have taken a large party on an Egyptian tour. But if that box contains what I think it contains, Lady Maccon will want it as soon as possible. I am charged to send important items on to her. They are traveling by steamer in deference to Lord Maccon's, er, health."

"Ah, mail by dirigible has ample opportunity to bisect their journey? A most acceptable proposal, Mr. . . . ?"

"Oh, dear me, my sincerest apologies, sir. Sandalio de Rabiffano. But everyone calls me Biffy."

"Ah, the newest member of the London Pack. Genevieve wrote of your metamorphosis. A matter of some scientific interest not to mention political unrest. Not my field, of course." Knowing he was conversing with a member of Lord Maccon's pack seemed to relax the Frenchman. Yet France was not progressive in its approach to the supernatural.

"You are not afraid of me, Monsieur Trouvé?"

"My dear young man, why should I be? Oh, ah, your unfortunate monthly condition. I admit before meeting Lady Maccon I might indeed have been taken aback, but a werewolf came to our rescue on several occasions, and of wonderful use he was, too. Now vampires, I will say, I have little use for. But werewolves are good to have on one's side in a fight."

"How kind of you to say."

"Here is the box for her ladyship. The contents are quite durable, but I should not like to see it lost."

"Certainly not. I will ensure it is transported safely."

The twinkle reappeared from the depths of all the facial hair. Biffy dearly wanted to recommend the man the services of a good barber but thought this might be taken as an insult. So he bent his head to examine the package—a plain thing of untreated wood, cut thin like a cigar box.

"There is one other matter."

Biffy looked up from his inspection expectantly. "Yes?"

"Major Channing, is he also out of town?"

Biffy's good breeding took over, hiding his surprise. "No, sir, I believe he is at the pack's town residence." He tried to hide the curiosity in his voice, but the Frenchman seemed to sense it.

"Ah, that werewolf I spoke of, the one who came to our rescue. We ended up traveling through Europe together. Decent fellow."

At a complete loss, Biffy told him the pack address. He and the Gamma had very little to do with one another. Biffy showed the major his neck on a regular basis, and the major took control as needed and ignored him the rest of the time. But never before had anyone described Major Channing Channing of the Chesterfield Channings as a *decent fellow.*

The French clockmaker continued this surprising line of conversation. "I believe I will pay him a call, seeing as the ladies are away. Thank you for your time, Mr. Biffy. Good evening to you."

"I hope the rest of your London visit is more productive, Monsieur Trouvé. Good night."

As soon as the man left, Biffy popped open the long, skinny wooden box to look inside. It was terribly out of form, of course, to inspect someone else's mail. But he argued himself into believing it was to check on the safety of the contents, and he *was* now a member of Lady Maccon's Parasol Protectorate. It granted him, he felt, certain rights of familiarity.

He gasped in horror at the contents. Lady Maccon had carried with her many rather ill-advised parasols over the course of their association, one of which had been a good deal *more*. There was something to be said for such a weapon. But the parasol in the box before him was a travesty. Apart from everything else, it was utterly plain and undecorated except for the stitching of the supposedly *hidden* pockets. It was made of drab olive canvas! It was probably quite deadly, and there was no doubt the bobbles on the handle housed hidden dials and debilitating poisons. It was certainly heavy enough to do any number of things. But if such a thing could be said of a parasol, it looked like the kind of object a sportsman would carry, all function and no beauty. The brass handle positively clashed with the olive color. It looked—Biffy shuddered in utter horror—like an . . . umbrella!

He checked the delivery schedule. He'd have to place it on the early morning Casablanca-bound post in order for it to cross Lady Maccon's path as soon as possible. With a determined gait, he returned to the front of the shop and flipped the CLOSED sign. He had only six hours to rectify the situation. Taking the hideous thing in hand, he made room upon the counter. He pulled out all the laces, silk flowers, feathers, and other trims, dumped them all around him, found a needle and thread, and went to work.

The P & O's Express Steamer was constructed with luxury in mind. Built to take advantage of the new craze in antiquities collecting and Egyptian tours, the line was an attempt by the shipping industry to compete with dirigible carriers. Dirigibles had the advantage of being faster and more frequent, but a steamer had more space and carrying capacity. Lord and Lady Maccon's first class cabin was quite as large as Lord Akeldama's closet, perhaps even bigger, and outfitted with two portholes—an improvement on the closet, which had no windows at all. Of course, the portholes could be covered over with thick curtains, as the one clientele liners could guarantee was werewolves.

Lord and Lady Maccon knocked on the adjoining cabin, which they had rented for Ivy's nursemaid and the children, and deposited the sleeping Prudence into a small cot there. They could hear Ivy, still chattering to her husband in a distressed tone over the loss of her hat, in the cabin on the far side.

In the interest of limiting numbers, they had not included a butler, valet, or lady's maid among their personnel. This was an embarrassing breach in propriety, should the information get out. Alexia was nervous because it meant Conall had to help her with her toilette, but she supposed she might call upon the theatrical troupe's wardrobe mistress in dire emergencies. Her hair would simply have to be stuffed under a cap as much as possible. She had a few of Ivy's hairmuffs on hand as well, suspecting that the deck of a steamer got just as cold as that of a dirigible, possibly more so.

Being of the supernatural set, and rather confirmed in their habits and ways, the Maccons defied the breakfast bell and all tenets of fellow traveler obligation by undressing and taking to bed. Alexia figured the acting troupe was also likely to keep to nighttime hours, and as their visit in Egypt was to pay court on a vampire, she saw no reason to alter the entire pattern of her married life merely because of a sea voyage. No doubt the crew was accustomed to such idiosyncratic behavior. She left very clear orders with regard to meal times and postal deliveries. It was daylight, so even if Prudence did awaken, the infant couldn't cause more harm than any ordinary precocious toddler. Thus Alexia felt comfortable falling gratefully into Conall's welcome embrace. The world outside could await her pleasure.

Lady Maccon awakened late that afternoon. She dressed herself as much as she was able and left the cabin without disturbing her husband. Poor Conall, he looked as though he'd been hit by a train.

The designated nursery was quiet and still, but a certain waving of arms and burbling indicated that Prudence was awake, although not inclined to cry and unsettle her companions. Lord Akeldama had noted, on more than one occasion, that while Prudence's peculiar abilities made her somewhat of a handful, she was a very good-natured child. He then flattered Alexia by saying this rather reminded him of her.

Alexia made her way over to the cot and looked in.

"Mama!" announced Prudence, delighted.

"Shush," admonished her mother. "You will awaken the others."

The nursemaid came up behind Alexia. "Lady Maccon, is everything all right?"

"Yes, thank you, Mrs. Dawaud-Plonk. I think I'll take Prudence down with me, if you don't mind seeing to the necessities?"

"Of course, madam." The nursemaid whisked Prudence off behind an Oriental screen in one corner of the cabin. The infant emerged moments later wearing a fresh nappy and a pretty dress of cerulean muslin with a fur cape for warmth and a French-style hat. She looked quite smart and a little mystified by the rapidity with which she had been dressed. So, indeed, was Alexia. Such efficiency in relation to her daughter was a miracle of the highest order.

"I see why Ivy values your services so highly, Mrs. Dawaud-Plonk."

"Thank you, Lady Maccon."

"You aren't, by any chance, related to my butler, Mr. Floote, are you?"

"I am afraid not, madam."

"I had no idea there could be more than one."

"Madam?"

"Oh, nothing. I should warn you, as you are likely to have care of my child as well as the twins over the next few weeks, that Prudence has some very unusual habits."

"Madam?"

"Special."

"Every child is special in his or her own way, madam."

"Ah, yes, well, Prudence can be *quite* special indeed. Please try to keep her from touching her father after sunset, would you? She gets overly excitable."

The nursemaid didn't even flinch at such an odd request. "Very good, madam."

Alexia propped Prudence on one hip and together they went to explore the ship.

Up top, the day proved still dreary. The wind was running fierce and cold and there was nothing to see but whitecaps atop a darkened ocean. Alexia merely wished to ascertain that they were still going in the correct direction.

"Brrr," was Prudence's eloquent comment.

"Indeed, most inclement weather."

"Ptttt."

"Exactly, let us adjourn elsewhere."

She switched Prudence to her other hip and made her way to the forward section of the steamer, in front of the first smokestack, where the dining room and the library were situated.

Unsure as to the wakefulness of her party, Lady Maccon visited the library first for some light reading so that if she did have to dine alone, she might have some kind of intellectual discourse. Prudence was not quite yet up to her mother's standard of debate. The library was of questionable curation, but she found a scientific manual on human anatomy that she thought might prove absorbing, if not entirely appropriate to dining. The cover was innocuous enough, and there were some rather graphic pictures within that intrigued Prudence. Alexia was enough her father's daughter to relax some standards of propriety so long as scientific inquiry was the result. If Prudence was interested in anatomy, who was Alexia to gainsay her?

Despite it being very nearly teatime, the eatery was empty save for one gentleman in the far corner. Lady Maccon was about to settle on the opposite side of the room, feeling it a standard of common decency not to inflict a child on anyone, least of all a lone gentleman, when the gentleman in question rose and nodded at her, revealing that he was Madame Lefoux.

Reluctantly, but not wishing to appear rude, Alexia wended through the chairs and tables to join her.

Lady Maccon settled Prudence on her lap. The infant stared at Madame Lefoux with interest. "Foo?"

"Good afternoon, Miss Prudence, Alexia."

"No," objected Prudence.

"It's her latest word," explained Alexia, distracting her child with the book. "I'm not entirely certain she knows what it means. How have you settled in, Genevieve?"

A steward appeared at Lady Maccon's elbow with a small scrap of paper on which was printed the comestibles on offer.

"Interesting approach to food service," she said, fluttering the pamphlet about. Prudence grabbed at it.

"Saves the bother of having to hold everything in stock for the entirety of a journey and at the whims of passengers," replied the Frenchwoman.

Alexia was not interested in commerce, only tea. "A pot of Assam, if you would be so kind. One of the apple tarts and a cup of warm milk for the infant," she said to the hovering man. "Do you have any cinnamon sticks by chance?" The steward nodded. "Infant, do you want cinnamon?"

Prudence looked at her mother, her tiny rosy lips pursed. Then she nodded curtly.

"Shave some cinnamon on top for her, would you, please? Thank you."

The steward moved smoothly off to see to her needs.

Alexia snapped open a monogrammed serviette and tucked it into the neck of her daughter's dress. Then she sat back and took in her surroundings.

If not exactly decorated with Lord Akeldama's flair, the dining hall at least bowed to Biffy's taste. There was gilt and brocade aplenty, if judiciously applied. The room seemed to have been made by enclosing a deck, rather like a greenhouse, for there were large windows all around showing the gloomy outside.

"So what do you make of the SS *Custard*?" Madame Lefoux asked, pushing aside her papers and favoring Alexia with a dimpled smile just like the old days.

"It's rather posh, isn't it? Although I shall reserve judgment until I have sampled the comestibles."

"As you should." Madame Lefoux nodded, sipping her own beverage from a tiny demitasse teacup.

Lady Maccon sniffed the air. "Hot chocolate?"

"Yes, and a very good showing, by my standards."

Alexia rather preferred to drink tea and eat chocolate, but Genevieve was French and had to be allowed some measure of European behavior.

The steward arrived with her tea and tart, both of which proved to be well above average. Alexia began to think she might actually enjoy the crossing. Prudence was quite taken with her warm milk, spending a good deal of time dabbing at the cinnamon sprinkles on the top with her finger and then sucking them off. Terribly undignified, of course, but as yet the infant-inconvenience had shown very little interest in the proper use of utensils, her attitude seeming to be that fingers had come first in her life, so why mess with a good thing? Alexia kept an eye on her but didn't otherwise interfere. It was amazing what having a toddler had done to her much-vaunted principles.

"So, how are you, Genevieve?" Alexia asked finally, determined not to be made to feel embarrassed. After all, Madame Lefoux was in the wrong, not she.

"Better than could be expected. It is not so bad as I had feared, working for the hive."

"Ah."

"And Quesnel is enjoying himself, getting plenty of attention and an excellent education. Say what you will about vampires, they value knowledge. And an entire hive of vampires and drones actually keeps my boy in check. Although, that said, they have not managed to impress upon him any interest in fashion."

"Dama?" Prudence wanted to know.

"Exactly, Prudence," answered her mother.

"No," said Prudence.

Alexia remembered Quesnel as a scamp with a predilection for grubby workman's clothing that rendered him, in appearance, much like a newspaper boy. "So you both may survive until he has reached his maturity?"

Prudence finished her warm milk and shoved the cup away petulantly. Alexia caught it before it fell off the table. The child switched her attention to the printed menu that the steward had unwisely left behind. She flapped it about happily and then spent some time folding the corners.

Madame Lefoux's dimples reappeared. "We may. It is strangely restful, having the responsibility for his well-being partly removed, although there have been"—she paused delicately—"discussions with the countess. I can but temper their influence. I suppose it must be similar for you and Lord Akeldama."

"Thus far, Prudence seems perfectly capable of making up her own mind on most things. He does favor frilly dresses but I could hardly expect practicality from a vampire. Prudence doesn't seem to mind. Conall and I are happy to have the help. The werewolves have a saying. Do you know it? 'It takes a pack to raise a child.' In this case, a pack, Lord Akeldama, and all his drones may just possibly be sufficient to handle my daughter."

Madame Lefoux gave a doubtful look. The child looked about as innocent as a werewolf with a pork chop. She was content with the pamphlet, quietly humming to herself.

The Frenchwoman finished the last of the chocolate in her cup and poured herself another helping from the pot. "You have an easier time letting go than I."

"Well, I am less motherly than you, I suspect, and Lord Akeldama is my friend. We share sympathies and interests. Fortunately, he is *very* motherly."

"Not so the countess and myself."

Lady Maccon smiled into the last of her tart before probing gently. "Although I understand you do share *some* tastes."

"Why, Alexia, what could you possibly be implying?"

"Mabel Dair, perhaps?"

"Why, Alexia." Madame Lefoux brightened. "Are you jealous?"

Alexia had only meant to needle, now she found herself drawn into flirting and became embarrassed as a result. She should never have even broached such a scandalous topic.

"You would bring things back around to that."

Madame Lefoux took Lady Maccon's hand, becoming serious in a way that made Alexia quite nervous. Her green eyes were troubled. "You never even gave me a chance. To determine if you liked it."

Alexia was surprised. "What? Oh." She felt her body flush under the constriction of stays. "But I was married when we met."

"I suppose that is something. At least you saw me as competition."

Alexia sputtered, "I . . . I am very *happily* married."

"Such a pity. Ah well, that's one of us sorted. I guess you could do worse than Conall Maccon."

"Thank you, I suppose. And things cannot be so off with the hive and Miss Dair, or you would not be so forthcoming about it."

"Touché, Alexia."

"Did you think that while you were studying my character, I was not studying yours? We have not been much in each other's company these last few years, but I doubt you have changed that much." Alexia leaned forward. "Formerly Lefoux said to me, before she died, that you loved too freely. I find it interesting that you can be so loyal to the individual and to your much-vaunted technology yet be so unreliable where groups and governments are concerned."

"Are you accusing me of having my own agenda?"

"Are you denying it?"

Madame Lefoux sat back and let out a silvery tinkle of laughter. "Why should I wish to?"

"I don't suppose you are going to tell me to whom you are reporting on this particular trip. Order of the Brass Octopus? Woolsey Hive? Royal Society? French government?"

"Why, Alexia, didn't you just say I work only for myself?"

This time it was Alexia's turn to be amused. "Very nicely turned, Genevieve."

"And now, if you will excuse me, I have some business to attend to in my quarters." Madame Lefoux stood, made a little bow to both ladies. "Alexia. Miss Prudence."

Prudence looked up from her careful mutilation of the menu. "No."

The inventor retrieved her jacket and top hat from a stand by the door and made her way out into the blustery corridor.

"Fooie," said Prudence.

"I couldn't agree with you more, infant," said Lady Maccon to her daughter.

Alexia remained in the dining hall a goodly while. She enjoyed the ambiance, the constant supply of tea and nibbles, the efficiency of the staff, and the fact that it afforded her a general inspection of the other passengers. Everyone, after all, had to eat. Their fellow pilgrims were the expected assortment. She spotted several sets of pale ladies—invalids in search of health. The two emaciated fellows who were all floppy hair and elbows with ill-cut jackets could only be artists. The tweed-clad jovial chaps intent on drinking the steamer's entire stock of port before they reached port were obviously sportsmen keen upon crocodiles. There was a wastrel in black Alexia first thought might be a statesman, until he whipped out a notebook, which made her think he was that lowest of the low: a travel journalist. There were various unfashionable gentlemen with battered headgear and too much facial hair, either antiquities collectors or men of science.

Of course, her main reason for staying was that Prudence seemed equally content to sit, mutilating the menu pamphlet, and there was no point in messing with a good thing. Which was how it was that her husband found her still at tea even after sunset.

He arrived trailing Mr. and Mrs. Tunstell, the nursemaid, the twins, and two members of the troupe, all looking bleary-eyed but dressed for dinner.

"Dada!" said Prudence, looking very much like she would appreciate some affection from her father. Alexia set her bare hand carefully on the back of her daughter's neck and then nodded at her husband.

"Poppet." Conall buzzed his daughter exuberantly on the cheek, making her giggle, and then did the same to his wife. "Wife." This elicited an austere look, which they both knew was one of affection.

Alexia supposed she ought to retire and dress for dinner herself, but she was terribly afraid of missing something interesting, so she remained, only transferring to a larger table so that the others could join her and Prudence.

"I do believe I might enjoy ocean transport even more than floating," pronounced Ivy, sitting next to Alexia without regard for proper table arrangement or precedence. Alexia supposed such standards had to be relaxed when traveling. Lord Maccon sat on Ivy's other side, keeping a good deal of room between him and his daughter.

"Is it the space or the fashion that appeals?"

"Both. Now, Percy, love, the furniture is not for eating." Baby Percival was busy gumming the back of the dining chair, arching over his father's arm in order to do so.

"Ahhouaough," said Primrose from her position on the nursemaid's lap. She had not yet developed the capacity for consonants.

This behavior, peaceable though it was, appeared to be too much for Mrs. Tunstell. "Oh, take them away, Mrs. Dawaud-Plonk, do. We will have a nice supper sent down to you. This simply isn't the place for children, I'm afraid."

Mrs. Dawaud-Plonk looked worried, faced with the logistical prospect of having to carry three toddlers. But Prudence, seeming to agree with Ivy that it was high time to leave, jumped down from her chair, removed the serviette from about her neck, handed it carefully to her mother, and stood waiting patiently while the nursemaid loaded herself up with twins. The little girl then preceded the nursemaid from the room, as though she knew exactly where she was going.

Ivy looked after, impressed. "I do look forward with pleasure to the time when mine are walking with greater stability."

"I wouldn't, if I were you. She gets into everything." It was a matter of some discussion in the Maccon–Akeldama household that Prudence seemed to walk sooner and with greater efficiency than was expected in an infant. It was generally thought that this might be because of her alternate forms—her vampire one being far faster and her werewolf one stronger. Together they probably bettered her burgeoning understanding of bipedal motion.

Ivy commenced to chatter about her experiences aboard the ship, for all they had been at sea only half a day, as though steamers were her life's work and main passion. "The windows in my cabin are actually *round*. Can you believe it?" The meal proceeded without incident, if the phrase *without incident* might be used to describe such an ordeal as objections to the type of sauce, the quality of the meat, and the color of the jellies. Lady Maccon began to suspect actors of being far more choosy in their preferences than even Lord Akeldama. She felt that the meal, comprised of giblet soup, fried turbot, beef shoulder, minced veal and poached eggs, corned pork, pigeon pies, croquettes of mutton, jugged hare, ham and tongue, and boiled potatoes was all that one might hope for aboard ship. And the seconds, always her favorite, far excelled such expectations, as they included both blackcap and rice puddings, jam tartlets, and a platter of excellent cheeses.

Lord Maccon declined after-dinner drinks and cards. Lady Maccon declined a stroll about the decks. Together they made their way back to their private quarters instead. Alexia, thinking of her filched book on anatomy, suggested they take advantage of the comparative peace of travel with no muhjah or BUR duties to distract them. Conall wholeheartedly agreed but seemed to believe books had no part in this activity.

They compromised. Alexia took out the book on anatomy and

used Conall as a study specimen. She was taken with trying to determine where different organs were situated from the outside, which involved prods and pokes with her fingers. Since Conall was ticklish, this led to a small tussle. Eventually, Alexia lost possession of the book, her clothing, and her heart rate, but the study session was declared, by Conall at least, to be a resounding success.

CHAPTER EIGHT

Alexia Makes an Unexpectedly Damp Discovery

The sea voyage was an oddly peaceful affair. This made Lady Maccon nervous. Because they kept to supernatural hours, the Maccons, the Tunstells, the collective progeny, and the acting troupe had nothing to do with the other travelers except at suppertime. During those convocations, when Alexia and her compatriots were commencing their waking hours, and the others their evening's amusement before bed, all travelers were required to socialize. The steamer was outfitted with only first-class compartments, unlike some of the less dignified Atlantic lines, and Alexia was delighted to find passengers behaving as first-class frequenters ought. Everyone was civil and politics never came up at table. The actors provided much needed entertainment, either through the acceptable avenues of conversation and the occasional musical interlude or through more dramatic means, like engaging in mad, passionate affairs with some dish on the menu and then having the vapors when the cook ran out or stealing the skipper's hat for a scandalous dance routine. They behaved themselves as much as could be expected and did not stray so far away from the upper crust as to commit any prank not already enacted by the young men of Oxford or Cambridge. Although one memorable evening of bread roll cricket certainly stretched the boundaries of propriety.

Trouble, when it inevitably came, originated in the most likely quarter—her husband and her daughter and her daughter's favorite toy, a large mechanical ladybug.

Early on in Prudence's life, Lady Maccon had written to her friend the clockmaker Gustave Trouvé, with an order for one of his mechanical ladybugs, only larger, slower, and less deadly. She'd had this outfitted with a small leather saddle and had, inadvertently, started a new craze in children's toys that kept that good gentleman busy for the next year. Lucrative, as it turned out, the market for rideable ladybugs.

Prudence showed this particular toy such favor as to make it entirely necessary to pack the thing for any trip—let alone one of several weeks—despite its bulky size. Alexia and Prudence had taken to occupying the first-class lounge and music room every evening after supper, Alexia with a book and a weather eye to her daughter, and Prudence with her ladybug and a gratifying willingness to wear herself out by running after it, or on top of it, or, on several occasions, under it. Sometimes one or two of the actors would join them to play the piano. Either Prudence or her mother might pause in their respective activities to listen, Lady Maccon sometimes driven to glare in disapproval when songs strayed too far toward the "Old Tattooed Lady" and the like.

It was when Lord Maccon joined them on the third night and Prudence, in a fit of excitement, ran her ladybug into his foot and fell against him that things went askew. They had been very careful, but it was so unexpected that even Lord Maccon's supernatural reflexes were not fast enough. This was compounded by the fact that, being a father, his instinct was to reach out and catch his daughter before she hit the floor, not, as it ought to have been, to leap away.

Prudence fell. Lord Maccon caught. And a werewolf cub dashed about the lounge causing chaos and panic. Prudence had been wearing a pretty pink dress with multiple frills, a nappy, and lace pantalettes. The nappy and the pantalettes did not survive the transition. The dress did. Prudence remained wearing it in wolf form, to Alexia's unparalleled amusement.

Prudence's werewolf nature seemed less driven by the need to hunt and feed than it was to run and play. Alexia and Conall had discussed whether this was a product of her youth or her metanatural nature. She also made for a very cute wolf cub, if Alexia did say so herself, so no one in the music lounge was *afraid* of her, but the unexpectedness of the cub's appearance did cause surprise.

"Gracious me, where did you come from, you adorable little fuzzball?" exclaimed Mr. Tumtrinkle, the gentleman playing the villain in *The Death Rains of Swansea*. He made a grab for said fuzzball, missed, and flew forward, crashing into the well-endowed lady soprano sitting at the piano. She shrieked in surprise. He grappled for purchase and ripped the bodice of her raspberry and green striped dress. She pretended a faint from embarrassment, although Alexia noted she kept an eye on a nearby steward to ensure her corseted assets were fully appreciated, which, from the young man's crimson blush, Alexia assumed they were.

Prudence the wolf cub made a circuit of the room, jumping up on people, trying to squirm under furniture and overturning it, and generally causing the kind of mayhem expected of an extremely energetic puppy wearing a pink frilly dress and confined to a small area. She completed her tour at her father's feet, at which point, operating on some infant memory, she attempted to try to ride the ladybug that had caused the accident in the first place, all the while avoiding her parents' grasp.

They probably would have caught her at some point. It was a large lounge, but it wasn't *that* large. Unfortunately, a deck steward opened the door, carrying a long package under his arm.

"Lady Maccon? This package just arrived for you by dirigible. And this letter. And here is a missive for you, Lord Maccon, and—Oh my goodness!"

Which was when Prudence made a break for freedom between the unfortunate man's legs.

"Catch her!" ordered Alexia, but it was too late. Prudence was off down the corridor. Alexia ran to the door, just in time to catch sight of the tip of her daughter's fluffy tail as it disappeared around a corner.

"Oh, dear."

"Lady Maccon," said the lounge steward sternly from behind her, "unregistered animals are not allowed on board this vessel! Even well-dressed ones."

"Oh, er, yes, of course. I will naturally pay any fine for the inconvenience or damages, and I assure you everything will be rectified the moment I get my hands on her. Now, if you will excuse me. Are you coming, Conall?"

With which Lord and Lady Maccon went dashing after their errant child.

Everyone left behind was very confused, especially when they found a torn child's nappy next to the forgotten ladybug and no evidence of little Lady Prudence anywhere in the lounge.

"You look tired, Professor. No insult intended, of course. And you make it intentionally difficult to tell, but I am beginning to believe that that little wrinkle about the pocket of your waistcoat indicates exhaustion."

"How very wise of you, young Biffy, to note my mood from the state of my waistcoat. Have you noticed anything else significant occurring around town of late?"

Biffy wondered if this was some kind of werewolf test to assess his skills of observation. Or perhaps Professor Lyall wanted to know what information Biffy might impart to a fellow pack member, or whether he would keep his own council, or whether he would tell Lord Akeldama, or whether he would tell Lady Maccon. He would, of course, tell all parties. He wouldn't tell them all everything, or even all the same thing, but he would tell them all *something*. What other point could there be in gathering the information in the first place? In this, he and his former master disagreed. Lord Akeldama liked to know things for their own sake. Biffy liked to know things for the sake of others.

He answered Professor Lyall in a roundabout way. "London's rove vampires are acting up. I had one in the shop this very evening, throwing his weight around like he was a queen. It's a good thing the contrivance chamber is hidden. His drones were nosing about after something, and it wasn't hats."

Lyall looked Biffy up and down, assessing. "You're coming along nicely, young Biffy. You'll make an excellent replacement."

"Replacement for what?"

"Ah, as to that, patience is a virtue, my dear boy. Now, this thing with the roves, how long has it been going on would you say?"

"They've been getting worse over the last few years, but it's gone quite tannic indeed since our Alphas left. Why, one rove accused me of purposefully not stocking gaiters. Made quite a fuss over it. I never stock gaiters! And just this evening I saw one of them feeding in the street. Assuredly, it *was* down near the embankment. But still, in the open air? I mean to say, that's almost as bad as picnicking in the park. Eating in *public*! It's simply not done."

Lyall nodded. "And the rove parties are getting rather wild as well. Do you know BUR had a missive from Queen Victoria on the subject? Bertie was seen at one of the Wandsworth events. She is a progressive, our dear Regina, but she is not all *that* progressive. Her son fraternizing with a hive on a regular basis—not at all acceptable. I understand the potentate got an earful on the subject."

"Oh, dear. Poor Lord Akeldama." Biffy brought all his new werewolf culture and his old vampire training to bear on the situation. "Is all this vampire ruckus because we werewolves are living inside their urban territory?"

"That is one theory. Any others?"

"Is it because Countess Nadasdy is no longer in Mayfair? There is no queen for London central. Could that be causing dissonance?" Biffy watched Professor Lyall's face closely. He would never have called the Beta handsome, but there was something very appealing in the mildness of his expression.

"That is a thought. Lord and Lady Maccon and their Alpha nature might have held them back somewhat, but London is missing a queen, and the Grande Dame of Kentish Town is simply too far away to oversee matters in Westminster and the south side of the Thames."

Biffy knew a little of London's northern queen. "She also cares very little for the affairs of society. Not even fashion."

"There are some vampires," Lyall said, "very few, but *some*, gone off like *that*." He sniffed in a way that suggested the odor of rotten meat that undercut the scent of all vampires.

If Biffy understood nothing else, he understood significant emphasis in speech. "What can we do about it?"

"I shall have BUR keep a close eye on the roves, call in the rest of our pack if I have to, but full-moon revels are likely to be overly fervent this month. And there is little I can do then. We can but hope that Lord and Lady Maccon complete their business quickly and return home before a second full moon, as one alone may tax us to our limits."

Biffy said, off the cuff, "Or we could find a replacement queen."

"Volunteering for the position?"

"Why, Professor, is that wittiness I detect?"

"Only for you."

"Charmer." Biffy tapped him on the arm playfully.

Professor Lyall started slightly and then actually looked embarrassed by the casual contact.

Prudence led them on a merry dance about the ship, ending her jaunt hidden in a lifeboat on the port side of the promenade deck. Conall managed to catch her. Despite her supernatural strength, he also managed to hold on to her long enough to transfer her to his wife.

"Mama!" said the wriggling girl who resulted from this transaction. And then, as they were on the outer deck and she was wearing only a pink party dress, "Brrrr!"

"Yes, well, dear, you have only yourself to blame for that. You know you have to avoid your father at night."

"Dada?"

"Yes, precisely."

Lord Maccon waved shyly at his daughter, standing a good distance away to forestall any additional accidents.

"Oh, now, Prudence, look at that," said her mother, pointing up.

"No," said Prudence, but she looked up.

Above them was the postal dirigible, lashed to the moving steamer and being dragged along as deliveries were transferred between the two. Mail was dropped down a taut silk chute. Alexia thought it looked like fun and wondered if people ever came aboard in such a manner.

"Any mail for Casablanca?" the assistant deck steward yelled, marching to-and-fro. "Mail for Casablanca? Departure in ten minutes! Any mail?" He continued his call and went down to the lower decks.

The floating post was a good deal different-looking from the passenger dirigibles Alexia was accustomed to utilizing. Prudence was duly fascinated. Lord Maccon took it as an opportunity to skulk off in pursuit of port in the smoke room, and possibly a nice game of backgammon.

"Bibble!" was Prudence's opinion. The infant was excessively fond of air flight, although she had yet to try it personally. There was some fear that, like her father and other werewolves, she would fall victim to airsickness. Her fondness was merely exhibited in pointing at dirigibles and squeaking whenever she happened to spot one above the town or when she was taken on a walk to Hyde Park. Occasionally, she was even allowed to sit in Lord Akeldama's private air transport, *Dandelion Fluff Upon a Spoon*, when it was at rest upon the roof of the vampire's town house. And, of course, she had multiple toy dirigibles, including one that was an exact replica of *Dandelion Fluff Upon a Spoon*.

The postal dirigible was very sleek and stealthy in appearance. Alexia and her daughter were riveted. Its balloon section was narrowed for speed. It had six aether current propellers, and its barge section was mainly one massive steam engine. Any other available space was utilized by the post itself and a small number of passengers, mostly businessmen, who were willing to trade luxury and comfort for speed.

Prudence was enthralled and might have stayed a good deal longer, but her teeth started to chatter. Lady Maccon noticed and took her daughter to the nursemaid for a new nappy and some warmer clothing. It was some time before Alexia remembered that the deck steward had attempted to deliver mail to her.

Lady Maccon went in pursuit of her deliveries, finding them in good time and then, suspicious of the contents, went to find her husband. She guessed well what it was from the shape of the box and supposed Conall might want to witness the opening of her new parasol.

She found him at the backgammon tables, delivered to him his missives—one in Lyall's tidy block lettering and the other in Channing's untidy scrawl—and then turned her attention to her own mail. In addition to the box, there was a letter from Biffy. The front of this was addressed as required for float mail, but on the back, below the seal, the young werewolf had written, *To be opened before the box!* in block lettering.

Conall, dear man, got all bouncy when he saw the package. "Capital! It has arrived at last!"

Alexia had enough sensitivity not to blurt out her certain knowledge as to the contents. "I have a communication from Biffy. Silly boy seems to believe it important that I read his letter first."

"By all means," said her husband magnanimously, although his eyes were caramel colored with excitement.

Alexia duly seated herself, despite glares from various gentlemen at the presence of a *female* in the *smoke room*, and cracked open the seal. Inside, Biffy detailed not only the current state of the murder investigation (no appreciable change), Lord Akeldama's latest waistcoat purchase (navy and cream striped with gold braid), and Floote's odd behavior on the subject of roasted pheasant (dismissed from the larder forthwith), but also a visit from Gustave Trouvé (beard of substantial magnitude). He went into a colorful and very detailed description of her new parasol upon its initial arrival. And then into even more specificity over the improvements to its appearance that he had felt compelled to make. He apologized profusely for opening her mail without permission but articulated that he felt his actions were duly excused, as they spared her the horror of ever having to encounter the parasol in its original state. He signed the missive with his real name, but Alexia knew this was because this particular letter contained nothing delicate nor Parasol Protectorate related, aside, of course, from the parasol itself.

Thus forewarned, Lady Maccon *opened the box*.

What lay before her was as dissimilar a creature to Biffy's description of the original as could be imagined. The talented boy had taken the monstrosity in hand and subdued it with as much finesse as might be brought to bear upon drab olive canvas.

He had covered the exterior with black silk. There were delicate white chiffon ruffles along the ribs and three layers of fine embroidered lace ruffles at the edge of the shade, completely disguising the multiple pockets hidden there. He had managed to drape the fabric overlay in such a way that when the parasol was closed, it puffed out, disguising any suspicious bulges. At the top, near the spike, was another bit of white lace and then a great puff of black feathers, cleverly hiding the springs and arming mechanism that allowed the tip to open and shoot various deadly objects and substances. Unfortunately, he'd had very little to work with on the handle. It was brass, very simple, with three nodules, the twisting of which, according to Gustave Trouvé's notes, would cause different results. He hadn't Madame Lefoux's predilection for fancy hidden buttons or carved handles. Biffy, however, had fought back against the simplicity by wrapping pretty ribbon at various points about the handle, hopefully not interfering with its primary function. He had completed his decoration by lining the interior with white chiffon ruffles and looping two black pom-poms about the handle, which acted decoratively and, Alexia realized with delight, would allow her to fasten the accessory to her person so she might not misplace it.

It was a bit loud for her taste, but the clean black-and-white color scheme added an air of refinement, and all the additional froofs would better disguise the secrets within.

"Oh, Conall, isn't it perfectly lovely? Didn't Biffy do a splendid job?"

"Oh, yes, if you say so, my dear. But what of Mr. Trouvé?"

"What, indeed? To praise his side of the work, I must put it through its paces, must I not?"

Lord Maccon looked around at the still-glaring gentlemen whose peaceful card games and cigar puffs had been inexcusably disturbed by the brash Lady Maccon and her frivolous mail.

"Perhaps elsewhere, wife?"

"What? Oh. Of course, somewhere private, and in the open air. There's no knowing what might come flying out of this little beauty." Alexia stood eagerly.

They exited the smoking room, only to run into Mrs. Tunstell in the hallway.

"Alexia! Lord Maccon! How fortuitous! I was looking for you. Mrs. Dawaud-Plonk has put the children down, and Tunny and I were wondering if you would like to join us for a game of whist?"

"I don't play whist," said Conall, rather shortly.

"Oh, don't mind him," dismissed his wife at Ivy's offended expression. "He's difficult about cards. I might be able to, in a quarter of an hour or so, but I just this moment took delivery of a new parasol, and Conall and I are off to the promenade deck to test it."

"Oh, how topping. But, Alexia, it isn't sunny."

"Not that kind of testing." Lady Maccon gave Mrs. Tunstell a wink.

Ivy was taken aback for only a moment. "Oh! Ruffled Parasol?"

"Exactly, Puff Bonnet."

Ivy was enthralled. "Oh, *I say*." She raised her hand to her face and made a little finger wiggle toward the tip of her pert little nose. This was her not-so-subtle gesture for secrets afoot. Alexia counted her blessings. Ivy's first suggestion had been that they each hop about in a small circle when they had clandestine information to impart, and then stop, face one another, and point both fingers at the mouth in a most ridiculous fashion.

Still, Lord Maccon was fascinated by Ivy's absurdly wiggling fingers.

Lady Maccon poked him in the ribs to get him to stop staring.

Ivy stopped her odd gesture. "Can I see *it*?"

Lady Maccon proffered up the accessory.

Mrs. Tunstell was appropriately enthusiastic. "Black and white, very modish! And is that chiffon? Now, that is something *like*. Nicely done. Of course, you know scarlet and yellow are far more *the thing* for spring."

Alexia gave her a look that said she was on very dangerous ground.

Ivy backpedaled hurriedly. "But black and white is more versatile, of course, and you want this one to last."

"Exactly so."

"May I join you on deck?"

"To view its anthroscopy?"

"Its anthro-what? No, my dear Alexia, to witness its"—Ivy paused and blushed, looking around to see if they were being overheard—"*emissions*."

"That's what I said."

"Oh, did you? Well?"

Alexia figured Ivy was officially part of her inner circle, and this parasol was that circle's defining feature. "Of course you may, my dear Ivy."

Ivy clapped her blue-gloved hands in excitement. "I'll go fetch a wrap and my hairmuffs."

"We shall see you up top." Lady Maccon took her husband's arm and led him away.

"My dear, what is the meaning of that . . ." Conall waved his fingers at his nose in a fair imitation of Ivy's wiggle.

"Oh, let her have her fun, Conall."

"If you say so, my dear. Odd behavior, though. Like she had a fly about her snoot."

Accordingly, a good fifteen minutes later, Ivy, complete with wardrobe change, joined a shivering Alexia and an annoyed Lord Maccon on the promenade deck.

Ivy now sported an outrageous set of hairmuffs that Alexia had no doubt had been specially designed. They exactly matched Ivy's hair and consisted of multiple corkscrew curls in the Greek style falling about her ears and a coronet of plaits. Gold braid was woven throughout, with a gilt dagger over the left ear with a spray of leaves and gold fruit falling at the back. It looked more like a headdress for a ball than anything else. It was all of a piece and worn like a helmet over Ivy's own hair.

Because the hairmuffs entirely covered her ears as well as her head, Mrs. Tunstell was warm but also rather deaf.

"Ivy, finally, what could possibly have taken you so long?" Lady Maccon wanted to know.

"You want a song? I couldn't possibly serenade you on an open deck. Perhaps later, in the lounge. You are meant to be anthropomorphizing the workings of that parasol, remember?"

"Yes, Ivy, I know. We have been waiting for you."

"What are you to do? Well, I assume the accessory came with instructions. It can't possibly be all that different from your original emissionous parasol."

Alexia gave up and turned to proceed with her experiments. She stripped off her gloves and passed them to Ivy, who took them gravely and tucked them into her reticule. Alexia consulted the instruction sheet.

Of the three nodules on the handle, the first, when twisted, appeared to do nothing whatsoever. As she was pointing the parasol out to sea, and this was the magnetic disruption emitter, this was the best that could be hoped for. Even Alexia was not so bold as to trot aft and try the parasol on the steamboat's engine.

"Nothing happened," objected Ivy in disappointment.

"Shouldn't with the emitter."

"Mittens? I suppose that is sensible in case of snow," replied Ivy.

The middle nodule, turned to the left, caused a silver spike to jut out, and to the right, a wooden one. Unlike Lady Maccon's previous parasol, both could not pop out at once.

Alexia wasn't certain about that change. "What if I need to fight off both vampires and werewolves together?"

Lord Maccon gave her a very dour look.

"Ooh, ooh, ooh!" Ivy was practically bouncing in excitement over some kind of revelation. "I had a thought," she said, examining the edge of the wooden stake with interest.

"Oh, yes?" encouraged Alexia loudly.

Ivy stopped and frowned, her pert little face creased in worry. "I said I *had* one. It appears to have vanished."

Alexia returned to her examinations. The bottom nodule, closest to the shade and nested in the puff of black feathers, was slightly more detailed. Alexia consulted her sheet and then opened and carefully flipped the parasol around. A twist to one direction and a fine mist spouted forth from the ends of the parasol's ribs. From the smell and sizzle of the liquid as it hit the deck, that was lapis solaris diluted in sulfuric acid. A twist in the other direction and lapis lunearis and water came out, causing a brown discoloration to the already pockmarked deck.

"Oops," said Lady Maccon, not very apologetically.

"There, you see, emissions! Really, Alexia, is there no more dignified approach?" Ivy stepped back from her friend and wrinkled her nose.

Finally, Alexia reached the very last point on Monsieur Trouvé's list of instructions.

Gustave Trouvé had written: *"My esteemed colleague included the two spikes in her original model, but I thought we might make additional use of them. Please ensure that you are well braced for this feature, my dear Lady Maccon, and that you have pointed the parasol at something substantial. Twist the nodule closest to the shade sharply clockwise while holding the parasol pointed steadily at your target."*

Alexia backed up, leaning against the railing of the ship, and pointed the parasol at the wall on the other side of the promenade deck. She handed Conall the instruction sheet, braced herself, gestured Mrs. Tunstell well out of the way, and fired.

Later, Conall was to describe to her how the parasol's tip shot completely off, twisting slightly as it flew and pulling behind it a long, strong rope. The spike sank into the wall of the cabin and held. Alexia was to comment that this might have been quite useful the time she nearly fell off of the dirigible or out of the hive house. However, Gustave Trouvé had not exaggerated when he instructed her to be well braced, for the parasol jerked back against her violently, quite destroying her stability. Alexia let go of it in surprise.

Unfortunately, the railing was just low enough not to accommodate a woman of Lady Maccon's stature, girth, and corsetry. She overbalanced entirely, flipped in graceless splendor backward over the railing, and plummeted down into the ocean below.

Alexia screamed in surprise and then in shock at the coldness of the water. She came up sputtering.

Without hesitating, her husband dove in after. He could swim better and catch up to her faster in wolf form, so he changed as he fell, hitting the water a massive brindled beast instead of man.

As the steamer churned swiftly away, Alexia heard Ivy screaming, "Woman overboard! Wait, no, man *and* woman overboard. Wait, no woman and *wolf* overboard. Oh, dash it, help! Help us please! Stop the ship! Man the lifeboats. Help! Summon the fire brigade!"

Conall arrowed through the icy black sea toward Alexia, his fur slicked back, seal-like. After only a few moments, he reached her.

"Really, husband, I can swim perfectly well. There's no need for both of us to get all salty," instructed Alexia tersely, although she was already shivering and she well knew the real danger in being cast adrift came not from drowning but from cold.

Conall barked at her and swam closer.

"No, *don't touch me*! Then you'll be human, too. Then we'll both shiver to death. Don't be silly."

Ignoring her, the wolf came up next to her and wormed his way under one arm, clearly intending to help her stay afloat.

He did not change.

Not even slightly.

Alexia had removed her gloves for parasol examination and was gripping him reflexively with one bare hand. Nothing. He remained a werewolf.

"Well, would you look at that!"

Conall's wolf face looked shocked. But then again, the markings about his eyes and muzzle often caused that expression, so there was no way to tell if he was truly registering the peculiarity or still acting on instinct to protect her. Whatever the case, at least he did not give in to his werewolf nature and try to eat her, which for the first time in their long association he might have been able to do.

Alexia's teeth started to chatter. Conall was doing most of the work to keep them afloat. She figured she might as well let him, as he still had all his supernatural strength.

She cogitated upon this amazing occurrence, thinking back over her life and every preternatural touch: those times when she had been forced to use her naked flesh, and those times when it had functioned even through fabric.

"Wat-t-t-t-ter!" she chattered. "It's all wat-t-t-t-ter. Just like ghosts and t-t-tethers."

Conall appeared to be ignoring her, but Alexia was having a scientific breakthrough and being stranded somewhere near the Strait of Gibraltar in the Atlantic Ocean wasn't going to stop her epiphany. "It all makes per-r-r-fect sense!" She wanted to explain but she was chattering so hard she could no longer understand herself. Also her extremities were going numb. Science would have to wait.

I'm going to freeze to death, she thought. *I have figured out one of the greatest preternatural mysteries and no one will know the truth. It's so very simple. It was there all along. In the weather. How annoying.*

"Oh! There she blows!" she heard Ivy sing out in the dark night. A wave of displaced water crashed over her, and a second later a wooden box with handles splashed down next to her for her to latch on to. The box was followed by a knitted hammock she could use to pull herself inside.

Conall changed into his human form and pulled himself in next to her.

"Cover yourself with my skirts," hissed his wife through still-chattering teeth, pushing the ruination of her evening gown at him.

Her husband only looked at her, mouth agape. "What just happened?"

"We have made a g-g-g-reat discovery! We may have to p-p-p-publish," announced his wife, waving her goose-pimpled arms about. "Scientif-f-f-ic-c-c break-k-k-through!"

Conall threw his arm around her, hugging her close, and they were lifted to safety. By the time they reached the deck, he was mortal.

CHAPTER NINE

Biffy Experiments with Flirting and Felicity

Everything ought to have proceeded smoothly with the investigation—or as smoothly as possible with Lady Kingair's brand of Alpha obnoxious interference. Biffy genuinely believed they were doing well, even after calling in at the eighth ball in an attempt to track down various private dirigible owners. Lucky for him, in the manner of all wealthy enthusiasts, the owners were quite willing to talk about their floating conveyances to the exclusion of all else, even with a slight young man to whom they had only recently been introduced. Biffy learned how the *Great Mitten Slayer* earned its name, where it was berthed, how often it was used, and what security measures were in place that prevented lone assassins from floating it to Fenchurch Street and killing werewolves. He ascertained similar details about *Her Majesty's Truss*, the *Lady Boopsalong*, and several others with names less easily recalled. He also learned that those gentlemen equipped with the means and inclination to purchase personal flotation devices were not so interested in tying their cravats with finesse. Dirigibles brought out the worst in people.

It was Professor Lyall's plan of inquiry. Biffy was to handle the high-society elements, while the professor looked in at registration offices and sequestered paperwork on pilots' credentials and private dirigible sales from Giffard's. Lady Kingair was of very little use, so they left her to stew at the house, pacing about the library and pouncing upon whoever stumbled in. Floote kept her in line as well as he was able with a constant supply of chewing tobacco, Scotch, and treacle tart. Just like Lady Maccon, she seemed to have an unholy passion for the dratted stuff. Biffy had never liked treacle tart, even as a human; he simply couldn't respect any kind of food that left a residue.

He came home from the eighth party, and yet another failed lead, to find Floote waiting for him in the hallway looking rather more concerned than he had previously thought Floote capable of looking, even after an entire evening spent with sticky, treacle-eating werewolf she-Alphas. The hallway smelled of roses.

"Is something wrong, Floote?"

"It's Miss Felicity, sir."

"Lady Maccon's sister? What could she possibly want with me?"

"Not you, sir. She called here to see Lady Kingair. They've been sequestered in the back parlor for over an hour."

"Good gracious me! They know each other from when the ladies visited Scotland, but I did not think they were on terms of any intimacy."

"No, sir, I don't believe they are."

"You think Miss Loontwill is *up to something*?"

Floote inclined his head. As much as to say, *Isn't she always?*

Biffy took off his hat and gloves, placing them both on the hall table and checking the state of his rebellious hair in the looking glass above it. Tonight it was frizzy. He sighed. "But what could Miss Loontwill possibly want with Lady Kingair?"

"Is that Professor Lyall?" came a roar from the back parlor. The door crashed open, revealing Lady Kingair in a towering fury.

Biffy, noting the rage, inclined his head, tugging down on his cravat to expose his neck.

This submissive stance only seemed to aggravate her further. "Oh, it's *you*. Where is Lyall, the little weasel? I'll see him flayed alive. You see if I don't."

Biffy glanced up through his lashes, trying to keep as unthreatening a demeanor as possible.

Felicity followed Lady Kingair out into the hall. She was wearing a dress of pale blue satin with royal blue velvet trim and a smug expression. Biffy had no idea why, but that expression terrified him more than Lady Kingair's rage. He wasn't particularly taken with the dress, either. Blue on blue always looked damp.

Lady Kingair came close enough for his hackles to rise, even in human form. "Did you ken, pup?"

"Know what, my lady?" Biffy kept his voice mellow.

"Did you ken it was him? Did you ken what he did?"

"I'm sorry, my lady, but I have no idea to what you are referring."

"Did you ken what he did to *my pack*? Stole Gramps away from us! Lyall, that jackass. Stole him! Organized everything. Played us all like we were bally puppets. Got my pack to attempt treason and Gramps to feel betrayed so he would up and run to Woolsey. Do you ken what that did to my life? A *child* left to clean up dross? Have you any inkling what it was like? Did he give us a single thought? Destroy one pack to save another, will he? Bollocks to that! I'll skin him alive!"

Biffy could only shake his head, trying to understand, trying to put everything together. "This is all before my time, my lady."

She lashed out at him, backhanding him hard across the face, all werewolf strength and Alpha rage at anyone who would threaten her pack, past or present, real or imagined. The force of the blow thrust Biffy back against the wall and down to one knee, blood spattering the perfect points of his white starched collar.

Felicity gave a little squeak of alarm.

The pain was intense but fleeting. Biffy could feel the cut on his lip healing even as he regained his feet. It had taken him a long while to become accustomed to the sensation of flesh knitting back together again, like skin darning. He pulled out his handkerchief, lilac scented, and dabbed the spatter off of his cheek. He could feel the hunger starting, the need to consume bloody flesh to compensate for the blood he had lost. Felicity, standing so still behind the vibrating Lady Kingair, smelled delicious, even through the lilac of his handkerchief and the rose of her perfume—werewolf urges were so embarrassing.

"Now, Lady Kingair, there's no call for that kind of behavior. We are all civilized here, if you would just—"

But the Alpha was already away, ripping the dress from her own body and changing to wolf form there in the hallway. She went charging out into the night. Floote had enough presence of mind to open the front door wide or she might have crashed through it.

Biffy was frightened for Lyall and momentarily at a loss given the suddenness and violence of the preceding few minutes. He knew he should warn the Beta somehow, but first he had to ascertain the particulars. He turned to face Felicity.

Out of the corner of his eye, he saw Floote subtly replacing a tiny pearl-handled gun into his inner coat pocket with his free hand. The butler must have armed himself when Lady Kingair turned violent. Biffy wasn't certain how he felt about this. Should butlers be hiding small firearms about their personage? Didn't seem very domestic.

Felicity tried to make her way to the now-open door.

Biffy moved supernaturally fast. He would never be as quick as Lord Akeldama, but he was certainly faster than Felicity Loontwill. He signaled Floote with a sharp gesture, and the butler, understanding perfectly, closed the door firmly in the young lady's face. In the same instant, Biffy took Felicity by one arm.

His hands—slender and fine and once so well suited to his preferred mortal pastime, playing the piano—were now more than equipped with the strength to waylay one frivolous female.

"I didn't know you knew Lady Kingair."

"I didn't until I met her."

Biffy glared.

Felicity started to prattle. "Why, Mr. Rabiffano, I've hardly seen you out in society at all since I returned from abroad. I'm finding private balls about town so very undiscriminating these days. They'll let practically *anyone* attend. Then again, you were at the Blingchesters last night, weren't you? Talking to Lord Hoffingstrobe about his new dirigible?"

Biffy decided, under the circumstances, it was not too rude to interrupt her. "Miss Loontwill, stop gargling, please. I think you had better tell me what, *exactly*, you just told Lady Kingair."

After being warmed by multiple hot water bottles and then cleaned of brine in the plushest of the SS *Custard*'s bathhouses, Lady Maccon was once more able to carry on a conversation without chattering.

"Alexia," Ivy reprimanded most severely once she was back in her friend's presence, "you had my heart in my chest! You really did."

Alexia disposed of Ivy's panic and solicitude by sending her off in search of comforting and obscure foodstuffs and took to her bed merely because it seemed the safest way to keep the gossipmongers at bay. Ivy had proved resourceful under such extreme circumstances as her favorite friend and patroness falling overboard. After calling for help, she had extracted the two parts of the new parasol, coiling the grapple about the tip like yarn about a spindle. She even spent time scuttling and hopping about, managing to stomp on the instruction sheet before it flew overboard.

"You see," said Alexia to her husband as Ivy dashed off to see about custard éclairs, "I told you she had hidden depths."

"Do you think it's only saltwater immersion that has this kind of effect?" Lord Maccon was far more interested in their recent revelation. Ivy's peculiarities of character were nothing on his wife's peculiarities of ability.

Alexia was most decided on this point. "No. I believe it is any water. Even moisture in the air narrows the scope. Did you never wonder why the Kingair mummy's effect was so wide in London and so small when we reached Scotland? It was raining in Scotland. Also, there must be some kind of proximity and air contact as well, for I was only affected by the preternatural mummy when I was in the same room with it, unlike you, who could not change into a werewolf within a larger-ranging area."

"We have always known preternaturals and supernaturals functioned differently. Why should we not react differently to an alien agent in our midst? Werewolves are affected by the sun and moon; preternaturals are not."

"And it's clear the water was not enforcing your form?"

"Absolutely. I can change in water. Have done so many times."

"So it definitely limits preternatural touch."

"We know your abilities are related to ambient aether. We should not be so very surprised."

Alexia looked at her husband. "I wonder how wet I have to be."

"Well, my darling, we will have to perform a series of scientific tests . . . by bathing together." Lord Maccon waggled his eyebrows at her and leered.

"Could soap be a factor?" Alexia was willing to play his game.

"And how about underwater kisses?"

"Now you're getting silly. Do you think that's why our Prudence hates bath night so much?"

Conall sat up and stopped flirting. "By George, that *is* an idea! Perhaps she feels a limiting of her abilities, or perhaps she has a way of sensing others out of the aether that she relies upon that is shut off by water."

"You mean she feels blinded? Goodness, bathing would be quite a torture, then. She does always seem to notice when someone new is in the room before anyone else."

"That could simply be excellent powers of observation."

"True. Oh, dear, I wish she would acquire complete sentences. It would be so much more efficient to ask her these questions and get a sensible answer."

"Our curiosity will have to wait a few years."

Alexia worried her lower lip. "It's all to do with the aether in the end."

"Very poetical, my dear."

"Was it? I didn't know I had it in me."

"Well, do be careful, my love. Poetry can cause irreparable harm when misapplied."

"Especially with reference to our daughter."

Very little made Biffy lose his poise or posture, but after Felicity's story, he was practically slouching. "Let me see if I have this quite clear: Professor Lyall was responsible for Kingair losing Lord Maccon as Alpha?"

Felicity nodded.

"But how could *you* possibly know a thing like that?"

Felicity flicked a curl of blond hair over one shoulder. "I overheard Alexia accusing him of it when I was staying here. He didn't deny it and they agreed to keep the whole thing from Lord Maccon. I don't think that's right. Do you? Keeping secrets from one's husband."

Biffy was sickened, not so much by the information, as he could readily believe such a thing of Professor Lyall, who would do anything for his pack, but by Felicity's duplicity. "You have been sitting on this information for several years, waiting to distribute it until it could do the most damage. Why, Felicity?"

Felicity huffed out a little breath of aggravation. "You know, I told Countess Nadasdy. I told her! And she did *nothing*! She said it was a matter of werewolf internal politics and domestic relations, and none of her concern."

"So you waited, and when you heard Lady Kingair was in town, you decided to tell her? Why?"

"Because she will react badly and tell Lord Maccon in the worst possible way."

"You may, quite possibly, be evil," said Biffy in a resigned tone.

"It's always been Alexia: better, smarter, special in that way of hers. Alexia who married an earl. Alexia who visits the queen. Alexia who lives in town. Alexia with a baby. Who am I to be left behind by my great lump of a sister? Why is she so wonderful? She's not pretty. She's not talented. She has none of my finer qualities."

Biffy could hardly believe such pettiness. "You did this to destroy your sister's marriage?"

"Alexia had me exiled to Europe for *two years*! Now I'm too old for the marriage mart. But what does she care for my problems? She's well set up. Wife of an earl! She doesn't deserve to have any of it! It should be *mine*!"

"Why, you horrible little creature."

"No wife should keep a confidence from her husband like that." Felicity struggled to find the moral high ground.

"And no thought of what this will do to Professor Lyall or this pack?"

"What do I care for a middle-class professor or a gaggle of werewolves?"

Biffy suddenly couldn't stand to even look at the girl. "Get out."

"What?"

"Get out of my house, Miss Loontwill. And I hope never to see you again."

"What do I care for your ill opinion, either, Mr. Rabiffano? A mere hat-shop owner and a low-ranked werewolf."

"You may not care for mine, Miss Loontwill, but I still enjoy the friendship of Lord Akeldama, and I will see he knows exactly what you have done. Lady Maccon is his *very dear friend* and he will see you ostracized from polite society because of this. Rest assured, Miss Loontwill, you will become a social pariah. I recommend you plan an emigration of some kind. Perhaps to the Americas. You will no longer be welcome in any parlor in London."

"But—"

"Good evening, Miss Loontwill."

Biffy didn't know what good he thought it might do, but it was quarter moon—enough for him to change without difficulty and not so full he might lose control. Not that he did *that* much anymore. He was getting better and better at the shift, almost like adjusting to a new haircut or cravat. It still hurt like nothing else on earth, which made it less cravatlike than one would prefer, but at least now when he was a wolf, he was still himself. There had been some doubt of that once.

He had only one advantage over Lady Kingair. He already knew where Professor Lyall was supposed to be. He did not have to track him through the city. He ran straight there, a lean chocolate-colored wolf with an oxblood stomach and a certain mottling about his neck that was almost, Lady Maccon had kindly noted, cravatlike. He used the back alleys and side streets so as not to disturb anyone. Most of London knew they now boasted a werewolf pack residing in the city center, but there was a difference between knowing and meeting a wolf face-to-face when engaging in an evening constitutional. That said, he did encounter a group of sporting blunts at their cups, who all politely raised their hats to him as he passed.

The Bureau of Unnatural Registry occupied the first few stories of an unassuming Georgian near the *London Times* offices and generally kept itself to itself in the manner of all semisecret government operations. Tonight, however, there was clearly something afoot even from outside the building. Had not the bright lights and rapidly shifting shadows given this indication, the yells loud enough for even a normal human to hear would have. Not to mention the fact that the front door was wide open and hanging askew on its hinges.

Biffy nosed his way inside.

The hallway was filled with running men, demands for numbing agents, calls for the constabulary, and arguments over whether they were authorized to interfere.

"Clearly a personal werewolf matter!"

"Oh, you think so, Phinkerlington? Then why bring it to BUR?"

"Who knows the ways of werewolves? Ours is not to question pack protocol."

"But . . . but . . . but Professor Lyall *never* fights!"

"This is a matter of enforcement. BUR must enforce!"

At that juncture, the collective in the hallway noticed Biffy slinking in among them.

"Oh, spiffing, here's another one!"

"Now, now, perhaps he can help."

"They're in the stockroom, Mr. Werewolf, sir, and we may not have a stockroom soon if they don't quiet down."

Biffy was not all that familiar with the layout of BUR, but he could follow his ultrasensitive hearing, which directed him up the stairs toward a large cavernous room. The door to this room was also open, although unbroken, and crowded round it stood a group of BUR officers and agents watching a battle within. Money was exchanged as wagers were taken on the outcome, and now and then a cry of distress went up as something particularly dramatic occurred.

Biffy forced his way through the onlookers' legs and entered the room, still not certain what good he might do but determined to try.

Professor Lyall and Lady Kingair were faced off against one another. Professor Lyall was not doing well.

If one were to pass the professor in wolf form in the countryside, one might mistake him for some kind of overgrown off-color fox. He was a slender, elegant creature and not one to inspire confidence in battle. Biffy had learned since joining the pack that Professor Lyall's skill lay in his ability to fight smart and in his quickness and dexterity. He was almost beautiful as he battled the Alpha of Kingair, his movements lithe and graceful, calculated, yet impossibly swift.

But he was only a Beta. He simply wasn't strong enough. He was holding his own, but his body was ripped open in a thousand places and he was fighting pure defense. Every good general knows that defense will never win.

Biffy couldn't help himself. Instinct took over. He'd been learning his werewolf instincts for two years now, so he was cogent enough to analyze their meaning. One urged him not to face an Alpha, but it was balanced out by another that urged him to help his packmate, to protect his Beta. That second instinct was the one that won.

Biffy launched himself at Lady Kingair, going for her face. As a human, he would never contemplate such a thing—to hit the face was ungentlemanly and to hit a lady unpardonable—but werewolves measured victory in challenge by the destruction of the eyes. Eyes were one of the few things a wolf could bite that took time to heal, rendering continued roughhousing impossible. There was also death, of course. It wasn't common, but it did happen, usually when an Alpha faced a much weaker opponent, or two Alphas fought in daylight.

Lady Kingair dodged easily out of Biffy's way. Professor Lyall barked at him, an order to stay out of it, but Biffy wasn't going to let him take on an enraged Alpha all alone. He charged Lady Kingair again.

The Alpha swung her head around and sliced at the side of his cheek, tearing it open with her teeth. Biffy felt the burning sting of profound pain and then the equally agonizing knitting sensation as his body repaired itself. Everything, he had realized shortly after his metamorphosis, was pain for werewolves. Which was probably why they were so mean—general buildup of peevishness.

Lady Kingair was on him again. Biffy realized what Professor Lyall was up against. The female Alpha was vicious in battle. She gave no quarter and had no mercy. Oh, she was smart about it, as smart as Lord Maccon in a fight, but she was a lot less nice. She was almost taunting them, never going in for a kill strike or the eye mark that would bring about victory. She wanted the torture, like a cat with mice. She wanted Professor Lyall to suffer, and now that Biffy was there, she wanted him to suffer, too.

Biffy and Professor Lyall exchanged yellow-eyed looks. They really had only one option. They had to either exhaust Lady Kingair, or they had to keep her occupied until sunrise. A tall order indeed, but there were two of them.

For the next three hours, Biffy and Lyall traded off fighting Lady Kingair. They never once let her rest, while managing to grab a few minutes to flop down and pant one at a time, catch a breath, and heal slightly. Even two of them acting together could not defeat her or injure her enough to make her yield. She was far too much of an Alpha for that. So they simply kept fighting her. Hoping her anger would run dry. Hoping she might collapse in exhaustion. Hoping the sun might rise. Her anger was inexhaustible, as was her speed and abilities. And the sun refused to rise.

Biffy was beginning to flag. The loss of blood was catching up with him in a quintessential werewolf way. He wanted to turn upon the humans crowding the doorway and feed almost as much as he wanted to fight. But some lingering sense of gentlemanly behavior would not allow him to abandon his Beta. He fought on until all his muscles were shaking, until he thought he could not lift another paw. He could only imagine what poor Professor Lyall felt, who must have been fighting Lady Kingair at least an hour longer than he.

Yet she kept right on going, her claws wicked and fast, her teeth impossibly sharp.

She got that great jaw of hers around Biffy's hind leg and began biting down. She was no doubt strong enough to snap the bone in half. Biffy hoped Professor Lyall was prepared to jump in while he took the time needed to knit that bone back together. He also hoped he was prepared for the pain. When the bone broke, it was liable to be excruciating, and he'd hate to howl with all those men watching.

Except it became suddenly clear that *all* the bones in his body were involuntarily breaking, fracturing, and re-forming. Fur was moving toward his head, the feel of stinging gnats crawling up his skin. He was left lying, limp and panting, naked in the utterly destroyed stockroom of BUR headquarters.

The sun had peeked its cheery head above the horizon.

"I'll thank you, Lady Kingair, to remove my ankle from your mouth," he said.

Sidheag Maccon did so, looking exhausted, and spat in disgust.

"I took a bath recently," said Biffy in mild rebuke.

Professor Lyall crawled over to them, his wounds far greater than either Biffy's or Lady Kingair's. They would be slow to heal, now that the sun was up. But at least the fighting was over. Or so Biffy thought.

"You nasty, manipulative little maggot," said Lady Kingair to Professor Lyall, her words more rancorous than her tone, which was fatigued.

The Beta looked over at the door full of curious BUR employees. "Haverbink, close the door, please. This is none of BUR's concern."

"Oh, but, sir!"

"Now, Haverbink."

"Well, here you go, sir. Figured you might need these." The aforementioned Haverbink, a strapping lad who looked like he ought to be milking pigs, or whatever it was they did in the Yorkshire dales, tossed some blankets and three large muttonchops into the room. Then he shut the door, no doubt leaning his ear to the outside.

Despite the gnawing, raging hunger, Biffy reached for a blanket first, dragging it to cover over his lower half, for modesty's sake.

"Good lad, Haverbink," commented Lyall as he bit into a chop. He handed one to Biffy, and in exchange Biffy tucked half the blanket around Lyall solicitously, noting that Professor Lyall had very nice thighs.

Biffy took the meat gratefully, wishing he had a knife and fork. And a plate, for that matter. But the meat smelled so good he turned aside so the others couldn't quite see and took as delicate bites as he could.

Lady Kingair gave the Beta a long look when he offered her the last chop and then took it with a muttered "thanks." She tore into the bloody meat without regard for anyone's finer feelings.

Lyall was looking at Biffy with an odd expression in his hazel eyes. "Biffy, my dear boy, when did you learn to fight with soul?"

"Um, what do you mean, Professor?"

"Just now, you knew who you were, who I was, and what we were doing the entire time."

Biffy swallowed his mouthful. "Isn't that part of controlling the shape-shift?"

"Goodness no. It's a rare thing for a wolf to fight smart. Alphas, of course, and a few lucky Betas, and some of the oldest of the pack regulars. But most everyone else goes on instinct. It's quite a gift to have learned so young. I'm proud of you."

Biffy could feel himself blushing. Never before had he received a compliment from Professor Lyall, not even a fashion-related one.

"Och, how sweet." Lady Kingair's lip curled. "But perhaps the compliments could wait until you have explained yourself, *Beta*."

Lyall finished his repast and collapsed against an overturned stack of metal slates. Biffy pressed his back slightly against his Beta's legs, taking comfort from the contact, and leaned up on one elbow to look at Lady Kingair. The Alpha propped herself into a full seated position, using a massive box of ammunition. She looked tired, but still angry. They all stared at one another.

Finally Professor Lyall said, "I'll admit I did not see it from your perspective, my lady. And for that I extend my sincerest apologizes. But you have no idea what he was like. No idea."

Sidheag Maccon looked much like her great-great-great-grandfather as she popped the last bite into her mouth and gave the Beta an austere look. When she finished chewing, she said magnanimously, "I ken he went mad. I ken he was violent. I dinna think that's an excuse."

"He killed Alessandro."

"Aye? Well, Templar training will only get a man so far. And after, what? You planned for years to get your revenge. At my expense. At poor old Gramps's expense. He was happy in Scotland. What werewolf wants to come to England when he has the rolling green of the Lowland to run? You stole him against his will. Against our will."

The Beta fished about for a scrap of paper and cleaned his hands of blood as though with a handkerchief. "I provided the temptation. Your pack need not have followed it."

"Na good enough, Randolph Lyall. Na good enough."

Professor Lyall took a deep breath as though to fortify himself. Biffy felt a soft touch on his shoulder, and he craned his neck about to find the Beta leaning toward him. "You needn't have come, pup, although I'm glad you did. But I do wish you didn't have to hear what comes next."

But Biffy did hear, every messy, degrading, disgusting detail as Professor Lyall told Lady Kingair exactly what life had been like under the Alpha Lord Woolsey. Servicing him as Beta near the end had been humiliating—for five and a half long years. Lyall's face was deadpan as he relayed the details, as those who are tortured or raped will become when they retell the pattern of abuse. Biffy began crying quietly and wishing, indeed, that he did not have to hear it.

Lady Kingair lost much of her anger in the telling, but her sympathies were not entirely swayed. She could understand that Lyall had found himself in a situation with no possible way out except the one he took. But she could still not forgive that her pack had suffered the consequences of his choice.

"Oh, aye, and is that to be my lot as well? Tae be going all over abusive and deranged? Will poor old Gramps face the same fate?"

"Not all Alphas go bad the way Lord Woolsey went bad. He already had the tendencies. It's simply that when he was sane, he acted with the consent of his partners. Take comfort, my lady—most Alphas die before the opportunity arises."

"Oh, aye, much obliged I'm sure. Verra comforting, that is. What now, Professor?"

"Well, in an odd way, I am glad it is known. But Lord Maccon will never forgive me or trust me again. I take it you wrote him the details?"

"Oh, aye."

"Poor Lady Maccon. She didn't want to keep my secret. Now she will have to handle Conall finding out."

"You telling me you're prepared to make reparations?" Lady Kingair looked less angry and more contemplative, examining Professor Lyall through half-lidded eyes.

Biffy, wary of that look, leaned in against his Beta. Relishing the intimacy, feeling oddly proprietary.

Professor Lyall squeezed his shoulder reassuringly. "Of course."

"And you ken what I will want of you?"

The Beta nodded, looking resigned.

Lady Kingair took a deep breath and looked down her nose at the slight, sandy-haired gentleman. And Professor Lyall was still a gentleman, Biffy realized, even without a stitch of clothing, lying on the floor of a stockroom.

"I'm thinking Kingair's needing a Beta right about now."

"No!" Biffy couldn't help the exclamation. He reeled away from Lyall, turning so that he faced him fully.

Professor Lyall only nodded.

"And you, for all yon manipulations, are one of the best. Possibly because of them."

Professor Lyall nodded again.

"Oh, no," Biffy cried. "You can't abandon us! What will we do without you?"

Professor Lyall only looked at him with a little smile. "Oh, now, Biffy, I think you will do very well."

"Me!" squeaked Biffy.

"Of course. You have the makings of an excellent Beta."

"But I . . . I . . . ," Biffy stuttered.

Lady Kingair nodded. "That'll do nicely. Now dinna worry, pup, we won't keep him for all time—only until we find someone better."

"There is no one better," said Biffy with absolute confidence.

They were interrupted by a knock on the door. Haverbink stuck his head in without being summoned.

"Didn't I order you to stay away?" asked Professor Lyall placidly.

"Yes, sir, but it was so quiet I wanted to make certain you were all still alive."

"As you see. And?"

"And a massive gilt carriage has just pulled up out front. Lord Akeldama sent it with his compliments." Haverbink produced a mauve-colored scrap of paper. Lilac scent wafted into the room. "Said you would need a nice dark ride back home to get some sleep, and what were you *fluffy darlings* all doing still out and about?"

"How could he have known to send such a thing? He himself should already be comatose." Lyall blinked in mild confusion and looked to Biffy for an explanation.

"He would have left orders with his drones."

"Nosy vampire neighbors," sniffed Lady Kingair.

Afterward, Biffy could only just recall that ride back home, stumbling into the house and up the stairs, he and Professor Lyall leaning against one another in exhaustion. But he remembered perfectly the Beta's face, a single sharp look when they reached the door to his chamber, almost frightened. It was a look Biffy recognized. He had neither the strength nor the interest in allowing loneliness to pillage anyone else's peace of mind.

So he made the offer. "Would you like company, Professor?"

Professor Lyall looked at him, hazel eyes desperate. "I wouldn't . . . that is . . . I couldn't . . . that is . . . I'm not all that . . . capable." He gave a weak little flap of a gesture indicating his still-wounded state, his fatigue, and his disheveled appearance all in one.

Biffy gave a little puff of a chuckle. He had never seen the urbane professor discombobulated before. Had he known, he might have flirted more in the past. "Just company, sir. I should never presume even if we were both in perfect health." *Besides, my hair must look atrocious. Imagine being able to attract anyone in such a state, let alone someone of Lyall's standing.*

The corner of his Beta's mouth twitched, and he withdrew behind a veil of dispassionate hazel eyes. "Pity, pup? After you heard what Lord Woolsey did to me? It was a long time ago."

Biffy had no doubt Professor Lyall was as proud, in his way, as any other man of good breeding and refined tastes. He tilted his head, showing his neck submissively. "No, sir. Never that. Respect, I suppose. To survive such things and still be sane."

"Betas are made to maintain order. We are the butlers of the supernatural world." An analogy no doubt sparked by the advent of Floote, who glided down the hallway toward them, looking as concerned as it is possible for a man to look who, so far as Biffy could tell, never displayed any emotion at all.

"You are well, gentlemen?"

"Yes, thank you, Floote."

"There is nothing I can get for you?"

"No, thank you, Floote."

"Investigation?" The butler arched an eyebrow at their fatigued and roughened state.

"No, Floote, a matter of pack protocol."

"Ah."

"Carry on, Floote."

"Very good, sir." Floote drifted away.

Biffy turned to make his way to his own sleeping chamber, assured now that his overtures had been rejected. He was forestalled by a hand on his arm.

Lyall had lovely hands, fine and strong, the hands of an artist who practiced a craft, a carpenter, perhaps, or a baker. Biffy had a sudden fanciful image of Lyall with a smudge of flour on his face, going comfortably into old age with a fine wife and brood of mild-mannered children.

The sandy head tilted in silent invitation. Professor Lyall opened the door to his bedroom. Biffy hesitated only a moment before following him inside.

By the time the sun set that evening, they were both fully recovered from the ordeal, having slept the day away without incident. Fully recovered *and* curled together naked in Lyall's small bed.

Biffy learned, through careful kisses and soft caress, that Lyall was not at all disturbed by messy hair. In fact, his Beta's hands were almost reverent, stroking through his curls. Biffy hoped that with his own touch he could convey his disregard for Lyall's past actions and suffering, determined that none of what they did together should be about shame. Most of it, Biffy guessed, was about companionship. There might have been a tiny little seed of love. Just the beginnings, but a tender, equality of love, of a kind Biffy had never before experienced.

Professor Lyall was as different from Lord Akeldama as was possible. But there was something in that very difference that Biffy found restful. The contrast in characters made it feel like less of a betrayal. For two years, Biffy had held on to his hope and his infatuation with the vampire. It was time to let go. However, he didn't feel that Lyall was edging Lord Akeldama out. Lyall wasn't the type to compete. Instead he was carving himself a new place. Biffy might just be able to make the room. Lyall was, after all, not very big, for a werewolf. Of course, he worried about Felicity's story of Alessandro Tarabotti, about whether Lyall was capable of loving him back, but it was early yet and Biffy allowed himself to revel in the simple joy that can only be found in allaying another's loneliness.

When Lyall lay flush against him, nuzzling up into his neck, Biffy thought they fit well together. Not matched colors so much as coordinated, with Lyall a neutral cream satin, perhaps, and Biffy a royal blue. Biffy said nothing concerning any such romantic flights of fancy. Instead he asked a more practical question.

"You truly intend to become Kingair's Beta, even after all you sacrificed for this pack?"

"I must make amends." Lyall did not stop his nuzzling.

"So far away from London?" *So far from me?*

"It won't be forever. But I'll have to stay away, at least until Lord Maccon retires."

Biffy was floored. He stopped smoothing the hair at Lyall's temple. "Retires? Retires from being Alpha?" *As though it were a position in a tradesman's firm?* "You think that is something he's likely to do?"

Lyall smiled. Biffy could feel the movement of his cheek against his chest. "Ah, Biffy, you think Lord Maccon is any less aware of the fate of Alphas who get too old than we are?"

Biffy's hand went involuntarily to his throat in shock. For there could be only one possible implication from such a statement. Lord

Maccon intended to kill himself before he went mad. "Poor Lady Maccon!" he whispered.

"Now, now, not to worry. I shouldn't think it'll be all that soon. Decades or more. You must really learn to think like an immortal, my sweet Biffy."

"Will you come back here after?"

"I will try."

"So we must wait until Lord Maccon dies? How macabre."

"Much of immortality, you will find, is in surviving the deaths of others. And the waiting has not started yet. We have some time before our Alphas return." He began kissing Biffy softly on the neck.

"By all means, let us not waste time."

Which was how Biffy missed his last window to send a message by dirigible post, warning Lady Maccon of Lady Kingair's letter to Lord Maccon. Which was why he used rather more colorful language than he ought upon realizing that he had mucked the timing up quite royally and would not have an opportunity to contact his mistress again until *after* she landed in Alexandria.

Timing, he realized, could work hard against one, even when one had, theoretically, all the time in the world.

CHAPTER TEN

Wherein Our Intrepid Travelers Ride Donkeys

It was Sunday tea aboard ship and the Tunstells had been persuaded to perform their rendition of *Macbeth* to rousing applause and much comedic effect in the dining hall when the port of Alexandria was sighted. Ten days of familiarity will make strangers traveling together more friendly with one another than an entire season of town socialization. Alexia was not certain how she felt about such familiarity—it led to homegrown theatricals while *at table*, but the other passengers were enjoying themselves.

Ivy was dressed in a corseted medieval gown and lamenting her blood-covered hands—beet juice from a most excellent stewed vegetable tureen—and wearing a blond wig of epic proportions and ratty state. She was giving the tragedy her all, in a rather misguided and decidedly impressionistic take on the famous knife scene. Tunstell lay prone over a potted plant stage right—also known as the kitchen entrance. Mr. Tumtrinkle, sporting a substantial fake mustache and a waistcoat so tight it was near to popping over his well-padded circumference, was tiptoeing across the stage wielding another potted plant, Macduff with Birnam Wood, and carrying a baguette sword.

The diners were riveted. Particularly by the antics of the waitstaff, who had to dodge through the climactic fight scene carrying scones and jam.

It was no wonder, then, that Alexandria snuck up on all of them. The first thing that signified the momentous event was a slowing in their speed and a loud tooting noise. The captain hurriedly excused himself, tea unfinished, and the Tunstells stopped their antics and stood about dumbly.

The proximity bells clanged out and everyone made busy finishing their conversation and foodstuffs without the appearance of excitement or hurry, although clearly under the influence of both.

"Have we arrived?" Alexia asked her husband. "I do believe we have."

Conall, for whom high tea was an exercise in futility, there being little protein on offer and too many small fiddly sandwiches expressly designed to thwart a man of his ilk, stood without prompting. "Well, come along, my dear, to the upper deck!"

Alexia took up Prudence, who was ostensibly the excuse for awakening early and attending the tea. The toddler had yet to experience such an occasion as Sunday tea in a public assembly on a steamer, and Alexia had thought she might enjoy the treat. Prudence had indeed, although her good behavior might be better attributed to the performance than the comestibles. Prudence found the Tunstells' rendition of *Macbeth* more fascinating than anyone else, possibly because the antics were right about her education level or possibly because life with Lord Akeldama had given her to expect a certain degree of extravagant theatricality.

Prudence was particularly taken with the idea that Mr. Tumtrinkle now answered to the name Macduff, possibly because she could say Macduff but not Tumtrinkle. She was also hypnotized by his mustache, a fact made clear as they climbed out onto the promenade and the actor stood behind them. Prudence somehow ended up leaning over her mother's shoulder, misappropriating the mustache and wearing it rather proudly on her own tiny, fat face.

"Oh, really!" was her mother's comment, but she did not try to remove it.

Madame Lefoux came up next to them and gave Prudence a green-eyed look of approval. "Child after my own heart."

"Don't you start," said Alexia, possibly to both of them. "Prudence, darling, look: Egypt!" She pointed before them as the rays of the slowly setting sun caught the beige buildings of the last great Mediterranean port. The first thing to appear was the famous lighthouse, rising above the level of a colorless line of coast. Although, to Alexia's mind, it seemed a little smaller than one would hope.

"No," said Prudence, but she looked.

The steamer chugged to a halt, disappointing everyone.

"We have to wait to take a pilot on board," explained, of all people, Ivy Tunstell.

"We do?" Alexia looked down at her friend, mystified. Ivy had come to stand next to them still garbed in her medieval dress and long blond wig.

Ivy nodded sagely. "The channel into the harbor is narrow, shallow, and rocky. Baedeker says so."

"Well, then, it must be true." They spotted a small tug chugging through the water toward them. A sprightly, dark-skinned fellow in very ill-fitting and baggy clothing was allowed aboard. He saluted the watching passengers in a casual manner and then disappeared toward the captain's lookout.

Moments later, the steamer puffed back up into rumbling action and began making its way sedately into the port of Alexandria.

Lady Maccon was pleased to say the city quite lived up to her expectations. While Ivy prattled on about Pompey's Pillar, the Cape of Figs, the Arsenal, and various other guidebook sights of note, Alexia simply absorbed the quality of the place: the subdued tranquility of exotic buildings, broken only occasionally by the white marble turrets of mosques or the sharp knitting-needle austerity of an obelisk. She thought she could make out ruins in the background. It was mostly sand colored, lit up orange by the sun—a city carved out of the desert indeed, utterly alien in every way. The thing it most resembled was a sculpture made of shortbread.

Ivy excused herself, remarking that they, too, ought to go below, or at least in out of the sea air. "Too much sea air can detrimentally affect the mental stability, or so I've read."

"Why, Mrs. Tunstell, you must have traveled by boat before," said Lord Maccon.

Lady Maccon stifled a chuckle and returned her attention to the shore. She felt the heat for the first time as well, rolling at them off the land. True, it had been getting hotter over the last few days, but this heat brought new smells with it.

"Sand, and sewage, and grilled meat," commented her husband, rather ignoring the romance of it all.

Alexia shifted against him and took his hand with her free one, bracing Prudence against the railing.

The baby frowned at the city, which loomed larger and larger as they moved in to dock. "Ick," she said, and then, "Dama."

Alexia wasn't certain if the toddler was simply missing her adopted father or if somehow the ancient city reminded Prudence of the ancient vampire. The little girl shivered despite the heat and buried her mustachioed face in her mother's neck. "Ick," she said again.

As complicated and difficult as it had been getting on board the steamer, it was twice as problematical getting off of it. Of course, it was intended that passengers spend that last night aboard, to awaken the next morning in a new land and begin their adventures well rested and fully packed. But Alexia and her party were on a night schedule and had no intention of wasting precious evening hours by staying on the ship. They hurried back to their respective rooms and threw a collective tizzy gathering up attendants to help them pack, tracking down multiple missing items, paying steward's fees, and eventually disembarking.

Even after they were safely ashore and getting their land legs back, Ivy Tunstell had to return to her quarters no less than three times. The first under the impression that she had misplaced her favorite gloves—they were in a hatbox with her green turban, as it turned out. The second because she was assured her Baedeker's was left on the bedside table, only to discover it in her reticule. The third because she panicked, convinced she had forgotten Percy, asleep in his bassinet.

The nursemaid, who had charge of the twins, safely ensconced in a rather impressive sling contraption, held Percy up for his frantic mother to see, at which juncture the baby spit up on the strikingly large turban of a native gentleman as he injudiciously cut through their assembled party.

The gentleman made a very rude gesture and said something rapid-fire in Arabic before dashing on.

Ivy tried desperately to apologize to the man's retreating back. "Oh, my dear sir, how terrible. He's only a very little boy, of course, not yet under his own power so far as the proper operation of the digestive centers. I am so very sorry. Perhaps I could—"

"He is long gone, Ivy dear," interrupted Alexia. "Best turn our attention to our hotel. Where are we headed?" She looked at Conall hopefully. It really was rather a bother to travel without Floote; nothing went smoothly, and no one seemed to know exactly what to do next.

Madame Lefoux stepped into the breach. "The custom house is over there, I believe." She gestured at an ugly square building to their right, from which a military-looking group of local gentlemen were charging in their direction. Alexia squinted, attempting to discern the details of the group. The sun was mostly set at this point, the exotic buildings around them blanketed in shadow.

The customs officials, for that is what they proved to be, practically crashed into them and began garbling unintelligibly in Arabic. Ivy Tunstell whipped out her travel guide and began trilling some, quite probably, equally unintelligible phrases in, for some strange reason known only to Ivy, a lilting falsetto and what appeared to be Spanish. Tunstell began prancing about trying to be helpful, his red hair attracting a good deal of unwarranted attention. When one of the men tried grabbing at

Mr. Tumtrinkle's carpetbag, Lord Maccon began yelling and gesticulating in English, descending rapidly into Scottish as he became increasingly annoyed.

During the hubbub, Madame Lefoux sidled up to Lady Maccon.

"Alexia, my dear, might I recommend relocating your gun to an inaccessible part of your apparel and opening the parasol as though the sun were quite up?"

Lady Maccon looked at the inventor as though she were mad. It was now evening, no time for a parasol, and Ethel was tucked away in her reticule, where any good firearm should be.

Madame Lefoux nodded significantly at one of the customs men just as he upended Mr. Tumtrinkle's carpet bag onto the dock, much to that gentleman's annoyance, and produced a prop musket triumphantly from within. Mr. Tumtrinkle's efforts to demonstrate that the firearm was, in fact, a fake did not meet with any kind of approval. Quite the opposite, in fact.

Using Prudence's body to hide her actions, Lady Maccon took her own tiny gun out of her reticule and shoved it down the front of her bodice. Then she reached for her parasol, dangling from a chatelaine hook at her waist, and opened it above her head. Prudence clung on dutifully while she did this and then insisted on holding the parasol handle herself. This delighted Alexia, as now it appeared as though the parasol were up at her daughter's childish whim, rather than her own eccentricity.

Lord Maccon was becoming red in the face as he argued violently with the customs officials over the rudeness of actually opening and looking through their luggage right there in public. The men were not intimidated by Lord Maccon's size, rank, or supernatural state. The first being the only thing they had any direct contact with, the second being irrelevant in Egypt, and the last virtually unknown. It was quite dark, and Conall looked to be in imminent danger of losing his temper altogether when the most curious savior appeared.

A medium-sized, medium-girthed native fellow arrived in their midst. He wore voluminous dark bloomers tucked into suede boots, a high-neck dark shirt of muslin, a wide yellow sash about his waist, and a fez upon his head with a long tassel. He had a beard neatly trimmed into sharp pointed aggressiveness and a serious expression. Alexia wasn't sure about the beard, nor the bloomers, but she did think that with a different hat and a very long sword, he would look most appealingly piratical. Except that with his figure, that would be more along the lines of a banker at a masquerade.

The newcomer introduced himself politely as Chancellor Neshi in perfect English. He interposed himself between Lord Maccon's bluster and the customs official's efficaciousness. Alexia saw her husband's nose wrinkle in a telltale way and noticed that slight wince that he never could hide if he wasn't anticipating a bad smell. She sidled up next to him, careful not to touch him just in case they needed all of his supernatural abilities.

"Vampire?" she whispered into his ear.

He nodded, not taking his eyes off of the stranger.

Chancellor Neshi said something in rapid staccato fashion to the officials and they instantly backed away and stopped fussing.

"This must be Lady Maccon? And the miracle progeny?" Their savior leaned forward a little too close for Alexia's comfort, staring hard at Prudence, and then looked away as though he could not tolerate the sight of the child.

The toddler pursed her little lips in consideration. "Dama," she said with certainty.

Alexia would wager her right glove that her daughter was picking up on the man's vampire nature and utilizing the only word in her vocabulary capable of articulating it. So she said, "Yes, my dear, very like."

Prudence nodded. "Dama Dama duck!"

"Queen Matakara has sent me to be your guide to Alexandria. One might say, perhaps, your dragoman. This is acceptable? I will see you through this business of customs and then safely to your hotel. I have arranged for your audience, and performance, later tonight. If that's not too soon?" He looked at the actors around him. "This is the famous troupe, I take it?"

Ivy and Tunstell pushed forward.

Alexia said, "Yes, indeed, Chancellor. This is Mrs. Tunstell and Mr. Tunstell, owners, performers, and artists extraordinaire. Your queen is in for a treat."

Tunstell bowed and Ivy curtsied. "She commands the performance right away? It is a good thing we have been practicing on the journey."

The dumpy man took in Ivy's hat and Tunstell's trousers and could only nod. Ivy had selected a gray felt chapeau with steel braid around the crown, a long gray feather, and a turned-up brim that showed off a turban of striped surah silk wound underneath. That went around her head to form a bow over the left ear, ending in a fringe down the back. The hat, Ivy no doubt felt, went with the Egyptian aesthetic, and it was her way of honoring their host country. Although, Alexia thought, looking about at the peasants and dockworkers engaging in various tasks around them, it was a little off the mark. Tunstell's trousers were, naturally, of a very aggressive purple and teal plaid and quite tight enough to be a second skin.

They were led into the custom house at that point and permitted to take seats in comparative comfort. Despite their objections, they then had to witness their bags, hatboxes, and trunks opened and examined in detail. The dragoman explained that it was best not to protest and that everything would be put back except for items of contraband. Apparently they were looking particularly for cigars and chewing tobacco, which was subjected to a high tariff. Prudence held on to the parasol firmly. No one gave it a second glance. They also did not check the gentlemen's hats, which was where, Alexia had no doubt, her husband had stashed his sundowner and Madame Lefoux her more nefarious gadgets.

Madame Lefoux's hatbox, full of tools and mysterious widgets, did cause some consternation. Until, with her usual aplomb, the Frenchwoman produced papers claiming she had special dispensation from the Pasha to work on water pumps in Asyut. The officials seemed either to not know or not care that she was a woman dressed as a man. The vampire dragoman referred to her as Mr. Lefoux and spoke and addressed her as though she were male. He also continually referred to her as a Hawal, whatever that meant.

Ivy's many hats and some of the props and costumes came under close scrutiny, until the dragoman explained at great length about Queen Matakara's request for a performance. Or Alexia assumed that was what he was doing. Queen Matakara's favor acted as some kind of oil to soothe the balm of quarantine, for it was only another hour more of questions before they were permitted to leave. One of the younger officials was particularly taken with one of Ivy's hats, a large straw affair, covered in silk fruit, grapes, strawberries, and a large knitted pineapple. He seemed to find it not so much suspicious as fascinating. Eventually, Alexia took off her own hat, a practical little brown bowler meets pith helmet, and put the fruity one on to demonstrate its proper use.

This gave the customs man in question a case of the giggles, and they were waved off with much good humor and goodwill. Alexia had a quick word with Ivy, promising reparations, and gifted the hat to the gentleman in question. Laughingly, he put it atop his own turbaned head. Then he bowed and kissed Lady Maccon's hand. Alexia was left with the distinct feeling that she had made an ally for life.

The street outside was an entirely different world from the dockyard. It was bustling with humanity. People walked, talked, dressed, and interacted like no people Alexia had ever seen before. She had traveled through Europe, but this . . . this was a different world! She was instantly and completely in love.

Ivy was equally enthralled. "Oh my goodness, look at all the men in gowns!"

There were old-fashioned oil streetlamps about, and even a few torches, but no gas, and it was now dark enough to make any estimation of color difficult. Nevertheless, Lady Maccon had a feeling that the clothing about them was quite as colorful as the buildings were monotonously drab.

Lord Maccon sniffed and then gave a little cough.

Alexia's own senses were so assaulted she could only imagine what her husband smelled. There was the intoxicating scent of honey, cinnamon, and roasted nuts. There was also a rather noxious gas emanating from various water-based smoking devices, hoarded by elderly men crouching on stone steps to either side of the narrow street. Underneath the other smells came the unmistakable odor of sewage, not unlike that of the Thames during a hot summer.

Conall turned to her with a wide grin on his handsome face. "That smells like you!" he said as though he had made some great discovery.

"Husband, I do hope you aren't referring to that noxious smoke nor the scent of bodily waste."

"Of course not, my love. Those pastries over there. They smell like you. Would you like to try one?" He knew his wife so well.

"Is Ivy fond of hats? Of course I would *love* to try one!"

The earl moved with alacrity over to the cleanest looking of the street vendors and in short order returned bearing a small sticky, flaky object. Alexia popped it into her mouth without hesitation, only to have her sense of taste assaulted by honey, nuts, exotic spices, and crisp flakes of some impossibly thin pastry.

She chewed in silence. It was far too sticky for anything else. "Amazing!" was her official pronouncement once she had finally swallowed. "Remember what it is called, would you, dear? Then I can order more when we arrive at the hotel. I'm delighted you think I smell like something so delicious."

"You are delicious, my dear."

"Flatterer."

The dragoman took charge of their highly distracted and distractible party and shepherded them toward a long string of donkeys with companion donkey boys who stood waiting under a nearby awning.

"Oh, aren't they perfectly sweet!" exclaimed Mrs. Tunstell.

"They *are* very fine donkeys, aren't they, Ivy? Such long velvet ears. Look, Prudence." Lady Maccon directed her daughter's attention to the string.

"No!" said Prudence.

Ivy shook her head. "No, Alexia, I mean the donkey boys. Look at those lovely almond-shaped eyes and such thick lashes. But, Alexia, is their skin meant to be so dark?"

Alexia didn't dignify this question with an answer.

At which point Mrs. Tunstell came upon a realization that proved even more startling. "Are we expected to *ride* those donkeys?"

"Yes, Ivy dear, I do believe we are."

"Oh, but, Alexia, *I don't ride*!"

Despite Ivy's protestations, which continued vociferously, there commenced a great round of strapping bags onto donkeys and climbing aboard donkeys, while Alexia and the other ladies of the party attempted to negotiate sidesaddle. The toddlers were popped into woven baskets, which the donkeys wore like panniers. The Tunstell twins were suspended together in one set, and Prudence in another, counterbalanced by her mechanical ladybug, which peeked its little antennae over the edge of the basket coyly. Mr. Tumtrinkle went on one side of his donkey and immediately off the other, so that he, like the luggage, had to be strapped into place. After seeing his wife safely up top, Tunstell threw his leg over easily enough, for he was quite nimble and athletic. Unfortunately, his trousers were not so flexible. They ripped loudly, exposing much of his scarlet drawers to the evening air and causing his wife to shriek in horror and faint forward onto the neck of her donkey. Lord Maccon guffawed loudly. Prudence clapped in appreciation. Madame Lefoux made her way genteelly to a nearby stand where she purchased one of the robes so favored by the locals. This Tunstell donned with all the enthusiasm and amiability of an actor accustomed to odd apparel in front of a large audience.

Ivy awoke from her swoon, noted her husband now wore what amounted to a dress, in public, and fainted again. The donkey beneath her was composed and unimpressed by her histrionics.

Conall refused donkey transport, as did their vampire dragoman. Even donkeys, placid creatures as they were, preferred not to carry werewolves or vampires. Lord Maccon perfectly understood this. After all, he was a good deal faster on four paws anyway, so the very idea was preposterous, and he would far rather snack upon the beast than ride it—particularly at this moment with ten days at sea and no live meat the entire time. Lastly, riding a donkey was pointless even when he had been mortal, for his long legs would touch the ground on either side of the wee thing. So he and the guide walked at the front, leading the way and chatting in a forced manner that had nothing to do with the fact that they were from different cultures and everything to do with the fact that one was a vampire and the other a werewolf.

As they trundled through the street, it became clear that they were as much a spectacle for Alexandria as Alexandria was for them. The great port city had been made much of over the last few decades, and the British army called there regularly, but high lords and ladies, small pale children, and troupes of English actors were practically unheard of and quite enthralling as a result.

Many Egyptians came to watch them. The natives pointed with interest at the ladies' hats, the gentlemen's top hats, Alexia's parasol, the odd shapes made by wardrobe and props, as though they were some kind of circus come to parade among them.

Alexia spent a good deal of her time trying to absorb every aspect of the city in the dim light of evening. They arrived at their abode, Hotel des Voyageurs, all too quickly for her, and she could not wait until the next day when she might see Egypt in all its glory. There was the expected chaos once more that saw them all, after much discussion and exchange of moneys, settled into a single floor of the hotel. The ladies took to their rooms for tea and rest, the children went down for naps, and the gentlemen retired to either the nearest bathhouses or the hotel's dubious smoke room, as suited their individual natures.

Lord Maccon helped his wife disrobe, merely raising one eyebrow when a gun dropped out of her corset and clattered to the floor. One became accustomed to such things when one was married to Alexia. Then he reacquainted himself with every aspect of her body, as if he had not just done so onboard the SS *Custard* that morning. Alexia threw herself wholeheartedly into the activity, having learned early on in their marriage that this was an exercise she found both enjoyable and entertaining. It also left her, generally speaking, relaxed and pleased with the world. Not so her husband. Not on this particular night, for even lying next to her on what had proved to be quite a resilient bed, he was what could only be described as *twitchy.*

"Conall, my love, what is the matter?"

"Foreign land," he said curtly.

"And you don't know the lay of it?"

"Exactly so."

"Well," she said with a supportive smile, "go on, then. We shall be fine without you for a few hours."

"Are you quite certain, my dear?"

"Yes, quite."

"You aren't trying to get rid of me?"

"Now, Conall, why would I want to do a thing like that?"

He grunted noncommittally.

"You will be careful, won't you?"

"Of what, precisely?"

"Oh, I don't know, random God-Breaker Plagues running amok? We only just arrived. I'd greatly prefer you not go missing or die quite yet."

"Aye-aye, Captain."

With which her husband gave her a passionate kiss, sprang naked from the bed, and exited their room rather spectacularly by way of the balcony in wolf form. Alexia wrapped the woven blanket about herself and made her way across the room rather less precipitously. She looked to see if she could spot him dashing through the streets off into the desert, but he was already out of sight. It was quarter moon, but he was restless from little exercise on board and he needed to hunt. She tried not to imagine what poor mangy desert creature he would end up eating. As the wife of a werewolf, one had to ignore certain unsavory aspects of cuisine and ingestion.

Lady Maccon felt only a slight twinge of concern. Conall Maccon could certainly take care of himself, and the one thing Alexandria boasted of in plenty was stray dogs. Her husband would simply look like a very large version thereof.

Alexia, thus consoled, drank her tea, which turned out not to be tea at all but that most ghastly of beverages, coffee. It was served with a great deal of honey, which rendered it drinkable if not entirely palatable. She then managed to dress herself. In honor of her trip, she had ordered up a nice mushroom-colored muslin blouse and matched tiny bowler hat, with a duster-style puff of brown feathers. The blouse was designed to be cool in hot weather, while still preserving her modesty. The fastenings at the back gave her some trouble, and the corset underneath could not be laced tight at all. But the draped brown overskirt and modest bustle went on easily enough. Her hair, in response to the desert heat, refused to obey any commands, coiling into great loglike curls. She fussed with it for a bit and then, figuring she was abroad where certain standards might be allowed to slip, pinned it half up and left the rest to flop about as it will.

Downstairs, supper had commenced and the front entrance to Hotel des Voyageurs was empty as all the residents descended upon the comestibles.

"Any messages for Lady Maccon?" she inquired of the desk clerk.

"No, my lady, but there is one for a Lord Maccon."

Alexia took it, noted that the handwriting was not one she recognized, and figured it was a BUR report. She tucked it into her reticule.

"Can you arrange an aetheric transponder connection appointment for me? I have my own valve frequensors, but I understand there is only one transmitter for public access in the city."

"Indeed, my lady. We are a little overtaxed as a result, but I am certain your rank will guarantee access. You'll want the Boulevard Ramleh's west end, opposite the street leading to the Exchange."

Alexia determined she would have to borrow Ivy Tunsell's guidebook in order to make sense of these directions, possibly attached to Ivy herself, but she made a mental note of the details.

"Thank you, my good man. I'll need to book to send a message for just after sunset London time, from here to England. Can you arrange such a thing?"

"Certainly, my lady. That should be something on the order of six o'clock in the evening. But I will ascertain the particulars and make the appointment for you."

"You are most efficient." Alexia, missing Floote quite dreadfully, gave the man a generous gratuity for his pains and wandered into the dining room to see if any of her party were about yet.

Ivy, Tunstell, the nursemaid, and the children were all there causing a ruckus at one of the larger tables. Prudence had her mechanical ladybug and was trundling about banging into people's chairs in a most indiscriminate manner. Alexia was mortified by such behavior. What was the nursemaid thinking, allowing the infant to bring the ladybug to a public eatery? Tunstell was explaining, in large expansive gestures, the thrilling plot of *The Death Rains of Swansea* to some poor unfortunate tourists at the adjoining table. Ivy was fretting over her Baedeker's guidebook, and the nursemaid was busy with the twins.

Lady Maccon scooped up her errant child.

"Mama!"

"Have you eaten, poppet?"

"No!"

"Well, food, then. Have you tried one of those cinnamon pastry thingamabobs?"

"No!"

Still unsure if *no* was Prudence's new favorite word or if she actually knew what it meant, Alexia guided the ladybug with her foot and made her way, baby on hip, to the Tunstells' table.

"Oh, Lady Maccon, how delightful!" extolled Tunstell upon seeing her. "Lady Maccon, may I introduce our new acquaintances the Pifflonts? Mrs. Pifflont, Mr. Pifflont, *this* is Lady Maccon."

One is never sure, upon being introduced, whether one should trust in the arranger of the association, particularly when that arranger was Tunstell. Nevertheless, it was Lady Maccon's business to be gracious, so gracious she was. The Pifflonts turned out to be antiquities experts of some amateurish Italian extraction, quiet and well mannered and exactly the type of people one would like to meet in a hotel. Careful inquiry, and control over Tunstell's exuberance, turned the conversation to the couple's journey through Egypt, which was nearing its close. They were about to return home, abiding only one or two more days before catching a steamer to Naples.

The following unexpectedly intellectual discourse was interrupted by the advent of Lord Conall Maccon wearing a cloak and, so far as Alexia could tell, nothing else. She was horrified. First her daughter went around bumping into people with a ladybug and now her husband appeared without shoes. *Well, there goes that acquaintance!* She couldn't even bear to look at the faces of those nice Pifflonts.

She stood and scuttled swiftly to the earl where he loomed in the doorway.

"Conall, *really*!" she hissed. "At least pull on some boots so you have a facade of decency!"

"I require your presence, wife. And the bairn."

"But, darling, at least a top hat!"

"Now, Alexia. There is something I wish you to see."

"Oh, very well, but do go away. There's blood at the corner of your mouth. I can't take you anywhere."

Lord Maccon vanished around a corner of the hall and Alexia hurried back to the table. She made their excuses and scooped up Prudence, despite her daughter's protestations.

"No! Mama. Nummies."

"Sorry, darling, but your father has discovered something of interest he wishes us to see."

Mrs. Tunstell glanced up. "Oh, is it a textile shop? I hear they produce the most lovely cottons in this part of the world."

"Something more along the lines of ruffled parasols, I believe."

Ivy was thick but not so thick as all that. "Oh, of course," she said immediately, winking in a very overt manner. "*Ruffled parasols.* Naturally. Now, my dear friend, you won't forget we have a private show in only a few hours. And while I know you are not integrated into the performance, your presence is desirable."

"Of course, of course. This shouldn't take very long."

"Carry on, then," said Mrs. Tunstell, although her friend was already trotting hurriedly away. Alexia heard Ivy say, "Lady Maccon is our particular patroness, don't you know? Such a very gracious and grand lady."

She was met outside the hotel by a large wolf. In order to make more of a thing of it, Alexia purchased a donkey rope off an obliging, though confused, donkey boy. This she clasped about Conall's brindled neck, quite a feat of loops and twists, as she could not touch him and had to keep hold of Prudence. Eventually she was successful and it looked as though she were taking a very large dog for a walk.

Lord Maccon gave her a baleful look but submitted to the humiliation for the sake of propriety. They wended their way through the still-vibrant city; sunset seemed more an excuse to visit than an ending to daily activities. He led her a long way, due south down the Rue de la Colonne, past the bastions, through the outer slums of the city until they reached the canal. Alexia was beginning to worry about the time, concerned they might not make it back by the vampire visiting hour. Conall, in his wolf form, had little estimation of distance, and while Alexia was a great walker and never one to shirk exercise, traversing an entire city in the course of only an hour was really rather extreme, especially when carrying a disinterested toddler. Eventually, they developed a method by which Prudence rode astride her father, with Alexia gripping one hand firmly so as to keep everyone in their correct forms and fur.

The earl stopped imperiously at the bank of the canal, and it took Alexia only a moment to surmise they must cross it.

"Oh, really, Conall. Couldn't this wait until tomorrow?"

He barked at her.

She sighed and waved over a reluctant-looking lad in command of a kind of reed raft obviously utilized to cross the canal.

The raft boy refused, with many shakes of the head and wide eyes, to allow the massive wolf into his little craft but was charmed into unexpected delight when said wolf took to the water and simply dragged his raft across. He had no need of the pole normally employed for the crossing. Lady Maccon forbore to say anything on the subject of the cleanliness of the water.

Alexia gave the lad a few coins and gesticulated in such a way as she thought might convince him to wait for them, while Conall shook out his coat violently.

Prudence clapped and giggled at her father's antics, twirling about in the spray of dirty water. Alexia caught her daughter's hand before she touched him.

Alexia thought it a good thing the locals were accustomed to the eccentricities of the English, for such a thing as Lady Maccon alone in the baser end of a foreign city with her only daughter and a large wolf should never be tolerated in any other part of the empire.

Nevertheless, she followed her husband dutifully, reflecting that this was one of the reasons she had married him, with the certain knowledge that life would never be dull. She often suspected it was one of the reasons he had married her as well.

The sensation was barely recognizable at first, but then she began to feel it—a tingling push, a little like the aether breezes against her skin when she floated. Only this sensation felt like the reverse. Aether tingling was like very mild champagne bubbles against the skin; this felt as though those bubbles were being generated by her own flesh. It was a faint sensation and it was almost pleasant, but it was odd. Had she not been alert for some new experience, she might not have even noticed.

Waving her arms about excitedly, Prudence said, "Mama!"

"Yes, dear, odd, isn't it?"

"No." Prudence was very decided on this. She patted Alexia on the cheek. "Mama *and*—" She waved her arms about. "Mama!"

Alexia frowned. "Are you saying that to you the air feels like me? How very odd."

"Yes," agreed Prudence, using a word Alexia hadn't until that moment realized she possessed.

"Conall, is that what I think it is?" Alexia asked the wolf, her attention still on her wiggling daughter.

"Yes, my love, I believe it is," said her husband.

Lady Maccon nearly dropped Prudence in startlement, looking up to confirm that her ears were not playing tricks on her and that her husband was standing a short distance away, fully naked and fully human.

Lady Maccon set down her daughter. The child toddled eagerly over to Conall, who scooped her right up, without fear. No need of it—Prudence remained her own precocious human self.

Lady Maccon went to stand next to him. "This is the God-Breaker Plague?"

"Indubitably."

"I thought I should feel more repelled by it."

"So did I."

"On the other hand, when the mummy was in London—do you recall?—and caused half the city to come over all mortal, I didn't register any sensations at all. This is almost as mild. It was only when I was in the same room as that awful mummy that I felt true repulsion."

The earl nodded. "*Sharing the same air.* I believe that was the Templar's phrasing for two preternaturals in the same place."

Alexia looked out over the low mud brick houses of Alexandria's poorest residents to the wide low black of nothingness beyond. "Is that the desert?"

"No. Desert has more sand. I believe that used to be a lake, all dried up now. It's wasteland."

"So there once was water and now there is none. Is it possible that the God-Breaker Plague has moved close to the city only since then? After all, we know preternatural touch is affected by water."

"That is a thought. Hard to know. Of course, it is also possible that the city has expanded toward it. But if it has moved closer, you can bet the local vampires would not be happy about it."

"Matakara's real reason for summoning us?"

"Anything is possible with vampires."

CHAPTER ELEVEN

In Which Prudence Discovers Sentences

The Maccons made it back to the hotel in time to change and make themselves presentable before being taken to Queen Matakara and the Alexandria Hive. Chancellor Neshi was waiting for them expectantly in the lobby.

The Tunstells and their troupe were soon to follow, trotting down the stairs lugging set pieces and already dressed in their costumes for the first act, although the gentlemen were all sporting top hats for the journey. If their arrival at the hotel had been remarked upon with interest by the natives, their departure was even more noteworthy. Mrs. Tunstell's dress was silver satin with an enormous quantity of fake pearl jewelry. Mr. Tunstell was attired as any fine gentleman about town except that his suit was of crimson satin and he had a short gold cape buttoned over one shoulder like a musketeer. Mr. Tumtrinkle, villainous from spats to cravat, wore black velvet with diamanté buttons, blue leather gloves, and a cloak of midnight blue satin that he swooped and swirled about like wings as he moved.

This time there was no need of donkeys. The hive queen had sent them a steam locomotive, a massive contraption worthy of even Madame Lefoux's interest. The inventor, however, was nowhere to be found, having disappeared about her own business more hastily than Alexia had ever expected. Alexia felt, it must be admitted, rather abandoned and unimportant. After all, she had surmised that Madame Lefoux was sent along to Egypt to spy on *her*, and here she found herself the least of the Frenchwoman's attentions.

The locomotive was a rangy, rumbling beast, a little like a stagecoach in shape but open topped. The flat back end was piled high with rushes, presumably for the comfort of the occupants, as there were no seats. As the thing rumbled down narrow roads and alleys designed with donkeys in mind, the straw did very little good. Never before had Alexia experienced such a bumpy ride. The locomotive belched bouts of steam high into a dark evening sky out of two tall smokestacks and was so loud that polite conversation was impossible.

Prudence, ghastly child, enjoyed the whole arrangement. She bounced up and down excitedly with each bump and rattle. Alexia was becoming horribly afraid that her bluestocking tendencies had transferred to her daughter, in spades. The infant was taken with anything remotely mechanical, and her fascination with dirigibles and other forms of transport was only increasing.

The Alexandria Hive house was situated off of the Rue Ibrahim within sight of Port Vieux on the eastern side of the city. The facade of the building was Greek in style. It was two levels high, the first level sporting widely spaced, large marble columns, and the upper level showcasing a colonnade of smaller supports open to the air in one long balcony. Inside, however, it was more as Alexia imagined one of the famous rock-cut tombs of the Valley of the Kings. There were doorways leading off of a vestibule, without doors, and woven reed mats spread on the floor. Basalt statues of ancient animal-headed gods stood all about like sentries at a masquerade. The walls were painted with more animal gods engaging in brightly colored and beautifully articulated myths. There was sinuously carved wood furniture here and there, but it was all quite primitive in shape and without adornment. The very starkness and lack of opulence was almost as awe-inspiring as the overabundance of riches that so characterized the vampires of Alexia's homeland. Here was a hive that knew its wealth was purely and simply in the world it had created, not in the objects it had managed to accumulate.

The Tunstells and troupe trailed in behind Lord and Lady Maccon and stood in reverent silence, the atmosphere subduing even them for a short time.

Chancellor Neshi clapped loudly—Ivy started and emitted a little "Oh, my!" of surprise—and near on twenty servants appeared from one of the darkened doorways, all handsome, dark-eyed young men wearing white loincloths for the sake of modesty and nothing else. Each crouched expectantly at the foot of a visitor. Alexia glanced at Chancellor Neshi and realized, with a good deal of shock, that these young men were expecting to remove her shoes. Not only hers, but everyone's! The gentlemen, each caught in the act of removing his outside topper, replaced the hat hurriedly and looked wide-eyed at one another. Realizing they would take their cue from her, Alexia lifted her foot to the young man's knee and permitted him to unlace and pull off her sensible brown walking boots. Following Lady Maccon's lead, the party allowed themselves to be divested of footwear. Alexia shuddered to see that her husband wore no socks and that Tunstell's were mismatched. Only Prudence was delighted to have her shoes removed, not being a very great fan of shoes to begin with.

Chancellor Neshi bustled off, presumably to herald their arrival, at which juncture Mrs. Tunstell broke the hush with a startled, "My goodness gracious, would you look at that god creature there? Its head is nothing but a single feather."

"Ma'at," explained Alexia, who had a particular interest in ancient mythology, "goddess of justice."

"One would perhaps call her feather-head?" suggested Tunstell to much general hilarity. The spell of the ancient world around them was broken.

Chancellor Neshi returned. "*She* is ready to see you now."

He led them up a set of cold stone stairs to the second level of the house, full of more cool, dark, windowless stone rooms, tomblike and torch-lit. From the upper vestibule, they were led down a long hallway that ended in a small open doorway that let onto an enormous room.

They entered. The room was certainly big enough to stage a play. Against the wall directly opposite the hallway door and halfway down on each side stood a series of low wooden divans with red cushions. The floor was spread with more intricately woven reed mats and the walls were again painted. These were done in a similar style to the ancient-looking images below but depicted a wide range of current events, from the Turkish invasion to the incorporation of Western technology, from the great Nutmeg Rebellion to the antiquities trade and tourism. It was a record of Egypt's modern history in bright pigment and perfect detail. It was odd to see the figures of bustled and trussed Europeans, British uniforms and army ships, all in the awkward childish style of papyrus paintings.

On the divans against either wall sat a string of striking and somber young persons who could only be the drones of the hive. They wore native dress but, Alexia noted with interest, both the men and women, in defiance of all she had observed so far, had their heads uncovered. She supposed this must be a kind of rejection of native religion in favor of worshipful loyalty to queen and hive.

Directly opposite the door in the position of greatest importance was what looked to be a large parasol. It was suspended from the ceiling, with great swaths of silken cloth hanging from around the edge. Richly colored and strikingly beautiful, the drapes formed a kind of tent, just large enough for one person to stand within. Alexia couldn't help feeling that whoever was inside could probably see out and was watching her every move.

To one side of this shrouded parasol sat four vampires. There was no doubt that they were, indeed, vampires. For, out of some custom alien to England, they were all showing their fangs to the guests. Vampires in London rarely showed fang without prestated, postintroduction intent. To the other side sat one more vampire, whom Chancellor Neshi went to join. Next to the dragoman were two empty spots.

After a moment of silently watching the odd crowd of mixed aristocracy and overdressed thespians, all six vampires rose to their feet.

"The entirety of the Alexandria Hive," whispered Lord Maccon to his wife.

"We are honored," said his wife back.

A stunningly lovely drone stepped forward, moving with liquid grace across the wide, empty floor until she stood before them. Her features were strong without being manly, her brows heavy, her mouth generous, her lips stained dark red by skilled artifice. She wore full, wide black trousers that ballooned well out and then came in at the ankles. Over this was a long black tunic, nipped in tight along arms and torso with a wide swath of fabric at the wrists and hem, floating away from the hips like a gentleman's frock coat. The wider parts of the tunic and the bloomers were patterned in gold leaves, and she wore a great quantity of gold jewelry about fingers, wrists, neck, ankles, and toes.

"Welcome," she said in perfect Queen's English, making a graceful gesture with her arms, like a dancer, "to the Alexandria Hive." Her large, dark eyes, lined heavily in black, swept over the crowd of actors before her.

"Lord and Lady Maccon?"

Alexia wanted desperately to take her husband's hand, but she thought he might need his supernatural abilities at any moment. So she shifted Prudence more firmly on her hip, taking strange comfort from the presence of her child, and stepped forward. Out of the corner of her eye, she watched Conall also segregate himself from the group.

The dark-eyed drone came closer. She looked to Conall first. "Lord Maccon, you are welcome to Alexandria. It has been many centuries since a werewolf visited this hive. We hope it will not be so long before the next one graces us with his presence."

Lord Maccon bowed. "I suspect," he said, because he had no tact, "that will rather depend on the course of this evening's events."

The drone inclined her head and turned dark eyes to Alexia.

"Lady Maccon, soul-sucker. You, too, are welcome. We do not judge the daughter by the father's actions."

"Well, thank you I'm sure. Especially as I never knew him."

"No, of course you didn't. And is this *the child*?"

Prudence was quite riveted by the beautiful lady. Perhaps it was all the gold sparkles and jewelry, or the liquid way the drone moved. Alexia hoped it wasn't all the face paint; the last thing she needed was a daughter with a keen interest in feminine wiles. She would have to cede all such training to Lord Akeldama.

"Welcome to the Alexandria Hive, stealer of souls. Your kind we have never had the pleasure of entertaining before."

"Remember your manners, dear," said Alexia to her daughter without much hope.

Prudence proved unexpectedly equal to the challenge. "How do you do?" she said, enunciating very clearly and looking quite directly at the lady drone.

Alexia and Conall exchanged raised eyebrow looks. *Very good*, thought Alexia, *we got ourselves a peppery one.*

The drone stepped aside and waved one graceful hand, offering the two empty spots on the divan next to Chancellor Neshi. "Please, be seated. The queen desires the performance to begin directly."

"Oh," protested Ivy, "but she is not here! She will miss the opening act!"

Tunstell put an arm about his wife's waist and hustled her to one corner of the room to prepare.

The drone clapped her hands and once more dozens of servants appeared. With their assistance, the actors managed to set up one half of the room as a stage, screening off the doorway in the middle. They had the servants move all of the many torches and lamps to that side of the room, throwing the other, where drones and vampires sat in perfect silence, into eerie darkness.

The Death Rains of Swansea was not a performance that improved markedly upon a second viewing. Still there was something appealing if not entertaining about Ivy and Tunstell's antics. Mr. Tumtrinkle pranced his evil prance, and twirled his dastardly fake mustache, and swirled his massive cloak most voraciously. Werewolf hero Tunstell strode back and forth, trousers ever in great danger of ripping over his muscled thighs, coming to the rescue as needed and barking a lot. Ivy fainted whenever there was cause to faint, and swanned about in hats of such proportions it was a wonder her head didn't collapse like a griddle cake under the weight. The supporting cast was, of course, much diminished in size, playing both vampires and werewolves as script demanded.

In order to save time, but causing no little confusion as to the plot—no matter what their character at the moment—they wore both the fake fangs and the large shaggy ears tied about their heads with pink tulle bows.

The bumblebee dance went off a treat, the watching vampires and drones almost hypnotized by the spectacle. Alexia wondered if the allegory was wasted on them, or if they, like her, had an appreciation for the ridiculous. Of course, Alexia had only heard Chancellor Neshi and the beautiful drone speak, so it was also possible none of the others understood a word of English.

At the end, vampire queen Ivy returned to werewolf Tunstell's arms after much separation and anxiety, and all was sweetness and light. The torches were dimmed and then raised, and the servants brought in extras to fill the room with an orange glow.

Alexia and the actors waited with bated breath. And then, oh, and then, the assembled vampires and drones rose to their feet crying out in adoration, trilling their tongues in a great cacophony of vibratory sound that could only be utter appreciation. Alexia even observed one or two of the vampires wipe away sentiment, and the beautiful drone with the amazing dark eyes was weeping openly.

The lady drone stood and rushed forward to congratulate Ivy and Tunstell with open arms. "That was wonderful! Wonderful! We have never seen such a performance. So complex, so brilliant. That dance with the yellow and black stripes, so perfectly articulating the emotion of immortality. How can words even begin to describe . . . so moving. We have been honored. Truly honored."

Tunstell and Ivy and the entire troupe looked quite overwhelmed by such an enthusiastic reception. Both Tunstells blushed deeply and Mr. Tumtrinkle began to blubber in an excess of emotion.

The drone wafted over to Ivy and embraced her warmly. Then she linked one arm with Ivy's and the other with Tunstell's and guided them gently from the room. "You simply must tell me the meaning of that interpretive piece in the middle? Was that an illustration of the soul's perpetual struggle with infinity, or a social commentary on the supernatural state in continuing conflict with the natural world as both host and food supply?"

Tunstell replied jovially, "A bit of both, of course. And did you notice the series of tiny leaps I performed stage right? Each one a hop in the face of eternity."

"I did, I did, I did indeed."

Thus agreeably conversing, they wandered down the hallway. There was a brief rustle of activity, and Ivy came bustling back, having extracted herself from her escort. She hurried into the room and made for Lady Maccon.

"Alexia," she said in a significantly hushed tone. "Have you your *ruffled parasol*?"

Alexia, did, in fact, have her parasol with her. She had found over the years it was always better to be on the safe side when visiting a hive. She gestured to her hip where it dangled off of a chatelaine at her waist.

Ivy tilted her head and winked significantly.

"Oh," said Alexia, making the connection. "Pray do not concern yourself, Ivy. Do go enjoy a well-earned repast. The parasol is fine."

Ivy nodded in a slow, suggestive way. Feeling that her secret society duties had been satisfactorily discharged, she went bustling after her husband.

After a moment's hesitation, the rest of the drones moved forward and introduced themselves, those who spoke English at least, to the acting troupe. After an exchange of pleasantries, mention of coffee was made, and they, too, were guided expertly from the room. This left Lord and Lady Maccon behind with Prudence and the six vampires.

Chancellor Neshi stood. "Are you ready now, My Queen?" he asked of the curtained off area.

No verbal response emanated from within, but the draped cloth twitched slightly.

Chancellor Neshi said, "Of course, my queen." He gestured for Lord and Lady Maccon to stand and come to face the front of the draped parasol. Then he pulled aside the curtains, tying them back with gold cords to each side.

Had Alexia not spent a good deal of time in Madame Lefoux's contrivance chamber prior to it being repurposed as a werewolf dungeon, she might have been startled by the contraption revealed. But she had seen an octomaton rampage through London. She had been attacked and then rescued by mechanical ladybugs. She had flown in an ornithopter from Paris to Nice. This was nothing by comparison. And yet, it was probably the most grotesque invention of the modern age. Worse than the disembodied hand in a jar under that temple in Florence. Worse than a dead body in an afterlife extension tank. Worse even than the wax-face horror of the Hypocras automaton. Because those creatures had all been dead or manufactured. What sat in the raised dais behind that curtain was still alive or still undead—at least in part.

She, for Alexia assumed it must be a she, sat atop what could only be called a throne. It was mostly made of brass. Its base was some kind of tank housing two levels of liquid, the bottom a bubbling mess of yellow that heated the upper composed entirely of a viscous red fluid that could only be blood. The arms of the throne were fitted with levers, nozzles, and tubes, some under the emaciated hands of the occupant, others going into or coming out of her arms. It was as though the woman and the chair had become one and not been separated for generations. Some parts of the chair were bolted directly into her flesh, and there was a bronze half mask covering the lower part of her face from nose to throat, presumably providing a constant supply of blood.

Only Lady Maccon's good breeding kept her from committing the vile act of involuntary purging right then and there on the reed mat. There was something particularly horrific about knowing that, because the queen was immortal, all those places where the chair speared into her flesh must be constantly trying to heal themselves.

Chancellor Neshi did a most humiliating thing. He knelt upon the floor and bowed forward all the way to the ground, touching his forehead to the reed mat. Then he stood and waved Alexia and Conall farther forward. "My Queen, may I present Lady Maccon, Lord Maccon, and Lady Prudence. Maccons, may I present Queen Matakara Kenemetamen of Alexandria, Ruler of the Ptolemy Hive ad Infinitum, Lady Horus of Fine Gold in Perpetuity, Daughter of Nut, Oldest of the Vampires."

With the lower half of her head concealed, it was difficult to determine Matakara's exact appearance. Her eyes were large and very brown, too large in that emaciated face. She had the dark complexion of most native Egyptians, grown darker as it shrunk in against the bone, like that of a mummy. She had a blue wig atop her head and a snake coronet made of gold set with turquoise eyes on top of that. Over the parts of her body not attached to the throne, she wore simple white cotton draped and pleated stiffly and a quantity of gold and lapis jewelry.

Despite the grotesqueness of the contraption and the pathetic appearance of the woman confined within it, Alexia was hypnotized by those huge eyes. Rimmed in black kohl, they stared fixedly at her. Alexia was convinced the queen was trying to communicate with her a message of great import. And she, Alexia Maccon, was too thick to comprehend it. The expression in those eyes was one of immeasurable desperation and eternal misery.

Lord Maccon made his bow, removing his hat in a wide, sweeping gesture and doing a creditable job of it. He did not look as surprised by the queen's appearance as Alexia felt, which made her wonder if BUR had received some kind of prior warning. She believed that she made a decent effort at disguising her own shock as she curtsied. Prudence, standing quietly by her side, hand firmly gripped in Alexia's, glanced back and forth from monstrosity to mother before performing her own version of a half bow, half curtsy.

A sound of disgust emanated from the queen and her contraption.

"She wants you to bow," hissed the chancellor.

"We just did."

"No, Lady Maccon, all the way."

Alexia was quite shocked. "Like an *Oriental*?" Her gown would barely permit kneeling and her corset certainly would not permit her to bow forward.

The earl looked equally taken aback.

"You are in the presence of royalty!"

"Yes," Alexia agreed in principle, "but to kneel on the *ground*?"

"Do you know how many strangers the queen has allowed into her presence over the last few centuries?"

Lady Maccon could hazard a guess. After all, if *she* looked as bad as Matakara did . . . "Not a lot?"

"None at all. It is a great honor. And you should bow, properly. She is a great woman, an ancient lady, and she deserves your respect."

"She does?"

Conall sighed. "When in Rome."

"That's just it, dear, we aren't. We are in Alexandria."

But it was too late; her husband had already swept off his hat a second time, knelt, and bowed forward.

"Oh, Conall, the knees of your trousers! Don't put your head all the way down. We don't know where that floor has been! Oh, now, Prudence, you don't have to follow Daddy's example. Oop, there she goes."

Prudence had nothing like her mother's reticence. Frilly yellow frock notwithstanding, she pitched forward and put her head to the ground with alacrity.

Feeling she was the last holdout, Alexia glared at her husband. "You'll have to help me back up. I can't possibly manage on my own without ripping my dress." So saying, she knelt slowly down and tilted herself forward as much as her foundation garments would allow, which wasn't very much. She nearly overbalanced to her left. Her corset creaked under the strain. Conall hoisted her back up, turning human for that one moment.

Chancellor Neshi went to stand next to his queen, on a pedestal of just the right height to bring his ear to her mouth area but ensuring he was no higher than she. The vampire queen spoke to him in a whisper. Alexia looked at her husband inquiringly, wondering if his supernatural hearing picked up anything.

"No language I know," he said unhelpfully.

"The queen says that Europeans do everything wrong, writing from left to right, uncovering the head to enter a room yet leaving the feet confined." Chancellor Neshi stood stiff-backed to state this, like a town crier, acting the mouthpiece for his queen. Then, without waiting for an answer to these accusations of backward behavior, he turned to listen once more.

"My queen wishes to know why all foreign children look the same."

Alexia gestured with her free hand at her daughter, who was standing in unusual docility by her side. "Well, this particular child is Prudence Alessandra Maccon Akeldama."

"No," said Prudence. No one listened. Prudence was to find this all too common in her young life.

Chancellor Neshi continued to speak for his queen. "Daughter of a hellhound, named for a soul-sucker and a bloodsucker. The queen wishes to know if she works."

"Pardon?" Alexia was confused.

"Is she a Follower of Set? A Stealer of Souls?"

Lady Maccon considered. It was a fair question, of course, but Alexia was too much a scientist to answer in the affirmative. Instead she said carefully, "She manifests the abilities of a supernatural creature after having touched him, if that is what you are asking."

"A simple yes would have sufficed, soul-sucker," said the chancellor.

Lady Maccon looked hard into Queen Matakara's sad eyes. "Yes, but it would not be true. Your names for her are not my names for her. Have you called my daughter and me here, Venerable One, simply to insult us?"

Chancellor Neshi bent to listen and then seemed to engage in a brief argument. Finally he said, "My queen wishes to be shown the truth."

"What truth, exactly?"

"Your daughter's gifts."

"Oh, now wait a moment there!" interjected Conall.

"It can be tricky," hedged Alexia.

Queen Matakara's finger twitched on the arm of the chair, lighting a small spark of flame for a brief moment. This seemed to be a signal, for one of her hive darted forward and, in a flash of smooth movement, scooped Prudence up. Prudence let go of her mother's hand and was otherwise untroubled. Alexia let out a cry of anger. The vampire in question, however, instantly dropped the toddler because he had unexpectedly lost the strength he had no doubt enjoyed for centuries. He probably possessed the ability to maintain his grip, but the surprise was overwhelming. His fangs vanished. Prudence hit the ground with a thud but, being now immortal, sustained no injury. She leaped up, little fangs bared, grubby hands reaching. She was intrigued by the bronze chair with all of its switches and levers. Prudence was one to manhandle first, ask questions later. Much *later*, perhaps when she was grown up and could formulate a complete study. Most of the time this was mere childish enthusiasm and no more disconcerting than Baby Primrose's constant groping for trim and feathers, but now Prudence was a vampire, and she had more than enough strength to do some serious damage to that chair.

Lady Maccon dove forward. Luckily, Prudence was so fascinated she did not bother to flee. Alexia got a hand around her arm in quick order, averting catastrophe.

The vampires, all frozen in startled horror for those brief, awful minutes, jumped to their collective feet and placed themselves between the Maccons and their queen. They were all shouting accusations at Alexia and Prudence in rapid, high-volume Arabic.

One of them nipped forward, hand back to strike Alexia full across the face.

Holding Prudence in both hands, Alexia could not go for her parasol, even had she been fast enough. She flinched away, curling protectively about her daughter, shielding Prudence from the blow.

Suddenly, standing between Alexia and the vampire was a very large, very angry brindled wolf. His hackles were raised, his huge white teeth were bared, and saliva dripped down from the pink of his gums.

It was a terrifying thing to confront for any creature, let alone those who had not seen a werewolf in hundreds of years.

Lord Maccon interposed himself between his wife and the hive and backed up until he was flush against the fabric of Alexia's skirt.

Alexia took the opportunity, with the vampires' attention now focused on this new threat, to switch Prudence firmly to one hip and release the parasol from the chatelaine with her free hand. She raised it up, arming the tip with a numbing dart. At the same time, understanding the meaning behind her husband's consistent furry pressure against her legs, she began backing slowly toward the door.

One of the vampires feinted in the earl's direction. At the same time, another made a lunge for Alexia. Without break for thought, the werewolf charged the first, grabbing him about the hamstring and hurling him hard into the other vampire. Both vampires crumpled to the floor for a short moment before bouncing back to their feet. Alexia, without pause, shot one of them with a numbing dart. He fell right back down again, and this time stayed there for a while before reeling groggily to his feet.

Alexia began backing with greater intent toward the doorway, not shifting her attention from the milling clot of angry vampires. Conall stuck close, maintaining a snarling, barking, growling ferocity that encouraged space between the vampires and his wife and daughter.

Chancellor Neshi stepped forward, slowly and with empty hands held up in supplication. "Please, Lord Maccon, we are unused to such antics."

Conall only growled, low and furious.

If Alexia had expected an apology at that juncture, she was sorely disappointed. The man, showing not insignificant bravery, only inched closer and gestured the wolf toward the door like a porter. "This way, my lord. We thank you for your visit."

Taking that as a statement of permission, Alexia turned and strode from the room with all haste. No sense in dawdling where one was unwanted. After a moment's hesitation, Conall followed.

Prudence struggled mightily in her mother's arm, but Alexia had had enough of *that* for one night and gripped her tightly.

The infant cried out, "No! Mama, no. Poor Dama!" in her high treble and strained back to the room.

Feeling her daughter's attention shift and possessed by the same compulsion, Alexia paused and turned to look back. The hive vampires stood in a huddle before their mistress, but the dais raised Queen Matakara high enough for Alexia's eyes to meet those of the vampire queen above the crowd. Alexia was struck once again by the profound unhappiness there and by the belief that Matakara wanted something of her, wanted it enough to bring her all the way to Egypt. *How can I help you with anything?* Alexia felt a tug at her dress and saw Conall had his teeth firm about her hem and was tugging her into motion. She did as she was bid.

Chancellor Neshi had to jog to catch up. After a moment's thoughtful regard, the vampire directed his conversation at Alexia, rather than her now-hairy husband. As if nothing unbecoming had happened, he inquired politely, "May we offer you some coffee before you leave?" They walked down the cold stone stairs to the entrance.

"No thank you," responded Alexia politely. "I think we had better depart."

"Mama, Mama!"

"Yes, my dear?"

Prudence took a deep breath and then said slowly and carefully, "Mama, get her out."

Alexia looked to her daughter in startlement. "Are we speaking in complete sentences now, Prudence?"

Prudence narrowed her eyes at her mother suspiciously. "No."

"Ah, well, still, that is an interesting theory. Trapped, you think. Against her will? I suppose anything is possible."

Biffy and Lyall spent that night much as though nothing of significance had happened in the previous one. They met with Lady Kingair and proceeded with the investigation as if there had been no fight, no life-altering decision, and no beginnings of a romance.

Lady Kingair sniffed and then glared at the two men suspiciously when they entered the room, but apart from that, made no comment about any change in state. If she noticed they were more relaxed around one another or the little touches they sometimes exchanged without quite realizing, she made no comment.

Biffy was sure Floote knew, because Floote always seemed to know such things. The butler attended to their requirements with the same solicitous efficiency as always. Perhaps more so, as it seemed that without Lady Maccon's demands to occupy his time and attention, he was ever on hand to help them with anything they might need.

Lyall spent his time looking over all the evidence they had gathered on the owners of private dirigibles in London. He compared these to political and tradesmen's concerns in Egypt but was unable to come up with any connections. Lady Kingair delved into the manufacture and distribution of sundowner bullets, trying to determine who might have access and why, but this also seemed fruitless. Biffy concentrated his efforts on Egypt and what Dubh might have found there. The man had clearly been inside the God-Breaker Plague zone to have emerged so weakened. Biffy gathered together passenger manifests on trains and steamers out of Egypt, attempting to access baggage information on the theory that, due to his emaciated state, Dubh must have been traveling in the company of at least *part* of a preternatural mummy on the voyage home. He must have disposed of it, or it had been stolen, as no supernatural creature in London had experienced ill effects upon his return.

Biffy was not one to get easily distracted, but after several hours immersed in manifests of one kind or another, he found himself drawn into an obscure treatise on the nature of the God-Breaker Plague written some fifty years ago. That, in turn, referenced a different report from the very first antiquities expeditions some hundred and twenty or so years prior. Something in the two documents struck him as odd, though he could not pinpoint the particulars. This sent him into a flurry of activity, pulling books on Egypt down from the library and sending Floote off to collect reports from the foreign office on the subject. The God-Breaker Plague was of peculiarly little interest to daylight folk and of particular secrecy to vampires and werewolves, so there was very little substantial information.

"Biffy, I don't mean to disturb your readings, but you appear to be getting a tad distracted from our original objective."

Biffy looked up at his Beta, rubbing his eyes blearily. "Mmm?"

"You seem to be delving further and further back in time. Away from our murder investigation. Are you tracking something of relevance?"

"There is something *peculiar* going on with this plague."

"You mean aside from the fact that it exists at all, a pestilence of unmaking affecting only supernatural folk?"

"Yes."

"What, exactly, are you on to, my boy?" Lyall crouched down next to Biffy, where he sat on the floor, surrounded by books and manuscripts.

Lady Kingair looked up from her own papers.

Biffy pointed at a line in one of the older texts. "Look here, one hundred and twenty years ago, reports of the plague being situated as far as Cairo. See here, particular mention of the pyramids being *clean*."

Lyall tilted his head, a sign Biffy was to continue.

"And here, a similar mention. No one seems interested in charting the exact extent of the plague, possibly because it would take a werewolf interested in scientific investigation, and willing to turn mortal on a regular basis as he walked through the desert. But so far as I can tell, fifty years ago, the God-Breaker Plague stretched from Aswan to, still, Cairo."

"Well?"

Biffy shook out a map of the Nile River Valley. "Taking into account topography and allowing water features and territory markers, much as werewolves and vampires do themselves, the plague would have extended like so." He drew a loose circle on the map with a stick of graphite. "So far as I can tell, the initial extent, here, remained fixed for thousands of years, ever since werewolves were divested of their rule and the plague began."

Lyall bent over the map, intrigued. "So what has you worried? This all seems to be as the howlers sing it. Ramses, the last pharaoh, who lost the ability to change and became old and toothless because of the God-Breaker Plague."

"Yes, except sometime after this last report, the one dated 1824, it moved."

"What! What moved?"

"Well, perhaps not moved. Perhaps *expanded* is a better word. Look at the more recent reports on the plague BUR got hold of, dated a few decades ago. Admittedly they come out of the Alexandria Hive and one loner wolf who braved the desert out of some kind of religious fervor. But I would say, at a conservative guess, that the God-Breaker Plague has expanded some one hundred miles in the last fifty years." Biffy drew a second larger circle on his map. "Here. It now includes Siwah and Damanhúr and stretches all the way to the outskirts of Alexandria."

"What!"

"Something happened five decades ago that caused the plague to start up again."

"This is not good," stated Professor Lyall baldly.

"You think our Dubh might have been carrying this information back to us?" wondered Lady Kingair.

"He was sent looking for preternatural mummies. What if he found more than any of us had wagered on?"

"Why be so obsessed with contacting Lady Maccon on the subject?" Lady Kingair seemed to find this point particularly aggravating.

"Well, she *is* a preternatural," said Biffy.

"We must send them an aetherogram immediately with this information. Do you have an appointment scheduled with Lady Maccon, Biffy?" asked Lyall.

"Yes, I . . . How did you know?"

"Because it's what I would have done in your place. When is it?"

"Tomorrow at sunset."

"You must relay this information to Lady Maccon."

"Of course."

"And you must warn her of . . . you know . . ." Lyall gestured with his head at Lady Kingair.

"Yes, that your secret is out, that our pack is about to change. I know."

"You are still not resigned to the change?" Lyall cocked his head to the side and lowered his voice.

"You will leave me, and you will leave me with a great deal of responsibility." Biffy looked up at him out of the corner of his eye, pretending further interest in the map of Egypt so as to disguise any sentiment.

"I believe you might have just proven how well placed my faith is in you."

"Well, gentlemen," interrupted Lady Kingair, "how about you prove Lord Maccon's faith and figure out who shot my Beta?"

CHAPTER TWELVE

Wherein Alexia and Ivy Meet a Man with a Beard

Lady Alexia Maccon awoke midafternoon. The light was rich and golden, peeking around the edges of the heavy curtains. She checked her husband's slumbering face, handsome and innocent in sleep. She trailed one fingertip down his fine profile and giggled when he snuffled a little snore at the familiarity. Sometimes she allowed herself to wallow in the sentimentality of knowing that this wonderful man, overbearing, impossible, and werewolf though he might be, was hers. Never in her old days as spinster and social outcast could she have imagined such a thing. She had thought that some kind, unassuming scientist might be persuaded to take her, or some midgrade clerk, but to have landed such a man . . . her sisters must envy her. Alexia would have envied herself, had that not proved logistically rather complicated. She kissed the tip of her husband's nose and climbed out of the bed, eager to investigate Egypt in the daylight.

She was not, however, to enjoy the pleasures of such an exploration alone. The gentlemen were still abed, but Mrs. Tunstell, the nursemaid, and the children were all awake and enjoying coffee in the room dedicated as the nursery.

"Mama!" came Prudence's excited cry upon seeing Lady Maccon in the doorway. She slid down off the chair and toddled over excitedly. Alexia bent to pick her up. Prudence grabbed her mother's head, one chubby hand to each cheek, and directed her attention at her own intent little face. "Tunstellings! Silly," she explained. "Eeegypttt!"

Alexia nodded slightly. "I agree with you on all points, my darling."

Prudence stared seriously into her mother's brown eyes, as though trying to determine whether Alexia was addressing the matter with due attention to the important details. "Good," she said at last. "Go go go."

Mrs. Tunstell stood back politely while Lady Maccon and her child conversed. At this she said, "Alexia, my dear, are you perhaps pondering what I am pondering?"

Alexia replied, without hesitation, "My dear Ivy, I very much doubt it."

Ivy took no offense, possibly because she did not perceive the insult, only saying, "We were considering a little stroll about the town. Would you be interested in joining us?"

"Oh, indeed. Do you have your Baedeker's? I need to get to the local aethographor by six o'clock or thereabouts."

"Oh, Alexia, do you need to *transmit* something significant? How exciting!"

"Oh, nothing of any material consequence, simply a matter of coordination. You have no objections to us making it one of the objectives of the excursion?"

"Certainly not. Taking the air is so much more enjoyable when one has purpose, don't you feel? I ordered up a donkey. Would you believe they don't have perambulators in this part of the world? How do they transport infants in style?"

"Apparently by donkey."

"That," stated Ivy most decidedly, "is *not* style!"

"I thought we could pop Primrose and Percival into those adorable little basket panniers, and Prudence here might like to try to ride."

"No!" said Prudence.

"Oh, come now, darling," remonstrated her mother. "You come from a long line of horsewomen, or so I like to believe. You should start while you are young enough to get away with riding astride."

"Pttttt," said Prudence.

A polite tap came at the open door and Madame Lefoux stuck her head in. "Ladies"—she tipped her elegant gray top hat—"and Percy," she added, remembering that one, at least, was a very minor gentleman.

Percy burped at her. Primrose waved her arms about. Prudence nodded politely, as did Alexia and Ivy.

"Madame Lefoux," said Mrs. Tunstell. "We were about to head out on an exploratory expedition around the metropolis. Would you care to join us?"

"Ah, ladies, I should ordinarily be quite eager, but I am afraid I have my own business to attend to."

"Ah, well, don't let us detain you," said Alexia, quite burning with curiosity as to the nature of Madame Lefoux's business. Was the Frenchwoman acting for the Order of the Brass Octopus, Countess Nadasdy, or herself? Lady Maccon wished, not for the first time, she had her own team of BUR-style field agents she could set to tail suspicious individuals at will. She looked with consideration at her tiny daughter, who was occupied playing with a curl of Alexia's hair. *Perhaps I should train Prudence in covert operation procedures? With an adopted father like Lord Akeldama, half my work will already be completed.* Prudence blinked at her and then stuffed the curl into her mouth. *Perhaps not just yet.*

Madame Lefoux made good her escape, and Alexia, Ivy, and the nursemaid dressed and mobilized the three infants. They made their way down and out the front of the hotel where a docile, soft-eared donkey and companion boy stood awaiting them. The twins took up basket position with little fuss, Percy being given a bit of dried fig to gnaw upon and Primrose a length of silver lace to play with. Both wore large straw hats, Primrose looking quite the thing with her dark curls peeking out and her big blue eyes. Percy, on the other hand, looked rather uncomfortable, like a fat, redheaded boatman unsure of the high seas.

Prudence, set astride the donkey, drummed her chubby legs and grabbed the creature's neck like a seasoned professional. What little sun she had experienced aboard ship had turned her skin a faint olive. Alexia was horribly afraid her daughter had inherited her Italian complexion. This spectacle, of three foreign children dressed in all the frills and lace of England's finest, plus donkey, caused a stir in the streets of Alexandria. It was just as well, since they couldn't move very quickly without Prudence falling off. The nursemaid walked alongside, keeping a watchful eye to them all, neat as a new pin in her navy dress, white apron, and cap. Mrs. Tunstell and Lady Maccon strode at the front, leading the way, parasols raised against the sun. Lady Maccon was dressed in a fabulous walking gown of black and white stripes, courtesy of Biffy, and Mrs. Tunstell in a complementary day dress of periwinkle blue and maroon plaid. Periodically they would pause to consult Mrs. Tunstell's little guidebook, until this took too long, at which juncture Lady Maccon would simply pick a direction and stride on.

Alexia fell deeply in love with Egypt on that walk. There really was no other way of putting it. As suggested by Ivy's Baedeker, Egypt had no concept of bad weather in the winter months, giving them instead a mild summer. The sandstone and mud brick buildings basked under the friendly orange glow, and the slatted rushes high above their heads made crisscrosses of shade at their feet. The flowing garb of the locals provided an endless shifting of bright colors against a muted monotone background. The native women carried baskets of food balanced upon their heads. Ivy, at first, thought this a peculiar kind of hat and was very interested in procuring one for herself, until she saw a woman lift the basket down and dole out bread to an eager donkey boy.

The gentlemen and ladies of Egypt seemed to possess a self-respect and innate gracefulness of manner, regardless of societal rank, that could only be thought engaging. That said, they also seemed inclined to sing while they worked, or sat upon their heels, or stretched out upon a mat. Alexia was not a particularly musical person, and her husband, a noted opera singer in his human days, had once described her bath time warblings as those of a deranged badger. But even she could recognize complete tunelessness, coupled to a certain rhythmic vocalization. The resulting renditions seemed a means of lightening labor or sweetening repose, but Alexia thought them monotonous and displeasing to the ear. However, she learned, as she had done with the harmonic auditory resonance disruptor, to disregard it as mere background hum.

As they tottered happily along, Alexia felt compelled to stop at many a small shop and one or two bazaar stands to investigate the goods on offer, mainly drawn, as was her wont, by delicious and exotic foodstuffs. Ivy and the child-burdened donkey trailed in her wake. The nursemaid paid due attention to her charges and was properly shocked by the foreignness of the city about them the rest of the time. "Oh, Mrs. Tunstell, would you look at that? Stray dogs!" or "Oh, Mrs. Tunstell, would you believe? That man is sitting cross-legged, on his front step, and his legs are bare!"

Mrs. Tunstell, meanwhile, became increasingly addlepated over their getting lost in a foreign land.

Prudence held on with all her might, and after taking in her surroundings with the jaundiced eye of a seasoned traveler, tilted her little head back, nearly losing her hat, and cooed in delight over the amazing sight of the many massive colorful balloons that hovered above the city. Egyptians were not yet proficient in dirigible travel but had for many hundreds of years played host to the balloon nomads of the desert skies, bronzed cousins to the Bedouin. The first of the English settlers named them Drifters, and the moniker stuck. A vast number hovered above Alexandria during the day, having come in for the markets and the tourist trade. They were every color of every hat Ivy had ever possessed, many of them patchwork or striped. As fascinating as the daily life of the natives might be, Prudence was lured by the promise of flight high above. She warbled her glee.

Thus pleasantly entertained, the group made its way through the city, pausing overlong only once, in one of the bazaars when Alexia was particularly taken by a fine display of leatherwork. Looking up, she noticed that the man seated behind the goods attractively arrayed on a colorful striped rug was not the same in looks as all the others they had encountered thus far. He had a different garb and bearing. His sharp, bearded features and steady gaze betokened firmness, resolution, and an autocratic nature. He was also *not singing*. This was no Alexandrian local but one of the Bedouin nomads of the desert, or so Alexia believed at first. Until she noted that a long rope ladder was tied to the building behind him, a ladder that stretched all the way up into the sky above, attached to the basket of one of Prudence's beloved balloons. The man was uncommonly handsome, his dark eyes intent, and he stared hard at Alexia for a moment.

"Leather for the pretty lady?" he asked.

"Oh, no thank you. Simply looking."

"You should look farther south. The answers to your questions lie in Upper Egypt, Miss Tarabotti," said the Drifter, his accent thick but his meaning unmistakable.

"Pardon me. What did you just say?" Alexia was startled into asking. She looked for Mrs. Tunstell. "Ivy, did you hear that?" By the time she had turned back, the man was gone, shimmying up his rope ladder into the sky with remarkable dexterity and speed, almost supernaturally quick—impossible, of course, as it was still daylight.

Alexia watched him go with her mouth slightly open until a new voice said, "Leather for the pretty lady?" and a small boy, in typical Alexandrian garb, looked hopefully up at her from the exact place the man had just been.

"What! Who was that bearded man? How did he know my name?"

The boy only blinked his fringe of lashes at her, uncomprehending. "Leather for the pretty lady?"

"Alexia, are we finished here? I hardly see what you would want with such goods."

"Ivy, did you see that man?"

"What man?"

"The balloon nomad who was just here."

"Oh, really, Alexia, it says right here in my little book—Drifters don't fraternize with Europeans. You must have imagined it."

"Ivy, my dearest boon companion, have I ever *imagined* anything?"

"Fair point, Alexia. In which case, I am very sorry to say that I did not observe the interaction."

"A disappointment for you, I'm sure, for he was a remarkably fine specimen."

"Oh, my, Alexia, you shouldn't say such things! You're a married woman."

"True, but not a dead one."

Ivy fanned herself vigorously. "La, Alexia, such talk!"

Lady Maccon only smiled and twirled her parasol. "Ah, well, I suppose time is of the essence. We should press on." She tried to memorize the stall's location and the color of the man's balloon, a patchwork of varying shades of deep purples.

With no further disruptions, they made their way to the west end of Boulevard Ramleh, arriving by six o'clock exactly. Alexia left her party in ecstasies over Port Neuf, glittering rich and blue under the low light of the late afternoon sun. She strode swiftly inside and, finding it was English run and quite up to snuff, had her own valve in place exactly on time to transmit a message to Biffy. At least she hoped it was the right time; so many things could go wrong with aethographors.

"Ruffled Parasol in place," her message ran. "Booking this time this location until departure." She then added the Alexandria codes and waited with bated breath. Within moments, as ordered, there came a reply. Unfortunately, it was not the reply Lady Alexia Maccon would have wished.

Biffy's sleep was troubled and not only by the fact that Professor Lyall boasted rather a small bed for two occupants. While neither of them was very large, Biffy was a good deal taller than his companion, which caused his feet to dangle off the end. Still neither would even think to suggest that they sleep apart, not now that they had discovered each other. Besides, once the sun rose fully, they both slept solidly enough to be thought dead, limbs wound together, breathing soft and deep. Nevertheless, Biffy's dreams were colored by missed appointments, canceled events, and forgotten messages.

Channing Channing of the Chesterfield Channings had caught Biffy following Lyall into his room that morning. He raised one blond eyebrow in silent criticism but said nothing. However, they both knew they were due to come under a good deal of teasing that evening, for all the pack would be informed. Werewolves were terrible gossips, especially about their own. Vampires preferred to talk about other people's business; werewolves were a tad more incestuous in their interests. Knowing that their new arrangement, as yet unformed in the particulars, was public fodder for the rumor mill allowed Biffy to give his claviger instructions to see him awakened a few minutes before sunset *in Lyall's chamber*.

"Sir, sir, wake up." As ordered, Catogan Burbleson, a nice boy with considerable musical talent, shook Biffy hard some fifteen minutes before sunset. It took a good deal of force to rouse a werewolf before sundown, especially one of Biffy's youth.

"Everything all right, Mr. Burbleson?" Biffy heard the Beta whisper.

"Yes, sir. Mr. Biffy asked me to see him up before sunset, something about not missing an important appointment."

"Ah, yes, of course."

Biffy felt a nuzzle at the back of his neck and then sharp teeth as Lyall bit him hard on the meat of his shoulder.

He stopped pretending to be asleep and said, "Now, now, Professor, save that for later. Naughty man."

Lyall laughed, actually laughed, and poor Catogan looked horribly embarrassed.

Biffy rolled out of bed and his claviger helped him into a smoking jacket, silk trousers, dressing gown, and slippers. Under ordinary circumstances, he would not leave his room, nor Lyall's for that matter, in anything less than shoes, spats, trousers, shirt, waistcoat, cravat, and jacket. But there was no time to waste, and he would have to complete his toilette at leisure later. He only hoped he should not encounter anyone with fixed opinions on his foray to the aethographor—a faint hope in a den of werewolves.

Thus informally attired, he hurried up to the attic of the house, where Lady Maccon had had her aethographic transmitter installed. The device looked on the outside to be nothing more than an enormous box, large enough to house two horses, raised up off the floor via a complex system of springs. The exterior was quilted in thick blue velvet to prevent ambient noise from reaching its interior. The box was divided into two small rooms, each filled with a precise arrangement of machinery. As he was supposed to be waiting for the Alexandria codes from Lady Maccon, Biffy took up vigil in the receiving chamber.

With everything switched to the on position, he sat as still as possible. Utter silence was necessary or the receivers might be disrupted in their response to aetheric vibrations. He watched intently and just as the sun set—he could feel the sensation in his werewolf bones—a message came through. Before him were two pieces of glass with black particulate sandwiched between, and a magnet mounted to a small hydraulic arm hovering above began to move. One by one, letters formed in the particulate. "Ruffled Parasol in place. Booking this time this location until departure." And there came a short string of numbers. Biffy had an excellent memory, so he simply made a mental note of the codes and then dashed out and over to the transmitting chamber.

As quickly as supernaturally possible, he dialed the aetheromagnetic setting into the frequency transmitters. Lady Maccon had insisted on commissioning only the latest and most sophisticated in aethographors. Biffy needed no companion valve on his end. That done, he double-checked his numbers and then picked up an acid stylus and an etching roll. He composed his message, careful to print each letter neatly in a grid square. This first communication was simple and had to be sent immediately. "Wait," it said, "more follows. Wingtip Spectator." He slotted the metal slate into the brackets and activated the transmitter. Two needles passed over the grid squares of the slate, one on the top side and the other underneath, sparking whenever they were exposed to one another through the etched letters.

Without waiting for a reply, he bent to compose his second message, the one carrying the bulk of his recent discoveries. It was a lot of vital information to transfer in code, but he did his very best. Once more he activated the aetheric convector. Barely breathing, he watched the sparks fly and hoped against hope that the message was away and that he was not too late.

"Wait," Biffy's message said, "more follows. Wingtip Spectator." Lady Maccon looked from the clerk to the scrap of papyrus paper he had passed to her and then back again.

"Is the receiving chamber booked just now?"

"Not for another few minutes, madam."

"Then allow me the privilege of renting it for one additional message." Alexia passed over a generous amount of money. The clerk's eyebrows rose.

"As you wish, madam." He hurried off, back to the Alexandria aethographor's receiving chamber, graphite pencil in one hand, a fresh scrap of papyrus in the other.

He returned a few moments later with another message. Alexia snatched it from him. The first part said, "50 years ago GBP start expand." Alexia puzzled over this for only a moment before she realized that Biffy must have figured out that the God-Breaker Plague was increasing and that this expansion had commenced some five decades ago. A fact that confirmed what she and Conall had surmised. She wished she knew how much and with what rapidity but guessed it must be quite significant for Biffy to think it important enough to mention. Also, Biffy had given her a time frame—fifty years. *What happened in Egypt fifty years ago? This must have something to do with Matakara's summons. But what good can I do? Or Prudence, for that matter. Neither of us can stop a plague.* Given that Biffy had determined the rate of expansion, Alexia wondered if he had also determined a possible epicenter. *If the plague moves far enough into Alexandria, I suppose Queen Matakara will have to swarm.* Could a vampire in her condition, grafted into a chair, afterlife supported by artificial means, still swarm? Then again, someone had once said that the older the queen, the shorter amount of time she had to swarm. Was Matakara simply too old to manage it at all? Had she lost the capacity?

Troubled by these thoughts, Lady Maccon almost didn't notice that there was a second scrap of paper with another message.

It read, "Lady K knows PL past. Wrote Lord M."

Alexia Maccon felt her heart sink down and lodge somewhere in the vicinity of her stomach where it caused no little upset. Her cheeks tingled as the blood drained out of her face, and she was certain, had she been the kind of woman to faint, she would have done so right then and there. But she was not, so she panicked instead.

The message was cryptic to be sure, but it could only mean one thing. Lady Kingair had somehow found out that Professor Lyall had rigged the Kingair assassination attempt and she had written to Conall informing him of Lyall's duplicity. This should not, ordinarily, upset Alexia all that much. Except, of course, that she, too, had known. And in knowing such an awful thing, she had also chosen for the last few years to keep it secret from her husband. A wifely betrayal she had hoped would not be revealed in her lifetime. For Conall would find it difficult to forgive such subterfuge.

At that moment, Lady Maccon remembered the innocent little letter, the one with the handwriting she had not recognized. The one she had picked up from the hotel clerk the other evening and placed upon Conall's bedside table, thinking it a missive from one of his BUR operatives.

"Oh, my giddy aunt!" she cried, crumpling the little scraps of paper in her hand and dashing out without further conversation. The surprised clerk had not the time to even wish her a good evening, merely bowing to her retreating back.

"Ivy! Mrs. Tunstell! Ivy! We must return to the hotel directly!" Alexia yelled upon exiting the offices.

But Ivy and the children, having grown tired of waiting in the street, were busy exploring the exotic world around them. Some species of little old lady in black robes, her face wrinkled into obscurity, was telling an animated story to a highly appreciative audience on the far side of the street. The crowd participated and responded to her words with cries of excitement. Ivy stood among the watchers, with Primrose on one hip and Percival on the other. Behind her was the nursemaid and the donkey with Ivy's parasol and the babies' hats. Prudence, however, was nowhere to be seen.

Seized by additional panic, Alexia dashed over, narrowly missing being hit by a cart full of oranges. The vendor hurled obscenities at her. Alexia shook her parasol at him.

"Ivy, Ivy, where is Prudence? We must return to the hotel directly."

"Oh, Alexia! This lady is an *Antari*, a singer of tales. Isn't she marvelous? Of course, I can't understand a word, but simply listen to the verbal intonations. And her projection is one of the finest I've ever experienced, even on the London stage. Such somnolence. Or do I mean resonance? Anyway, would you look at this crowd? They are riveted! Tunny would be so intrigued. Do you think we should go back to the hotel and wake him?"

"Ivy, *where is my daughter*?!"

"Oh. Oh, yes, of course. Just there." Ivy gestured with her chin. When Alexia still looked about frantically, she said, "Here, hold Tidwinkle," and passed Primrose off to her.

Alexia adjusted the little girl in her arms, and Primrose became fascinated by the white ruffles on the hem of her parasol. Alexia gave it to her obligingly to hold.

One arm now free, Ivy pointed into the crowd to the very front, where Alexia could just make out her daughter, sitting cross-legged and hatless in the dust of the road, exactly like the Antari, absorbing the story with great interest.

"Oh, really, has she no decorum at all?" wondered her mother, relieved beyond measure, but also back to frantic rushing, in the hopes that she might make it to the hotel in time to stop Conall from reading that letter.

Alexia was making her way back to the nursemaid to deposit Primrose so she could go scoop up her own daughter when something unpleasant happened. A group of white-clad, turbaned men descended upon her and surrounded her. Their faces were all veiled like those of Egyptian females, and their intent was clearly hostile. They were grabbing and pulling at her, trying to separate her from Primrose, or perhaps from her purse or parasol; it was difficult to tell.

Primrose set up a thin wail of discouragement and wrapped her chubby arms more firmly around Alexia's parasol like a good little assistant accessory guardian. Alexia used her free hand to beat off their attackers, exclaiming in anger and whirling about as much as possible, making it difficult for any to find purchase on her or the baby. It was not good odds, and she seemed to have no free moment at all to grab the parasol and bring the full capacity of its arsenal into the fray.

Help came from a most unlikely quarter. Perhaps it was motherly instinct, or perhaps being an actress had somehow expanded her gumption over the intervening years, or perhaps she felt it more appropriate as a member of the Parasol Protectorate, but Ivy Tunstell waded into the fray. Clutching Percy with one arm, she screamed her version of obscenities. “How dare you? You ruffians!” And, “Cads! Unhand my friend.” And, “Can’t you see there is a child involved? Behave!”

The nursemaid, donkey in tow, also joined the kerfuffle. She was wielding Ivy’s parasol with a skill Alexia quite admired, bashing at the men and also yelling.

The storyteller paused in her recitation when it became clear that a pair of foreign ladies with children were under assault. No decent person, not even a native of this wild land, would condone such a thing in the middle of the street.

Their entertainment curtailed, the crowd pressed back against the men. The street was alive with flying limbs and staccato Arabic shouting. Alexia, fist flying, elbows prodding, did her best to keep herself and Primrose from being injured or separated, but there were many men all constantly grasping at her with brutal intent.

Suddenly she found herself seized by the shoulders and dragged out of the milling throng into the comparative safety of an alleyway. She looked up, panting slightly from the exertion, to thank her rescuer, only to find she was face-to-face with the balloon nomad from the bazaar. She would recognize that handsome face with its neatly trimmed beard anywhere. He nodded at her once, in a friendly manner.

Alexia took stock of her situation. She seemed to have only a few bruises to show for the battle. Primrose was still crying but was safe in her arms, parasol firmly clasped to her little breast.

Alexia felt a weight against her legs and looked down to see that Prudence had glommed on to her skirts and was looking up at her with wide, frightened eyes. “Whoa, Mama,” she said.

“Indeed.” *Well that is two accounted for.*

The Drifter dove back into the crowd, robe flapping behind him, while Alexia extracted her parasol from Primrose and armed the tip. One of the white-clad men broke away and made for her, murder in his eyes, and Alexia shot him in the chest without compunction. The numbing dart was only partly effective on supernatural creatures, but it brought that daylight thug down before he took even one more step in their direction. He crumpled in a heap of white fabric to the dirty street. Then her mysterious savior reappeared, dragging behind him a screaming and thrashing Ivy Tunstell.

“He seems to be on our side, Ivy. Do stop fussing.”

“Oh, oh, dear, Alexia. Can you believe? Why I never, in all life’s flutterings!”

Ivy looked a little worse for wear. Her hat was gone, her hair loose, and her dress torn. Percival was red-faced and crying like his sister, but otherwise both seemed unbowed. The nursemaid, still with donkey—remarkably placid and undisturbed by the ruckus—came behind them.

Ivy plunked her squalling child into one of the panniers and Alexia did the same with Primrose. The twins continued their thin treble wails of distress but remained inside their respective baskets.

Alexia bent and lifted Prudence up. Her daughter was sobered by the experience, although much less overset by the excitement than the two younger infants. Not a tear tracked down the dust covering her face. In fact, her eyes glittered with hidden excitement.

"Oh-ah Eeegypt!" she said as a kind of commentary.

"Yes, dear," agreed her mother.

Ivy leaned back against the donkey, fanning herself with one gloved hand. "Alexia, I am quite overset. Do you realize we were attacked! Right here, in a public thoroughfare. Really, I feel quite faint."

"Well, can it wait? We must make for safety."

"Oh, my, yes, of course. And I could hardly faint with a bare head in a foreign country! I might catch something," Ivy exclaimed.

"Exactly."

Their bearded savior gestured. "This way, lady."

With no other options—Ivy having dropped her guidebook in the excitement—they followed.

The Drifter set a brisk pace through hidden streets and alleys, up small sets of stone steps in a direction Alexia could only hope was toward their hotel. She was beginning to worry that they might have gone from boiler to steam engine, trading one danger for another. She shifted so that her parasol pointed at the man's unprotected back, wary that she still did not recognize the city around them.

Then at long last, they burst out onto a familiar square and saw the front entrance to Hotel des Voyageurs sitting in peaceful serenity before them across a bustling bazaar. Alexia glanced over to thank their guide, but the man had melted off into the crowd, leaving the ladies to make their way this last little bit without escort.

"What a mysterious gentleman," commented Alexia.

"He probably had to make it back to his balloon."

"Oh?"

"Baedeker says that the balloons heat during the early part of the day and rise up. Most Drifters allow them to sink back down at night as they cool, wherever they are in the desert, until the morning heat again. He said that once the balloon is up, a Drifter will never allow it back down again until evening," Ivy explained as they pushed their way through the milling throng.

"How very ingenious."

"So, you see, his home is probably sinking. He has to go meet it or he wouldn't know where it landed."

"Oh, Ivy, I hardly think . . ." Alexia trailed off.

Lord Conall Maccon stood in the doorway to the hotel, holding a letter in one hand, and he did not look pleased.

CHAPTER THIRTEEN

In Which Idle Letters Waste Lives

Alexia Maccon adored her husband and she should never wish to cause him any pain. He was a sensitive werewolf type, unfortunately, for all her efforts, prone to extremes in emotion and with a particular, perhaps even obsessive, regard for such noble concepts as honor, loyalty, and trust.

"Wife."

"Good evening, husband. How was your repose?" Alexia paused at the threshold to the hotel, trying to angle herself to the side so they did not entirely block the entranceway. Given her husband's bulk, this was no mean feat.

"Never mind repose. I have received a most upsetting letter."

"Ah, yes, well. I can explain."

"Oh, ho?"

"Do you think we might repair to our room to discuss the matter?"

The earl ignored this entirely sensible suggestion. Alexia supposed she was in for a well-deserved bout of public humiliation. Behind Conall's looming form, in the foyer of Hotel des Voyageurs, she could see guests turn to look at the tableau in the doorway. Her husband had raised his voice rather more than was common, even for Alexandria.

Lord Maccon boasted a barrel chest and companion booming vocalization at the best of times. As this was the worst of times, he could have roused the undead—and probably did in some areas of the city. "Randolph Lyall, that squirrelly snot-nosed plonker, rigged the whole darn thing: caused Kingair tae betray me, got me tae come tae Woolsey, saw me eliminate his old Alpha. All of it! He never saw fit tae tell me this little fact." The earl's tawny eyes were narrowed and yellow in fury, and it looked as though a bit of canine was showing out the corners of his mouth.

His voice went very cold and clipped. It was terrifying. "Apparently, *you* know all of this, wife. And you dinnae tell me. I canna quite ken tae such a thing. But my own great-great-great-granddaughter assures me of the truth of it, and why should she lie?"

Alexia raised her hands, placating. "Now, Conall, please look at this from my perspective. I didn't *want* to keep it secret. I really didn't. But I saw how upset you were about Kingair and that betrayal. I couldn't bear to see you hurt again if I told you about Lyall. He didn't know you intimately way back when. He had no thought to your loss. He was trying to save his pack."

"Oh, trust me, Alexia. I ken what old Lord Woolsey was like. And I ken verra well what Lyall was up against. I can even ken what love and loss drove him tae do. But tae keep such a secret from me even after we became kin? After I had grown tae trust him? And worse, that you should do the same! You who have nothing like his excuse."

Alexia bit her lower lip, worried. "But, Conall, even knowing how awful it was for him, Lyall and I both knew you would never trust him again. And you need him—he is a good Beta."

Lord Maccon looked at her, even more coldly than before. "Make no bones about it, Alexia. I *need* no one! Least of all a wife like you and a Beta like *that*! If you owe me naught else in this marriage, you owe me truth about pack! I wouldna ask for truth in anything else. But *my pack*, Alexia? It was your duty tae tell me the moment you found out!"

"Well, to be fair, at the time I had other things on my mind. There was an octomaton, and Prudence to be born—you know, little trifles like that." Alexia tried to smile weakly, knowing there could be no real excuse.

"Are you making light of this, woman?"

"Oh, dear. Conall, I *wanted* to tell you! I really did. I simply knew you would react . . . well, you know."

"Do I?"

She sighed. "Badly. I knew you would react badly."

"Badly! You have no idea how bad this is going to get."

"See?"

"So you thought you might wait it out, that I shouldna find out?"

"Well, I thought perhaps, since I'm a mortal, I might at least die first."

"Don't go playing the sympathy card with me, woman. I know verra well you'll be dying afore me." Then he sighed.

The earl was such a massive man, yet as Alexia watched in concern, he seemed to shrink in upon himself. He leaned back against the side of the door, old and tired. "I canna believe you would do this tae me. Alexia, I *trusted* you."

It was said in such a small, little boy voice that Alexia felt her own heart contract in response to his pain. "Oh, Conall. What can I say? I thought it was for the best. I thought you would be happier not knowing."

"You thought, you thought. Never did you *think* it might be better tae have been told by you than to have you ally against me? You have made a chump of me. To hell with the lot of you." With that, he crumpled the letter and tossed it to the street before striding off into the crowded city.

"Where are you going? Please, Conall!" Alexia called after him, but he only raised one hand into the air in disregard and strode away.

"And with no top hat," came a small addendum comment from behind her.

Alexia turned in a daze, having entirely forgotten until that moment that Mrs. Tunstell, the nursemaid, the children, and the donkey—all of them grubby, sunburned, and tear-stained—stood waiting patiently to enter the hotel, except the donkey, although he probably wouldn't have minded going inside.

Alexia could only blink down at Ivy, experiencing a kind of emotional distress heretofore alien to her makeup. Oh, Conall had been angry at her in the past, but to the best of *her* knowledge, he had never been in the right before. "Oh, Ivy. I am so very sorry. I forgot you were there."

"Goodness, that doesn't happen often," replied Ivy. Although she had heard much of the conversation, she was ignorant as to the significance of the tirade, for she asked at that juncture, looking with concern into her dear friend's ashen face, "Why, Alexia, my dear, are you quite well?"

"No, Ivy, I am not. I do believe my marriage may be in ruins."

"Well, it's a good thing we are in the land of such things, then, isn't it?"

"What things?"

"Ruins."

"Oh, Ivy, *really*."

"Not even a smile? You must truly be afflicted by sentimental upset. Do you feel faint? I've never known you to faint, but I suppose one is never too young to start trying."

Then, much to Ivy's shock and Alexia's horror, the bold-as-brass Lady Maccon—paragon of assertive behavior and wielder of stoicism, parasols, and the occasional cryptic remark—burst into tears, right there on the front step of a public hostelry in central Alexandria.

Mrs. Tunstell, horrified beyond measure, wrapped one consoling arm about her friend and hustled her quickly inside Hotel des Voyageurs and into a private side parlor where she called for tea and instructed the nursemaid to see that the children were cleaned and put down for a nap. Alexia had just enough presence of mind to babble out that under no circumstances was anyone to attempt to bathe Prudence.

Alexia continued to blubber incoherently and Ivy to pat her hand sympathetically. Mrs. Tunstell was clearly at a loss as to what else she might do to allay her friend's anguish.

Tunstell appeared in the doorway at one point, riding atop Prudence's mechanical ladybug—he had always been fond of ladybugs—his knees up by his ears and grinning like a maniac. Even that failed to cheer Alexia. Ivy sent her husband off with a quick shake of her head and a stern, "Tunny, this is a serious matter. Bug off. We are not to be disturbed."

"But, light of my life, what has happened to your hat?"

"Never mind that now. I have an emotional crisis on my hands."

Tunstell, shaken to the core by the fact that his wife was clearly not disturbed by the loss of one of her precious bonnets, elected to take Alexia's tears seriously and stopped smiling. "My goodness, what can I do?"

"Do? Do! Men are useless in such matters. Go see what is delaying the tea!"

Tunstell and the mechanical ladybug trundled away.

Finally a beverage did arrive, but it was once again honey-sweetened coffee, not tea. This only made Alexia cry harder. What she wouldn't give for a cup of strong Assam with a dollop of quality British milk and a piece of treacle tart. Her world was crumbling around her!

She sobbed. "Oh, Ivy, what am I to do? He will never trust me again." She must have been feeling quite undone to ask Mrs. Ivy Tunstell for advice.

Ivy clasped Alexia's hand in both of hers and made sympathetic shushing noises. "There, there, Alexia, it will all be all right."

"How will it be all right? I lied to him."

"Oh, but you've done that heaps of times."

"Yes, but this time it was about something that matters. Something he cares about. And it was wrong of me to do it. And I knew it was wrong but I did it anyway. Oh, blast Professor Lyall. How could he get me into this mess? And blast my father, too! If he hadn't gone off and gotten himself killed, none of this would have happened."

"Now, Alexia, language."

"Right when I have important information about this plague and I need Conall here to help me figure out the particulars. But, no, he has to go storming off. And it's all destroyed, all lost."

"Really, Alexia, I've never known you to be fatalistic before."

"Too many viewings of *The Death Rains of Swansea*, I suppose."

There came a bustle at the door and another familiar face peeked in. "What on earth has happened? Alexia, are you well? Is it Prudence?" Madame Lefoux came hurrying into the room. Tossing her hat and gloves carelessly aside, she dashed over to the divan and sat next to Alexia, on the other side from Ivy.

Lacking Mrs. Tunstell's natural British reticence, the Frenchwoman scooped Alexia into a full embrace, wrapping her bony arms around her friend and pressing her cheek to the top of Alexia's dark head. She stroked Alexia's back up and down in long, affectionate caresses, which reminded Alexia of Conall and made the tears, which were almost under control, start up once more.

Genevieve looked at Ivy curiously. "Why, Mrs. Tunstell, whatever could cause our Alexia to be so overset?"

"She has had a most trying argument with her husband. Something to do with a letter, and Professor Lyall, and a trifle, and some treacle, I believe."

"Oh, dear, it sounds gummy."

The absurdity of Ivy's interpretation was the boost Alexia needed to rein in her runaway sentimentality. *Really*, she thought, *there is no point in wallowing. I must get myself in order and come up with a way to fix this.* She took a deep, shaky breath and a long sip of the horrible coffee to calm her nerves. She then developed a bad case of the hiccoughs, because, as she could only surmise, the universe was against her retaining any dignity whatsoever.

"Old history," she said at last. "With werewolves, it is never so very well buried as one might hope. Suffice it to say that Conall has discovered something and I am to blame in part for his not knowing it to start with. He is not happy about this. Sticky, indeed."

Genevieve, sensing Alexia was beginning to recover, let her go and sat back, pouring herself a cup of coffee.

Mrs. Tunstell, wishing to provide some distraction while Alexia composed her emotions, began prattling on about their adventures at the bazaar in highly embellished terms. Madame Lefoux listened attentively and gasped in all the right places, and by the time the telling was complete, Alexia was feeling better, if not entirely up to snuff.

Alexia turned the full focus of her attention onto the French inventor.

"And how about you, Genevieve? I trust your explorations about the metropolis have proved more enjoyable than ours?"

"Well, they were certainly less exciting. I had a matter of business to conduct. It seems, however, to have opened up more questions than it answered."

"Oh?"

"Yes."

Alexia took a gamble. "While I know that ostensibly the countess sent you along to keep an eye on me and figure out what Matakara wants with Prudence, I don't suppose your true purpose in visiting Egypt is to investigate the expansion of the God-Breaker Plague for the OBO. Is it?"

Genevieve dimpled at her. "Ah. I see. You've noticed it, too, have you?"

"Conall and I suspected as much the evening we arrived, and a missive from Biffy recently confirmed it. Some fifty years ago, or thereabouts, it began an accelerated push."

Madame Lefoux tilted her head in acknowledgment. "Actually, we are thinking that it was more like forty."

"You have an idea of what might have set it into motion?"

"Well . . . ," Madame Lefoux hedged.

"Genevieve, we have been through this before. Don't you think it wiser simply to tell me what you are thinking? It saves burning half of London and having to build weapons of immense tentaclization."

The Frenchwoman pursed her lips and then nodded. She stared for a moment at Ivy out of suspicious green eyes and then finally said, "I suppose. It's not that we know exactly what caused it, more that there is a terrible coincidence. How to put this? You see, Alexia, your father happened to be in Egypt right about that time."

"Of course he was." Alexia wasn't surprised in the slightest by this information. "But, Genevieve, how would you know a thing like that? Even with all your contacts."

"Ah, yes, that. Well, that's the problem. Alessandro Tarabotti was working for the OBO at the time."

"It was after he broke with the Templars? Go on. There must be more."

"Well, yes, yes, there is. He came here and something happened, and he abandoned the OBO with no warning."

"That sounds like my father. He wasn't particularly loyal to any organization."

"Ah, but he took half the OBO underground information network with him."

Alexia had a sinking sensation. "Dead?"

"No, turned. They stayed alive, only working for him instead of us. And we never did get them back, even after he died."

Alexia felt a slight wiggle of butterflies in her stomach, which she was beginning to label her *sensation of significance*. Something was, quite defiantly, *up*.

"It's sealed under the Clandestine Scientific Information Act of 1855." Professor Lyall sat down with a thump next to Biffy on the small settee in the back parlor. He shoved him over gently to make room. Biffy bumped back against him affectionately but moved. Lyall had just returned from BUR and he smelled like a London night, etching acid, and the Thames.

"Have you been swimming?"

The Beta ignored this to continue his complaint. "It's all sealed."

"What is?"

"Records to do with Egypt, for a period of twelve years, starting right about the time the plague began to expand. Familiarity with clandestine-level scientific secrets is beyond my rank and authority. Especially mine, as no supernaturals, drones, clavigers, or persons with suspected excess soul are allowed access. I was working for BUR at the time, and I didn't know anything about the Clandestine Scientific Information Act until after it had passed into law." Professor Lyall seemed mildly annoyed by this. It wasn't that he was particularly troubled by not knowing, in the way of Lord Akeldama, it was more that he did not approve of anything that upset the efficient running of pack life or BUR duties.

Biffy thought back to some bits of information that Lord Akeldama had once let slip. "Wasn't the Clandestine Act linked to the last of the intelligencers before they were disbanded?"

"Under the previous potentate, yes. It also had something to do with the Great Picklemen Revolt and the disposal of patents of domestic servitude. What a mess things were in those days."

"Well, that's that, then." From what Biffy could recall, very serious action had been taken and there was nothing even the hives could do to countermand the restrictions that were put into place as a consequence.

"Not entirely. All this material about Egypt is locked under a cipher, and that cipher is linked to the code name of a known provocateur. A provocateur whose loyalties were unreliable and true allegiance unknown."

"Yes?"

"Fortunately, his is a cipher I know, without having to go up against the Clandestine Act."

"Oh?" Biffy sat up a little straighter, intrigued.

"He went by Panattone, but his real name was Alessandro Tarabotti."

Biffy started. "Again? My goodness, your former amour certainly had his fingers in many pies."

"Preternaturals are like that. You should know their ways by now."

"Of course—worse than Lord Akeldama. He has to know everyone's business. Lady Maccon has to know everyone's business *and* interfere in it."

Professor Lyall turned to face Biffy fully on the small couch, placing his hand on the young werewolf's knee. His calm demeanor might have been slightly shaken, although not a hair was out of place. Biffy wondered if he might persuade him to share this secret.

"The thing is, he was there. I *know* Sandy was there. It's in his journals—several trips to Egypt starting in 1835. But there is nothing about what he did while he was there nor the name of his actual employer. I knew he was involved in some pretty dark dealings, but to require an official seal?"

"You think it might have something to do with the God-Breaker Plague, don't you?"

"I think preternaturals, mummies, and the God-Breaker Plague go together better than custard and black-currant jelly. Alessandro Tarabotti was one powerful preternatural."

Biffy wasn't comfortable with Lyall talking about his former lover in such a reverent tone, but he kept his mind on the business in question, finding reassurance in the fact that Lyall's hand was still on his knee. "Well, I have only one suggestion. And Egypt is not exactly his forté. But you know . . ."

"We should see what Lord Akeldama has to say on the matter?"

"You suggested it, not me." Biffy tilted his head and examined Lyall's sharp vulpine face for signs of jealousy. Unable to discern any, he stood and offered the Beta a quite unnecessary hand up. *Any excuse for a touch.*

The two men clapped top hats to their heads and made their way next door to call upon the vampire in question.

Lord Akeldama's house was in an uproar. A very frazzled-looking drone opened the door a good five minutes after they had yanked on the bell-pull for the third time.

"Werewolf on the loose?" asked Professor Lyall casually.

Biffy pretended to blush, remembering just such an incident a few years back when he had broken into his former master's abode. He had written a long letter of apology but had never quite recovered from the humiliation. Lord Akeldama had been decent about the whole incident, which somehow made it worse.

"No, not so bad as that, but something untoward certainly has happened." Biffy looked around, eyes bright with curiosity.

A gaggle of excited drones rushed through the hallway at that juncture, carrying various-sized empty jam jars. Two of the drones were wearing large brown leather gloves.

"What ho, Biffy," called out one excitedly.

"Boots, what's afoot?" Biffy asked.

Boots separated from the gaggle and slid to a stop before the two werewolves. "Oh, it's all go around here! Shabumpkin let loose a lizard in the front parlor."

"A lizard? Whatever for?"

"Just because, I suppose."

"I see."

"Can't seem to catch the darn thing."

"Big lizard is it?"

"Huge! Almost the size of my thumb. No idea where Shabumpkin got it. Cracking teal color."

Then came a crash from said front parlor and a deal of squealing. Boots hastily excused himself and went dashing after the sound.

Biffy turned to Professor Lyall, grinning. "A lizard."

"Massive one," agreed the Beta, pretending seriousness.

"It's all go at Lord Akeldama's place."

"As if I would have it any differently!" sang out the vampire himself, wafting in to greet them on a wave of lemon pomade and champagne cologne. "Did you hear what that *silly* boy let loose in my house? A reptile of all things. As if I should admit any creature *born out of an egg*. I don't even like poultry. *Never* trust a chicken—that's what I say. But enough about my little problems. How are you, my *fuzzy darlings*? To what do I owe the honor of this visit?"

Lord Akeldama was wearing a black-and-white-checked jacket with black satin trousers, the beginnings of what might have been subtle and elegant evening dress. Except that he had paired this with a burnt umber waistcoat and orange spats.

He received them with every sign of pleasure and led them into his drawing room with alacrity. Once seated, however, his bright blue eyes darted back and forth between the two werewolves with a hint of suspicion. Had the opportunity presented itself, and had it not been a delicate and highly personal matter, Biffy might have tried to tell his former lord of his new sleeping arrangements. But the opportunity did not arise, nor was it likely to. One did not, after all, gossip about oneself. It was simply *not done.*

Lord Akeldama's drones, however, would be pretty poor spies if they had not already informed their master as to the Beta's new chew toy, which meant that Lord Akeldama's odd expression was one of a man hunting for confirmation. It wounded Biffy deeply to know that he might be causing his former master emotional pain, but it had been two years, and he was tolerably assured that Lord Akeldama had moved on to better, younger, and more mortal morsels himself. Werewolves also liked to gossip about their neighbors.

As was often the case with Lord Akeldama, while he seemed to be doing a good deal of the talking, in the end Biffy and Lyall found themselves transferring to him the bulk of the information. Professor Lyall was not happy with this, but Biffy was comfortable knowing that the vampire enjoyed collecting information, but rarely did he put it to any concrete use. He was rather like a little old biddy who collected demitasse teacups that she then set upon a shelf to admire.

Biffy found himself telling Lord Akeldama all about Egypt and the expansion of the God-Breaker Plague. Lyall was convinced to tell him what he could about Alessandro Tarabotti and his trips to Egypt and how they all might be connected.

Once they had relayed all they could, the two werewolves stopped and sat, looking expectantly at the thin blond vampire as he twirled his monocle about in the air and frowned up at his cherub-covered ceiling.

Finally the vampire said, "My furry *darlings*, this is all very interesting indeed, but I fail to see how I could possibly be of any assistance. Or how this might connect to that tiny upset the Kingair Pack experienced. Losing a Beta. So sad. When was it? Last week or the week before?"

"Well, Dubh did say something to Lady Maccon about Alessandro," said Lyall.

Lord Akeldama stopped twirling the monocle and sat up straighter. "And there is Matakara to consider. The hive queen wanted to meet *my little puggle.* And the puggle is your Alessandro's granddaughter. You are correct to be suspicious, Dolly dear. But there are so many threads, and it is not so much that you are trying to untangle them, as weave them back into a pattern someone else already set."

The vampire stood and began to mince around the room. "You are missing something key, and while I should hate to mention it, given his *most excellent* service, there is only one person who knows what happened—*what really happened*—to your Sandy when he was in Egypt, my dear Dolly."

Biffy and Lyall looked at one another. They both knew to whom Lord Akeldama was referring.

Lyall said, "It's always difficult to get him to talk."

Biffy said, "I've often wondered if he could say anything more than the obligatory 'yes, sir.' "

Lord Akeldama smiled, showing his teeth. "So, lovely boys, in this instance it is not me you want for information. Who knew I should ever be outclassed by a butler?"

Professor Lyall and Biffy stood, bowing politely, knowing that what Lord Akeldama said was true and that they might be facing, for the first time in their collective careers in covert inquiry, a true challenge: convincing Floote to talk.

They tracked Lady Maccon's butler down to the kitchen where he was overseeing the menus for next week's repasts.

Biffy had never really looked at Floote before. One didn't, as a rule, examine one's domestic staff too closely. They might think it interfering. Floote was the perfect servant, always there when needed, always knowing what was desired, sometimes before the sensation registered in his employers.

Professor Lyall said softly, "Mr. Floote, might we have a moment of your time?"

The butler looked up at them. A nondescript man with a nondescript face, he could outdo Professor Lyall at his own game. Biffy noticed for the first time how weather-beaten Floote's skin was and that there were deep wrinkles about his nose and mouth and the corners of his eyes. He noticed that the butler's shoulders, once ramrod straight, were beginning to curve with age. Floote had acted as valet to Alessandro Tarabotti, so far as Biffy knew, since Alexia's father first appeared in the Bureau's official registry. Floote had worked for Alexia after that. *He must be*, thought Biffy, *well over seventy years of age!* He'd never even thought to ask.

"Of course, sirs," said Floote. There was some wariness in his tone.

They adjourned into the back parlor, leaving the cook and the housekeeper to finish the menu without Floote's input. Floote did not seem happy with this arrangement.

Professor Lyall gestured with one of his fine white hands, his vulpine face pinched. "Please, take a seat, Mr. Floote."

Floote would do nothing of the kind. To sit in front of his betters? Never! Biffy knew the man's character well enough to know that. So did Lyall, of course, but the Beta was trying to make the man uncomfortable.

Lyall asked the questions while Biffy simply crossed his arms and observed the butler's behavior. He had been trained in just such a skill by Lord Akeldama. He watched the way Floote's eyebrows moved slightly, the dilation of his pupils, and the shifting of weight in his knees. But very little changed about the butler during the course of the questioning, and Floote's responses were always abbreviated. Either the man had nothing to hide, or Biffy was in the presence of a master whose skills far exceeded his own powers of observation.

"Sandy was in Egypt at least three times, according to his journals, but he makes few comments as to his business there. What happened the first time?"

"Nothing of consequence, sir."

"And the second?"

"He met Leticia Phinkerlington, sir."

"Alexia's mother?"

Floote nodded.

"Yes, but what else did he *do* in Egypt? He can't have gone merely to court a girl."

No response came from Floote.

"Can you tell us who he was working for, at the very least?"

"The Templars, sir. It was always the Templars, right up until he broke with them."

"And when was that?"

"After you and he . . . sir."

"But he went to Egypt after that. I remember his going. Why? Who was he working for then? It wasn't us, was it? I mean, England or BUR. I know Queen Victoria tried to recruit him. She offered him the position of muhjah. He turned it down."

Floote blinked at Professor Lyall.

The Beta began to get a little frustrated.

"Floote, you must give us something. Unless . . . Are you, too, sealed into silence under the Clandestine Act?"

Floote nodded the tiniest of nods.

"You *are*! Of course, that would make perfect sense. You couldn't talk to any of us, not even Lady Maccon, because we are all enemy agents under the terms of that act. It prevents supernaturals and their associates, including preternaturals, from access to certain scientific information. Or that's the rumor. I don't know the particulars, of course."

Floote only gave one of his little nods again.

"So Sandy discovered something in Egypt so severe it was included under the act even though it was outside the homeland. For the good of the Commonwealth."

Floote did not react.

Professor Lyall seemed to think they would get nothing more useful out of the butler. "Very well, Floote, you may return to your menu planning. I'm certain Cook has made a botch of it without your supervision."

"Thank you, sir," said Floote with a hint of relief before gliding quietly out.

"What do you think?" Lyall turned to Biffy.

Biffy shrugged. He thought that Floote still had more information. He also thought that Floote didn't want to tell them, even if he could. He thought there was something else going on—that it wasn't just acts of parliament and games of politics and science. He thought that Lyall would want to believe the best of Lady Maccon's father, no matter how unworthy the gentleman. If Alessandro Tarabotti had been doing good deeds during any one of his visits to Egypt, he, Sandalio de Rabiffano, would eat his own cravat. Under the Templars, the OBO, or his government, Mr. Tarabotti was a nasty piece of work.

Instead of any of these things, Biffy said, "Mr. Tarabotti broke with the Templars out of love, not principle. Or so I thought. But you would understand the man's character far better than I."

Professor Lyall hung his head and looked like he might be hiding a small smile. "I see your point. You think that something more than a major act of parliament would be required to influence Sandy."

"Don't you?"

"So while Floote may be obeying the law, something else was keeping Sandy silent about Egypt for those few years we had together before he died?"

Biffy only raised his eyebrows, allowing the Beta time to think through what he had known of his former lower.

Lyall nodded slowly. "You are probably right."

CHAPTER FOURTEEN

Wherein Alexia Loans Mr. Tumtrinkle Her Gun

The Tunstells had been encouraged by Chancellor Neshi to perform an encore of *The Death Rains of Swansea* at a local theater for the benefit of the public. The theater was open air, much in the manner of Ancient Rome. Alexia was persuaded to attend and endure a third viewing of the dratted spectacle in an effort to distract her from her worries. Lord Maccon was still off in his huff when they departed for the theater.

The play was as much admired by the masses as it had been by the vampire hive. Or at least Lady Maccon *believed* it was much admired. It was difficult to determine with any accuracy, when praise was heaped upon the theatricals in a tongue entirely alien to all. However, the approbation did seem genuine. Lady Maccon, patroness, waited for Mr. and Mrs. Tunstell afterward, but so, too, did a collection of excited Egyptians, eager to touch the hero and heroine of the play, press small gifts into their hands, and in one extreme case kiss the hem of Ivy's gown.

Ivy Tunstell took such accolades in stride as her due, nodding and smiling. "Very kind" and "Thank you very much" and "Oh, you really shouldn't have" were her pat responses, although no one understood her any more than she them. Alexia thought, if she was reading body language properly, that the locals were convinced that the Tunstells' Acting Troupe a la Mode represented some species of prophesiers of the American tent-preacher variety. Even the secondary actors, like Mr. Tumtrinkle, seemed to have gained unexpected notoriety and companion acclaim.

Alexia congratulated her friends on yet another fine performance. And, since it looked like otherwise they might never leave, the group wended their way back to the hotel on foot, followed by a collective band of sycophants and admirers. They made quite the raucous crowd through the otherwise quiet streets of Alexandria.

It was only a few hours before dawn, but Alexia was not surprised to find, when she inquired after her key at the hotel, that Lord Maccon had not yet returned. Still angry, she supposed.

They were making their farewells for the evening, Mrs. Tunstell solicitous in her care for Lady Maccon's low spirits, particularly in light of the buoyancy that admiration had given her own. The hotel was busy trying to eject the legion of Tunstell devotees, when a vision of horror came down the stairs and into the hotel reception area.

No one would have described poor Mrs. Dawaud-Plonk as attractive, even at the very best of times. The Tunstells' nursemaid had not been selected for her looks but for her ability to tolerate twins plus Mrs. Tunstell, while not crumbling under a strain that would have felled lesser females. She was old enough to be mostly gray, but not so old that her limbs had been sapped of the strength needed to carry two infants at once. She wasn't particularly tall, but she was sturdy, with the arms of a boxer and the general expression of a bulldog. Mrs. Dawaud-Plonk, Alexia supposed, had some species of hearty leather armchair somewhere in her ancestry. However, the Mrs. Dawaud-Plonk who came down those stairs that early morning was far from sturdy. In fact, she looked to have cracked at last. Her face was a picture of horror, her normally tidy pinafore was wrinkled, her cap was askew, and her graying hair fell loose about her shoulders. She clutched Percival to her breast. The baby boy was crying, his face as red as his hair.

Upon catching sight of Lady Maccon and the Tunstells' party, she cried out, raising her free hand to her throat, and said, on great gulping sobs of terror, "They're gone!"

Alexia broke free of the crowd and went up to her.

"The babies, the babies are gone."

"What!" Alexia brushed past the distraught nursemaid and charged up the stairs to the nursery room.

The chamber was in an uproar, furniture overturned, probably by the distraught nursemaid in her panic. The Tunstells' two bassinets were empty, as was Prudence's little cot.

Alexia felt her stomach wrench up into the most tremendous knot and a cold, icy fear trickled through her whole body. She whirled away from the room, already calling out instructions, although the hallway was empty behind her. Her voice was hard and authoritative. Then she heard, from behind her, a querulous little voice say, "Mama?"

Prudence came crawling out from under the bed, dusty, tear-stained, but present.

Alexia ran to her, crouching down to wrap her in a tight embrace. "Prudence, my baby! Did you hide? What a good, brave girl."

"Mama," said Prudence seriously, "no."

Alexia let her go slightly, grabbing on to her shoulders and speaking at her straight on. Grave brown eyes met grave brown eyes. "But where is Primrose? Did they take Primrose? Who took her, Prudence? Did you see?"

"No."

"Bad men took the baby. Who were they?"

Prudence only tossed her dark curls, pouted, and burst into unhelpful tears. Partially a response to her mother's frantic behavior, Alexia supposed, trying to calm herself.

"Dama!" the little girl wailed. She broke free of her mother's grasp and ran to the door, turning back to look at her mother. "Dama. Home. Home Dama," she insisted.

"No, dear, not yet."

"Now!"

Alexia marched over to her daughter and scooped up the child's struggling form. She strode back down the stairs into the hotel reception room, where all was still chaos.

Mrs. Dawaud-Plonk began to weep openly upon seeing Prudence clutched safely in Lady Maccon's arms and dashed over to coo over the toddler.

"Prudence hid under the bed, but it does look as though they took Primrose," announced Alexia baldly. "I am so very sorry, Ivy. Who knows why or what they want from a baby, but she is definitely gone."

Mrs. Tunstell let out a high keening wail and fainted back into her husband's arms. Tunstell looked as though he, too, might be in favor of fainting. His freckles stood out starkly against his white face and he stared at Alexia with desperate green eyes.

"I don't know where my husband is," replied Alexia, guessing at the nature of the plea in those eyes. "Of all the times for him to be off in a huff!"

The Tunstells were well loved by their troupe, so this misfortune threw all the other actors into sympathetic paroxysms of distress. The ladies fainted or had hysterics, whichever better suited their natures. Some of the gentlemen did the same. One ran out into the night with a fake sword, determined to track down the dastardly culprits. Mr. Tumtrinkle began stuffing his face with those little honey pastries and blubbering into his mustache. Percival was busy screaming his head off, only pausing to spit up all over anyone who came near.

Lady Maccon really could have used her husband's booming voice at that juncture. However, knowing the onus fell on her, and relieved her own daughter was accounted for, she took charge. Alexia was quite worried for Primrose's safety, but she was also clear on two fronts. Either the baby had been kidnapped in order to extract a ransom, in which case they could expect contact relatively soon, or they had the wrong baby, in which case they could expect her return momentarily. After all, why would anyone want the daughter of an actress? No matter how popular said actress was in Egypt.

Alexia cast a desperate look about for the only other person who might still have as level a head as she under such circumstances, but Madame Lefoux was nowhere to be found. She inquired of the hotel clerk, interposing herself in front of the poor man as he attempted to control the bedlam in his reception chamber.

"My good man"—Lady Maccon pulled him away from one of the hysterical actresses—"have you seen Madame Lefoux? One of our fellow travelers, the Frenchwoman inventor who dresses as a man. She might be useful at this juncture."

"No, madam." The man bowed hurriedly. "She's gone, madam."

"What do you mean *gone*?" Alexia did not like this turn of events. Now two ladies were missing! Well, Primrose was barely half a lady and Madame Lefoux dressed as a man, so Alexia supposed together they made up only one whole lady, but— Alexia shook herself out of spiraling thoughts and returned to the clerk.

"Left the hotel, madam, not one hour ago. Moving rather quickly, I must say."

Lady Maccon turned back to the pandemonium, a little floored. *Gone, Genevieve, but why?* Had she perhaps sent the kidnappers? Or was she on their trail? Or could it be that she was the kidnapper herself? *No, not Genevieve.* The Frenchwoman might build a massive octopus and terrorize a city, but that had been because someone kidnapped her own child. She would hardly put another mother through such an ordeal. *I suppose it could be coincidence?*

Still puzzling over the matter, Alexia stopped dead in the center of the room and took stock of her situation. "You—fetch smelling salts, and you—get cold compresses and wet towels. Everyone else—do be quiet!"

In very short order, she had the staff trotting to her bidding. She ordered them not to touch the nursery, as the offenders could have left clues behind. She had them set up the still-hysterical nursemaid in a new room, one with very secure windows and better locks. She left her there with Prudence, Percy, Ivy, Mr. Tumtrinkle, and several other actors now restored to sense and ready to do battle. She gave Mr. Tumtrinkle her gun, as he assured her he had pointed many a prop firearm at many a hero in his day and shooting a real one could hardly be much different. Alexia assured him that she would be back as soon as possible and to please make certain he ascertained the truth of any enemy attack before shooting Ethel at *anyone*, particularly a hero.

She sent Tunstell to alert the local constabulary, the other actors and actresses back to their rooms, and the now-rather-worried-looking collective of Tunstell Troupe admirers off about their business. She had to use gesticulations, shushing sounds, and, eventually, a broom in order to accomplish this last.

The sky was beginning to pink and things were finally calm at Hotel des Voyageurs, when a dark shadow loomed in the doorway and Lord Maccon, wearing only a cloak and a sour expression, entered the room.

Alexia hurried up to him. "I know you are still angry with me, and you have a perfect right to be. It was beastly of me to keep the information from you, but we have a far more serious problem that needs your attention now."

The frown deepened. "Go on."

"Primrose appears to have been baby-napped. She was taken from her room several hours ago while the Tunstells were engaged in a performance. I was with them. Madame Lefoux has also vanished. Apparently, the nursemaid was asleep and when she awoke, she found both Primrose and Prudence had disappeared."

"Prudence is gone, too?!" Lord Maccon roared.

The clerk, dozing fitfully behind his desk, snapped to attention with the expression of a man near to his breaking point.

Alexia put a hand on her husband's arm. "No, dear, do calm down. It turned out ours had taken refuge under a bed."

"That's my girl!"

"Yes, very sensible of her, although she seems to be having some difficulty describing the kidnappers to us."

"Well, she is only two."

"Yes, but as she really must learn coherent phrasing and syntax eventually, now would be an excellent time to complete the process. And she *has* let forth a complete sentence lately. I was hoping . . . never mind that now. The fact is, Primrose is gone and so is Genevieve."

"You believe Madame Lefoux took the baby?" The earl was frowning and chewing on his bottom lip in that darling way Alexia loved so much.

"No, I don't. But I think Madame Lefoux may be chasing the kidnappers. She was around the hotel at the time, and the clerk said she left in a great hurry. Perhaps she spotted something out her window. Her room is near the nursery."

"It's a possibility."

"I've sent Tunstell to the local authorities. I haven't let anyone into the room. I thought you might be able to smell something."

Lord Maccon nodded crisply, almost a salute. "I'm still angry with you, wife. But I can't help but admire your efficiency in a crisis."

"Thank you. Shall we go check the scents?"

"Lead on."

Unfortunately, up the stairs and in the nursery, the earl smelled nothing of significance. He did say he thought he caught a whiff of Madame Lefoux and that it was possible she had grappled with the assailants or perhaps simply stuck her head in to see what had happened. It was also possible that it was a lingering remnant from the previous evening. He said he smelled a trace of the Egyptian streets about the place, but nothing more than that. Whoever had taken Primrose had hired ruffians to do it. He traipsed back out into the hallway, still sniffing.

"Ah," he said, "there is Madame Lefoux again—machine oil and vanilla. And here." He began walking back down the steps. "You know, wife, I do believe I have a fresh trail. I'm going after her." He dropped his cloak, revealing an impressive bare chest matted with hair, and shifted form. Luckily the lobby was deserted but for the extremely harried clerk who watched, openmouthed, as his esteemed guest, a real British earl, changed into a wolf right there in front of him.

The poor man's eyes rolled up into his head and he followed in the path of many a young lady that evening and fainted dead away behind the desk.

Alexia watched him fall, too dazed to make any effort to help him, and then turned back to her husband, now a wolf, carefully picking up his discarded cloak with his mouth.

"Conall, really, the sun is almost up. Do you think you'll have time . . . ?"

But he was already gone, dashing out the door, nose lowered before him like a scent hound after a fox.

Lord Conall Maccon returned well after sunup. Alexia was coping with an utterly distraught Mrs. Tunstell. She had finally convinced Ivy to take a dram of poppy to quiet her nerves. At which point both Ivy and her nerves became rather floppy and confused.

Ivy managed to raise her head from where it bent low over Percy, asleep in her lap, when Lord Maccon tapped quietly at the door.

Mr. Tumtrinkle, seated facing the door with Alexia's gun in his lap, started violently and fired Ethel at the earl. Lord Maccon, slower than usual after a long evening's run and a good few hours dashing about as a human under the scorching heat of an Egyptian sun, ducked too late, but the bullet missed him.

Alexia tsked at the actor and put out her hand for the return of her pistol. The man handed it over, apologized profusely to Lord Maccon, and resumed his chair in embarrassed silence. Lady Maccon noted, however, that he did take one of the rapiers, tipped for use in stage fights and thus rather useless, and placed it to hand. Alexia supposed he could ferociously poke someone if he tried hard enough.

"Osh, Lord Maccon!" cried out Ivy, head lolling back and eyes rolling slightly. "Ish that you? Hash you any . . . indigestion . . . no . . . information?"

The earl gave his wife a pained look.

"Laudanum," explained Alexia succinctly.

"Not as such, Mrs. Tunstell. I am very sorry. Wife, if you could spare me a moment?"

"Aleshia!"

"Yes, Ivy dear?"

"We should go dancing!"

"But, Ivy, we're in Egypt and your daughter is missing."

"But I can't see myself from here!"

Alexia stood up from where she was seated next to her nonsensical friend, experienced some difficulty in convincing Ivy to let go of her hand, and followed her husband out the door.

He spoke in a hushed voice. "I traced Madame Lefoux to the dahabiya docks. A peculiar sort of place. Lost the scent there. I'm afraid she may have boarded a ship. I'm going to go ascertain how Tunstell is getting on with the local authorities. Then I think we might need to notify the consular general. Bad publicity, very bad, a missing British baby on his watch."

Alexia nodded. "I'll go back to the docks, shall I? See if I can work my womanly charm and discover who accepted Madame Lefoux's fare and where she might be headed."

"You have womanly charm?" The earl was genuinely surprised. "I thought you simply harangued a blighter until he gave in."

Alexia gave him a look.

Lord Maccon snorted. "Only one direction to head if one is going by dahabiya."

"Up the Nile to Cairo?"

"Indeed."

"Well, they might at least tell a female if a passenger had a baby. They might even be convinced to say if she was chasing after someone."

"Very well, Alexia, but be careful, and take your parasol."

"Of course, Conall. I shall require a parasol, as the sun is up. Don't tell me you hadn't noticed."

"Yes, very amusing, wife."

Neither of them mentioned sleep, although Alexia was feeling the strain of having been awake since four the previous afternoon. Bed would have to wait; they had a baby to catch and a Frenchwoman to trace.

Biffy awoke before sunset and, after struggling with his hair for a quarter of an hour, returned to the maps he'd laid out of Egypt and the expansion of the God-Breaker Plague. He'd awakened with a certain feeling that he was missing something. He went back to the circles he'd drawn and reviewed notes on times indicating the plague's expansion and general location. He began to extrapolate inward, trying to determine its course. What if the plague had always been expanding, very slowly? What if there was a starting point?

He got so distracted he very nearly missed his appointment with Lady Maccon and the aethographor. He took the maps with him to the receiving chamber to await any missive, studying them carefully.

It was while he was waiting alone in that tiny attic room that he came upon the missing piece of the puzzle. All signs pointed to the fact that the epicenter for the God-Breaker Plague was near Luxor, at one prominent bend in the Nile River close to the Valley of the Kings. His books said very little on the archaeology of the area, but one report indicated that the bend housed the funerary temple of the expunged and vilified Pharaoh Hatshepsut. He had no idea how this might tie into the plague, but he resolved to send Lady Maccon the information, should she contact him that evening.

He was about to creep out and gather together some acid and a metal slate when the receiving chamber activated, the metal particles between the receiver panes shifted about, and a message appeared.

"Ruffled Parasol. Conall upset. Primrose kidnapped. Uproar."

Biffy recoiled. What interest could Egyptian kidnappers possibly have in Mr. and Mrs. Tunstell's daughter? The child of thespians. How odd. He awaited further information but nothing more came through. He moved next door, dialed in the appropriate frequensor codes, and sent his message back.

"GBP center is Hatshepsut's temple, Nile River, Luxor. Wingtip Spectator."

Silence met that and after a quarter of an hour, Biffy supposed his message had been received and there was nothing else to relate. He shut down the aethographor, made certain his own missive was tucked securely away, and ate the scrap of paper on which he'd scribbled Lady Maccon's. He'd witnessed Lyall do so in the past with delicate information and figured it was a werewolf tradition he'd better uphold. Then he went to find his Beta, not certain he was authorized to relay either bits of information.

It was in thinking about this, and wondering who might kidnap Primrose and how Lady Maccon might be coping with this new crisis—violently, he suspected—that Biffy came upon another realization. Following that realization to its inevitable, horrible conclusion, he detoured toward the servants' quarters.

Floote was sitting alone at the massive table in the kitchen, polishing the brass candlesticks, a sturdy apron tied about his waist. His jacket was off and draped over the back of a nearby chair. The moment he saw Biffy, he made a move toward it, but Biffy said hastily, "No, Floote, please don't trouble yourself. I simply had a question."

"Sir?"

"When Mr. Tarabotti traveled in Egypt, did he visit Luxor?" Biffy came casually over to Floote's shoulder, standing a little too close, pretending to inspect the polishing. He bent down as though particularly interested in one of the candlesticks and with one hand behind his back, quick as any vampire, snaked the tiny little gun out of the inside pocket of Floote's jacket.

Biffy tucked the gun up his own sleeve, wondering that there weren't more werewolf and vampire conjurers; sleight of hand was easy when one had supernatural abilities.

Floote answered him, "Yes, sir," without looking up from his polishing.

"Well, ahem, yes. Thank you, Floote, carry on."

"Very good, sir."

Biffy escaped to his own room where he locked the door and immediately took out the gun.

It was one of the smallest he had ever seen, beautifully made with a delicate pearl handle. It was of the single-shot variety popular some thirty years ago or more, outdated in this age of revolvers. It must be sentiment that urged Floote to keep it, for it wasn't the most useful of weapons. Difficult to hit anything at more than five paces and it probably shot crooked. Biffy swallowed, hoping against hope he wasn't about to find what he predicted. With a twist, he opened and checked the chamber. It was loaded. He tipped the bullet out into his hand. Such a small thing to damn a man so utterly. For that bullet was made of hardwood, capped in metal to take the heat and caged in silver. It was not quite the same as the modern ones, of course, but still undoubtedly a sundowner bullet.

At first Biffy didn't want to believe it, but Floote *had* been at liberty the night that Dubh was shot—with all his employers out of the house. Floote had access to Lord Akeldama's dirigible, for no drone would comment on Lady Maccon's butler coming and going from Lord Akeldama's house. Floote owned a gun that was loaded with sundowner bullets of exactly the kind with which Dubh was shot. Then later, when Lady Maccon rushed in with the injured man, Floote had been left alone with Dubh, and Dubh had died. Floote certainly had the opportunity. But why? Would the butler really kill to protect his dead master's secrets?

Biffy sat for a long time, rolling the bullet about in his hand and thinking.

A polite knock disturbed his reverie. He stood to open the door.

Floote walked quietly in, his jacket back on.

"Mr. Rabiffano."

"Floote." Biffy felt strangely guilty, standing there holding Floote's gun, which was obviously very precious to him, the damning bullet in his other hand.

Biffy looked at Floote.

Floote looked at Biffy.

Biffy knew, and he knew that Floote knew he knew—so to speak. He handed the butler his gun but kept the bullet as evidence, tucking it into his waistcoat pocket.

"Why, Floote?"

"Because he left his orders first, sir."

"But to kill a werewolf on a dead man's orders?"

Floote smiled the tiniest of half smiles. "You forget what Alessandro Tarabotti was, sir. What the Templars trained him for. What he trained me to help him do."

Biffy blanched, horrified. "You have killed werewolves before Dubh?"

"Not all werewolves, Mr. Rabiffano, are like you, or Professor Lyall, or Lord Maccon. Some of them are like Lord Woolsey—pests to be exterminated."

"And that's why you killed Dubh?"

Floote ignored the direct question. "Mr. Tarabotti gave his orders, sir," the butler repeated himself, "long before anyone else. I was to see it through to the end. That was my promise. And I've kept it."

"What else, Floote? What else have you been keeping in motion? Was Mr. Tarabotti responsible for the God-Breaker Plague expanding? Is that what he was doing over there?"

Floote only moved toward the door.

Biffy went after him, hand to his arm. He didn't want to use his werewolf strength and was horrified by the idea that he might have to, on a member of Lady Maccon's domestic staff! A longtime family retainer, no less—the very idea!

Floote paused and stared at the floor of the hallway, rather than at Biffy. "I really must see that carpet cleaned. It's disgraceful."

Biffy firmed up his grip.

"He left me with two instructions, sir—protect Alexia and protect the Mandate of the Broken Ankh."

Biffy knew from the way the butler's face closed over that he would get no more out of Floote that evening. But Biffy also could not afford to be wrong. Even knowing that it would disrupt the smooth running of the household, even knowing there was danger both at home and abroad, even knowing that Floote was elderly, even knowing that there would be werewolves traipsing around with badly tied cravats as a result, Biffy stuffed down his scruples. He drew back his fist and with supernatural speed and strength, tapped the butler on the temple hard enough to knock him senseless.

With a very sad sigh, the dandy flipped Floote's limp body easily over one well-dressed shoulder and carried him down to the wine cellar. There he removed the man's guns—there were two, as it transpired—from his pockets, searched for anything else of interest, and locked him in. It was ironic that the wine cellar had originally been fortified as a prison to hold Biffy only two years ago.

Biffy didn't feel victorious. He didn't feel as though he had solved some great mystery. He was simply sad. He was also grateful it would be up to Lyall to sort this mess out. His dear Beta would have to decide whether to tell Lady Kingair or not. Biffy did not envy him that conversation. With the heavy heart of a man burdened with unpleasant news, Biffy went looking for Lyall.

Alexia didn't want to awaken Conall—he was catching up on a few hours of sleep after a very hectic day—but she had news to relate and she was near to dropping from exhaustion herself.

She'd been awake over twenty-four hours with no trace of poor Primrose. No ransom note, no trail, nothing. The sun would set in less than an hour, and Alexia felt like she'd been at her inquiries for an age.

"Conall!"

He snuffled into the pillow.

She reached out to touch his bare shoulder with her bare hand, turning him human. Even that didn't awaken him. He was knackered. Lord knows what he had been up to, gallivanting around angry and then tracing the baby and dealing with politicians. He had probably expended a lot of energy. *And* the sun was very hot and bright in Egypt.

"Conall, really. Wake up."

The earl blinked tawny eyes open and glared at her. Before she could react, he gathered her in against him in a warm embrace. Always amorous, her husband. Then he seemed to remember that not only was there a crisis, he was still angry over her siding with Professor Lyall.

He pushed her away petulantly, like a small child. "Yes, Alexia?"

Alexia sighed, knowing he needed time to forgive her, if he ever would, but finding it hard not to be able to hold him under such nerve-wracking circumstances. "I've just had a message from Biffy. Or, better said, I remembered at the last minute my standing aethographor appointment. I managed to relay to him the current crisis, not that he could do anything, but I thought home ought to know. He sent a note back. Then I had to stop. The transmitter was booked and they booted me off. *Me!* Now, of all times! You know, I tried to extend the time, but the little old lady behind me in the queue had a terribly important message for her grandson and would not be reasoned with!"

"Someday, Alexia, *you* will be that little old lady."

"Oh, thank you very much, Conall."

"The message?" her husband prodded.

"Biffy says that he has traced the epicenter of the God-Breaker Plague to one particular bend in the Nile River, near Luxor."

"And this relates to Primrose how?"

"It might. Because I managed to, well, um, bribe a few of the dahabiya captains down at the dock."

The earl raised an eyebrow.

"Madame Lefoux definitely hired a boat, one of the fastest and best on the line, to take her upriver. But not to Cairo, only *by way* of Cairo. No, her fare was for Luxor, or that's what one man said, based on the amount of money he observed changing hands. She had a mysterious bundle with her and she asked a lot of questions. So what do you think?"

"Very suspicious. I think we should go after her."

Alexia bounced slightly. "Me too!"

"How are Mr. and Mrs. Tunstell?" Lord Maccon switched topics.

"Coping tolerably well. Tunstell, at least, has been responding to direct questions. Ivy is difficult but then that is Ivy for you. I think we can leave them for a few days and follow Genevieve up the Nile."

"Right, then. The sooner we set out the better." Conall lurched out of bed.

Alexia tried to be practical. "But, my love, we both need rest."

"Still mad at you," he grumbled at her using an endearment.

"Oh, very well. But, *Conall*, we still need rest."

"Ever the pragmatist. We can rest on the train to Cairo. I think we can still catch one. It won't be as fast as Madame Lefoux, not if she hired one of the new steam-modified dahabiyas. But it will put us only a day behind her."

Alexia nodded. "Very well, I'll pack. You tell the others. And get Prudence, please. She's asleep in the nursery. I'm not leaving her behind with a baby snatcher on the loose."

The earl lumbered from the room, shirt hanging loose about his wide frame and his feet bare, before Alexia could stop him and make him dress. She supposed Ivy and Tunstell would be too distraught to take umbrage. She began a whirlwind of packing, throwing everything she could think of into two small cases. She had no idea how long they might be but figured they ought to travel as light as possible. Prudence would have to leave her mechanical ladybug behind.

Lord Maccon returned a quarter of an hour later with a sleeping Prudence tucked casually under one arm and Tunstell trailing behind.

"Are you certain I can't accompany you, my lord?" The redhead was looking frazzled. His trousers were not as tight as usual.

"No, Tunstell, it's best if you stay. Hold down the home front. It's possible we could be on the wrong track, that Madame Lefoux isn't the culprit or isn't following the culprits. Someone with a reasonable sense of responsibility must remain here to deal with the authorities, keep making a stink, keep them hunting."

Tunstell's face was serious, no smiles for once. "If you think it best."

Conall nodded his shaggy head. "I do. Now, don't hesitate to bandy my name about if you need the authority."

"Thank you, my lord."

Alexia added, "If Ivy feels up to it, there are messages coming in for me at the aethographor station every evening just after six. Here is a letter of permission granting Mrs. Tunstell the authority to receive them in my stead. Even so, they may not accept a substitute without my presence, but it's the best I can do at short notice. Only if she feels up to it, mind you."

"Very well, Lady Maccon, if you're certain I won't do?" Tunstell was clearly falling back on his claviger training in order to deal with this crisis.

"I'm afraid not, Tunstell my dear. The individual sending the messages from London will only respond to me or Ivy."

Tunstell looked puzzled but didn't question Lady Maccon further.

"Good luck, Tunstell. And I *am* sorry this has happened to you and Ivy."

"Thank you, Lady Maccon. Good luck to you. I hope you catch the bastards."

"As do I, Tunstell. As do I."

CHAPTER FIFTEEN

In Which We Learn Why Werewolves Don't Float

There were no more trains to Cairo that day, which meant Lady Maccon and her husband were forced to return to the dock and hire river transport. It was easier said than done. Despite the fact that they were now familiar with Lady Maccon and her autocratic demands, the captains did not want to set out until the following morning. Then there was the price to negotiate. Very few dahabiyas carried any kind of modern conveniences—augmented small-craft outboard steam propellers or tea kettles, for example—making them mere pleasure vessels designed to be pulled slowly up the river by mule or, worse, human power!

"It's all so very primitive!" huffed Alexia, who might ordinarily have enjoyed such a leisurely mode of transport.

Her excuse for such bad behavior must be that she was, at this juncture, exhausted, dusty, worried about Primrose, and tired of carrying Prudence. It was after sunset and the toddler was entirely in her charge. Under such circumstances, everyone's tempers were fraying, even Prudence, who was hungry. The quintessential Egyptian lack of urgency and insistence on haggling and negotiation was driving the efficient Lady Maccon slowly insane.

It was almost midnight and they were talking with the eighth captain in a row when a tap came on Alexia's shoulder. She turned around to find herself face-to-face with an extraordinarily handsome man, his features familiar, his beard cut neat and sharp—their Drifter rescuer from the bazaar.

"Lady? You are ready now, to right the wrong of the father?" His voice was deep and resonant, his words clipped by an Arabic accent and limited English.

Alexia looked him over. "If I say yes, will that get me any closer to Luxor?"

"Follow." The man turned and walked away, his dark blue robe a swirl of purpose behind him.

Alexia said to her husband, "Conall, I believe we may have to follow that gentleman."

"But, Alexia . . . what?"

"It has worked in my favor before."

"But who on God's green earth is the man?"

"He's a Drifter."

"Can't be—they don't fraternize with foreigners."

"Well, this one does. He rescued us at the bazaar when we were attacked."

"What? You were *what*? Why didn't you tell me?"

"You were busy yelling at me about Professor Lyall's manipulations."

"Oh. So tell me now."

"Never mind, we have to follow him. Do come on." Alexia firmed up her grip on Prudence and dashed after the rapidly disappearing balloon nomad.

"Oh, blast." Conall, bless his supernatural strength, hoisted all of their luggage easily and trundled after.

The man led them toward the Porte de Rosette. Eventually he veered off and, rounding a corner in the street, came upon a medium-sized obelisk carved of red rock that glittered in the moonlight. He was using it as a mooring, a heavy rope wrapped about the base, and his balloon hovered above like—Alexia tilted her head back—well, like a big balloon. The man stopped and made a move to take Prudence from Alexia. She jerked back but when he gestured at a rope ladder significantly, she nodded.

"Very well, but my husband goes first."

Conall was looking with white-faced horror at the swinging ladder. Werewolves do not float. "No, really. I'd prefer not, if you don't mind."

Alexia tried to be reasonable. "We must get to Luxor somehow."

"My dear wife, you have seen nothing in your life so pathetic as a werewolf with airsickness."

"Do we have a choice? Besides, with any luck we'll be flying into the God-Breaker Plague zone soon. At which point you should be fine and human once more."

"Oh, you think that, do you? What if the plague doesn't extend upward?"

"Where's your spirit of scientific inquiry, husband? This is our opportunity to find just such a thing out. I promise to take lots of notes."

"That's very reassuring." The earl did not look convinced. He eyed the ladder with even greater suspicion.

"Up you go, Conall. Stop dawdling. If it's that bad, I can simply touch you."

Her husband grumbled but began to climb.

"There's my brave boy," said his wife condescendingly.

Being supernatural, he heard her but pretended not to, eventually making it over the edge and into the balloon basket.

Alexia noticed that the balloon was much lower than the first time she had seen it, during the day. She was grateful for this—less ladder to climb.

The Drifter shimmied up, Prudence strapped to his back in a sling. The toddler squealed in delight. She, unlike her father, was very excited by the prospect of floating.

After a moment's hesitation, Alexia followed suit.

A little street urchin, all unobserved until that moment, darted forth and unwound the rope from the obelisk mooring. Alexia found herself unexpectedly climbing a free-floating ladder drifting down the street. This was not quite so easily done as one might think, particularly not in a full skirt and bustle, but no one had ever called Lady Maccon a spiritless weakling. She hung on for dear life and continued to make her way up by slow degrees, even as the ladder on which she clung headed for a very large building at a rate rather more alarming than reassuringly dignified.

She made it up into the basket just in time, somewhat hampered by the restrictions proper dress imposed upon the British female. She thought, not for the first time, that Madame Lefoux might have the right of it. But then she simply could not get around the idea of wearing trousers, not as a female of her proportions. The Drifter met her at the top with a strong hand of assistance, quickly hauling the rope ladder up after her.

So it was that the Maccons found themselves floating low above the city of Alexandria in one of the famous nomadic balloons completely at the mercy of a man to whom they had not been formally introduced.

The earl, with a muttered oath, lurched to the basket edge and was promptly sick over the side. He continued to be so for a good long while. Alexia stood next to him rubbing his back solicitously. Her touch turned him human, but it seemed that he was a man ill suited to travel by air, immortal or no. Eventually, she respected his dignity and his mutters of "do shove off" and left him to his misery.

The Drifter unstrapped Prudence from his back and set her down. She began to toddle around investigating everything—she had her mother's curiosity, bless her. The crew of the balloon, Alexia surmised after a short while, must be the man's family. There was a wife, upon whom the harsh features of the desert were not quite so attractive but who seemed more ready to smile than her dour husband. This lent her an aura of beauty, as is often the case with the good-natured. The woman's many scarves and colorful robes wafted in the slight breeze. There was also one strapping son of perhaps fourteen and a young daughter only slightly older than Prudence. The entire family was amazingly tolerant of Prudence's curiosity and evident interest in trying to "help." They pretended to let her steer with the many ropes that dangled in the center of the basket, and the boy held her up high so she could look out over the edge—an action that was met with peals of delighted laughter.

The balloon remained rather low, especially for a lady accustomed to dirigible travel. Alexia remembered Ivy's comment about the Drifters ordinarily landing at night because of the cold and then rising up with the heat of the day. It made her wonder.

With the initial flurry of float-off past, Alexia left her self-imposed position of noninterference, checked once more on poor Conall, who was still expunging, and made her way slowly to their rescuer. It was difficult to walk for, while the sides of the basket were made of wicker, the floor was a grid of poles with animal skins stretched between—not the easiest thing for a woman of Alexia's girth and shoe choice. Add to that the fact that her moving about shook the entire basket most alarmingly.

"Pardon me, sir. It's not that I'm not grateful, but who are you?"

The man smiled, a flash of perfect white teeth from within that trimmed beard. "Ah, yes, of course, lady. I am Zayed."

"How do you do, Mr. Zayed."

The man bowed. Then he pointed in turn. "My son, Baddu; my wife, Noora; and my daughter, Anitra."

Alexia made polite murmurs and curtsied in their direction. The family all nodded but did not leave their respective posts.

"It is very kind of you to offer us, a, er, lift."

"A favor to a friend, lady."

"Really? Who?"

"Goldenrod."

"Who?"

"You do not know, lady?"

"Evidently not."

"Then we will wait."

"Oh, but . . ."

The man's face closed down.

Alexia sighed and switched topics. "If you don't think it interfering, may I ask? We are very low—how can we float at night?"

"Ah, lady. You know some of our ways. Let me show you." He made his way over to the middle and threw several blankets off what looked to be a container of gas, of the kind used for lamp lighting back home in London. "For special, we have this."

Alexia was instantly intrigued. "Will you show me?"

The man flashed a brief grin of excitement and began unhitching and hooking in various tubes and cords. He hoisted the canister so its mouth pointed into the massive balloon.

While he was busy fussing, Alexia took a moment to take in her surroundings.

The balloon was utterly unlike the British-made dirigibles Alexia had utilized in the past. She had traveled in both small pleasure-time floaters and the larger mail post and passenger transports—the company-owned monsters. This balloon was similar to neither. For one thing, the balloon part itself hadn't the shape of a dirigible and was entirely made of cloth. It was guided by means of opening and closing flaps rather than by a propeller of any kind. For another, the basket was bigger than a personal jaunt dirigible but much smaller than one of the larger cross-country behemoths. It was twice the length of a rowboat but basically square. In the center was the mooring for the balloon and all the associated straps and contraptions required to see it float and directed properly. As the basket slowly spun with the balloon, there seemed to be no particular front or back. There was an area clearly used for sleeping, another for cooking, and one tented corner that Alexia could only assume was meant for doing one's private business. She supposed that the family lived in the basket and that the various hanging sacks over the edge and from the base of the balloon—which she had assumed were ballasts—were probably goods and supplies.

Prudence went wobbling past, the Drifter girl on her tail, both of them giggling madly and having a grand old time. Alexia made her way to Conall, to defend him from possible contact with his daughter. The last thing they needed was an airsick werewolf pup dashing about the craft. Better to have a large airsick man instead.

A blast of flame and a whoop of delight from the boy, Baddu, and the balloon began a stately rise upward, fuel from the gas giving them a boost of speed high toward the aethersphere. There was no lurching sensation; in fact, the movement hardly registered except that the ground retreated below them and Alexia's ears popped.

Alexia knew in principle what the Drifters were aiming for. If they could get the balloon up and into an aether stream, they could hook into a current that would carry them south, up the Nile. It was a tricky maneuver, for should the balloon rise too much into the aether, there was a possibility of it getting torn apart, or caving with the sheer of crosscurrents, or the gas flame blowing out, causing them to drop out and down toward the desert.

Alexia tried not to think about it, instead looking down as Alexandria fell away under them.

Poor Conall, at this point reduced to dry heaving and little whimpers of distress, had his eyes tightly shut and his big hands white-knuckled about the side of the basket. Alexia wondered if she shouldn't get Prudence to take on wolf form. Perhaps they could trap her as a pup in the corner? Prudence didn't seem to feel the pain of werewolf shift, so perhaps she didn't get airsick either? She certainly wasn't suffering from the affliction now. She was having a wonderful time. And, Alexia noted with pleasure, always stopping politely should any of their hosts wish to show her the correct anchoring of a cord or explain to her the thermodynamics of floating—in Arabic, mind you. If Lord Akeldama did nothing else, he was instilling in his adopted daughter the very best manners.

Soon they had risen high enough to turn Alexandria into a spot of faint torchlight. Below and ahead, Alexia could see only the dark of the desert, here and there a lonely fire, and, glinting under the moonlight, the hundreds of long silver snakes that made up the Nile Delta. A sudden flurry of activity in the basket, and Alexia looked over to see Zayed hauling hard on one of the ropes while Baddu offloaded some weight. Then there came a jerk and a woof noise, and the top of the balloon caught an aether stream. Zayed turned up the gas and angled the canister toward the cave-in and the balloon rose up fully into the aether stream. It immediately began to float, with much greater speed, due south. Despite this change in pace, Alexia felt almost nothing. Unlike a dirigible, there were no breezes; the balloon was moving with the currents.

Conall straightened, looking markedly better and less green.

Alexia patted him sympathetically. "Human?"

"Yes, but that doesn't do much good. I think I simply got everything, well, out. If you know what I mean?"

Alexia nodded. "Could it be our current proximity to the aether?"

"Could be. Well?"

"Well, what?"

"Are you going to make a note of it, wife? Seems that the God-Breaker Plague reaches all the way up to the aether."

"Either that, or the aethersphere itself counteracts your supernatural abilities."

"Well, if that were the case, scientists would have figured that out by now, wouldn't they?"

Lady Maccon took out a tiny notebook from one of the secret pockets of her parasol and a stylographic pen from another. "Oh, yes? And how would they have done that? Vampires can't float up that high, because they are tethered too short. And werewolves don't float at all, because they get sick."

"You can't tell me no one has transported a ghost and body via float before?"

Alexia frowned. "I don't know, but it's worth researching. I wonder if Genevieve and her deceased aunt came via float or ferry when they left Paris for London."

"You'll have to ask her when we catch up." They paused in their conversation, awkward for a moment; then Conall asked, "Can you feel the plague?"

"You mean that odd tingly sensation I felt at the edge of Alexandria?"

He nodded.

"Difficult to tell, since the feeling was already similar to that of aether breezes." Alexia closed her eyes and leaned her arms out of the balloon basket, embracing the air.

The earl immediately grabbed her shoulder and pulled her backward. "Don't *do* that, Alexia!" He was looking green again, this time with fear.

Alexia sighed. "Can't tell. Could be the plague, could be proximity to the aethersphere. We'll simply have to wait and see what happens as we move farther toward the epicenter."

"Did no one ever tell you, wife, that it's rather dangerous to do scientific experiments on oneself?"

"Now, dear, don't fuss. To be fair, I'm doing them on you as well."

"How verra reassuring."

Biffy knocked politely on Lyall's office door. He sniffed the air while he waited to be bidden entrance. He smelled the usual odors of BUR—sweat and cologne, leather and boot polish, gun oil and weaponry. In the end it was most similar to a soldier's barracks. He did not scent another pack. Wherever she was at the moment, Lady Kingair was not there.

"Enter," came Lyall's mild bidding.

Biffy was shocked by how warm simply the sound of that voice made him feel. Almost reassured. Whatever they were building together,

Biffy decided at that moment that it was *good* and worth fighting for. Which, being a werewolf, he supposed might actually be more of a literal than figurative way of putting matters.

The young dandy took a breath and entered the room, his pleasure subdued under the weight of the information he had to impart. The burden of a spy, Lord Akeldama always said, was not in the knowing of things but in knowing when to tell such things to others. That and the fact that creeping around could be dusty work, terrible on the knees of one's trousers.

Biffy felt that there was no point in barking about the dell. "I know who killed Dubh, and no one is going to like it." He moved across the room, pausing only to remove his hat and place it on the stand near the door. The poor hat stand was already overloaded with coats and wraps and chapeaus as well as a number of less savory items—leather collars with gun compartments, Gatling straps, and what looked to be a plucked goose made of straw.

Once he stood across the cluttered desk from Lyall, Biffy removed the bullet from his waistcoat pocket and slapped it down on the dark mahogany.

Professor Lyall put aside the papers he had been studying and picked up the bullet. After a moment of close examination, he tipped a pair of glassicals down from where they perched atop his head and studied the bullet even more carefully through the magnification lens.

He looked up after a long moment, the glassicals distorting one hazel eye out of all proportion.

Biffy winced at the asymmetry.

Lyall took the glassicals off, set them aside, and handed the bullet back to Biffy. "Sundowner ammunition. Old-fashioned. Of the kind that shot Dubh."

Biffy nodded, face grave. "You'll never guess who from."

Professor Lyall sat back, vulpine face impassive, and raised one dark blond eyebrow patiently.

"Floote." Biffy waited for a reaction, wanted one.

Nothing. Lyall was good.

"It was all Floote. He had opportunity. He was free at the time of the initial attack at the train station. He had access to Lord Akeldama's dirigible, which he could fly back, setting part of London on fire to delay Lady Maccon. Do you recall, Dubh mentioned something to her ladyship about not wanting to go with her home? He said it wasn't safe. I believe that was because he knew Floote would be there. Then when Lady Maccon brought the wounded Beta back, who did she leave him alone with in the sickroom for those few minutes?"

"Floote."

"And what happened?"

"Dubh died."

"Exactly."

"But opportunity is not motive, my dear boy." Professor Lyall, for all his passivity, was unwilling to believe.

"I confronted him, but you know Floote. He claimed it was something to do with Alessandro Tarabotti, orders left behind when he died. Something wasn't supposed to get out. Lady Maccon wasn't supposed to know. Of course, she left for Egypt anyway. You know what I think? I think Alessandro Tarabotti somehow set the God-Breaker Plague into motion, and Floote has been seeing that it continues to expand. Those were the orders Mr. Tarabotti left, and Floote's been secretly conducting a long-distance supernatural extermination mandate ever since. I think Dubh simply got in the way and Floote had no other choice."

"Ambitious, but what do you—" Lyall paused and sniffed the air. "Oh, dear," he said succinctly.

Biffy sniffed as well. He caught a whiff of open fields and country air, although not of the kind he might be familiar with from his own pack. This was a damp, lush, impossibly green field leagues to the north—Scotland.

Biffy whirled and ran to the door, throwing it open, only to see Lady Kingair's graying tail tip disappear out the front entrance of BUR and into the night, at speed.

He felt Lyall's presence next to him. "What did you do with Floote, my dandy?"

"Locked him in the wine cellar, of course."

"This is not good. Given half a chance, she'll kill him before we extract any additional information out of him."

"Not to mention that it's a bad idea to eat one's domestic staff."

The two men looked at one another and then, by mutual accord, began to strip out of their clothes. At least, Biffy consoled himself, BUR agents were accustomed to such eccentricities.

Professor Lyall gave up about halfway through and simply sacrificed his wardrobe to the cause. Biffy watched him run after the Alpha. He hoped fervently they weren't in for another fight with the she-wolf; he didn't think he had it in him. However, Biffy did spare a few moments to divest himself of his favorite waistcoat and cravat before shifting form. The trousers and shirt could be replaced, but not that waistcoat; it was a real pip.

Biffy took off after Lyall, pushing himself hard, so hard he caught up to the slighter wolf just before they reached the pack's town house. Professor Lyall was reputed to be one of the fastest fighters in England, but Biffy still had enough muscle mass on him to catch up in a straight race. He was inordinately proud of himself.

They pushed in the open door to the Maccon's town house to find Lady Kingair snuffling about, dashing frantically from room to room, evidently having started her hunt for the butler on the top floor in the servants' quarters. Luckily, she had not yet reached the wine cellar. Floote's scent was so prevalent throughout the house it must be throwing her off.

Biffy and Lyall looked at one another, yellow eyes to yellow eyes. Then they both leaped toward the angry Alpha and backed her into the front parlor by dint of surprise, rather than power.

Biffy lashed out with his tail, slamming the door closed behind them.

Professor Lyall changed form, standing before the furious she-wolf. "Lady Kingair, don't you think we might talk about this civilly, just this once?"

The rangy wolf sat back on her haunches, as though considering this proposition, and then, after a moment, the graying fur of her coat retreated, and she stood before Lyall.

Sidheag Kingair was a fine figure of a woman for all she had been converted later in life. She crossed her arms, utterly unself-conscious. "Professor, I dinna want tae be civil. If that man killed my Beta, 'tis my right tae take his blood."

"If."

She looked at Biffy, now sitting back on his haunches, tongue out and panting after such a run. "But I heard him say that—"

"You heard him speculate. Nothing has been proven."

"That dinna sound like speculation tae me."

Biffy wondered if he, too, should change his form, or if such a thing would be wasted on the Alpha's rage. He wanted to have some input, however, aside from wagging his tail and twitching his ears, so he sought out his reserves of courage, faced the pain, and shifted.

"We need to act within the confines of British law, Lady Kingair, as well as pack protocol. The first thing to do is confront the man and inquire further."

Lady Kingair's lip curled. "Inquire? If you insist."

Professor Lyall turned to Biffy. "If you would like to lead the way?"

Biffy would not like, but he did as he was told by his Beta, moving with a certain amount of embarrassed poise through the house in full view of half the servants.

Thus they trooped down to the wine cellar—to find the door slightly open with no sign of being forced and the cellar itself completely empty.

Floote was gone.

Lady Kingair erupted into immediate fury. "He's escaped!"

Professor Lyall shook his head. "Not possible. We secured this room to hold werewolves."

"Then *someone* must have let him out. Or not locked the room down properly." She snarled at Biffy.

Biffy was affronted. "I assure you, it was securely locked, and I searched his person for tools."

"You must have missed something, pup!"

"Perhaps I missed the utterly ridiculous idea that a butler could pick locks!"

"Perhaps you did, you little—"

Professor Lyall stepped in. "Now wait just a moment, Lady Kingair. Did you search Floote's room just now when you were looking for him?"

The Alpha shrugged, the long fall of her thick hair shifting against her naked breasts. She still glared at Biffy.

Unashamed, knowing he had done all that could be asked of someone in his position, Biffy pretended to examine his manicure. For some reason, shifting forms played hell on the cuticles.

Lyall continued his questioning. "Had he taken his belongings?"

Lady Kingair wasn't interested in figuring out the minutiae of Floote's disappearance. She was interested in blaming someone for it—Biffy.

Biffy turned away to poke about the cellar, trying to find any clues that might represent Floote's ability to escape a heretofore impenetrable wine cellar.

He did not see her shifting forms. The only warning he got was Lyall's shout.

Afterward, Biffy was never quite certain what he did or why it happened. He reacted out of instinct, but there were two instincts in place—the werewolf one that wanted to shift forms out of self-preservation and the Biffy one that hated the pain of shifting more than anything, more than a badly cut jacket or a loose cravat. Those two instincts went to battle against each other as the great vicious she-wolf charged toward him.

He shifted.

He simply didn't quite manage to shift everything.

Only his head went over.

That action stopped Lady Kingair in a way that nothing else possibly could. She halted her charge, stood on four legs stiffed in surprise, and stared at him.

Biffy didn't understand what was going on. He still felt like himself, and there was very little pain, but his head felt swollen and heavy, as though he had caught a cold, and his senses were suddenly far more acute.

Professor Lyall moved forward, brushed past Lady Kingair, and stood quietly in front of him. The Beta's mouth was open ever so slightly in shock, not an expression Biffy had ever thought to see on his lover's face.

He tried to ask, "What's going on?" But all he could manage was a bit of a whine and a small bark.

"Biffy," said Professor Lyall softly. "Did you know you had an Anubis form?"

Biffy barked at him again. He was beginning to shake slightly. It was from the fear and the stress, not from being naked in a cellar. Werewolves rarely felt cold even in human skin. Or half-human skin.

Lady Kingair shifted back into her *fully* human guise. She was still looking angry and impatient, but she also seemed far less inclined to fight him than she had mere moments before.

"He dinna *act* like an Alpha."

All Lyall's attention was on Biffy; he barely glanced at the Kingair Alpha. "He does in some areas," he replied.

Biffy argued he must look beyond ridiculous. The head of a wolf, all fuzzy and yellow-eyed, on the lean pale body of a dandy. *I don't want to be an Alpha*, he cried out internally. *I don't want to spend half my time fighting challengers. I don't want to have the responsibility of a pack. I don't want to die early or go mad. Make it go away!*

But again, all he could do was whine.

"It's all right, pup," soothed Lyall. "You simply shift it back. At least I think that's how it works." He frowned to himself. "I've served several Alphas and I never thought to ask if Anubis worked any differently than full wolf fur. Some professor I am."

Biffy only whined again. He was trying. He was reaching for that place deep inside that could force the shift, that tingling pressure of bones re-forming. It wasn't working. He couldn't go either direction, couldn't return to wolf or human. He was trapped in the in-between of Anubis state.

"Oh, dear. Are you stuck?" asked Lyall.

Smart man. Biffy nodded his shaggy head vigorously.

"Och, I've nae time for this! We must catch that blighter Floote."

Lady Kingair was at her limit. Clearly Biffy's predicament was merely an added insult to her evening.

She went up the stairs. Preparing, no doubt, to chase after Floote into the night. "Where would he go?" she shouted back at the two werewolves.

With a shrug, Lyall and Biffy followed.

The Beta said, "If he was still working for Sandy, and if he was operating under that agenda all along, we must assume that it is an antisupernatural agenda. Sandy promised me . . ." The Beta winced slightly at this, an old lie only now uncovered. "Never mind what he promised. If the plan all along was to expand the plague, then it may be that even I couldn't change his mind."

Lady Kingair concurred. "I guess you weren't as alluring as you thought, Beta. So where would he go?"

Biffy came to stand close behind Lyall, placing a supportive hand on the man's shoulder. He wanted to reassure Lyall that he found him alluring, but he could only growl in annoyance.

Biffy knew what he would do were he in Floote's situation. Were he a mortal man with werewolves on his tail, there was only one truly safe place—the air. And Floote, loyal to the last, would try to get to Lady Maccon to explain his actions to her. To see that she was safe, as that, too, was part of Alessandro Tarabotti's mandate. Biffy might have said all these things, but he had no proper mouth and his neck was part wolf as well, including, apparently the voice box. *Good Lord*, he thought, *what if I'm permanently stuck like this? I'll never be able to carry off a pointed collar again!* Then he realized with relief that Anubis was wolf form, at least in part, and wolf form would not survive the sunrise. *Only a few more hours, then.*

Lyall had reached the same conclusion as Biffy regarding Floote's probable course of action. "He'll head to the nearest dirigible."

Lady Kingair dashed off.

Biffy whined and gestured with his wolf head at the stairs. The stairs that led to the second-story hallway that ended in a balcony that had a secret drawbridge to Lord Akeldama's house. If Floote wanted to take to the air quickly, he'd go for *Dandelion Fluff Upon a Spoon.* After all, he'd used Lord Akeldama's private dirigible before.

Lyall concurred, but he didn't try to stop Lady Kingair. He allowed her to rush off into the night, presumably toward the ticket stations of the larger public dirigibles at the green. She was not a woman accustomed to London and its extravagances. It had not even occurred to her that there might be a *private* dirigible nearby.

The Beta began making his way upstairs to cross over into the vampire's abode.

Biffy held back.

"Don't you want to see if you're correct? See if he did manage to steal Lord Akeldama's dirigible a second time?" Lyall goaded him gently.

Biffy gestured down at his naked body and furry head with one fine white hand.

Professor Lyall understood perfectly. "You're embarrassed?"

Biffy nodded.

"Don't be foolish. This is something to be proud of—very few werewolves boast Anubis form, not even all Alphas. And it's highly unusual in a pup so young as you. Generally, it takes a decade or more to manifest. This is brilliant."

Biffy whined in a sarcastic manner.

"Don't be silly. It really is."

Biffy gave a huffy bark that he hoped sounded like a snort of derision.

"Trust me, my dandy, this is a *good* thing. Now, do come along."

With a sigh, Biffy did as ordered and followed his Beta across the small drawbridge and into his former master's house.

Only three years earlier, all would have been chaos at the sight of two naked men, one of them with a wolf head, wandering the halls of Lord Akeldama's domicile. Several of the drones, possibly Biffy included, might even have had the vapors.

It was not that Lord Akeldama and his boys objected to nudity; in fact, all were coolly in favor of it—in the boxing ring, for example, or the bedroom. But wandering the hallways underdressed, let alone undressed, was frowned upon unless cursed by extreme inebriation or emotional instability. And a werewolf was not to be tolerated in the house of a vampire except when socially mandated. All that had shifted when Lady Maccon installed herself in Lord Akeldama's closet. For where Lady Maccon went, Lord Maccon was soon to follow, and that good gentleman had somewhat improved the general outlook of Lord Akeldama's household on the subject of nudity and wolves, particularly in combination.

It was universally held among the drones that Lord Maccon had a particularly fine physique, and there had been quite the scuffle over who would be allowed to dress him in the evenings. After Floote assumed that role, it became a trickster's challenge to ascertain who among the boys could arrange such little incidences as would cause the London Alpha to bluster out into the hallway in the altogether of an afternoon.

As a result, the entire Akeldama household was markedly tolerant of Lyall's and Biffy's unexpected appearance and absent attire, although they did give Biffy some odd looks. Many of them had never seen Anubis form. Biffy took great solace in the fact that, as his head was that of a wolf, none of them knew it was him. Until, of course, they ran smack dab into Lord Akeldama, coming out of his aethographor chamber as they were making their way up onto the roof.

The vampire was dressed in an outfit that most closely resembled the waters of some tropical island, varying shades of turquoise, teal, and blue, accessorized with pearls and white gold. His effeminate features were screwed up in concentration over some small scrap of paper on which was scribbled, no doubt, an aetheric message of grave political, social, or fashionable import.

Lord Akeldama took a long look at Professor Lyall's physique and then gave him a little nod of academic approval. Then he directed an even longer look at Biffy.

Finally he said, "Biffy, my *darling* boy, what *have* you done to your hair? Something new for the evening?"

Biffy inclined his wolf head, dreadfully mortified. Of course, there was no chance of Lord Akeldama needing to see his face to recognize him; the vampire had a long, and somewhat inconvenient, memory for body parts.

Lord Akeldama smiled ever so slightly, the hint of a fang peeking out one corner of his mouth. "Now, my dear Dolly, did *you* know this would happen? You are a fortunate werewolf as well as a fortune man, now, are you not? Anubis form could be the solution to all your problems given some patience and a few well-placed suggestions."

Professor Lyall only inclined his head.

"But of course, you would have known *that* the moment he manifested."

The Beta's expression did not alter.

Lord Akeldama smiled fully, his fangs sharp and bright and fierce, as pearly as the cravat pin about his neck. "I don't trust serendipity, Professor Lyall. I don't trust it at all." No one missed the fact that the vampire was, for once, using someone's proper name.

Biffy's wolf head swayed back and forth between the combatants, wondering at all the unspoken undercurrents.

"I never underestimate the same man twice," said Lord Akeldama, fiddling with his cravat pin with one hand while he surreptitiously tucked the bit of paper with the aethographic message away with the other.

"You give me too much credit, my lord, if you thought I could anticipate this." Professor Lyall nodded at Biffy's altered state.

"Well, Biffy, what do you have to say on the subject?" The vampire regarded his former drone, his expression friendly, if a little distant.

"He's stuck, my lord." Lyall came to Biffy's rescue.

"Goodness, how unnerving."

"Indeed. Imagine how Biffy must feel."

"That, my dear Dolly, is beyond even *my* capacities. And now, how may I help you gentlemen? Do you require *garments*, perhaps?"

Professor Lyall rolled his eyes slightly. "Shortly. We were hoping if first we might ascertain the condition and state of your lordship's dirigible."

"*Buffety*? I believe she's moored up top. Haven't sent her out in many a moon. No need with my dear Alexia right here, I suppose. Why?"

"We believe she might have been used for nefarious purposes."

"Really? How wonderfully *salacious*! I can't believe I wasn't invited."

Professor Lyall said nothing.

"Ah, are you perhaps here in your BUR capacity, Dolly, my pet?"

Professor Lyall knew better than to give Lord Akeldama any more information than strictly necessary.

"No? Pack business, then? Has my little *Buffety* something to do with that unfortunate incident concerning *the other Beta*?" The vampire tsked around his fangs. "So sad."

With still no response from Professor Lyall and none possible from Biffy, the vampire waved an aqua-gloved hand magnanimously at the ladderlike staircase that led up onto his roof. "By all means."

The three gentlemen climbed up to find that the *Dandelion Fluff Upon a Spoon* was, indeed, no longer in residence. They could see it, some distance away, floating high in the aether stream heading in a southwesterly direction. Lyall and Biffy were unsurprised. Lord Akeldama pretended outrage, although he was surely warned there might be something amiss.

"Why, I do declare! How unsporting, to purloin a man's dirigible without asking! I suppose you two have a very good idea who borrowed my beauty?"

The werewolves exchanged looks.

"Floote." Lyall no doubt figured Lord Akeldama would discover the truth soon enough.

"Ah, well, at least I know he'll take good care of it and return it in first-rate condition. Butlers are like that, you know? But where's he taken it? Not *too far* I trust—my little darling isn't made for long distances."

"Probably to try to make an in-air transfer to one of the postal dirigibles."

"Going after my darlingist of Alexias, is he? To Gyppie?"

"Most likely."

"Well, well, well."

"So you say."

"She'll be cast adrift, poor thing. I had better alert the authorities, let them know she's gone missing, so as I'm not held responsible if she drifts into anything *important*. Unless you, *my dear Dolly*, being BUR might count as . . ."

The Beta shook his head.

"Ah, well, so I shall send Boots to the local constabulary. Our beautiful boys with the silver pins."

Professor Lyall nodded. "That is probably a good plan. Although, I shouldn't think they need know who took it. Not just yet. Right now all we have is coincidence and speculation."

The vampire regarded Lyall up and down in a very considering sort of way. "Look at you, Dolly, controlling information like an old intelligencer. One would almost think you vampiric. And, of course, *my darling Alexia* wouldn't like it, not her butler with a police record."

"Exactly. We must take into account Lady Maccon's feelings on the matter."

"I suppose . . . Lady Kingair?" Lord Akeldama twiddled his fingers casually in the air.

The Beta only lowered his eyes.

"Indeed, werewolf business. Just so. Well, Dolly my love, I *do* wish your werewolf business hadn't absconded with *my dirigible*."

"I do apologize about that, Lord Akeldama."

"Well, never you mind. Nice to have something for my boys to do. London has been awfully quiet without Lady Maccon. And now I see the sun will be rising soon, if you gentlemen will excuse me?" The vampire made a little bow at Professor Lyall. "Beta," and then to Biffy, pointedly, "*Alpha*."

Biffy and Lyall stayed, naked, on the roof of Lord Akeldama's town house watching the sunrise. As the sun eased itself up over the horizon, Biffy found himself inching closer and closer to Lyall's slight frame, until they stood, shoulders touching. When the first rays peeked over the horizon, he knew Lyall could feel the shudder of change that wrenched him back from Anubis to fully human.

The sunlight felt harsh, causing the sensation of dry and stretched skin. It was a condition, Biffy had learned, that was the price werewolves paid for being out during the day. But it was a relief to experience it once more, pulling at his nose and eyes. He reached up a tentative hand to feel, finding his own face instead of the wolf's.

"I do not want to be an Alpha," was the first thing he said, testing out his vocal cords for functionality.

Lyall bumped closer against his shoulder. "No, the best ones never do."

They continued to stand, not looking at one another, staring out over the awakening city, as though trying to see a small dirigible long since gone.

"Do you think he made it to the post?" Biffy asked at long last.

"It's Floote. Of course he made it."

"Poor Lady Maccon, a butler who murders, a father who betrays, and a husband who wants to die."

"Is that why you think Lord Maccon was so eager to visit Egypt?"

"Don't you? What man wants to go mad. It seems to me the God-Breaker Plague is an excellent solution to the problem of Alpha immortality." Biffy was, of course, thinking of his own future now.

"An interesting way of putting it."

"I cannot believe no werewolf has thought to use it so before."

"How do you know they have not? Who do you think gathered that data you were so interested in, on the extent of the plague?"

"Ah."

"Ah, indeed. Are you reassured by this?" The Beta turned to face him. Biffy could feel those concerned hazel eyes fixed on his profile. He kept resolutely facing the far horizon. *At least I have a good profile*, he consoled himself.

"You mean now that we know I am an Alpha?" Biffy considered the question. To be reassured that he had a safe place to die as a werewolf when once, an age ago now, he had thought to live forever as a vampire? He gave a tiny sigh. "Yes, I suppose I am." He paused. "How long do I have?"

Professor Lyall gave a little huff of amusement. "Oh, a few hundred years at least, possibly more, if you settle well. You still have to do military service, of course. That's always a risk."

"Learn to fight?"

"Learn to fight. I shouldn't worry, my dandy. Lord Maccon will make an excellent teacher."

"You think he's coming back?"

"Yes, I do. If only to yell at me over the sins of the past."

"Optimistic."

"I think, in this matter, young pup, I know our Alpha better than you."

"He will tolerate my presence, even with . . . ?" Biffy gestured at his head.

"Of course. You are young yet and certainly no challenge to an Alpha of his standing."

"Funny, I was beginning to feel rather old."

Professor Lyall gave a tiny smile. "Come on, then, to bed with us, and I will remind you, in the best possible way, how young you really are."

"Very good, sir."

"Ah, Biffy, I rather think that *now* that is my line."

Biffy laughed and straightened his spine, grabbing the Beta by the hand. "Right'o, come along, then."

"*Very* good, sir." Professor Lyall managed, somehow, to make his reply sound like a change in rank, a promise of wickedness, and the approval of a favorite teacher, all in one simple phrase.

CHAPTER SIXTEEN

The Curative Properties of Nile Bathing

Alexia, Conall, and Prudence were five days with the balloon nomads of Egypt floating south. Five days drifting at speed above the long rope of the Nile River, a deep, dark blue-green during the day and a silvered strand at night. During those five days, the full moon came and went, with Conall, for the first time in hundreds of years, unaltered by its presence. The earl could freely play with and, much to Lady Maccon's delight, take care of his daughter any time of the day or night without repercussions. He also grew a very large and scruffy beard, with which she was far less delighted.

"A man's virility is in his beard," he insisted.

To which Alexia replied, "And a woman's is in her décolletage. Yet you don't see me allowing mine to get out of control, now, do you?"

"If wishes were balloons," was his only response.

Drifting was, thought Alexia, a most agreeable pastime. True, the accommodations on board left something to be desired and were rather cramped, but there were some wonderful moments that could only be experienced on a trip by way of balloon. For two days they linked up with what appeared to be most of Zayed's extended family. They, too, sported bright balloons, mostly of a purple color, which drifted up close to Zayed's, then floated a short distance off and hitched in to the same aether current. Zayed cast out a massive circular net, and as each new balloon arrived, they would pick up a section of net, until there they were, all linked together, with a kind of immense hammock dangling under and between them. This became the walkway by which certain matters of business were conducted and a playground for the children. Conall, still mostly uncomfortable with being up high at all, refused point-blank to even test it, but Alexia was never one to shirk a new experience when it presented itself with such appeal. She set forth, even knowing that should anyone on the ground have binoculars they might very well see up her skirts. Soon enough, she found herself bouncing and tumbling across the wide net. It was not so easy to traverse as it looked. She was entirely unable to effect the smooth bobbing walk of the Drifter women, who managed to go from basket to basket, in an odd reflection of the British housewife paying a social call, with great mounds of food balanced atop their heads.

Prudence, of course, took to the new sky-high transport like a newly minted vampire to blood, springing about with little Anitra, who was her new favorite person in the world. Alexia was tolerably assured that Anitra, who had been raised on such folderol as nets in the aether, knew more than the average child about falling. Alexia also noticed that there always seemed to be older children or mothers about with a watchful eye to the net's edge, and so she relaxed some of her own vigilance. Not so Conall, whose eyes stayed fixed in horrified terror on first his daughter and then his wife. Each of whom he would yell to in turn. "Now, Prudence, don't jump so high!" "Alexia, if you fall off, I shall kill you!" "Wife, look to our daughter!" Prudence, blissfully uncaring of her father's concern, continued to bounce. Alexia ignored his rantings as those of a man whose feet, two or four, ought to always be on the ground.

During their five days of travel, they landed only once, on the evening in which they were linked to the other balloons. Zayed insisted that they needed to rest and restock both fuel and water. They drifted down slowly after the sun had set, pulling the net in as they went and coming to ground by a little oasis. The tingly feeling of the God-Breaker Plague was much stronger in the desert. It was almost uncomfortable for Alexia, as it had not been while floating. She felt the beginnings of that odd little push, that physical repulsion she had first experienced in the presence of one very small mummy, decorated with a broken ankh. Prudence, too, wasn't happy grounded. "Up," she kept saying. "Mama, up!" Only Conall was pleased, rolling about in the sand like a puppy before stripping down to bathe in the oasis. Alexia supposed not even the God-Breaker Plague could really get the wolf out of Lord Conall Maccon.

Two days later, they arrived at the bend in the Nile.

Alexia was hypnotized by the spot as they floated over it. It was the early evening, so their descent was slow and measured. From the sky, the place looked oddly familiar, the wide curve of the river forming a shape in the desert that Alexia was certain she recognized. But it was like trying to see a figure in the clouds. Then, as they dropped down closer and closer, she realized what it was.

She beckoned autocratically at her massive husband. "Conall, do come over here. Do you see that?"

The earl gave his wife a very dour look. "Alexia, I am trying *not* to look down." But he made his way over to her.

"Yes, but, please? Just there. Zayed, if you could spare a moment? What *is* that?"

Their host came over to where the Maccons stood, Alexia leaning over the basket's edge, looking down intently.

He nodded. "Ah, yes, of course. The Creature in the Sands."

Alexia pointed it out for the benefit of her husband, even though Conall clearly wasn't interested. "See there, the curve of the river? That is its head, and there, stretching out in ribbons into the desert, those are its legs. Are those pathways, Zayed?" The earl, unwilling to study further the ground he would probably describe as *rushing* toward them, went over to lie down on a pile of colorful blankets, shutting his eyes.

Zayed confirmed Alexia's assessment. "Ghost trails into the desert."

"Really, made by actual ghosts? Before the plague, I assume?"

"So they say. Not just any ghosts, lady. Ghosts of kings and queens and the servants of kings and queens. Must be ghosts, lady. What living man would walk voluntarily into the desert sands?"

"Eight trails, eight legs," ruminated Alexia thoughtfully. *It is an octopus. But an upside-down octopus? Of course, because the Nile runs backward!* She continued interrogating her host. "And that spot there? The one that represents its eye?"

"Ah, lady, that is, how you might say, a temple."

"For which of the many Ancient Egyptian gods?"

"Ah, no, not for a god, lady. For a queen. A queen who would be king."

Alexia knew enough of Egyptian history to know that could mean only one person. "Hatshepsut? Indeed. How *very* interesting."

Zayed gave her a very funny look. "Yes, lady. What might she say to you visiting here?"

"Goodness, why should her opinion matter? Has it been properly excavated yet, that temple?"

Before Zayed could answer, several things happened at once. The balloon lost altitude, as the air began to cool with proximity to the river, dropping down toward the very point under discussion—the Eye of the Octopus. Alexia felt a sensation of total repulsion, one she had only experienced heretofore from a preternatural mummy. Only this time it was ten times worse. She felt as if she were being pushed, literally pushed, by hundreds of invisible hands. All of them were trying to press her skin inward so that it melted back into flesh and bone. It was a horrible sensation and she wanted more than anything to beg Zayed to take the balloon back up into the aether. But she also knew that the answers to all her many questions lay down below.

At the same time, Conall said, "Oh, I feel much better," and sat upright.

Prudence cried out, "Mama, Mama, Mama. No!"

Alexia, dizzy from the repulsion, sank forward, tilting over the edge of the basket slightly, and spotted, moored near that fateful octopus eye, a large modern-style dahabiya.

Oblivious to the internal chaos of his lady passenger, Zayed answered Alexia's question. "One should never disregard the opinion of a queen. But *that* queen changed the pathways of the world."

Alexia felt as though she were missing something. As though the earth were spinning away from her, as fine and silvery fast as the Nile in full flood. The pushing came on harder and harder until it was as though she were being suffocated in a vat of molasses.

The balloon bumped down not ten paces from the Temple of Hatshepsut, but Alexia knew none of this. For only the second time in her adult life, she had fainted dead away.

Lady Maccon awoke to the sensation of cool water being splashed on her face and cool water surrounding her body.

Someone had thrown her into the Nile River—fully dressed.

She sputtered. "Oh my goodness, what?"

"It was my idea." Genevieve Lefoux's mellow, slightly accented voice came from behind Alexia's head. The Frenchwoman seemed to be supporting her by the shoulders so that she could float with the current.

Her husband's worried face appeared, blocking out the stars in the evening sky far above. "How do you feel?"

Alexia assessed the situation. The pressure was still there, the sense of repulsion, but mostly around her head and face now. Where her body was fully immersed in water, she felt nothing at all. "Better."

"Well, good. Don't scare me like that, woman!"

"Conall, it wasn't my fault!"

He was truculent. "Still, quite un-Alexia of you."

"Sometimes even I behave unexpectedly."

He was not to be mollycoddled. "Don't do it again."

Alexia gave up; there was no way he would be reasonable. She tilted her head back to look at Madame Lefoux, upside down. "It was a good idea, Genevieve. But I can't stay here in the Nile indefinitely. I have an octopus to investigate." Then she remembered something. "Primrose! Genevieve, did you steal Primrose and bring her with you?"

"No, Alexia. I did not even know she was missing until your husband asked me that same question not ten minutes ago."

"But we thought . . ."

"No, I am sorry. I was in a rush to leave the hotel because I had uncovered some very telling information and wanted to make my way here as quickly as possible. I had no idea there was a kidnapping. I do hope the little girl is all right."

"Don't we all? Blast it, we were hoping you saw something and were on the trail of the kidnappers. What was so interesting, then?" Alexia had no subtlety.

The Frenchwoman sighed. "Well, as you are here now, we might as well combine forces. Perhaps you are in possession of some missing pieces of my puzzle."

"How do you know it's not the other way around?" interjected the earl.

Genevieve continued as though he hadn't interrupted her. "I found myself in the company of Edouard Naville, a burgeoning archaeologist."

"An OBO member? I knew you had some other reason for visiting Egypt."

Madame Lefoux made no acknowledgment of any connection to the Order of the Brass Octopus. That, in and of itself, was an admission. "He has recently received the concession for Deir el-Bahri."

"Oh, indeed," encouraged Alexia, understanding none of this. She paddled frantically to right herself, touching her feet down into what she was certain was a filthy river bottom, but as she still had her walking boots on, it was impossible to tell. She stayed crouched down to keep as much of herself immersed as possible.

Conall offered his assistance with the maneuver. Alexia made note that while they had not bothered to remove *her* dress, Conall was quite naked, and Genevieve was wearing some kind of gentleman's undergarment as a bathing costume. Behind her, on the shore, Alexia could make out Zayed's balloon, mostly deflated, and a party of human shadows that must be made up of Zayed's family and the crew of Genevieve's dahabiya. They were engaging in some kind of trade, or meal, or both. Alexia could hear Prudence, with her usual lack of interest in water, shrieking with laughter. The infant was utterly unperturbed by her mother's ailment or resulting damp predicament.

Madame Lefoux gestured behind her at the shore. "*This* is Deir el-Bahri. You can make out some of the ruins of the temple behind our party. Beyond it is the Valley of the Kings. But this . . . this is the Eye of the Octopus."

Alexia nodded. "Yes, I had figured as much."

"Naville is young yet, but he hopes eventually to excavate here. I was sent to investigate, you know, *the source*."

Alexia was one step ahead of her. "The source of the God-Breaker Plague. You too?"

Lord Maccon interrupted, "Whose temple did you say it was?"

"I didn't, but Monsieur Naville believes it to be the mortuary temple of Queen Hatshepsut."

At which Conall, quite unexpectedly, busted out with a great crack of booming laughter. It echoed out over the river. "Well, well, well, I'm certain she won't like us visiting."

Alexia frowned. "Mr. Zayed said much the same thing."

Her husband continued. "And it could hardly be a mortuary temple. A metamorphosis temple, perhaps, but not mortuary."

Alexia began to comprehend what he was getting at, almost falling backward into the Nile in her surprise. "Are you telling me . . . ?"

"Matakara is Hatshepsut's other name. Well, one of the many. You didn't know?"

"Of course I didn't know! Why should I? And why didn't you *tell* me? My goodness, she really is *very* old!"

Lord Maccon tilted his handsome head in that annoying way of his that was meant to be coy. "I dinna think it was of particular import."

"Oh, *dinna* you? Wonderful. And now, do you think it might be important *now*?" Alexia thought even harder, difficult to do with the sense of repulsion pressing in against her brain. She splashed her head back down into the river, immediately feeling better. She resurfaced, wondering at the no-doubt-horrible state of her hair, pleased that someone at least had thought to remove her hat and parasol before her dunking. "But, Conall, didn't you once tell me that Ancient Egypt was ruled by werewolves?"

"Only inasmuch as Ancient Rome was ruled by vampires. There were still vampires around Egypt, even then. Hatshepsut was quite an upset. Made some people very angry. Tuthmosis, of course, put everything to rights again. He was one of *ours*."

"It makes no sense. Why would Matakara's temple be the epicenter of the God-Breaker Plague? Why would a vampire be involved in such a thing? Her kind, too, would be exterminated."

Genevieve Lefoux said, "May I suggest we look to the scientific evidence, and the reality of the situation first, and speculate afterward?"

"I take it you haven't yet explored the temple?" Alexia was surprised.

"I only recently arrived here myself. We were mooring when your balloon touched down. How did you, by the way, manage to convince a Drifter to carry you?"

"I am supposed to right my father's wrong," replied Alexia cryptically, twisting up her face in disdain.

"Goodness, which of the many?" the inventor wanted to know. "Anyway, the temple is completely unexcavated, so it is still filled with sand. It would take years to dig it out. I wouldn't know where to start."

Alexia splashed at her. "My dear Genevieve, I don't see that our answers are going to lie inside the temple."

"No?"

"No. Remember what we have found out, that preternatural touch requires air—preferably dry air—to work? Don't you think dead preternaturals might function the same way?"

"Dead preternaturals? Is that our source?"

Alexia only pursed her lips.

"How long have you known that might be a possibility?"

"Since Scotland."

"The artifact of humanization was a mummy?"

"Of a preternatural, yes."

"But why didn't you *tell* me?"

Alexia gave her sometime friend a very funny look.

Madame Lefoux clearly understood. Alexia could not reveal such a dangerous scientific fact to a member of the OBO. "You think we should look for the epicenter outside the temple?"

"Indeed I do."

"Can you manage it?"

Alexia frowned. "I can manage anything if we get some answers at the end of it."

Thinking of the fact that she had recently fainted, Conall said, "We'll bring water along and keep your dress as damp as possible. That might help."

"Oh." Alexia felt guilty for maligning her husband's actions in her head. "Is that why you chucked me into the Nile fully clothed?"

Lord Maccon made a funny face. "Of course, dear."

They paddled to shore and climbed out onto the muddy bank. The moment she was free of the river, Alexia began to feel that awful sense of repulsion against her skin.

"I think I may have to sleep in the river tonight," she said to no one in particular.

"You've done stranger things, I suppose," was her husband's reply.

Early the next morning, before the heat of the sun, Lady Maccon, Lord Maccon, and Madame Lefoux climbed up the hill above Hatshepsut's temple—or squelched up in Alexia's case. She was all pruned from a night spent in the river, a kind of hammock having been made to support her while she slept. It had not been very restful at all, and she was peevish and annoyed as a result. A trail of Egyptians followed in their wake, each carrying a large urn or canteen of river water. At Alexia's signal, one would step forward and splash her with it, rather too enthusiastically and much to Prudence's amusement.

"Mama, wet!"

"Yes, darling." Alexia could almost hear her daughter's adult commentary behind the baby phrases: *Sooner you than me, Mother.*

The sand-covered hill they scaled formed the back part of the roof of the temple, where it had been carved into the side of a cliff. Alexia took the lead, despite her damp dress hindering her stride, her parasol raised against the vicious sun. Then came Genevieve, and then Conall and Prudence. They left Zayed and family back at camp.

It was there, on the top of that hill, they began to see the bodies. Or to be more precise, the mummies. Or to be even more precise, it was where Lord Maccon accidentally stepped on a long-dead preternatural.

It made a sad, dry, cracking noise and let out a little puff of brown dust.

"Conall, do be careful! Inhale one of those and you could be mortal forever! Or something equally nasty."

"Yes, dear." The earl wrinkled his nose and shook off his boot.

Madame Lefoux held up a hand and they all stopped walking and simply looked. They could see down the sloping back side of the hill the eight long pathways out into the desert.

"Ghost trails," said Alexia, repeating Zayed.

"I hardly think so. Quite the opposite." Madame Lefoux was crouched down examining one of the bodies.

They were all mummies, or at least they looked to be mummies. As they followed along one of the trails down the hill, they eventually came across unwrapped bodies, baked and charred into a mummylike state by the dry desert sun. A thin coating of sand covered most of them, but once brushed aside, it became clear that it was these bodies that formed the octopus's tentacles. Hundreds of mummies, stretching out into the desert, spaced farther and farther apart. Maximizing the expansion, perhaps? Each one was marked by a headstone, some made of carved rock or wood. They bore no legend or the names of the dead.

They were all carved with the same shape—or to be precise, two shapes, an ankh, broken.

Alexia looked out over the tendrils extending off into the sands, disappearing from sight. "My people."

Madame Lefoux stood up from where she had crouched down to examine yet another mummy. "Preternaturals, all of them?"

"That would do it."

"Do what, exactly?" The Frenchwoman goaded her into saying it out loud.

"Cause the plague. Dry desert air combined with hundreds of dead preternaturals, basically—oh, I don't know how to put it properly—*outgassing*."

"That's a lot of dead preternaturals," said her husband.

"Collected from all around the world for hundreds and hundreds of years, I suppose. There aren't that many of us to start with. Could also be that originally they were all piled up and that forty years ago *someone* decided to start spreading them out."

Lord Maccon glanced over at Genevieve. "That would take quite an operation."

Alexia added, "Two operations: one to get it started originally and another to start it up again forty years ago."

Madame Lefoux looked back at them, her dark head twisting between the two and her green eyes grave. "It isn't me! This is the first I've heard of it, I promise you!"

"Yes," agreed Alexia, "but it is the kind of thing that might require a secret society. A massive underground secret society, of scientists, perhaps, who might not get so squeamish as others about handling the dead and collecting them from all over the world."

"You think the OBO is doing this!" Madame Lefoux rocked back on her heels, genuinely surprised by the idea.

"It is an *octopus*." Alexia was having none of that kind of silliness.

"No, you mistake me. The Order did spawn the Hippocras Club. I read the reports. I know we are capable of monstrous things. I simply don't believe this is us. To have such knowledge, to know what the body of a dead preternatural could do and not tell any other members? It is all very well to have a secret society of geniuses, but to keep such information secret from the members defeats the purpose. It's ridiculous. Think of the weapons I could have devised against vampires and werewolves had I known this. No, not the Order. It must be some other operation. The Templars, perhaps. They certainly have the infrastructure and the inclination."

Alexia frowned. "Don't you think the Templars might have done more with such knowledge? Might have developed weapons, as you say, from the technology. Or more likely, have collected the bodies in Italy to protect the homeland there. Move the God-Breaker Plague rather than expand it."

Conall Maccon joined the fray. "You know what I think?"

Both ladies turned to look at him, surprised that he was still there. Alexia's husband had their daughter propped on his hip. He was looking scruffy and hot. Prudence was inordinately quiet and somber, faced with all the bodies. She ought to have screamed and cried with fear, like any ordinary child, but instead she had merely looked at them, muttered, "Mama" in a very humble way, and buried her face in her father's neck.

"What do you think, oh, werewolf one?" asked Alexia.

It was hard to make out her husband's expression behind all that beard. "I think Matakara started it all those thousands of years ago. I think she started it to get rid of the werewolves and it got out of hand. She might even have done it at Alexander's behest. After all, when the Greeks came to Egypt and took over, they were very antisupernatural. She might have struck up a deal. A deal that left her the lone vampire in Alexandria and everyone else gone."

"It's as good a theory as any," agreed his wife.

"And then what?" Madame Lefoux wanted to know.

"Someone figured out what she did. Someone who wanted to expand it."

Alexia could guess that one. "My father."

Madame Lefoux picked up the story. "Of course. Alessandro Tarabotti had the contacts. The OBO tried to recruit him after he broke with the Templars. There were a number of people throughout Europe, including my father, who he might have turned to such a cause as this. Can you imagine? The promise of mass supernatural extermination? Start up a worldwide preternatural bodycollecting scheme."

"How macabre." Alexia did not approve of this stain on the family name. "Why does my father always have to be so difficult? He's dead after all. Couldn't he have left it at that?"

"Well, you must have gotten the inclination for trouble from someone," ruminated her husband.

"Oh, thank you, darling. Very sweet." Alexia felt the repulsion building up, pressing against her skin. The sun had risen and it was already doing its best to see her dry and suffering. She turned to one of the Egyptians. "Splash, please."

He made a gesture down at the nearby mummy.

"Oh, yes, I suppose water would damage it." She moved away from the bodies, and the man doused her thoroughly.

"Lady," he said, "we are running out of water."

"Oh, dear. Well, I suppose that means I, at least, had better head back." She looked pointedly at her husband and the French inventor. "Are you coming? I don't think there is much more to learn here." Another thought occurred to her. "Should we stop it?"

Lord Maccon and the inventor looked at her, not quite understanding.

"End the plague, I mean to say. We could try. I'm not certain how. My parasol's acid worked on the mummy in Scotland, but I've nowhere near enough for all these. Water might work, dissolve some of the mummies. It's the dry air that keeps them preserved. Just think, we might destroy the God-Breaker Plague right here and now."

Madame Lefoux looked conflicted. "But the loss of all the mummies. The science, I don't . . ." She trailed off.

Alexia said, with a tilt to her head, "Do I need to remind you that you are indentured to the Woolsey Hive? You must consider the best interests of your queen."

The Frenchwoman grimaced.

Lord Maccon interjected. "I think we should wait, Alexia. It is enough to know."

His wife was suspicious. "Why?"

"The plague has its uses."

"But to allow it to expand?"

"I didn't say *that* was a good idea. It might be a moot point anyway. Your father might not have known about the disruption of water. Will the plague even be able to cross the Mediterranean?"

"But if we can visit this location and discover the truth, so can others."

The earl was not about to give quarter. "It's important to have a part of the world that is free of supernaturals."

"Why is that?" Alexia was even more suspicious. It wasn't like her husband to argue against destructive behavior. She felt the repulsion building against her skin and decided it was an argument they might continue back at camp, preferably in the Nile. "We can discuss it later. Shall we?"

Madame Lefoux looked reluctant. "I should like to take a few samples, to see what . . ." She trailed off again, her eye caught by something behind them, up the hill above the temple.

A man was standing there, waving at them madly.

"Laydeeee," the man called out, "*they* are coming!"

"Is that Zayed? What is he . . . ? Oh my goodness gracious!" Alexia turned to look in the direction Zayed pointed, and there across the desert, running low and fast, a *thing* was moving toward them. It was a thing straight out of one of Madame Lefoux's sketches. In principle it resembled an enormous snail, its eye stalks belching gouts of flame into the air. It couldn't possibly operate on steam power, for where would one get the water in the desert? It must have multiple wheels, like those on farming equipment, under its shell. It was made of brass and glinted in the sun.

The snail was fast in a way that, given its form, Alexia found rather insulting. Riding atop its head and neck and hanging down the sides of its back were a number of men. They were dressed in white robes and turbans.

Alexia, Conall, and Genevieve stood for a moment, transfixed by the snail sliding across the desert.

"High-pressure, air-compressed sand buggy operating on methane fumes, unless I miss my guess."

"What was that, Genevieve?"

"A gastropod transport. We've hypothesized about them, of course. I didn't think anyone had actually built one."

"Well, it looks like someone did." Alexia shielded her eyes against the glare.

As the contraption neared, spitting up a wake of sand to either side, it slurred between the tentacles of the octopus so as not to disturb the bodies laid out there.

"That's not good," said Alexia.

"They know what's going on here," said Genevieve.

"Run!" said Conall.

Alexia took off, as ordered, throwing her modesty to the wind. She snapped closed her parasol and clipped it to the chatelaine. Then she picked up her skirts high, showing ankle but not caring for once, and took off up the hill.

"Alexia, wait! Here, take Prudence," Conall called after her.

Alexia paused and held out her free arm.

"No!" yelled Prudence, but she clung like a limpet to her mother after the transfer, wrapping her chubby arms and legs tight about Alexia's corseted frame.

Alexia looked into her husband's face; it was set and determined. "Now, Conall, don't do anything rash. You're mortal, remember."

Lord Maccon looked hard at this wife. "Get our daughter to safety and protect yourself, Alexia. I don't think . . ." He paused, clearly searching for the right words. "I'm still mad, but I do love you and I couldna stand it if . . ." He let the sentence trail off, gave her a blistering kiss as hot and as fierce as the Egyptian sun, and turned, charging toward the oncoming snail.

The snail spat a blast of fire at him. He dodged it easily.

"Conall, you idiot!" Alexia yelled after him.

She ignored his instructions, of course, reaching for her parasol.

Madame Lefoux came up to her, pressing a firm hand to the small of her back, almost pushing her up the hill.

"No, here, take Prudence." Alexia passed the little girl off once more.

"No, Mama!" remonstrated Prudence.

"I have my pins and my wrist emitters," said Madame Lefoux, looking like she, too, might disobey orders.

"No, *you* get her to safety and get Zayed to inflate the balloon. Someone has to see to that dunce of a husband of mine." Alexia was white with fear. "I think he's forgotten he could *actually* die."

"If you're certain?"

"Go!"

Madame Lefoux went, Prudence shrieking and struggling under her arm. "No, Mama. No, Foo!" There was no way the toddler could break free. Madame Lefoux might be bony and tall, but she was wiry and strong from years of hoisting machinery.

Lady Maccon unhooked and flipped her parasol about and turned to face the gastropod.

CHAPTER SEVENTEEN

A Gastropod Among Us

Whoever they were, they were less interested in guns and hurling fire than in scrapping hand to hand with the big man who stood alone before them. They'd stopped their snail in front of Lord Maccon and were leaping off it to attack him. Alexia's husband stood, waiting for them, arms akimbo.

I married an idiot, thought his loving wife, and she rushed down the hillside.

The idiot glowered at the gastropod enemy. His hair was a shaggy mess, his face covered in a full beard, his expression ferocious. He looked like a mountain man come to raise hell among the desert folk.

The first of the white-clad men charged him.

Conall lashed out. He might be mortal but he still knew how to fight. What Alexia worried about was his remembering he wasn't nearly so strong nor so durable in his nonsupernatural state.

She came dashing up just as he engaged two more robed men in combat. She drew back her parasol, took aim, and fired a numbing dart at one of the opponents.

At this action, the attackers paused and fell back to regroup behind the snail, nattering at each other excitedly in Arabic.

"Guess they weren't expecting projectiles," said Lady Maccon smugly.

"I told you to leave!" The earl was not pleased to see his lady wife.

"Be fair, my love. When have I ever done as ordered?"

He snorted. "Where's Prudence?"

"With Madame Lefoux, getting the balloon up, I hope." Alexia braced herself next to him, reaching into one of the secret pockets of her parasol. She pulled out Ethel and handed the small gun to him.

"Just in case." Even as she said it, they heard the sound of a gunshot, and sand near Conall's foot spat up sharp pellets at them.

Alexia and her husband both dove forward. They had the advantage of higher ground, but they also had no shelter.

Alexia opened her parasol defensively in front of them, trying to remember if this new one had armor.

Lord Maccon took careful aim and fired the gun.

A loud *ping* indicated the bullet had hit the metal of the gastropod's shell harmlessly.

"This is very decidedly not good," said Alexia.

Conall looked at her, his expression ferocious. "We are stuck on a hill, outmanned and outgunned."

Another barrage of shots came at them, this time narrowly missing Conall's head. Alexia and her husband began to squirm backward, up the hill. Alexia's bustle wiggled back and forth suggestively as she squirmed. Her skirts began to ride up scandalously high, but she had other things to worry about.

Lady Maccon was not happy about the situation. Not happy at all. She was also drying out, the sun beating relentlessly down, and all her water carriers had run off at the first sign of the gastropod. The pressure of the mummies around her was beginning to leak in and distract. Her entire being felt as though it were being pushed. All she could think was that she wasn't meant to be there. The dead didn't want her there. And neither did the living, if the white-clad snail men were anything to go by.

Another barrage of bullets came at them. Conall let out a sharp cry as one lucky shot hit the meat of his upper arm.

"See, what did I warn you of?" Alexia was concerned. In Alexia, concern, nine times out of ten, came out of her mouth as annoyance.

"Not now, wife!" Lord Maccon yanked off his cravat, and Alexia wrapped it quickly about his arm while he transferred Ethel to his other, working, hand.

"Should I?" she asked, offering to take the gun back.

"Even with the wrong hand I can still shoot better than you."

"Oh, thank you very much." Alexia glanced back up the hill and saw the purple rise of Zayed's balloon peek up behind it.

"He won't come get us," she said. "Not with bullets flying. The balloon would be at risk."

"Then I suppose we had better get to it."

Alexia was peeved enough to reply, "Well, yes. Couldn't you have done that in the first place?"

"I was trying to buy you ladies some time to escape. Precious little good it's done you."

"Oh, *very* gallant. As if I would let you take on a gastropod alone without any kind of weaponry."

"Must we argue right now?" Another round of gunfire spit the sand up around them.

They continued squirming up the hill and exchanging fire with the snail. Or Conall did; Alexia was out of the numbing darts.

Alexia closed the parasol so she could see where she was aiming. She reached for the first nodule on the handle and twisted it, activating the magnetic disruption emitter. Some of the gastropod must have been comprised of iron components, for the engine seized up, much to the bewilderment of the shouting driver.

Taking advantage of the confusion, Alexia and Conall jumped to their feet and dashed up the hill toward the balloon, the earl pushing his wife before him.

They almost reached the top. The balloon was higher now, and Alexia could make out the long rope ladder dangling down and trailing toward them in the sand. She ran to it, faster than she had ever thought possible. The repulsion pressure was bearing down on her hard, there being far more mummies at the top of the hill. She could feel the blackness closing in—too many dead preternaturals pressing against her skull.

I can't faint again. Now is not a good time, even if I were the fainting type, she remonstrated with herself.

Conall paused, turned, and fired. The snail was in motion again, the disruption worn off, but some of the men had given up waiting for it and had taken off after them on foot up the hill. When Conall paused to shoot, so did they.

Alexia heard her husband cry out and he jerked backward against her. The bottom fell out of her world as she turned frantically, half supporting his massive weight, desperately looking to this new injury. A bloom of red appeared over his ribs, staining the shirt. He wasn't wearing a waistcoat.

"Conall Maccon," she cried, shaking off the blackness, "I forbid you to die."

"Don't be ridiculous, woman. I'm perfectly fine," he replied, dropping Ethel to clutch at his side, gasping and terribly pale under the beard.

Alexia bent to scoop up her gun.

"Leave it. We're out of ammunition anyway."

"But!"

Conall began climbing up the hill, bent almost double against the pain.

Alexia turned to follow, only to find herself seized about the waist by one of the white-clad enemy. She screamed in rage and swung her parasol up and back hard, hitting the man squarely atop the head.

He let go of her.

She was out of numbing darts but there was more than that in her accessory's arsenal. She twisted the nodule closest to the shade, hoping she had the correct direction for the correct liquid. Either the acid for vampires or the silver nitrite for werewolves would work on humans, but the acid was nastier. She couldn't remember which was which, so she simply hoped.

Alexia met the man's eyes over the top of the parasol and felt a brief flash of recognition. She had seen him before, on the train to Woolsey back in England.

"What?" she said, pausing in her action. Then remembering her husband's wounds, she let loose the spray.

The man, as shocked as she, leaped backward out of harm's way, tripped on his long robe, and tumbled down the hill before regaining his feet. Instead of continuing his pursuit, he whirled about, running back toward the gastropod waving his arms wildly in the air.

Alexia couldn't understand a word he said except one. He kept repeating something that sounded Italian, not Arabic: "Panattone."

The peace brought about by this startling reversal didn't last long for, despite his gesticulations, the other white-clad men continued to fire. One or two ran past their erstwhile companion and continued after her.

Conall, who had reached the ladder and was holding on to it, had turned back at Alexia's yell. He was looking even whiter, and there was a good deal more blood running down his side than Alexia had ever seen spilling out of anyone.

Her world was closing in. It was like being inside a black tunnel, the repulsion pressing against the corners of her eyes. Pushing herself, slogging that last short distance to her husband took herculean effort. But then she was there, and Conall was pressing the rope into her hands.

"Go on!" he yelled, pushing up on her bustle as though he might hoist her into the air. He was nowhere near strong enough for that in his current state.

Alexia stuffed the cloth of her parasol into her mouth, holding it with her teeth, and began to climb. She paused halfway up to glance back, making certain her husband was following her.

He was, but he did not look well. His grip must be very weak, particularly with that injured arm.

The moment they latched on to the ladder, Zayed, blessed man, gave the balloon some heat, and it floated up.

Below them they could hear more guns firing. Alexia felt one whiz past her ear and heard a thunk as it lodged itself in the wicker of the basket.

Madame Lefoux and Prudence's heads poked over the edge. They both looked terrified. There was nothing they could do to help.

"Genevieve, take Prudence to cover!" Conall yelled.

The heads disappeared for a moment and then only the inventor's reappeared.

Madame Lefoux had one of her deadly little wrist darts out and was aiming it down. Startled, Alexia thought she was pointing it at her or Conall. In that moment, she wondered, yet again, if she had misjudged the Frenchwoman's loyalty.

Genevieve fired. The dart hurtled past Alexia's ear. There came a cry, and it hit the man Alexia hadn't even realized was there. A man in white robes dangling off the very bottom of the ladder let go and fell, screaming.

The balloon lifted again, and Alexia felt a lightening of that horrible sensation of repulsion, the black tunnel receding from around her vision. She wished the balloon would go faster, but they were at the mercy of the sky now.

Finally, after what felt like an age, bullets whizzing by all the while, Alexia attained the basket lip and tumbled in. She spat out her parasol and instantly turned to see to her husband.

Conall was still some ways behind her, slowed by his wounds. Below him she could see the gastropod, tracking them across the sands, still close enough to be a danger. Alexia went for her parasol, prepared to use the grapple attachment.

The firing continued but the balloon was out of range.

Then, one of the enemy pulled out a different kind of gun, a huge fat rifle that looked like it was designed for large game. He fired. Whether he was aiming to bring down the balloon or not, he hit Lord Conall Maccon.

Alexia wasn't certain where he was hit exactly, but she could see her husband's face, already ashen under the beard, turned up toward her. A ghastly expression of profound surprise suffused his handsome visage and he let go and fell. Desperate, Alexia shot the parasol grapple at her husband and missed. Conall fell for what seemed leagues, silent, not screaming, not uttering a sound, to land in a broken heap in the desert far below.

Biffy was worried. He wasn't a man to let slide his training—the many years under Lord Akeldama, the few under Professor Lyall. His training taught him to be practical, to look to the evidence, to watch and observe, never to assume, and always to be stylish about it. But he was still worried, for something was wrong. He had received no message from Lady Maccon in three sunsets. He had faithfully, every evening, climbed to the attic aethographic chamber and waited, at first only for a quarter of an hour or so, but as the days passed, he waited longer and longer.

He mentioned his concerns to Professor Lyall and the Beta made sympathetic murmurs, but what could they do? Their orders were to remain in London, keep things in check. That was difficult enough with Lady Kingair convinced they should send someone after Floote and Channing convinced they were lying about Biffy's new state.

"Prove it!" Major Channing said the moment Lyall made the announcement to the pack. "Go on. Show me Anubis form!"

"It's not like that. I can't control it yet." Biffy spoke calmly.

The Gamma was unconvinced. "There's no way you're an Alpha. You're a ruddy dandy!"

"Now, now, Channing. I saw it. So did Lady Kingair." Professor Lyall's voice was mellow and calm.

"I dinna ken what I saw," said that lady most unhelpfully.

"See? Do you see?" Channing turned back to Biffy, his shapely lip curled in disgust. His face, though handsome, was disagreeably set and his blue eyes icy. "Go on, then. Can't show me the head? Fight me for dominance." The Gamma really looked as though he might strip right there in the dining room and change to a wolf, simply to prove Biffy was lying.

"You think I desired this state?" Biffy was outraged at being accused of making such a thing up. "Do I look like the kind of man who *wants* to be Alpha?"

"You don't look like an Alpha at all!"

"Exactly. Look at Lady Kingair and Lord Maccon—clearly being Alpha plays hell with one's wardrobe!"

Professor Lyall stepped in again. "Stop it, both of you. Channing, you will have to take my word for it. You know how long it takes to control wolf form, let alone master a second one. Give the pup a chance."

"Why should I?" The white wolf was petulant.

"Because I said so. And because he might be your Alpha someday. Wouldn't want to get off on the wrong paw, now, would you?"

"As if Lord Maccon would allow any such thing."

"Lord Maccon is in Egypt. You take your orders from me."

Biffy had never heard Lyall sound so forceful before. He rather liked it. It worked, for Channing backed down. He was willing to fight Biffy, but not Lyall; that was clear.

"Such an unpleasant fellow, and so attractive; it makes it that much worse," commented Biffy to Lyall later that night.

"Now, don't you worry about Channing. You'll be able to handle him eventually. Attractive, is he?"

"Not so much as you, by any means."

"Right answer, my dandy. Right answer."

Someone was screaming.

It took Alexia a long time to realize it was her. Only then did she stop, turn, and charge across the balloon to Zayed.

"Go back down! We must go back for him!"

"Lady, it is full sun. We cannot go down in daylight."

Alexia gripped his arm desperately. "But you must! Please, you must."

He shook her off. "Sorry, lady, there is only up now. He is dead anyway."

Alexia staggered back as though physically struck. "Please, don't say such a thing! I beg you."

Zayed only looked at her calmly. "Lady, no one could survive that fall. Find yourself a new man. You are still young. You breed well."

"He isn't just any man! *Please* go back." Alexia tried to grab at his hands. She had no idea how the balloon worked but she was willing to try.

Madame Lefoux came to her, pulling her gently off of Zayed. "Come away, Alexia, please."

Alexia shook Genevieve off and stumbled to the side of the basket, craning her neck to see, but they were rising fast. Soon they would hit the aether currents and then there really would be no going back.

She saw Conall lying in the sand. She saw the gastropod give up chasing the balloon and stop next to her husband. The men in white jumped down and surrounded his broken form.

Alexia opened her parasol. Perhaps it would help if she jumped; perhaps somehow it would catch the air and slow her fall.

She climbed up onto the edge of the basket, parasol open.

Madame Lefoux tackled her and yanked her back inside the basket.

"Don't be an imbecile, Alexia!"

"Someone has to go back for him!" Alexia struggled against her friend.

Zayed left off supervision of the balloon to come and sit on Alexia's legs, immobilizing her. "Lady, don't die. Goldenrod wouldn't like it."

The Frenchwoman grabbed Alexia by the face, one hand to each cheek, forcing her to look deep into her green eyes. "He's dead. Even if the fall didn't get him, he was badly wounded, and there was that shot from the smoothbore elephant gun. No mortal could survive both. It'd be hard for a werewolf to survive such a thing and he's no werewolf anymore."

"But I never told him I loved him. I only yelled at him!" Alexia felt as if there was nothing securing her to reality but Genevieve's green eyes.

Genevieve wrapped her arms about Alexia. "For you two, that *was* loving."

Alexia refused to believe he was gone. Not her big strong mountain of a man. Not her Conall. The desert warmth surrounded her. The sun shone bright and cheerful. The sensation of repulsion had lifted at last. But she was cold; her face felt sunken in against the hollows of her cheeks, and her mind was blank.

A small, soft hand pressed against her freezing cheek. "Mama?" said Prudence.

Alexia stopped thinking that her parasol might allow her to jump out of an air balloon. She stopped feeling like she was splitting in half, like her soul, if she had had one, was being wrenched down through her feet, a tendril, a tether to the man far below.

She stopped feeling anything at all.

The balloon jerked, catching first the southern current that had brought them to Luxor, and then after a few masterful manipulations from Zayed, floated up into a higher western current, one that, Alexia vaguely heard him say to Genevieve, would connect them to the northern route.

Even though they spoke directly above her head, Genevieve still holding her close, Prudence still cuddled up against her, the little girl's eyes huge and dark and worried on her mother's face, it all seemed to be occurring far away.

Alexia let it. She let the numbness take over, immersed herself in the lack of feeling.

Five days later, in the darkness several hours before dawn, they landed in Alexandria.

CHAPTER EIGHTEEN

The Truth Behind the Octopus

Everything was still chaos around her, but Lady Alexia Maccon sailed through it all on a sea of profound numbness. She allowed Madame Lefoux to take charge. The French inventor told the acting troupe about Lord Maccon's death. She explained what had happened using scientifically precise language. She also informed them that they had failed to find Primrose.

For ten days, Ivy and Tunstell had waited, with no contact from the kidnappers, their hopes pinned on Alexia and Conall discovering the whereabouts of their daughter. Now Lady Maccon had returned with the earl dead, and Primrose still missing.

And Lady Maccon? Lady Maccon was also missing. Nothing seemed to reach her. She responded to direct questions but softly, quietly, and with long pauses. She was also uninterested in food. Even Ivy was shaken out of her own worry enough to be upset by this.

But Alexia did cope. Alexia was always one to cope. She did what needed to be done, once someone pointed it out to her.

Ivy, between tears, managed to explain that she had been unable to convince the aethographor to give her Lady Maccon's messages. So Alexia went to bed, slept most of the day away with dreams full of Conall's face as he fell, woke up, dressed automatically, and went to get the messages herself. There were nine of them from Biffy, one for every sunset she had missed. The more recent were merely worried notes of "Where are you?" but the earlier ones told such a depressing truth that Alexia was almost glad she was too numb to be affected by it.

Not Floote.

Not *her* Floote.

Not the man who had always been there for her. Always provided her with the necessary cup of tea and a soothing, "Yes, madam." Who had changed her nappies as a baby, who had helped her sneak out of the Loontwills' house as a young woman. Not Floote. Yet, it made horribly perfect sense. Who else but Floote would have had all the necessary contacts? Who else but Floote would have the training in how to kill a werewolf? Alexia had seen him take on vampires firsthand; she knew he had the ability.

Lady Maccon returned to the hotel, clutching her stack of messages in one hand, moving like an automaton through the bustling city streets that only a week and a half earlier she had found more friendly and charming than any other. In the hotel, she caught sight of Madame Lefoux and Ivy in one of the private parlors off the reception area. She floated past, not even realizing that she should extend an evening greeting. There was nothing left in her for even the social graces. She felt, in fact, very absent from herself. Adrift, as if nothing might bring her back again. Not even tea.

But at Madame Lefoux's summoning gesture, she wandered into their private boudoir and, in answer to her friend's polite inquiry as to her health, said, "As it turned out, it was Floote."

Genevieve looked confused.

Ivy gasped and said, "But he was *here*. Floote was here, looking for you. We sent him down the Nile after you. I thought . . . Oh, silly me, he isn't with you? I thought he would have caught up. Oh, I don't know what I thought."

Even that didn't pull Alexia back to the here and now. "Floote was looking for me? He probably wanted to explain himself."

Madame Lefoux pressed for details. "Explain what, exactly, Alexia?"

"Oh, you know, the God-Breaker Plague. Killing Dubh. That kind of thing." Alexia tossed Genevieve the little stack of papyrus papers from the aethographor station. "Biffy says . . ." Alexia trailed off, standing quietly while Madame Lefoux read over the notes.

Ivy said, "Oh, Alexia, do sit down!"

"Oh, should I?" Alexia sat.

Prudence came running in. "Mama!"

Alexia didn't look up.

The little girl grabbed at her hand. "Mama, bad men! Back."

"Oh, yes? Did you hide under the bed again?"

"Yes!"

The nursemaid came in, clutching Percy to her trembling breast. "They came back, Mrs. Tunstell! They came back!"

Ivy stood, face pale, clutching at her throat with both hands. "Oh, heavens. Percy, is he all right?"

"Yes, madam. Yes." The nursemaid passed over the redheaded infant to Ivy's clutching embrace. Percy, unperturbed, burped contentedly.

"See," said Prudence, still trying to get her mother's attention.

"Yes, dear, very wise. Hiding under the bed, good girl." Alexia was busy staring off into space.

"Mama, see!" Prudence was waving something in front of her mother's face.

Madame Lefoux took it from her gently. It was a roll of heavy papyrus tied with cord. The inventor unwound it and read the missive aloud.

"'Send Lady Maccon for the baby, alone. Tonight, after sunset.'" She added, "And they provide an address."

"Oh, Primrose!" Ivy burst into floods of tears.

Alexia said, "I suppose they were waiting for me to return."

"Do you think they wanted you all along?" Madame Lefoux looked upset.

Alexia blinked. She felt as though her brain were moving like a snail—a real snail, slow and slimy. "That's possible, but then, they kidnapped the wrong infant, didn't they?"

The Frenchwoman frowned in deep thought. "Yes, I suppose they did. What if that's it? What if they were after Prudence? What if they are taking you as a substitute? What if they still think they have Prudence, not Primrose?"

Alexia was already standing and wandering toward the door, her footsteps slow and measured.

"Where are you going?"

"It's after sunset," said Lady Maccon, as though it were perfectly obvious.

"But, Alexia, be sensible. You can't simply trot to their orders!"

"Why not? If it returns Primrose to us?"

Ivy, trembling, could not speak. She looked back and forth between Alexia and the Frenchwoman. Her hat, a mushroom-puff turban affair with a peacock-style fan of feathers out the back, quivered with a surfeit of emotion.

"It could be dangerous!" protested Madame Lefoux.

"It's always dangerous," replied Lady Maccon flatly.

"Alexia, don't be a peewit! You can't *want* to die. You're not one for melodrama. Conall is *gone*. You have to keep on going without him."

"I am going. I'm going right out to find the kidnappers and retrieve Primrose."

"That's not what I meant! What about Prudence? She needs her mother."

"She has Lord Akeldama."

"That's not quite the same thing."

"No, it's better—mother and father all rolled into one attractive package, and he doesn't look to be dying anytime soon."

"Oh, goodness, Alexia, please, wait. We must talk about this, devise a plan."

Alexia paused, not really thinking out her next maneuver.

The hotel clerk came in to the parlor at that moment.

He approached Genevieve. "Mr. Lefoux? There is a gentleman for you. A Mr. Naville. Claims he has some important information to impart."

Genevieve rose and brushed past Lady Maccon. "Just wait a few minutes, please, Alexia?"

Alexia merely stood, unresponsive. She watched as the Frenchwoman strode across the reception room to a small gaggle of gentlemen. One of them was very young. Another was carrying a leather case stamped with the image of an octopus. She watched Madame Lefoux tilt her head, lift up her short hair, and pull down her cravat and collar, exposing the back of her neck. She was showing them her octopus tattoo. Alexia's brain said, *Those are members of the Order of the Brass Octopus.* Her practical side said, *I hope she doesn't tell them about the preternatural mummies. There will be a race to the bodies, to use them in munitions, to shift the balance against immortals.* Her even more practical side remembered that there were men dressed in white willing to defend those mummies to the death. Her husband's death.

The rest of her kept walking, in defiance of Genevieve's request. She had her parasol hanging from its chatelaine at her waist. She had the address of the location on a scrap of paper. She moved across the reception room and out into the street, Genevieve unaware of her movements.

There Alexia hailed a donkey boy and told him the address. The boy nodded eagerly. With very little effort at all, she climbed astride, the boy yelled to his creature in Arabic, and they started forward.

The donkey took her into an unfamiliar sector of the city, a sad and abandoned-looking structure behind the customs house. She slid off the animal and paid the boy generously, sending him away when he would have waited. She climbed the step and pushed through the reed mats of the doorway into what looked to be some kind of warehouse, possibly for bananas, if the sweet smell was to be believed.

"Come in, Lady Maccon," said a polite, slightly accented voice out of the dim echoing interior.

With a flitter of speed customary to the breed, the vampire was right up next to her, almost too close, showing his fangs.

"Good evening, Chancellor Neshi."

"You are alone."

"As you see."

"Good. You will explain to me why the child isn't working."

"First let me see that Primrose is safe."

"You thought I would bring her here? Oh, no, she is left behind, and she is safe. But I thought the abomination's name was Prudence? You English and your many names."

"It is Prudence. Did you want my daughter? You got the wrong child."

The chancellor reeled back and blinked at her. "I did?"

"You did. You got my friend's baby. She has not been happy about that."

"Not the abomination?"

"Not the abomination."

There was a long pause.

"So might we have her back, then?" Alexia asked.

The vampire went from confused, to angry, to resolved. "No. If I cannot use the abomination, I will use you. She cannot be let to suffer any longer."

"Is this about Queen Matakara?"

"Of course."

"Or should I say Queen Hatshepsut?"

"To use that name, you should say *King* Hatshepsut."

"What does *your* queen want with *my* daughter?"

"She wants a solution. An easy solution. One that could be smuggled in and then back out with none of the others noticing. But, no, this had to be difficult. There had to be two black-haired English babies, and we got the wrong one. Now I am stuck with you."

"I am not easy to smuggle."

"You most certainly are not, Lady Maccon."

"Yes, but why?"

"Come with me and you will learn why."

"And Primrose?"

"And we will return to you the useless baby."

He led her from the building and together they walked toward the hive.

It was a long, quiet walk through the city. Lady Maccon allowed herself to drift on that sea of absence.

Despite this, she found herself eventually thinking about Queen Matakara. Trapped in that chair, her eyes as sad as anything Alexia had ever seen or felt until now. They were the eyes of someone who wanted to die. She could sympathize.

"It's Matakara," she said into the silent night, stopping in her tracks.

Chancellor Neshi stopped as well.

"She set the God-Breaker Plague originally *and* she started it up again. She and my father." Alexia talked out her revelations. "They struck a deal."

The chancellor continued for her. "He broke with the OBO without telling them what he found. He agreed not to tell the Templars either. In return he got to continue the plague's expansion with the certain knowledge that eventually it would take my queen, too."

"Why not just bring a preternatural mummy into the room with her? Wouldn't that work?" Alexia began walking once more.

The vampire said, exasperated, "Do you think I haven't tried? But your father left iron orders. None of my people ever seem to be able to get to a preternatural body fast enough. It's like they are networked. It's like there is someone in charge who keeps an eye on all the preternaturals in the world. He won't let me break the original agreement, even from the grave."

Alexia wondered if Floote had done as he said and had her father's body cremated, or if Alessandro Tarabotti was one of those who lay exposed above Hatshepsut's Temple. "Why not simply ask me to do it? I was right there. I would have been happy to touch her."

"Not in front of the others. They can't know that their queen wants to die. They can't possibly know. Done at the wrong time, they would swarm—swarm without a queen. That is not pretty, Lady Maccon. I could sneak a child in and out easily enough, but you, Lady Maccon, are *not* sneaky. Besides, if Lady Maccon, English, killed Queen Matakara, it would cause an international incident."

"Why not simply stick with the plan and wait for the plague to expand? It's already reached the edge of Alexandria."

"The OBO found out. A concession to excavate at the temple was issued. Our time has run out. When I heard of your child, I thought she would be an easy solution. I could sneak her in and my queen would be free at last. Done quietly, before dawn, and my drone could have her back out again and no one the wiser."

"But why you, Chancellor?"

"The queen trusts me. I am almost as old as she. I, too, am ready to die. But the others, they are young yet."

Alexia paused again in her walking. "Is that what would happen? I didn't know. When a queen dies, all her hive goes with her?"

"And go quietly if it is timed correctly."

"You were willing to do that to your hive?"

"It is the pharaoh's way. To travel with servants into the afterlife. Why shouldn't we all die together?"

Alexia could understand what came next. He would get her in to the queen, he would arrange for her to touch Matakara, and she would die. So, too, would Alexia, as the other vampires in their pain and loss would kill her outright, and baby Primrose as well.

"Have you thought this through, Chancellor?"

"Yes."

"You are cursing me to die with this last desperate gambit."

"Yes."

"You know, you could still borrow Prudence? She's small enough to sneak in and out."

"Too late, Lady Maccon."

"I thought things were never too late for an immortal. Isn't that the point? All you creatures have is time."

Chancellor Neshi only led the way into the hive house.

Alexia followed. She couldn't think of anything better to do.

It was much the same as before. A crowd of servants descended upon them to remove their shoes, and the chancellor went off to alert his queen as to Lady Maccon's presence.

However, Alexia was much less welcome without her actor escort. She couldn't understand what the other drones and vampires said to Chancellor Neshi when she appeared at the throne room entrance, but it was said very loudly and angrily.

Above them, Queen Matakara sat on and in and within her throne of blood and watched everything with tortured eyes.

Alexia inched toward her.

Chancellor Neshi went and retrieved Primrose from some hidden sanctum. The baby seemed perfectly unharmed. She waved chubby arms at Alexia, in one fist clutching a large necklace of gold and turquoise.

One of the drones noticed that Lady Maccon was moving toward his queen and launched himself at her. He was a slender fellow, but wiry and muscled, plenty strong enough to hold her.

Alexia thought of going for her parasol. She thought of diving at the queen, getting her bare hand to the woman's exposed forehead. She thought of grabbing Primrose and running away from them all. She thought of struggling against her captor. She could probably break free; she'd had enough experience with *that* by now. For a proper Englishwoman, she was adept at the application of elbows and feet to delicate anatomy. She thought of doing many things, but she actually did none of them. She pushed herself back into the numbness and let it wash over her, for the first time in her life inclined to do nothing at all, to wait and see.

The arguing continued.

Then there was a tumult in the hallway and two drones brought in a struggling Madame Lefoux.

"Alexia! I thought you would be here."

"You did? Oh."

"It was the only logical explanation. Once I removed the idea that a vampire wants to live forever, I was left with the answer. Matakara started the plague, both times. First against the werewolves and later against the vampires and herself. And if she wanted to die that badly, she'd try to get either you or Prudence to touch her."

"And how could you blundering in here now possibly help?" Alexia was confused but not angry. She didn't have enough emotion left to be angry.

"I brought reinforcements."

At which juncture a mechanical ladybug trundled into the room with Prudence riding atop it. "Mama!"

At that, Alexia did get angry. "Genevieve, what were you thinking! To bring my daughter into a hive of vampires, one of them a kidnapper who wanted her in the first place? A hive whose queen wants to die. A hive that will go mad if that happens."

The Frenchwoman smiled. "Oh, I didn't bring *only* her."

Bustling in after Prudence came the acting troupe. The thespians wore identical expressions of seriousness and were armed with the stage swords and props of their trade. They were led by Ivy Tunstell and her husband. Ivy wore an undersized admiralty hat in white and black with a particularly large ostrich feather out the top, and Tunstell's trousers, while tight, were made of leather for battle.

The practical part of Alexia thought that an acting troupe was hardly reinforcements against a hive of vampires.

The advent of this crowd of theatrical invaders caused a tizzy. There were colorful fabrics and people flying everywhere, as the actors employed stage fighting, tumbling, and, in the case of one young lady, ballet to dodge their opponents. There was a good deal of shouting and one operatic war cry from Mr. Tumtrinkle.

Tunstell began quoting Shakespeare. Ivy charged for her daughter, parasol wielded in a manner Alexia felt did her proud. The drone holding the infant stood with mouth slightly open for sufficiently long enough to allow Ivy to bop him hard on the head and yank her daughter away. Alexia half expected her dear friend to then faint at her own audacity, but Ivy Tunstell stood firm, child on hip, parasol at the ready. The tiny part of Alexia that was not numb was outlandishly satisfied.

With uproar continuing and the vampires and drones distracted, Alexia resumed creeping toward the hive queen. Matakara wanted to die. Matakara who had started everything. Matakara who was responsible for *her husband's death*. Well, Lady Alexia Maccon would see her dead. And gladly!

Alexia made it to the base of the platform upon which the gruesome chair stood. She caught Chancellor Neshi's eye and he nodded, encouraging her, before continuing his argument with one of the other vampires. Alexia wondered if anyone else even understood what was going on.

Just as she was about to climb up, a vampire grabbed her around the waist. He lost his strength upon contact but maintained his grip. He yanked her around and bore her down to the floor. As she fell, Alexia could see all was not going well for Madame Lefoux's would-be invasion.

Ivy, clutching Primrose, was fending off two drones with her parasol, but soon enough their surprise at her attire would wear off and she would succumb. Gumption only got a girl so far. Tunstell had Prudence's ladybug held high and was bashing it about. Mr. Tumtrinkle was faced off against a vampire and not doing well, as might be expected. Even all his fancy fencing tricks from *Hamlet and the Overcooked Pork Pie—a Tragedy* were not fast enough nor strong enough, or, quite frankly, deadly enough for an immortal.

A scream diverted Alexia's attention. A vampire launched himself at Ivy, going for her neck. The drone attacking her fell back.

Alexia unhooked her parasol, took aim, and then realized she was out of numbing darts. She turned the middle nodule right and out popped the wooden stake at the tip. She began bashing about with it. She dared not use the lapis solaris; the acid would surely do just as much damage to one of her actor defenders.

Prudence, who had taken initial refuge from the kerfuffle under a small table, emerged at Ivy's terrified scream. She charged the vampire attacking Mrs. Tunstell and beat at his ankle with her tiny fists. It was enough contact to turn her vampire, and him not. He was left gnawing uselessly on Ivy's bloodied neck, and Prudence turned into a bouncing blur of excited infant with supernatural abilities. She was of very little help as she merely bucketed about, not knowing her own strength, hurling everyone aside whether vampire, drone, or actor. Behind her, Ivy crumpled to the floor, still managing to support Primrose but suffering from shock or loss of blood, or both.

And then, leaping up to the balcony from the street below and charging into the room via the open window came a massive beast. And atop the wolf, looking as dignified and butlerlike as might be possible for a man riding a werewolf, was Floote.

Alexia stopped trying to touch Queen Matakara and turned in a slow, ponderous manner. She felt as though she were seeing and experiencing everything underwater.

"Conall Maccon, I thought you were dead!"

Lord Maccon looked up at his wife from where he had his jaws about a vampire's leg, let go, and barked at her.

"Do you know how I've been suffering for the last week? How could you? Where have you been?"

He barked again.

Alexia wanted to throw herself at him and wrap both arms and legs about him. She also wanted to whack him over the head with her parasol. But he was there and he was alive and everything was suddenly working again. The numbness vanished and Alexia took in the world around her. Her brain, somewhat absent for the better part of a week, returned to full capacity.

She looked to her butler. "Floote, what have you done?"

Floote only pulled out a gun and began shooting vampires.

"Prudence," Alexia called sharply, "come to Mama!"

Prudence, who had been, until that moment, busy trying to suck the blood out of the arm of a very surprised drone, stopped and looked over at her mother. "No!"

Alexia used *that* tone of voice. The voice that Prudence rarely heard but knew meant trouble. "Right this very moment, young lady!"

For Prudence, currently a vampire, *right this very moment* was very fast indeed. In a veritable flash, she was at Alexia's side. Alexia grabbed her daughter, turning her human once more, and then, without any kind of compunction at all, lifted her up and set her in the lap of Queen Matakara of Alexandria.

Prudence said, "Oh, Dama," in a very somber voice and looked deep into the tormented eyes of the ancient vampire. Her little face was as grave and gentle as any nurse ministering to the wounded on a battlefield. She stood up on the frail woman's lap and reached for her face.

Madame Lefoux, having somehow determined what was happening, even through the chaos, appeared on the other side of the aged queen. The inventor assessed the situation. In a few quick movements, she flipped several toggles and snaps at the bottom of Queen Matakara's mask. The awful thing fell away, exposing the vampire's face fully to Prudence's metanatural touch.

Under the mask, Matakara's skin was sunken against the bones of her chin, but it was clear she had once been quite beautiful. Her face was heart shaped with an aquiline nose, broadly spaced eyes, and small mouth.

Prudence, drawn by the newly exposed flesh, placed one small, chubby hand to the vampire's chin. It was a sympathetic, intimate gesture, and Alexia couldn't help but imagine that her daughter somehow knew exactly what she was doing.

Complete and total pandemonium resulted.

All the vampires in the room turned as one, leaving off whoever they had been fighting with or feeding on. They charged. This only frightened Prudence who, now a vampire once more, leaped nimbly out of the way and dashed about the room pell-mell.

Matakara, mortal and still attached to her chair, jerked against the straps and tubes, letting out a silent scream of agony.

One of the vampires turned to Alexia. "You! Soulless. Make it stop!"

Lord Maccon, still a wolf, mouth dripping with old dark vampire blood, leaped to his wife's defense. His hackles were up, his teeth bared in a snarl.

"She cannot die," cried out one of the vampires. Clearly more of them spoke English than Alexia had previously supposed. "We have *no new queen*!"

"So you, too, will die." Lady Maccon was unsympathetic.

"More than that, we will go mad. We will take Alexandria with us. Just think of the damage even six vampires can do to one city."

Alexia looked around. Madame Lefoux had lost her hat but otherwise stood strong. She was tussling with the beautiful female drone on the opposite side of the throne. Mr. Tumtrinkle lay fallen in one corner. Alexia wasn't certain he still breathed. Several of the other thespians were looking worse for the wear. One of the younger, prettier actresses bled copiously from multiple neck bites. Floote stood in the midst of the melee, wooden knife in one hand, an expression of utterly unbutlerlike ferocity on his face. When he caught Alexia's eye, his customary impassivity immediately returned. Then, coming from the far side of the room, Alexia heard a strangled choking sound and saw Tunstell sobbing, his red head bent over the crumpled form of Ivy.

Alexia's friend lay broken and bloodied, her neck a ruin of torn flesh. Baby Primrose, unharmed, lay squalling in the crook of Ivy's flaccid arm. Tunstell scooped the child up and clutched her to his breast, still sobbing.

A shout distracted Alexia from the tragic scene—one of the other vampires managed to capture Prudence. He ran toward Alexia with the toddler's struggling form held out at arm's length, as if in an egg-and-spoon race. Alexia knew he would try to hand her the child. She dodged away. Not that she didn't love her daughter, but right then she certainly didn't want to touch her.

Lord Maccon snarled and intercepted the attack, perfectly understanding Alexia's predicament.

"Wait!" yelled Alexia. "I have an idea. Chancellor, what if we could get you a new queen?"

The vampire stepped forward. "That is an acceptable proposal, if Matakara has the strength to try and we have a volunteer? Who do you suggest?"

Alexia looked thoughtfully at Madame Lefoux.

Even in the middle of grappling intimately with the beautiful drone, the Frenchwoman shook her head madly. The inventor had never sought immortality.

"Don't worry, Genevieve, I had someone else in mind."

Around her everything stilled as Alexia walked across the room to where Ivy Tunstell lay. Her bosom companion's breathing was shallow, her face unnaturally pale. She did not look long for this world. Alexia was familiar enough with death to know when it stalked a friend. She swallowed down hard on her own unhappiness and looked to Ivy's beloved husband. "Well, Tunstell, how would you like to be married to a queen?"

Tunstell's eyes were red but it took him no time at all to make the decision. He had once been a claviger and had spent his life on the fringe of immortal society. He had sacrificed his own bid for metamorphosis to marry Miss Ivy Hisselpenny. He had no compunctions or reservations. If Ivy were to be dead or a vampire, he would rather her be a vampire. Tunstell was the most progressive man Alexia had ever met.

"Try it, Lady Maccon, I entreat you."

So Alexia signaled to one of the vampires in that utterly autocratic way of hers. The vampire came to do her bidding, when only a few minutes earlier he might have killed her where she stood. He carried Ivy over to drape her on Matakara, setting the actress on the queen's lap like a ventriloquist's doll and arranging her to lie back so Ivy's neck was near Matakara's mouth. Ivy's head lolled back.

Chancellor Neshi pulled a set of leather belts with chain links attached and strapped them over Ivy, lashing her tightly against his queen. Then he turned and nodded at Lady Maccon.

Alexia took Prudence into her arms.

Queen Matakara turned back to a vampire.

She began spouting a string of words, ancient-sounding words, not Arabic at all but some other language. Her voice was commanding, melodic, and very direct. Chancellor Neshi leaped to her side and bent to her ear, whispering frantically. The other vampires stilled, waiting.

Alexia wasn't quite certain what they thought was happening. Would they know that their queen was still destined to die? Did they know the bargain the chancellor was striking? Did they understand the ancient tongue, or did they still think there was a chance?

Chancellor Neshi leaped back down and approached Alexia. When Conall growled and would not let him near, Alexia said, "All is well, husband. I do believe I know what he wants."

Chancellor Neshi sidled past the still-bristling wolf. "She desires your assurance, Soulless, that you will see the deed done, whether this metamorphosis is successful or not."

"You have my word," said Alexia. She was thinking of Countess Nadasdy, a younger and stronger queen. The countess had *failed* to metamorphose a new queen. Yet here Alexia was wagering all their lives on Ivy Tunstell having excess soul and Queen Matakara enough strength to draw it out of her.

CHAPTER NINETEEN

How to Retire to the Countryside

Chancellor Neshi nodded, once, to the ancient queen. At his signal, Matakara bent forward, opening her mouth wide. Unlike Countess Nadasdy, she didn't appear to need any kind of drinking cup for preparation. Her fangs, Alexia noted, were particularly long—her makers even longer than her feeders. Perhaps it was a factor of her age. Perhaps when queens got too old, all they could do was try to make a replacement queen. Perhaps that was the problem: Matakara needed to breed more than she needed to eat. She had been kept alive long past that time. *Her hive should have been doing nothing but giving her girls to try to change over,* thought Alexia. Then again, she probably would have gone through a large number of girls that way. Local authorities wouldn't have been too chuffed.

The ancient vampire sank both sets of fangs deep into the flesh of Ivy's already-lacerated neck. Matakara could not move her arms to hold Ivy. She kept herself attached by the strength of her jaw and with the aid of the straps that held Ivy against her. The queen's dark eyes, visible over the fall of Ivy's black hair, had lost a little of their eternal sorrow and looked almost contemplative. She moved not one muscle as she sucked, except that like Countess Nadasdy, there was a strange up-and-down fluttering in her emaciated neck.

Ivy Tunstell remained limp for a very long time. Everyone in that room held their breath, waiting. Except Conall, of course, who paced around growling at people. The earl had very little sense of gravity in any given situation.

Then Ivy's whole body jerked and her eyes popped open, wide, startled, looking directly at Alexia. She began to scream. Tunstell made a lunge toward her but one of the other vampires grabbed him and held him back. Ivy's pupils dilated, darkening and extending outward until both her eyeballs were a deep bloodred.

Alexia knew what came next. Ivy's eyes would begin to bleed, and she would continue to scream until those screams became garbled by the blood pouring from her mouth. *Of course Ivy doesn't have excess soul! Stupid of me to even think it.*

Except that Ivy's eyes did not start to drip blood. Instead, the darkness in them began to recede, until eventually they were the velvety brown of her true self. Ivy stopped screaming, closed her eyes, and began to jerk violently from side to side as though undergoing a kind of fit. Her copious dark ringlets bobbed about her face and her tiny admiral's cap gave up its grip upon her hair—after enduring so much during the battle—and tumbled to the floor, its white plume sagging sadly.

Ivy opened her mouth once more, but not to scream this time. Oh, there was blood dripping out, but it was blood from the fangs, four of them, as they broke through her gums and extended forth, shining in the candlelight. Ivy's face, already fashionably pale, became ashen white. Her hair took on an even bouncier and glossier sheen, and she opened her eyes once more. With a tiny shrug, she threw off the thick leather and metal straps, snapping them easily as if they were no more than gossamer silk. She leaped down from the throne to land, light and easy on the floor of the chamber.

She lisped around her new teeth, "What an odd sethathion. Tunny dathling, did I faint? Oh, my hath!" Bending, she retrieved her admiral's hat and popped it firmly back upon her head.

Behind her, Queen Matakara looked even more sunken and bloodless than ever before. She slumped forward, only the artifice of the chair keeping her upright.

Chancellor Neshi said to Alexia, "Your promise, Soulless?"

Alexia nodded and moved forward, this time unhindered by any vampires. She climbed upon the dais and pressed her hand to the ancient vampire's arm in one small spot where the skin was free of straps and tubes.

Queen Matakara, King Hatshepsut, last of the Great Pharaohs, Oldest Vampire, died right then and there at Alexia's touch. There was no fanfare, no screaming in pain. She let out a tiny sigh and slipped out of her immortal cage at last. It was both the worst thing Alexia's preternatural state had forced her to do and the best, for the expression in those dark eyes was, for the very first time, one of absolute peace.

In the silent stillness of wonder that followed, while drones and vampires adjusted themselves and their tethers to a new queen, Chancellor Neshi picked up Prudence. Prudence turned, yet again, into a vampire, and before anyone could stop him, the chancellor dashed on chubby legs out the window to the balcony and jumped over the edge, falling to his death in the street below.

The moment he died, Prudence turned back into a normal baby. Or as normal as she got. Alexia filed that little fact away; apparently something else canceled out her daughter's powers besides her mother, sunlight, and distance—death.

There was a good deal of cleanup to be done, a number of explanations and arrangements to be made, and discussions to be had. Not to mention several formal introductions and a few broken bones and bloody necks to medicate. The five remaining vampires looked at one another and then, as a body, rushed to surround their new queen, chattering at her in Arabic and gesticulating excitedly.

Ivy, confused—head bobbling back and forth between them, white feather puffing about—finally raised her voice in a most un-Ivy-like way and ordered silence. She looked to her husband—who was standing, crying, clutching Primrose to his breast—and then turned to Lady Maccon for assistance.

"Alexia, pleath ethplain whath ith going on?"

Lady Maccon did, to the best of her ability. The pretty female drone who spoke English translated the explanation for the benefit of the vampires. Soon it became clear to everyone that Ivy had both a husband and children, which caused much consternation, as such a thing was taboo among those seeking metamorphosis. At which Ivy protested she hadn't sought it, so she couldn't possibly be blamed. Alexia stated categorically that what was changed was changed, and like spilled blood, there was no point going on about it. Mrs. Tunstell was a vampire queen now and they had all better make the best of the husband and twins that came with the package.

Ivy said she felt remarkably restless and wanted to know if she had to stay in Alexandria for the rest of her life.

Alexia remembered Lord Akeldama once mentioning something about new queens having several months to resettle. *How else would vampires have spread over the world?* Ivy said, good, in that case she wished to return to London *immediately*.

The Egyptian vampires protested. Alexandria was their home, had been for hundreds of years! Ivy would have none of it. London was *her* home, and if she had to spend eternity anywhere, it was going to be in the place where one could get a decent hat! She batted her eyelashes and lisped out girlish pleas, her character clearly not so much metamorphosed as her soul. Yet her tactic worked despite her lack of autocratic tendencies. In remarkably short order, everyone was dispersing. Those drones who wished to ally with a new queen and relocate were to pack and meet at the departure dock for the steamer the next morning. The vampires, looking slightly panicked, dashed off to gather belongings and then, sticking close to Ivy, escorted her, her husband, her daughter, and her acting troupe back to the hotel.

Alexia was left in the hive house with Matakara's dead body, Madame Lefoux, Prudence, and Lord Maccon. Her daughter was exhausted beyond her childish capacities and was sitting in a sobbing heap. Her husband was still a wolf. During Ivy's metamorphosis, Floote had disappeared.

Madame Lefoux gave Alexia a long look and then climbed up to examine the vampire queen's body and chair with studied interest, pointedly leaving Alexia to work out her family affairs on her own.

Alexia went over and scooped up Prudence, cuddling the sobbing baby close. She simply stood like that, glaring at her husband, tapping one foot.

Finally, Lord Maccon shifted form.

"Explain yourself," said his lady wife in a very decided tone of voice.

"Floote found me badly injured and imprisoned among his men and tended to me until he could get me out of the plague zone," Lord Maccon explained.

Alexia thought about her former butler. "His men? Ah. While I am very grateful to him for seeing to you, wayward husband, it does seem to me that it was his men who caused all the fuss in the first place."

Lord Maccon said, "According to Floote, they didn't know who you were. He has given them new instructions."

"I should hope so." Alexia paused, considering her next move. "Do you think we'll ever find him?"

Lord Maccon shook his head. "Not if he doesn't want to be found. Floote has a whole network here, and familiarity with the terrain, and no werewolves to track him in the God-Breaker Zone."

"I suppose that saves us from determining what to do with a butler who goes around killing people. It certainly reflects badly upon our domestic staff. Still, I shall miss him. There was a man who knew how to brew a good cup of tea." Alexia was sad to lose her dear old companion, but she also knew it was for the best. She should hate to have to put him on trial or turn him over to Lady Kingair.

"Did Floote tell you it was all based on a deal my father made with Matakara?"

"He did."

Alexia asked her husband, "What are we to do about it?"

Lord Maccon came over to her tentatively, unsure whether she forgave him yet for dying on her, unsure whether he forgave her yet for lying to him.

Alexia could sense his uncertainty. She was having none of any such silliness anymore. She closed the gap between them and curled herself against his nakedness, bracketing Prudence against his large form so that the baby was in close contact with both her parents.

Prudence gave a little murmur of approval.

Conall sighed, giving over his resentment, and wrapped his family tight in his strong arms. He pressed small kisses against Alexia's temple and against his daughter's head.

The earl cleared his throat, still holding Alexia tight against him. The words rumbled in the massive chest so close to her ear. "I have been giving some thought to my retirement."

"Indeed, how very unusual of you. From BUR, or from the pack?"

"Both. I purchased property, in Cairo, shortly after we arrived."

Alexia tilted her head back and looked to her husband in confusion. "Conall, what is this?"

"A strategic retreat, my love. I thought, when Prudence has grown, we might return here, together. Take long walks, eat pastries, play, uh, backgammon or whatnot."

"In the God-Breaker Zone . . . but you'll grow old and die!"

"As will you." Conall began stroking her back in a soothing manner.

"Yes, but I was *always* going to grow old and die!"

"Now we can do it together."

"My love, that's a very chivalric thought, but there is no need to be nonsensical in matters of the heart."

The earl stopped petting his wife and leaned a little away from her so he could look down into her upturned face. His tawny eyes were serious. "My dear, I am getting old. Older than you think. I will not allow myself to become one of *those* Alphas. Two Betas have already betrayed me—I must be losing some measure of control. In another decade or so, it will be time to let go gracefully. Can you think of a better way than relocating here?"

Alexia, practical to the last, actually considered this. "Well, no. But, dear, are you quite certain?"

"You like it here, don't you, my love?"

Alexia tilted her head. "Well, it's warm, and the food is tasty."

"That's settled, then."

Lady Maccon was not one to give in so easily as that. "We will have to bring a great deal of tea with us when we relocate." She was quite firm on *that* point.

"We could start a tea-import business," suggested her husband. "Something to keep you entertained in your old age."

"Trade! Really, I don't know . . ." Alexia trailed off thoughtfully.

Madame Lefoux, all forgotten until that moment, jumped down off the throne platform to join them. "It's very romantic, his wanting to die with you."

"*You* would say that."

"Can I come and join you as well?" She sidled up to Alexia and winked at her.

"Genevieve, you don't know when to give up, do you?"

Conall wore a very amused expression.

"Can you imagine the things I could build without supernatural or governmental interference?"

"Good gracious me, what a terrifying thought. You may visit us, Genevieve, but that is all."

"Spoilsport."

"Shall we?" suggested Conall, gesturing at the exit.

The four of them filed out of the now-abandoned hive house. Alexia paused to turn and look at it thoughtfully. They might make use of it as well. After all, Alexandria was a port city. If they were going to import tea . . . "Oh, dear, Prudence, I'm already thinking like a tradeswoman."

"No," said Prudence.

Conall stepped out into the street. Alexia considered reminding her husband he was naked and then gave up. In Alexandria, they were bound to be a spectacle whatever they did.

She shifted her daughter to her other hip. The baby's eyes were half closed and she was nodding off, the victim of an exciting night. "Come along, then, Prudence, my dear."

"No," muttered Prudence softly.

Madame Lefoux said, "Have you ever considered that she might be saying no because she doesn't like her name? She never says no when you use an endearment."

Alexia stopped, floored by the idea. "Do you think? Is that true, my little puggle?" She used Lord Akeldama's favorite moniker for Prudence.

"Yes," said Prudence.

"Prudence?"

"No!" said Prudence.

"Goodness, Genevieve, you may be on to something. What should we call her, do you think?"

"Well, she has an excessive number of names. Why not wait until she's a little older? She can choose for herself. Can't you, sweetheart?"

"Yes!" said Prudence, most categorically.

"There, you see? Takes after her mother already."

"What could you mean by that?" queried Alexia archly.

"Likes her own way, doesn't she?" suggested the Frenchwoman with a dimpled smile.

"I don't know what you're talking about," replied Lady Maccon with a great deal of dignity. With which she took off at a brisk pace, keeping an eye to her husband's rather distinguished backside as it wandered down the street under the waning Egyptian moon.

CHAPTER TWENTY

In Which Times Shift

After a sea journey only slightly less exciting than the first, Lord and Lady Maccon, their daughter, the Tunstells and their twins, the acting troupe, one nursemaid, five vampires, and seven drones arrived at the port of Southampton on a blustery day in late April of 1876. Such a crowd had mostly taken over the ship and proceeded, in remarkably fine fettle after such an extensive journey, to take over the train to London.

London was ill prepared for such an invasion. It was also not quite the same London as when they had departed.

Lord Maccon, for one, returned to his pack to find that his previous Beta had emigrated to Scotland for an unspecified indenture and that a young dandy of an Alpha waited tentatively in his place.

Biffy handed him a letter from Professor Lyall, tears in his eyes. Alexia, unabashed, read it over her husband's arm.

"My dear sir. I have no means of making amends. Even an apology would be more an insult, of that I am well aware. I have trained young Biffy to the best of my abilities. He will make a fine Beta, even though, as you may now already have smelled, he has manifested Anubis form. I thought, perhaps, you might take over training him for his next role—your replacement—contingent upon such a time as you leave us for Egypt and a well-earned retirement."

Upon reading that, Alexia asked, "How did he know your plans? You didn't discuss it with him ahead of time, did you?"

"No, but that's Randolph for you."

They continued with the letter.

"Our Biffy is part of this modern age. Shifting times require a London dandy for a London Pack. Try not, my dear lord, to see him in light

of your own abilities as Alpha. He will never be that kind of wolf. I believe he is what our pack will need in the future, regardless."

Alexia looked up at Biffy. The young werewolf seemed to be feeling a more intense emotion over Professor Lyall's abandonment than she might have predicted. What had happened while they were in Egypt?

"Biffy," asked Alexia, because she had no subtlety, "did something significant occur between you and Lyall while we were away?"

Biffy hung his head. "He promised he would come back to me eventually. When we were all ready. Ten, twenty years, he said. Not so long for an immortal. Shifting times, he said."

Alexia nodded, feeling old. "But it feels like a very long time?" *Ah, young love.*

Biffy nodded sadly.

The earl, sensitive to his pack member's feelings, drew Alexia's attention back to Lyall's letter before she could continue interrogating the young dandy.

The letter continued.

"Don't tell Biffy yet. He isn't ready to know his future. Not the one that I envision for him. But he is ready to learn how to lead a pack, and you, my lord, will be an excellent teacher. Despite everything, I remain faithfully your friend, Professor Randolph Lyall."

"Ah, so," said Alexia, looking back and forth between the two gentlemen, their eyes down-turned. "It is an elegant solution," she said at last.

"He was always verra good at elegant solutions," said Lord Maccon softly. Then he bucked up. "Well, young Biffy, I suspect with you as my Beta, I'll never again be allowed out without a cravat."

Biffy was aghast. "Certainly not, my lord!"

"Good to know where I stand from the start." Conall grinned amiably at the boy.

Rumpet stuck his head in. Rumpet had been brought out of retirement to take over for Floote as pack butler. He'd set up as an innkeeper in Pickering after the vampires took over Woolsey but jumped at the chance to return to his old position. Pickering and innkeeping, as it turned out, were not all he had hoped.

"Lady Maccon, there's a gentleman to see you." The butler had a certain curl to his lip that in Alexia's experience could only mean one man.

"Ah, show him into the front parlor. If you will excuse me, husband, Biffy, I'm certain you have much to discuss. There is Channing to consider, if nothing else."

"Oh, blast it. Channing," muttered Lord Maccon.

Alexia let herself out.

Lord Akeldama sat waiting for her in the front parlor, one silken leg crossed over the other, blue eyes bright and slightly accusatory. He was wearing pea green and salmon this evening, a pleasant swirl of spring colors to counteract the gray weather they'd been experiencing of late.

"Alexia, my *darling* toggle button!"

"My lord, how are you?"

"I am here to reclaim my dearest little daughter."

"Of course, of course. Rumpet, fetch Prudence for his lordship, would you? She's sleeping in the back parlor. Did you miss her, my lord?"

"Like a hat misses a feather, darling! The droney poos and I have been bereft, quite bereft I tell you!"

"Well, she was very useful, in her way."

"Of course she was. And Matakara—are the rumors true?"

"Where do you think Ivy acquired her new hive?"

"Yes, Alexia, pigeon, I mean to discuss that little incident with you. Did you have to bring them *all*?"

"A new queen, plus five Egyptian vampires and assorted drones? You object to my bringing souvenirs back from Egypt? Everyone brings back souvenirs from their travels abroad, my lord. It is the *done thing*."

"Well, dewdrop, I don't object *as such*, but . . ."

Alexia smiled craftily. "Ivy has chosen somewhere in Wimbledon for her hive's location. A little too close for comfort, my lord?"

The vampire arched a blond eyebrow at her haughtily. "Countess Nadasdy is *not* amused."

"She wouldn't be. Someone is essentially taking on her old role in society."

"*Ivy Tunstell*, no less." Lord Akeldama frowned, one perfect crease marring the white smoothness of his forehead. "She is terribly interested in fashion, isn't she?"

"Oh, dear." Alexia hid a smile. "That, too, is your territory. I see."

"An *actress*, my little blueberry. I mean, really. Have you *seen* her hats?"

"You paid a call?"

"Of course I paid a call! She is a new queen, after all. Etiquette *must* be observed. But really"—he shuddered delicately—"those hats."

Alexia thought of Professor Lyall's letter. "It is the modern age, my dear Lord Akeldama. I think we must learn to accept such things as a consequence of shifting times."

"*Shifting times*, indeed. What a very werewolf way of putting it."

Rumpet opened the door and Prudence toddled sleepily into the room.

"Ah, *puggle precious*, how is my darling girl?"

Alexia grabbed her daughter's arm before she could launch herself at the vampire. "Dama!"

At Lady Maccon's nod, the vampire bent to embrace his adopted child, Alexia maintaining a firm grip the entire time.

"Welcome home, *poppet*!"

"Dama, Dama!"

Alexia looked on affectionately. "We've learned a few things about our girl here, haven't we, Prudence dear?"

"No," said Prudence.

"One of them is that she doesn't like her name."

"No?" Lord Akeldama looked very thoughtful. "Well, there you have it. I couldn't sympathize more, puggle. I don't *approve* of most people's names either."

Alexia laughed.

Prudence took sudden interest in Alexia's parasol, sitting next to her on the settee.

"Mine?" suggested Prudence.

"Perhaps someday," said her mother.

Looking at his adopted daughter thoughtfully, Lord Akeldama said, "Shifting times, my dear *Ruffled Parasol*?"

Alexia did not bother to ask how he might know her secret code name. She only looked him straight on, forthright as always. "Shifting times, *Goldenrod*."

Meet the Author

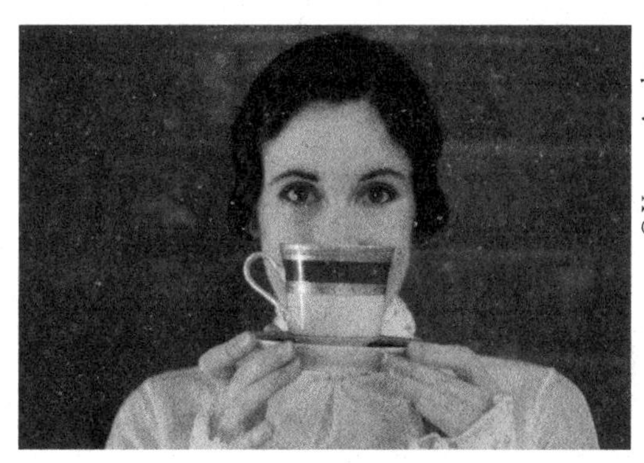

© Vanessa Applegate

Ms. Carriger began writing to cope with being raised in obscurity by an expatriate Brit and an incurable curmudgeon. She escaped small-town life and inadvertently acquired several degrees in Higher Learning. Ms. Carriger then traveled the historic cities of Europe, subsisting entirely on biscuits secreted in her handbag. She now resides in the Colonies, surrounded by fantastic shoes, where she insists on tea imported directly from London. She is fond of teeny-tiny hats and tropical fruit. Find out more about Ms. Carriger at www.gailcarriger.com